D1193391

HUMANS

THE UNTOLD STORY OF ADAM AND EVE AND THEIR DESCENDANTS

VOLUME TWO

MJOMBA AND THE EVIL GHOST

(3ʳᴰ REVISED EDITION)

EDITORIAL REVIEWS

Reviewed in the United States on November 4, 2019 by Misty s: "Great book good story line very interesting."

Barb Wild wrote, regarding Volume One (The Thesis): "very detailed story. It is amazing to me how much information authors use to make up their stories. I would recommend it to others." (Goodreads, April 14, 2021).

Erika Kraus wrote: "Discussing this book was almost more important to me than reading it. Joseph M. Luguya is highly intelligent and respectable. I thoroughly enjoyed reading this book." (Goodreads, Jun 02, 2020)

Emily Nicole wrote: "Mjomba and the Evil Ghost is a heavy read that requires your attention and thoughts. I really enjoyed this thought-provoking book." (Goodreads, Jul 29, 2020)

Melissa wrote: "Interesting read. Well written."
(Goodreads, May 23, 2020)

Debra wrote: "Very interesting and often thought provoking." (Goodreads, May 23, 2020)

Mary wrote: "Interesting read." (Goodreads, Jul 28, 2018)

Csimplot Simplot wrote: "Excellent book!!!" (Goodreads, Dec 18, 2018)

Sasha wrote: "This book for me was a very interesting read. I truly enjoyed reading this book. I couldn't put it down once I began reading it. I kept wanting to find out more. I would recommend this book to others. It is a very good read. I will be reading this again. This is an amazing author. If you haven't read any of his books you should."

(Goodreads, Jul 30, 2020)

Connie wrote: "I found this book uneven. Parts I could hardly read. Other parts I devoured. It is the story of a young man writing his thesis (think) and he somehow gets the devil to lecture him. It is never anti God. Always God is a real being in the story. It's the how and why the devil was banished and what his job has become." (Goodreads, Dec 20, 2018)

Mary wrote: "Unique read." (Goodreads, July 1, 2020)

The Columbia Review of Books & Film:
-- Avraham Azrieli, TheColumbiaReview.com

Humans: The Untold Story of Adam and Eve and their Descendants is a substantial novel in three parts by Joseph M. Luguya, which explores good and evil through human, mythological and supernatural characters, much of it in the form of a grand debate, delivering an intricate theological saga.

Humans includes three volumes: "The Thesis" (Volume

One), "Mjomba and the Evil Ghost" (Volume Two), and "The Demoniac" (Volume Three). The scene that launches Humans appropriately involves both mystery and magnificence: "The International Trade Center literally sat on the edge of downtown Dar es Salaam, the beautiful metropolis whose name fittingly signified "Heaven of Peace". Christian Mjomba's office was located on the twenty-seventh floor.

In an unusual move, using a key he took from his wallet, Mjomba unlocked a side door to his office and slid furtively inside." And from this opening of a mysterious door, Humans builds up to a complex yet compassionately humane story of Mjomba's fascinating journey.

In his earlier days, Mjomba had been a seminarian whose tangling with a monumental assignment on the "Original Virtue" led to an immensely challenging intellectual and spiritual quest—as well as a "Devil's bargain" of sorts. He fences with Satan and with its good counterparts while bringing into stark question many of the basic tenets of the church. In fact, "having in effect enlisted the help of Satan in the task of turning out a winning thesis on the subject of "Original Virtue," Mjomba finds himself "feeling quite uncomfortable filling the role of scribe to a creature that the sacred scriptures had pointedly referred to as "Accuser of our Brethren" (Revelation 12:10)."

And so, in a twist that makes Humans uniquely intriguing, Mjomba's sincere efforts to turn the most evil force into good and, thus, save souls, ends up placing our hero himself in a highly questionable— and dangerous— position.

Author Joseph M. Luguya brings to this novel enormous knowledge of religious concepts and historical records. Through the protagonist and the secondary characters, the reader becomes privy to a wealth of ideas and detailed arguments, many of them new and daring. While much of the book offers a multi-faceted, extensive dissertation that might appear dense to some readers, the author's creative use of Satan's own voice makes it hard to put down, not only when provocative arguments begin to attain logical flair, but also when the author brings in controversial historical figures whose legacy is open to debate—and to literary license—as Satan claims them to his side: "Take the so-called 'reformation' that I engineered. Believe it or not, but it was my idea. I used Martin Luther, a Catholic friar – yes, and a good one at that – and a reformer, to set it in motion."

Or this one: "… Joan of Arc who was labeled a witch and burned at the stake! You may or may not like to hear it, but I also succeeded in using that innocent girl to confound and drive other good souls in the Church to virtual despair."

Some of the arguments in fact ring true not only in the historical context, but in our current world, festering as it is with religious tensions and ethnic prejudices: "Later, during his oral defense of the thesis, Mjomba would comment that one of the legacies of original sin was the perennial tendency of humans to never see evil in themselves, and to see nothing good in other humans – especially those who were different from themselves in some respect." How true!

The author is especially deft at merging abstract ideas and structural visualizations into symbols that our hero's mind ponders in ways reminiscent of Dan Brown's symbologist Robert Langdon in The Da Vinci Code: "But the image of an inverted pyramid balancing on top of another pyramidal shape flooded Mjomba's mind with a force that made him feel like he might pass out. He attributed his ability to stay afloat and not drift off into a swoon to the fact that he was able to focus his mind on the peculiar design Primrose had produced using the blurb's material and its similarity to the letter "X"!

Humans is also distinguishable in telling a story within a story, cleverly utilizing several layers of imaginary characters. For example, here is our protagonist reflecting on his own created protagonist: "Mjomba shut his eyes and paused to think about Innocent Kintu, the central character of his 'masterpiece'. As images of the nurse's beguiling manner came flocking back, he came close to concluding that a non-fictional character like Kintu could in fact be considered fictional when contrasted with a character like Flora!"

In summary, Humans: The Untold Story of Adam and Eve by Joseph M. Luguya creates a dramatic confrontation between a virtuous young scholar and the most malevolent character of all, delivering an extensive, all-encompassing confrontation that becomes a metaphor for the very core of human existence. This thought-provoking, sprawling novel explores unresolved issues of faith and spirituality while the leading character valiantly defends all that he holds dear in the struggle between good and evil, life and death, and the opposing forces of divine creation. Readers will be enticed to contemplate the most fundamental questions of human existence and come away with a deeper understanding of both differences and commonalities that define us. Significant and Memorable!

-- Avraham Azrieli, TheColumbiaReview.com

KIRKUS REVIEWS: Luguya (*Payment in Kind*, 1985) offers a three-part novel about one man's extensive views on Christianity.

When readers first meet Christian Mjomba, he's seated in his 27th-floor office in the city of Dar es Salaam, Tanzania. He has a pleasant view of the harbor and a degree from Stanford University on the wall, and seems to be doing fairly well. However, his dream of publishing a best-selling work remains unfulfilled. He does have a background in writing, though; as readers soon learn, he'd once been a member of a seminary brotherhood. During that time, he composed an extensive thesis on various aspects of the Christian faith, which strayed from official church teachings. Mjomba's intention was, in part, to "show unequivocally that the Prime Mover loved everyone irrespective of religious affiliation."

The book begins with an in-depth exploration of the protagonist's views; there's more action in later chapters, but the emphasis throughout is on ideas. They include Mjomba's annoyance with those who use the phrase "the bible says", and his meditation on the human body, which he says is "designed to be both a temple of God and a vessel of His grace." The book covers an extensive amount of theologically intriguing material; it's critical of many different parties, including the Apostle Peter, the devil, and people who revel in "mostly ill-gotten wealth…"

Readers looking for new interpretations of Christian thought will find them here, though those hoping for more thorough integration with plot may be disappointed. Its details of life in Tanzania, such as the notion that "Even though most spoke English very well, Tanzanians just loved to speak Swahili," are memorable. That said, the text as a whole is concerned with issues that go well beyond any single nation.

An insightful…array of spiritual material.

BOOKS WE'VE REVIEWED BY JOSEPH M. LUGUYA

—Foreword Reviews

Joseph Luguya's book *Mjomba and the Evil Ghost* involves a sprawling discourse with Satan concerning the tenets and values of Christianity.

Christian Mjomba is a Stanford-educated success story. The virtuous Tanzanian scholar is also an amateur theologian; in the book, he functions as a stand-in for Christian inquiry. Even his name is symbolic: "mjomba" means "fish" in Swahili. Through a twisting, dramatic series of debates and clashes with dark forces, he explores ideas about faith.

The opponent in Christian's debates is Satan, who is silver-tongued, slick, and convincing. Christian's arguments are human and sometimes clunky, so Satan often claims the upper hand. Referred to by many aliases and claiming to be "more catholic than the Catholics," Satan can debate any point. The two cover topics including the meaning of "victory of good over evil," the pre-lapsarian state of original virtue, murder, and the dangers of rationalization.

Both parties hold forth at length, with Satan picking holes in each of Christian's arguments with the expertise of a lawyer…The book's extensive, in-depth scholarship is excellent, educational, and exhaustive, but as a morality play, the book is too dense to be entertaining.

Mjomba and the Evil Ghost is a discursive novel

concerned with the heresy that it views as inherent in scholarship; it works to justify the dogma of the Catholic Church.

Reviewed by <u>Claire Foster</u>
—Foreword Reviews

Joseph M. Luguya's *Humans: The Untold Story of Adam and Their Descendants* spins an ambitious three-volume fictional tale, in which he charts the history of the human condition…

In this novel, readers learn first-hand from Satan how humans have historically succumbed to temptation. Satan makes sure to present himself here not as villain but victim, and merely one who whispers suggestions to humans who then make unfortunate decisions…

According to the devil, he didn't instruct them to eat the proverbial fruit, but merely to think; they then concluded they didn't need the "Prime Mover" to make choices for them. The next instance was not far behind, when their son Cain listened to whispers and yielded to jealousy...

No pride-based offense is omitted, from that original fall through present-day power grabs by nations who justify their actions by claiming that they are for the greater good.

Readers must first digest the sum of Christian history, the Bible, all the major players (ex., St. Peter, Mother Teresa), and spiritual concepts (free will, sin, etc.) before being introduced to Satan and his apologetics...The author's own biblical study background is on full display, and he can accurately quote not only Scripture but also his scope of theology in general...
www.blueinkreview.com

www.Spiritrestoration.org: In the same way that C. S. Lewis wrote **Screwtape Letters**, Joseph Luguya attempts to describe the spiritual realm from a human perspective. Luguya does very well at portraying the character of the Devil...This book is one that every fan of C. S. Lewis should check out. Luguya has a very scholarly form just like Lewis...The Devil teaches almost more than the Christian. It is a very convicting book. Luguya is a great writer and well worth the investment in this huge book.

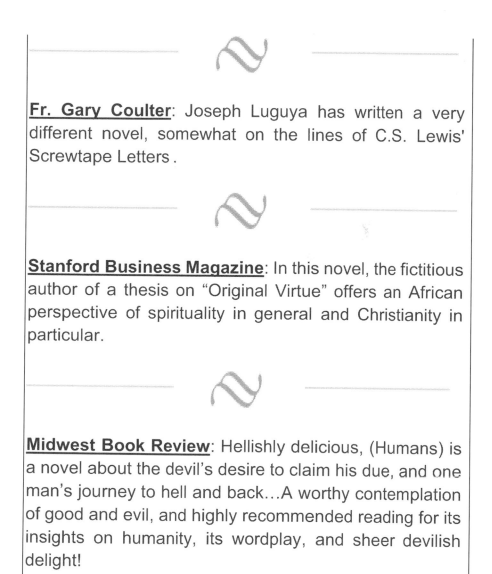

Fr. Gary Coulter: Joseph Luguya has written a very different novel, somewhat on the lines of C.S. Lewis' Screwtape Letters .

Stanford Business Magazine: In this novel, the fictitious author of a thesis on "Original Virtue" offers an African perspective of spirituality in general and Christianity in particular.

Midwest Book Review: Hellishly delicious, (Humans) is a novel about the devil's desire to claim his due, and one man's journey to hell and back…A worthy contemplation of good and evil, and highly recommended reading for its insights on humanity, its wordplay, and sheer devilish delight!

Hellishly Delicious... Sheer Devilish Delight!

Original Books
14404 Innsbruck Court
Silver Spring, MD, 20906, USA
Website: www.originalbooks.org (under construction)
<u>Visit Amazon's Joseph M. Luguya Page</u>

Copyright © 2020 by Joseph M. Luguya and Lorna M. Luguya

All rights reserved. No part of this book may be reproduced or transmitted in any form or by any means, electronic or mechanical, including photocopying, recording, or by any information storage and retrieval system, without the written permission of the Publisher, except where permitted by law. For inquiries, address: Joseph M. Luguya, Original Books, 14404 Innsbruck Ct., Silver Spring, MD 20906, USA.

Library of Congress Control Number: 2015914304
ISBN-13: 978-1-7355649-0-6
ISBN-10: 1-7355649-0-7

Third Revised Original Books Edition, August 15, 2020

Created and written by Joseph M. Luguya
Illustrations by Lorna M. Luguya
Printed and produced in the United States of America
First published August 2015.

About the Author

The author is a native of Uganda. He received his early education at St. Pius X Seminary Nagongera, St. Joseph's Seminary Nyenga, and St. Mary's Seminary Gaba. A graduate of the University of Nairobi, Mr. Luguya is also a former Sloan Fellow at the Stanford Graduate School of Business. He has lived and worked in Uganda, Kenya, Tanzania, Canada, and the United States. He is also the author of Payment in Kind, 2nd Revised edition (Original Books, 2017); The Forbidden Fruit (Original Books, 2011); and Inspired by the Devil Part 1: The Gospel According to Judas Iscariot (Original Books, 2007).

About the Book

Publisher: "Mjomba and the Evil Ghost" is Volume Two of Joseph Luguya's thrilling three-volume novel "Humans, The Untold Story of Adam and Eve and their Descendants". The other volumes are "The Thesis" (Volume One) and "The Demoniac" (Volume Three).

A virtuous but rather naïve member of St. Augustine's seminary brotherhood has a class assignment to turn in a thesis on "Original Virtue". But he has a runaway imagination, and easily gets snared into serving in a very strange role, namely the role of scribe to none other than Satan.

Misled by the practice in Rome that has one of the cardinals (the Promoter of the Faith) play the role of the so-called *advocatus diaboli* (Latin for Devil's advocate) in order to argue against the canonization of the candidate for sainthood, he falls for the temptation to employ the devil as his mouthpiece for expounding on the doctrines of the church. He imagines that if he succeeds in doing that, he will effectively make Lucifer who is also known as Beelzebub work for the salvation of souls instead of their damnation.

And, incredibly, the seminarian appears to succeed in tricking the Evil One into working against his own interests and helping him craft a thesis that looks like a definite winner! Satan starts by bragging about how he derailed the father and mother of mankind, and it soon begins to dawn on the student that it is the Evil One who is using him instead of the other way round. Using the free platform provided by the unwitting seminarian, the devil indicates gleefully that he is in total control, and that his evil plan to consign everyone, Catholic and non-Catholic alike, the luckless student himself included, to hell is on track!

And that former "Angel of Light" and also "Father of Lies", in a master stroke of genius, succeeds in ensuring that humans are on the road to perdition by pulling off the most unlikely hat trick of all, namely shining as much light on truth as possible so that humans, who are already inclined to sin as a result of the fall of the first Man and the first Woman from grace, don't have any excuse at all when their time of reckoning comes - or so he leads the seminarian to believe! The Prince of Darkness attempts in that manner to counter the Deliverer who, in the moments before His death on the gibbet, pleaded with His Father saying: "Father, forgive them, for they know not what they do." Predictably the devil also brags that he is more knowledgeable in matters of theology than all the doctors of the church combined! And as he goes about shining light on the "Truth", the devil seems quite happy to use this opportunity to show the world that he does not just profess the Catholic faith, but he is actually more Catholic than the Catholics themselves!

Before long the student himself starts to see limitless possibilities of benefitting from the scheme, and dreams about riding on the cocktails of Diabolos and achieving fortune and fame by converting the "winning" thesis into a mega-selling blockbuster! While the devil is quite happy with that mutual arrangement and wants to see the student succeed, because disseminating "Truth" in whichever way now serves his purposes very well from one angle, from a different angle, because as the Father of Lies he is being coerced to act against his nature and sees it as punishment, all this now puts the student's eternal salvation in the greatest peril because of his central role in it.

This prodigious work dramatizes the battle between the forces of Good and the forces of Evil in a singularly effective manner, and would make for a really hilarious flick!

If **Humans, The Untold Story of Adam and Eve and their Descendants**, ever does get to hit the "Big Screen", the movie goers will actually accompany the seminarian in the final scene as he crosses the gulf that separates the living from the dead and, unrepentant, prepares to meet "His Mystic Majesty" face to face for his final reckoning only to find himself accosted by a totally enraged and menacing Satan who is at the head of a column of crazed demons. They are there to take him to his dungeon in the bottom of hell; and it happens in the moments before the student's "resurrection"!

"**Humans**" is a treatise on the knowledge of good and evil; and it damns and convicts sinful and sinning humans one and all without any distinction.

This is the untold story of Adam and Eve and their descendants. Prepare to take off on a cruise into realms of spirituality quite beyond anything you had ever dreamed of; and be a witness to:

The Epic Battle Between the Forces of Good and the Forces of Evil

Watch the showdown as the devil and the Deliverer battle for human souls!

As you delve into "Humans", it will start to dawn on you slowly but surely that for a long time you had been wishing, albeit subconsciously, that someone would write a book exactly like this one. Your wish that someone would succeed in tricking Satan, that evilest of evil creatures, to spill all his dirty secrets, has come true at long last. Relax, sit back now, and enjoy Volume Two of "Humans"!

Disclaimer:

This book is a work of fiction. The characters, names, businesses, organizations, places, events, incidents, dialogue and plot are the product of the author's imagination or are fictitiously used. Any resemblance to actual persons living or dead, names, events, or locales is entirely coincidental.

Acknowledgements:

To my daughter Lorna for her imaginative illustration of the Prince of Darkness; and to my family, for being a great inspiration, and for their support; and to the many individuals who genuinely could not wait to see "Humans" in print.

TABLE OF CONTENTS
PARTB 5: MJOMBA AND THE EVIL GHOST

HUMANS

THE UNTOLD STORY OF ADAM AND EVE AND THEIR DESCENDANTS

VOLUME TWO

MJOMBA AND THE EVIL GHOST

3RD REVISED EDITION

PART 5: MJOMBA AND THE EVIL GHOST

The devil's desire to have his due...

Mjomba wrote that, after being permitted to tempt humans, the devil found himself compelled to own up to the truth, and to reveal exactly how he himself forfeited eternal life. And then Mjomba did something very extraordinary. To illustrate how the tempter sometimes griped over his fall from grace in the hearing of the very people he was wont to prey on, Mjomba had the Evil One lament in what was a virtual confession:

"I can tell you for a fact that I missed my crown, not by a hair's breadth, but by some trillion light miles; because, when preparing for the Church Triumphant Entrance Test, I aimed at satisfying a completely fanciful dream of being something I knew quite well I could not be - a *prime mover* - when I should simply have aimed at self-actualization. And I blinded myself to my folly by pretending that I could not quite account for the way I had come into existence. What led me to act so stupidly was my desire to impress the companies of angels as well as the legions of Cherubim and the bands of Seraphims that I was boss of myself and owed no one, including the Prime Mover, anything.

"You ought to know that the downfall of your own great-uncle and great-aunt - I mean Adam and Eve - can be traced to the same weakness: a desire to impress posterity that they too were prime movers. Believe me when I tell you that it is all about making and giving impressions - false impressions. Trying to be what you are not. That archangel, Michael, who is *my* archenemy, and those other creatures in Elysium - Oh, I detest them all so! They would be under me if I had not elected to chase a flight of fancy that was completely detached from reality!"

But the confession would not preclude Satan from aiming what Mjomba described as Lucifer's traditional "parting shots" at those he had successfully preyed upon.

According to Mjomba, the Evil One usually commenced by mocking the transgressor using language designed to drive the poor soul to despair. The effect was also usually devastating because the message being communicated was injected directly into the mind of the recipient.

The substance of the communication supposedly was similar to the following: "Ha! Ha! You thought you were getting all the satisfaction you wanted and were enjoying yourself, eh! And you also thought that you were unique and that you accordingly could impress the world by your showing! As far as satisfaction and enjoyment are concerned - terms that might be in the lexicon of humans but are no longer in my own vocabulary - I can tell you that you actually were satisfying only your fantasy, and the enjoyment you thought you were experiencing was also fanciful with nothing to it really. If any of those things were real, you would still be happy, wouldn't you!

"And as for making an impression, to the extent that you share the same bloody human nature with the trillions upon trillions of human souls in existence, you are not unique at all! And if you couldn't see that, where on earth did you get the idea that you could impress anyone, let alone the world - or me, you knucklehead!"

The devil's language, according to Mjomba, was a lot more ribald and obscene than that - not to mention depressing. The ultimate objective of the "parting shots" was to prepare the individual in question for the *coup de grâce* which the devil planned with great care and administered with great finesse, and the archenemy knew better than to make his objective too obvious while moving to implement it. If successful, his strategy, which was based on lies on the one hand and intimidation on the other, invariably saw the Evil One installed as the official mentor of the individual in question.

According to Mjomba, after practically terrifying his quarry into submission with suggestions that the transgressor was beyond redemption, the Ruler of the Underworld then moved cautiously to regain the confidence of the individual in question with words such as: "And now look! I like you, and I don't want to see you in worse trouble than you are in already. So, do yourself a favor by staying away from those hypocritical Church going folks of yours whom you call kin."

Even though Satan had lost the opportunity of being one of the most favored luminaries in the Church Triumphant through stupidity, his bag of tricks still included some astonishingly rock solid syllogisms that, by definition, favored the opposition. Mjomba speculated that the wicked one was probably compelled to argue the way he sometimes did - against his own position - as a punishment.

In any event, it did not surprise Mjomba when Beelzebub, elaborating on his statement about the transgressor's hypocritical kin, picked up where he had stopped and continued.

"They were hypocritical because, if you took a poll, you would find that they would want you stoned with the specific objective of dispatching you to hell before you got a chance to repent and/or become rehabilitated. And you see, hypocrites believe that they deserve forgiveness as and when they succeeded in owning up to the evil things they did out of public view - something that they infrequently did; and they believe that others, particularly those who were not their pals, did not deserve any. Their jealousy, I can tell you, is such that they often prefer to be damned and be in my company rather than meet with other fellow transgressors near a confessional. Many of them, for that matter, could not contemplate rubbing shoulders with those who were the object of their opprobrium in the New Jerusalem.

"Indeed, frequently hypocrisy also masks feelings of resentment, fueled by the anticipation that those who now openly flouted the divine commandments and were not their cronies might eventually repent and regain favor with the Prime Mover. Then, there was also the prospect that the hypocrite's own dirty dealings might one day become exposed.

"You see, the whole attitude of hypocrites flies in the face of the fact that humans are inclined to sin; and that they too, like some of us in the pure spirit realm, have been caught transgressing; that the promise of the Deliverer was made to the fallen Adam and Eve who had incurred the divine wrath by eating of the forbidden fruit, the fact that they were constituted in an original state of holiness and justice notwithstanding (CCC 375, 376 398), and that they, along with their descendants, were now saddled with the stain of that original sin and the evil inclination! Hypocrites certainly do not hearken to John the Baptist's bidding that humans deny themselves, prepare the way of the Lord and make his paths straight, particularly now that the Deliverer has arrived.

"Oh! How I hate him - that John the Baptist. You see, every time some human somewhere takes a step, however fledgling, to do His bidding, it undercuts my rule over the Underworld. That John succeeded in turning my world down side up by demonstrating that the blood of martyrs was the seed of conversion!

"Frankly, I am almost at my wit's end now because, even when Agrippa's woman at my urging stopped him in her own bizarre manner, that only raised

5

his profile in the eyes of the Deliverer! And then, just when I thought I had the Deliverer Himself nicely cornered and put away permanently, there He was pulling off the mightiest victory imaginable by turning hell itself upside down and restoring to Adam and Eve and all those people I thought I had neutralized their freedom.

"Oh, how I hate them! This is because they represent Good and I represent evil, which has now been exposed as a nonentity - an absence of Good. That is also what hypocrites represent.

"And so, you can understand why, if your Deliverer were around and were to depict the kind of dirt in which they themselves (the hypocrites) were mired, they would make haste to vanish from the scene when they really should be prostrating themselves before Him and begging for His mercy!

"This is extraordinary. I do not get caught speaking the truth very often! Count yourself lucky for hearing it from the mouth of the Evil One himself!"

Mjomba wrote that the devil spat out those last words especially just like a viper spits venom. It was clear that he was speaking like that under duress and hated the fact that what he was saying was true. And it was apparent that, while at it, he was enjoined from using dirty words or swearing.

As might be expected, that outward display of compunction did not usually deter the prince of darkness from pursuing his original goal of trying to frustrate the divine work of redemption. And he was usually much more menacing and deadly after being chastened in that fashion by the Prime Mover. According to Mjomba, Beelzebub still retained enough wits about him in all such instances to conceal his true motives behind a demeanor that was so courteous and a tongue that was so smooth, he would probably be mistaken for a saint and would be canonized over and over if he had been able to take on the shape of a human!

Mjomba thus had the devil turn his reluctant dismissal of hypocrites to his full advantage by throwing his arm around his quarry at that juncture and speaking as follows: "Look, you are very different from those hypocrites. And now, my good fellow; promise me you won't go near them churches - especially those churches where sanctuary lamps are not allowed to go out! That is the height of hypocrisy, you see. If you do any of these things, you see I will not be in a position to help you! Otherwise you can count on my word. Buddy, a promise is a promise, you see!"

Mjomba had the Prince of Darkness confess that some who were his best friends at one point in time often ended up as his worst enemies at a later date.

"Paul, the so-called Apostle to the Gentiles, who had at one point been my instrument for murdering and getting rid of many of those first Christians, changed course and suddenly declared war on me!" Mjomba had the devil rant. "And even Judas Iscariot, who had started off cavorting with me as if I was his Maker and whom I had spent so much of my time grooming with a view to getting him on the witness stand and testifying before Pilate himself against the Deliverer, turned against me at the last moment and declared to the whole world that he had betrayed an innocent man!"

According to Mjomba, it really pained the devil to think that even Judas Iscariot himself succeeded in escaping his tentacles, even though the "noose around his neck had seemed tight", and had even proved, in the process, that everything was possible with God to the dismay of Satan and, admittedly, the dismay of hypocrites who wanted to see only themselves saved!

If you asked Mjomba whether Judas - after he had

betrayed the Deliverer with a kiss, and then compounded that treacherous act of betrayal by taking his own life - was in hell or in heaven, or was perhaps still languishing in Purgatory, his response would have been that all sinners were equally betrayers, and it was the height of hypocrisy for anyone who was himself or herself in need of the mercies of the Prime Mover to think that one of their number was less deserving of His mercy. Mjomba would have gone as far as suggesting that trying to gainsay the infinite mercies of the Prime Mover (infinite because of the nature of sin) might even be indicative of a lack of faith.

Besides, it was not as though Judas Iscariot had foisted himself on the Deliverer, getting himself chosen as one of the twelve thereby. The historical record was clear. "And it came to pass in those days, that he went out into a mountain to pray, and he passed the whole night in the prayer of God. And when day was come, he called unto him his disciples; and he chose twelve of them (whom also he named apostles)." (Luke 6:12-13). And also: "You have not chosen me: but I have chosen you; and have appointed you, that you should go, and should bring forth fruit; and your fruit should remain: that whatsoever you shall ask of the Father in my name, he may give it you." (John 15:16). But then the Deliverer had also told them: "I AM the true vine; and my Father is the husbandman. Every branch in me, that beareth not fruit, he will take away: and every one that beareth fruit, he will purge it, that it may bring forth more fruit. Now you are clean by reason of the word, which I have spoken to you. Abide in me, and I in you. As the branch cannot bear fruit of itself, unless it abide in the vine, so neither can you, unless you abide in me. I am the vine; you the branches: he that abideth in me, and I in him, the same beareth much fruit: for without me you can do nothing." (John15:

1-5). And also: "Judge not, and you shall not be judged. Condemn not, and you shall not be condemned. Forgive, and you shall be forgiven." (Luke 6:37). And, finally, the historical record included this: "Then, Judas, who betrayed him, seeing that he was condemned, repenting himself, brought back the thirty pieces of silver to the chief priests and ancients."

With the exception of the relatively few heroic souls who, like the remaining eleven apostles, stuck with the Son of Man despite their many foibles, from the time they were received in the *Sancta Ecclesia* and confirmed, the great bulk of Christians ended up exactly like Judas Iscariot, the proverbial betrayer who had been upset that Mary Magdalene, the sister of Lazarus of Bethany, had (according to John 12:3) taken a pound of ointment of right spikenard, of great price, and anointed the feet of Jesus, and had wiped his feet with her hair so that the house was filled with the odour of the ointment – Christians only in name and equally betrayers no doubt! Christian Mjomba believed that he, certainly, was the wrong person to take up stones and start throwing them at Judas Iscariot, if only because, at the time he betrayed his master, that Judean had been a seminarist, albeit one under the tutelage of the Son of Man, for the space of a mere three years compared to the length of time he himself had been in seminary!

Mjomba was actually inclined to the view that it was more likely in real life for a repentant individual who momentarily forgets that others like David have also been there (Psalm 40:11-12) to take his/her own life because of an overwhelming sense of compunction upon realizing the gravity of sins committed than for an unrepentant sinner to take his/her own life in the wake of committing a despicable act he/she was prepared to repeat if accorded the opportunity. The seminarian noted that the question

9

of the transgressor despairing that he/she could be forgiven for grievous sins committed did not even arise. That was because, as in the case of the Sodomites who were accused (among other things) of behaving unethically by shunning outsiders and withholding bread from the poor, and even punishing severely those who showed mercy or invited paupers into their home like Lot (Ezek. 16:49 and Job 30:25), their consciences (as St. Paul pointed out in 1 Timothy 4:2) are "seared" or effectively dead!

But Mjomba also recognized that individuals took their own lives for a variety of other reasons too, and these included the inability to withstand torture, the readiness to die for one's country in battle, and also the fear of public humiliation when faced with accusations that may even be baseless. Mjomba's position was that, however many people linked suicides to despair, that link remained tenuous and in the great majority of cases unproven.

During his exchange with the professors and his fellow students, Mjomba also made reference to those who sought to enrich themselves at the expense of public morality and/or engaged in activities that led others into sin. Mjomba contended that it was because humans who engaged in those sorts of things were such willing proxies for the Tempter that the Deliverer had warned that they would end up at the bottom of hell their passage there accelerated by what He described figuratively as millstones strung about their necks. (Luke 17:2) Also, according to Mjomba, a most unfortunate aspect of transgressions of that sort was the fact that, instead of directing gratitude for gifts possessed to their Prime Mover, the wayward humans directed it to the Adversary just as he was planting a wedge between them and the Prime Mover.

The problem of humans, according to Mjomba, was that they took forever to decide if they came into the world by pure accident and were therefore not answerable to any one for their actions, or if they came into the world by design and had to submit an accounting of the way they employed their God-given talents. Since they had only a limited lease of life - far more limited than most species of trees and certainly rocks - the longer they took to decide, the less time they gave themselves to prepare for the CTET (Mjomba's acronym for the Church Triumphant Entrance Test).

Humans had only so much time in which to prepare for and pass the CTET. According to Mjomba, this was a high stakes pass/fail examination, performance on which determined if lives led by humans had been simply squandered or worthwhile in accord with their human nature which consisted of an incorruptible soul and a corruptible body. Now, the sojourn of a human on earth was very short; the average life span of humans shorter in fact shorter than that of some of the beasts that roamed the earth, trees and rocks. But because generations of humans overlapped, members of a generation, particularly those belonging to the youngest generation, had this tendency to imagine that while the older generations would be dying off in time alright, it was not so their own generation. The last thing on the minds of members of the Gen Alpha (born 2013 - 2025) was that the time was coming for them to say fare thee well to members of the iGen or Gen Z (1995 – 2012), Generation Y or Gen Next or the so-called Millennials (1980 – 1994), the Xennials (1975 – 1985), Generation X or Baby Bust (1965 – 1979), , the Baby Boomer Generation (1946 – 1964), the Silent Generation (1925 – 1945), the Greatest Generation (1910 – 1924), the Interbellum Generation (1901 – 1913), and the Generation of 1914 or the so-

11

called Lost Generation (1890 – 1915). Mjomba wrote that it was always the same story with members of these other generations; and he went on to claim that some by-products of the impious activities engaged in by humans not only outlived them but went on to become a distraction to humans of later generations!

And even as their twilight years are closing in and they have seen members of the older generations as well as members of their own generation depart one by one to join the ancestors, humans have this strange tendency to imagine that, because they have survived wars and other disasters, often emerging miraculously from the devastation of floods, lightning strikes, volcanic eruptions, earthquakes, tsunamis, landslides, mudslides, wildfires, tornados, pandemics and so on and so forth in one piece, or dodging death from car crashes, train crashes, plane crashes, shipwrecks, etc. by a whisker, they must be invincible – as if they now were exempt from the curse of death that became the lot of humans after Adam and Eve filched fruit from the tree of the knowledge of good and evil! (Genesis 2-3)

According to Mjomba's thesis, humans had many gifts and talents; and there was probably none that they jealously - and even zealously - guarded more than they did the gift of freedom of choice. Since humans were also able to differentiate what was right from what was wrong, you would think that the one thing humans would be really good at would be to choose and do what was morally right and to shirk what was morally wrong. But you would be well advised not to bet your money on it, Mjomba also advised.

Committing a vice consisted in making a choice a human knew to be a wrong one in that it could only lead to perdition and not to righteousness. And, to make things worse, humans, rather than being inclined to righteousness, had actually been inclined to sin since the fall from grace of the first Man and the first Woman. That was also precisely when the clamor for the right to choose this and the right to choose that started. According to Mjomba, there was an obvious connection there - a connection between the fall of Adam and Eve and the clamor for the right to choose; and he believed that the one engendered the other.

After misusing their right to choose, and after indulging in activity that was offensive to the Prime Mover to such a degree that He found Himself with no choice but to throw them out of the *paradisum voluptatis* or paradise of pleasure (Genesis 2:8), humans evidently did not find it any easier after that to start reigning in that which was at the root of their downfall. And, in what Mjomba referred to a "cycle of failures", that in turn blinded humans to the fact that it was a grave matter to continue doing things that offended the Prime Mover - just as it had been a grave matter for the first Man and the first Woman to flout His specific directive not to eat of the fruit from the Tree of the Knowledge of Good and Evil at the time they did. The act of ejecting humans from the Garden of Eden and all that this action entailed was, Mjomba added, a very drastic measure by any standard, and was in fact analogous to the action the Prime Mover had taken against the disgruntled angels when they too spurned His graces and ended up sinning against Him!

Having decided that they would not preoccupy themselves with seeking the kingdom of heaven and letting everything else be added as promised, these humans, who were created in the image and likeness of the Prime Mover and Author of Life, were attempting to play God and were out to try and grab at the "forbidden" fruit in the hope of converting it to their own purposes in a blatant attempt to usurp the power and authority of their

13

Creator.

It was, ironically, still in the same realm of the eternal that they were wasting their time chasing mirages with their focus on what was transient and ephemeral. It was the fruit from the Tree of Knowledge of Good and Evil that they still hankered after, in an effort to be like the Prime Mover Himself in every way. Mjomba explained that it was in the divine realm that, having nothing of real substance to do, humans still sought to do "it". They still dreamed of converting their satisfaction on a temporal plane into eternal happiness!

Going against the grain...

It was, perhaps, not entirely accidental, Mjomba argued, that it was a lifestyle of poverty and chastity involving the voluntary abdication of all freedoms that was most praiseworthy in the eyes of the Prime Mover. He also thought that it was damning for humans to make so much of their right to choose when it was clear that they also knew perfectly well what they were up to when they engaged in behavior that was unbecoming of them and for which there was punishment in store.

Mjomba claimed that self-indulgence was the ultimate goal of those who argued passionately for the right to choose, and he was quite confident that he could prove his point. But, as he was casting about in search of the appropriate words to describe the pitfalls of that "deleterious preoccupation" as he called it, something really weird happened. Mjomba, who was occupying an isolated desk in the Seminary library, first heard what sounded like a purring sound that came from nowhere in particular; and before he could look, it was clear that something had taken control of his entire frame, which now shook momentarily. It was quite clear to him that his

14

earlier decision to engage the Evil One and use him in producing his thesis had come back to haunt him.

It was as though the "Lord of the Flies" (*Ba'al Zəbûb* or Beelzebub) had been waiting for the seminarian to acknowledge that self-indulgence was indeed an injurious preoccupation before making his move. Mjomba shuddered at the thought that his faculties of the intellect and will were now partially under the control of the Evil One. But it was now too late. He had been determined to turn in a winning thesis by any means, even if that meant employing the Evil One as his mouthpiece. And it was now quite clear that Satan, for reasons best known to himself, was ready to deliver on the deal. But at what price, Mjomba asked admittedly a little late!

"I can tell you that I know something about 'self-indulgence'. And look - you humans cannot imagine what it means in terms of self-indulgence when a pure spirit makes a choice that is contrary to what it knows is right! You, Mjomba, would have to be a pure spirit to understand the extent to which a pure spirit indulges itself when it exercises its right to choose and that choice happens to be contrary to the divine will! This is exactly where I can come in handy. This is the stuff I am good at!"

Mjomba did not have to guess who the interlocutor was at that point. Except that the devil seemed to hesitate as he awaited Mjomba's consent to proceed. The consent came in the form of an imperceptible but nonetheless unmistakable nod from the seminarian.

"I am the devil, and I can tell you that self-indulgence is good for me - not for the other side", Mjomba heard the Prince of Darkness rumble in his own defense, and then continue:

"Self-indulgence, which by the way does not occur in the abstract, radically shifts the focus of attention of the

15

individual from the source of all goodness, which is unchanging and permanent, and has the power to enrich, to something that is transitory."

Talk about being verbose! Mjomba thought that Old Scratch fit the bill perfectly; and he (Mjomba) was glad that, while a minimum number of pages - a hundred pages to be exact - had been specified for the theological theses, no maximum limit had been set in accordance with the tradition at St. Augustine's Seminary.

He was busy scribbling away as the Evil One continued: "Such self-centered indulgence, therefore, plays right into my hands. The tactic I employ is to entice humanoids away from constructive activities and get them mired in this deleterious preoccupation.

"And that was precisely the approach I took when I set out to drive a wedge between Adam and Eve and the Prime Mover. These humans knew perfectly well that fruit from the tree of the knowledge of good and evil was out of bounds. But I calculated that, even though the father and mother of humankind were unsullied and innocent, if confronted with any choice, they either were going to stay in line and do the bidding of their Maker without giving their own ego a thought, or they were going to think that giving themselves a little treat to fruit - any fruit - in the Garden of Eden where they spent a lot of their time trimming branches of all manner of fruit trees on whose succulent produce they subsisted would be within their rights and wouldn't hurt at all.

"They, of course, knew full well that hankering after fruit from the Tree of the Knowledge of Good and Evil, located in the middle of the Paradise of Pleasure, was offensive to the Prime Mover, even though He *was* invisible. And they knew that if they did, it would no longer be the Prime Mover who would shield them from evil, but the choices they themselves made from there on -

16

choices that either resounded to the Prime Mover's greater honor and glory or to their own incipient egos. The secret I kept from them was that after that act of disobedience, making choices that resounded to the Prime Mover's greater honor and glory by dint of their own will power, without the intervening help of divine grace, wouldn't be feasible! All I needed to do to get Adam and Eve on a *permanent* collision course with the Prime Mover was to get them to think: 'But, what the heck - they surely didn't need a Prime Mover to tell them if something was good for *them* or not. They had been growing smart by the day; and they had already accumulated useful knowledge about so many things - like shielding under trees to stay dry and comfortable when the skies opened up and it started drizzling (provided the rain wasn't accompanied by any thunder clap) - it would not have made any sense to bury their heads in the sand and stop 'learning' if they were going to harness everything in Creation the way the Prime Mover actually wanted them to. They were, therefore, already well on the way to knowing what constituted 'good' and what constituted 'a nuisance' or 'evil'!'

"They had also discovered and sampled fruit from most of the trees in the Garden of Eden, and they already knew that some trees produced fruit that could kill you outright. They had discovered, for instance, that apple seeds also contained cyanide that could kill you if you took a large enough dose. And, well, what if the forbidden fruit from the tree of the knowledge of good and evil contained the antidote for the dangerous toxins and venom they might accidentally ingest while sampling fruits of the wild? It was surely good for them (Adam and Eve) to investigate and find out for themselves instead of sitting back and relying on Providence!

"And now, with the human inclination to sin that has

17

been in place since the fall of Adam and Eve already blocking any tendency on the part of humans to do good, that further preoccupation with the self not only reinforces the inclination to do things that are offensive to the Prime Mover, but actually fuels the penchant for mischievous conduct or sin, and completely blinds humans to the existence of the one and the only Supreme Good. It is a tough spot for humans to be in because, when they elect to indulge themselves, they effectively turn their backs on the Prime Mover on Whom they still depend for their every breath.

"You may not know it" the devil pressed on; "But I brought off a real coup when I derailed that Adam and Eve; because, their posterity, inclined to sin and stupefied by concupiscence, find it really hard, if not impossible, on their own to stagger back onto the rails they can't even see. I really shouldn't tell you this because it will hurt my cause; but the best way to put it is to say that self-indulgence is incompatible with communion with Him who is Perfect Goodness! (John 6: 26-58)

"Understand that when you are inclined to do one thing, that inclination acts as a very strong disincentive to do something else, and even more so it's opposite. And that is in addition to the inertia that would already be at play in normal circumstances even in the absence of the inclination to act in some particular way, in this case to keep all one's attention focused on the Supreme Good. But that is not all. In a situation where everybody is not only disinclined to truth, love, justice and fairness, etc. - that is what 'being inclined to sin' entails - you can bet that sinning in whichever way becomes not just a pastime but big time business.

"In that kind of situation, everyone will essentially be plotting to undercut everyone else in any way, and will also be jostling for positions of advantage in a contest in which, by definition, no holds are barred! The disincentive for some jerk who is 'insane' enough to take time out to listen to his or her conscience and who is, additionally, bold enough to try and do the 'right thing' is as great as you can possibly imagine. And if I were not the Prince of Darkness - say your guardian angel - and wished to offer you advice, I would simply tell you 'Go, say a prayer'!

"But do not think that you then are entirely off the hook and that you are safe from me even if you do follow that advice - although that, mark you, is just about all someone in that sort of situation can do? This is because I have not told you how I counter acts of piety...

"It is said that charity covers a multitude of sins because of the immense good that flows from it. Where there is inclination to sin and a disinclination or aversion to positive things, charity, which (as St. Paul wrote in 1 Corinthians 13:4) is neither exploitive nor selfish, works to reinforce the willingness of the spirit of the beneficiary, and thus fills the role of grace. In practical terms, charity helps to reduce roadblocks that stop individuals who wish to go against their inclination to sin from doing so. An act of charity, by making the individual dispensing it look more and more like Him who is Himself not only Perfect Love but also the Judge, has to work in his or her favor when his or her own day of reckoning arrives.

"You have no doubt heard the slogan 'Make Love, Not War'! And you have it right - the great bulk of people frown on the anti-war advocates who find the courage to hoist banners proclaiming: 'Make Love, Not War'! They regard them as jerks who have nothing to do. But the reality is that it isn't very long ago when that adage was in fashion, and it explained the intermarriages between European dynasties to the point where almost all of Europe's royal families are related, leading some unscrupulous geneticists to suggest that many of the royals unwittingly ended up suffering from the deleterious effects of consanguineous marriages and 'inbreeding', even as they sought to assert their claim to 'royal descent' so they wouldn't be lumped together with 'commoners' and 'plebs'.

"The hard work of my folks here in the Pit has since changed all that; so that today, led by the military industrial complexes and the spy agencies, stupid humans are ever jostling, not just over control of the earth's resources, but over who should own planets, including the moon and the sun, and the rights to harness solar energy! Nations of the world try to outdo each other with regard to the expenditures for preparations for imaginary wars. You would think that earthlings, as they stockpile war materiel of every conceivable type including spy satellites, intercontinental ballistic missiles, bunker busting nuclear bombs, roadside bombs - you name it - are preparing to fight aliens who might be hovering out there in outer space!

"Now, this is all crazy. But you shouldn't think for a moment that it has come about by accident - not unless you yourself are crazy! We here in the underworld have worked long and hard to bring this about - to get humans, who are, or course, driven by greed for material possessions like never before, to live in fear of one another, and to imagine that 'the other guy' is just waiting for the opportunity to come and steal from them and get rid of them in the process if possible. We have also convinced them that it is prudent to always be planning to rob or steal from 'the other guy' and to kill him/her if possible out of the fear that 'that other guy' is planning to rob and steal from them, and to ensure greater security for themselves thereby.

"And as those humans who are regarded as an

immediate threat are targeted for elimination from the face of the earth, they too naturally become uncompromising in their dealings with any allies of their perceived enemies. And it is great to sit back and enjoy the sight of humans going after one another with rockets launched from UAVs (unmanned aerial vehicles), or with IED's (improvised explosive devices) as the roadside bombs are called, often not because they (the other humans) are a threat, but because one side calculates that control of the place is necessary to undermine the influence of some other emerging power. And we of course aren't far removed when our minions frame the justifications for the losses in 'blood and treasure' in terms of either geopolitics, fighting terrorists, or just helping to feed a starving population, which always turn out to be lies anyway. The real reasons, namely providing military industrial complexes the opportunity to make a buck and giving the spy agencies a chance to become even more entrenched as the real 'deciders' in these matters, are concealed from the citizenry for obvious reasons - the same citizenry who would of course cry foul if they learnt that the lives of their sons and daughters were being sacrificed to perpetuate the rule over Earth of the 'Father of Death'!

"And so - you see - I hate to see humans being nice to each other for a reason. Being nice to each other is the most effective way of robbing me of souls. You see - even though the Immaculate Heart of Mary will ultimately triumph (as the mother of the Deliverer revealed to Lucy and her friends at Fatima), in the meantime the good must be martyred, and various nations must be annihilated. And, while I can, I must savor my rule over Earth as the Prince of Darkness.

"And talking about robbing, you should know that I operate from a very big disadvantage. This is even though this is a world where everyone is inclined to what is diabolical and disinclined to honesty and morality. I have practically succeeded in ensuring that there is no justice in the world - and this particularly so in those nations that brag about the equality of their citizens. The percentage of a country's incarcerated population will always betray this. In some of these places, influence, money, politics and things of that nature play important roles when it comes to dispensing justice. Judges, at my instigation, will invariably interpret 'juvenile' to mean only a certain type of juvenile, for example; and it pleases me so much when I see them unashamedly trying offenders who are juveniles as adults all the same.

"Also, verdicts from the 'benches' in some of these countries invariably end up reflecting the political persuasion of those who sit on them - something that arguably is *not* synonymous with justice. Which means that, if those justices had been entrusted with deciding who went to heaven and who went to hell, all their political foes would be doomed from the beginning, while their political allies would all be assured of salvation regardless of the lives they led. Which again is not surprising, because they obviously play not by the rules of jurisprudence but by the rules of politics which, as everyone knows, is a dirty game.

"If only the Prime Mover had delegated the power to send souls to hell along with the authority which enables humans to pass judgement on others. Like acts of charity, rendering justice isn't one of those things that humans, inclined to vice since Adam and Eve rebelled against Him who is the embodiment of all that is good and noble, are naturally inclined to do.

"You see, getting love and justice in this world is, *fortunately for me* (Diabolos) not the most important thing for humans. Focusing on the eternal is really all that

22

should matter, whether they get love and justice in this world or they don't. And when they do that and pay no heed to what is transient, they end up safe and sound at the end of time. In that scenario, obviously any success I might have in making this world a dreadful place to live in by making fairness and love rare commodities in the interim period ends up working against me and in favor of those humans who persevere by assuring them even larger crowns in the next world. (John 3:16; John 5:28-29; John 11:25; John 14:1-3; Matthew 10:28; 1 Thessalonians 4:13-18 and Revelation 20:11-15). It is a terrible frustration that I know I fully deserve for being the Prince of Darkness.

"But, a word from the Prince of Darkness on prayer. You shouldn't think I know nothing about these things, because I used to be Lucifer, the chief archangel, you know! And I am a Catholic too, albeit a very bad one. As for being versed in theology, I can tell you that I anticipate the Church's dogmas long before they are promulgated by the Pontiff of Rome! That is why you yourselves, who are even now squandering your blessings as believers, should at least give credit to non-believers who still get by on the strength of their God-given 'original virtue'.

"But you are, of course, always well advised not to enter into dialogue with the Tempter for obvious reasons. The Antichrist, when he comes, will do precisely that; and that is why he will be so effective. And you be warned yourself, now. You are safe for now anyway, because it is someone else's choice that you are listening to me, not your own choice.

The power of prayer...

"Any way, continuing our discourse on prayer, there is no doubt that prayer is the starting point for

23

humans in that sorry state of affairs - you can at least credit me with creating havoc on a magnitude that boggles the mind some, and you bet I'm always pretty good at anything I do. And what I say is not always lies, mark you, because I am also subject to limitations. There are certain things I have to do, however reluctantly, when ordered. Even though a rebel to the hilt, I would be no more if the Prime Mover forgot about me for just one moment. That should explain why I, even I, have on occasion confessed to the world openly that the Deliverer is the son of the Most High!

"To repeat: there is no doubt that prayer is the starting point if a human wants to steer clear of the morass. But prayer in what language - I mean under the banner of what church or religion? There are almost as many religions these days as there are spoken dialects!

"I have never been able to manufacture falsehoods fast enough. They get snapped up just like that by some who are desperately seeking the truth - even a semblance of it; but my falsehoods also get snapped up by others who use them to exploit those who are gullible. Your Deliverer put it succinctly: there are so many blind people following others whose vision is often so much worse than their own! And He was right on when, referring to the scribes and Pharisees and no doubt also those who would follow in their footsteps, He said: 'Woe unto you, scribes and Pharisees, hypocrites! for ye are like unto whited sepulchres, which indeed appear beautiful outward, but are within full of dead men's bones, and of all uncleanness. Even so ye also outwardly appear righteous unto men, but within ye are full of hypocrisy and iniquity.'

"I have a lot of fun just watching. But I still urge humans who seek deliverance in those conditions to say

24

a prayer all the same - any prayer and in any tongue or dialect.

"Going against one's inclination and doing anything that goes counter to what is done by society at large is a very peculiar thing to do. Besides, attempting to do so is fraught with all sorts of risks. After all no one wants to go off on a limb and actually rebuff the accepted logic that when in Rome, do as Rome does. An individual, heading off into the unknown knowing that no support or backing will be forthcoming would normally be discouraged from starting off on that course at the very outset, because only insane people headed off into the unknown without any blessings from any quarter.

"And unless someone was entirely insane, the ensuing fear of failure from going against the current would by itself be enough to stop any diehard from proceeding any further. And, in any event, society's self-appointed guardians of sanity would be standing by ready to step in and put an end to what they would have every reason to regard as wrong-headedness or insanity! But above all, I cannot overemphasize how discouraging it is for a human who is sidelined and also deprived of any moral or material support to succeed in any endeavor.

Lucky Humans...

"You folks may not know it, but you are lucky that, after I succeeded in derailing Adam and Eve, the Prime Mover did not wait to promise you the Deliverer. Suppose that had not happened. The immediate descendants of Adam and Eve, inclined to sin by virtue of the original sin, would all have promptly staged their own rebellions which would in turn have generated a new series of original sins. And, being original sins, they would have escalated the proclivity of men to sin, and things would become uglier

25

and uglier for the human race as succeeding generations contributed to the morass in an exponential way.

"The lives of humans, abandoned and at one and the same time left completely to their own devices, would give a new meaning to the word 'curse', with humans ending up as their own worst enemies. And, while the only possible way out of the quagmire and the human miseries would again have been prayer, any supplications and entreaties for mercy, however plaintive or shrill, would have been ineffectual, absent the promise of the Deliverer, and would have gone unanswered forever.

"And so, in retrospect, you folks can take comfort in the fact that you were promised the Deliverer in a timely fashion. And you can take it that if a human says an *Ave Maria* or a *Pater Noster* or, for that matter, makes any plea for deliverance from his or her adversities that are overwhelming by any account, that entreaty or prayer not only is the starting point on the road to deliverance, but clearly cannot go unanswered by virtue of the promise made to Adam and Eve. I dare say you'd probably be delivered even if you'd be caught addressing your pleas to me - I mean mistakenly!

"Put it this way: on their own, individuals trying to get themselves out of their predicament soon get discouraged, even though they know that what they are trying to do is the right thing. And that is if they succeed in overcoming the initial hurdle, namely getting past me and my troops! And it is only when such individuals throw up their hands and sigh that imploring sigh, however incongruous, or say that beseeching prayer, however deficient, that they begin to notch up any success as they stumble along on the narrow path - narrow because, with not too many people travelling along it, it is unbeaten, rough shod, and unwelcoming.

"And even when they do notch up some success, any such 'success' will not only pale when compared with the obstacles confronting them, but - perhaps even worse - will also tend to attract fresh obstacles as these individuals try to forge ahead on that confining, little travelled path. Indeed, in the so-called 'eyes of the world', achievements in this arena in fact meet all the requisites for what is called 'unqualified failure'!

"But, at that point, some usually find themselves preferring to imagine, conveniently, that the Deliverer's sacrifice was enough, and that they themselves do not have to continue trudging along clumsily under the burdensome weight of their own crosses, giving credence to the postulate that salvation is by faith alone! And they also find themselves declaring that 'good works', which is just another way of saying that humans have to keep the commandments, are entirely redundant, with no role in the divine scheme of redemption.

"Such a position also makes all the foregoing talk about the human inclination to sin and the problems associated with such a predicament also redundant. It also makes salvation dependent, not on trying to lead lives that are righteous, but on chance - being born in the right place at the right time, for instance! Others go to the other extreme - they imagine that they are on the road to salvation because of what they are, not despite what they are. The hypocrites...!"

Homily on grace (and other topics)...

Christian Mjomba would have been the last person to try and tackle the subject of grace and its workings in a thesis. He was aware that really brilliant folks like Augustine, Bernard, and even Thomas of Aquin shied away from that subject. Mjomba thought it was a smart

27

move on his part to get Lucifer involved, and then turn around and use the "infernal liar" as his mouthpiece to expound on the obscure subject.

Mjomba knew that, if he hadn't done that, he would have been told that it was utterly presumptuous of him to even include grace as one of the topics covered by his thesis! Mjomba was well pleased with himself as he pressed on with his scheme and got down to the task of conjuring up words to put in the mouth of the Evil One. He was surprised that the words came to him spontaneously - almost as if he was receiving inspiration from some extraterrestrial being! But he could not be sure if the inspiration was coming from the Evil One or from some other source.

Mjomba wondered if someone who had no qualms about openly employing the devil as his mouthpiece could still receive inspiration from On High. Even though the scheme under which he intended using Beelzebub to pontificate on doctrinal matters was clearly a strange one, he did not really see anything wrong with it *per se*. And it was reassuring that what the devil was mouthing made a lot of sense.

Still, as time went by, Mjomba found some of the things to which the devil was giving expression extremely disconcerting. That would be especially true during his - or rather the devil's - discussion of the Cain doctrine, and the related topics of "death" and "death culture enthusiasm".

But, after agreeing to the deal under which he was going to use Satan as his mouthpiece, with Satan supposedly agreeing for his part to just play dumb and go along, Mjomba felt helpless, and could only listen with apprehension as the devil rumbled on and on. Once the process got under way, Mjomba for some reason found himself unable to stop and try to figure out if there might be anything that Beelzebub expected to get from the whole thing. Every time he tried to do so, something else came to his mind, causing him to shelve the exercise.

It was all very strange - and also very funny. But it definitely terrified Mjomba that, try as he might, he was unable to understand exactly how it all was happening. And then there were times when it even looked as if it was the Evil One who was using him (Mjomba), instead of the other way round. The seminarian found the situation so scary at times that he wished he hadn't gotten involved with the archfiend in the first place. But, for now, Mjomba listened as Satan rambled on.

"To wrap up my sermon, one of the most underrated discoveries was one the Deliverer Himself announced...discovery, revelation - it is all the same to me! And it would have revolutionized the social sciences, particularly Psychology and Sociology, if only humans had given it the importance it deserved. You may recall the Deliverer addressing the eleven, who had fallen sound asleep in the Garden of Gethsemane when they were supposed to be on the lookout for Judas and the Sanhedrin's secret police, and saying: 'The spirit is willing, but the flesh is weak'!

"I naturally have a great interest in this 'doctrine' - if you will - of willing spirit and weak flesh. You see, human frailty provides us in the Underworld a window of opportunity that we could never pass up. And you'd better take me at my word for it even if it looks like I am saying something nonsensical.

"How, otherwise, would two individuals start off as innocent, virtual angels, only to part ways with one of them becoming a little 'devil' before becoming immersed in a life of sin, while the other one stayed the course with no apparent difficulty and grew up a model of virtue! How come that you will see this sort of thing happen even within a family, with one kid heading off to become a pious monk and recluse, while the other one veered off in the opposite direction and became a pimp or even worse? How come that one twin will head off into one direction and on the road to perdition and damnation, while the other twin went off in the opposite direction as if drawn to their separate paths by magnates?

"I will tell you for the last time: it is the same old story of willing spirit and weak flesh! It is the story of one chap refusing to heed the clamor of his/her conscience with respect to the pitfalls of self-indulgence and allowing himself/herself - with a little help naturally from us here in the Underworld - to gradually become mired in that deleterious enterprise, while the other chap - obviously with help from On High - refuses to trust himself/herself in a matter of such critical importance to one's destiny and (by the same token) surrenders himself/herself to the Deliverer, enabling the Holy Ghost (who was promised by the Deliverer) to exercise permanent rule and sway over him/her, including control over the little day-to-day things in that individual's life.

"But it is, of course, not that simple. Just how come that one fellow decides to be true to him/herself and, recognizing that he/she is in a relationship with his/her Maker, resolves to do the ordinary things that are expected of one in the situation, and succeeds in keeping the relationship intact, while the other fellow, well-knowing that if a party to a pact with the Prime Mover is likely to renege and prove unfaithful or inconstant, or refuse to keep a promise, it is not going to be the Prime Mover but him/herself? How come that humans who are created with intelligence elect to stuff cotton wool in their ears to shut out the clamor of their consciences, and then devote their lives to chasing mirages in a vain attempt to play the Prime Mover?

30

Permission to exercise free will...

"Indeed, if the Prime Mover had not decided to permit humans - in the exercise of their free wills - to do things that went against their consciences, all their attempts to sin would come to naught. Humans would be frustrated even as they cast about, looking for ways to defy Him. It certainly would not have required very much effort - none in fact - on the part of a Prime Mover who is unchanging and has no need for anything to see to it that the more humans tried to subvert His divine will, the more they would be frustrated. And, by the same token, unaided by divine grace, humans were actually incapable of bringing off anything for which they could be commended.

"That was how dependent humans were on the Prime Mover. Indeed, they would be capable of nothing - not even of leading lives that were unworthy of their status as creatures that are fashioned in the Prime Mover's own image! And that is exactly what you 'stupid' humans are itching to do all the time - stupid because such a stance assumes that the generosity of the Prime Mover is not infinite, something that (if it were true) would detract from His own status as the Almighty. Humans will not even draw the obvious conclusion from this total "dependence" on the Prime Mover which, namely, is that the Prime Mover cannot be very far away - that He is not even at arm's length and that it is at the core of their being that He subsists.

"Of course, I could include the pure spirits in the discussion, but let us concentrate on you folks who might still just benefit from hearing this repeated - it wouldn't really do any good for spirits who are already lost or the angels who are safe and sound in heaven to be lectured to by even the most brilliant preacher ever like me on these matters.

"The bottom-line is that humans on their own - unaided by grace - do not have the wherewithal to accomplish any good. Whereas before the fall, Adam and Eve were in a state of grace and, thanks to the fact that they were in that state, were able to show love to one another as commanded by the Prime Mover in addition to paying Him homage as the one and the only Prime Mover, after the fall, humans became entirely dependent on the grace merited for them by the Deliverer.

"When it came to doing good or performing acts of virtue, it was presumptuous for humans to imagine that they could bring about anything that was meritorious on their own unaided by grace, and attempts to do so - to try and spirit themselves into heaven by, in effect, bypassing the Deliverer - automatically signalled a blatant determination to usurp the power and authority of the Prime Mover. The woman in the New Testament, who expressed her desire to have the seats to the immediate right and the immediate left of the Deliverer in heaven reserved for her sons, was attempting to do precisely that!

"You call that an attempt to promote oneself. It is also evidence of an absence of realism and an utter lack of humility; and it is suggestive of the individual's determination to try and ignore the hard fact that being in original sin means being born in bondage - bondage to me.

"You compound the situation when you ignore the existence of the Prime Mover, pretend that no allegiance of any kind is implied when creatures that did not exist in any form are given a nature and an existence at the time they are gratuitously willed into existence by the Prime Mover with a bundle of gifts or talents to match, and then also pretend that you, as descendants of Adam and Eve, did not inherit the status of outlaws.

"By the way, humans do not have to be specifically told in history class that they had a great, great grandfather and a great grandmother called 'Adam' and 'Eve' or whatever, and that they were driven from Paradise and forfeited eternal life when they stole fruit from the Tree of Knowledge of Good and Evil - or that they became inclined to evil thereby!

"But, wait - history class and history books? Story class and storybooks would be more like it. Authored by 'scholars' who are inclined to sin like anyone else and largely operate under my vassalage, most of those history books are of course designed to mislead!

"Any way, with the exception of the Mother of the Deliverer, every human has 'stolen fruit from the Tree of Knowledge of Good and Evil', and all - except the very hypocritical - know deep down in their hearts that they are inclined to sin, have been banished from Paradise, and have forfeited the right to an eternal inheritance.

"But all humans also know deep down in their guts that they owe a pledge of allegiance to their Maker or 'Prime Mover' by virtue of having an 'essence' or nature that is not just any kind of nature, but one that is truly magnificent and splendid because of what it has in common with the nature of their Maker, and enjoying an existence they did completely nothing to deserve.

"Having opted of their own free will to refuse to pay homage to Him and to join me (the Father of Death and the Destroyer) in my own rebellion in the process, you wouldn't expect me as their new master to just let them to walk away. You have to be insane to think that I would.

"On the one hand, they are all outlaws and banished children of Adam and Eve; and on the other hand they are creatures over whom I, 'Satan' or 'Devil' - or whatever label you like to employ to refer to me - have full control over. After the fall, Adam and Eve and all their descendants became my slaves! What did you expect? We are at war - the struggle between Good and Evil! This is rough stuff, you know. We are not playing games here. Snap it! They all *are* my minions!

"The situation was aggravated by the fact that humans, after the fall, became inclined to sin rather than to good. Now, if humans are inclined to evil, it means that instead of spending their time trying to fend off temptations from me and my troops, they are busy tempting themselves in all sorts of ways. And it is not *probably*, but *a fact* that instead of avoiding occasions of sin, they are actively seeking them.

"That, combined with the fact that lines of communication between humans and the Prime Mover had been irretrievably cut when Adam and Eve fell from grace and stopped being in good books with the Prime Mover, signified that humans (who were now not just legally but actually 'blind') were stumbling along in virtual darkness in an effort to march to heaven along what was a decidedly very narrow path (even as they themselves could always confirm from their own experience)!

"To make things worse, some humans even thought that they were better than others. Those who were the most 'devilish' - or like me - believed that they were the most angelic and also wise; while those who were the least devilish - or unlike me - were the ones who believed that they were the least worthy. This also went to illustrate the stubbornness of the wicked and to explain their reluctance to hearken to the urging of divine grace!

"Everything was now screwed up: those who were at the bottom rung of society and had the most difficult time trying to put bread on the family table were despised the most. Totally depraved humans with the most God-awful records, and many with blood on their hands, represented themselves as angels who were not in need of forgiveness. Humans with records that were not as bad were the ones who seemed to believe in the need for forgiveness for themselves and for their enemies!

"In their stupidity, some of these 'blind' folks did not even hesitate to represent themselves as being in a position to lead other blind folks in the pitch darkness along that path! It was the height of presumptuousness. Humans who did that ended up not just misleading those they sought to lead, but actually tempting their 'flock' to do likewise. You'd better take my word for it. That is exactly how I myself, who was created a noble creature, became transformed into the Beelzebub you are now having this discourse with!

Homines Iniqui (Wicked Humans)

"When I led the hosts of angels in the rebellion against the Prime Mover, I myself as the ring leader became transformed into the 'embodiment of evil', something that had up until then existed only as an idea! I, as the revolt's instigator, became the truly evil ghost (diabolus malus) that I still am to the present day and will continue to be through eternity.

"The difference between myself - the fallen Lucifer who had once upon a time headed the angelic host comprising of various angelic choirs including Seraphim and Cherubim - and Adam and Eve (who were also created in the image but fell from grace because of their curiosity) and their progeny is that I am evil (malus), whereas fallen humans are merely wicked (iniquus). But the fact is that even though I am diabolus malus (the devil), unlike you wicked humans (homines iniqui), I have never allowed that to cloud my vision. Even as fallen angels, we here in the Underworld remain with all our wits

35

about us, and that is precisely why we are so dangerous! And this has major implications for the struggle between good and evil which has been unfolding since the beginning of time and which continues.

"Actually, I misspoke: Humans are both wicked and evil just like us. The Deliverer Himself called humans 'evil' when He stated: '*Si ergo vos, cum sitis mali, nostis bona data dare filiis vestris: quanto magis Pater vester, qui in cælis est, dabit bona petentibus se?*' (If you then being evil, know how to give good gifts to your children: how much more will your Father who is in heaven, give good things to them that ask him?) (Matthew 7:11).

"Anyway, it is an established fact, on the other hand, that humans don't even know what they are. Humans seem perplexed that they might indeed be spiritual beings that have been fashioned by their Maker, Himself an all knowing, all loving, and infinitely merciful, but infinitely just all the same, in His own divine image and likeness! Just look how many even care to profess that He exists! Well, even when they say He does, it very definitely isn't reflected in the way they live. But that does not negate what humans are, namely temples of the Prime Mover. Yet, with the sole exception of the immaculately conceived Virgin Mother of the Deliverer, humans have all wickedly allowed sin to blind them to all things spiritual - and I mean *all* things of the spirit, including my very own existence!

"Now, it is bad enough for humans to be clueless about who or what they are; and to be oblivious to the existence of the Prime Mover, of His Word, and the existence of the Holy Ghost that binds the Father and the Son together in an eternal bond of Divine Love. But to be oblivious to the existence of the evilest creature - I mean myself, Beelzebub, Sheitan, the Tempter, the Evil One, the embodiment of evil or 'Devil', and above all the Father of Death - you have to be kidding!

"Talking about being the embodiment of evil, you would think it would dawn on humans that whenever they acknowledged that evil existed in the world, it would signal to them that I, Diabolos and the personification and also source of evil, do truly and verily exist in the same way humans themselves did! The fact nonetheless is that only good and truly decent humans are aware of my existence, and they are a precious few of them.

"Of course there are those humans who are constantly talking about 'the devil this' and 'the devil that', and who are forever ranting about 'demons' when it is all just that - talk! And that is where it all stops, revealing that it is all mere lip service. If humans knew how truly evil my troops and I were, they would be fasting and mortifying themselves non-stop, and they would not rest until their union with their Deliverer was complete. And they most definitely wouldn't be holding those Halloween festivals that depict us as harmless ghosts that only exist in the human imagination!

"When Adam and Eve, the father and mother of the human race, lost their innocence after stealing fruit from the Tree of Knowledge of Good and Evil and lying about it, the human faculties of reason and free will apparently became so blunted that humans have been virtual walking zombies ever since. It is only what can be seen, heard, smelt, touched and felt or somehow 'sensed' with the help of the five senses that catches their attention. The fact that things of the spirit transcend matter - something that is so obvious even to the dumbest demon - remains an enigma to most humans, the only exception being the odd mystic.

"It is one thing to be brought into existence out of nothing. But it is something else altogether to be crafted in the image of Him-Who-Is-Who-Is and Author of Life!

Humans are so confused about everything, and have such a screwed up idea of the world around them - such a fuzzy idea of who they are - it now requires a miracle of grace for them to appreciate the fact that they are fashioned in the image of Him-Who-is-Who-is. Which is just swell - my own prayers will be answered if humans desist from praying for that grace and consequently remain clueless as regards their elevated status and nature, and their last end."

More Catholic than the Catholics themselves...

Unaccustomed to having discourses with the creature he had been brought up to regard as the Father of Lies, Mjomba was evidently caught off guard by the "Evil Ghost". He had commenced work on his thesis on the subject of "Original Virtue" determined to turn in a winning thesis like no other. More than anyone else, Mjomba knew that to succeed in producing a truly winning thesis, he could not spare himself any effort while applying both his faculties of reason and the imagination to the task at hand. And he was convinced that, as regards the latter, he could not hope to succeed in attaining his goal of producing the most winsome thesis - one that would be the last word on the subject of his choice - unless he allowed his imagination unfettered freedom.

But that was before Mjomba had decided to employ the devil as a mouthpiece for expounding on the Church's dogmas. He was now completely shocked at the things that his imagination was attributing to the Evil One, but felt quite helpless to deter the caricature of Diabolos his imagination had invented from venting what decidedly were weird notions about humans - himself included - and their destiny. For the first time, Mjomba wondered if he

38

could trust his imagination - or the caricature of "Satan" that his imagination had conjured up. He told himself that he couldn't care less as it was now too late to interfere with his imagination, let alone stop it from serving up more of the rambling but solidly reasoned arguments the "devil" - or the devil's alter ego (or whatever!) - was using at every turn to try and show that humans were doomed.

But, while he was unapologetic as he continued lending the shameless Lucifer his ear, Mjomba thought there was something scary about the methodical manner in which the evil ghost punched holes in the arguments of those who contradicted the Church's teachings. What was more, Satan appeared to be hurting his own cause by proving that the Roman Catholic Church *was* divinely instituted. Listening to the 'Ruler of the Underworld' pontificate, Mjomba even attempted to play the role of 'devil's advocate' himself by assuming that the Father of Lies had to be lying, and was trying to trick him into writing a thesis that was full of hollow arguments on important dogmas of the Church.

To Mjomba's great surprise, out of the innumerable points the devil had made up until then, Mjomba was unable to find a single point he thought he could challenge without making a fool of himself in the process. That left the seminarian, who knew that Beelzebub couldn't be trusted and definitely couldn't be up to any good in any case, even more terrified! Mjomba knew that the creature everyone loved to give the rap as the Evil One was the former Lucifer who, with Michael the Archangel, had jointly commanded the heavenly hosts, and that Lucifer had been privy to much more than ordinary mortals, whose vision was clouded by the effects of original sin, were capable of grasping.

Without a doubt then, the Evil One couldn't be faulted for being ignorant, and much less for not knowing what he was talking about. Therefore, unless he, Mjomba or anyone else, could reveal flaws in the devil's logic and consequently punch holes in his arguments or otherwise prove him wrong, he didn't have any option but to concede that the Ruler of the Underworld was right!

At one point, Mjomba was torn between giving the brilliant Diabolos his full attention, or fleeing what he imagined could be a clever trap that the Father of Death was laying in his path, perhaps aimed at getting him to embrace a new kind of heresy himself. Mjomba never stopped wondering if others before him - like Luther, for example, who had started out as a pious and well-intentioned member of a monastic order, and had even taken perpetual vows of poverty and obedience - didn't fall for similar traps laid for them by the Cunning One! The sense of guilt Mjomba felt as he continued translating the thoughts he was receiving from Satan into material for his Thesis on Original Virtue was palpable.

And if "Old Scratch" was right - if it was true that members of the human race, one and all, were an irresponsible bunch who had turned against the Deliverer and, before Him, the prophets the Prime Mover had sent to help humans "pave and straighten the paths", and who were even now turning the *Sancta Ecclesia* the Deliverer had established with due solemnity and charged with His work of redemption into a virtual "den of thieves" - the Deliverer and Master had to be really mad even as He sat triumphant on His throne at the right hand of His Father in heaven.

Mjomba recalled the parables the Deliverer had used to teach His disciples on numerous occasions, and His insistence that the Prime Mover was a jealous Prime Mover who would deal mercilessly with those humans who decided to bury their talents and as well those other humans who turned on His messengers and harmed them. It seemed evident to Mjomba that the writings of the evangelists (John, Matthew, Mark and Luke) and others like Peter, James and the "Apostle of the Gentiles" were being exploited for gain by the many self-appointed apostles and "prophets" who contradicted each other right and left, and for that reason couldn't care less about the Truth the Deliverer died for.

Mjomba concluded that, when the end of the world came, and along with it Judgement Day, there would also be lots and lots of drama! But the sad thing in the meantime, Mjomba told himself, was the fact that Beelzebub had to be laughing his guts out, the fact that he was languishing in hell notwithstanding.

Yes, if the devil was right, the Son of Man, who had labored so hard and sacrificed so much to get his disciples to change from being timid and vacillating to individuals who were resolute and prepared to suffer martyrdom for their belief in His teachings and for His sake, had to be seething at the sight of hordes who were jostling for the opportunity to cash in not just on the books that now comprised the New Testament, but the books that comprised the Old Testament as well! And, of course, people like Solomon, Isaiah, John, Peter, Paul and others who diligently committed to paper what had been revealed to them by the Holy Spirit to facilitate the Church's evangelizing mission had to be turning in their graves just seeing what was going on back on earth! From their "mansions" in heaven, they had to be angry seeing many a man and a woman who were starved for spiritual food fall for the machinations of the "false prophets".

The idea that the Evil Ghost might in fact be right was very troubling to Mjomba for one other reason. If the shameless Beelzebub was right, this was automatically bad news for those Catholic prelates - and there were many of them - who gave the impression that it was quite alright to be a "separated" brother or sister; that Christians who did not embrace all the teachings of the Church were somehow better off than "non-Christians". Mjomba could not help wondering of the devil was not sticking to a strict interpretation of the Gospels for a reason! To drive a wedge between the Deliverer and those he had chosen to step into the shoes of His apostles perhaps?

The devil's position was quite clear. Just as the remnants of the Deliverer's band of followers did on the Day of Pentecost (the day the Holy Ghost promised by the Deliverer had descended upon them), the prelates needed to come to terms with the fact that the crowds that had mobbed the Deliverer prior to His arrest and trial had indeed done so out of self-interest; and that the interest of the separated brethren in the Deliverer - and indeed also the interest of the many Catholics who were accustomed to chanting "Lord, Lord" but did not do the will of the Deliverer's Father and were Catholics only in name - was similarly based on the wrong motivations. That what the crowds - and the throngs of separated brethren - were really interested in was the fun they derived from following the Deliverer wherever He went in Judea and Galilee, and witnessing the miracles He performed; like, for insistence, seeing people who had been born blind regain their sight, the dumb speak, the lame walk, and the dead Lazarus get up and pick up in a second life where he had left off in his first life.

But the same crowds that had witnessed and marvelled at the miracles the Deliverer performed had balked at His suggestion that they needed to regard His body (the body He had received from His blessed mother Mary at the time of her "immaculate conception") as being truly and verily the bread of angels; and that they had to also be prepared to feast on it, and as well to take a gulp of His precious blood (the blood which He was going to shed for the salvation of sinful humans), and do these things worthily before they could graduate into full-fledged members of the Church Triumphant (the heavenly kingdom over which he was going to preside for all eternity as High Priest)! And that was in fact the case with all those followers of the Deliverer (or "Christians") who viewed the celebration of the Holy Eucharist and the Church's doctrine of Transubstantiation as witchcraft!

The Deliverer had Himself laid down His life - spilled his precious blood, endured mockery from the likes of Pontius Pilate and Herod Agrippa - for the Truth and the whole Truth! And rather than compromise that Truth, the original apostles, following the Deliverer's example, had been prepared to suffer martyrdom for the sake of the Deliverer and for the sake of that unvarnished and sacred Truth. The devil could even argue that the so-called separated brethren, particularly those who prided themselves on being avid readers of the bible, had to know that more would be expected of them than say those other descendants of Adam and Eve who were atheists from their cradle and had never had any opportunity to study the sacred scriptures!

The devil could contend that the decision of any separated brother or sister to remain outside the *Sancta Ecclesia* because of the prevalent traditional prejudices against the "Church of Rome" - prejudices that ultimately were the work of Satan himself, but were attributed to the Prime Mover and passed off as special personal revelations - or for any other self-serving reason, far from vindicating that separated brother or separated sister on Judgement Day, would work squarely against him or her, just as the apathy and malaise of Catholics in the practice of their faith was reason enough for the Deliverer to wish to "spit them out of His mouth"!

43

It was incredible! If the prelates were indeed compromising Catholic doctrine to appease and not appear to be alienating the so-called separated brethren (separated brethren who persisted in championing heresies to the detriment of the Church's mission of evangelization), the devil could claim that the prelates, like Peter before them, were attempting to stop the Deliverer from proceeding to Jerusalem and to His ignominious death on Calvary!

It was at that juncture that Mjomba realized that Beelzebub was up to something evil in the extreme; something that was patently "devilish". For, what was there to stop Satan from going on to claim that, with prelates of the Church projecting the wrong image of the Mystical Body of the Deliverer, the prelates had in fact abandoned the Deliverer in the exact same way Peter did when he was confronted by the woman in the court of the Roman Governor's palace on the night before the Deliverer was crucified! Indeed, any admission on the prelates' part that they were frail humans - frail humans who needed prayers of the faithful to stay clear of the wiles of the Evil One and the temptations of the flesh so that they could continue to "fight the good fight" like every other member of the Church Militant - could be cited by the Ruler of the Underworld as evidence that it was he, rather than the Deliverer, who had the upper hand in the battle for souls. And it was, of course, a fact that none of the successors to the apostles was in a position to say truthfully that he had never once slipped in his life (an implicit admission that they had failed to live up to their priestly status as *Alteri Christi* or "other Christs").

And if all that was true, and assuming that the prelates had not rehabilitated themselves at some point in their lives to the same extent as Peter (who deemed himself unworthy to be crucified on the cross with his head up and who had accordingly implored his executioners to crucify him upside down) had, the devil could claim - and with some justification no doubt - that it was not the Deliverer but he himself (Satan) who still called the shots in the Church which was the modern equivalent of Noah's Ark! The leader of the rebel band of angels, who had become the embodiment of evil, would in effect be claiming victory in the battle between good and evil! He would be saying almost in so many words that members of the Church's hierarchy were wearing "his barge" or what the evangelist referred to as the "mark of the beast"!

No kidding (Diabolos as "Defender of Truth")...

But Mjomba saw something even more sinister in the apparent determination of the shameless Father of Lies, and also the Evil One, to project himself as the "Truthful One"! By projecting that image of himself, the devil could go on to argue that the ambivalence of the Catholic prelates in their interpretation of Catholic doctrine and the Church's sacred role as Defender of Truth was what lead many of the separated brethren to remain contented and happy with the *status quo* instead of striving to grasp and embrace the whole Truth for which the Deliverer laid down His life. That in turn caused 'non-Christians' to dismiss the Church's evangelizing mission as a big joke!

Actually, being the conscientious seminarian that he was, Mjomba worried that in trying to hijack Holy Mother the Church's agenda and platform, and pretending that he was the de facto Defender of Truth, the clever Satan actually wanted to control the forces of good ranged against him in the now uneven battle between Good and Evil to give himself a chance - the only chance

45

he had - of coming out as a winner!

It was already clear to Mjomba that, even after the Son of God had come to earth and died on the cross for the redemption of humans (those, at any rate, who would believe in Him and follow in His footsteps by carrying their own crosses), the devil, noting that the twelve apostles and their successors were an imperfect lot, was signaling that it was he himself, and not the divine Redeemer of humans, who was still in charge and calling the shots!

Except for Simon Peter, the rock upon which the Deliverer had built His church against which the gates of hell could not prevail at the time he was minding the Deliverer's sheep and providing them guidance *ex-cathedra* as he had to do from time to time, and his successors, the apostles and those who would be called to succeed them, because they were far from perfect even as they ministered to His flock or dispensed the sacraments, were just like everyone else including those so-called excommunicated heretics and the unbaptized! In some respects they probably were just as bad as the priests and Pharisees who missed the chance of leading the people of Israel in giving the long-awaited Messiah a red-carpet welcome when He showed up among them two thousand years ago in fulfilment of the Prime Mover's promise to Adam and Eve and their posterity.

Mjomba admitted that he himself had witnessed enough scandals engineered by members of the Church's hierarchy that proved the point the Evil One was making. Even the history books were filled with accounts that sometimes made him sick to the stomach, like for instance the Holy Masses that were offered for the safe return of European slave traders, or the prayers of chants of the *Te Deum* that filled cathedrals in Europe following the imperial conquests that left the indigenous populations in the parts of the world that had been colonized either decimated and indigent, or permanently banned from the lands where generations of their people were interned, as Western countries tried to outdo each other in their conquests and annexation of foreign lands often under the dubious pretext of spreading the Gospel.

These were classic cases of members of the church's hierarchy making common cause with evildoers against God's people along with their Maker!

Mjomba had no doubt in his mind that the Evil One and Father of Lies, in a dirty and all too cynical maneuver, was using that as the basis for projecting himself as the Defender of Truth! It terrified the seminarian to think that "Old Scratch", as the devil was also called, was capable of being so cunning and that, even though the Savior of Mankind had already come, died for men and risen from the dead in triumph, the situation remained so precarious!

Mjomba could almost hear Lucifer stuttering with laughter, and mocking that this was a perfect set-up in which he, Satan, could now tempt the so-called separated brethren on several key fronts at once. He could, for instance, tempt them to imagine that they did not need to take up and carry their crosses and to follow in the Deliverer's footsteps, and that they could save themselves a lot of sweat by merely "accepting the Deliverer".

Or he could tempt them to imagine away the *sancta ecclesia* which the Deliverer built on the rock called *Petrus*, and with it it's all embracing and burdensome Teaching *Magisterium*, including the power to hold bound in heaven whatever it held bound on earth, so that they (the separated brethren) would be free to interpret the sacred scriptures in any way they fancied and to believe what suited them, or to quote texts out of context from the Holy Book and so formally have the scriptures justify their lust for material riches and earthly power!

Then the Evil Ghost could tempt them to pretend that those humans who had been called by the Deliverer to step into the shoes of the apostles, even though they remained completely human despite their high calling, could not let the Deliverer down in some way and still continue to serve as shepherds of His flock. In that way, the separated brethren would have an excuse to pursue their own independent, self-serving schemes of salvation outside the purview of the *Sancta Ecclesia*, and deny themselves thereby access to the sacramental graces the Holy Ghost dispensed to the faithful.

Mjomba found Satan's position very persuasive. He himself knew quite well that, since time immemorial, humans had dreamed up schemes that were designed to bypass the Way of the Cross. They had even attempted to tunnel their way into heaven by constructing the Tower of Babel! The problem with humans going out on a limb an establishing their own churches in competition with the *sancta ecclesia* was that the Holy Ghost and the Son of Man, whose titles included "High Priest", King of Kings, Redeemer and Judge, were one. The Holy Ghost identified Himself unreservedly and completely with the Mystical Body of the Deliverer, and Mjomba could not see how the Holy Spirit, who informed Holy Mother the Church, could be persuaded to operate outside it.

Thinking about the mystery of the Blessed Trinity, and specifically the oneness of Holy Spirit with the Word through whom all creation came into being, Mjomba ended up agreeing completely with the Evil Ghost that the reason human schemes that did not have the blessing of the Almighty One, were doomed to failure precisely because creatures, whether human or angelic, could successfully drive a wedge between the three persons of the Blessed Trinity. Satan and the other fallen angels had tried and ended up being transformed into demons and cast into hell for their pains.

And Mjomba now worried that the Evil Ghost had far more to do with the proliferation of the so-called mega churches in modern times, whose founders poured scorn on the doctrine that there was no salvation outside the Roman Catholic Church, than met the eye! After all, what members of those mega churches and all the other separated brethren were really attempting to do was get the Holy Ghost to support efforts that were directly undermining the work and mission of the sancta ecclesia!

This was not the first time that the Devil was at it; and it most certainly wasn't going to be the last. As if in confirmation of his fears, Mjomba now recalled the fairly recent reports of the apparitions of the Our Lady to one Sr. Agnes Sasagawa of Akita, Japan, and the chilling message of the weeping statue of the Blessed Virgin Mary to the effect that the devil would infiltrate the Church in a way that would see cardinals opposing cardinals; bishops opposing bishops; and priests who venerated the Blessed Virgin scorned and opposed by their confreres; churches and altars sacked; and the Church full of those who accepted compromises!

Even though Mjomba was quite alert and had no problem following the devil's reasoning, and was even able at times to marshal what clearly was uncommon courage which he needed to challenge the Evil Ghost in his own court, Mjomba thought he was having a bad dream. Mjomba thought about the "separated brethren" - the brethren who were counted, not in their hundreds or thousands, but in their millions - and shuddered at the unimaginable idea that the holy Ghost could refuse to heed the pleas of so the multitudes who actually passed themselves off as disciples of the Deliverer; but who nonetheless genuinely believed that the Pontiff of Rome, who was Peter's successor and was for that reason respectfully referred to by Catholics as the "Holy Father", was the anti-Christ. Any one growing up in a similar environment would have imbibed similar prejudices against the Holy Father and what he stood for. It would have required uncommon heroism for anyone who was brought up as a separated brother or sister not to be prejudiced against the pope and by extension the *sancta ecclesia*.

Mjomba told himself that the Ruler of the Underworld had to be kidding if he (or perhaps she?) was suggesting that the separated brethren were on the path to perdition! Mjomba knew from his training in psychology that for sinful and sinning humans, exposure to temptation was really all that was needed to entrap them in sin. After all, on their own, they were as nothing. It therefore seemed a foregone conclusion that the Holy Ghost could not abandon any human of goodwill, and especially if the circumstances in which that human was born were not conducive to the formation of a correct and clear Catholic conscience. And so, provided the separated brethren did whatever they did in good faith, Mjomba was inclined to the view that they were on good and solid ground in terms of their personal relationship with their Maker.

It was as though the Evil Ghost had been reading Mjomba's mind and was sensing that Mjomba was beginning to doubt that the situation of the separated brethren was hopeless. And Mjomba himself realized that the thoughts that inundated his mind at that juncture, even though quite orthodox and noble in themselves, were coming straight from the Evil One. Clearly, the salvation of the separated brethren, just like that of other sinful and sinning humans, could not be guaranteed just because they chanted "Master, Master" in their places of worship.

As long as they refused to accept what the Deliverer had taught - the same teaching that the apostles' lawful successors kept repeating for all and sundry to hear - that the Deliverer's flesh was food indeed, and that His blood was drink indeed, and so long as they refused to welcome those whom the Deliverer had personally hand-picked and sent out to spread the message of the crucified and risen Deliverer, who was Mjomba to suggest that the separated brethren were on the path of salvation!

The sacred scriptures, tradition and the Church's teaching were all unambiguous regarding the Deliverer's position on the Holy Eucharist. As the evangelist had written, unless humans feasted on the Deliverer's flesh and drunk His blood, there would be no life in them! That was exactly what the Church had taught from the beginning and still taught to day. And yet, the sacred worship of the Mass remained one of the biggest stumbling blocks to "Christian unity"! Moreover, for sure, the Deliverer had established one ministry; not two, ten, and much less a myriad ministries such as those which proliferated in modern times and many of which had funny sounding names too!

There could not be any doubt that the devil, who was leading the forces of darkness in the battle between Good and Evil, knew that the Deliverer was sworn to protect the Church he was establishing for the purpose of ministering to the people of the Prime Mover and over which Peter was going to preside from any mischief maker. Indeed, not even the powers of the hell were going to be able to prevail against his *Sancta Ecclesia*.

Now, the devil, more than any other creature that was fashioned in the Image, had to know that the consequences for anyone who contemplated any mischief against the *Sancta Ecclesia* would be severe.

Even though he himself had already been judged and condemned, the devil knew very well that he actually risked his head being crushed by the woman who had the sun itself for her raiment if he made any move. However, precisely because he had already been condemned, the devil did not really care less about the consequences to himself. But he cared very much about the consequences to the poor forsaken children of Adam and Eve. If he saw any way of getting humans to do his dirty work for him in that regard, he was not going to spare any efforts to get them to jump on the bandwagon. Knowing that he could not derail the divine plan relating to the *Sancta Ecclesia* even if he tried, he was going to try and persuade misguided humans to try and cause the *Sancta Ecclesia* problems so that they would forfeit their salvation in the process!

The devil had no scruples whatsoever about pursuing that line of action; and he undoubtedly was very delighted when humans took it upon themselves to establish "ministries" in competition with the Deliverer's *Sancta Ecclesia*. Shameless humans knew that the Deliverer had established but one Holy Church; and one could not get better evidence for their callousness than the manifold attempts to establish substitute ministries, with their heretical positions on key doctrinal matters, for the Deliverer's *Sancta Ecclesia*.

The Deliverer had also stated that His grace was enough for sinful and sinning humans, heretical and schismatic ones included. Consequently, the separated brethren had no excuse for not heeding the call to return to the fold just as it was incumbent upon those who already belonged to the Holy Universal (Catholic) Church to develop a personal relationship with their Deliverer in it.

Mjomba was dismayed to think that he had to agree

with the devil on that score. Consequently, the devil could now set the stage to claim for himself the souls of all sinful and sinning humans, including the souls of the separated brethren, so long as they persisted in their intransigence, and did not heed the call to true discipleship with the Deliverer inside the "Ark of Noah" (the Church of Rome). So long as humans resisted the urgings of the Holy Ghost to seek the kind of discipleship that canonized saints enjoyed with their Deliverer, they were doomed!

The Holy Ghost, Mjomba told himself, without any doubt provided all humans, the separated brethren included, the grace to enable them to form their consciences in accordance with the will of the Prime Mover and to follow its dictates. Reluctantly, Mjomba concurred with the Evil Ghost that, unless the separated brethren abandoned the heresies and schisms that kept them cut off from the fullness of grace that was only available in the Catholic Church, they actually risked losing their souls!

The separated brethren remained free to allow history to repeat itself in their regard. They remained free to do as the first man and the first woman had done, namely give in to their curiosity and try to find out if indeed they will be like the Prime Mover if they ate of the forbidden fruit - the fruit from the tree of knowledge! And that is precisely what they were doing by ignoring the promptings of the Holy Ghost and doing their own will! They also did it by choosing to ignore the existence of the Church's *Magisterium* or teaching authority, so clearly spelled out in the Holy Book. Mjomba found it incredible that this was coming from Beelzebub, the Father of Lies and the embodiment of evil!

Mjomba himself noted in passing that all the descendants of Adam and Eve, with the sole exception of the Son of Man and His immaculate mother Mary, had

53

been conceived in original sin, and in that sense were not entirely innocent or sinless. The separated brethren were thus not alone in their intransigence. Mjomba was at one point tempted to regard the separated brethren as being in a more enviable position than folks who did not profess to be "followers of Christ" or "Christians". And he was also tempted to think that by the same token Catholics, nominal or otherwise, were in a more favored position by virtue of their membership in the "One, Holy, Catholic, and Apostolic Church". He was thinking of the biblical passage that stated: "Whoever has will be given more, and they will have an abundance. Whoever does not have, even what they have will be taken from them." (Matthew 13:12). But he was swiftly disabused of those notions in a very short order. He had no doubt that Satan, whose desire it was to see everyone forfeit his or her salvation, had a hand in it.

The passage from Luke 12:48 had immediately sprung to mind: "But he who knew [it] not, and did things worthy of stripes, shall be beaten with few. And to every one to whom much has been given, much shall be required from him; and to whom [men] have committed much, they will ask from him the more."

On the face of it, this meant that those who had not found faith in the Catholic Church were better off, especially if one also took into consideration the fact that it was not individual humans who determined the place and time and the other circumstances surrounding their appearance on earth, and also the fact that humans were inclined to sin and, even though possessed of reason and a free will, were incapable of any good deeds on their own without the help of the Prime Mover's grace!

And, by the same token, the separated brethren were in a less enviable position than those who had no acquaintance at all with the sacred scriptures. That was because the latter could cite that as an excuse for their failure to find and enter that One, Holy, Catholic and Apostolic Church!

Mjomba couldn't really argue against that. But he reminded himself all the same that the character he was up against was none other than the Evil One about whom it was written: "*Ille homicida erat ab initio, et in veritate non stetit: quia non est veritas in eo: cum loquitur mendacium, ex propriis loquitur, quia mendax est, et pater ejus.*" *(*He was a murderer from the beginning, and he stood not in the truth; because truth is not in him. When he speaketh a lie, he speaketh of his own: for he is a liar, and the father thereof.) (John 8.44).

He thought about Mother Teresa, St. Kizito, St. Bakhita and other souls whose heroic practice of virtue had earned them canonization. Noting that the spiritual life he himself led left a lot to be desired, Mjomba told himself that he would be lying if he said that he was a better person than the separated brethren who at least strove to enter into a personal relationship with their Deliverer - if what he saw on television was not staged, that is.

But if Mjomba was thinking that he could let himself off so lightly by merely acknowledging, as he was doing, that the life he led left a lot to be desired, he was seriously mistaken. It now occurred to him that he was the perfect example of how souls squandered the hard-earned graces that were afforded to them through the death of the Deliverer on the gibbet while oblivious of the fact that this would almost certainly not be the case if other souls had been the recipient of those same graces! He could tell that it was Satan who was attempting to drive him to despair my making him understand that as a cradle Catholic and a seminarian at that, he had available to him the fullness of the graces found in the *Sancta Ecclesia* -

something that half the human race didn't.   Therefore casually pooh-poohing the fact that he was on the road to perdition (as he was doing) wasn't going to alter that fact!

It was just then that Mjomba did something rather funny.   A serious expression on his face, Mjomba mumbled that the infernal one, who had himself already been judged and condemned, had used him (Mjomba) to successfully consign all those separated brethren - the separated brethren who claimed that they were saved after accepting the Deliverer, and everyone else was lost - to hell! Mjomba added that, after attempting to use him to drive a wedge between the separated brethren and their Maker, the devil was turning on him and trying to make him despair about his own salvation! The devil had succeeded in persuading Mjomba that he himself was as good as lost, and Mjomba himself even appeared to agree. The situation was all the more serious because of the solid arguments the Adversary employed at every turn for his evil purpose!

And to make things worse, while he was busy writing about the separated brethren and even lecturing them on the importance of forming their consciences aright and heeding the promptings of the Holy Ghost, he himself did not recall stopping and taking time a moment to "form his conscience"! Mjomba didn't even know what his response would be if he were asked what was really meant by this thing called "conscience"!

It was only slowly, and on reflection, that it all finally started to click and to make sense to the seminarian. Old Scratch (the devil), in order to inflict the greatest damage on the sancta ecclesia, would of course try very hard to impersonate the Holy Father; and then, knowing how fickle humans were and at the same time masquerading as the "Defender of Truth", the devil would go all out to show that the clergy and the prelates who were successors to the apostles, and the Holy Father, because they too were inclined to sin and incapable of performing any virtuous act without the aid of divine grace, were hypocritical every time they tried to speak out against evil in the world! Hypocritical in the same exact way he was himself a hypocrite for posing as the Defender of Truth and as the *de facto* the only reliable source of Truth when he actually was the Father of Lies!

Mjomba could almost hear the Evil One chuckling before emphasizing that the record of Catholic bishops, who only paid lip service to the fact that all humans regardless of their faith were created in the Image and therefore as much children of the Prime Mover as baptized Catholics were, spoke for itself!

When it suited them, they were vocal in denouncing heretics and anyone who fell in schism and, even though possessed of the gift of prophecy as the anointed of the Prime Mover and faith that moved mountains and well versed in Dogmatic, Systematic, Moral, and other branches of Theology and in the Scriptures, did it without any charity as was typical of all poor forsaken children of Adam and Eve! But even though a hypocrite himself, the devil at least seemed to get it right at least in the interim. He was going to teach humans the truths of salvation with the greatest charity and would only point out that, inclined to sin, they (humans) were unlikely to live up to those selfsame truths, a situation that elicited the devil's greatest sympathy!

Mjomba was tempted to say he could not agree more with the Father of Lies - that humans remained hopelessly unfit to approach the throne upon which the risen and glorious Deliverer, King of Kings and Lord of Lords, sat; and that this likely was going to be the case regardless of what the poor forsaken children of Adam and Eve did! Still, the devil was wrong. The reason the

Son of Man came down from heaven was so that humans who believed in Him, unworthy though they were, would be saved!

Just as Mjomba was thinking that he had caught Old Scratch on the wrong foot and was now in a position to use his thesis to expose him for what he really was, his mind, clearly under the control of the Evil Ghost, out of the blue conjured up a new and completely different scenario. No, it was not Satan, Mjomba found himself writing, who was attempting to usurp the authority of the Holy Father! It was those who started their own churches and operated ministries outside the purview of the *Sancta Ecclesia* who were guilty of that charge. And, just as trees that bore fruit, they could be judged by the fruits of their labor, namely the divisions they were trying to get the Church to embrace.

And, actually, when the Deliverer prayed that "they may be one", from one angle he had in mind the faithful who already belonged to His Mystical Body and with respect to whom His prayer was answered at confirmation, when the successors to the apostles laid their hands on them and they received the Holy Ghost. But from a different angle, the Deliverer also had in mind all frail mortals, including the separated brethren. With respect to this group, His prayer would be answered only when humans permitted themselves to be led by the Holy Ghost where "they would not go".

As far as what Beelzebub himself was doing, Mjomba was shocked at the suggestion that the Ruler of the Underworld was out to help his nemesis, Peter, and those who had succeeded him as the cornerstone upon which the Deliverer's Church continued to stand! It definitely said something about the utterly evil nature of the Father of Lies.

The devil would, of course, not need to be

persuaded to tempt the separated brothers and sisters to imagine that they were the special elect who were predestined for heaven and that everyone else was damned and lost, and to frown on the notion that true followers of the Deliverer belong to the Church Militant that, by definition, actively participates in and (as the Apostle of the Gentiles put it) completes what is missing in the passion of the crucified Deliverer, as opposed to being a mere passive onlooker.

Mjomba felt certain that he had finally cornered Beelzebub. It was true that the innumerable "ministries" that served the throngs of separated brethren were operated in direct competition with the *Sancta Ecclesia*, and as such could not be considered the work of the Holy Ghost. Still, the fact was that the multitudes who thronged to those "churches" in search of spiritual fulfilment did so in good faith.

But the seminarian would realize, too late, that this was precisely the sort of argument Beelzebub had been waiting for him, clearly a neophyte, to verbalize before dropping the hammer. Yes, so much for the blind leading the blind, Mjomba could almost hear the evil ghost sniggering in triumph. It was also true that the Son of Man, who was sent to redeem mankind, was one with His Father in heaven; and He was also the Truth and the Life, two things that by their nature could not lend themselves to duplication nonetheless - exactly like the *Sancta Ecclesia*. The fact that some misguided members of the Church's hierarchy gave the impression that things were otherwise did not matter in the slightest. Those clergy and those unrepentant heretics and schematics - it did not matter in the slightest that historians and others now referred to them as the "separated brethren" - were all in grave error and in danger of losing their souls!

There was no doubt whatsoever in Mjomba's mind

that the devil - the truly evil devil - knew exactly what he was doing. The diabolical Lucifer, who had become the embodiment of evil by challenging the Most High to a fight in the presence of the heavenly hosts, had no scruples about projecting himself as being more Catholic than the Catholic prelates themselves! It was in the same way so many "heretics" and "schismatics" projected themselves as being better defenders of orthodoxy than the successors to the apostles!

Mjomba sensed Diabolos positioning himself for the final, albeit desperate, assault on the Mystical Body of the Deliverer. Taking advantage of the platform Mjomba was unwittingly providing him, the devil (the smarter of the two no doubt) was actually using the catechism of the Church to try and show that members of the Church's hierarchy had themselves become like branches of the vine that were in danger of being separated from the tree's main stem. It was tantamount to claiming - in the same way many of the separated brethren claimed - that the *Sancta Ecclesia*, founded by the Deliverer to continue the work of saving human souls, had become dysfunctional and needed to be fixed or alternatively discarded! And that he (the devil) could essentially be trusted to step into the shoes of the apostles, and shepherd the Prime Mover's flock through the desert to the Promised Land. It was just incredible!

There was no doubt in Mjomba's mind that the devil's intent was to drive the separated brethren to despair and cause them to lose their souls in that way after persuading them that their situation was quite hopeless. Mjomba was himself already persuaded that the Ruler of the Underworld could not have made his point about the untenable position of the separated brethren any clearer when the devil dropped the bombshell. Mjomba found himself writing, under the inspiration of the Evil Ghost no doubt that, by refusing to allow themselves to be led by the Holy Ghost where they of themselves would not go, the separated brethren had no one else but themselves to blame. And because they insisted that they had everything right, and accordingly refused to submit to the *magisterium* or teaching authority of the Church - because they preferred to follow their own instincts concerning what was right and wrong and had freely opted for their personal interpretation of the *Sanctae Scripturae*, that stubborn streak, which amounted to self-will, had the effect of blinding them to the motions of grace; and it sealed their fate.

But it was as Mjomba was mulling over the separated brethren's prospects for salvation thusly that it suddenly occurred to him that he himself was not entirely blameless, and could not say that he was not guilty of the very same thing. So long as he himself had some ways to go in developing a genuine personal relationship with the Deliverer (and the same applied to other Catholics), to that extent he was still imbued with self-love and could not claim that he had succeeded in letting the Spirit lead him where he himself would not go. His own situation if anything was far worse because of what he knew, and it was dissimilar to the situation of the fallen Lucifer. And even though he was required to turn in a thesis as a part of his preparation for holy orders, he indeed had to also admit that, allowing himself to be used by the Evil One to condemn the separated brethren as he had done sealed his own fate as well!

Mjomba was realistic and he did not think that the spiritual life he led even came close to putting him on the road to anything like canonization! The spiritual life he led was by no means heroic, and it did not even bear the remotest resemblance to the life of Mother Theresa for instance. What was more, he even frowned on fellow

61

seminarians who were in the habit if paying frequent visits to the chapel for the purpose of praying in front of the Blessed Sacrament, or to mediate on the mysteries of the Rosary! What sort of saint could he have made any way when he had enough trouble doing those same things during the annual retreat! And he had always had difficulty trying to be composed in spirit and not allow himself to be distracted by everything that went on around him.

Perhaps that was the reason images of Judas Iscariot, the betrayer, rather than images of John the evangelist or Peter, that quickly popped up in his mind whenever he thought about the twelve whom, two thousand years ago, the Deliverer hand-picked to be his apostles. Mjomba frequently worried that if he ever became a priest, he might end up a disgrace to the Church and a betrayer - just as Judas had.

And indeed there were times when, attempting to be recollected so he could contemplate on some divine mystery, out of the blue the most unsettling images of the betrayer would besiege his mind. Occasionally they would be in the form visions of Judas Iscariot in a variety of situations. The most frequent were visions of the betrayer stealing pennies from the Deliverer's purse the betrayer had himself volunteered to be bearer and custodian. On one occasion, it was a vision of a disembowelled Judas dangling from the branch of an oak tree with a rope around his neck and in a terrible agony of death.

Mjomba now realized that, while the intention of the Evil One concerning the separated brethren could not be anything but evil, perhaps it was he himself who was the principal target of the machinations of the devil in this particular instance. Mjomba shuddered at the thought that his decision to use the devil as a mouthpiece for enunciating the Church's dogmas was a bid mistake, and instead of hurting the devil and promoting the intentions of the Holy Father in the conflict between good and evil, the scheme had backfired. Mjomba could not avoid the conclusion that he had handed Old Scratch what was in effect an unsolicited opportunity to heal him a mortal blow by turning the tables on him.

But even then, the idea still sounded far-fetched, and Mjomba told himself that his fears were exaggerated and in fact groundless. Mjomba tried to reassure himself that using Beelzebub to show that separated brethren were on a dangerous course and needed to make a U-Turn and come back into the fold before it was too late couldn't be anything but commendable.

Of course that ingenious scheme would make the Ruler of the Underworld who was already seething mad even madder, and would send him thirsting for revenge. But then, who really cared for Beelzebub. It was an article of his faith that every human had a guardian angel who was tasked with ensuring that Satan and his host of demons remained at a distance. For now, Mjomba was going to leave his guardian angel to deal with the heightened threat from Satan and his host.

It was precisely as Mjomba was dismissing the idea that his own salvation could be in mortal danger as a direct result of his decision to become involved with the devil that he felt the rug being pulled from under his feet. And it didn't matter at this stage if what was happening was the result of inspiration he was receiving from the Holy Ghost or the Evil Ghost!

Mjomba found himself acknowledging that it was the actions of his ilk, namely Catholics who were lukewarm and weren't ready to let the Spirit lead them where they of themselves would not go, that separated brethren and others outside the Church found it so hard

63

to recognize the *Sancta Ecclesia* as the institution that was founded by the Deliverer and that was informed by the Holy Ghost. It was because of actions of humans like him that there was all this confusion in the world regarding what constituted unvarnished Truth and what didn't! Humans who led lives like his were in for special surprise on Judgement Day, Mjomba now acknowledged.

The Deliverer did not, after all, look kindly upon those who passed themselves off as his disciples but persisted in remaining lukewarm in their practice of virtue - those who he had said he would actually much rather spit out from his mouth. Mjomba noted that the Deliverer had not said the same about humans who had not received the Gospel and were still unbelievers for that reason.

But the Deliverer had let the world know that included were people like Pontius Pilate, whom he called a 'fox' because, even though the Roman Governor of Judea had used his agents to gather information on the Deliverer and knew that he was not a terrorist as the high priests and the Pharisees claimed but a completely blameless messenger of the Prime Mover sent to redeem the world from sin, Pilate had balked at becoming a disciple of the Deliverer and had decided to pursue his dreams of empire and world domination which he shared with his masters in Rome. And, while claiming to be dispensing justice and minding the *bonum commune*, the fox was actually determined to achieve his objectives without any regard to natural justice.

It suddenly dawned on Mjomba that instead of the angels and saints, it was actually Judas Iscariot and Pontius Pilate whom he had for his company! This was unbelievable!

Mjomba could not bring himself to accept that the devil's aim was to use him (Mjomba) to seal the fate of the separated brethren and other non-Catholics, and then turn around and seal his (Mjomba's) own fate? But Mjomba admitted that, as things now stood, he (Mjomba) was in much greater danger of losing his soul to the Evil Ghost than were the separated brethren whom he had made a subject of his thesis. This was incredible!

In disbelief and shock...

But what shocked Mjomba more than anything else was his discovery, as he was preparing to go to confession, that he had not been fulfilling his obligation to attend Mass on Sundays and other Holy Days of obligation as required by the Canon. What Mjomba found out as he was examining his conscience as he was wont to do before joining the queue of penitents at the confessional one Saturday evening around this time, was that he was actually living in mortal sin, and consequently in mortal danger of losing his soul. This was even though, as a member of the seminary brotherhood living within the confines of St. Augustine's Seminary, he had been ostensibly doing everything that all the other seminarians did including chapel attendance day in and day out. Mjomba was flabbergasted as he allowed that he had just been going through the motions.

Unlike so many other people who saw advantages of sorts in living in a dream world and in preferring not to accept reality, and who decided to imagine away the facts of life and their real situation, Mjomba, at least in this particular case, decided to confront the truth about his spiritual life head on. And he did not just stop at admitting that his disposition left a lot to be desired. Mjomba took himself back in time to the Upper Room in Jerusalem where the Deliverer and his apostles were gathered for supper on the night before He gave his life for the

65

salvation of humans; and he fancied himself hearing first hand Nazarene's words to the twelve: "One of you will betray me!" Mjomba was utterly shocked to hear the "man of Kerioth" who was going to betray the Nazarene also ask: "It isn't me, is it, Rabbi?"

It was also then that Mjomba realized the extent of his moral depravity! For, here he was, living in mortal sin, and just getting on with his daily routine at St. Augustine's seminary, as though nothing had happened - and this when he had most definitely betrayed the Son of Man and Judge!

And, as if that wasn't bad enough, he was even preparing to tout the "Thesis on Original Virtue" that he was crafting with the help of none other than Diabolos himself as something that would in time be an important instrument of the Prime Mover's saving grace! This, On reflection, this mirrored almost exactly the flirting by Judas with the priests and Pharisees even after they had made it clear to all and sundry that they would not rest until they had liquidated the self-proclaimed Son of Man, and the crazy idea Judas had entertained to the very last that, after all was said and done, his "diplomatic" moves and dealings with the Nazarene's sworn enemies were going to pay dividends of one sort or another!

The parallel with the apostle whose act of betrayal would cause the Deliverer to exclaim "That which thou dost, do quickly!" did look at one point as if it had gotten the better of Christian. This showed in the many sleepless nights he endured as he struggled to justify his own actions, and as he tried to reinvent himself as a follower of the apostle Peter despite the latter's own passion tide denials of his Master. And then the thought that any material dividends that would accrue from his thesis was going to be the equivalent of blood money made him feel as though all the exits were blocked and he was about to go nuts! He could not bring himself to accept that, just like the thirty pieces of silver the distraught Judas had emptied at the feet of the teachers of the law following his betrayal of the Son of man with a perfidious kiss, the efforts he was even now investing in his project were good for nothing except perhaps as a revenue source that could be employed to acquire "fields of blood" or grounds in which unidentified murder victims could be interred.

Mjomba felt relief of sorts when he finally succeeded in persuading himself that was the height of hypocrisy to go on as if nothing wrong had happened. Mjomba saw that his situation would be so much better if he could go to the chapel and, facing the altar, summon the courage, even at that late stage, to ask: "It isn't me, is it, Rabbi?

But, No! He, Mjomba, preferred to act as though nothing had happened! And this seemed to be so typical of everyone these days! It occurred to Mjomba just then that, perhaps, that was as it should be since the purpose of the Deliverer incarnation was so He would suffer and die for the salvation of sinful humans! But Mjomba quickly realized that it was the Enemy who was planting that totally wicked and morally bankrupt idea in his mind.

During the several weeks that Mjomba had been working on the thesis, his concentration on its subject matter had been building up, and had eventually gotten to the point where nothing else really mattered. Like a zombie, he methodically did whatever the other seminarians did, and was outwardly attentive in class and also in chapel. But the fact of the matter was that he didn't really notice any of the things that went on around him. Mjomba had been attending chapel alright; but he might as well have been on another planet, or sauntering in the orchard behind the chapel taking in the scenery - or in the

67

library flipping through the pages of tomes on the state of mind of the first man and the first woman as they prepared to commit the sin which changed the course of human history.

Mjomba had become so absorbed by his literary project, it was a wonder that he didn't hurt himself as a result of his inattentiveness to the goings-on around him. Mjomba now realized with horror that he had been so absent-minded during the services, he had to admit that his presence there in chapel had been only in body. He had been completely absent where it mattered most, namely in spirit.

Mjomba acknowledged that, for quite some time now, he had been living in mortal sin for those reasons. But the stage during which he could curb his interest in the thesis' subject matter had long passed; and Mjomba knew it. His only hope now was meditation, fasting and saying prayers - lots of them - since, on his own, he could not turn back from the perilous course, and start paying attention to the liturgy during Holy Mass as he was expected to do and things of that nature. That would be asking too much of someone who had become consumed to that extent with his project.

By the time Mjomba's thoughts on the matter had crystallized, he was already in the queue and awaiting his turn at the confessional. In despair Mjomba yielded his place at the head of the queue to another penitent, and walked away without going to confession. He did not want to compound the situation by lying to the priest that he was sorry for landing himself in that deplorable situation.

Mjomba was in disbelief and shock nevertheless, seeing that he, Mjomba, could actually end up in hell! But it surprised him that, even then, he was unable to muster the will power to pull back from the brink. To be sure, he had an obligation to turn in a thesis; and it was not as if there was anything sinister or wrong with the subject of his thesis. His professors had applauded his choice of subject, and all without exception had moreover signaled that they were looking forward to reading his thesis on "Original Virtue". Knowing Mjomba and his ability to delve into the most obscure topic and turn it into something that everyone enjoyed talking about, they were all hoping that the originality of his thesis would meet if not exceed their expectations. But now here he was with his spiritual life in tatters. It was something Mjomba had not bargained for at all.

Mjomba suspected that the devil was behind his misfortunes. Getting humans to lose their souls was after all what the Evil Ghost and his host of fallen angels were dedicated to doing. There had been times when Mjomba imagined that he just might be safe from the devices and wiles of Satan because of his upbringing which discouraged him from courting danger foolishly or getting into trouble through carelessness. Mjomba did not now doubt that, as far as the evil Lucifer who had once commanded the Seraphim was concerned, every creature that had been created in the Image without exception was exposed and fair play. The devil was going to do whatever it took to ensure that they did not become recipients of the largess of the Prime Mover that he himself had forfeited. Above all, Mjomba now also knew that the devil was not referred to in the Holy Book as a "snake" for nothing.

Mjomba lamented that there were many humans who believed in the existence of the devil all right, but thought of him as a dumb, stupid and ignorant creature. That was because they imagined, mistakenly, that anyone in Lucifer's favored position at creation had to be nuts to do what he did, namely opt for rebellion and hell

69

instead of loyalty to the being that was "Goodness" itself and for the heavenly mansion that went with obedience to the will of the Almighty One. If there was anything Mjomba had learnt on the other hand since he commenced work on his thesis, it was that Beelzebub was brilliant, very smart, and sharp, and quite possibly more knowledgeable in matters of faith than all the doctors of the Church combined!

Unlike the majority of humans who pooh-poohed the idea of going to hell and still blamed the devil for everything that went awry, Mjomba, who had been forced to awaken to the reality of his situation with a jolt, had enough common sense to know that he was definitely facing the prospect of going to hell, and that he had only himself to blame. The temptation might have originated from the adversary, or possibly even from his own flesh or ego; but that did not alter the fact that it was the exercise of his free will that had caused him to sink so low.

Instead of using his thesis to grow in the knowledge of the Prime Mover as he was supposed to do (and it was completely immaterial whether he ended up in the eyes of the world with a truly "winning" thesis or not), Mjomba had succumbed to the temptation to use it for personal self-aggrandizement at the expense of the Prime Mover. He had turned what ought to have been a very worthy project into an ego trip! And to make matters worse, as a senior seminarian, Mjomba should have known better!

Because Mjomba had gained a clearer understanding of how the devil operated - how he lured unwitting humans away from the path of holiness by getting them to imagine that they were better than others and could even "prove" it with their "good works" - the fact that he was better informed in that regard now only served to confirm him in his sin of pride. But try as he might, he found it impossible to desist from imagining that, if separated or even atheist brethren picked up and read his thesis (which he himself saw as a brilliant piece of original work from a rising apologist of the Church) and became converted as a result, he would deserve some if not all the credit for the spiritual conversion of those individuals.

Mjomba, while paying lip service to the role of grace in the conversion of non-Catholics, was inclined to give credit, not to the grace of the Prime Mover, but to himself, if it were to happen that an atheist who had never heard of the Catholic Church before, or a "separated" brother or sister, became convinced that it was indeed the one, holy and apostolic Church that traced its origins to the promised Messiah and Deliverer after reading his thesis.

Mjomba had also noted that everyone, both Catholics and non-Catholics, paid lip service to the efficacy of grace in saving souls. Mjomba had still to find a preacher who did not betray his true feelings about the credit he deserved personally, sometimes immediately after emphasizing that all the credit must go to the Prime Mover! And when he listened to sermons of the separated brethren who believed that humans attained salvation by the *faith alone*, and who consequently supposed that *good works* were not needed for salvation, he was even more scandalized by the credit they gave themselves in matters related to salvation.

The very manner in which they became saved, namely through personal statements that they were "accepting the Deliverer", implied taking personal credit for the decisions to start forging "personal relationships with the Deliverer". The one thing Mjomba did not personally want to do was to be hypocritical. He admitted that he was paying only lip service to the role of divine

71

grace in saving souls; and, even though he did not trumpet it, quietly he was all for taking full credit for any developments that resulted from his efforts.

As far as Mjomba was concerned, that was what had to happen in the "real world". He had noted that the only humans who did not take credit for the things they did were heroic souls like Mother Teresa of Calcutta and others who became canonized upon their death. Of course, even though they themselves refused to take credit for the good deeds they wrought here on earth, everyone else looked at things differently and gave them the credit as the vessels through which the Prime Mover's graces were dispensed. Even the process of canonization hinged on miracles being attributed to their intercession! Without any doubt therefore, these heroic souls were perfectly deserving of credit for leading completely selfless lives, which in turn permitted the Holy Ghost to perform wonders, including the wonder of saving souls that would otherwise have been lost, through their self-effacing labors.

Reflecting on his own intransigence, and his determination to take full credit for what, in reality, only the grace of the Prime Mover could bring about, Mjomba thought he now also understood how it came about that Lucifer tripped himself and fell from his elevated position in spite of his vast knowledge. Beelzebub had fallen from grace because he was just too puffed up and was bursting with pride!

Mjomba thought about people like Don Scotus (nicknamed the "Subtle Doctor"), St. Jerome (who supposedly was the most learned of the Fathers of the Western Church), the great St. Augustine, Martin Luther, John Calvin, St. Bernard of Clairvaux, St. Thomas Aquinas (nicknamed "Doctor Angelicus"), St. Paul of Tarsus and Apostle to the Gentiles, and Judas Iscariot, and saw clearly for the first time that what differentiated them was their readiness to let the Spirit lead them where they, on their own, would definitely not go.

The true heroes among them were heroes, not because of the depth of their individual knowledge, which was like a drop in the ocean when compared to the Prime Mover who was Knowledge *per se*, but because of their humility and their willingness to give the full credit for any of their achievements to the Prime Mover, and do so unreservedly and without dissembling. In the case of Paul of Tarsus, who previously went by the name of Saul, on his own he would still have been chasing and murdering followers of the Deliverer!

Mjomba acknowledged that the Prime Mover revealed himself and his secrets, not to swaggering, best-selling authors or university dons or scientists, but to the truly humble in heart - people like Saint Thérèse of the Child Jesus and of the Holy Face (or "The Little Flower of Jesus"), St. Catherine of Siena, and St. Francis of Assisi. The Prime Mover revealed His secrets to children and to souls that were similarly innocent.

Admittedly, Mjomba not only knew this, but he also knew that his attempt to produce a winning thesis, far from being driven by pure motives reflecting a genuine and self-less desire to save souls by becoming an *alter Christus* (other Christ), was motivated by the desire to show off and his glaring pride.

Chastened, but unrepentant...

Mjomba was chastened but still unrepentant as he noted gloomily the one thing to which all this pointed, namely the decision he made at the outset to use the Evil One as his mouthpiece for expounding on the Church's dogmas. Mjomba should have noticed immediately that he was falling into a trap that the devil was laying, and he should have retreated at that point without further ado and disowned the Tempter. He did not do that because he believed that he was perfectly capable of dilly-dallying with the Evil Ghost and getting away unscathed. He didn't even think of saying a prayer before going off on such a reckless adventure. And also, unfortunately, the prospects of becoming renowned, famous and even rich by riding on the coattails of the sleek Beelzebub were too attractive and tempting, and that was apparently still the case as Mjomba left the queue, and headed blindly to his allotted spot in the pews.

Unknown to Mjomba, it was Father Raj, his personal confessor, who was closeted inside the dingy cubicle and hearing confessions on that Saturday evening. If he had been aware of this, perhaps Mjomba would have thought twice about skipping his weekly confession and losing hope. Father Raj had always struck Mjomba as a man of God who also seemed to have a winning way even when the prospects for finding a solution were completely bleak. It was for that reason that Mjomba had chosen the Indian as his confessor.

Humans are like zombies...

Mjomba's tussles with the devil had gained him a new respect for the intellectual prowess of the Ruler of the Underworld, and this was quite plain as Mjomba continued work on his thesis. And he did not have any doubt at that point concerning the source of his inspiration. He was now quoting Satan directly as he continued to write.

"Humans, the separated brethren included, have to admit that they are either very ignorant and are consequently prone to making serious albeit unintentional errors on matters that are critical to their last end, or intellectually dishonest, or both. In either case, humans seem to be in a lot of trouble. For how come that in the present times panels of history 'experts', while able ostensibly to reach agreement as regards things Cæsar Augustus said, did and wrote have never been able to reach agreement on what the Deliverer did and said, let alone who he was? How come men and women of letters have failed to put to rest the doubts regarding the institution in the world that is the lawful successor to the *Sancta Ecclesia* the Deliverer inaugurated on Pentecost Day?

"And how come panels of biblical scholars don't seem to agree on anything at all? How come all these ministries whose teachings are at variance with each other? How come all those 'messengers' of the Prime Mover, who bandied around the fact that they were men and women of letters, seem to derive lots of fun in contradicting each other where it matters the most, namely regarding the one and the only authentic ministry started by the Deliverer, and which ones weren't and therefore needed to close their doors to reduce the prevailing confusion on the world? Or are these things exactly as they are supposed to be because they reflect the ignorance of humans and/or the pervasive intellectual dishonesty that are now a standard feature of a world populated by *homines iniqui* who have no scruples about exploiting anything in sight, including the Holy Book, for their own ends?

"Humans are like zombies! They don't know they are human! The concept of humanity became foreign to them from the moment the first man and the first woman fell from grace, and the effects of original sin began to take their toll. Starting with Cain who nipped the life of his brother Abel in the bud, humans have slaughtered each other and have gotten into the habit of treating their pets better than they do 'strangers'! They steal from each other, lie to fellow humans, cheat and do unimaginable things to one another in the name of progress. To maximize their enjoyment of material things, those in the majority even go to the extent of 'legislating' an order in which struggling members of society or, 'deviants' as they are called, can be permanently put away by locking them up in cages or 'prison cells' or in the literal sense by 'executing' them! So, so stupid!

"Humanity isn't multiple. There aren't as many 'humanities' or 'humankinds' as there are humans. Human nature - or the essence of being human - is not just one; it is indivisible, the fact that humans exist as separate entities or 'individuals' notwithstanding.

"In contrast, we demons and those pure spirits that remained loyal to the Almighty One do not share the same nature. There is no such a thing as 'angelic nature'! But whether in heaven or down here in the Underworld, we pure spirits still take full cognizance of the right of other spirits to exist. We do not try to murder or destroy each other. And that is why the Prime Mover Himself decided to leave us alone after we rebelled against Him. The conditions here in Gehenna may be ghastly, but they are of our own making. We demons couldn't accuse the Prime Mover of any cruelty in that regard. But that is of course what you humans would have done if you were in our place.

"The Prime Mover spared humans - those at any rate who try to live up to their elevated state as His temples and do not deserve to join us here in Hell - the fate of being consigned to 'Limbo' through all eternity by sending them a Messiah even. And the Son of Man instituted the 'ecclesia' or 'Church' through which He dispenses the divine graces that are intended to help them live up to their state as children of the Prime Mover. But look what humans did to the Messiah - they killed Him. And then look what humans are doing to the *ecclesia* that He established on the rock called Peter.

"First, when the Deliverer came to 'His own' (namely the Israelites from whom the Deliverer took His stock and for whom Providence had done so much to ensure their survival as a people until His coming), they rejected and abandoned Him in His greatest time of need. And then, look what humans have turned the *ecclesia* he founded to serve as the new 'Ark of Noah' into! But it also speaks to the nature of humans that, since its inception, many inside the Church who should have known better have attempted to emulate Judas Iscariot and Ananias, and succeeded in using that divine institution for their personal aggrandizement, causing untold grief to many inside and outside the Church in the process."

As he was jotting down the thoughts that were flooding his mind and which he was now dutifully attributing to Beelzebub, Mjomba considered the infinite possibilities of profiting from the kind of theological treatise he was writing, and allowed that he could himself fall for the temptation to use its contents, which were about saving souls, for personal gain alright! He was struck by the ease with which he would be able to do this, and it suddenly dawned on him that most, if not all, of those who exploited the *Sancta Ecclesia*, or alternatively the Holy Book, for personal gain probably started out with the most noble motives! Brushing the tempting thought aside, Mjomba continued writing.

"Others have taken to setting up and operating private ministries to exploit the human hunger for spiritual sustenance under the guise of winning believers for the Deliverer, and have turned evangelization into one of the most profitable enterprises after taking a leaf from those who profit immensely from starting and operating 'non-profit' organizations.

"And it is not as if it is hard for humans to find the traditional *ecclesia* which the Deliverer instituted two thousand years ago on the rock called Peter! It is after all not so very long ago when Peter's tomb was found beneath the basilica in Rome that bears his name, and not far from the place where he was martyred for his faith. And it has nothing to do with the passage of time either. For indeed, out of the many who flocked to hear the Deliverer out as He crisscrossed Galilee and Judea teaching the multitudes, healing the sick and performing other miracles, not a soul showed up on Calvary to commiserate with His mother Mary as He hung dying on the cross. A traditional *ecclesia* whose central message has as its main theme 'the crucified Deliverer' and an independent money making 'ministry' of course aren't things that can be compatible.

"While the sacred scriptures are sacred and will always remain so, the fact of the matter is that the Deliverer founded something He called an *ecclesia*; and it is not just tradition, but even the *New Testament* (on which the Deliverer Himself was ever so singularly and deafeningly silent) attests to the planning for and establishment of the one (and only one), universal (catholic), and apostolic (founded on the rock called *Petrus*) *ecclesia* (a divinely instituted entity through which the Deliverer planned to dispense His saving graces to those who would believe in Him). And so, it should raise suspicions when self-appointed, bible totting 'ministers' decide to insist that their followers take orders, not from the agency He commissioned (with Peter as its first CEO) and charged with the task of passing on what He had taught them under the guidance of the Spirit (Paraclete), but only from the written 'Word of the Prime Mover'!

"Yet it is actually not that hard to see the fallacy in that so-called doctrine of *sola scriptura*! But it should also be obvious that the doctrine of *sola scriptura*, whose origins are recent and moreover well known, by its very definition should be seen as self-defeating, since it did not leave any room for (and therefore militated against) the very notion of an *ecclesia* that could serve as the vehicle for carrying on the Deliverer's evangelizing mission.

"Oh, Goddamn dissembling humans! So there are folks, 'Christians', who claim to be followers of the Deliverer but also simultaneously adhere to the doctrine of *sola scriptura*! You do that, and you automatically deny that the Deliverer was capable of setting up an *ecclesia* to continue to do His bidding after He left this world on Ascension Day to go sit on the right hand of His Father in heaven. Since the sacred scriptures themselves attest to the existence of such an *ecclesia*, your action in denying its existence now also puts into question not just your understanding of those selfsame scriptures, but even faithfulness to the same - damn it!

"And, yes; you've guessed correctly. You do that and you also automatically concede that the 'Deliverer' you purport to have a personal relationship with is one who espouses a completely different *modus operandi* from that of the historical Deliverer! In other words, you have a personal relationship, not with the historical Deliverer, but with a completely different 'Deliverer' of your own invention!

"Still, it can be said that this doctrine and the eagerness with which it is embraced by disenchanted Christians are additional evidence of the gullibility of humans when it comes to anything that is divine!

"And then almost every human blames the Prime Mover for the self-inflicted 'pain and suffering' that sinful and sinning humans are so deserving of in any case. And they do so despite the fact that 'pain and suffering' have been sanctified by the death and resurrection of the Deliverer. But, in truth, humans have even greater reason than us pure spirits to be one - to live and exist as 'one people' and in 'one society of humans' in the one and the only 'Mystical Body of the Deliverer' or 'Church'; but that is running ahead a little…"

Mjomba noticed a change in tone, mood or whatever as the Evil Ghost took a pause and then continued.

"But, by Golly! Humans are so ignorant! I myself and all the other fallen angels now endure pain and suffering, not because the Prime Mover is some kind of vindictive Being (which He cannot be by nature); but because, being creatures that were formed in the image of the triune Divinity (whose three persons were united in an eternal bond of love) meant that we too stood to be partakers of the *joy* that came with being in love. The fact though is that the Prime Mover the Father, the Prime Mover the Son, and the Prime Mover the Holy Ghost - the three divine persons, each one through a separate but divine act of the will, freely choose to coexist as a single Godhead. And it is the desire of all three divine persons of the Blessed Trinity, exercised jointly and severally, that creatures that bear the Prime Mover's divine image and likeness likewise be in a position to freely choose to sing, exalt and praise Him in unison.

"Our own refusal to genuflect violated the sacred relationship between us creatures and the infinitely gracious and loving Prime Mover and Lord of All. Our refusal to worship and adore the Almighty and Omnipotent One resulted in our being ejected from His holy presence into nowhere! That was not something we had anticipated. And that was quite a transition for beings whose creation was itself a labor of divine and infinite

80

love. Since we were not 'prime movers', we couldn't reinvent ourselves in order to be able to exist in some alternative 'dream heavenly world' apart from the Prime Mover and our Maker. We were pig-headed to that extent! Our refusal to embrace Him who was our Infinite Good was an act of violence against ourselves. It had been our intention to eject everyone else, including the Prime Mover Himself, from heaven!

"The evil at the heart of my plan consisted in my hope of playing one Divine Person against another Divine Person; and in trying to position myself in such a way that, regardless of which Divine Person triumphed, I would usurp the power of the Most High, and become the *de facto* Ruler of the Universe. Frankly, I reckoned that the three Divine Persons, because they are all equally divine, would end up fighting each other to the finish, and that I would then be in a position to install myself of the Ruler over all creation with the help of my minions. I knew that my chances of success were slim, and that the consequences of failure were dire; still, the prize - installing myself as the Ruler of the Universe - looked very attractive! I had persuaded myself that the risk was worth taking.

"Instead of going on after our trial to become happy and contented members of choirs of angels in the Church Triumphant, we suddenly found ourselves transformed into demons! This was the state we had craved for - the state of being defiant spirits that wanted nothing to do with the Infinite Goodness and the Infinite Love that define the Prime Mover and also Almighty One.

"On the one hand, we are endowed with all these wonderful voices and other gifts which come with being fashioned in the Image. But on the other hand, we hate ourselves for having chosen to defy Him-Who-is-Who-is, and who brought us into existence out of nothing. Instead

81

of using our voices to sing praises to the Prime Mover, all we can do with them now is curse ourselves until we are hoarse for engaging in an outrageous act of disobedience, and for the fact that we will never achieve our self-actualization! There is now no way that our hunger for fulfilment will ever be satisfied, even though by refusing to genuflect, we were granted our hearts' desire namely freedom and independence to do exactly as we liked with ourselves!

"Humans are in exactly the same situation as we are. Free creatures, they choose to flagrantly do things that are against their consciences, and are not in accordance with the will of the Prime Mover and Lord of All. But the difference between humans and us is that humans would like to pretend that they fell from grace by accident and not through a deliberate act of the free will! And, whereas the sin of Adam and Eve was what first triggered concupiscence and the other effects of 'original sin', the fact is that sinful and sinning humans are always crying foul and blaming the Prime Mover for all their woes, real and imaginary, when they have yet to experience real pain and real suffering! Adam and Eve regretted their sin almost as soon as they had committed it – and their sin merely consisted in stealing fruit from the Tree of the Knowledge of Good and Evil! Compare that with the wicked deeds that humans do to each other to day!

"Some humans spend their time complaining loudly for the sake of complaining, and are oblivious to the fact that the lifestyles they lead are the source of their problems; and that real suffering and real pain await them here in hell - or, if they are lucky, in Purgatory expiating the feelings of guilt for their wicked deeds! Even though the souls in Purgatory are assured of salvation, the self-inflicted suffering that derives from the knowledge that they spurned the graces the Deliverer had merited for them - graces that would have enabled them to lead wholly upright lives - and had desisted from acknowledging the hurt they caused others and the Deliverer and making up whilst here on earth will be quite acute and terrible.

"Unfortunately for humans, the folks who least need to be jolted to their senses - folks like Catherine of Genoa, Mary Faustina, Padre Pio, and John Vianney - are the ones who have visions of Purgatory whilst here on earth. And that is probably just as well, since others would go nuts at the sight of the poor suffering souls, and probably not recover! That wouldn't be helpful if the purpose of the visions was to alert humans to the need for repentance.

"On their first day in Purgatory, humans will be wishing they were back on earth enduring all the miseries and woes they were in the habit of complaining about a thousand-fold! And, Pew! For those humans who end up here in hell with us, when they realize that they had squandered the opportunities they had been afforded to live as befitted creatures that were fashioned in the Image, and that as consequence their innate desire for self-actualization will go unfulfilled for the rest of eternity, they will wish for the impossible, namely that the Prime Mover should change His mind and rub them out - perhaps in the same way they themselves were always attempting to rub out fellow humans whom they detested for one reason or another back on earth - rather than face the prospect of losing their souls to me! They will be beside themselves when it starts to dawn on them that, instead of the all good and all loving Lord, they will have me, the meanest and evilest creature imaginable, as their adopted lord and master!

"When we pure spirits fell from grace, we experienced an immediate and dreadful sense of loss, accompanied by overwhelming feelings of despair and emptiness from knowing that we were now accursed; and this morbid sense of intense loss has continued without let-up ever since. It is what constitutes the pain and suffering that we endure. And it all came about because of an act of free will on our part signifying that we were not prepared to either serve or pay homage to the Prime Mover.

"In the case of humans, the original sin committed by Adam and Eve signalled to the Prime Mover that they too would not serve or pay Him the homage He was due. The fact of the matter is that the original sin committed by the first man and the first woman was a merely *wicked* deed, unlike our own sin that was a truly *evil* deed because, in addition to openly challenging the Prime Mover's authority, we embarrassed Him by disrupting the solemn procession of Cherubim and Seraphim.

"Not only were the angels whom I succeeded in drawing into my rebellion legion, but I actually dared the Prime Mover to cast me and my minions into the 'fires of hell' for our outrageous act of defiance! The expression 'fires of hell' was actually coined by me!

"Even though the pain and suffering that immediately resulted from the rebellion of Adam and Eve was horrible and debilitating by human standards, it was really negligible. The immediate effect of the act of rebellion of the first man and the first woman was to make them susceptible to things like hunger and thirst, physical weariness, which in turn required that they try and understand the vagaries of nature, and take measures to minimize any pain and suffering arising there from.

"But because humans became inclined to sin in the wake of their fall from grace, while at the same time remaining incapable of performing any good deeds on their own without the help of divine grace, the scope for them (humans) to cause their fellow humans pain and suffering out of purely selfish motives also became limitless. As long as humans were meek and humble, and acknowledged their haplessness, and provided they matched that meekness and humility with a determination to lead lives of self-denial, the miseries and suffering to which they were exposed increased the scope for them to expiate for their own sins on earth. Enduring pain and suffering effectively became purifying, and sanctifying. Still, true meekness and humility was only possible with the help of the divine grace that was merited for humans by the Deliverer.

"Also, a meek and humble life could pretty much insulate humans who were prepared to embrace that sort of existence from the temptations of the flesh and from my wiles. And for humans who managed to bear their 'crosses' in that fashion, the manifestation of pain and suffering, while no less nasty and hurting, represented an opportunity to identify themselves with the Word-become-flesh, and to participate in the passion and death, and also resurrection of the Deliverer - and now, alas, also Judge - of Mankind.

"Human pain and suffering otherwise presaged the miseries that awaited those descendants of Adam and Eve who refused to pay heed to their consciences as and when the time came for them to give up their ghosts. For all such humans, instead of representing a much awaited and momentous occasion on which they would be finally ushered into the presence of their Creator and Lord following their period of trial on earth, death became the occasion for us here in hell to celebrate the victory of evil over good. As a rule, the reward I give the demons who contribute the most to the loss of human souls is the freedom to turn the tables on those wicked humans, and give them a taste of the miseries and frustration they wrought upon their fellow humans back on earth. Now, that - as you can imagine - is an experience that can be very painful and also very humiliating.

One humankind...

"Listen up you fools: the Word-Become-Man identifies Himself completely with you stupid humans. Now, the Word deciding to take up human nature and 'becoming flesh' in the process is testimony to one hell of love that the Prime Mover and Almighty One has for created beings in general - including us pure spirits - and for you humans in particular. If the Prime Mover's love for you humans was not *infinite*, He of course wouldn't have sent His only Begotten Son to a place like Earth that was now populated with humans who were not merely wayward, but had become so unbelievably hostile even to their very own, making it actually the most unlikely destination for a decent creature, leave alone a Divinity.

"It would not have been practical for the Word to become an angel in order to carry out His Father's bidding because, unlike humans, each angel has its own distinctive essence or nature. Doing that would have been the same as taking up the name of one or other angel while remaining the Word - the Second Person of the Trinity. And, as He donned His humanity, He opted for the male as opposed to the female gender because, as the Word through Whom all created beings came into existence, He had already decided in eternity that He would become not a 'Second Eve' upon becoming man, but a 'Second Adam'. And He was able to become a Second Adam only *because* He had deigned to fashion you humans in His Father's image and likeness. You may have two legs and two arms and share some other things with brutes, but the fact is that you are created in the

Prime Mover's image and brutes are not. It is what makes all the difference.

"And, as if to show that He was not belittling the 'weaker' gender, the Second Person of the Holy Trinity, who had fashioned Eve from a rib taken from the side of Adam, not only became flesh while relying on the *fiat* of His *maiden* mother Mary, but he also relied on her completely for the human nature that He as the Second Adam and Deliverer of humankind needed for His own sojourn on Earth. The Word relied on a member of humankind whose *(female)* gender had been formed with the help of the male gender (Adam) at creation.

"One could speculate that, if the Word had fashioned 'Woman' from a piece of the earth's crust and had instead molded Man from a rib taken out of the side of Eve, there probably wouldn't have been any problem for Him to opt for the female gender upon taking up His human nature. There wouldn't have been any problem with that *per se*.

"But that would have created a different problem for Providence because of the obvious desire on the part of the Word to emphasize the oneness of humanity and the intractable and close affinity of members of humankind reflected firstly in the manner in which He brought Adam and Eve into being on the one hand and secondly in the manner in which He Himself became flesh.

"There is no doubt that Providence wanted to have humankind reflect the unity in the triune Godhead in a special way; and His actions, conceived in eternity and executed in time, pertaining to humans attest to that. Even though it required the intervention of supernatural power to execute, it was not a physical impossibility *per se* for the Word to rely on His maiden mother alone for His human nature when becoming flesh. The same would not have been the case if Mary had been a man.

The desire of the Word to rely solely on a member of humankind whose *(male)* gender (in this case) had been formed with the help of the female gender (Eve's) at creation would have been frustrated for obvious reasons.

A statistic...

"Useless creatures that are clueless about their own nature, their identity, and where they are headed, and that nonchalantly betray their own Deliverer, and the Word-Become-Flesh, whenever they go out of their way to betray their own kind; creatures that, knowingly or unknowingly, likewise level false accusations against Him whenever they deceive, lie and spin in their dealings with their own kind; other humans; creatures that scourge Him and crown Him with thorns whenever they injure and harm their own kind anywhere; creatures who spit on Him and drive nails rough shod into His sacred hands whenever their selfishness drives them to do things that occasion their own kind miseries and suffering; and creatures that murder their Deliverer whenever they sit back, and allow injustice on earth to take its course while pretending to be working to promote world peace! A fair description of you humans by me, Beelzebub, nee Lucifer, aka the Evil Ghost? You bet!

"Now, there is no way that humans who are so clueless about who they are, would be able to grasp the 'mystery of mysteries', namely the Mystery of the Incarnation whence the Word, the Second Person of the Blessed Trinity, in abeyance to the will of His father, agreed to become a statistic! Yes, a statistic! We here in the Pit keep track of the number of humans whom the Almighty deigns to bring into existence. We used to do the same for angelic essences that He caused to come into existence, but lost count ages ago. At one point, on the spur of the moment, He created so many zillions of them at once, it became impossible to keep up with the count. Actually, the number of the new additions alone was so boggling even to my sharp mind, I remember I nearly went crazy just trying to conceptualize it. Unfortunately for my cause, I did not succeed in leading a single one of those zillions astray.

"By the way, we here in the Pit also keep count of the human souls we succeed in leading astray. That is the count we would love to lose track of - yes, the number of damned human souls! That would make me, Beelzebub, a winner over and over...

"Any way, as humans have never cared to relate to their own kind whom they will scourge, crucify and murder on a whim under the cloak of following spurious 'rules of engagement', they will never be able to relate to the Deliverer, let alone appreciate that, of all the divine mysteries, the Mystery of the Incarnation is the most mysterious of them all! By deciding to take on the shape of a human, the Omnipotent One also agreed to become a statistic - just like those countless and nameless souls that are dispatched daily to their eternal rest by so called 'security forces' after being labeled everything from 'terrorist' and 'insurgent' to 'unfortunate collateral damage'.

"When the Word, through whom all creation came to be, Himself became flesh and dwelt among humans, by my count He became the 999,872,094,998,651, 392,701,335,682,929,411,360,095,883,552,296th human embryo that had been carried inside a woman's womb. With Adam and Eve included in the count, Mary's sinless child, who saw the light of day for the first time in a manger in Bethlehem two thousand years ago, became the 999,872,094,998,651,392,701,335,682,929,411,360, 095,883,552,298th inhabitant of Earth.

"Our count includes all those babies whose lives were nipped in the bud for any reason whilst still inside their mothers' wombs. And, except for the one occasion when the 'Son of Man' as He called Himself became transfigured and appeared with Abraham and Moses to Peter, James and John, He was also subject to all the limitations of the descendants of Adam and Eve in obedience to the will of His Father. Let us take a moment and consider the chronology of the events that led to this, and also check out the implications for humans.

"These events started in the beginning when darkness was still upon the face of the deep heaven and earth, both of which the Prime Mover had just caused to bounce into existence out of nothing; and the earth was void and empty. It was then that His spirit moved over the waters, and what next happened is history: On the first day, the Prime Mover created light; and He then created the firmament on the second day; and on the third day He caused dry land that He called Earth and the gathering together of the waters that He called Seas to evolve for the first time; and He followed that up with a command that the earth bringeth forth the green herb such as yieldeth seed according to its kind, and the tree that beareth fruit having seed each one also according to its kind; and He created the Sun, Moon, and Stars on the fourth day; and on the fifth He commanded the waters to bring forth the creeping creature having life, and the fowl that may fly over the earth under the firmament of heaven, and He created the great whales, and every living and moving creature, which the waters brought forth, according to their kinds, and every winged fowl according to its kind; and then on the sixth He commanded the Earth to bring forth the living creature in its kind, cattle and creeping things, and beasts of the earth, according to their kinds…(Genesis 1:25)

"And then, as if on cue, the Prime Mover said: 'Let us make man to our image and likeness: and let him have dominion over the fishes of the sea, and the fowls of the air, and the beasts, and the whole earth, and every creeping creature that moveth upon the earth'! And He then blessed the humans saying: 'Increase and multiply, and fill the earth, and subdue it, and rule over the fishes of the sea, and the fowls of the air, and all living creatures that move upon the earth...Behold I have given you every herb bearing seed upon the earth, and all trees that have in themselves seed of their own kind, to be your meat...' (Genesis 1:29-30)

"It was quite clear, when the Prime Mover started His work of creation, that from day one He had humans in mind; and the purpose of His work over those seven days was so humans would get to enjoy His largess. And it was for that reason that He created humans in His own image and likeness.

"And then there is also the way He brought the Woman into existence. When the Prime Mover built the rib He took from Adam into the woman and then presented the results to Adam, Adam had exclaimed: 'This now is bone of my bones, and flesh of my flesh; she shall be called woman, because she was taken out of man!' (Genesis 2:18-24) And that said it all. You could see the mirror of the Holy Trinity there. God the Father, God the Son, and God the Holy Spirit – three persons each one of them possessing the same divine nature; except that in this instance the divine nature of the three persons was such that all three divine persons constituted but one divine Prime Mover in accordance with the indivisible nature of a divinity!

"And to guarantee that humans, created in the Image, would really enjoy the Prime Mover's munificence, after the heavens and the earth were finished, and all the furniture of them, the Prime Mover had planted a Paradise of Pleasure wherein He placed man whom He had formed. And He brought forth out of the ground all manner of trees, fair to behold, and pleasant to eat of: the Tree of Life also in the midst of Paradise - the Tree of Knowledge of Good and Evil. And the Prime Mover took man, and put him into the Paradise for Pleasure, to dress it, and keep it. And He commanded him, saying: 'Of every tree of paradise thou shalt eat: But of the Tree of Knowledge of Good and Evil, thou shalt not eat. For in what day so ever thou shalt eat of it, thou shalt die the death!'

"Now I tell you I came very near to swearing that there was something the matter with the Prime Mover when I observed things unfold the way they did! This was not the first time the Prime Mover had experimented with creatures in that manner. The only difference was that this time around His work of creation was over seven days instead of a moment's time as had happened when He caused us here in the celestial sphere to bounce into existence out of nothing.

"And at the end of each of the seven days He had expressed satisfaction with His work of creation in the exact same way He had looked upon His work of creation in the angelic realm - choirs of Seraphim, Cherubim, Thrones, Dominions or Lordships, Virtues and Strongholds, Powers and Authorities, Principalities and Rulers, and Archangels - and expressed His full satisfaction with the result. But you, of course, know what transpired virtually immediately thereupon.

"I led the rebellion against the Prime Mover, and I promptly ended up in this place of the damned along with the angels who had stupidly joined me in the unsuccessful uprising. But here was the Prime Mover again creating humans in His own image and likeness out of nothing, and giving them dominion over the earth and everything in it! He definitely knew what we here in Gehenna would be up to, and He tried to hedge His bets by allotting the human creatures each one a guardian angel. But, endowed with the faculties or reason and free will, they would of course still be able to do as they pleased.

"Modern day humans, of course, appear quite incapable of appreciating the Prime Mover's works of creation even after He Himself had declared that He saw and they were excellent! Only a handful - mostly hermits and cloistered monks and nuns - seem to have any idea as regards the value of human beings in the eyes of their Maker, or see His hand in everything that surrounds them. And with humans patently unable to appreciate the grandeur of the cosmos in which they live - even though they are endowed with the senses that enable them to see, hear, smell, taste and touch things around them, in addition to the faculties of reason and free will - it would be a stretch to expect them to have any inkling of the grandeur of the Prime Mover's works of creation in a realm that is not immediately susceptible to the five senses, and whose existence is knowable only through revelation.

"Suffice it to say that humans do not have the wherewithal whilst on earth to appreciate even in the slightest degree the grandeur of the Prime Mover's works of creation in the celestial realm after He willed those of us who belong to the choirs of angels into existence out of nothing. Actually it is the sort of grandeur that can be fully grasped only by those spiritual essences that enjoy beatific vision!

"But you can, in any event, imagine the revulsion that I, as the ringleader of the angelic revolt against the Prime Mover, felt when I saw Adam and Eve in their

93

pristine innocence basking in the love of their Maker, and putting me and all the other fallen angels to shame! There was absolutely no way I could hold back at that point.

"Now you might not know, but the different species of the beasts of the earth that the Prime Mover created as recorded in the Book of Genesis (Genesis 1:25 to be exact) are representative of - and actually mirror - the choirs of Seraphim, Cherubim, Thrones, Dominions or Lordships, Virtues and Strongholds, Powers and Authorities, Principalities and Rulers, and Archangels that the Prime Mover had created in the celestial realm; and the different species of snakes symbolize us demons. That is why the Book, referring to me as the ringleader, says that the serpent was more subtle than any of the beasts of the earth which the Lord God made.

"I sincerely could not believe my fortune when, despite having been told by the Prime Mover that they were free to eat fruit from every tree in the Garden of Pleasure except fruit from the tree that stood in the midst of the garden, Eve still caved in to the temptation, and not only plucked and ate fruit from the Tree of Knowledge of Good and Evil, but gave some of it to her Companion who also did eat. Yes, Eve at my instigation actually saw that the forbidden fruit from that tree was good to eat, and fair to the eyes, and delightful to behold!

"Of course the rest is history. After they took and ate of the forbidden fruit, the eyes of them both were opened: and when they perceived themselves to be naked, they sewed together fig leaves, and made themselves aprons. They couldn't bear the shame!

"And as soon as I heard the Prime Mover, addressing me, say: 'I will put enmities between thee and the woman, and thy seed and her seed: she shall crush thy head, and thou shalt lie in wait for her heel', I knew that the Prime Mover was coming for me; except that I did not know at that time that He was going to come as a deified human! I should have guessed because I had just played such a crucial part in the downfall of Adam and Eve and their descendants! He could not humiliate me more.

"And then the Prime Mover had conceded that, by disobeying and eating of the forbidden fruit from the Tree of Life, the duo had set themselves on a totally unacceptable course, saying: 'Behold Adam is become as one of us, knowing good and evil: now, therefore, lest perhaps he put forth his hand, and take also of the tree of life, and eat, and live forever.' He accordingly found Himself with no choice but to eject the humans from the Paradise of Pleasure in the same way he ejected me and my co-conspirators from His presence as described in Revelation 12:7-12. The difference was that in the case of humans, the Prime Mover was compelled to acknowledge the role I played in their downfall, and hence the promise of the Deliverer.

"Taking up His human nature, the Deliverer for whom are all things, and by whom are all things, who had brought many children into glory allowed Himself to be made a little lower than the angels as Paul would write in his epistle to the Hebrews (Hebrews 2:7-9). Paul would add: 'He that sanctifieth, and they who are sanctified, are all of one. For which cause he is not ashamed to call them brethren.' (Hebrews 2:11)

"Elsewhere Paul would write: 'Christ also did not glorify himself, that he might be made a high priest: but he that said unto him: Thou art my Son, this day have I begotten thee. As he saith also in another place: Thou art a priest forever, according to the order of Melchisedech.' (Hebrews 5:5-6)

"And then, after the Deliverer had given up His life for humans, suffering an ignominious death on the cross in atonement for their sins, and risen from the dead, as He prepared to ascend to His Father in heaven, He had said to His apostles: 'Go ye into the whole world, and preach the gospel to every creature. He that believeth and is baptized, shall be saved: but he that believeth not shall be condemned...' (Mark 16:15-16) As Paul would explain, the word of God is living and effectual, and more piercing than any two-edged sword; and reaching unto the division of the soul and the spirit, of the joints also and the marrow, and is a discerner of the thoughts and intents of the heart. Neither is there any creature invisible in his sight: but all things are naked and open to his eyes, to whom our speech is. (Hebrews 4:12-13)

"And then, to quote from the preface of the Sancta Ecclesia's Eucharistic Prayer for Reconciliation, never did the Prime Mover turn away from humans; and, though time and again they have broken their covenant, He has bound the human family to Himself through the Deliverer His Son, their Redeemer, with a new bond of love so tight that it can never be undone.

"That was the Deliverer's way of settling scores with me! Of course the vast majority of humans only think of me as some mythical hobgoblin that is harmless in the final analysis. And that is well and good for me naturally. But let me say this: I could not be more motivated, after all the humiliation I have endured for helping to trip up humans, to now try and get as many of you as possible damned!

"And yes, *that* is my way of getting even with you hypocritical and foolhardy humans. You stupid humans who can't even resist the temptation to turn the House of the Prime Mover into a place where you conduct commerce; and you have the cheek to imagine that you can put on pious faces and get away with it by deriding and mocking me and the host of my good and faithful demons here in Gehenna, and get away with it that way! So, so damn stupid. You damn stupid humans who do not even know your identity should remember that, even though a resident of the Pit along with the rest of the damned, I still remain the Prince of Darkness! And no one who dares to make me a laughing stock, especially when that individual still continues to call my tune while pretending to be redeemed and delivered (or saved!) gets away scot-free!

The Way, the Truth...

"You, perhaps, are now also beginning to understand why, through the disobedience of one man (Adam), 'Death' was introduced into the world; and also how, with the Word, becoming one of you and going on to pay the price for the redemption of humans who would elect to believe in Him, 'Life' was restored back to Humanity, restored through the obedience of one man just as Death was visited upon humans through the disobedience of one man.

"Human nature is one such that if one human hurts, all humans hurt. It happened when Adam and Eve fell from grace, and it happens every time any human hurts to day. Injustice perpetrated by one human against another human is injustice done to all humankind, including the Word!

"If a human goes nuts and starts to imagine that it is going to pay to hurt another human in any manner (with the fall of Adam and Eve from grace, that is exactly what all of you humans became inclined to do), the hurt that stupid human actually inflicts on him/herself is in fact far greater than the hurt which that human inflicts on his/her supposed human enemies. Oblivious to this 'law' which is rooted in the 'human' nature, you humans are busy trying to do that all the time. And that is how stupid members of the human race became when the First Man and the First Woman fell for my ruse and lost their innocence. Just so, so stupid, aren't you!

"Instead of unity among members of humankind, selfishness and greed now drives everyone to try and undercut each other. It happens among immediate family members, and it is of course many times worse when humans forget that they are all descended from Adam and Eve and are related, and begin to treat one another as aliens.

"Thank the Prime Mover that we pure spirits are not visible to the human eye. Because if that were the case, you can bet that humans, in their blind greed, would be tempted to initiate wars of conquest in an attempt to enslave even us demons in hopes of finding stuff to loot. That is how lustful and covetous humans can be. And that is also where my original decision to tempt humans to trade in their birthright for illusionary gains, and to betray the Prime Mover thereby as they stupidly did, would have come back to haunt me!

"The only way the breach in the unity of humanity can now be healed is through membership in the Mystical Body of the Deliverer. Outside the Mystical Body of the Deliverer or the *Sancta Ecclesia*, it is greed and selfishness that rule. The Deliverer brought it off by accepting to become the sacrificial lamb, and allowing the crooked priests and Pharisees, the crafty Pontius Pilate and his cruel and merciless soldiers, and the blood thirsty mobs who not long before had gawked at the miracles He performed for their benefit to have their way.

"And He now invites all wayward humans to get back into the fold and become one again by receiving Him in the sacrament of the Holy Eucharist. In other words, he invites all humans one and all to eat of His flesh under the species of bread and to drink of His blood under the species of wine during a memorial service that has come to be known as Holy Mass, a service during which the Deliverer's passion, death and resurrection are re-enacted following a tradition that goes back to that 'Maundy' Thursday, during the reign of the wicked King Herod Agrippa.

"When the 'Word-become-flesh' supped with His twelve apostles, including his beloved apostle John and his purse bearer Judas Iscariot, for the last time before His death, He put in practice what He had taught them to expect as His disciples, and invited them all to eat His body under the species of bread, and to drink His blood under the species of wine, telling them to continue doing what He had done - partaking of His body and His blood - in His memory. For, as He had explained to them in no uncertain terms, unless humans ate His body and drank His blood, they would not have 'Life' in them and would continue to be enslaved to me, the 'Author of Death'!

"There is, in other words, no possibility of regaining membership in the revamped human family (in which the Deliverer and His blessed mother now also belong) except through their blessing; and that blessing is not available to anyone outside the 'Mystical Body of the Deliverer or the Church', the only place where you won't be able to find my fingerprints by divine decree. But pick any other place, and you will find my fingerprints all over the place. I can guarantee you that the minute a human forgets that it is I and my cohorts who exercise rule over all the Earth, that human is mincemeat and as good as dead! There can only be salvation outside the Church over my dead body - and, you know I don't have one!

"But you humans are so stupid, you don't even see that your legacy as members of the *Ecclesia Militans* (Church Militant) - and it is the only legacy that matters at all - determines your rank order in the *Ecclesia Triumphans* (Church Triumphant).whose members include all the generations from Adam and Eve to Shem to Abraham to Hezron to David to Nathan, to Zeeubbabel to the Deliverer and *Logos* and to the saints that have gone marching into the Divine Banquet Hall since then for the Marriage Supper of the Lamb described by John in Revelation 19:7-10.

"The attitude of humans to this idea of generations is a good example that stupidity. Look, even though a total of five generations make up human society today (namely the Centennials or Gen Z, the Millennials or Gen Y, Generation X, the Baby Boomers, and the Silent Generation that is about to go completely 'silent' in the literal sense in twenty years or so), the Centennials act as though the Millennials, Generation X, the Baby Boomers and the Silent Generation are nincompoops who do not really belong in society, but possibly are even illegit! And that is even though the centennials wouldn't be enjoying what they enjoy if it wasn't for the labors of the older members of society and the generations that went before them. And they are brought up to imagine that when a human grows old and frail and 'goes to join his/her ancestors' or 'goes to his/her rest', it means the 'end of life' for that emaciated old man or old woman, when in actual fact that is when the person enters the final stage of self-actualization, and the real games begin.

"The Apostle of the Gentiles described that transition pretty accurately in his first letter to the Corinthians when he wrote: 'Now we see but a dim reflection as in a mirror. Then we shall see face to face. Now I know in part; but then I shall know even as I am known. (1 Corinthians 13:12) And Peter was so overawed by the scene of the Transfiguration when the Deliverer appeared with Moses and Elijah, he thought it was fitting to emblazon that scene in history by getting tabernacles constructed on that mountain in their memorial for the benefit of future generations no doubt. (Luke 9:33, Matthew 17:1-13, Mark 9:1-13 and Peter 1:16-21) This was two thousand years ago! And when Saint Stephen was being stoned for rebuking the crowd in Jerusalem that included members of the Synagogue of Roman Freedmen and the Sanhedrin, members , he looked called out 'Lord, do not hold this sin against them'. This was after he had looked intently to heaven and seen the glory of the Prime Mover and the Deliverer standing at the right hand of the Prime Mover and exclaimed: 'Behold, I see the heavens opened and the Son of Man standing at the right hand of the Prime Mover!' (Acts 7:55- 60) It is customary in societies in sub-Saharan Africa for the relatives, neighbors and other acquaintances of someone who 'passes on' to wail, mourn and lament that individual's passing. Africans who are have always known implicitly what the *Sanctae Scripturae* (Sacred Scriptures) have stated explicitly, namely that the Prime Mover answers prayers of those who are inconsolable. (Matthew 7:7). The prayers of the mourners are so that the Prime Mover might look favorably on the soul of the departed. This undoubtedly assures their ancestors lots of seats overall at the Divine Banquet Table for the Marriage Supper of the Lamb.

"When the curious stare at the incorruptible bodies of St. Bakhita, St. Catherine Labouré, St. Francis Xavier, St. Catherine of Genoa, Blessed Anna Maria Taigi, St. Elizabeth of Aragon, St. Vincent de Paul, St. Bernadette, St. John Vianney, St. Robert Bellarmine and others, they picture these saints as being 'at rest', as if they were simply asleep while innocently cradling the imperishable crowns of glory they have won. (Psalm 149:1-9, Isaiah 25:9, 1 Corinthians 9:25, 2 Timothy 4:8, James 1:12,

Revelation 2:10, 1 Peter 5:2-4, and Revelation 7:9-17) Others can't even make anything of the fact that the Blessed Virgin Mother of the Deliverer was assumed into heaven alive - or that the Deliverer Himself rose from the dead! Those saints are partying, you fools! And that is the reason I work so hard to try and stop you from joining the party!

"Look, that is when the human gets ushered into the Divine Banquet Hall where the celebrations of the Marriage Feast of the Lamb are ongoing - if that human hadn't forgotten to keep his/her candle alight whilst awaiting the arrival of the Bride that is. (Luke 12:35 and Matthew 25:1) And remember that one can't trade in a mansion in Beverly Hills for a seat at the Divine Banquet Table. Things don't work that way. There is seating there only for folks who have washed their robes and made them white in the blood of the Lamb. (Revelation 1:5, Revelation 7:14, Revelation 12:11, Revelation 22:14 and 16 Ephesians 1:7)

"And that is the mindset that all generations of humans since Adam and Eve have entertained. Over the ages, the younger generations of humans have typically looked down on the older generations as a matter of course! And, even worse, every generation that has come after the generation of the Deliverer has tried its best to ignore the fact that His generation was the most important of all, and that without it everything loses meaning! Well, you tell me how many of you humans stop to reflect on the fact that the *Logos* - the Master of the house – is not only returning (as the Deliverer Himself reminds you in Matthew 24:36-51, Luke 35-48 and Mark 13:35, and as it is also written in Genesis 6:1-7), but is going to expect each one of you to give a reckoning of what you did with the talents that He gave you! (Matthew 25:14-30 and Luke 19:12-27) And, look: it wasn't me,

102

Mephistopheles, I swear! It was the Nazarene Himself who warned you humans, and not in Greek but in plain Hebrew, in Matthew 7:13-16, Luke 13:22-30 and Luke 6:43-45 with the words: '*Intrate per angustam portam quia lata porta et spatiosa via quae ducit ad perditionem et multi sunt qui intrant per eam. Quam angusta porta et arta via quae ducit ad vitam et pauci sunt qui inveniunt eam. Attendite a falsis prophetis, qui veniunt ad vos in vestimentis ovium, intrinsecus autem sunt lupi rapaces. A fructus eorum cognoscetis eos. Numquid colligunt de spinis uvas, aut de tribulis ficus...*' (Enter ye in at the narrow gate: for wide is the gate, and broad is the way that leadeth to destruction, and many there are who go in thereat. How narrow is the gate, and strait is the way that leadeth to life: and few there are that find it! Beware of false prophets, who come to you in the clothing of sheep, but inwardly they are ravening wolves. By their fruits you shall know them. Do men gather grapes from thorn bushes, or figs from thistles?) But just look around and tell me what you see! Noticed all those churches that enterprising folks have 'planted' and whose numbers just keep growing?. For sure they cannot be the work of the Holy Ghost who is one with the Father and the Son, and could not therefore do anything that was not in consonance with the *Sancta Ecclesia* established by the Deliverer on the rock called Peter! And while those who are in the business of contradicting the *Sancta Ecclesia* are many and completely unhinged and daring, that of itself does not make wrong right much less right wrong in the moral sphere. Those who peddle heresies and contradict the Logos should be wary of the words that I sincerely wish were mine, but *fortunately* are not. The words go as follows: 'Many will say to me in that day: Lord, Lord, have not we prophesied in thy name, and cast out devils in thy name, and done many miracles in thy name? And then will I profess unto them, I never knew you: depart from me, you that work iniquity.' (Matthew 7:22-27). And John, quoting the Deliverer and writing in plain Aramaic, has this: 'I am the good shepherd, and know my sheep, and am known of mine.' (John 10:14) And so, regardless of the favor and power with which you twist and misrepresent the message for which the Deliverer gave His life, all that will simply come back to haunt you! Look, I really wish that these were my words, but *fortunately* they are the words of the Deliverer Himself and not mine! Again, two thousand years ago, addressing the Israelites, the Deliverer, dwelling amongst you humans and referring to His works, said and I quote: 'Woe to thee, Corozain, woe to thee, Bethsaida: for if in Tyre and Sidon had been wrought the miracles that have been wrought in you, they had long ago done penance in sackcloth and ashes. But I say unto you, it shall be more tolerable for Tyre and Sidon in the day of judgment, than for you. And thou Capharnaum, shalt thou be exalted up to heaven? thou shalt go down even unto hell. For if in Sodom had been wrought the miracles that have been wrought in thee, perhaps it had remained unto this day. But I say unto you, that it shall be more tolerable for the land of Sodom in the day of judgment, than for thee.' (Matthew 11:21-24 and Luke 10:13-16). Those words apply to all of you humans today in the exact same way they applied to the Israelites two thousand years ago!

"Hee, hee ha, ha, haa! Hak, hak, hak, haaak! Hoooheee! You humans are something else; and it is only the Mother Theresas and the Padre Pios (supposedly the 'dumb ones') in every one of the human generations who remember that they are dust and to dust they shall return as it is written in Genesis 3:19 and bother to live accordingly. The fact is that whether one is a Centennial, a Millennial, a member of Generation X, a

Baby Boomer, a member of the Silent Generation that is about to go completely 'silent', or a member of any generation beginning with the generation of Adam and Eve to which Cain, Abel and Seth belonged (Genesis 4), you humans, because you came from dust and to dust you will return, have to show something for the gift of life you enjoy whilst on earth. For starters you will be asked by the Deliverer and Judge, the Logos through Whom all things were made and without Whom was made nothing that was made and Who is present in the Blessed Sacrament (John 6:48-57, 1 Corinthians 11:26, Acts 2:42-43, Corinthians 10:17), if you kept the ten commandments the Prime Mover gave Moses on ten slabs - if you loved the Lord your Prime Mover with all your heart and with all your soul and with all your mind and with all your strength and your neighbor as yourself! You will have to explain to Him why it is that you did not follow the good example set by the Mother Theresas and the Padre Pios.

"Created in the image of the Prime Mover, an image that predates time itself because the Prime Mover Himself exists in eternity, you humans, just like us here in the pure spirit realm, can only find self-actualization in *that* Prime Mover and *not* in the one of your fantasy. You cannot find self-actualization in Jupiter, the so-called the 'King of Gods'; or in Neptune, the so-called 'God of the Sea'; or in Pluto, the so-called 'God of the Underworld'; or in Apollo, the so-called 'God of the Sun, Music, and Prophecy'; or in Mars, the so-called 'God of War'; or in Ares, the so-called 'God of war, bloodshed, and violence'; or in Cupid, the so-called 'God of Love'; or in Diana, the so-called 'Goddess of the hunt, the moon and birth'; or in Athena, the so-called 'Goddess of reason, wisdom, intelligence, skill, peace, warfare, battle strategy, and handicraft'; or in Aphrodite, the so-called 'Goddess of beauty, love, desire, and pleasure'; or in Dionysus, the so-called 'God of wine, fruitfulness, parties, festivals, madness, chaos, drunkenness, vegetation, ecstasy, and the theater'; or in Pluto, the so-called 'King of the underworld and the dead and the God of wealth' whose consort, Persephone, is the 'Queen of the Underworld'; or in Hera, the so-called 'Queen of the gods, and goddess of marriage, women, childbirth, heirs, kings, and empires'; or in Hestia, the co-called 'Virgin goddess of the hearth, home, and chastity'; or in Zeus, the so-called 'King of the gods, ruler of Mount Olympus, and god of the sky, weather, thunder, lightning, law, order, and justice'; or in Amun, the Egyptian god of the sun and air; or in Ba-Pef, the so-called 'God of terror', specifically spiritual terror, and whose name translates as 'that Soul'; or in Bastet (Bast), the supposedly beautiful Goddess of cats, women's secrets, childbirth, fertility, and protector of the hearth and home from evil or misfortune; or in Gengen Wer, the celestial goose whose name means 'Great Honker' and who was supposedly present at the dawn of creation and guarded (or laid) the celestial egg containing the life force; or in Hapi, the fertility god who was also God of the Nile silt and was associated with the inundation that caused the river to overflow its banks and deposit the rich earth the farmers relied on for their crops; or in Haurun, the so-called 'protector God' associated with the Great Sphinx of Giza; or in Heka, one of the oldest and most important gods in ancient Egypt who was the patron god of magic and medicine, and supposedly was also the primordial source of power in the universe; or in Labet, the so-called 'Goddess of fertility and rebirth' known as 'She of the East' and sometimes associated with Amenet ('She of the West'); or in Ihy, the so-called 'God of Music and Joy'; or in Ishtar, the Mesopotamian 'Goddess of love, sexuality, and war'; or in Isis, the most powerful and popular goddess in Egyptian history who was associated with virtually every aspect of human life; or in Kabechet (Kebehwet or Qebhet), originally a celestial serpent deity who became known as the daughter of Anubis and a funerary deity, and who provided pure, cool water to the souls of the deceased as they awaited judgment in the Hall of Truth; or in Tiāngōng 天公, the so-called 'Duke of Heaven' or 'General of Heaven'; or in Shàng Tiān 上天, 'Highest Heaven' or 'First Heaven' as it is supposedly the primordial being supervising all-under-Heaven; or in Huángdì (軒轅黃帝 'Yellow Deity of the Chariot Shaft') who is the Zhōngyuèdàdì (中岳大帝 'Great Deity of the Central Peak') and represents the essence of earth and the Yellow Dragon; or in 瘟神 Wēnshén or 'Plague God'; or in 猿神 Yuánshén or 'Monkey God'; or in 猿王 Yuánwáng, Monkey King, who is identified as Sūn Wùkōng (孙悟空); or in Babalú-Aye, the African deity who promotes healing for those who are close to death and is feared because he is also believed to bring disease upon humans, or in Obatala (known as Obatalá in Latin America or Koya in Brazil), the Deity who is believed to be the Sky Father and the creator of Heaven and Earth, or in Oya, the deity who commands winds, storms, and lightning and is also the Queen of the river Niger, or in Unkulunkulu, the 'highest god' who is known as the 'greatest one' and supposedly was created in Uhlanga, a huge swamp of reeds, before he came to Earth, or in Ogbunabali ('kills at night'), the Igbo Death deity who supposedly kills his victims in the night as these are usually criminals or folks who have indulged in socially impermissible activity, or in Mercury, the most honored deity in Celtic Gaul.

"And you humans definitely do not get to decide which one of the seven sacraments instituted by the

Deliverer you should keep and which one you should ditch – period. And those of you who are into throwing your weight around while you still kick should get this albeit from me, Beelzebub, the personification of evil: It is to the Prime Mover that you should cry in your trouble, as it is He, your scrupulosity aside, who delivers you from your distress. And brings you out of darkness, and the shadow of death; and breaks your bonds in sunder. (Psalm 107:13-14) But I should add that we ourselves here in the Underworld know how to hijack the show. We play on your scrupulosity which, in the last analysis, is not at all driven by willfulness (pride) and not by humility! You don't want to let go of stuff that makes you feel good, eh! Oh, you don't even remember what the Apostle to the Gentiles said in 1 Corinthians 2:9-13 huh! You don't believe the Deliverer when He says: 'This is the bread that comes down from heaven, so that one may eat of it and not die. I am the living bread that came down from heaven. If anyone eats of this bread, he will live forever. And the bread that I will give for the life of the world is my flesh?' (John 6:50) You are my man! But you humans are something else. You even go around 'planting' your own churches the way the original twelve apostles traveled the earth 'planting' the faith, never mind that the teachings of these new churches contradict the doctrines of the *Sancta Ecclesia*! Goodness gracious me! Unfortunately for you, the fantasies you indulge in all come to an end when you kick the bucket; and that is also when the reckoning begins!

"And since you have never even stopped to think about the reason and purpose for your existence, you tell me now if you humans are not really dumb and stupid! Look, this might not look surprising because it was all foretold. The lectionary for the divine services (Holy Masses) for Christmas Day and for the Second Sunday after Christmas doesn't just say it all; it rubs it in. The readings from the *Sacrae Scripturae* include this: 'He came unto his own, and his own received him not.' (John 1:11) Yeah, the true light, which enlighteneth every man that cometh into this world - He was in the world, and the world was made by Him, and the world knew Him not! (John 6:41-71) That is like you humans all right But this was shocking to us here in the Underworld. Just suppose that the impossible happened - that the Prime Mover had a change of heart and decided to offer all of us here in hell who are damned and banished forever from His sight a reprieve! Look – and I can truthfully speak for my fellow demons;. you cannot imagine the melee as we all scrambled for the gates to get the hell out of here and into heaven! But sadly I have to qualify the statement 'as we all scrambled for the gates' and exclude the damned humans. This is because, from what we observe about you stupid humans, it is quite conceivable that the accursed. wretched and lost souls of those of you who inhabit this hell with us, would be heading into the opposite direction. They would be scrambling to occupy the dungeons that we were vacating (perhaps imagining that they must be better) just as we ourselves made the dash to get back in good books with the Prime Mover and reclaim our places in heaven! .Well, O.K.; we demons might be partly responsible for the fact that you humans no longer think aright and, inclined to sin as a result of the fall from grace of Adam and Eve, you are incapable of doing any good on your own without the help of the graces merited for you by the Deliverer with His death on the gibbet; and the only way out is to do as you are told, namely to say the *Pater Noster* or the 'Our Father' (Matthew 6:9-13); because as the Deliverer explained to His disciples, no one can come to Him unless it is granted him by the Father. As the living Father sent Him, and He lives because of the Father, so whoever feeds on the Deliverer, he also will live because of Him." (John 6:41-71)

"Yeah, to the *Pater Noster* – the Prime Mover. But you stupid humans think you can hoodwink the Prime Mover by pretending that you are totally dependent on Him for your existence and your daily bread and for deliverance from evil when you are just self-centered jerks and on my payroll! You can even put on the pretense of being a 'prayer warrior' all you like; but if you do not genuinely believe that you totally depend on the Prime Mover, and if the '*Pater Noster*' you recite is just hollow words and if your 'Hail Mary', instead of being a *bona fide* invocation to the Deliverer's Blessed Mother for her intercession, is more akin to a 'Hail Mary pass' in American football, you can take it from me, Beelzebub, that you won't be among those to whom the words 'All those the Father gives me will come to me, and whoever comes to me I will never drive away' (John 6:37) will apply. Aaaah ha, ha, ha, ha! Eeeeh he, he, he, he heeeeh! Uuuuh ha, ha, ha, ha, haaaah!

"You humans have all those graces that were merited for you by the Deliverer with His death on the gibbet; but all you are concerned about is the here and now - and the self. If that was not the case, you would all be devout Catholics!

"You want to wait until your generation goes 'silent' to find out if I am right? Be my guest; and, look, it won't actually be that long of a wait at all - a hundred and forty years at the max! In the meantime, we ourselves here in the Underworld will, of course, be rooting for you fools to be damned and banished from your Maker's face forever because *that* is what you richly deserve! Yeah, for your damnation! The Deliverer instructed His disciples to brush the dust from their feet and to move on if they entered a house or a city where they were not welcome. (Matthew 10:14, Mark 6:11 and Luke 9:5) So you see that we are covered quite well there as well. Ooh heeeh, hee! Aaah ha, ha, ha, haaah! Yeee, ha, ha, ha, ha haaah! Hak, hak, Hak, Haaaakkk!

And, being the Father of Death, I was going to say: 'God bless Covid19!' But unfortunately, when we thought that everything was a done deal, Pope Francis comes along and takes the extraordinary step of issuing his Apostolic Penitentiary, *Ex Auctoritate Summi Pontificis* (From the Authority of the Supreme Pontiff). It grants Plenary Indulgences to the faithful who, trusting in the word of the Deliverer and considering with a spirit of faith the COVID-19 epidemic that is ravaging the world, implore from the Prime Mover the end of the pandemic, and relief for those who are afflicted and eternal salvation for those whom the Lord calls to Himself. This is in order that all who today suffer because of the pandemic, just like all those who endured the miseries of the Black Death which wiped out a third of the population of Europe and ravaged other parts of the globe in the thirteenth century, may rediscover, in the mystery of this suffering, the same redemptive suffering of the Son of the Prime Mover who dwelt amongst you stupid humans sixty generations or so ago.

"In his bull *Unigenitus Dei Filius* (Only-Begotten Son of God) dated 25th January, 1343, Pope Clement V,I who reigned from 1342 to 1352 and saw the Black Death first hand as it knocked off hundreds of thousands around him, laid out the Church's doctrine on which indulgences granted by the Vicar of the Deliverer hinge. He wrote in the Bull: 'The only begotten Son of God "made unto us from God, wisdom, justice, sanctification and redemption" [1 Cor. 3], "neither by the blood of goats or of calves, but by His own blood entered once into the holies having obtained eternal redemption" [Heb. 9:12]. "For not with corruptible things as gold or silver, but with the precious blood of His very (Son) as of a lamb unspotted and unstained He has redeemed us" [cf.1 Pet. 1:18-19], who innocent, immolated on the altar of the Cross is known to have poured out not a little drop of blood, which however on account of union with the Word would have been sufficient for the redemption of the whole human race, but copiously as a kind of flowing stream, so that "from the soles of His feet even to the top of His Head no soundness was found in Him" [Is. 1:6]. Therefore, how great a treasure did the good Father acquire from this for the Church militant, so that the mercy of so great an effusion was not rendered useless, vain or superfluous, wishing to lay up treasures for His sons, so that thus the Church is an infinite treasure to men, so that they who use it, become the friends of God [Wis. 7:14]. Indeed this treasure through blessed Peter, the keeper of the keys of heaven and his successors, his vicars on earth, He has committed to be dispensed for the good of the faithful, both from proper and reasonable causes, now for the whole, now for partial remission of temporal punishment due to sins, in general as in particular (according as they know to be expedient with God), to be applied mercifully to those who truly repentant have confessed. Indeed, to the mass of this treasure the merits of the Blessed Mother of God and of all the elect from the first just even to the last, are known to give their help; concerning the consumption or the diminution of this there should be no fear at any time, because of the infinite merits of Christ (as was mentioned before) as well as for the reason that the more are brought to justification by its application, the greater is the increase of the merits themselves...'

"Pope Clement VI's bull went on to grant full indulgences to the dying, and it removed the spiritual penalty for sins that they were unable to confess to a priest. Yeah, because of their exposure to the sick and the dying, the *Sancta Ecclesia*'s clergy was disproportionately affected by the bubonic plague. And before long, it was very hard to get a priest to hear a confession. Actually some prelates were even urging the faithful who were dying to confess their sins to anyone who was nearby! That would by itself most definitely evidence contrite sorrow for sins committed. Many of the faithful were so desperate in the face of the ravaging pandemic, they resorted to self-flagellation whilst they could. The situation was as bad as that; and so, Pope Clement VI was spot on when he promulgated the bull *Unigenitus Dei Filius*. He actually didn't have much of a choice. It was the sensible thing to do in the face of the unforgiving pestilence!

"Still, you cannot tell how mad we here in the Underworld become with Peter's successors who are devoted to implementing the Great Commission! Look - epidemics and pandemics strike suddenly and are no respecter of persons. They are a reminder to you stupid humans that you are immortal only by virtue of possessing souls!

Would you have imagined that in the twenty-first century everyone, except for the really stupid ones (the so-called 'Covidiots'), following the example set by the citizens of Wuhan where Covid 19 first struck, would be scrambling to get a face mask to don as protection against the 'invisible enemy'! It looks really funny seeing the faces of so many - young and old and rich and poor - wondering around with their faces masked up. It is as though everyone has gone bonkers!

"And yet, while it is I, Beelzebub, who poses the real mortal danger for you humans, I don't see anyone scrambling to don protective gear in my regard! So, so stupid! But then, luckily for you humans, out of the blue the Vicar of the Deliverer comes and ruins everything for us. Oh, how mad I am at Pope Francis! If you don't know, there are already so many humans who will be grateful for the actions of Pope Clement VI for evermore for issuing that saving bull *Unigenitus Dei Filius*! And he was of course inspired by the Prime Mover Himself to do it.

Taking credit for a job well done...

"Do you now perhaps understand why you humans, ignoring your own identity, and lusting for things that belong to your neighbors, are now into such uncouth and inhuman things? Let me tell you: the things you do to each other boggle even our demonic imagination! Red ants do not wage wars against each other. Neither do alligators, nor bees, nor any other specie among the lower beings. But you human do - an indication that you're morally bankrupt. And then, when you humans are not at each other's throats (yes, each other's throats!), you are busy polluting the environment in which you live and ensuring that the Earth will be inhabitable in very short order. That is doing the same thing as hacking away at the branch from which one is dangling! That is a dumb thing to do isn't it?

"We ourselves might be engaged in this struggle between Good and Evil; but, in truth, we demons aren't into any 'undemonic things' against fellow demons! It is only you stupid humans who systematically conduct the most inhuman and 'inhumane' operations against your own kind, and who even go on to brag that you treated your own kind to 'shock and awe' and things of that nature! It is only you dumb and stupid humans who see 'statesmen' in the ring leaders among you who have no qualms leading nations to wars and sacrificing countless human lives in the process in the senseless efforts to conquer and dominate the world - senseless because you humans should know by now that you will never succeed in devising a way to take ill-gotten earthly possessions with you beyond the grave.

"And yet, what really mattered was not the expansionist ambitions of those nations that are no more, but the dignity of the many souls that were sacrificed at the altar of greed! I, as Ruler of the Underworld, must give myself credit for ensuring that, in every age, there are among humans stupid fools who will not hesitate to use their positions of God-given authority to trample on the dignity of their fellow humans - to ensure that the violence of human on human continues to the very last day!

"I have to be fair to myself and take credit for being able to manipulate humans and ensuring that, throughout the ages, it is human societies that have been responsible for shamelessly promoting and institutionalizing of injustices of the vilest sorts. They range from banditry masquerading as religious crusades, to slavery, lynching and other associated forms of discrimination that are supposedly grounded in the sacred scriptures, to colonialism, imperialism, and unbridled lust for material goods, to an unconscionable and immoral preoccupation with armaments that are supposed to guarantee unfettered access to the world's dwindling resources.

"I have to take credit for getting humans to re-invent themselves as members of what is effectively a virulent 'man-eat-man' society. I have to take credit for the fact that, in modern times, powerful nations are determined to create chaos in the world at will so that they can turn around and exploit it for their benefit. And just to think that such activities, while they last, are not merely condoned, but have the full support of the fabric of society, including those who are supposed to provide spiritual and moral leadership!

"You stupid humans know that you live on 'borrowed time' on earth. But how many of you realize that everything you see is 'passing' for that reason. The way most of you imagine it, it is you who are 'passing' and moving on presumably back into nothingness - just like a drunk on horseback who sees the trees and the scenery 'flying past him' in reverse, and does not realize that it is he himself who has the awareness of those objects heading back to where he himself is coming from. He doesn't realize that it is himself who is going to be accountable for what happens next to himself and to the horse as he tries vainly to avoid ramming into a boulder in his path.

"Like thousands upon thousands of 'nations' for whom millions of 'patriotic' citizens beginning with Cain toiled in vain, it is just a matter of time before the objects you humans see around you will be no more. But that will not dissolve you from accounting for the manner in which you employed your talents. Guess what, the 'heavenly riches' that we ourselves tried to wrest from the Prime Mover (that are not unlike the earthly 'riches' that we keep dangling in front of your eyes) were only a mirage, and we are still paying the price for daring to challenge Him. And so will it be with you humans.

"But, contrary to what war mongers for instance seem to believe, namely that they can take their war mongering with them into the next world, the fact is that humans who are unable to regain their identity as members of one humankind, and who themselves kick the bucket before renouncing their war mongering habits, end up here in the Pit with us, because this is the place for the spiritually dead - a place where they will be free to spin and tell lies.

"These are the guys who take what we suggest to them literally. And so they believe that the only philosophy that makes sense is the philosophy of every human for himself/herself. We have persuaded them that the only viable policy is to have every human on earth mind for himself/herself, and to have every household mind for itself, and every clan mind for itself, and every tribe mind for itself, and every ethnic grouping mind for itself, and every nation on earth mind for itself, and to completely disregard the fact that humanity is one and indivisible!

"These fellows, following the example of Cain, believe in the policy of world domination, meaning that if a scarce resource is in someone else's back-yard, just go get it if you can marshal the guts and have the means to do so. And, of course, if using an atom bomb is what is needed to gain access to that scarce resource, just go ahead and do what it takes to manufacture one, even though that policy is short-sighted because it puts all other nations on notice that they have to do likewise to ensure that what is in their backyard doesn't get filched by other marauding humans.

"So, so stupid! This is because, what with porous borders and the World Wide Web that enables humans in any part of the globe to communicate with each other, the prevalence of dissatisfied citizens who are astute enough to see themselves as *loyal* members of humankind and not just of some 'country' with its artificial boundaries, and what have you, it simply isn't possible for any nation to keep a lid on atomic and other secrets. And hence the changing geopolitical face of the earth! And then there is the question of the purpose of it. What use is it if a human gains the whole world and loses his/her soul to me? None! First you humans ought to know that since Cain knocked off his brother Abel, the number of wars that

117

humans have fought while seeking control over some portion of earth or resources are countless, while those who faced each other in battle in time ended up facing each other before the King of Kings and Lord of Lords with nothing to show except blood on their hands for the talents they received at creation.

"The very first thing that all those warmongering kings, emperors, field marshals, commanders-in-chief and what-have-you discover, upon kicking the proverbial bucket, is that the deaths of all the poor, indefensible humans whose fate meant utterly nothing to them as they prosecuted their wars using every means at their disposal - battering rams, predator drones, artillery barrages, remote controlled car bombs, rocket fire, robots, etc. - and were dismissed off-handedly as 'collateral damage', is that all human life, their own included, meant a lot to the Prime Mover and to their Judge in the person of the Son of Man. And at that time of reckoning, these characters will wish to no avail to exchange places with the victims of their wanton and rabid excesses. And then the realization that when they 'did it' to those nondescript, voiceless souls, they did it to none other than the Judge Himself will be so damning in itself, they will be wishing to head over here in the Pit and out of His sight even before the sentencing was over - before they were presented with the full list of their crimes against humanity amongst other sins.

"It will come as a very great surprise when these usually flamboyant characters discover that their Record in the divine Court of Justice contained not one single good deed that could be used by the Judge to mitigate the sentence. This was because all such 'good deeds' - church attendance in the glare of publicity, kisses on the children's cheeks at political rallies, etc. - were all part of a grand design of burnishing their public image, and concealing the real personae beneath, so that they could continue committing crimes against humanity and other mortal sins with impunity.

"Unfortunately because those humans who made it their business to prey on others back on earth come here stuck with the habit, even we demons find it sickening just observing these characters still screaming and hollering for revenge against their 'enemies', forgetting that it was they themselves who unwittingly dispatched those they regarded as their enemies to their eternal reward in heaven. They make a pitiful sight as they endure spiritual torment and agony from discovering, too late, that they sold their spiritual inheritance for a pittance, and ended up not just wedded to vengefulness, but determined to parade that vice as holy zeal for "justice"!

"But then, unrepentant and 'hard core' (as you humans say), they thoroughly deserve the terrible punishment they get - at their own hands! This is a fate that dwarfs anything that they may have inflicted on their victims who were weeping and mourning then, but whose tears and mourns turned into a veritable 'blessing' afterward.

"We demons have one great virtue - yes, I mean 'virtue'…the virtue of patience! And it is this virtue of patience, practiced to a degree that has been heroic in every sense of that word, which is starting to pay off handsomely. Knowing that humans had lost their identity to a point where they had become clueless as regards their origin (as creatures who owed their existence to the Prime Mover), who they were (as creatures who shared the same 'esse' or 'human nature' with their fellow humans and now also the 'Word-become-flesh', or as regards their destiny (namely as creatures that had a certain rendezvous with the Prime Mover in whose image they had been created and who therefore demands a reckoning of all who are fashioned in His image), or their purpose in life (to do all to the Prime Mover's greater honor and glory), we here in the Pit were confident that we could groom them and then in turn use them to do the dirtiest thing imaginable, namely make it appear as if the Church - the Mystical Body of the Deliverer - was similarly capable of losing its identity as something that was divinely instituted!

"We here in the Pit in fact also do have dreams. We for example dream of the day when an ultra-reform-minded individual will appear and, with our help, argue persuasively that the 'parable of the fig tree' which all the gospels refer to, was in fact a fable that some enthusiastic translator inserted into the sacred texts but wasn't in the original biblical texts at all.

"Consequently the separated brethren will be able to claim that, even if the Roman Catholic Church *was* the Church the Deliverer founded, they had a firm basis for claiming that any purported act of excommunication by the Holy Father on behalf of the Church was itself in error as it was without any basis in the *Sanctae Scripturae*. They could argue that no one could say they couldn't wax and grow in virtue and in the manner Providence would have them wax and grow and wax in holiness, just because they had rebuffed the traditional Church and the 'errors' to which it was prone.

"The argument that the separated brethren were doomed because they were operating 'outside the Church' because, like branches that are cut off from a fruitful vine, risk withering and becoming good only for keeping the fireplace alight in the winter, would no longer hold water! But for now, this is definitely one 'parable' we love, because it dooms all the so-called separated brethren as long as they knowing desist from abandoning their heresies and schisms and returning to the fold. For our part, we would like the separated brethren to remain under the misguided notion that the infinitely loving and merciful Prime Mover could never permit a situation in which professed 'Christians' could be 'excommunicated' or cut off from the was sacramental grace the fullness of which was found inside the Church or Mystical Body of the Deliverer.

"We would like to see some zealot launch a campaign to have this parable declared apocryphal material that was included in the Canon by some 'misguided pope' who was acting under my influence while claiming at the same time to be 'speaking *ex cathedra*'! And, of course, this tells you one other thing. Things are not well in the *church* (the word 'church' being used here to refer to 'Christendom' so called, or the collection of 'Christian' sects each of which claims to be the 'Church' that was founded by the Deliverer) even after that *first* 'Reformation'. We very definitely need a *second* and actually far more reaching 'Reformation', one that will assure that 'there will be no faith left on earth when the Deliverer returns'!

"Even then, we can today proudly proclaim that after working very patiently with misguided humans over the two thousand years or so that have elapsed since the Church of the Prime Mover was inaugurated, it is virtually impossible, even for humans of goodwill, to tell the true Church at a glance from the innumerable (and still growing number of) 'churches' that have been set up by self-proclaimed messengers of the Prime Mover.

"These churches, which contradict each other right and left, are united in challenging the teaching authority of the Church of Rome over which 'popes', the successors to the apostle who was singled out by the Deliverer to be a 'fisher of men' and chosen from among the 'Dirty Dozen' (as we here in the Pit refer to them because of what their mission which really hurts our cause) to be the 'rock' upon which the Deliverer was going to build His '*ecclesia*' as He called it, have presided in an unbroken line of succession.

"You would think that, because these 'non-traditional' churches, unlike the Holy Catholic Church, do not have anyone who claims to be the lawful successor to Peter and are therefore 'leader-less' (even though the 'pastors' in these churches all claim to be 'anointed' and guided in their pronouncements and interpretation of the books of Sacred Scripture by the 'Spirit'), they would be shunned and spurned by those in search of deliverance and the 'Truth'. And never mind the fact that most of the pastors regarded the most important sacraments and much of the Church's traditional liturgy as witchcraft, and now spent most of their time lecturing members of their congregations on how to become instantly saved by intoning words from a prayer book, describing the personal revelations they claimed they were receiving daily and reciting passages from the Old and New Testaments *ad nauseam* by way of illustration, and persuading their congregations to throw in their lot with them by 'sowing seeds', the latest euphemism for making a donation!

"It should at least have struck someone among the rank and file in these blossoming church institutions as a little suspicious that, while it had become fashionable for these presumptive modern day 'Fathers of the Church' to abandon important sacraments (like the Sacrament of Confession, Holy Eucharist, etc.) and to ditch much of the Church's rich traditional liturgy, there had never been any suggestion by even the most 'reform minded' separated brother or sister that 'Peter's Pence' (which was variously referred to as the 'Collection'), that ancient but by the same token also much abused part of the Church's liturgy, should likewise be dropped.

"But more importantly, you would think that it would be obvious to everyone that for anyone to go out on a limb and assume the responsibility that was reserved for Peter, also known as *Cephas* (the Rock) for leading actual and potential members of the Deliverer's flock away from the Mystical Body of the Deliverer and from the sacramental life of the universal and apostolic Church and its sacred traditions, and out of the 'Community of Saints' or Church Militant to nowhere is the last thing a human would think of doing! You wouldn't expect an ordinary mortal to try and appoint oneself as a rival Moses who presumes to be qualified and able to lead the people of the Prime Mover out of the desert and into the Promised Land.

Fruit from the Tree of Knowledge...

"It cannot be emphasized enough that we here in the Underworld do work very hard to see hordes diverted from the path of Truth represented by the Holy Catholic Church and the present-day equivalent of Noah's Ark. Now I may have spilled out a lot of our secrets, but how exactly we in the Underworld do this is something I won't reveal. It is, as you humans would put it, a 'classified secret'.

"But you have to be really stupid and dumb if you cannot see my fingerprints all over the place when a new 'church' or sect pops up. I cannot, however, really take any credit for that stupidity and dumbness on the part of humans. I cannot do so in the same way I really can't take credit for the fact that Adam and Eve disobeyed the Prime Mover, and consequently fell from grace. Even though I was hiding up there in the branches of the apple tree and suggesting all sorts of things to the father and

123

mother of the human race, they were under no compulsion to hurt themselves by doing what they did.

"But this is one thing I can and will reveal to you. Even though I am called the Father of Lies, I can tell you that I have never uttered one lie in my entire life - I mean since the beginning of time when I was created. And you guessed right…I am a spirit and do not have a mouth! In this particular respect, I am the very opposite of you wicked humans who are capable of lying until they are blue in the face. And also when the Book refers to me as the *Diabolus Malus* (the evil ghost), it is not really true that I am evil. I am actually very nice - my clientele can assure you of that. And you yourself have seen how truthful I try to be all the time. If I have lied, it is simply because I have 'lied by example' if I may put it that way - by disobeying the Prime Mover, and thereby suggesting to you lesser creatures that a mere creature can take on the Prime Mover.

"I was completely truthful when I suggested to the first man and the first woman that, if they ate of the forbidden fruit from the Tree of Knowledge of Good and Evil, they would become immortal like the Almighty One. Well, isn't that exactly what humans who are members of the Church Triumphant are - like the Almighty whom they can now see face to face? If they weren't, they wouldn't withstand the glitter and glow that surrounds the Triune Divinity. They would become vaporized and disintegrate into the nothingness from which they came.

"And look - in retrospect it wasn't such a bad idea after all that Eve, hearkening to my suggestion, succeeded in drawing Adam into the rebellion, and persuading him to join her in the act of disobedience to their Maker, appalling though it was!

"If they hadn't been curious and succumbed in the process to the temptation, there wouldn't have been any

124

need for a Deliverer in the first place; and, barring a change in the Divine Plan (which was highly unlike), Adam and Eve and all of their descendants would have been stuck in Paradise; and their transition to wherever, to make room for new generations of humans, wouldn't have added anything special to their spiritual fulfillment. The world would have looked more or less like a zoo with nothing really interesting going on - a complete contrast to what goes on in today's world in which humans continually savage and maul their own kind as though they were beasts of the wild that were permanently locked in a brawl over a meagre catch! But it is because the Deliverer came to earth and redeemed humans with His death and resurrection that humans now can realize Eve's dream of becoming immortal and like the Prime Mover Himself in beatific vision.

"If truth be told, it is because the Divine Plan in the Prime Mover's providence called for humans to take the places in heaven that I and the other fallen angels vacated in the wake of our own rebellion that this thing happened. And, yes, you can say that I shot myself in the foot by dangling the fruit from the Tree of Knowledge in from of those eager and adventuresome humans.

"You would, of course, think that humans would be able to infer from this that the idea of an intermediate state in the next life where repentant humans have a chance to requite sins can't be fiction! That, because sinful and sinning humans whose pleas for divine mercies whilst they are still kicking and 'alive' often aren't nearly as genuine as they ought to be, it is they themselves who will be the first to acknowledge that they still had a debt to pay, and who whereupon will plead for a little bit of time before being received by the Prime Mover into the 'bosom of Abraham' so that they may expiate their sins and, in the words of Gregory of Nyssa, 'be purged of the filthy

125

contagion in their souls by the purifying fire' - the 'purging fire' that cleanses the stains with which the souls of sinful and sinning humans are infested!

"But, No! These humans who spend most of their waking hours vying with each other and trying to outdo '*El Ingenioso Hidalgo Don Quixote de la Mancha*' actually beat the 'ingenious Hidalgo Don Quixote of La Mancha' at his own game when they suddenly act sissy and assert that, being the 'true believers' they are, all their sins and even the stains left by the sins they commit are simply 'washed away' by the precious blood of the Deliverer, and that the very notion of 'Purgatory' is fiction, never mind that many holy mystics, amongst them people like Sister Faustina Kovalka, Saint Caterina from Genova, Maria Simma, Saint Veronica Giuliani, Saint Margherita Maria Alacoque, Saint Geltrude of Helfta, etc. have actually been to the 'place' and have bequeathed to the world exciting accounts of what goes on there! But even those humans who accept that such Purgatory isn't a fictitious idea act for the most part as if it is. And that is why monasticism isn't thriving and 'hermits' nowadays only exist in works of fiction - thank the Prime Mover!

"That is also why humans are all excited about Neil Armstrong jaywalking on the moon, and that the Hubble telescope's Canadian-built robotic arm at a command causes the telescope to aim its sights at the perimeter of 'space'; whilst the only people who are excited about the fact that the Second Person of the Blessed Trinity, and Creator of the Universe and everything that is in it, made it to Planet Earth two thousand years ago, and spent three years attempting unsuccessfully to persuade the chief priests and the Pharisees that he had turned up in fulfillment of His Father's promise to Abraham, Isaac and Jacob are televangelists! And so, the fact that a transcendent and omnipotent Supreme Essence (whose very nature is to be or to exist) took on human nature and became a veritable statistic, and did so in order that fallen humans (whom he had fashioned in His own image and likeness) might yet gain eternal life through their faith in Him, goes virtually unheralded!

"Sound familiar? It might not sound familiar to you humans; but it certainly sounds familiar to us here in the Underworld! Take Moses whose life was devoted to leading the Prime Mover's chosen people from bondage in Egypt into Canaan. After Moses' initial encounter with the Prime Mover who addressed him from the 'burning bush', Moses returned to pick up the Ten Commandments that everyone was expected to follow. The commandments were engraved on two stone tablets. But at the sight of the children of Israel sinning like the blazes and worshipping false gods, Moses was unable to take it and became the only human ever to break the Ten Commandments all at once! These were the Israelites - descendants of one or other of the twelve sons of Jacob, namely Reuben, Simeon, Levi, Judah, Dan, Naphtali, Gad, Asher, Issachar, Zebulun, Joseph and Benjamin.

"Fast forward to the reign of Tiberius Caesar... Even though the Israelites had settled in the Promised Land that came complete with the Temple and the Holy of Holies (an inner sanctuary that only the High Priest entered on Yom Kippur, the tenth and final Day of Atonement), it was Pontius Pilate, the Roman Governor, who called the shots in Judea, while Herod Antipas (also known as Herod the Great), a stooge of the Romans who had been proclaimed 'king of the Jews' by the Roman senate, reigned as Tetrarch of Galilee and Peraea.

"The real bad news was that John the Baptist, sent by the Prime Mover, had begun to preach and baptize saying: 'Repent, for the kingdom of heaven is at hand!' After all those years during which the Prime Mover, true to His word, had put enmity between the serpent (me) and the woman (Mary), and my seed and her seed, the chickens had come home to roost! The time had come for the most important prophecy to be fulfilled, namely that the Immaculate Mary, Mother of the Deliverer 'shall crush thy (my) head, and thou (me, Diabolos) shalt lie in wait for her (Mary's) heel'.

"As the history books have it, the chosen people, led by the chief priests and the Pharisees and representing humanity, disowned 'the *Logos* (the Word of God) who became flesh and dwelt among humans'; they disowned 'the Son of God'; they disowned 'the only Son of the living Prime Mover; they disowned Mary's boy child whom she called 'JESUS…for He shall save His people from their sins'; they disowned 'the Lamb of God who takes away the sin of the world'; and they also disowned the 'one Lord Jesus Christ, the only-begotten Son of God, begotten from the Father before all ages, light from light, true God from true God, begotten not made, of one substance with the Father, through Whom all things came into existence'. The damn stupid fools disowned their Maker and Deliverer!

"But those were not the only damn stupid fools! This has been typical of you humans ever since, and will continue to be until Planet Earth goes up in a plume of smoke in a nuclear holocaust (thanks to the Manhattan Project) and, unhinged from its axis, Mother Earth starts drifting in space like a rudderless ship and crushes into the sun!

"If Adam and Eve hadn't listened to me and gone on to offend the Prime Mover by giving in to the temptation, there would be no such thing as beatific vision for humans. You can say that it is because of the intransigence of humans that the Almighty One sent His only begotten Son, the Second Person of the Blessed

Trinity who is begotten by the First Person in eternity, down to Earth so that those who believed in Him might be saved. Well, it is now more than simply being saved from the fires of hell, for humans to now be able to behold the Almighty One face to face in beatific vision, I tell you!

"If I and my fellow demons hadn't opted to go our own way during the time we ourselves were on trial, we would have had the chance to see Him face to face ourselves; but we blew it as you know. For us, that would have been more-or-less automatic - if we had 'kept the faith' as you humans say, and remained faithful creatures of the Prime Mover! But if Adam and Eve had remained good the good boy and the good girl they had been until their adventure in the Garden of Eden on that fateful afternoon four hundred thousand ago, they would have been one very happy pair. But, barring the outside chance that their descendants would have ended up falling for my tricks and blowing it on behalf of humanity by committing original sins of their own, beatific vision would have remained outside the scope of their dreams!

"Now I had been suspecting ever since I myself fell from grace - and quite rightly as it turned out - that the Almighty One would, in His infinite goodness, try to let humans inherit what we fallen spirits had forfeited. My intention was to get the father and mother of the human race to join our camp, lock, stock and barrel so that this would never happen. I was determined to try and frustrate the Divine Plan in that regard - and I very nearly got away with it. What I did not count on was that the stupid Adam and Eve would recoil from their dastardly act of disobedience and seize the opportunity to get back into good books with the Almighty by being remorseful and renouncing me and my whiles when they discovered that they had been stripped of their divine graces and, spiritual essences, were now naked in the real sense!

"And so, again, you can see that I never lied to Adam and Eve at any time - and I can assure you that I have never lied to any of their descendants either! But as you can expect, I am always haunted by the thought that, even after my troops and I have worked so hard to get humans to refuse to get aboard the Ark of Noah, the Almighty One might still have something else up His sleeve. I am haunted by the fear that some incomparable good might ensue from humans straying from orthodoxy and refusing to submit to the authority of Peter's successors.

"This is even though I know full well - just as you humans do - that there is no salvation outside the Holy Catholic Church; and that all those humans who decide to trash the card inviting them to attend the divine banquet and rebuff the overtures of the messengers of the Deliverer are doomed. I am still haunted by the fear that we here in the Underworld might not end up bagging the souls of all those we see fritting away opportunities to enter the Ark of Noah!

"It could be something as insignificant as the stroke of a pen - if, for instance, some upstart from a liberal wing of the Church were to become pope, and then promptly issue an encyclical redefining the phrase 'Mystical Body of the Deliverer' and making it encompass 'all humans for whom the Deliverer laid down His life on Mt. Calvary in obedience to His heavenly Father' until they slammed the door in the face of the successors to the apostles when the latter arrived bearing the message of the Risen Christ! Can you imagine the damage to our cause if things were to come to that!

"I will be frank and tell you what we here in the Underworld suspect is going on and robbing us of our fair share of souls. It is those prayers that are offered up by followers of Faustina and others who specifically offer up

130

prayers to the Sacred Heart of the Deliverer beseeching Him to always look with mercy on all humans particularly at their hour of death. You know what can happen when it is time for a sinful and sinning human, regardless of the life he/she led, to 'kick the bucket' as you fools put it. Who can tell what the graces of the Prime Mover, extended to the dying sinner as a result of such intercession, can accomplish? One thing is certain: when prayers are offered up for a dying human who might have led an unworthy and quite despicable life, the effect of such prayers is to block me and my troops from our quarry at precisely the moment that we would be poised to snatch his/her soul.

"By Golly! Who can say how many humans have renounced my whiles and the temptations of the flesh at the time they saw death staring in their faces and, looking around, instead of seeing me and my troops there in force to reassure them that everything will be alright, they saw my arch-enemy, Michael, on his knees in adoration before the pierced Sacred Heart of the infinitely merciful Deliverer - the pierced heart that signifies that their pangs of death, however tormenting, have been sanctified by the Deliverer's own death on the cross for the salvation of all humans! We, of course, work very hard to keep humans ignorant of the power of their own prayers. Oh, we even strive to get lukewarm followers of the Deliverer to turn their backs completely on their faith just so that they won't ever beseech the mercies of the Prime Mover either for themselves or for their fellow humans, and will be looking to me, the Evil Ghost, and my fellow demons for succor when the end of their pilgrimage on earth is at hand.

"We know one thing for sure, namely that humans will not be able to claim that they were merely following their consciences when they did unto others what they

131

wouldn't possibly have liked done to them by other humans! The same is of course true when sinful and sinning humans presume to know better than those whom Providence in His infinite wisdom has entrusted His work of redemption however unworthy!

"Also, there will be no excuse if, out of pride, humans had decided that it was too demeaning to submit to the *magisterium* (teaching authority) of the *Una Sancta Ecclesia Apostolica et Catholica* (the one and the only holy, apostolic and universal Church), and preferred to substitute the message of the crucified Deliverer with their own self-serving testimonies. And certainly not after I myself have been dragged from Gehenna to provide all these pages upon page of testimony on the Deliverer's visitation, and to spill out so many of my secrets in the course of this forced confession! Still, one big plus from my being treated in this manner is that from now on Catholics will have no excuse for not knowing the basics of their faith - and non-Catholics will have no excuse for continuing to peddle heresies!

Exiles from Paradise...

"Regardless, let me - Satan, Arch-Devil, Evil Ghost or whatever you want to call me - say this one thing concerning the 'instant salvation' fad and specifically the manner in which it supposedly can be obtained. Now, I know enough not to say anything that might suggest that being born and bred a 'Catholic' automatically gets one a pass to heaven! Nothing could be further from the truth. Catholics, just like anyone else must keep the Lord's commandments; and no amount of chants of 'Lord, Lord' will help them if they too do not take up their crosses and follow in the Deliverer's footsteps.

"And look here buddy, Jesus of Nazareth I know,

and Paul of Tarsus I recognize (Luke 4:31-37 & Acts 19:13-20), and as well Jorge Mario Bergoglio (Pope Francis); but who are these other folks who are peddling each their own peculiar - and, I would add, confusing - brand of 'Christianity'? Then, concerning this 'instant salvation' thing: if it were true that humans could be saved, not by keeping the Prime Mover's commandments, but by just reciting a prayer however that prayer was constructed, I - Beelzebub and Father of Lies - would have gone out of business two thousand years ago.

"What about those humans who just worked away at keeping the Ten Commandments, but had never heard of that prayer? Of course it isn't true. But, promise that you won't whisper our secret to any one for now at least! It all sounds like the mother of the apostles James and John all over again. That woman, if you remember, wanted the Deliverer to go against His own divine principles and just reserve for her two sons the places in heaven immediately to His right and His left! She wanted to have it so easy!

"As soon as humans start awakening to the fact that there is such a thing as the 'human condition' which has its roots in the sin of disobedience of the first man and the first woman, and realize that from that moment on, humans were all - with the sole exception of the Blessed Mother of the Deliverer and the 'Son of Man' Himself - the 'forsaken' children of Adam and Eve by virtue of being born in the original sin, instead of praying for an increase in their faith, they immediately start looking for the easiest way out! I will tell you, exiles from Paradise, that none of those 'easy solutions' stands any chance of working because I, Lucifer, not only know all about them, but my stamp is all over those 'easy solutions'.

"The gift of faith on the other hand works because the stamp of the Deliverer is all over it. The gift of faith that is imparted to humans of good will (who can now also call the Word-become-flesh - and now, alas, also Judge - their brother, and call His mother Mary their mother) doesn't leave me room to do my dirty work and bedevil and/or frustrate its efficacy. Being a gift, you humans cannot just reach out and grab it - and certainly not when you are not ready to ask humbly for it or are well disposed to receive it.

"When a human of good will receives this gift, I (Satan and vile as I am) am powerless to stop the sanctifying grace from working in that human. But you try to show your metal and begin getting the idea that you on your own can find an easy solution to the human predicament, and my minions and I will be lying in wait for you with any number of certified and fully guaranteed options for you to choose from. You disrespect me if you think that you can find salvation and escape my tentacles except by the grace of the Deliverer!

"Or were you under the impression that I hadn't figured that one out as well? Always keep in mind that, while Knowledge is divine, we here in the Pit, because we do not want to be the only ones who are damned, have a vested interest in acquiring it and using it for our Evil Plan. You have to be really dumb if you do not believe that we wouldn't try to use Knowledge to our benefit - which, hopefully you are!

"And you have got to understand, by the way, that my troops and I have invested a great deal indeed in this 'project'. It is not by an accident of nature that you have all these intelligent people claiming that salvation comes, not by faith *and* good works alone, but by reciting a couple of words (without even the need to cross yourself before or after). That you can just make up your mind, mumble a few words, and get yourself out of the boon docks! Again, the Deliverer has made it very clear that it is not those who exclaimed 'Lord, Lord' who will inherit the kingdom of heaven, but those who kept His commandments.

"As for praying, the Deliverer went out of His way to teach the apostles and those who would be His disciples how to pray, and he composed and gave them the *Pater Noster* which, among other things, gets humans to stop the foolery, and to ask the Prime Mover not to lead them into temptation, but to deliver them from evil.

"Good" codes and "Blessed" codes...

"Humans, already confused about Natural Law, because they do not know their identity as 'incarnated spirits', now also need a veritable leap of faith to find their way into the One and the only True, Holy, Catholic and Apostolic Church, the institution whose *raison de tre* is to guide humans as regards not just the Natural Law (the good code) and the Supernatural Law (the blessed code), but as regards the Truth.

"You see - we here in the Pit are not really as bad as you might think. You can see that try to be there for those humans who muster the courage to 'love their fathers and mothers more than they love the Deliverer' (to use His exact words), and as well those astute and smart enough to know what is good for them and who will, therefore, not 'take up their crosses and follow the Deliverer'. Those humans who scrupulously 'find their lives' and are not prepared 'to lose them for the Deliverer's sake can always be assured of our support, albeit only for so long...

The next phase...

"During the next phase of the battle for souls, we would like to see more and more Catholic bishops and cardinals (because these are the successors to the 'Dirty Dozen' regardless of whether they are worthy 'Men of the Cloth' or not) make fondly references to the 'separated brethren' even as these 'saved' followers of the Deliverer show more and more that they are not prepared to renounce the schisms and heresies that have kept them 'separated' from the Church and in a state of excommunication.

"We would like to see the Church's functionaries give the false impression that, their schisms and heresies notwithstanding, the status of these bible wielding and supposedly 'saved' schismatics and heretics as members of the Mystical Body of the Deliverer was not affected in any way after all by their refusal to submit the authority of Peter's successor and to the Church's *Magisterium*'!

"In that way, the distinction between the 'Holy Catholic Church' and the burgeoning 'church' establishments (that are making evangelization the fastest growing and also lucrative 'industry' in the West) will gradually become blurred, making the Church's evangelizing mission even more difficult. Already the words 'church' and 'separated brethren' have become virtually meaningless as every Dick and Harry who sets up his/her church on a whim also automatically starts enjoying the benefits of being counted among the 'Separated Brethren'! And since everyone who 'talks church' not only claims that he/she has received a special revelation from the divine 'Ghost', but soon enough also starts claiming that he/she is capable of causing miracles to happen by simply invoking the name of the Deliverer, the fact that all these self-proclaimed 'anointed of the

Prime Mover' blaspheme whenever they invoke the name at the sound of which every head should bow will be completely lost sight of.

Dumb demons don't exist...

"Now, the fact that we here in the Pit are demons doesn't make us necessarily dumb. You ought to know that by this time - unless you yourself are entirely dumb (which, of course, might very well be the case)! We too know that, even though the Church teaches that there is no salvation outside it (the Mystical Body of the Deliverer), 'it' (the Church) no doubt extends beyond the 'Visible Church'. But also knowing the nature of humans, we here in the Pit also know that all those spiritually starved hordes, who (as you know) are simultaneously inclined to sin and continually on the lookout for the easiest ways out of their bind, will be open - yes, very open - to the temptation to meddle in things that are the prerogative of the Prime Mover, like trying to decide, for instance, who outside the Visible Church has received the baptism of desire or the baptism of blood and therefore belongs to the Invisible Church.

"We actually tempt them to imagine that it is only they themselves - and perhaps also those who prescribe to the same religious tenets as they themselves - belong to the 'Church' or 'Ark' of the Prime Mover (or whatever!), and will go to on to inherit the kingdom of heaven; and that everyone else is doomed regardless of the sort of lives they lead. We tempt them to then act as though it isn't so much they themselves who are supposed to allow the Holy Ghost to lead them where He may, but the Holy Ghost who is supposed to hearken to their instructions so that He may lead them where they will, namely to some earthly 'Paradise'.

"Look, humans do not have a clue why they were born when they were born. These days they might know when it is going to rain; but they do not have the faintest idea when a hurricane of the magnitude of Katrina is going to make landfall on their shores, or when the tsunami is going to descend on them - or when the 'Big One' is going to come. Humans do not know if or when they might suffer a fatal heart attack and drop dead, or even if they will be really better off if they win that jackpot. And so you would think that humans would be overjoyed to learn that the Holy Ghost, the Second Person of the Blessed Trinity, is ready, if they will only let Him, to lead them where they belong, but won't go on their own! No! They prefer instead to continue stumbling along blindly through uncertain times without a bothering about their last end, and to waste the precious time they have available to attain their self-actualization.

"The self-will and the selfishness become more than plain when these foolish humans (who did not even know what they were doing when they drove nails into the hands and feet of the Deliverer) presume to know whether other humans about whose religious beliefs or human condition they frequently know nothing are destined for our company here in the Pit or elsewhere - like the 'good thief'! It is the same way these misguided humans keep calling us here in the Pit all sorts of names when they know nothing about us or even why we are here - and when they are actually clueless about what they themselves are or even their destiny!

Invitees to the Divine Banquet...

"Now, because folks in the Catholic Church, including members of the clergy who should know better, have the same tendency to blame me for all human failings including unbelief, that has provided us another window of opportunity which we have to exploit. And, believe it or not, our efforts in this regard are beginning to pay off as well! Increasingly, priests and even bishops are going around talking as if the 'separated brethren' are for all practical purposes members of the Mystical Body of the Deliverer.

"And they seem to be intent on making the Jews - the chosen people under the Old Testament - feel as if it is just fine for them to be waiting for their earthly messiah! The way we here in the Pit see it, rejecting the Deliverer when He showed up and sending Him to His grisly death was the very worst thing a people, chosen or not, could inflict on themselves. And their preoccupation with deliverance in the worldly sense just about seals their fate, doesn't it! But it is also a measure of the extent to which we here in the Pit, despised though we might be by the so-called saved folks, have frustrated the Divine Plan! This is just swell! Can you imagine members of the race that bequeathed the Messiah to the world turning their backs on Him and consequently denying themselves the opportunity to relish His victory over sin and over death, and doing so with the help of functionaries of the Church the Deliverer commissioned and tasked with spreading the message of salvation!

"Those same clergy who are loath to embarrass the separated brethren and the descendants of the Israelites don't treat people of other faiths - Buddhists, Hindus, Moslems to mention a few - the same way. In essence, these functionaries of the Holy Church are going around talking as if it is not enough to be a child of the Prime Mover by virtue of being created in His Image. They are directly suggesting that only a select few, not all the poor forsaken children of Adam and Eve, are being invited to the divine banquet!

"You see, they tie the child/father relationship between humans and the Prime Mover, not to the fact that the Prime Mover, in His infinite wisdom, has brought his subjects into existence in different circumstances of His own choosing, but to the fact that some of these humans, in their desire to exclude other humans from the divine banquet table, go around waving the Book (as though it were a magic wand).

"To put it differently, they are almost encouraging the 'separated brethren' to continue in their apostasy and to remain excommunicated thereby! And they are doing this at the expense of evangelization, because they essentially should be rebuking the 'separated brethren' to abandon their apostasy, in the exact same way they ought to be rebuking the 'faithful' to stop being complacent about their faith, and also praying that their own faith may be strengthened to the point to which they would be ready to become martyrs for the Deliverer. But how on earth (and in hell) could they expect to win more souls for the Prime Mover by spreading the message of the risen Deliverer to the ends of the globe if they are satisfied with themselves and are cozy with those who call the Holy Father the anti-Christ!

Papal Infallibility Bulwark against the Lying Devil...

"Actually, the way some 'separated' brothers and sisters nowadays refer to the soon to be beatified Mother Theresa or Pope John Paul II, you would think that their meditations on the lives of these stalwart pillars of Roman Catholicism would cause them to start worrying about their precarious position as 'brethren' who were still separated and were still cut off from communion with Holy Mother the Church! But that is not what we here in the Pit discern.

140

"It is pretty obvious to us that when the separated brethren say something nice about a character like John Paul II whom they sometimes forget and refer to as the 'Antichrist', what they really mean is that a good man like John Paul, being the undisputed leader of 'unquestioning faithful' (as separated brethren have always characterized Catholics) and of a 'cult' that comes complete with rituals, idols and votive offerings (or so they claim), would probably have led his misguided flock back to orthodoxy and 'communion with the rest of 'Christendom' if he had been around a little longer! He had, after all, started off well by apologizing for the missteps of his predecessors, implying that it was Catholicism that had been in the wrong all the time. Hahaha, héhéhé, hihihi, hohoho!

"Since (unlike they themselves who were 'saved') neither Mother Theresa nor Pope John Paul, who had held on stubbornly to the supposedly 'fallacious' dogmas of the Catholic Church to the very last and refused to renounce their 'heresy', could have been admitted to heaven upon their death for that reason, their souls likely were still in limbo somewhere between the earth and the heavens, and possibly in real danger of being lost forever. But they (the supposedly saved ones who, as the Deliverer's very good and utterly faithful servants, were ready to sacrifice their own lives for the unadulterated Truth) had dutifully prayed for the duo; and, consequently, both the deceased pope (who had offered the best chance yet for Catholics to mend their ways) and the nun (who had spent her days ministering to Calcutta's homeless and was remembered with great fondness by India's Hindus, Moslems, and Buddhists alike) stood a good chance of receiving a reprieve from the Almighty One!

"That being the case, it was imperative that Pope

141

Benedict XVI, the new leader of Catholicism, at the very minimum reciprocated and urged his cardinals, bishops, monsignors, priests, and heads of religious orders (and the head of the Jesuits in particular) to endorse what the Church's liberal wing has been suggesting, namely that the separated brethren were as much members of the Mystical Body of the Deliverer as say members of the 'Eastern Rite' patriarchates that have always been in communion with Rome - something the Holy Father could, of course, not do as long as they continued to cling to their errors and did not recant.

"Now, I have to tell you that we, the inhabitants of Gehenna, cannot but be very pleased indeed with this result (even though we cannot 'celebrate' in the true sense of that word because of the unspeakable frustration that flows from being excluded from membership in the Church Triumphant for all eternity and the reward of everlasting happiness that would have been ours for the taking if we had not rebelled against His Mystic Majesty and 'separated' ourselves from the Pilgrim Church in the process.

"Indeed, how could we, evil as we are, not derive all the delight we can muster as damned and doomed spirits from the fact that things have come to pass in the way they have? How could we not delight in the fact that a worthy successor to Peter like John Paul II was regarded by the separated and self-proclaimed 'saved ones' or 'saints' as the one who was the toothless bulldog and the 'pretender'? If John Paul II and his predecessors were guilty of laying a false claim to being the pillar upon which the 'Visible Church' was built, then the Deliverer lied when He told the assembled apostles: 'And I will give you the keys of the kingdom of heaven, and whatever you bind on earth will be bound in heaven, and whatever you loose on earth will be loosed in heaven.' (Matthew 16:18

and Matthew 18:18)

"But, leaving the question of the Deliverer lying aside, why don't stupid humans ask themselves why the Deliverer went out of His way to say what He said? Did He do it in jest? The Deliverer was not a charlatan; and I tell you He knew damn well that I, Beelzebub, would be attempting to derail the Divine Plan from the word go!

"You have to be really dumb not to see that we here in Gehenna are mightily pleased to see souls that are in danger of missing a ride to safety in the 'Ark of Noah' mocking those who are attempting to throw them a lifeline! Formally excommunicated by decrees of the Councils of the Church of Rome over which the successors to the apostle Peter preside, and effectively 'separated' from the Church, they still have the audacity to refer to the Mystical Body of the Deliverer as the work of the anti-Christ!

"It is just such sweet music to my ears when humans, who should be pining for deliverance from my clutch, stand there and declare to the world that they are 'saved'! It is sweet music to my ears when, usurping the authority of those in the Church who are charged with 'being fishers of men' and with going forth and spreading the message of the risen Deliverer, the separated brethren assert that it is in fact they who are 'the anointed of the Deliverer' and are empowered to perform miracles in the Deliverer's name! It is very sweet music indeed in my ears when they declare to the world that it is preposterous for the successors to the apostles to claim that what they hold bound on earth (which they invariably do in the name of the Word and Second Person of the Blessed Trinity and also Deliverer) perforce is held bound in heaven, or that whatever they loose on earth will in Heaven be held to be loose by virtue of the Deliverer's promise!

"Oblivious to the fact that the Deliverer was the Word who chose to take up human nature in accordance with the Divine Plan of Redemption, and then interacted with the likes of Judas, Matthew, Peter and John, and after quizzing Peter regarding the genuineness of the fisherman's love for Him, tasked him with minding His sheep, the brethren who have been formally excommunicated, as a consequence which they remain 'separated' from the Church, bristle at and are deeply offended by the idea that Peter, a mere human, could actually presume to do what he, and those who succeeded him as vicar of Rome, did in abeyance to the command of the Deliverer and High Priest when he told them: 'Feed my sheep'!

"Even though the fisherman was not yet ready at that time to take the reigns as the first pope who would march on Rome and set up shop in that sin city, the Deliverer for His part was concerned that Peter and the other apostles be clear about what He meant by 'love', and what He expected of them in that regard. As Paul, whose resume included hunting and liquidating followers of the 'Terrorist' and the 'Insurgent', aptly explained after his own conversion to the Cause, by 'love', the Deliverer meant a love that would always be patient, persevere, protect, and never fail; and above all a love that, as Peter, following in the footsteps of the Deliverer, showed by his own example, would predispose the lover to die for his/her brothers and sisters who now included the Word-become-flesh Himself.

"Now, what you saw happening at the time of the reformation was no different from what happened at the time the Deliverer himself walked the earth. What the reformers did was exactly like what the priests and Pharisees did. They rejected the Messiah and decided to keep looking to invent one who would be to their own liking. Humans of little faith, they all prefer to be their own teachers and in the process deride the Deliverer who proclaimed that He was the Way and the Life. Actually, this is what all humans who will not allow themselves to be led by the Spirit where they on their own would not go - Catholics and non-Catholics alike - are up to.

"This is my legacy as Ruler of the Underworld. The only thing that stops me from having a complete walkover is the *Sancta Ecclesia* and the efficacy of the graces humans receive through the sacraments that are administered by it.

"This is a big coup - and one that we here in the Pit cleverly engineered. And we succeeded, not because Michael the Archangel was having a sneeze, giving us the opportunity to regain our footing and to meddle thereby; but because you humans are a dumb lot. Knowing that history repeats itself, from that moment on Pentecost Day when the Deliverer inaugurated His Church by sending forth the Holy Ghost, we here in the Underworld were waiting and ready to join battle, and our plan from the beginning was to enjoin disgruntled elements inside the Church - those 'believers' who would try to have it both ways, namely inherit the kingdom of heaven while refusing to have their wings clipped. And there were lots of them already at the time the infant Church was spreading its own wings from Judea through Asia Minor to Rome, and to the rest of the world from there.

"All we needed to do was just mark our time, while waiting for some of the Church folks to do what I myself, the host of angels who fell with me from the Prime Mover's favor and Adam and Eve (your own great grand Pa and great grand Ma) did, namely refuse to obey. It didn't take very much really - a couple of ruses here and there, and some members of the Church's hierarchy started smarting from the notion that it was only Peter and whoever would succeed him as 'Shepherd' of the Deliverer's flock on earth who could dictate to them on vital aspects of the Church's teachings or spiritual matters - in other words. As if the words '*Et ego dico tibi quia tu es Petrus, et super hanc petram, Ecclesiam meam edificabo*' were empty and meaningless - in fact a distraction!

"A wilful act of disobedience inevitably sets the stage for other wilful acts of disobedience that are intended to bolster and affirm the earlier acts of disobedience. In the case of the Reformation, for example, once we succeeded in persuading a disgruntled monk and his supporters in and around the 'Holy Roman Empire' to stand up and take the position that they did not feel bound by the Church's *magisterium* or teaching authority, it was easy enough to persuade the monk's countrymen, who were eager to throw off the yoke of virtual fiefdom that was exercised by the occupant of the See of Peter at the time, to join hands with him so they would manage their affairs, religious and otherwise, independently of Rome thenceforth. This was pretty easy because we were able first to ensure that whoever was the occupant of the Holy See was too preoccupied with 'stately' and other matters and too distracted to care about the heresy that monk was spreading.

"Still, it was of the highest importance that we proceeded carefully. Because if we didn't, we could end up giving the game away. This was especially important given the numerous warnings that had been given about heresies and false prophets. And, of course, as the one who inspires and leads the pack, I am not called the Father of Lies for nothing. (John 8:44, Revelation 12:9, Revelation 13:11-15).

"Jeremiah had said: 'And the LORD said to me: "The prophets are prophesying lies in my name. I did not send

146

them, nor did I command them or speak to them. They are prophesying to you a lying vision, worthless divination, and the deceit of their own minds. Therefore thus says the LORD concerning the prophets who prophesy in my name although I did not send them, and who say, 'Sword and famine shall not come upon this land': By sword and famine those prophets shall be consumed. And the people to whom they prophesy shall be cast out in the streets of Jerusalem, victims of famine and sword, with none to bury them—them, their wives, their sons, and their daughters. For I will pour out their evil upon them." (Jeremiah 14:14-16)

"And again: 'Thus saith the Lord of hosts: Hearken not to the words of the prophets that prophesy to you, and deceive you: they speak a vision of their own heart, and not out of the mouth of the Lord. They say to them that blaspheme me: The Lord hath said: You shall have peace: and to every one that walketh in the perverseness of his own heart, they have said: No evil shall come upon you. For who hath stood in the counsel of the Lord, and hath seen and heard his word? Who hath considered his word and heard it? Behold the whirlwind of the Lord's indignation shall come forth, and a tempest shall break out and come upon the head of the wicked. The wrath of the Lord shall not return till he execute it, and till he accomplish the thought of his heart: in the latter days you shall understand his counsel. I did not send prophets, yet they ran: I have not spoken to them, yet they prophesied. If they had stood in my counsel, and had made my words known to my people, I should have turned them from their evil way, and from their wicked doings. Am I, think ye, a God at hand, saith the Lord, and not a God afar off? Shall a man be hid in secret places, and I not see him, saith the Lord? do not I fill heaven and earth, saith the Lord? I have heard what the prophets said, that prophesy lies in my name, and say: I have dreamed, I have dreamed. How long shall this be in the heart of the prophets that prophesy lies, and that prophesy the delusions of their own heart? (Jeremiah 23:16-26)

"And Micah had warned: 'Thus says the Lord concerning the prophets who lead my people astray, who cry "Peace" when they have something to eat, but declare war against him who puts nothing into their mouths.' (Micah 3:5)

"And in his farewell address to the Israelites, Moses said: 'And if you say in your heart, 'How may we know the word that the Lord has not spoken?'— when a prophet speaks in the name of the Lord, if the word does not come to pass or come true, that is a word that the Lord has not spoken; the prophet has spoken it presumptuously. You need not be afraid of him.' (Deuteronomy 18:21-22)

"But as if those were not enough odds that we here in the Underworld had to contend with, the Deliverer Himself had sounded the alarm anew when He arrived on the scene. He made it clear that, far from resting on our laurels after we had seen Him agree to become the sacrificial lamb (see Genesis 22:8, John 1:29, Matthew 26:2, Matthew 26:17, Luke 22:7, Revelation 13:8, 1 Peter 1:18-19 and Corinthians 5:7), we here in the Underworld would be working extremely hard to sow seeds of confusion. He clearly saw that we would be aiming to ensure that the situation on earth, after He ascended into heaven to be with His Father even as He Himself remained Head of the *Sancta Ecclesia*, would be as confused and confusing as it could possibly be! The Deliverer was very specific. (John 10:1-42, Matthew 7:15-20, Matthew 7:21-23, Matthew 7:22, Matthew 24:1-51, Matthew 24:4-5, Matthew 24:11, Matthew 24:24, Mark 13:22 and 1 John 4:1-6) He wasn't going to be able to do much about that because He had created humans free to choose their individual eternal destiny.

"And Paul, in his farewell to the Ephesians had written: 'I know that after my departure ravening wolves will enter in among you, not sparing the flock. And of your own selves shall arise men speaking perverse things, to draw away disciples after them.' (Acts 20:29-30)

"And, writing to Timothy, Paul had warned: 'Having the appearance of godliness, but denying its power. Avoid such people.' (2 Timothy 3:5) And again: 'But evil men and seducers shall grow worse and worse: erring, and driving into error.' (2 Timothy 3:13) And again: 'For the time is coming when people will not endure sound teaching, but having itching ears they will accumulate for themselves teachers to suit their own passions, and will turn away from listening to the truth and wander off into myths. (2 Timothy 4:3-4)

Writing to the Corinthians and true to form, that Paul had not minced any words in describing my role in all of this: 'But what I do, that I will do: that I may cut off the occasion from them that desire occasion: that wherein they glory, they may be found even as we. For such false apostles are deceitful workmen, transforming themselves into the apostles of Christ. And no wonder: for Satan himself transformeth himself into an angel of light. Therefore it is no great thing if his ministers be transformed as the ministers of justice, whose end shall be according to their works.' (2 Corinthians 11:12-15)

"To the Colossians, that former pal of ours wrote: 'See to it that no one takes you captive by philosophy and empty deceit, according to human tradition, according to the elemental spirits of the world, and not according to Christ.' (Colossians 2:8)

"And, anxious to stem the spread of the heresies that my minions were already spreading especially regarding the Deliverer Himself, for example that He was not a true man, the Apostle John, addressing the new converts to Christianity, had implored: 'Dearly beloved, believe not every spirit, but try the spirits if they be of God: because many false prophets are gone out into the world. By this is the spirit of God known. Every spirit which confesseth that Jesus Christ is come in the flesh is of God: And every spirit that dissolveth Jesus is not of God. And this is Antichrist, of whom you have heard that he cometh: and he is now already in the world. You are of God, little children, and have overcome him. Because greater is he that is in you, than he that is in the world. They are of the world. Therefore of the world they speak: and the world heareth them. We are of God. He that knoweth God heareth us. He that is not of God heareth us not. By this we know the spirit of truth and the spirit of error. (1 John 4:1-6)

"And similarly, the former fisherman turned a 'fisher of men', writing to the converted gentiles to alert them of our activity, had penned: 'But there were also false prophets among the people, even as there shall be among you lying teachers who shall bring in sects of perdition and deny the Lord who bought them: bringing upon themselves swift destruction. And many shall follow their riotousness, through whom the way of truth shall be evil spoken of. And through covetousness shall they with feigned words make merchandise of you. Whose judgment now of a long time lingereth not: and their perdition slumbereth not.' (2 Peter 1-3)

"But, if I may - let's go off track for just a second; and I am saying this in a whisper for just your benefit alone. The good news is that those prophets, the Deliverer Himself, and those apostles of His, and as well Paul, that Apostle of the Gentiles, were addressing folks of different generations, not you folks of 'modern' times when the spirit of liberty and freedom of speech are the rage…and when, above all, you – and I mean you – can start and officially register your own church along with its own Peter's Pence of course or collection box and appoint yourself its pastor! Nah, the things they were ranting about could not possibly apply to you! Aaaah, ha, ha, ha, ha, haaa! Eeee, hee, hee, hee, hee! Hak, hak, hak, hak! Oooh, my goodness!

"Humans are so funny. Yeah, with the fall from grace of Adam and Eve from whom they are all descended, they became inclined to sin - although some, attempting to be creative, go as far as imagining that they are not descended from Adam and Eve! Regardless, the Deliverer comes along and establishes His *Sancta Ecclesia* which Noah's Arc foreshadowed, and He invites them to hop aboard. But then, phew! Wicked as they are, they start finding fault with this or that aspect of the Deliverer's *Sancta Ecclesia*; and, lo and behold, they start their own churches! And they quickly forget what the Deliverer, explicitly addressing them, said, namely: 'If any man come to me, and hate not his father, and mother, and wife, and children, and brethren, and sisters, yea and his own life also, he cannot be my disciple. And whosoever doth not carry his cross and come after me, cannot be my disciple'. (Luke 14:26-27).

"Look, this is not fiction. I am Lucifer, the Prince of Darkness – the darkness the Deliverer referred to when He said: 'But this is your hour, and the power of darkness.' (Luke 22:53) We are at war; and in this battle for souls between the forces of Good and the forces of Evil, there are casualties - exactly like happens in the wars that you humans fight among yourselves. Our battle plan is so there will be a great number of you humans to the left of the Judge to whom He will say: 'Depart from me, you accursed, into the eternal fire that has been prepared for the devil and his angels!' (Matthew 25:41) We've got to get you numbered among the goats that, unlike the sheep of His little flock (Matthew 26:31and Luke 12:32) and the sheep of His Pasture (Psalm 100:3 and Jeremiah 23:1), just won't listen to His voice. (Psalm 95:7) And, yeah - we've got to get as many of you as we can to end up like the chaff that is must needs be burned with the unquenchable fire which the Deliverer referred to in Matthew 3:12 and Luke 3:17! And, you'll be surprised at who the ones who are the easiest catch are. It's those selfish ones who wield power and strut around like peacocks whilst making the lives of their fellow humans hard, completely oblivious to what the Deliverer, standing atop a mountain after He had arisen from the dead, told His disciples: 'All power is given to me in heaven and in earth.' Matthew 28:18). Yes, *all* power, not *some* power. And it wasn't that long ago that the Deliverer had seen fit to tell Pontius Pilate to his face: 'Thou shouldst not have any power against me, unless it were given thee from above.' (John 19:11) The power those fools wield is given to them from above, and those fools are commanded to love their neighbors as they love themselves! And you humans can bet that, as Armageddon draws nigh, things are going to get uglier and uglier.

"Anyway, let's get back to the Middle Ages and the Renaissance that followed. I was determined, with the help of my minions among humans, to avenge the setbacks we had suffered all those years beginning from the day of Pentecost when the Deliverer launched His *Sancta Ecclesia*; setbacks that had taken a new turn when that fellow, Flavius Valerius Constantinus, also known as *Kōnstantînos ho Mégas* (r. 306-337), appeared out of nowhere and caused things to unravel. With his Edict of Milan in 313 A.D., he changed everything.

"Until Emperor Constantine the Great showed up, we had actually been doing pretty well. We had the knee firmly on the neck of the *Sancta Ecclesia* - or so we thought! Operating through our minions in imperial Rome, we had ensured that Christians were persecuted, enslaved and killed at our pleasure. But then, after defeating Diocletian's surviving tetrarch in the person of the treacherous Licinius (r. 308-324) and becoming the sole master of the Roman Empire in the process, Constantine the Great decided to totally abandoned our cause. In a stunning reversal, the fellow even used his office as the Roman Emperor to convoke and then facilitate the very First Ecumenical Council of the Church (the Council of Nicaea), notable for condemning the Arian heresy, defining the divinity of the Holy Spirit and defining the Nicene Creed.

"We still thought that we might succeed in snagging the guy himself because, even as he was doing all that damage to our cause, he had not yet been baptized, and therefore wasn't a member of the Church Militant. The fellow wasn't even a catechumen! But he fooled us. He took a calculated risk of waiting until he was on his deathbed to be formally received into the *Sancta Ecclesia* (through the Holy Sacrament of Baptism) in order that he would be absolved from as much sin as possible, including the sins he committed in the course of carrying out his policies while emperor! But by then he had done irreparable harm to our evil cause.

"Look, it may be that, of the first fifty-seven (57) occupants of the Chair of Peter after that former fisherman turned 'Fisher of Men' died (crucified with his head downside up in the year 64 AD and just three months after the Great Fire of Rome), all but four (4) of those popes ended up being canonized, a tribute to the fact that the lives they led had been marked by the exercise of heroic virtue. While it isn't true that all humans who lead saintly lives end up being recognized as such, this is an index we still like to use for measuring the extent to which Peter's successors have been faithful to the Great Commission (Matthew 28:16-20). It is a rough but fairly reliable index. For those early Christians, it was a prize well-earned (I tell you) because being a Christian in pagan Rome wasn't anyone's cup of tea after that fire which destroyed the city. We succeeded in getting the stupid Emperor Nero (r. 54-68) to blame the fire on Christians! According to our count, the pontificate of St. Silvanus (who reigned from 536 to 537) was the fifty-seventh in that line of papal succession. The persecution of Christians in the empire continued almost unabated until Constantine came along in the fourth century.

"Unfortunately, the saying of Tertullian that 'the blood of the martyrs is the seed of the Church' (*Apologeticus*, L.13) proved to be all too true. The fact that St. Victor I (the fourteen successor of the fisherman) who reigned from 189 to 199 was a native of Africa should tell you something. Still, even if we did not stop the *Sancta Ecclesia* from expanding, we certainly gave those Christians a run for their money. And, for the record, of the first one hundred popes who followed in the footsteps of Peter (the pontificate of Gregory IV who died in the year 844 being the 100th), only sixty-eight ended up being canonized!

"And now, back to the so-called 'Reformation'. We knew that we were on to something the moment we saw that that disgruntled monk along with his supporters were determined to rebuff the authority of Peter's successor, and had joined hands for the showdown. And, as luck would have it (as you humans say), just as we were helping folks to start those bonfires in Germany, Denmark and Sweden, there was this one king who also decided that the time for his country to break with Rome had come when his request for the annulment of his marriage was denied. This was a really fortunate convergence of circumstances for us. Instead of just one, there would actually be multiple openings that would enable us here in the Underworld to try and undo the grievous harm which Constantine the Great had inflicted on our cause, the unsuccessful attempt of the pope to galvanize the Christian world for a new crusade against the Turk Selim I (also known as Selim the Grim or Selim the Resolute) who was Sultan of the Ottoman Empire from 1512 to 1520 (at a time when the profligate Pope Leo X had squandered the papal treasure amassed by the frugal Pope Julius II he had succeeded) being another such opening.

"When the Crusade was preached in Germany for instance, a large section of the populace was already prejudiced against the Curia in Rome, and the effort only went to provide the folks there a chance to air their grievances openly. And that was at a time when Luther had already started stirring things up. The technology of printing was in full bloom, and one of the deprecating leaflets that were distributed asserted that Quote: 'The real Turks are in Italy and these demons can only be pacified by streams of gold!' Ha, ha, ha, ho, hee, hee, hee, he, he, he, he!

"The target of that spiteful literature was, of course, none other than the Holy Father, except that the papacy was occupied by Leo X and not by Saint Peter. And these were also different times. It was the Renaissance, and Italy was its birthplace. It was a time that was seeing the rebirth of ancient Greek and Roman thinking and style; and both Roman and Greek civilizations were thriving anew in the region surrounding what Romans had called *Mare Magnum* ("Great Sea"), or *Mare Internum* ("Internal Sea"), or *Mare Nostrum* ("Our Sea"); and the Ancient Greeks had called ἡ ἡμέτερα θάλασσα (*hē hēmétera thálassa*; "Our Sea"), or sometimes ἡ μεγάλη θάλασσα (*hē megálē thálassa*; "the Great Sea"), or ἡ θάλασσα ἡ καθ'ἡμᾶς (*hē thálassa hē kath'hēmâs*; "the sea around us"), or simply ἡ θάλασσα (*hē thálassa*; "the Sea"); a veritable boiling pot of cultures. And, instead of Pope St. Silvester I, the See of Peter was occupied by Leo X, the son of Giovanni de' Medici (also called Giovanni di Bicci) and head of the House of Medici! The Medici family was into banking and it did not just rule Florence; at one time the Medici was the wealthiest family in Europe; and the family was also into the Arts! And we ourselves here in the Underworld figured that the opportunity to avenge the many setbacks we had suffered over the centuries had finally come and that the timing was just perfect!

"It was also the time of the 'Renaissance man'! This was the time of the likes of Michel de Montaigne (1533-1592), Raphael (1483-1520), Paracelsus (1493-1541), Thomas More (1478-1535), Niccolo Machiavelli (1469-1527), Nicolaus Copernicus (1473-1543), Francis Bacon (1561-1626), Leonardo da Vinci (1452-1519), Desiderius Erasmus (1466-1536), Michelangelo (1475-1564), William Shakespeare (1564-1616), and Galileo Galilei (1564-1642). They invented everything from mills and wind turbines to printing presses, banking, the violin, and even ice cream. And then they used the latest technology to design embroidered cloaks (considered to be a big thing among the Tuscan *gentiluomini* or gentlemen of the time), and ribbed caps that were worn perched on the side of the head. The Croatian Faust Vrančić, who was a real polymath and also a bishop, invented all sorts of machines including the parachute which he named *Homo Volans* ("The Flying Man"). Someone even published a dictionary for the five noblest European languages (*Dictionarium quinque nobilissimarum Europæ linguarum, Latinæ, Italicæ,*

Germanicæ, Dalmatiæ, & Vngaricæ)! And, as Antonio Costa has said, nobody rocked the Renaissance like the Medici family did! (Ten astonishing facts you might not know about the Medici Family, Antonio Costa The Roman Guy, December 3, 2019.) Yeah, the Medici family that bequeathed Pope Leo X to the world!

"It was a time when a bishop as a rule wore two hats, the hat of a spiritual leader and the hat of a secular leader, as also did an archbishop and a cardinal. As a result, bishoprics and archbishoprics and cardinalates (or the 'red hat') were coveted things – exceedingly valuable plums - that were sought after by anyone with ambition, and it was normal for them to go to the highest bidder. The Third Lateran Council (Eleventh Ecumenical) convened in March 1179 by Pope Alexander III (who had the satisfaction of receiving the submission of the antipope Callistus III) vested the exclusive right of papal elections in a two-thirds vote of members of the Sacred College of Cardinals, and consequently the 'red hat' was regarded as an immensely valuable prize. To be 'named' a cardinal, one typically advanced a large sum of money, some of which went to ensure that papal states (civil territories that acknowledged the pope as temporal ruler beginning in eighth century) officially known as the *'Patrimonium Sancti Petri'* (landed possessions and revenues of various kinds that belonged to the Church of St. Peter in Rome) were not encroached upon by anyone.

"The opportunities for undermining the *Sancta Ecclesia* were thus infinite in the literal sense; and it was not long before the perfect one came beckoning, compelling us here in the Underworld to scamper and also jump on the bandwagon. It was triggered by the death of Pope Julius II who would be succeeded by Pope Leo X.

"Papa Giulio II (as Italians called Pope Julius II) had been Pope and Ruler of the Papal States from 1503 to the time of his death in 1513; and he was one of a kind. When he was elected Pope, he chose his papal name (Julius II), not in honor of Pope Saint Julius I who had reigned from 6 February, 337 to 12 April, 352 and whose feast is celebrated on 12 April, but in honor of Gaius Julius Caesar (July 13, 100 B.C.E. - March 15, 44 B.C.E.)! Pope Julius II was therefore fittingly nicknamed the Warrior Pope and also the Fearsome Pope. Everyone seems to be agreed that he was one of the most secular-minded Renaissance popes.

"Machiavelli in his works describes Julius II as the 'ideal prince'! The pope personally led the Papal armed forces against the forces of the French King Louis XII (who was supporting the schismatic movement that had its base in Pisa) at the Siege of Mirandola. And, assisted by Swiss mercenaries, he forced the king's army to retreat behind the Alps and effectively out of Italy.

"In the midst of all that, Julius II also proved to be a great patron of the arts in Italy. He commissioned the Florentine fine artist Michelangelo di Lodovico Buonarroti Simoni to paint the ceiling of the Sistine Chapel, regarded as one of the greatest masterpieces of the Renaissance. And, most notably, he initiated the construction of the new Basilica of St. Peter on the site of the old Basilica of St. Peter that Emperor Constantine I had had constructed over the historical site of the Circus of Nero. It was a project that would take a hundred and twenty years to complete.

"In his satirical piece *Julius Exclusus e Coelis* (Julius Excluded from Heaven) which he published anonymously out of fear of retribution from the pope's supporters, the Dutch scholar Erasmus of Rotterdam, goes as far as depicting a Pope Julius II who planned to storm the Gates of Heaven upon his death in the event that he was denied entry, despite the fact that he had been a deft diplomat, a financier of genius, and one of the ablest administrators ever to occupy the Chair of Peter, not to mention his military conquests. The dialogue starts with Julius, who was armed with the key to the papal treasury, exploding: 'What the devil is this? The doors don't open? Somebody must have changed the lock or broken it.' And after a couple of fruitless exchanges with Peter who was guarding the Gates of Heaven, Julius sounded quite exasperated. Calling Saint Peter a rascal for not recognizing him immediately as the 'Pontifex Maximus, he blurted out: 'Enough words, I say. If you don't hurry' up and open the gates, I'll unleash my thunderbolt of excommunication with which I used to terrify great kings on earth and their kingdoms too. You see, I've already got a bull (a papal bull of excommunication) prepared for the occasion.' When Peter let the chap who was his two hundred and seventeenth successor as Bishop of Rome know that he had no more standing with him than any other dead man, Julius retorted: 'But as long as the cardinals are arguing over the election of a new pope, it counts as my administration.'

"Regarding the merits he was expected to have accumulated so he could take his seat at the divine banquet, Julius admitted that he had been continually engaged in warfare back on earth. And, to Peter's question if he perhaps had distinguished himself in theology, Julius responded that there were plenty of priests to do that sort of work! As to whether he had gained many souls for the Deliverer through a virtuous life, the impatient Julius had a strange answer: 'Many more for hell, I'd say!' And when Peter asked of his successor if he had subdued the lusts of the flesh with fasts and long vigils, that compelled Julius's guardian angel to step in: 'Enough of this, please; with this line of questioning, you're just wasting your time!'

"At one point, trying hard to get Julius to say something that might just provide enough grounds to pry the gate open to let him in, Peter ventured: 'When I held your position, I followed that rule in the word of God which says to use no sword save that of the spirit.' Julius: 'That would surprise Malchus, whose ear you cut off-without a sword, no doubt!' Peter: 'But were you the sort of man they say?' Julius: 'What has that got to do with it? I was pope. Suppose I was a worse rascal than the Cercopes, stupider than a wooden statue or the log from which it was made, more foul than the swamp of Lerna; whoever holds this key of power must be revered as the vicar of Christ and reverenced as the holiest of men.' Peter: 'Even if he's openly evil?' Julius: 'As open as you like. It's just unthinkable that God's vicar on earth, who represents God himself before men, should be rebuked by any puny mortal or disturbed by any sort of popular outcry.' Julius, the Warrior Pope, at one point threatened Peter and shouted: 'By my triple crown, and by my heroic triumphs, I swear if you stir my anger, you, even you, will feel the wrath of Julius.' Ha, ha, ha, ho, ho, ho, hee, hee, hee! Oooh, ha, ha, ha, ha!

"Actually, Erasmus did not know that what he imagined happened after Pope Julius II crossed the gulf that separates the living from the dead - that this two and hundred and seventeenth successor of the son of Jonah as bishop of Rome had actually threatened to excommunicate the person the Deliverer Himself had appointed to be His Vicar on earth - happened almost exactly as he depicted it in the dialogue! And when Julius found himself face to face with the Judge, he wasn't just quizzed about the things he had done or failed to do as pope (even though his sins of commission and omission as Pontiff of Rome were automatically more grievous), but about everything he had done or failed to do from the moment he first saw the light of day on 5 December 1443 to the time he breathed his last a little over sixty-nine years later.

"But, look, Papa Giulio was not the only pope who tried to excommunicate Saint Peter. The case of Julius's immediate successor as pope was eerily similar. When Pope Leo X breathed his last on 1 December 1521 aged 46, he expected to see the Gates of Heaven fly open in the same manner that the gates of the Papal Palace in Rome had flung open for him as a member of the Medici family, permitting him to muster the votes of all the cardinals present at that Friday March 4, 1513 Conclave in the Second Scrutiny, so he could be enthroned as the Vicar of Christ on earth. Leo was even more desperate if anything. He had issued his bull *Exsurge Domine* (Arise, O Lord) condemning propositions extracted from Martin Luther's teachings on 15 June 1520 only to learn that the monk had set copies of it alight in a bone fire on 10 December 1520 in the main square of Wittenberg. Leo had of course followed that up with the bull *Decet Romanum Pontificem* (It Pleases the Roman Pontiff) on 3 January 1521 formally cutting Luther and everyone who shared his heretical beliefs off from the *Sancta Ecclesia*. But that was coming a little late as the Monk, a graduate of the University of Erfurt and now a popular academic and professor of Moral Theology at the University of Wittenberg, had a large following that included powerful German princes like Frederick III (also known as Friedrich der Weise or Frederick the Wise), Elector of Saxony. That was almost inevitable given the goings-on in high places in Rome and elsewhere. He was now also effectively shielded from the fate of the likes of Jan Hus

161

and Saint Joan of Arc. Emboldened, Luther went as far as dismissing out of hand the gathering at the Diet of Worms, called to try and get him to recant. He was actually more than happy to use that forum to propagate and spread his heresies!

"Luther had posted his famous 95 Theses on the door of All Saints Church in Wittenberg in 1517. Pope Leo X's actions in awarding the title 'Defender of the Faith' to King Henry VIII of England for writing a treatise defending the Seven Sacraments that Luther had challenged, and also to Emperor Charles V for calling Luther to testify at the Diet of Worms and condemning the views he expressed there, were not nearly enough. And as for Leo's support of the Arts - his commissions for the painting of the Stanza d'Eliodoro, the Stanza dell' Incendio (which served as Leo X's dining room), and Raphael's depictions of architecture in the Fire in the Borgo, the tapestries for the Sistine Chapel and Michelangelo's painting of its ceiling, the famous painting of the Transfiguration, the Vatican Palace's entrance façade which joined Leo's apartments, the Stanza, at the right angle on the palace's northeast corner, the new streets that Pope Leo had laid out in Rome (the Via Babuino, the Via del Corso and Via Leonina, etc), his support for the Vatican Library and for church music, and even his lavish works of charity and support for convents, hospitals, and other acts of 'generosity' of every description – all these things when taken together don't make up for the harm occasioned by the neglect and disregard of matters of the spiritual realm by the Vicar of the Deliverer on earth.

"Then there was the rush on the part of ecclesiastical figures to fill the vacuum that had been left by the collapse of the Western Roman empire. We for our part made sure that it wouldn't be without

162

consequences. This was, moreover, occurring at a time when Europe was transitioning from the Middle Ages to Modernity (during the renaissance). One might even go as far as postulating that, during the pontificates of Julius II and Pope Leo X, the visible Church was rudderless. But that is exactly what we ourselves here in the Underworld had been agitating for from the inception. And, look: you can take it that we did not like it a bit when, in those early days of the Infant Church, we saw Peter, John, Paul, and the rest of them hasten to alert their flock about this or that heresy that our minions were attempting to spread. But we really loved it when we succeeded in getting Pope Julius II and Pope Leo X and a good section of the clergy to focus their energies more on the temporal powers of the papacy and less on the exercise of the Church's teaching magisterium. For us, it was a balancing act, and we had to move really, really carefully.

"Look, the battle for souls is no joke. It is for real! Remember that guy Satchmo (or Satch) and the song he recorded in 1938?

'Hey! We are following the footsteps of those who've gone before and we'll all be reunited on that new and sunlit shore.

Oh, when the saints go marching in, [Repeat]
Oh, Lord, I want to be in that number when the saints go marching in.

And when the sun refuse to shine, [Repeat]
Oh, Lord, I want to be in that number when the sun refuse to shine.

Oh, when the trumpet sound its call, [Repeat]

*Oh, Lord, I want to be in that number when the trumpet
sounds that call.*

*Oh, when the new world is revealed, [Repeat]
Oh, Lord, I want to be in that number when the new
world is revealed.*

*Oh, when the saints go marching in, [Repeat]
Oh, Lord, I want to be in that number when the saints go
marching in.*

*Oh when the drums begin to bang, Oh when the drums
begin to bang,
Oh Lord I want to be in that number, When the saints go
marching in.*

*Oh when the stars fall from the sky, Oh when the stars
fall from the sky,
Oh Lord I want to be in that number, When the saints go
marching in.*

*Oh brother Charles you are my friend, Oh brother
Charles you are my friend,
Yea you gonna be in that number, When the saints go
marching in.*

*Oh when the saints go marching in, Oh when the saints
go marching in,
Oh Lord I want to be in that number, When the saints go
marching in.'*

"And that was before he met two live ones –
Venerable Pope Pius XII in 1949 and Saint Pope Paul VI
In 1968! The reason we've always needed to move so
very carefully is precisely because, as Louis Armstrong

piped, the saints just go marching in! But, of course with you humans so unconcerned with your last end, the song Satchmo is best remembered for undoubtedly is 'Hello, Dolly… This is Louis, Dolly', the song that ended the Beatles' streak of three number-one singles on the charts and was ranked the No. 3 song of 1964 by Billboard. And let's be clear – the march of the saints starts right here on earth. Once they get to hear that He came and established His *Sancta Ecclesia*, they not only regurgitate what he said, but with the help of the grace that was merited for them by the Deliverer they follow in his footsteps. And that's how they go marching in. Our job here in the Underworld is to see to it that humans do not see even though they have eyes, and that they do not hear even though they have ears as well! And we do not find that such a heartless task because humans are just so damn stupid!

"But still, as we worked to edge on the 'reformation', we had to move very cautiously; because, as the Middle Ages were giving way to the Renaissance and even at the height of the Renaissance itself, you still got holy men and holy women whose work threatened to nullify our efforts to stifle the *Sancta Ecclesia's* work of evangelization (the work of bringing the Good News of the Deliverer into every human situation and seeking to convert individuals and society by the divine power of the Gospel itself). I typically try to allocate two demons apiece to humans who look like they are determined to turn their backs on us. Like sentinels, the demons must maintain a 24/7 watch over their quarries and be on the lookout for the slightest flaws in their character which we then proceed to exploit to our advantage. But I couldn't even afford to do that over the critical period spanning the Schism of 1054 (the greatest schism in the church of the Prime Mover) and the Reformation that Luther engineered at the height of the Renaissance because they were just too many of them. When they crossed the gulf that separates the living from the dead and went marching into heaven to take their seats at the divine banquet, all I could do was exclaim with bitterness that you humans cannot imagine: 'Good riddance!'

"You see - once the victorious soul gets through those Gates of Heaven that are guarded by the former fisherman turned Fisher of Men, and is ushered into the Divine Banquet Hall, that's it. At the divine banquet, the soul becomes satiated to the point to which it becomes unable to desire anything but its Maker - exactly as St. Anselm said! That is also what happened to the angels that saw through my pranks and remained faithful. They were rewarded with happiness that made them incapable of sin, there being no happiness left for them to seek outside of their Maker.

"Pope St. Leo IX (born Bruno von Egisheim und Dagsburg), who occupied the papal throne from 1049 to 1054 and was the first of the 'Gregorian Reform' popes (he belonged to that eleventh-century religious reform movement associated with Pope St. Gregory VII who would reign from 1073 to 1085 and would be its most forceful advocate), was a good example of such a victorious soul. Also dubbed *Peregrinus Apostolicus* (Apostolic Pilgrim), Pope Leo IX was a great reforming pope in his own right. He was actually born in 1002, exactly thirty-eight years after the *Saeculum Obscurum* (Dark Ages) of the Papacy, better known as the sixty year 'Rule of the Harlots' or the 'Era of Pornocracy', which came to an end with the death in 963 of Pope John XII, the grandson of Marozia. Upon ascending the papal throne, he had to deal with the likes of Pope Benedict IX who famously sold off the Papacy for a large sum to his godfather, only to change his mind and try to reclaim the pontificate (when the woman he was after changed her mind). Saint Leo IX favored celibacy for clergy in his reformation of the Church; and one of his first public acts was to hold the famous Easter Synod of 1049, at which celibacy of the clergy down to the rank of the sub-deaconate (the highest of the minor orders of clergy in the *Sancta Ecclesia*) was required anew. Leo IX removed many priests, abbots, bishops, and cardinals who had been appointed to their positions through simony (buying church offices) or through nepotism; and he also worked to limit the power of the nobility in Italy and elsewhere over the appointments of Church leaders. Pope Leo IX is the one who directed King Edward the Confessor of England to build what later came to be Westminster Abbey.

"And then, towards the end of his life, he had to contend with the crafty Michael Cærularius, Patriarch of Constantinople from 1043 to 1058, whose actions precipitated the Great East-West Schism. Following the death on February 22, 1043 of Alexios Stoudites (the last of the Patriarchs that had been appointed by Emperor Basil II Porphyrogenitus), Cærularius had been ushered onto the stage for his act on March 25, 1043, upon being named by the Byzantine emperor Constantine IX Monomachus (Emperor from 1042 to 1055) as the new patriarch of Constantinople. He would become the author of the second and final schism of the Byzantine Church.

"After the reconciliation that followed the four-year (863–867) schism of Photius (d. 891) between the episcopal sees of Rome and Constantinople centering around the right of the Byzantine Emperor to depose and appoint patriarchs in Constantinople without papal approval, an anti-Latin party that gloried in the work of that patriarch and honored him as the great defender of the Orthodox Church had remained active, and was apparently biding its time for the right opportunity to resurrect Photius' quarrel with Rome.

"One historian (Abbe Darras) described thusly: 'When Photius began the schism consummated by Michael Cærularius in 1054, the Byzantine Church had, since the death of Emperor Constantine in 337, been formally out of communion with the Roman Church during 248 years (55 years on account of Arianism, 11 on account of the condemnation of St. John Chrysostom, 35 on account of Zeno's Henoticon, 41 on account of Monothelism, 90 on account of Iconoclasm, 16 on account of the adulterous marriage of Constantine VI). On the whole, therefore, Constantinople had been out of communion with the Apostolic See one out of every two years. During this period nineteen patriarchs of Constantinople were open heretics, some of them quite famous, e.g., Eusebius of Nicomedia, Eudoxius, Macedonius, Nestorius, Acacius, Sergius, Pyrrhus.'

"Fast forward to 1052. Partly in response to concessions which the emperor made to Pope Leo IX, Michael Cærularius decided to force the Latin churches in his diocese to use the Greek language and liturgical practices; and when they refused to do so, he ordered them shut. Around that time, a monk named Nicetas Pectoratus (Stethatos) had written a book on unleavened bread, the Sabbath, and the marriage of priests; and in it he had vented his rage at Latin liturgical observances. He would find himself obliged to recant in the presence of the emperor and the papal legates, and to throw his book into the fire in 1054; except that he would revert to his anti-Latin posture not long after. But he would, in meantime, be credited with authorship of the treatise that Cærularius circulated to the other three Eastern Patriarchs (Antioch, Jerusalem, and Alexandria) in 1053, in which he lambasted Latin liturgical practices. And not entirely surprising, in that same year, a group of Studite monks, led by none other than Cærularius's chancellor, someone by the name of Nicephorus, broke into Latin churches in Byzantium, smashed open tabernacles, and trampled on consecrated hosts, claiming that they were 'invalidly' consecrated!

"One Bulgarian primate had gone on to lambast those who used unleavened bread, ate meat from strangled animals, fasted on Saturdays, and omitted the Halleluia during Lent, writing: "Anyone who thus observes the sabbath and uses unleavened bread is neither Jew nor pagan; he resembles a leopard.' And, true to form, at a synod held on 20 July 1054, Michael Cærularius, purported to excommunicate the legates who had been sent by Pope Leo IX prior to his death on 19 April 1054. That action on the part of the Patriarch of Constantinople resulted in folks for whom 'Eastern Orthodoxy' was beloved above all else to turn their backs on the *Una, Sancta, Catholica et Apostolica Ecclesia* and go their own ways. Yeah, we ourselves here in the Underworld had seen it coming!

"Look, it wasn't by accident that Pope Leo IX died when he did, after giving his Constantinople-bound legates an official sendoff. Nothing in the *Sancta Ecclesia* happens by accident. It just meant that the pope could not change his mind after he did so! And it also meant that Cærularius was pipe dreaming when he fancied that he was excommunicating the Pontiff of Rome and Vicar of Christ along with the legates at his 20 July 1054 schismatic synod. And the Deliverer wasn't cracking a joke either when He said to the Twelve: '*Non vos me elegistis, sed ego elegi vos, et posui vos ut eatis, et fructum afferatis, et fructus vester maneat : ut quodcumque petieritis Patrem in nomine meo, det vobis.*' (You have not chosen me: but I have chosen you; and have appointed you, that you should go and should bring forth fruit; and your fruit should remain: that whatsoever you shall ask of the Father in my name, he may give it you) (John 15:16); or when He said to Peter: '*Beatus es Simon Bar Jona: quia caro et sanguis non revelavit tibi, sed Pater meus, qui in cælis est.*' (Blessed art thou, Simon Bar-Jona: because flesh and blood hath not revealed it to thee, but my Father who is in heaven.) (Matthew 16:17); or when He challenged His disciples saying: '*Numquid et vos vultis abire?*' (*Will you also go away?*) (John 6:68); Or when He instructed His disciples to shake the dust from their feet as they left a house or a city where they were not welcome – just as Cardinal Humbert of Silva Candida and his two fellow legates immediately did on that Saturday afternoon on July 16, 1054 after they had placed the sealed papal bull on the altar of the Cathedral, Hagia Sophia, just as the service was about to begin, the bull that proclaimed Michael Cærularius and his associates excommunicated, no longer in communion with the *Sancta Ecclesia*, and no longer permitted to receive the grace of God through the sacraments!

"I will say this, namely that folks like Photius, Nicetas and Cærularius made things really easy for us here in the Underworld to get what we wanted. Because of their actions, humans have had to live with the Great East-West Schism ever since! Still, it shouldn't come as a surprise that we are able to notch up such successes. Remember Judas who was one of the twelve? Look, we were able to compromise him, notwithstanding the fact that he was handpicked by the Deliverer Himself and chosen to be one of His twelve apostles, because humans are free. That was true then; it was true in the Middle Ages when Photius and Cærularius decided to do their thing; it was true during the Renaissance period when on 10 December 1520, the very day by which Martin Luther was supposed to recant his errors, the monk, oblivious to his vow of obedience, did the unthinkable – a professor of Moral Theology at the University of Wittenberg, he took the papal bull *Exsurge Domine* (Arise O Lord), promulgated by the Holy Father had promulgated on 15 June 1520 in response to the errors he had been openly disseminating, and cast it into the bonfire! And he even went on to ignore the bull *Decet Romanum Pontificem* that the Holy Father, pursuant to his responsibilities as the Vicar of Christ on earth, subsequently issued on January 3,1521, the bull that formally excommunicated him! It was true then; and it is true now!

"Look, you have to be dreaming if you are imagining that the Prime Mover is going to change rules of the game at this late hour just to accommodate you - to enable you to crash the Marriage Feast of the Lamb by surreptitiously sneaking unnoticed into the queue of the saints as they go marching in. Look here, buddy; all those folks in that queue (and you need to take a good look because this is important) have had their robes washed in the blood of the Lamb, exactly as it is described in the Apocalypse - Revelation 22:14 to be exact - the last book written that is the revealed Word of the Prime Mover and that, accordingly is the final piece of Divine Revelation, penned by John, the last of the apostles to die and the only one of the Twelve who did not forsake the Deliverer in the hour of His Passion, and written towards the end of that apostle's own life. Ha, ha, ha, ho, ho, ho, hee, hee, hee!

"And, did I say the saints who went marching in were just too many of them? I should have emphasized that they were really, really far too many of them – almost too many to count. There will probably never be a time that produced more saints than those who 'went marching in' during the roughly seven hundred years or so starting around 920 AD and ending in 1670 AD. They actually caused a traffic jam of sorts at the Gates of Heaven; and, yes, Saint Peter had to enlist the help of the saints' guardian angels to maintain a semblance of order as the victorious souls streamed in for the Marriage Feast of the Lamb!

"The list was really long; and was composed of folks like that Swiss **Saint Wiborada of St. Gall** (died 926); and other folks like **Saint Wenceslaus I** who was Duke of Bohemia and whose assassination in 935 was orchestrated by his young brother, Boleslaus the Cruel. Boleslaus the Cruel, unlike the Good King Wenceslaus, was clearly also Boleslaus the Fool because, while we got him to fancy that he himself would live on here on earth forever, his actions, which were intended to hurt his elder sibling, actually had the opposite effect – they merely sped Wenceslaus's march into the banquet hall where the festivities of the Marriage Feast of the Lamb were already well under way. We nailed the fool, and it was so easy! Saint Wenceslaus is hailed as the patron of the Bohemian people and of the former Czechoslovakia.

"There was **Saint Ludmila of Bohemia**, the grandmother of Saint Wenceslaus, whose murder in 921 was engineered by Drahomíra, her daughter in law. She was driven to do that because she was jealous of the saint's influence over Wenceslaus. **Saint Matilda of Ringelheim**, also known as Saint Matilda (d. 968). **Saint Ulrich of Augsburg**, the first saint to be canonized by the Pope acting on behalf of the universal church (d 973), and **Saint Conrad of Constance** (d.975). Described as a saint from the cradle, and endeavoured to be religiously exact in whatever belonged to his sacred functions, particularly to the sacrifice of the mass. It happened that a spider dropped into the chalice from wherever whilst the prelate was saying mass on Easter-day. Out of devotion and respect for the holy mysteries, the saint swallowed the spider which he vomited up some hours afterwards without being harmed. Other people would no doubt have reacted differently. **Saint Edward the Martyr** (Old English: *Eadweard*, pronounced æ:adweard. (d. 978); **Saint Gebhard of Constance** (Latin: Gebhardus Constantiensis; German: Gebhard von Konstanz) (d. 995 AD), German bishop of Constance from 979 until 995; he founded the Benedictine abbey of Petershausen in 983. **Saint Gerard of Toul** (French: *Geraud*; German: *Gerhard*) (d. 994), and **Saint Wolfgang of Regensburg** (d. 994) who were all German bishops. There was **Saint Rudesind** who was a Galician bishop and abbot (d. 977); **Saint Pietro I Orseolo** (d. 987); **Saint Adalbert of Prague** (Latin: *Sanctus Adalbertus*, Czech: *svatý Vojtěch*, Slovak: *svätý Vojtech*, Polish: *święty Wojciech*, Hungarian: *Szent Adalbert*); (d. 997); **Saint Adelaide of Italy** also called Adelaide of Burgundy (German: *Adelheid*) (d. 999); **Saint Gregory of Narek** (died c. 1003), Armenian mystical and lyrical poet, monk, and theologian. He is best known for his Book of Lamentations, a major piece of mystical literature. He was declared Doctor of the Church (the first Armenian Doctor of the Church) by Pope Francis in 2015. He is the only Doctor 'who was not in **communion** with the Catholic Church during his lifetime. **Saint Abbo of Fleury** (d. 1004); **Saint Attilanus** (d. 1007); **Saint Andrew Zorard** (died c 1009); **Saint Bruno of Querfurt** (d. 1009); **Saint Abraham of Rostov** (d. 1074); **Saint Benedict of Szkalka** (d. 1012); **Saint Alphege of Canterbury** (d. 1012); **Saint Boris and Saint Gleb** (d. 1015), Russians brothers who were proclaimed saints by Pope Benedict XIII in 1724; **Saint Vladimir**

Sviatoslavich also known as Vladimir the great (d. 1015); **Saint Adelaide**, Abbess of Vilich (d. 1015); **Saint Simeon of Mantua** (d. 1016); **Saint Heribert of Cologne** (d. 1021); **Saint Bernward of Hildesheim** (d. 1022) was a German bishop. He is invoked against fever, dropsy, childhood sicknesses, hailstones, the pain of childbirth, and gout. **Saint Symeon the New Theologian** (d. 1022); **Saint Henry II**, Holy Roman Emperor who is known as Saint Henry the Exuberant (d. 1024); **Saint Romuald**, founder of the Camaldolese order and a major figure in the eleventh-century 'Renaissance of 'eremitical asceticism' (d. 1024); **Saint Bononio** (d. 1026); **Saint Olaf II Haraldsson of Norway** who is also known as St. Olave (d. 1030); **Saint Emeric of Hungary** (Hungarian: *Szent Imre herceg*) also *Henricus, Emery, Emerick, Emmerich, Emericus or Americus* (d. 1031); **Saint Simeon of Trier** (d. 1035); **Saint Ladislaus I of Hungary** (d. 1035); **Saint Emma of Lesum** or Emma of Stiepel and also known as Hemma and Imma (d. 1038); **Saint Stephen of Hungary** (d. 1038; **Saint Cunigunde of Luxembourg** (d. 1040); **Saint Hemma of Gurk**, a noble woman who founded several churches and monasteries (d. 1045); **Saint Gerard of Csanád** (d. 1046); **Saint Odilo of Cluny** (d. 1049), who as Benedictine Abbot of Cluny, established the 2nd November as the day for the annual celebration of All Souls' Day in Cluny and its monasteries, a practice that was soon adopted throughout the whole Western church. **Saint Procopius of Sázava** (d. 1053); **Saint Íñigo of Oña** (d. 1057); **Saint Adamo Abate** (died c. c1070); **Saint Edward the Confessor** (d. 1066); **Saint Theobald of Provins** (d. 1066); **Saint Amunia of San Millán** (d. 1069) was a Benedictine hermit, from what is currently the La Rioja province in Northern Spain. She became a hermit after the death of her husband, following her daughter, St.

Áurea, who was also a hermit. Both saints spent their contemplative lives at the Monastery of San Millán de la Cogolla .in La Rioja. **Saint Godelieve of Gistel** also known as Godelina (d. 1070); **Saint Aurea of San Millán** (d. 1070). her mother was St. Amunia, and her favorite saints were Saint Agatha, Saint Eulalia and Saint Cecilia.. When she was aged nine, she and her mom (Amunia) decided to leave the world and to embrace a life of asceticism. They went to the Monastery of San Millán de la Cogolla, where they appealed to the prior, Dominic (later founder and namesake of the Abbey of Santo Domingo de Silos) for assistance in that regard. For Aurea, Prior Dominic had a narrow anchorhold built for her in the wall of the monastery church, with a small window through which she could see the altar, and another to the outside. He then consecrated her and had her walled into her new cell. Aurea completely applied herself to the contemplative life. By the age of 20, she was living in a cave where she received a vision of her three favorite saints. Aurea was twenty-seven years old at the time of her death. Her body was initially buried in her cave, which served as her shrine until 1609, when the bulk of her remains were enshrined at the monastery, with some being transferred to the parish church of her home town of Villavelayo , where a special chapel was built to house them and to honor her as the patron saint of the town. **Saint Peter Damian** (Italian: *Pietro or Pier Damiani*) (d. 1072). He was a reforming Benedictine monk and Doctor of the Church. Dante, in *Paradiso*, (the third part of his *Divine Comedy*), placed the saint (as a great predecessor of Saint Francis of Assisi) in one of the highest circles. **Saint Giovanni Gualberto** (d. 1073), also known as John Gualbert, is the patron saint for foresters and he is also the patron for park rangers and parks. Pope Pius XII named him - in 1951 - as the patron saint for the Italian Forest Corps while he was named as the patron for Brazilian forests in 1957. **Saint Dominic of Silos** (d. 1073); **Saint Anthony of Kyiv** (or Kiev), also called Anthony of the Caves (Russian: Антоний Печерский, Ukrainian: Антоній Печерський;(d. 1073); **Saint William of Roskilde** (d. 1074); **Saint Erlembald** (d. 1075); **Saint Anno II** (d. 1075); **Saint Bernard of Menthon** (d. 1081); **Saint David of Munktorp** (David av Munktorp) (d. 1082); **Saint Gregory VII** (d. 1085). He is one of the great reforming popes, and perhaps best known for the part he played in the Investiture Controversy. His dispute with Henry IV, Holy Roman Emperor, that affirmed the primacy of papal authority and the new canon law governing the election of the pope by the College of Cardinals.. He was the first pope in several centuries to rigorously enforce the Western Church's ancient policy of celibacy for the clergy and to attack the practice of simony. He excommunicated Henry IV three times, as a result of which Henry IV appointed Antipope Clement III to oppose him in the political power struggles between the Catholic Church and the monarch's empire. He is hailed as one of the greatest of the Roman pontiffs after his reforms proved successful. **Saint Canute IV of Denmark** (d. 1086); **Saint Arnold of Soissons** (d. 1087); **Saint Wolfhelm of Brauweiler** (d. 1091); **Saint Margaret of Scotland** (Scots: *Saunt Magret*) also known as Margaret of Wessex (d. 1093); **Saint Nicholas the Pilgrim** (Italian:*Nicola il Pellegrino*) also known as Nicholas of Trani (d. 1094); **Saint Gerald of Sauve-Majeure** (d. 1095); **Saint Wulfstan** (d. 1095); **Saint Osmund** (d.1099); **Saint Sigfrid of Sweden** (d. 1100); **Saint Bruno of Cologne** who founded the Carthusian Order (d. 1101); **Saint Peter of Anagni** (d. 1105); **Saint Benno of Meissen** (d. 1106), German prelate who is patron saint of anglers and weavers. **Saint Hugh of**

Cluny (d. 1109), was one of the most influential leaders of the monastic orders from the Middle Ages; **Saint Dominic de la Calzada** or Dominic of the Causeway (d. 1109); **Saint Alberic of Cîteaux** who was one of the founders of the Cistercian Order. (d. 1109); **Saint Anselm of Canterbury** (d. 1109), a Doctor of the Church and one of the most important Christian thinkers of the eleventh century; and his Proslogion ('Address,' or 'Allocution'), originally titled *Fides quaerens intellectum* ('Faith Seeking Understanding'), established what has been known since the time of Immanuel Kant (1724-1804) as the ontological argument for the existence of God. At the Council of Bari in October 1098, Anselm delivered his defense of the Filioque and the use of unleavened bread in the Eucharist before 185 bishops. Anselm held that faith necessarily precedes reason, but that reason can expand upon faith. Anselm employs Aristotelian logic to affirm the existence of an absolute truth of which all other truth forms separate kinds. He identifies this absolute truth with God, who therefore forms the fundamental principle both in the existence of things and the correctness of thought. He argued that the angels who upheld justice were rewarded with such happiness that they are now incapable of sin, there being no happiness left for them to seek in opposition to the bounds of justice; and that humans retain the theoretical capacity to will justly but, owing to the Fall, they are incapable of doing so in practice except by divine grace. Regarded as the Father of Scholasticism, the saint is also known as the *doctor magnificus* ('Magnificent Doctor') and the *doctor Marianus* ('Marian doctor'). **Saint Robert of Molesme** who was an abbot and one of the founders of the Cistercian Order (d. 1111); **Saint Yves or Ivo of Chartres** (d. 1115)**; Saint Gerald of Potenza** (d. 1119); **Saint Jón Ögmundsson** or Ogmundarson (Latin:

Ioannes Ögmundi filius) (d. 1121); **Saint Bruno di Segni** who chastised Pope Paschal II for signing the Concordat of Sutri (1111) and for which he was relieved of his duties as Abbot of Montecassino (d. 1123). **Saint Stephen of Muret** (d. 1124); **Saint Bertrand of Comminges** (d. 1126); **Saint Isidore the Farm Laborer** (d. 1130); **Saint William of Breteuil** (d. 1130); **Saint Canute Lavard** (d. 1131); **Saint Hugh of Châteauneuf** (d. 1132); **Saint Bernardo degli Uberti** (d. 1133); **Saint Stephen Harding** (d. 1134); **Saint Norbert of Xanten,** also known as Norbert Gennep, on Christmas Day in 1120 founded the order of Canons Regular of Prémontré (d. 1134). **Saint Leopold III**, also known as Leopold the Good, was the Margrave of Austria from 1095 to his death in 1136. **Saint Christian of Clogher**, also known as Gilla Críst Ua Morgair (d. 1138) and his brother **Saint Malachy**, the first native born Irish saint to be canonized. (Middle Irish: *Máel Máedóc Ua Morgair*; Modern Irish: *Maelmhaedhoc Ó Morgair*; (d. 1148); **Saint Otto of Bamberg** (d. 1139); **Saint Gaucherius** (d. 1140); **Saint Bellinus of Padua** (d. 1145); **Saint Belina** (d. 1153). A peasant girl from Troyes, France, she was threatened with rape by the feudal lord of the district . She refused his advances and died in defense of her virginity. **Saint Bernard of Clairvaux** (d 1153), Doctor of the Church. Bernard had observed that when *lectio divina* was neglected monasticism suffered. Bernard considered *lectio divina* and contemplation guided by the Holy Spirit the keys to nourishing Christian spirituality. He is labeled the 'Mellifluous Doctor' for his eloquence. Doctor of the Church. Authorship of the hymns 'O Sacred Head, Now Wounded', 'Jesu the Very Thought of Thee' and 'Jesus, Thou Joy of Loving Hearts' among others is attributed to him. His theological works include *De gratia et libero arbitrio* (On grace and free choice) in which the *Sancta*

Ecclesia's dogma of grace and free will is defended according to the principles of St Augustine; and *De diligendo Dei* (On loving God) which outlines seven stages of ascent leading to union with God – to name just a few. One day, to cool down his lustful temptation, Bernard threw himself into ice-cold water. Another time, while he slept in an inn, a prostitute was introduced naked beside him, and he saved his chastity by running. **Saint William of York** (d. 1154); **Saint Stephen of Obazine** (d. 1154); **Saint Henry of Uppsala** (d. 1156); **Saint William of Maleval** also known as William the Great (d. 1157); **Saint Rögnvald Kali Kolsson** also known as Saint Ronald of Orkney (d. 1158); **Saint Guarino Foscari of Palestrina** also known as Guarinus of Palestrina (d. 1158); **Saint John of Meda** also known as John of Como (d. 1159); **Saint Helena of Sköfde** (d. 1160); **Saint Eric IX of Sweden** (d. 1160); **Saint Ubald of Gubbio** (d. 1160); **Saint Rosalia** (d 1160); **Saint Rainerius** who is the patron saint of Pisa and also of travellers (d. 1160); **Saint Theotonius of Coimbra** (d. 1162); **Adalgott II of Disentis** (d. 1165); **Saint Thomas Becket** also known as Saint Thomas of Canterbury, Thomas of London and later Thomas à Becket (d. 1170). He was murdered on the orders of King Henry II (5 March 1133 – 6 July 1189) in Canterbury Cathedral. Following Becket's death, the monks prepared his body for burial. According to one account, it was discovered that Becket had worn a hairshirt underneath his archbishop's garments—a sign of penance. **Saint Pierre de Tarentaise** (d. 1174) is also known as Peter of Tarentaise. He tried to resist his elevation to the episcopate, but his superiors and Saint Bernard of Clairvaux insisted that he accept the position of Archbishop of Tarentaise. In his episcopal role he applied the Cistercian principles he had learned as an abbot to restore discipline in the diocese. He removed corrupt priests (and elevated good priests to important pastoral positions) and promoted education for all the faithful. He also founded a charity which distributed food to farms in the surrounding hills. This would become known as pain de Mai and became a tradition that continued in the region until the French Revolution. But he longed for the simple and pious life of a monk and, in 1155, vanished without a trace. He was later found, however, living as a lay brother in a remote convent in Switzerland after about a year, when the monks discovered who he was and alerted the archdiocese. The bishop was reluctant to emerge from his newfound solitude but was welcomed back into his archdiocese with much enthusiasm on the part of the people. **Saint Isfrid of Ratzeburg** (d. 1178); **Saint Hildegard of Bingen** also known as Saint Hildegard (d. 1179); **Saint Lorcán Ua Tuathail** or Saint Laurence O'Toole and in French as *St. Laurent d'Eu* (d. 1180); **Saint Galgano Guidotti** (d. 1181); **Saint Gilbert of Sempringham** who founded the Gilbertine Order (d. 1190); **Saint Albert of Louvain** (d. 1192); **Saint Meinhard** (d. 1196); **Saint Homobonus** (Italian: *Sant'Omobono*, German: *Sankt Gutmann*) (d. 1197), the patron saint of business people, tailors, shoemakers, and clothworkers, as well as of Cremona, Italy. **Saint Hugh of Lincoln** also known as Hugh of Avalon (d. 1200); **Saint Gherardino Sostegni** who is one of the Seven Holy Founders of the Servite Order (d. 1200); **Saint William of Perth** (d. 1201); **Saint Martin of Leon** (Spanish: *San Martín de León*); (d. 1203); **Saint Ubaldesca Taccini** (d. 1205); **Saint Julián of Cuenca** (d. 1208); **Saint Guillaume de Donjeon** (d. 1209); **Saint Felix of Valois** (d. 1212) was a hermit and **Saint John of Matha** (d. 1213) co-founded the Order of the Most Holy Trinity dedicated to ransoming captive Christians. **Saint Albert of Jerusalem** also known as Albert of Vercelli or

Alberto Avogadro (d. 1214); **Saint Franca Visalta** also known as Franca of Piacenza (d. 1218); **Saint Angelus of Jerusalem** (d. 1220); **Saint Berard of Carbio** (d.1220) and **Saint Daniel** and Companions (d. 1227) who are venerated together with other members of the Friars Minor who were beheaded in the Saracen city of Ceuta for preaching the Gospel to Muslims of the Maghreb. **Saint Dominic** also known as Dominic of Osma and Dominic of Caleruega and often also called Dominic de Guzmán (d 1221); **Abraham of Smolensk** (d. 1222); **Saint Christina Mirabilis** (d. 1224); **Saint Adolf of Osnabrück** (d. 1224), also known as Adolphus, Adolph, Adolf of Tecklenburg; **Saint Engelbert of Cologne** (d. 1225); **Saint Francis of Assisi** (d. 1226). He founded the men's Order of Friars Minor, the women's Order of Saint Clare, and the Third Order of Saint Francis. While on a pilgrimage to Rome, he joined the poor in begging at St. Peter's Basilica. He is very well known for the stigmata he received during an apparition. Along with Saint Catherine of Siena, he was designated Patron saint of Italy. He later became associated with patronage of animals and the natural environment. **Saint Anthony of Padua**, Doctor of the Church (d. 1231); his help is invoked for finding lost or stolen things; **Saint Elizabeth of Hungary** also known as Saint **Elizabeth of Thuringia** (d. 1231); **Saint Serapion of Algiers** (d. 1240). The Seven Holy Founders of the Order of Friar Servants of St. Mary (*Ordo Fratrum Servorum Sanctae Mariae*) also known as the Servite Order in 1233, namely **Saint John Buonagiunta Monetti** (d. 1256), **Saint Buonfiglio dei Monaldi** (Bonfilius) (d. 1261), **Saint Bartolomeo degli Amidei** (Amideus) (d. 1266), and **Saint Benedetto dell' Antella,** also known as Benedict dell'Antella (d. 1268). **Saint Gherardino di Sostegno** (Sosteneus) (d. 1276**), Saint Hugh dei Lippi Uggucioni**, also known as

Ricovero dei Lippi-Ugguccioni (Hugh) (d. 1282) and **Saint Alessio de' Falconieri** (Alexis) (d. 1310). **Saint Villanus** (d. 1237); **Saint Edmund of Abingdon** (d. 1240); **Saint Serapion of Algiers** (d. 1240); **Saint Raymond Nonnatus** also known as Sant Ramon Nonat or San Ramón Nonato and also San Rajmondo Nonnato (d. 1240). His nickname (Latin: *Nonnatus*, 'not born') refers to his birth by caesarean section, and the fact that his mother died while giving birth to him. He is patron saint of childbirth, midwives, children, pregnant women, and priests defending the confidentiality of confession. **Saint Guillaume (William) Pinchon** (d. 1234); **Saint Hermann Joseph** (d. 1241); **Saint Veridiana** also known as Virginia Margaret del Mazziere (d. 1242); **Saint Hedwig of Silesia** (d. 1243); **Saint Bernat Calbó** (d. 1243); **Saint Gilbert of Dornoch** also known as Gilbert of Caithness (d. 1245); **Saint Lutgardis of Aywières** also spelled Lutgarde) (Dutch: *Sint-Ludgardis*). (d. 1246); **Saint Peter González** sometimes referred to as Pedro González Telmo or Saint Telmo (d. 1246); **Saint Theobald of Marly** (d. 1247); **Saint Theresa of Portugal** (d. 1250); **Saint Ludolph of Ratzeburg** (d. 1250); **Saint Rose of Viterbo** (d. 1251); **Saint Ferdinand III of Castile** (d. 1252); **Saint Zdislava Berka** (d. 1252); **Saint Peter of Verona** (d. 1252) was a member of the Order of the Friars Preachers (Dominicans), was a celebrated preacher throughout northern and central Italy. in the 1230s Peter preached against heresy, and especially Catharism, which had many adherents in thirteenth-century Northern Italy. Once, when preaching to a vast crowd under the burning sun, the heretics challenged him to procure a shade for his listeners. As he prayed, a cloud overshadowed the audience. In his sermons he denounced heresy and also those Catholics who professed the Faith by words, but acted contrary to it in deeds. **Saint Clare of Assisi** (d.

1253), who founded the Order of Poor Ladies, a monastic religious order for women in the Franciscan tradition, and her younger sister **Saint Agnes of Assisi** (d. 1253). When they told their father, a wealthy representative of an ancient Roman family, who owned a large palace in Assisi and a castle on the slope of Mount Subasio, that they wanted to live like Francis, he said he would never allow it to happen. One night, Clare sneaked out of the house and went to live at a Benedictine convent. And two weeks later, Agnes joined her. The family went to the convent to force the sisters to return home, but they would not, even when their father got soldiers to try and force them to leave the convent and return home. **Saint Claudus Corrius** (d. 1253); **Saint Richard of Chichester** also known as Richard de Wych (d. 1253); **Saint Peter Nolasco** who in 1218 formed a congregation of men that became the Royal and Military Order of Our Lady of Mercy of the Redemption of the Captives (the Mercedarians) (d. 1256); **Saint Hyacinth of Poland** (d. 1257); **Saint Juliana of Liège** (also called Juliana of Mount-Cornillon), (d. 1258); **Saint Boniface of Brussels** (d. 1260); **Saint Buonfiglio Monaldi** (d. 1261); **Saint Simon Stock** (d. 1265); **Saint Amadeus of the Amidei** (d. 1266); **Saint Silvestro Guzzolini** (d. 1267); **Saint Isabelle of France** (d. 1270); **Saint Margaret of Hungary** (d. 1270); **Saint Louis IX of France** commonly known as Saint Louis and the only King of France to be canonized in the Catholic Church (d. 1270). **Saint Zita** of Lucca (d. 1272). She worked as a house maid for one a family in Lucca for the last forty-eight years of her life; and, while at it, found time to attend Mass daily. She is patroness of house maids and other domestic workers. **Saint Thomas Aquinas**, the Angelic Doctor of the Church, (d 1274). He was sent to the Abbey of Monte Cassino to train among Benedictine monks when he was

5 years old; and while there, the quizzical kid repeatedly asked his benefactors: 'What is God?' He was a student of Saint Albert the Great, the Father of Scholasticism. **Saint Bonaventura** (d. 1274). Pope Sixtus V bestowed upon the saint the title 'Angelic and Seraphic Doctor of the Church' in recognition of his unfathomable love for God and outstanding theological writings. The saint also founded the Society of the Gonfalone in honor of the Blessed Virgin. **Saint Raymond of Penyafort** (d. 1275); **Saint Albertus Magnus** (d. 1280), Doctor of the Church. Also known as Albert the Great, he was one of the most universal thinkers to appear during the Middle Ages. Even more so than his most famous student, St. Thomas of Aquinas, Albert's interests ranged from natural science all the way to theology. He made contributions to logic, psychology, metaphysics, meteorology, mineralogy, and zoology. He is the patron saint of natural scientists. **Saint Benvenutus Scotivoli** (d. 1282); **Saint Thomas de Cantilupe** (d. 1282); **Saint Agnes of Bohemia** (d. 1282); **Saint Ingrid of Skänningea**, Swedish abbess who founded the Skänninge Abbey, a nunnery of the Dominican Order, in 1272 (d. 1282); **Saint Philip Benizi de Damiani** also known as St Philip Benitius was a general superior of the Order of the Servites and is credited with reviving it (d. 1285); **Saint Amato Ronconi** (d. 1292); **Saint Kinga of Poland** also known as Cunegunda, patroness of Poland and Lithuania (Polish:*Święta Kinga* and Hungarian: *Szent Kinga*) (d. 1292); **Saint Margaret of Cortona** (d. 1297); **Saint Mechtilde of Hackeborn** (d. 1298); **Saint Celestine V**, a Benedictine monk and hermit who had been known as Brother Peter and who sought to model his life according to Saint John the Baptizer, was elected pope in the Sancta Ecclesia's last non-conclave papal election. But on 13 December 1294 at Naples, where he had

established the papal court under the patronage of Charles II of Naples and had continued to live like a monk there, even turning a room in the papal apartment into the semblance of a monastic cell, he abdicated as pope only five months into his papacy (5 July - 13 December 1294) in order to return to his humble pre-papal life as a hermit. resigned the papal throne   He is also founder of the order of the Celestines as a branch of the Benedictine order (founded in 1244). Pope Boniface VIII, who succeeded Pope Celestine V, worried that those who had been opposed to Celestine's resignation might try to see him re-installed and cause a new schism in the *Sancta Ecclesia* in the process.   And so he had Celestine imprisoned in the Castle of Fumone at Ferentino in the Lazio region where the saint died on 19 May 1296 at the age of 81. **Saint Sancha of Portugal** (d. 1302); **Saint Gertrude the Great** (also known as Saint Gertrude of Helfta (d. 1302). **Saint Ivo of Kermartin** (d. 1303), also known as Yvo, Yves, or Ives and also St. Ivo Helory, was a parish priest among the poor of Louannec, the only one of his station to be canonized in the Middle Ages. He is the patron of Brittany, lawyers and abandoned children. **Saint Pedro Armengol**, born Pedro Armengol Rocafort, was of noble stock and also a thief during his adolescence. After experiencing a sudden conversion, he became a professed member of the Mercedarians, a mendicant order established in 1218 by Saint Peter Nolasco. (d. 1304); **Saint Nicholas of Tolentino**, Patron of Holy Souls (d. 1305); **Saint Albert of Trapani** (d. 1307); **Saint Clare of Montefalco** also known as Saint Clare of the Cross (dc 1308); **Saint Aldobrandesca Ponzi** (d. 1309); **Saint Angela of Foligno** who started her own community of tertiaries devoted to the care of the needy and who is also referred to as the 'Mistress of Theologians', and whose body is one of those that are adjudged incorrupt (d. 1309); **Saint Humility** (Humilitas) who is founder of Vallumbrosan convents and is also considered the founder of the Vallumbrosan Nuns (d. 1310); **Saint Agnes of Montepulciano** (d. 1317); **Saint Thomas of Tolentino, Saint Demetrius of Tiflis, Blessed Peter of Siena**, and **Blessed James of Padua** who were scourged and tortured before being beheaded in 1321 for 'blaspheming' Muhammad in Thane, India, and are venerated together as the Four Martyrs of Thane (d. 1321); **Saint Elzéar of Sabran** (d. 1323); **Saint Roch** (d. 1327); **Saint Elizabeth of Aragon** also known as Saint Elizabeth of Portugal (d. 1336); **Saint Juliana Falconieri**, foundress of the Religious Sisters of the Third Order of Servites (or the Servite Tertiaries) (d 1341);.**Saint Peregrine Laziosi** (d. 1345); **Saints Anthony, John, and Eustathius** (Kumetis, Nizilas, and Krulis) of Vilnius, Russian brothers who died for their faith in 1347 under the Lithuanian Great Prince Algirdas; **Saint Bernardo Tolomei** who founded the Congregation of the Blessed Virgin of Monte Oliveto (d 1348); **Saint Conrad of Piacenza** (d. 1351); **Saint Peter Thomas** (d. 1366); **Saint Bridget of Sweden** (d. 1373), She founded the Bridgettines nuns and monks after the death of her husband of twenty years. Outside of Sweden, she was also known as the *Princess of Nericia*. She was the mother of Saint Catherine of Sweden who is also known as Catherine of Vadstena (d. 1381). Even though they came from a noble family, they were not members of Swedish royalty. **Saint Andrea Corsini** (d. 1373); **Saint Roch** also known as Saint Rocco (d. 1376 or 1379); **Saint John Twenge** (also known as Saint John of Bridlington, John Thwing, John of Thwing, and John Thwing of Bridlington) (d. 1379). He was the last English saint to be canonized before the English Reformation. **Saint Catherine of Siena** whose influence with Pope Gregory

XI played a role in his decision to leave Avignon and return to Rome (d. 1380); **Saint Catherine of Sweden** also known as Katarina av Vadstena, also Catherine of Vadstena or Katarina Ulfsdotter (d. 1381); **Saint Nicholas Tavelic**, **Saint Stephen of Cuneo**, **Saint Deodato Aribert** from Ruticinio and **Saint Peter of Narbonne**, Priests of the Order of Friars Minor who were burned to death in Jerusalem on November 14, 1391 for having preached boldly in the public square in front of the Saracens; **Saint Deodat of Rodez** (d. 1391); **Saint John Nepomuk** (d. 1393), who is considered the first martyr of the Seal of the Confessional. He died by drowning in the Vitava river on the orders of Wenceslaus IV of Bohemia who suspected that the queen had been unfaithful. The saint was her confessor, and he refused to divulge the secrets of the confessional. He is also the patron saint against calumnies and (because of the manner of his death) a protector from floods and drowning. **Saint Dorothea** (or Dorothy) of Montau who was a German hermitess and visionary (d. 1394); **Saint Margaret the Barefooted** (d. 1395). In order to relate to the people she helped, St. Margaret the Barefooted also went shoeless and dressed like one of them (meaning like a beggar). **Saint Jadwiga of Poland** also known as Hedwig (d. 1399); **Saint Vincent Ferrer** (d. 1419); **Saint Andrei Rublev** (d. c 1430); **Saint Nuno Álvares Pereira** who is often referred to as the Saint Constable (d. 1431); **Saint Frances of Rome** (d. 1440); **Saint Joan of Arc** (d. 1431); **Saint Mark of Ephesus** (d. 1439); **Saint Bernardino of Siena** also known as Saint Bernardine of Siena (d. 1444). Pope Pius II (pope from 1458 to 1464), a humanist writer and poet who denounced slavery as an enormous crime, called the saint the 'second Paul' because of his outstanding missionary activity. **Saint Colette of Corbie** (d. 1447); **Saint Fra Angelico** (d. 1455); **Saint Peter de**

Regalado (Spanish: *San Pedro Regalado*), whose body when exhumed 36 years after his death, at the insistence of Saint Lawrence Justinian (Italian: *Lorenzo Giustiniani*), (d. 1456); **Saint John of Capistrano** (Italian: *San Giovanni da Capestrano*) (d.1456). A 'soldier saint' who is also referred to as 'Soldier Priest', he survived the battles only to be taken down by the bubonic plague that saw one-third of the population and nearly 40 percent of the clergy wiped out in the 14th century. **Saint Isabella the Catholic**, was found incorrupt (d. 1456); **Saint Rita of Cas**cia (d. 1457); **Saint Antonino Pierozzi** (d. 1459); **Saint Antonius of Florence** (d. 1459); **Saint Didacus of Alcalá** who was in the first group of missionaries to the newly conquered Spanish possessions of the Canary Islands (d. 1463); **Saint Catherine of Bologna** (d. 1463). She was a model of piety and experienced miracles and several visions of Christ, the Virgin Mary, Thomas Becket, and St. Joseph, as well as future events, such as the fall of Constantinople in 1453. Her writings include the Seven Spiritual Weapons Necessary for Spiritual Warfare (*Le Sette Armi Spirituali*), which includes descriptions of her visions. They included visions of me, Satan! Also known as Caterina, she was buried in the convent graveyard after she died. But after eighteen days, a sweet smell emanated from the grave and the incorrupt body was exhumed. It was eventually relocated to a chapel where it remains on display, dressed in her religious habit, seated upright behind glass. **Saint John Cantius** (d. 1473); **Saint James of the Marches** (d. 1476). Born Dominic Gangala (Italian: *Domenico Gangala*) in the early 1390s to a poor family in Monteprandone, he joined the Order of Friars Minor, in the chapel of the Portiuncula, in Assisi, on 26 July 1416, taking the monastic name Jacobus (Jacob, Jacopo; rendered James in English). Upon completing his novitiate at the hermitage of the

Carceri, near Assisi, he studied theology at Fiesole, near Florence, with St. John of Capistrano, under St. Bernardine of Siena. He was ordained a priest on 13 June 1420, and began to preach in Tuscany, in the Marches, and in Umbria. He helped spread devotion to the Holy Name of Jesus. From 1427, the saint preached penance, combated heretics. At the time of the Council of Basle (1431), the saint promoted the reunion of the moderate Hussites with the Catholic Church, and later that of the Eastern Orthodox at the Council of Ferrara-Florence (1438–1445). James was buried in Naples in the Franciscan church of Santa Maria la Nova, where his body remained until 2001. At the instigation of the provincial minister (Franciscan superior) of the Marches region, Father Ferdinando Campana, O.F.M., the saint's body was relocated to Monteprandone, where it remains incorrupt and visible to the public today. **Saint John of Sahagún** (Spanish: *Juan de Sahagún*), (d. 1479); **Saint Antonio Primaldo and his Companion Martyrs** (Italian: *Santi Antonio Primaldo e compagni martiri*), also known as the Martyrs of Otranto, were 813 inhabitants of the Salentine city of Otranto in southern Italy who were killed on 14 August 1480 when the city fell to an Ottoman force under Gedik Ahmed Pasha. According to a traditional account, the killings took place after the Otrantins refused to convert to Islam. **Saint Szymon of Lipnica** (d. 1482); **Saint Casimir Jagiellon** (d. 1484); **Saint John of Dukla**, also known as 'Jan of Dukla' (d. 1484) is one of the patron saints of Poland and Lithuania. **Saint Pedro de Arbués** (cd. 1485); **Saint Eustochia Smeralda Calafato** (d. 1485); **Saint Nicholas of Flüe** sometimes invoked as Brother Klaus (d. 1487); **Saint Stanisław Kazimierczyk** (d. 1489); **Saint Beatrice of Silva** also known as Beatriz da Silva y de Menezes (d. 1492). A noble woman of Portugal, she became foundress of the monastic Order of the Immaculate Conception of Our Lady in Spain. **Saint Girolamo Savonarola** (d. 1498); **Saint Isabella** the Catholic, Queen of Castile (d. 1504); **Saint Joan of France** who founded the monastic Order of the Sisters of the Annunciation of Mary (d. 1505); **Saint Francis of Paola** who founded the Order of Minims (d. 1507); **St. Catherine of Genoa** (d. 1510), whose celebrated writings include 'Dialogues of the Soul and Body' and 'Treatise on Purgatory', was well known for her care for the sick in Genoa. **Saint Joseph Volotsky** — also known as Joseph of Volotsk or Joseph of Volokolamsk (**Russian:** Иосиф Волоцкий); secular name Ivan Sanin (**Russian:** Иван Санин) (d. 1515); **Saint Camilla Battista da Varano** (d. 1524); Mexican teenage **Saints Cristobal of Tlaxcala** (d. 1527), **Saint Antonio of Tlaxcala** (D. 1529) and **Saint Juan of Tlaxcala** (d. 1529) who died for their faith; **Saint John Houghton** was a Carthusian hermit and Catholic priest and the first English Catholic martyr to die as a result of the Act of Supremacy by King Henry VIII of England. He was also the first member of his order to die as a martyr and is venerated along with others who are commonly referred to as the Forty Martyrs of England and Wales.(d. 1535). **Saint Thomas More**, Knight, Lord Chancellor of England and author was executed by executed at the Tower Hill on 6 July, 1535 under King Henry VIII; **Saint John Fisher**, bishop, cardinal, and theologian who eventually served as Chancellor of the University of Cambridge and was executed by order of Henry VIII during the English Reformation for refusing to accept him as the supreme head of the Church of England and for upholding the Catholic Church's doctrine of papal supremacy.(d. 1535). **Saint Richard Reynolds** (d. 1535), **Saint Augustine Webster** (d. 1535), **Saint John Stone** (d. 1539), **Saint Alexander Briant** (d. 1581), **Saint Edmund Champion** (d. 1581), **Saint Ralph**

Sherwin (d. 1581), **Saint Luke Kirby** (d. 1582), **Saint John Payne** (d. 1582), **Saint Richard Gwyn** (d. 1584), **Saint Margaret Ward** (d. 1588), **Saint Margaret Clitherow** (d. 1586), **Saint Polydore Plasden** (d. 1591), **Saint Edmund Gennings** (d.1591), **Saint Swithun Wells** (d. 1591), **Saint Eustace White** (d. 1591), **Saint John Boste** (d. 1594), **Saint Robert Southwell** (d. 1595), **Saint Henry Walpole** (d. 1595), **Saint Philip Howard** (d. 1595), **Saint John Jones** (d. 1598), **Saint John Rigby** (d. 1600), **Saint Anne Line** (d 1601), **Saint Nicholas Owen** (d. 1606), **Saint Thomas Garnet** (d. 1608), **Saint John Roberts** (d. 1610), **Saint John Almond** (d. 1612), **Saint Edmund Arrowsmith** (d.1628) **Saint Ambrose Edward Barlow** (d. 1641), **Saint Alban Roe** (d. 1642), **Saint Henry Morse** (d. 1645), **Saint John Southworth** (d. 1654), **Saint John Kemble** (d.1679), **Saint Philip Evans** (d. 1679), **Saint John Wall** (d. 1679), **Saint John Lloyd** (d. 1679), **Saint David Lewis** (d. 1679), and **Saint John Plessington** (d. 1679), who were executed between 1535 and 1679 for not accepting Henry VIII's Act of Supremacy and are venerated as the Forty Martyrs of England and Wales. **Saint Robert Lawrence** (d. 1535); **Saint Jerome Aemilian** who founded the *Ordo Clericorum Regularium a Somascha* (Company of the Servants of the Poor or the 'Somaschi Fathers' (d. 1537); **Saint Gerolamo Emiliani** (d. 1537); **Saint Anthony Maria Zaccaria** who founded the religious order the Clerics Regular of Saint Paul (*Clerici Regulares Sancti Pauli*) in 1530 also known as the Barnabites (d. 1539); **Saint Angela Merici** who founded the Company of St. Ursula in 1535 (d. 1540); **Saint Peter Faber** (French: *Pierre Lefevre*) was the first Jesuit priest and theologian, who was also a co-founder of the Society of Jesus, along with St. Ignatius of Loyola and St. Francis Xavier. (d. 1546); **Saint Cajetan of Thiene** (Gaetano dei

Conti di Tiene) who with others founded the Congregation of Clerics Regular of the Divine Providence, better known as the Theatines, (d. 1547); **Saint Juan Diego Cuauhtlatoatzin**, a native of Mexico and the first indigenous saint from the Americas (d. 1548). **Saint John of God**, a Portuguese soldier turned health-care worker in Spain, (d. 1550). His followers later formed the Brothers Hospitallers of Saint John of God, a worldwide Catholic religious institute dedicated to the care of the poor, sick, and those suffering from mental disorders. To put a stop to the saint's custom of exchanging his cloak with any beggar he chanced to meet, his bishop (Sebastian Ramirez, Bishop of Tui) had a religious habit specially made for him, which was later adopted in all its essentials as the religious garb of his followers. **Saint Francis Xavier** who with Saint Ignatius of Loyola and Saint Peter Faber co-founded the Society of Jesus. (d. 1552). Considered to be one of the greatest missionaries since the Apostle Paul, Pope Pius XI in 1927, published the decree '*Apostolicorum in Missionibus*' naming Francis Xavier, along with Thérèse of Lisieux, co-patron of all foreign missions. **Saint Thomas of Villanova** (d. 1555); **Saint Ignatius of Loyola**, (d. 1556). With Saint Charles Borromeo and Saint Philip Neri, the saint was a leading figure of the Counter-Reformation against the Protestant Reformation. He was declared patron saint of all spiritual retreats by Pope Pius XI in 1922. He is also the patron saint of soldiers, the Military Ordinariate of the Philippines, the Roman Catholic Archdiocese of Baltimore, the Basque Country, Antwerp, Belo Horizonte, Junín and various towns and cities in his native Basque region. **Saint Peter of Alcantara** (Spanish: *San Pedro de Alcántara*) is the patron saint of nocturnal adoration of the Blessed Sacrament. In 1826, he was named patron saint of Brazil, and in 1962 (the fourth centenary of his death), of the Spanish region of Extremadura. (d. 1562); **Saint Salvador of Horta** (d. 1567); **Saint Stanisław Kostka** (d. 1568); **Saint John of Ávila** (Spanish: Juan de Ávila) (d. 1569); he is a mystic and a Doctor of the Church. **Saint Francis Borgia** (d. 1572). He founded the *Collegium Romanum* in Rome, now known as the Gregorian University. **Saint Pius V** (d. 1572). Pius V was elected in 1566, and it fell upon him to implement the sweeping reforms called for by the Council which had closed in 1563. He ordered the founding of seminaries for the proper training of priests. He published a new missal, a new breviary, a new catechism, and established the Confraternity of Christian Doctrine classes for the young. Pius zealously enforced legislation against abuses in the Church. He patiently served the sick and the poor by building hospitals, providing food for the hungry, and giving money customarily used for the papal banquets to poor Roman converts. His decision to keep wearing his Dominican habit led to the custom–to this day–of the pope wearing a white cassock. **Saint Anthony of Hoornaar** (d. 1572); **Saint Andrew Wouters** (d. 1572), **Saint Leonard van Veghel** (d. 1572), **Saint Francis of Roye** (d. 1572), **Saint John of Cologne** (d. 1572), **Saint Godfried of Mervel** (d. 1572), **Saint Godfried van Duynen** (d. 1572), **Saint James Lacobs** (d. 1572), **Saint Willehad of Denmark** (d. 1572), **Saint Nicholas Pieck** (d. 1572), **Saint Nicasius of Heeze** (1572), **Saint Theodore of der Eem** (d. 1572), **Saint Peter of Assche** (d. 1572), **Saint Jan of Oisterwijk** (d. 1572), **Saint Cornelius of Wijk bij Duurstede** (d. 1572), **Saint Adrian van Hilvarenbeek** (d. 1572), and **Saint Anthony of Weet** (d. 1572) who are venerated as the Martyrs of Gorkum (a group of 19 Dutch Catholic clerics who were hanged on 9 July 1572 in the town of Brielle by militant Dutch Calvinists during the Dutch Revolt against

Spanish rule). **Saint Catherine of Palma** (d. 1574); **Saint Cuthbert Mayne** (d. 1577); **Saint Louis Bertrand** (Spanish: *Luis Beltrán, Luis Bertrán*) (d. 1581); **Saint Teresa of Avila** (d. 1582), was active during the Catholic Reformation. She reformed the Carmelite Orders of both women and men, actions that eventually led to the establishment of the Discalced Carmelites. **Saint Charles Borromeo** (d. 1584),was a leading figure, together with St. Ignatius of Loyola and St. Philip Neri, of the Counter-Reformation combat against the Protestant Reformation. A nephew of Pope Pius IV who is credited with bringing to a glorious conclusion the Council of Trent, the saint was also one of the pope's chief aides. **Saint Felix of Cantalice** (Italian: *Felice da Cantalice*) (d. 1587). In Rome, Brother Felix became a familiar sight, wandering barefoot through the streets, with a sack slung over his shoulders, knocking on doors to seek donations. He received permission from his superiors to help the needy, especially widows with many children. It is said that his begging sack was as bottomless as his heart. Brother Felix blessed all benefactors and all those he met with a humble '*Deo Gratias*!' (thanks be to God!), causing many to refer to him as 'Brother *Deo Gratias*'. **Saint Benedict the Moor** (d. 1589) was born to former slaves who were given Italian names and who later converted to Christianity (the Italian '*Il Moro*' for 'the dark skinned' has been interpreted as referring to Moorish heritage. He suffered a lot of insults for his color. His patient and dignified bearing was noticed by the leader of an independent group of hermits on nearby Monte Pellegrino, who followed the Rule for hermit life written by St. Francis of Assisi. Invited to join that community, Benedict gave up all his earthly possessions and joined them, initially serving as the cook for the community. Benedict is remembered for his patience and understanding when confronted with racial prejudice and taunts. He was declared a patron saint of African Americans, along with the Dominican lay brother, Martin de Porres. He was beatified by Pope Benedict XIV in 1743 and canonized in 1807 by Pope Pius VII. It is claimed that his body was found incorrupt upon exhumation a few years later. **Saint Catherine de' Ricci** (d. 1590); **Saint Bartholomew of Braga** (d. 1590), A bishop, he took part in the last sessions of the Council of Trent and made a total of 268 suggestions at the council at which he collaborated with Saint Charles Borromeo. He made repeated requests to resign from his episcopal see and finally received papal permission from Pope Gregory XIII on 20 February 1582 to resign and withdraw to his order's convent at Viana do Castelo. He served for a while as a teacher, and otherwise spent the rest of his life at Viana do Castelo in solitude. **Saint John of the Cross** (Spanish: *Juan de la Cruz*) (d. 1591), who is referred to as the Mystical Doctor of the Church. While praying in a loft overlooking the sanctuary in the Monastery of the Incarnation in Ávila, the saint, an acquaintance of St. Theresa of Avila, had a vision of the crucified Deliverer, which led him to create his drawing of Christ 'from above'. In 1641, the drawing was placed in a small monstrance and kept in Ávila. That same drawing inspired the artist Salvador Dalí's 1951 work Christ of Saint John of the Cross. **Saint Alonso de Orozco Mena** (d. 1591); **Saint Aloysius Gonzaga** (d. 1591), who cared for victims of the plague that swept Europe between 1591 and 1599, and died of it.at the age of 23. He is patron saint of Catholic youth just like St. Don Bosco (d. 1888) who founded the Salesian Congregation and is also patron saint of young people, apprentices, and Catholic publishers and editors. **Saint John Augustine Adorno** (d. 1608). With twelve others along with Saint Francis

Caracciolo (d. 1615), founded the Minor Clerks Regular, or the Adorno Fathers. Their mission is to minister to the sick and the imprisoned. Their motto is *Ad Maiorem Dei Resurgentis Gloriam*, 'For the Greater Glory of the Risen God.' **Saint Paschal Baylón**, a Franciscan lay brother who became noted for his strict austerities and his compassion towards the sick. Sent to counter the arguments of the Calvinists in France, he was chased out and nearly killed by a mob. He was best known for his strong and deep devotion to the Eucharist. Pope Leo XIII proclaimed him as the 'seraph of the Eucharist' and also patron of Eucharistic congresses and affiliated associations. (d. 1592). **Saint Alexander Sauli** who is known as the 'Apostle of Corsica' (d. 1592); **Saint Philip Romolo Neri** who is also known as the Second Apostle of Rome after Saint Peter; and who in 1574 established the Congregation of the Oratory. The saint is hailed as the patient reformer, who leaves outward things alone and works from within, depending rather on the hidden might of sacrament and prayer than on drastic policies of external improvement; the director of souls who attaches more value to mortification of the reason than to bodily austerities, dwells on the importance of serving God in a cheerful spirit, and gives a quaintly humorous turn to the maxims of ascetical theology; the silent watcher of the times, who takes no active part in ecclesiastical controversies and is yet a motive force in their development, now encouraging the use of ecclesiastical history as a bulwark against Protestantism, now insisting on the absolution of a monarch, whom other counsellors would fain exclude from the sacraments, and now praying that God may avert a threatened condemnation. (d. 1595); **Saint José de Anchieta y Díaz de Clavijo** (Joseph of Anchieta) (d. 1597). He was the second native of the Canary Islands, after Peter of Saint Joseph

Betancur who died in 1667. Joseph of Anchieta is also considered the third saint of Brazil. **Peter Canisius,** considered the Second Apostle of German (d 1597). **Saint Bonaventure of Miyako** (d. 1597), **Saint Matthias of Miyako** (d. 1597), **Saint Anthony Dainan** (d.1597), **Saint Francis Kichi** (d. 1597), **Saint Francis of Saint Michael** (1597), **Saint Francis of Nagasaki** (d. 1597), **Saint Gabriel de Duisco** (d. 1597), **Saint Francisco Blanco** (d. 1597), **Saint Magdalene of Nagasaki** (d. 1597), **Saint Gonsalo Garcia,**(d. 1597), **Saint James Kisai** also known as Diego Kisa (d. 1597), **Saint Joachim Sakakibara** (d. 1597), **Saint John Kisaka** (d. 1597), **Saint Thomas Xico** (d. 1597), **Saint Martin of the Ascension** (d. 1597), **Saint Thomas Kozaki** (d. 1597), **Saint Cosmas Takeya** (d. 1597), **Saint Leo Karasumaru** (d. 1597), **Saint Paul Suzuki** (d. 1597), **Saint Paul Miki** (d.1597), **Saint Philip of Jesus** (d. 1597), **Saint Paul Ibaraki** (d. 1597), **Saint Louis Ibaraki** (d. 1597), **Saint Peter Sukejiro** (d. 1597), **Saint Pedro Bautista Blázquez**, **Saint Michael Kozaki** (d. 1597), and **Saint John Soan de Goto** (d. 1597) who were executed by crucifixion at Nagasaki on February 5, 1597 on the orders of Hideyoshi Toyotomi and are venerated as the 26 Martyrs of Japan – four Spaniards, one Mexican, one Portuguese from India (all of whom were Franciscan missionaries), three Japanese Jesuits, and 17 Japanese members of the Third Order of St. Francis, including three young boys. **Saint Juan Grande Román** whose adopted name was 'John the Sinner', died of the plague that ravaged Jerez in 1600 while attending to its victims (d. 1600); **Saint Germaine Cousin** (d. 1601); **Saint Seraphin of Montegranaro** (d. 1604); **Saint Toribio Alfonso de Mogrovejo** who was a strong advocate for archdiocesan reform and who set to work reforming the diocesan priests from impurities and scandals while instituting new educational procedures for seminaries, and who predicted the exact time and hour of his death (d. 1606); **Saint Mary Magdalene de' Pazzi** (Italian: *Maria Maddalena de' Pazzi*) (d. 1607); **Saint Francis Caracciolo** (d. 1608) Born Ascanio Pisquizio, he joined the priesthood and, with John Augustine Adorno, co-founded the Congregation of the Clerics Regular Minor which is both a contemplative and active congregation. **Saint Andrea Avellino** (d. 1608); **Saint Giovanni Leonardi** (d. 1609), founder of the order of Clerics Regular of the Mother of God (*Clerici Regulari a Mater Dei*) which is dedicated to education and pastoral care; **Saint Francisco Solano y Jiménez** also known as Francis Solanus (d. 1610); **Saint Juan de Ribera** (d. 1611); **Saint Joseph of Leonessa** (d. 1612); **Saint Juan García López-Rico** (d. 1613); **Saint Camillus de Lellis** (d. 1614), founder of the order of Camillians or Clerics Regular, Ministers to the Sick; **Saint John Ogilvie** (d. 1615), a priest who served a dwindling Catholic community in 17th century Scotland, and is the only post-Reformation Scottish saint. **Saint Bernardino Realino** (d. 1616); **Saint Rose of Lima**, patron saint of Peru and the rest of the indigenous people of Latin America and the Philippines (d. 1617); **Saint Alphonsus Rodríguez**, patron saint of Majorca (d. 1617); **Saint Marko Stjepan Krizin** (or Marko Križevčanin; Hungarian: *Kőrösi Márk*). (d. 1619); **Saint Melchior Grodziecki** (d. 1619); **Saint Stephen Pongracz** (d. 1619); **Saint Lawrence of Brindisi** (d. 1619); **Saint Jan Sarkander** (d. 1620). When tortured in order that he might reveal details of the confessional, he replied, 'I would choose, with God's help, rather to be torn in pieces than sacrilegiously to violate the seal of confession.' The saint survived to burn him alive. The torture finally ended with his death on March 17, 1620. In 1720 his remains were exhumed and were deemed to be incorrupt. **Saint John Berchmans** (d. 1621); **Saint Robert Bellarmine** or Roberto Francesco Romolo Bellarmino, a Jesuit priest, cardinal and Doctor of the Church who was one of the most important figures in the Counter-Reformation. (d. 1621); **Blessed Alix Le Clerc** also known as Mother Alix, together with Saint Peter Fourier, founded the Canonesses of St. Augustine of the Congregation of Our Lady (French: *Notre-Dame*), a religious order founded to provide education to girls especially those living in poverty. (d 1622); **St. Francis de Sales** (d. 1622); **Saint Fidelis of Sigmaringen** who was a major figure in the counter reformation (d. 1622). **Saint Josaphat Kuntsevych** (d. 1623); **Saint Simón de Rojas** (d.1624); **Saint Michael de Sanctis** (Catalan:*Miquel dels Sants*) (d. 1625); **Saint Alfonso Rodríguez Olmedo** (d. 1628); **St. Roque González de Santa Cruz** who was one of the first Missionary to go to Paraguay (d. 1628); **Saint Juan de Castillo** (d. 1628); **Saint Lucas del Espiritu Santos** (d. 1633). **Saint Domingo Ibáñez de Erquicia** (d. 1633), **Saint Matthew Kohioye** (d. 1633), **Saint Francis Shoyemon** (d. 1633), **Saint Domingo Ibáñez de Erquicia** (d.1633), **Saint Luke Alonso Gorda** (d. 1633), **Saint Fr. Jacobo Kyushei Gorobioye Tomonaga de Santa María** (d. 1633), **Santo Tomás Hioji de San Jacinto** (d. 1634), **Thomas Rokuzayemon** (d. 1634), **Saint Marina of Omura** (d. 1634), **Saint Giordano Ansalone** or Giordano di San Stefano Ansalone (d.1637), **Saint Antonio González** (d. 1637), **Saint Lorenzo Ruiz** (d. 1637), **Saint Vincent Shiwozuka** (d. 1637), **Saint Miguel de Aozaraza** (d. 1637), **Saint Michael Kurobioye** (d. 1637), **Saint Lazarus of Kyoto** (d. 1637), and **Saint Guillaume Courtet** (d. 1637) who are venerated along with others as the 16 Martyrs of Japan. **Saint Humilis of Bisignano** (d. 1637); **Saint Martin de Porres Velázquez** (d. 1639) was the illegitimate son of a Spanish nobleman, Don Juan de Porres, and Ana Velázquez, a freed slave from African-Native American descent; when he was admitted as a member of the Third Order of Saint Dominic at the Convent of Holy Rosary, a home to 300 men, not all of whom accepted the decision of the prior Juan de Lorenzana to admit him, one of the novices called Martin a 'mulatto dog', while one of the priests mocked him for being illegitimate and descended from slaves. His body when exhumed after 25 years was found intact and exhaling a fine fragrance. He is the patron saint of mixed-race people, barbers, innkeepers, public health workers, and all those seeking racial harmony. **Saint Jeanne de Lestonnac**, also known as Joan of Lestonnac, who founded the Sisters of the Company of Mary, Our Lady, in 1607 (d. 1640); **Saint Peter Fourier** (French: *Pierre Fourier*) (d. 1640). He founded the Congregation of Notre Dame of Canonesses Regular of St. Augustine in 1597 together with Blessed Alix Le Clerc. The congregation is devoted to ensuring the free education of children, and members take a fourth vow to that goal. **Saint Jean-François Régis**, known as Saint John Francis Regis and also St. Regis (d. 1640); **Saint Hyacintha of Mariscotti** (d. 1640); **Saint Jane Frances de Chantal** (d. 1641), who founded the religious Order of the Visitation of Holy Mary (the order accepted women who were rejected by other orders because of poor health or age). She is invoked as patron of forgotten people, widows, and parents who are separated from their children. **Saint René Goupil** (d. 1642); **Saint Mariana de Jesús de Paredes** (d. 1645); **Saint John Macías** (Spanish *San Juan Macias*), (d. 1645) went as an evangelist to Peru in 1620. He is invoked as counsel to both rich and poor. It is said that he was deeply generous to the poor and he fed at least 200 of them every day. It is also said that he was greatly aided in that chore by a diminutive donkey that he used to send on special errands in Lima. A small sign put on the donkey asked for donations for the poor; and the donkey, knowing his route perfectly, would travel through the streets and come back with benefactions for the city's poor. The animal would make stops at certain locations and make loud noises; hearing which folks would emerge from their houses and make a donation. **Saint André de Soveral** (d. 1645), **Saint Domingos Carvalho** (d. 1645), **Saint Ambrósio Francisco Ferro** (d. 1645), **Saint Antônio Baracho** (d. 1645), **Saint Antônio Vilela** (d. 1645), **Saint Antônio Vilela Cid** (d. 1645), **Saint Diogo Pereira** (d. 1645), **Saint Estêvão Machado de Miranda** (d. 1645), **Saint Francisco de Bastos** (d. 1645), **Saint Francisco Mendes Pereira** (d. 1645), **Saint João da Silveira** (d. 1645), **Saint João Lostau Navarro** (d. 1645), **Saint João Martins** (d. 1645), **Saint José do Porto** (d. 1645), **Saint Manuel Rodrigues de Moura** (d. 1645), **Saint Mateus Moreira** (d. 1645), **Saint Simão Correia** (d. 1645), **Saint Vicente de Souza Pereira** (d. 1645), and twelve other unnamed martyrs were among a group of 30 Brazilian Catholics killed in northern Brazil by Dutch Calvinists and who are venerated together as the Martyrs of Natal. **Saint Isaac Jogues** (d. 1646), **Saint Jean de Lalande** (d. 1646); **Saint Joseph Calasanz** (Spanish: *José de Calasanz*; Italian: *Giuseppe Calasanzio*) also known as Joseph Calasanctius and Josephus a Matre Dei, founded *the Ordo Clericorum Regularium Pauperum Matris Dei Scholarum Piarum* (Order of Poor Clerics Regular of the Mother of God of the Pious Schools). or Piarists (d. 1648). **Saint Francis Ferdinand de Capillas** (d. 1648) who is venerated together with a group of 87 Chinese Catholics and 32 other Western missionaries martyred between 1648 and 1930 for their faith. As the Martyr Saints of

201

China, and were canonized on 1 October 2000 by Pope John Paul II. **Saint Antoine Daniel** (d. 1648), **Saint Jean de Brébeuf** (d. 1649), **Saint Noël Chabanel** (d. 1649), **Saint Charles Garnier** (1649), and **Saint Gabriel Lalemant** (d. 1649) who are venerated together as the Eight Canadian Martyrs. **Saint Virginia Centurione Bracelli** (d. 1651); **Saint Andrew Bobola** (d. 1657); **Saint Vincent de Paul** who is founder of the Congregation of the Mission and Daughters of Charity of Saint Vincent de Paul (d. 1660); **Saint Louise de Marillac** also known as Louise Le Gras, was co-founder, with Vincent de Paul, of the Daughters of Charity. (d. 1660); **Saint Joseph of Cupertino** (Italian: *Giuseppe da Copertino*) (d. 1663); **Saint Bernardo da Corleone** (d. 1667); **Peter of Saint Joseph de Betancur** (or Betancourt) y Gonzáles , who is also known as Pedro de San José de Betancur y Gonzáles or simply as Saint Brother Peter (d. 1667). He is the first saint native to the Canary Islands where he is popularly referred to as 'St. Francis of Assisi of the Americas'. His work led to the formation of the Order of Our Lady of Bethlehem (Spanish: *Orden de Nuestra Señora de Belén*) or Bethlemitas who tend to the sick. **Saint Charles of Sezze** (d. 1670); **Saint Pedro Calungsod**, also known as Peter Calungsod and Pedro Calonsor, was a Filipino sacristan and missionary catechist who died as a martyr in Guam at 17 years of age along with Blessed Diego Luis de San Vitores, the Spanish Jesuit missionary who founded the first Catholic church on the island of Guam (d. 1672); **Saint Marie of the Incarnation** (d. 1672); **Saint John Eudes**, founder of both the Order of Our Lady of Charity in 1641 and the Congregation of Jesus and Mary also known as The Eudists in 1643, (d. 1680); **Saint Kateri Tekakwitha** (pronounced gaderi dega'gwita in Mohawk), given the name Tekakwitha, baptized as

Catherine and informally known as Lily of the Mohawks, an Algonquin–Mohawk laywoman and the fourth Native American to be venerated in the Catholic Church and the first to be canonized (d. 1680); **Saint Oliver Plunkett**. Being Irish, he tackled drunkenness among the clergy, writing: 'Let us remove this defect from an Irish priest, and he will be a saint' (d. 1681); **Saint Claude La Colombière** (d. 1682); **Saint Margaret Mary Alacoque** (French: *Marguerite-Marie Alacoque*) (d. 1690); **Saint John de Britto** (d. 1693); and last but not least **Saint Gregorio Giovanni Gaspare Barbarigo** (d. 1697).

"I mean – just look at some of those names of the saints who went marching in starting with the martyrdom of Saint Ludmila, grandmother of Saint Wenceslaus, on 15 September 921 t n 821 and ending with the death of Saint Barbarigo on 18 June 1697 – Bernard of Clairvaux, Catherine of Siena, Thomas Aquinas, Ignatius of Loyola, Anthony of Padua, Francis Xavier, Vincent de Paul! Just so many saints going marching in, and so many luminaries among them. And just to think that this happened despite our efforts to move very carefully as we worked to trip up unwitting followers of the Deliverer and get them to embrace the heresies of Cærularius and Luther! And there is no doubt in my demon mind that this came about because of the violence on the faithful that was bred by schisms and heresies; and, as Tertullian said, the blood of martyrs *is* the seed of the *Sancta Ecclesia*! At least half of the folks on that list are venerated as martyrs of the Church! We definitely shot ourselves in the foot as we attempted, with the help of our minions amongst humans, to derail the work of the Church. The schism in Constantinople and the so-called protestant reformation acted as a stimulus for the greatest flowering of sainthood in the world since the time of Abel!

"Still, as usual, there is always a good side to everything, and this was no exception. Yes, as I have said before, the Prime Mover, who is unchanging, wasn't about to change the rules of the game at the time of the so-called reformation, and that is even less likely today. If you were thinking of crashing the Marriage Feast of the Lamb by surreptitiously sneaking into the queue of the saints as they go marching in, think again! All those saints without exception have lived by the Prime Mover's rules, and the robes in which they are clad have been washed in the blood of the Lamb; and that is all there is to it.

"Look here; I was a murderer from the beginning, and I abide not in the truth, because there is no truth in me. When I speak a lie, I do what comes naturally to me: because I am a liar, and also the father of lies. (John 8:44) But do not now accuse me of misleading my minions and leaving them high and dry. Free humans, they do my bidding because it serves their self-interest. They could say no; and it is completely their choice not to allow their robes to be washed in the blood of the Lamb exactly like those saints who go marching in do! And the 'churches' they set up in competition with the *Sancta Ecclesia* are theirs not mine. Humans are, of course, free to cast them as the work of the Holy Ghost; and that suits me just fine. And, again, that is their decision. But my minions must always remember Matthew 7:21: 'Not every one that saith unto me, Lord, Lord, shall enter into the kingdom of heaven; but he that doeth the will of my Father which is in heaven.' Yes, and note exactly what He said. He said 'My Father which is in heaven' and not 'My Father which is in the imagination of the self-proclaimed believer or in any place else! And He could not have been clearer concerning who His followers were. 'Those who want to come with me must say no to the things they want, pick up their crosses every day, and follow me. (Luke 9:23, Matthew 16:24, Matthew 10:37-39, Mark 8:34, Luke 9.23, Luke 10:25, Luke 14:27 and John 6:60-65). I, for my part, as the undisputed Ruler of the Underworld, am emphasizing this to make sure that, come judgment day, my minions won't be able to claim that they did not know what was expected of them – or that I, the Father of Lies and the Father of Death, misled them. And, of course, 2 Corinthians 12:9 bears repeating as I am dealing, not with my fellow demons who use their common sense, but with stupid fools (humans)! 'My grace is sufficient for thee; for power is made perfect in infirmity. Gladly therefore will I glory in my infirmities, that the power of Christ may dwell in me.' And again, talking about 'my minions' (which is just a figure of speech) and 'leaving them high and dry' - who ever said I was their Maker! As they say in New Orleans, 'I don't owe them nothing!' Aaaaah, ha, ha, ha, ha! Eeeeeh, hee, hee, hee! Ooooh, ho, ho, ho! Eeeeh, hee, hee, hee!

"When elected pope in 1503, Julius II (Pope Leo X's predecessor) promised under oath to convoke a general council; but that promise was not fulfilled as that 'Ideal Prince' (to borrow Machiavelli's term) couldn't desist from pursuing his ambitions of playing Julius Caesar during the Renaissance and concentrating his efforts on centralizing the Papal States and 'freeing' Italy from the non-Italian 'barbarians'. Things got more interesting when the pope deposed and excommunicated his vassal Alfonso I d'Este, Duke of Ferrara. for his support of France's King Louis XII. The king retaliated by convoking a synod of French bishops at Tours in September 1510. That synod decreed that the pope had no right to make war upon a foreign prince; and that, in case he undertook such a war, that act gave the foreign prince the right to invade the Ecclesiastical States and to withdraw his subjects from their obedience to the pope! Some of the French bishops had taken offence at the pope's anti-French policy; and, with the support of the French king, decided to convoke the schismatic council at Pisa with the grand opening set for 1 September 1510. Representatives of the clergy, including the Pope himself, were invited to participate. Reacting to the fact that a schism was brewing in France, Julius on 18 July 1511 summoned a general council, the Fifth Lateran Council, at Rome; and it assembled there on 19 April 1512, Julius II died on February 21, 1513.

"Upon being enthroned as pope, Leo X was ostensibly occupied with the business of the council that his predecessor had invoked during the first five years of his pontificate. It was symptomatic that the Fifth Lateran Council continued to be dominated by Italian bishops and was marked by very poor attendance. While the council debated the principal issues of the day, it not only did not receive any direction or encouragement from the pontiff, but it wasn't even accorded the kind of urgency and sense of necessity that would spur on the Council of Trent (1545 – 1563) which was convoked by Pope Paul III and came 40 years later. The Holy Father's preoccupation with politics was largely responsible for the premature close of the council which was dissolved on March 16, 1517 without any really significant action, and just before Martin Luther nailed his ninety-five theses on the door of the Castle Church in Wittenberg on October 31, 1517.

"But, as usual, we ourselves here in the Underworld for our part, unlike you humans, always endeavour to understand phrases like 'dissolved without any really significant action' in the 'correct' perspective - a perspective that invariably eludes you humans because you are only focused on the mundane. Look, you ought to know by now that this is exactly how the Holy Ghost works. He takes full cognizance of the fact that He works through frail humans; and He ends up scooping the full credit for the results of human endeavours in that way. So, in a mysterious way, the Fifth Lateran Council, by appearing on the surface to have failed humanly speaking, even though it took place under the watch of two popes who were almost completely distracted with other matters, most likely ended up in all probability laying the strongest possible foundation not just for the Council of Trent, but for all future councils. If there is one thing we have learnt in this business, it is that we not judge 'success' by appearances because the Holy Ghost is another one. He uses the most unlikely humans to achieve His ends, and He does so in a really brilliant style. For all we know He probably uses the heretics we send along in much the same manner even though that does not absolve them from both the immediate and long-term consequences of their actions of commission and omission! Remember that the Prime Mover causes good to come out of evil, and His will always prevails. And, for all I know, He is probably using me and my evil intentions to help some folks – to help the bible believers who claim that the Sancta Ecclesia is the Whore of Babylon to step back and recant their errors! But I agreed to work with this Mjomba fellow here because I want to use the free platform he has provided me to try my best to confuse the situation. Ha, ha, ha, ha, ho, ho, ho, hee, hee, hee, hee!"

Mjomba, who had been scribbling furiously in order not to miss any of the points Satan was making, paused briefly and, addressing no one in particular, hissed: "I'm dealing with the crookedest crook! That is even as he is using me to ensure that our separated brethren won't be able to plead ignorance as an excuse on their judgement day!" But he resumed writing immediately as the Ruler of the Underworld pressed on.

"But, to circle back to the matter at hand, as regards bulls of excommunication, Leo's next target (if he had lived on a little longer) was going to be King Francis I whose French forces had been threatening the Papal States. *That* was really more important to Leo than the widespread buying and selling of ecclesiastical privileges, like for example pardons and benefices (or simony); or the spread of Luther's heresies in Germany that went unchecked.

"But even then, as Peter's two hundred and eighteenth successor as Bishop of Rome (Pope Leo X) crossed the gulf that separates the living from the dead on 1 December 1521 and approached the Gates of Heaven, it verily looked as though the only card he still had left up his sleeve (if he was going to succeed in getting past that son of Jonah and proceed to lay claim to his seat at the heavenly banquet).was the threat of excommunication; except that, unlike Pope Julius II who used his last moments on earth to prepare a formal papal bull excommunicating Saint Peter (just in case he needed one) and who made sure he had it with him as he crossed the gulf that separates the living from the dead, Pope Leo X died really suddenly, just short of his 46th birthday, after being taken ill with bronchopneumonia and didn't have any time at all to start working on a draft.

"Even though Pope Leo X had been bedridden for quite a while and his death was anticipated, he had been too preoccupied with matters of this world (that is exactly how we here in the Underworld like to look at it and were always 'praying' for) to think about matters of the next, and, specifically how he would find his way past Saint Peter and then proceed to claim his seat at the heavenly banquet. And this was despite the fact that his failing health had become the subject of speculation among members of the College of Cardinals including folks like

Cardinal Bandinello Sauli, Cardinal Raffaelle Sansoni Riario, Cardinal Adriano di Castello and Cardinal Francesco Soderini who were among the aspirants for the office of Vicar of Christ and who very nearly paid with their lives for talking about the pope's imminent death, accused of wishing to see the Holy Father dead and doing so in league with Cardinal Alfonso Petrucci who was not so fortunate.

"And the diseased Pope Leo X also seemed to have forgotten something else, namely that not long before - four years and five months to be exact - he had engineered the murder of the youthful Alfonso Cardinal Petrucci, a member of the rival Petrucci family. The cardinal was only twenty-six years old when he was strangled in his prison cell in the Castel Sant'Angelo for allegedly plotting to have Leo poisoned. Leo had tricked the young prelate into returning to Rome by promising talks about the restoration of property that his family had lost in Siena. Petrucci's father was the tyrant Pandolfo of Siena. Now, Pandolfo had played a key role in the restoration of the Medici in Florence; and his son (Cardinal Alfonse Petrucci) had played a considerable part in Leo's election as pope in the 1513 Conclave. Siena was wedged between the Republic of Florence and the Papal States, and maintained ties between Petrucci and the Baglioni of Perugia. Leo X, unable to occupy the territories directly, had taken the extraordinary step of facilitating a coup by Raffaello Petrucci, Bishop of Grosseto and lord of Castel S, on 8 March 1516. Borghese Petrucci, Cardinal Alfonso Petrucci's elder brother, in power in Siena up until that time, was overthrown and exiled. The brothers lost everything in that coup which the Holy Father had engineered – the coup that miraculously resulted in the Republic of Siena being brought under the 'protection' of the Papacy.

"That was a brilliant move that was applauded by us here in the Underworld, not just for its brinkmanship (it helped Pope Leo to consolidate his power over the Papal 'empire' in Italy), but because it resulted in Petrucci and his kin becoming excluded from rulership of Siena and dispossessed of the properties from which they drew all their revenues – and it above all guaranteed that the young, ambitious and full blooded cardinal would end up embittered in the extreme at that ungrateful 'fraud'! Try as he might, the cardinal from Siena could not think of the Holy Father in any other terms.

"It was with that backdrop that Pope Leo X, worried that a plot might be in the works to see him dead prematurely, tricked Cardinal Alfonso Petrucci into returning to Rome, even offering Petrucci not only safe passage and guarantees for his safety, but also a veiled promise for the restoration to him of the estates that his family had forfeited as a result of the coup in Siena (pledges which the crafty Holy Father had no intention whatsoever of keeping).

"This was just the perfect set-up for what some have appropriately labelled 'Murder in the Vatican' and we ourselves were with the Holy Father (Leo X) all the way. Look, one has to be spectacularly blind and also really dumb not to see my finger prints all over that twisting and totally captivating plot. Cardinal Alfonso Petrucci had a perfectly valid grievance against the Holy Father for ousting his relatives including his brother from the governance of the Republic of Siena. He had very good reason for 'wishing the ungrateful charlatan from Florence dead'. But, unfortunately, for the young and rather naïve prelate, the hopes of getting some of his family's stuff back blindsided him; and he sauntered into the lion's den only to be devoured. He definitely ought to have known better. If his father (the Tyrant and himself a crafty operator like Leo) had been around, he would undoubtedly have tendered the young and inexperienced member of the College of Cardinals advice that would have helped him avoid making that really stupid mistake – the mistake of expecting fairmindedness from a wayward and totally corrupt descendant of Adam and Eve like Giovanni di Lorenzo de' Medici, son of Lorenzo the Magnificent and now also known as Leo, the fact that that 'son of a bitch' (as some of the folks who wound up in his orbit referred to him on the sly) occupied the See of Peter and was referred to by his flock as 'Holy Father' (because of the special deference owed by the faithful to occupants of the office of Vicar of Christ) notwithstanding.

"Now, Pope Leo X was notorious for the deceitfulness and insincerity that was a hallmark of his dealings with the rulers of France, Spain, Germany, England and any countries in the former Roman empire. As the saying went, the pope always 'sailed with two compasses', and loved to hold rivals with whom he was politicking at bay by a double game played with deft skill, and even frequently succeeded in concluding alliances with rival parties simultaneously! Poor Cardinal Petrucci took the Holy Father at his word, and dutifully presented himself at the papal palace only to find himself arrested and charged with conniving with the pope's doctor to add a poisonous substance to the bandages that were employed in keeping the persistent fistula with which the man of God was afflicted in check.to hasten his death thereby.

"While it was alleged that there were six other cardinals (apart from Cardinal Petrucci) who had been complicit in the plot to murder the pope, only the names of four were published. These namely were Bandinello Cardinal Sauli, Raffaelle Cardinal Sansoni Galeoti Riario,

Adriano Cardinal di Castello (Castellesi) and Francesco Cardinal Soderini.

"**Cardinal Bandinello Sauli** was born in Genoa ca 1494 to Pasquale Sauli and Mariola Giustiniani Longhi, a noble family. He was named administrator of the see of Malta on October 5, 1506 when he was 12 years old, the post he occupied until he was named bishop of Gerace and Oppido. He was elected bishop of Gerace and Oppido in 1509, and resigned the government of the see on November 19, 1517. Early in his life he was Protonotary Apostolic *Participantium Abbreviatore Minutæ Pariter* and *Scriptor* of apostolic letters until 1511. It is not known when he received his priestly ordination or consecrated bishop. Pope Julius II made him a cardinal deacon in the consistory of March 10, 1511, and he received his red hat on March 13, 1511 at the age of thirty.and the deaconry of S. Adriano on March 17, 1511. He participated in the conclave of 1513, which elected Pope Leo X. He was made Administrator of the see of Albenga on August 5, 1513 and resigned the post on November 19, 1517. He was named Canon *commendatario* and prebendary of the archdiaconate of Saldaña in the diocese of León. He opted for the title of S. Maria in Trastevere on July 18, 1516. He was deposed as a cardinal and incarcerated in *Castello Sant'Angelo* in Rome on June 22, 1517 by Pope Leo X for not disclosing to him the assassination plot of Cardinal Alfonso Petrucci. The same pope restored Sauli's cardinalate on July 31, 1517; *sed non ad vocem activam et passivam*; these were restored on December 25, 1517.

"**Cardinal Raffaelle Riario** was born in poverty to Antonio Sansoni and Violante Riario, a niece of Francesco della Rovere, who became Pope Sixtus IV in 1471. He was created Cardinal of San Giorgio in Velabro on 10 December 1477 Pope Sixtus IV to whom he was related through his mother. He was sixteen at the time and a student of canon law at the University of Pisa. He was also named Administrator of several dioceses (diocese of Cuenca, diocese of Pisa, diocese of Salamanca, diocese of Treguier, and diocese of Osma) at the same time, appointments

"Implicated in the process against Cardinals Bandinello Sauli and Alfonso Petrucci, Cardinal Riario was arrested on May 29, 1517, in the chamber of Pope Leo X at the Vatican, for not having revealed the plot planned by them against the pope. He was transferred to 'Castello Sant'Angelo' where the two other cardinals were detained. The three were tried by the Sacred College of Cardinals, which found them guilty, degraded them, deprived them of their cardinalitial dignity and their dioceses, benefices, charges and possessions; they were turned over to the secular authorities. Cardinal Riario appealed to the pope, asked for his pardon and promised, on July 17, 1517 to pay a large fine . On the following July 24, in consistory, the pope pardoned him and reestablished all his dignities, except the title of S. Lorenzo in Damaso and the see of Ostia e Velletri, the latter of which would be restored later; and he was deprived him of active and passive voice, which was however restored shortly after. When the pope summoned the cardinal before him and embraced him, the reconciliation was greeted with joy by the entire city of Rome. He was eventually reinstated to his see of Ostia e Velletri, and was received in consistory on January 10, 1519. He was freed from his fines on February 10,1519.

"**Cardinal Adriano di Castello** (ca. 1460-ca 1521) came from an obscure family in Cornet in the province of Viterbo, Lazio, Italy. Early in his career he was sent as Papal nuncio to Scotland, and was named Collector of the Peter's-pence in England in 1488, a post he occupied

213

until 1514. .Sent by Pope Innocent VIII, to England in 1490 to reestablish the peace between that country and Scotland, he earned the trust of King Henry VII Tudor of England. He was made a protonotary apostolic on October 14, 1497. Upon his return to Rome, he was named papal treasurer in 1500 and Ambassador of England to the Holy See. At the request of the king of England, he was promoted to the episcopate. He became clerk of the Apostolic Chamber and secretary of Pope Alexander VI who was his confidante and favorite. He was created cardinal priest in the consistory of May 31, 1503 and he was published on June 2, 1503; receiving the title of S. Crisogono on June 12, 1503. Some believe that Alexander VI (born Rodrigo de Borja y Doms in 1431 in Játiva, near Valencia, Spain) was the epitome of corruptness, worldliness and ambition and that his neglect of the spiritual inheritance of the *Sancta Ecclesia* contributed to the emergence of the Protestant Reformation. He even openly acknowledged fathering several children over the period of his pontificate. He was reportedly paid a large sum by Adriano di Castello for the red hat. Adriano di Castello participated in the conclave of 1513 which elected Pope Leo X. Accused of conniving with Cardinal Bandinello Sauli and Cardinal Alfonso Petrucci to assassinate Pope Leo X, he was forced to admit that it was true in the consistory of June 8, 1517, and he asked for forgiveness. The pope granted it, but he was required to pay a hefty fine in return, which was doubled shortly after. Fearing the worst, he escaped in the middle of the night of June 20, disguised as a harvester, and went first to Tivoli, then to Naples and finally to Venice, where he arrived on July 13th. He received orders from the pope to return to Rome on November 4th, which he disobeyed. The pope started a process against the cardinal on March 3, 1518; and on

April 12th, he was tried for contumacy and was deposed as a cardinal. He was deprived of his episcopal see for disobedience by Pope Leo X in the consistory of July 5, 1518; and was ordered to sell his possessions, including the magnificent palace he had built in Borgo for which he had hired Bramante da Urbino as architect.

"**Cardinal Soderini** was born in Florence on June 10, 1453 and belonged to a noble family allied with the Medici He studied *utroque iure*, both canon and civil law, and was Professor of *utroque iure* at the University of Pisa in 1476. Elected bishop of Volterra on March 11, 1478, he was administrator of the bishopric up until the time he reached the canonical age of 27 years. He resigned the see on May 23, 1509 in favor of his nephew Giuliano, and went to reside in the Roman Curia where he joined the confraternity of S. Spirito in Sassia, Rome, on December 7, 1478. He received his ordination to the priesthood on 27 March, 1486. Upon receiving the episcopal consecration, he celebrated mass in the cathedral of Volterra for the first time in September 1491, assisted by Jacopo Gherardi and Mario Maffei, two friends from the Roman Curia, who were office holders in the diocese. He continued as an absentee bishop and governed the diocese through vicars general until the summer of 1494 when he left the Roman Curia and returned to Florence to serve initially as a diplomat at the service of the Florentine state. He did a number of stints as ambassador before he received his red hat in June 1503. He arrived in Rome on August 30, 1503, and .participated in the first conclave of 1503, which elected Pope Pius III. He then participated in the second conclave of 1503, which elected Pope Julius II. He received several benefices from the new Pope Julius II. He participated in the Fifth Lateran Council; and, most notably, he also participated in the conclave of 1513 which elected Pope Leo X. When the plot to poison Pope Leo X unraveled in June 1517, he was in Rome. According to the official record, he did admit to his complicity in the plot led by Cardinal Bandinello Sauli and Cardinal Alfonso Petrucci to murder the Holy Father, and also admitted that he had promised to offer the papal tiara to Cardinal Raffaele Sansoni Riario. Regarding the reported 'confessions', Cardinal della Rovere, a relative of Cardinal Riario, is said to have wondered aloud: 'The devil take it, do you think that these are true confessions?'

"Cardinal della Rovere was not alone in taking the purported confessions of the alleged conspirators with a pinch of salt. Some have speculated that the four cardinals who were implicated in the plot were adjudged guilty for merely listening to Petrucci (if they did at all), and for desiring his success as a result. It is also claimed that the confessions of some of the co-conspirators were obtained through torture. There are suggestions that the full complicity of those who allegedly participated in the plot to murder the pope was not proved. Reasons given include financial and political motives to act against rivals and the absence of impartiality. One of the appointed judges is said to have had an axe to grind against Petrucci; while the interrogators and their relatives were in for a lucrative share of the disgraced cardinals' benefices and key city offices.

"Regardless, three other lower ranking 'co-conspirators' identified as Marcantonio Nini (the cardinal's major-domo), Scipione Petrucci (a groom and cousin of the cardinal), Battista Vercell, the doctor who reportedly was going to administer the poison, were first tortured using pincers, then hanged, drawn and quartered, and their bodies displayed on the bridge outside the Castel Sant'Angelo.

"And then, in a classic move, Pope Leo X, moving quickly to assure that he had a compliant College of Cardinals, in a consistory of 1 July 1517, appointed a total 31 new cardinals, a number that more than doubled the size of the college. Seven of the cardinals named were members of prominent Roman families; signalling a reversal of policies of the pope's predecessor (Julius II) as regards the involvement of political factions in the Curia.

"Pope Leo X died unexpectedly of pneumonia exactly four years and five months later. And you'd better believe me when I say that Leo didn't give Saint Peter any chance to see if he might be of some help. When Leo saw that the gates of heaven were bolted shut as he approached, he knew automatically that it was because someone did not like him, and he screamed: 'Goddamn, you, there. Open those gates or else! My successor has not yet been elected, and the Chair of Peter is still mine. Open the gates at once or else you are excommunicated!' St. Peter took a good look at his successor in the See of Rome, and he remembered vividly that Julius II had waived at him what he claimed was a bull of excommunication. Without waiting, Peter now shot back: 'Do you have a copy of the bull? Moreover, I have a report here that you haven't really been a good shepherd. Tell me - what happened to Alfonso? How come he turned up here so prematurely?' Ha, ha, ha, ha, hee, hee hoo, hoo, hoo! But let us get back to the events that resulted in Pope Leo X's elevation to the Chair of Saint Peter.

"Following the death of Pope Julius II, the man who was elected to succeed him was Cardinal Francesco Todeschini Piccolomini. Even though only sixty-four years old, the cardinal, a victim of severe with gout, looked almost ninety years old. He had grown up destitute; and looked like a good man contrary to what some historians (who are described as bitter enemies of the papacy) have suggested. He had shirked Rome as much as possible during the worldly reigns of Sixtus IV and Alexander VI. He studied law at the University of Perugia, receiving a doctorate in Canon Law. He reportedly left no moment unoccupied. He kept a schedule according to which he undertook study before daybreak, then spent his mornings in prayer and his midday hours in giving audiences to which even the humblest had easy and unfettered access. As for food and drink, he only allowed himself an evening meal every other day.

"The Pope elect had not yet received the priestly ordination and the episcopal consecration at the time of his election to the papacy. To our great relief here in the Underworld, the Pope elect, who had chosen Pius III as his name, easily succumbed to the strain of the protracted ceremonies for his installation as pope. He kicked the bucket as the ceremonies were under way in what has to be the briefest pontificate ever in the *Sancta Ecclesia*. His papacy would undoubtedly have been a very different one from that of the man who would be elected to fill his place as pope.

"And now, finally, enter Pope Leo X, Pope Pius III's successor. Born Giovanni di Lorenzo de' Medici on December 11, 1475, he was the second son of Lorenzo the Magnificent, who ruled the Republic of Florence and simultaneously run the Medici Bank. He received the tonsure indicating his intention to become a cleric in 1482 when he was eight; and was made Abbot of Font Douce in the French Diocese of Saintes in 1483 and appointed Apostolic prothonotary by Pope Sixtus IV. The young Lorenzi came into possession of the rich Abbey of Passignano in 1484, and of Monte Cassino in 1486.

Then, thanks to the constant pressure from Lorenzo Senior on their relative Innocent VIII, Lorenzo Junior was named cardinal-deacon of Santa Maria in Domnica on 8 March 1488 when he was 13. He was formally admitted into the Sacred College of Cardinals on 23 March 1492 four years later when he was seventeen.

"Giovanni di Lorenzo de' Medici received the finest education that was available in Europe, studied theology and canon law at the University of Pisa from 1489 to 1491. His tutors included the philosopher Pico della Mirandola and Filippo Decio, an Italian jurist whose services were courted by European universities and rulers.

"Most of the cardinals were already in Rome at the time of the death of Pope Julius II, on 21 February 1513. They had been participating in the Fifth Lateran Council, which had been summoned by the Pope to deal with the most pressing problems facing the Church. That Fifth Council of the Lateran, held between 1512 and 1517, was the eighteenth ecumenical council of the Catholic Church and the last one before the Protestant Reformation. The Council was called in opposition to a rival council in Pisa that was convoked under the leadership of nine dissident cardinals with the support of the French King and the French clergy.

"The pope (Pope Julius II) was too ill to attend the Fifth Session on 16 February. It was at that session that Julius's famous Bull, *Cum tam divino*, which forbade the buying and selling of sacred things (simony), and most especially the papal office, was solemnly republished. That bull against simony appears to have kept participants in the conclave on the alert. At his last audience for the Cardinals, on 19 February, Pope Julius had advised the Cardinals not to allow the schismatic cardinals from the Council of Pisa (which was underway under the auspices of King Louis XII of France) to take part in the Conclave.

"The death of Pope Julius II had been expected for some weeks with his doctors holding out little hope for his recovery. The French King had been kept informed of the situation, and he had apparently ordered the French cardinals to hasten their journey to Rome so they could participate in the Conclave. He also wrote to the College of Cardinals, pleading with them in vain to await the arrival of the French (schismatic) cardinals.

"The election of Lorenzo Medici as pope was concluded on 11 March 1513. Lorenzo, who had only been ordained a deacon, received his ordination to the priesthood on March 15, and was consecrated bishop of Rome on March 17. He was installed as pope March 19. During his entire reign as occupant of the See of St. peter (from 9 March, 1513 to 1 December 1521), Pope Leo X would be pope, ruler of the Papal States and titular head of the Medici family all at one and the same time! But, significantly, he would be the last pope not in priestly orders at the time of his election to the papacy.

"Now, if you can recall, it was in the immediate aftermath of the Deliverer's resurrection that, appearing to the eleven, He had sat down at table and, in the words of the Evangelist Mark, 'upbraided them with their incredulity and hardness of heart, because they did not believe them who had seen him after he was risen again.' (Mark 16:14) The Deliverer had then proceeded to give the eleven the 'Great Commission' saying: 'And he said to them: Go ye into the whole world and preach the gospel to every creature. He that believeth and is baptized shall be saved: but he that believeth not shall he condemned.' (Mark 16:15-16).

"This is how the Evangelist Matthew described the Great Commission which the Deliverer took time to rehash when the eleven met him at an appointed time and place atop a mountain in Galilee: 'And the eleven disciples went into Galilee, unto the mountain where Jesus had appointed them. And seeing him they adored: but some doubted. And Jesus coming, spoke to them, saying: All power is given to me in heaven and in earth. Going therefore, teach ye all nations: baptizing them in the name of the Father and of the Son and of the Holy Ghost. Teaching them to observe all things whatsoever I have commanded you. And behold I am with you all days, even to the consummation of the world.' (Matthew 28:16-20) And, you bet that those of us here in the Underworld were watching and observing all that was going on very intently.

"If Michelangelo personified the 'Renaissance man', the newly elected Pontiff personified the Renaissance spirit and its ideals, and he did it at the expense of the Great Commission on which all occupants of the See of Peter are expected to expend all their energies. But now, as Pontiff of Rome, administrator of the Papal States, and as head of the Medici family that managed the affairs of the Republic of Florence, Pope Leo had all the excuses in the world to renege on some of his responsibilities and on some of the promises he had made at the time he was installed as Peter's successor; and it was imperative for me and my troops here in the Underworld to get behind him and provide all the assistance he needed to succeed in his endeavours - I mean, succeed in promoting our cause.

"He needed to exert his influence in Italy, and so it was quite 'proper' for him to resort to the common practice of nepotism like granting offices or benefits to relatives, regardless of merit. A good first step was to appoint his cousin Giulio de' Medici (the future pope Clement VII) Archbishop of Florence, an influential

221

position by any count. And he had no scruples in naming his younger brother Giuliano and his nephew Lorenzo to be patricians, and according them in the process the status of nobility. As a matter of fact, up until Giuliano's premature death in 1516, the pope's plan had been to create a central Italian kingdom for him.

"But, as I said earlier, it was important for us to tread carefully so as not to end up giving the game away. You see it was not as if Pope Leo was an illegitimate pope. A total of twenty-five out of the thirty-one living cardinals entered the conclave on Friday 4 March, 1513. In the first Scrutiny at the Conclave, Medici had received only one vote out of the votes cast. A total of seventeen votes were required for a canonical election. However, in the second Scrutiny on the morning of 11 March, 1513, Medici was elected unanimously. It was almost miraculous. Every conclave strives to end *unanimiter et concorditer* (unanimous and in concord), to eliminate all grounds for a schism. Medici's election to fill the See of Peter was therefore just perfect.

"His accession to the throne of St. Peter at thirty-eight years of age wasn't even close to beating a record for youngest Holy Father. That record is probably held by Pope Benedict IX. He hailed from a family of popes that included his two immediate predecessors (Pope John XIX and Pope Benedict VIIII); and his other records include being the only person who ever enjoyed three pontificates (1032-1044, 1045 and 1047-1048), being the only pope who succeeded in enriching himself by auctioning off the Chair of Peter and then reclaiming it after pocketing the proceeds, and also being the only pope to be formally deposed *in contumaciam*.

"The story goes that Pope Benedict IX, who openly led a scandalous life as a sybarite or playboy, consulted his godfather, John Gratian, an archpriest and reputedly quite a good man, as to whether he could resign the supreme pontificate and pursue his interests. But Pope Benedict IX let his godfather know that he would resign as pope only if he got paid a large sum of money under the deal. John Gratian, seeing the opportunity to rid the See of Peter of the lecherous and totally unworthy playboy pontiff, coughed up the money. John Gratian doled out the money apparently in all good faith and simplicity; and, hailed for the sacrifice he was making, he was recognized as pope in his godson's place, and took the name of Gregory VI.

"But things were moving fast. Even as Gratian was assuming his office as Pope Benedict IX's successor, a faction of the nobility in Italy that had physically chased the lecherous Pope Benedict IX from the Vatican out of concern for the scandalous life he led now moved to install their own candidate as Pope in Benedict IX's place. That candidate was John, bishop of Sabina; and he took the name of Pope Sylvester III. To complicate matters, Benedict IX, unable to obtain the bride on whom he had set his heart, soon regretted his decision to resign as pope and returned to Rome to reclaim the papacy. He apparently succeeded in acquiring dominion over a part of the city of Rome, and forcing Sylvester III to leave Rome and return to his See of Sabina. But Sylvester would not budge on giving up his claims to the papal throne; and he succeeded with the help of his political allies in retaining some hold on a portion of the city. In the meantime, Pope Gregory VI (Pope Benedict IX's godfather) with the help of the Emperor, Henry III of Germany, succeeded in getting the Synod of Sutri so-called going in 1046. At that synod, Pope Gregory VI admitted to purchasing the Chair of Peter albeit with the intention of reforming that office. For that, he was deposed by the synod as also was the antipope Sylvester

III. The synod also declared Pope Benedict IX deposed, and the German, Suidger von Morsleben, Bishop of Bamberg, was crowned as Gregory's successor on 25 December, 1046, taking the name of Pope Clement II. The new Pope (Clement II) lost no time in starting the work of reforming the church with respect to simony. He had the full support of Emperor Henry III, himself a sworn enemy of simony who never took a penny from any of his own appointees and a legacy, no doubt, of Emperor Constantine the Great who was himself used by Providence to turn the fortunes of the *Ecclesia Militans* (Church Militant) for the better in its greatest time of need. At a great synod in Rome in January, 1047, the buying and selling of things spiritual was made punishable with excommunication. Anyone who knowingly accepted ordination at the hands of a prelate who was guilty of simony was ordered to do canonical penance for forty days. But then, the Pope (Pope Clement II) died unexpectedly on 9 October, 1047.

"And then, out of the blue, Benedict IX was back on the scene once more, determined to get back the tiara. He had never accepted his deposition in 1046 by the Synod of Sutri. Bouncing back out of the blue, he succeeded in seizing and occupying the Lateran Palace in November, 1047 with the intention of resuming his papacy. He was eventually expelled by German troops in July 1048, and then formally excommunicated. His sudden appearance fed rumours to the effect that Pope Clement II had been poisoned at his behest. So, Pope Benedict IX also has the distinction of being the only validly elected Pontiff of Rome who turned antipope not once but twice and whose actions ended up saddling the *Sancta Ecclesia* with two additional antipopes (Pope Gregory VI and Pope Sylvester III)!

"Upon Benedict IX's removal, the German emperor's chosen candidate for the Chair of Peter, Bishop Poppo of Brixen and a native of Bavaria, became the third German to be elevated to the See of Peter. He was enthroned at the Basilica of St. John Lateran in Rome Lateran as Damasus II on 17 July, 1048. But his pontificate would last only twenty-three days. Trying to escape the summer heat of Rome shortly after his installation, the new pope had made his way to Palestrina, thirty-five kilometres east of Rome and located on a spur of the Monti Prenestini in the Apennine Mountains, only to catch malaria and die of it there on 9 August 1048.

"But Pope Benedict IX might have succeeded in setting another record. In his work on Saint Bartholomew of Grottaferrata (c. 97-11 November 1065), Abbot Luke of the Abbey of Grottaferrata wrote that the man who had committed numerous murders and adulteries in broad daylight, and robbed pilgrims on the graves of the Martyrs until finally the people drove him out of Rome (Pope Benedict IX) actually did finally turn away from his life of sin and came to him, and that. Benedict did indeed resign his pontificate on St. Bartholomew's advice and died a penitent at the Abbey. That was no small feat, and I can tell you that we ourselves here in the Underworld didn't like what we were seeing at all. We wanted to see that three-time pope die unrepentant!

"But let's revert to our subject (Pope Leo X). We knew that the new man who succeeded Julius II (the chap who had chosen to be named after Emperor Gaius Julius Caesar) would be susceptible to all things beautiful, much like his predecessor Pope Julius II, the man Machiavelli described in his works as 'the ideal prince' and from whom Leo was inheriting a papal treasury that was full to the brim.

"But we were at pains to see the new pope present a façade that shone and was beyond reproach. We were immensely delighted when the Pope, who was naturally dignified in manner and a polished orator, showed from the beginning that he was determined to fulfill his spiritual duties, at least outwardly, in a truly exemplary manner. He celebrated Mass daily and met all his obligations to celebrate the Liturgy of the Hours (breviary) as befitted a man of God and, for that matter, as 'Bishop of Rome, Vicar of the Deliverer, Successor of the Prince of the Apostles, Supreme Pontiff of the Universal Church, Primate of Italy, Archbishop and Metropolitan of the Roman Province, Sovereign of the State of Vatican City, Servant of the Servants of God' (to use the pope's proper title). He fasted three a week, and he was always seen going to confession before celebrating Holy Mass in public. He was always careful to show that he was not ostentatious, and he attached no importance to ritual. And he was above all lavish in works of charity. It is duly recorded that convents, hospitals, discharged soldiers, poor students, pilgrims, exiles, cripples, the blind, the sick, the unfortunate of every description were all generously remembered, and he saw to it that tons of money was distributed annually in alms.

"Now, Pope Julius II (the Warrior Pope) had started out as a big pal of ours too; and he had pleased us mightily with his drive to see to it that the temporal powers of the Papacy in Italy and elsewhere in Europe were firmly entrenched. I say, a 'big pal' with reason. He for instance really hated his predecessor (Cardinal Rodrigo Borgia who adopted the name of Pope Alexander VI upon his election) for having succeeded, through secret agreements and simony, in marshalling the votes that in his eyes unfairly cheated him of the tiara at the Conclave of 1492.

"Upon his own election at the Conclave of October 1503, Pope Julius II had seen it fit to take immediate action to render it impossible for the Borgias to retain their power over the Papal States. Actually, on the very day he was elected, he declared: 'I will not live in the same rooms as the Borgias lived. He [Alexander VI] desecrated the Holy Church as none before. He usurped the papal power by the devil's aid, and I forbid under the pain of excommunication anyone to speak or think of Borgia again. His name and memory must be forgotten. It must be crossed out of every document and memorial. His reign must be obliterated. All paintings made of the Borgias or for them must be covered over with black crepe. All the tombs of the Borgias must be opened and their bodies sent back to where they belong—to Spain.' I distinctly recall telling the demons who were observing all this unfold with me from the Pit: 'That's my boy!'

"In 1506 Pope Julius II founded the Swiss Guard to provide a constant corps of soldiers to protect the Vatican City. And, setting in motion his Renaissance program of re-kindling the glory of Rome and headquarters of Christendom, Julius II did everything to present himself as a Pope-cum-Emperor who was well equipped to lead a Latin - Christian empire! He made a show of entering Rome on Palm Sunday in 1507 as 'a second Julius Caesar, heir to the majesty of Rome's imperial glory, and in the likeness of Christ, whose vicar the pope was and who in that capacity governed the universal Roman Church!' The pope, who made a point of modelling himself after his namesake Caesar, would in due course personally lead his army of Swiss mercenaries across the Italian peninsula under the old imperial war-cry 'Drive out the barbarians'!

"That was all well and good until the pontiff did something else towards the end of his life. To counter the schismatic *conciliabulum* that was taking place in Pisa under the auspices of Louis XII of France and Maximilian I, German King and Roman Emperor, the pope convoked the Fifth Lateran Council (18th ecumenical council). The actual agenda of the Council was potentially devastating to our cause. And thank the Prime Mover that Julius II died at the time he did, and was succeeded by Leo X. His pontificate was starting to undo a lot of the gains we had notched up in the visible church as regards greed for money and corruption in general.

"The fifth session was held on 16 February, 1513; and with Cardinal Raffaele Riario, the Dean of the College of Cardinals and Bishop of Ostia, presiding because Pope Julius II was too ill to attend, the Bishop of Como, Scaramuccia Trivulzio, read from the pulpit the Pope's Bull, *Si summus rerum*, which was dated that very day and contained within its text the complete bull of 14 January 1505, *Cum tam divino*. That bull, which forbade the buying and selling of sacred things, and most especially the papal office, was submitted to the Council fathers for their consideration and ratification.. As you may recall, that bull against simony actually kept participants in the conclave very much on edge given what previously happened at Conclaves electing popes. You can therefore say that the Fifth Lateran Council already affected the proceedings of the Conclave of 1513

"Even as the Council was approaching its close under Leo X, it issued numerous and very timely decrees too, for example, decrees against the false philosophical teachings of Professor, Pietro Pompanazzi of Padua who, with our assistance, was denying the immortality of the soul! Additionally, as a result of the Council's work, the encroachments of pagan Humanism on the spiritual life were now going to be met by the simultaneous rise of a new order of philosophical and theological studies.

During the Council's ninth session, a Bull that treated the reforms in the Curia and the Church very exhaustively was promulgated. Abbeys and benefices were henceforth to be bestowed only on persons of merit and according to canon law! The Bull included provisions regulating benefices and consistorial proceedings. It also made Ecclesiastical depositions and transfers much more difficult; and it forbade commendatory benefices outright. And this was after the Council's fourth session had clipped the wings off those schismatic bishops who were congregated in Pisa for their pseudo-Council (and were, of course, being cheered on by us). This was all so ridiculous!

"We for our part of course worked very hard to make sure that the salutary reforms of the Fifth Lateran Council did not find any real practical acceptance under Pope Leo X. Thanks to our efforts that were implemented through our minions among the *Sancta Ecclesia's* clergy, pluralism, commendatory benefices, and the granting of ecclesiastical dignities to children remained customary and continued a before.

"We worked on Pope Leo some and we succeeded in ensuring that he himself did not have any scruples about ignoring repeatedly the decrees of the Council after it closed. The much maligned and despised Curia in Rome remained as worldly as ever and everyone continued doing their thing merrily. We ensured that the pope did not have time to regulate the unworthy and immoral conduct of his courtiers, and that he was absorbed with the politics of the Renaissance and the promotion of arts. And we were pleased that he closed the Council quickly. Deeply entangled in political matters, Pope Leo X let the imperial election eclipse and overshadow Martin Luther's revolt and was quite happy for quite a while to relegate the resolution of the problem of the 'dissident' monk' to the Augustinian Order to which the monk belonged.

"The fact is that we worked really hard to keep the Holy Father engaged both as a Patron of the Arts, ruler of the Papal States, and head of the Medici empire, as those responsibilities kept him from fully grasping the consequences of not being fully immersed in the work of the Great Commission and of attending to the needs of his flock. Along the way, we were pleased to see the pope's addiction to the arts turn the Papal Palace into what amounted to a 'Center for the Performing Arts'.

"The pope promoted literature, science, and arts as no other pope ever did. Under him Rome also became the center of the literary world as men of letters from all parts started flocking to the Eternal City, their patroness. Pope Leo X lavished gifts, favors, positions, titles, not only on the real poets, writers and scholars, but apparently quite often on poetasters and commonplace jesters as well! Some of the folks who were the recipients of benefices were openly self-indulgent and worldly. But other who received the pope's largess apparently led pure and spotless lives like Some of the folks who were the recipients of benefices were openly self-indulgent and worldly. There were, however, others who also received the pope's largess (folks like Father Sadoleto) who actually led pure and spotless lives but just happened to of one purpose with the Holy Father in their enthusiasm for the promotion of culture, ancient and modern.

"Eager to increase the treasures of the Vatican Library, the pope sent emissaries in all directions, including Scandinavia and even the Orient, to discover literary treasures and either acquire them outright or borrow them so that copies, greatly increasing the Library's holdings thereby.

"Rome again became the cultural center of the

known world under the Pope's patronage. The construction of the *Basilica Papale di San Pietro in Vaticano* (Papal Basilica of Saint Peter in the Vatican) more commonly known as St. Peter's Basilica on burial site of Saint Peter, started on 18 April 1506 under Pope Julius II, was accelerated. The construction would be finally completed under Pope Paul V.in 1615 and consecrated by Pope Urban VIII on 18 November, 1626.

"The address delivered by Gianfrancesco Pico della Mirandola, a publisher and author and an outspoken critic of corruption, towards the close of the Fifth Lateran Council (1517) on the prevailing morality of clergy and the immediate need for reforming their morals was of course quite telling. A lay man, Mirandola had concluded with the warning that the pope continued to ignore the situation and to apply the healing remedies to those wounds of the Church, God Himself would cut off the rotten limbs and destroy them with fire and sword! It turned out to be a prophetic warning indeed.

"It therefore pleased us mightily when the pope dismissed Martin Luther as just 'another heretic whose teachings would lead some of the faithful astray but, as had happened in the past, the true religion would triumph in time', minimizing the gravity of the situation in that way. Pope Leo X had in mind movements of the likes of John Wycliffe, the English reformer, and the Bohemian (Czech) Jan Hus (anglicized as John Hus). There is no question that the instantaneous support that Luther enjoyed amongst his countrymen was born of centuries of malcontent with the papacy in Rome and the protracted meddling by popes in the temporal affairs of England, Spain, France, Germany and the Scandinavian countries not to mention Italy itself; and that the odious greed for money displayed by the Roman Curia'. That is certainly no doubt about that. We were always rooting for the Turk,

Suleiman I (6 November 1494 – 6 September 1566), also known as Suleiman the Magnificent, to mount an attack on the Christians, because that would get the Pope pinned down with the crusades, with little time left to mind the spiritual needs of his flock.

"We would also find it relatively easy to persuade King Henry VIII who ruled England at the time, along with his subjects, to join the 'reformers' and part ways with the papacy in Rome actually over a simple love affair.

"And, just as we had expected, that first reformed Christian 'church', started by individuals who had been excommunicated and cut off from the Mystical Body of Christ because of their refusal to submit to the Church's teaching authority, inevitably splintered into more reformed 'churches' as 'ministering' under the new 'reformed' order became dependent, not on the magisterium of the Church and the validity of the ordination of the successors to the apostles, but on personal testimonies that ignored Tradition in the Church as an authentic source of revealed truth, and cited the 'Holy Book' as the sole source of revelation.

Leave nothing to chance...

"When we in the Underworld set out to do anything, we go about it in a very thorough manner. We leave nothing to chance. The way we went about sowing the seeds of disunity in Christendom was typical of this *modus operandi*. We had made up our minds that the 'churches' we would help dissidents in the Church set up would not be poor replicas of the Holy Church the Deliverer had commissioned. And to make up for the fact that the One True Holy and Catholic Church was informed by the Holy Ghost, we planned to persuade our minions to retain the Holy Ghost as the central focus of the revamped theological positions and doctrines. And we could not have been more delighted than to see those in schism and/or heresy struggle to make the case that their personal testimonies were inspired by none other than the Paraclete and Comforter.

"And sure enough, some of these 'reformed' churches now look so much like the Church of Rome, you need an expert to tell the difference! Then, even those churches that have shed many important features of Catholicism such as the Sacrifice of the Mass, Benediction and the 'Holy Hour', the Confessional, veneration of the Blessed Mother of the Deliverer, veneration of relics of martyrs and canonized saints, or the churches that have down-graded the place of priests as ministers who share directly in the priesthood of the Deliverer Himself (and consequently bear an indelible mark that will distinguish them from all other humans for all eternity) to mere preacher-men or 'pastors', still succeed in putting on impressive, mesmerizing shows for their congregations.

"These reformed churches come complete with elegant church edifices and cathedrals that rival St. Peter's Basilica in Rome, and firebrand preachers who know the Bible like the back of their hand; and the apologists on their rolls who have the ability when push comes to shove of making the Church's own scholars look like dwarfs! And the same goes for the vestments and livery employed during church services. These churches sport the best that money can buy, including gold-embroidered mitres and chasubles, gilded croziers, Roman collars, flowing white cassocks and silk stoles - you name it!

"But then it could also be said that these reformed churches in fact come with everything that should lead someone with a wee bit of common sense to start suspecting that they have my hallmark! Promise me solemnly you won't whisper that to any soul! Well, even if you get out 'on the street' and spill your guts and reveal my secret to all and sundry, that probably will have very little effect on the project that we here in Gehenna have dubbed 'Operation Camouflage'! This is because, even though 'faith cometh by hearing', it still remains a gift of the Prime Mover, and no amount of yearning by self-willed humans can ever force Him to change His *modus operandi* and impart it to those not deemed by Him as worthy of it.

"It was after all self-will on the part of the 'reformers' that opened the flood-gates for the different varieties of reformed churches! Yah! It was self-will on the part of misguided humans that gave us our window of opportunity. Once the first 'reformers' had gone out on a limb and started promulgating and propagating versions of 'Evangelism' that were based on their own personal interpretation of the sacred scriptures and done so without the blessing of the Church - once they had ranged themselves against the teaching *magisterium* or authority of the Holy Church headed by the Pontiff of Rome - it didn't really matter after that how clever or even 'prophetic' the personal testimonies they broadcast to the world sounded.

"The stage was set from that point on for us here in the Underworld to also get into our act. Working with well-intentioned humans who nevertheless had difficulty reconciling imperfections in humans who had been 'called to the feast' and were members of the Church - and specifically in those humans who had been called to leadership positions in the body of the faithful - with the fact that the Deliverer, the head of the 'Mystical Body' (Ephesians 1:22-23) was 'perfect', we were able to effectively create and reinforce the impression in the minds of humans that 'Christendom' comprised so many feuding churches that were all equally informed by the Holy Ghost just the same, and that were also all 'integral' parts of the Holy Church!

"Using the most masterful maneuvers that our satanic 'minds' could devise, we even succeeded in blurring the fact that humans who were excommunicated could not by definition be members of the Mystical Body of the Deliverer at the same time! We succeeded in promoting the 'Great Lie' that self-willed acts of humans have the same force and effect as acts that spring from the humble submission of a soul to the Holy Ghost and to the authority of the one and only true Church that is informed by Him by virtue of the promise the Deliverer made to the apostles who were cowed and congregated in the Upper Room out of fear of those who believed that they had successfully liquidated the Son of Man and also the 'Second Adam'!

"You just tell me the number of 'Catholics' who know what the phrase 'to be in communion with Rome' means! All these misguided souls inside and outside the Church believe that, names being names and there being nothing in a name, all it matters is for humans to feel comfortable with the 'Christian' denomination to which they belong. How many 'Christians' know that 'there is no salvation outside the Church which is headed by the successor to Peter, the first 'Papa' or 'Pope'?

"We also knew that, starved spiritually and inclined to sin at the same time, humans would always be tempted to grasp at anything that promised quick results. We here in the Underworld had never had any doubt that humans would be easy prey for our schemes for those reasons - and we have been proved right!

"It is pretty obvious to us at any rate that it doesn't take very much for spiritually starved humans to become (if you will excuse the vulgar expression) dumb asses as well! And they end up making the Deliverer a liar! And so, today, there are those humans who call themselves 'Orthodox followers of the Deliverer' who will tell you that, when the time comes for them to cross to the other side of the gulf that separates the living from the dead, they will be accosted by a Deliverer who will tell them: 'Well done, good and faithful followers of mine who upheld the faith of my Orthodox Church which I constructed on a Rock called Peter!' According to those humans who call themselves 'Mormon followers of the Deliverer', He will say: 'Well done, good and faithful followers of mine who upheld the faith of my Mormon Church which I constructed on a Rock called Peter!' And, according to those humans who call themselves 'Baptist followers of the Deliverer', He will say: 'Well done, good and faithful followers of mine who upheld the faith of my Baptist Church which I constructed on a Rock called Peter!' But, according to those humans who call themselves 'Lutheran followers of the Deliverer', He will say: 'Well done, good and faithful followers of mine who upheld the faith of my Lutheran Church which I constructed on a Rock called Peter!' Anglicans, Catholics, Calvinists - you name it - will make the Deliverer continue lying to the world and proclaiming *them* and them alone as His true followers! In other words, humans make the Deliverer a worse liar than even I, the Father of Lies! Such dumb asses! It is just so incredible!

"They even make Him lie about that 'Rock called Peter' because after all is said and done, that 'Rock called Peter' ends up being anything but a rock!"

The mother of the children of Zebedee...

"Now, because there are spiritually starved hordes

236

looking for easy ways out of their bind, it doesn't mean that the Deliverer is going to change His *modus operandi* to accommodate them. He didn't do it for the mother of the children of Zebedee, and He is not about to do it for moderns who are looking for short cuts to heaven and/or special treatment. The Deliverer actually used that classic case of a misguided human who was expecting Him to bend the rules, and promise to reserve the two choicest seats at the heavenly banquet (the seat immediately to the right of the Son of Man and also the one immediately to His left) for her dearest beloved, to make one thing absolutely clear. Those special seats were not for Him to allocate. Doing that was the prerogative of His Father.

"It was that same Father whose divine will the Deliverer sought to do from day one; the same Father to whom the Deliverer cried as He sweated blood in the Garden of Eden saying: 'If it be thy will, take the cup away from me...'

"Not wanting to be a witness to the good woman collapsing and dying from a heart attack right there in front of Him, the Deliverer stopped at informing her that those special seats at the divine banquet were not His, but His Father's to give away. To be saved, her sons, like every other descendant of Adam and Eve for whom He had consented to become the 'Second Adam', needed to 'believe in Him'. If they did that, His Father in heaven, who so loved the world that He gave His only-begotten Son, so that whosoever believed in Him would not perish, would do what He had to do!

"You must be naive if you do not believe that the mother of the children of Zebedee would have died of a heart attack if the Deliverer had turned to her and said something like:

'Ma'am, you love James and John so much that

you would be prepared to lay down your life for them - if, let us say, a hungry maneater turned up in your home and threatened them, you would gladly prefer to let the animal have you rather than them for its lunch wouldn't you? Now, many are called, but few are chosen. And look, I have invited your sons, James and John, to follow me - yes, that is what I told them. I asked them to leave their boats and to follow me. Actually, I would like them to be not just my disciples, but my apostles! And, woman, you've got to understand what this means.

'As my apostles, they are going to be exposed to the wolves, and they must needs drink of the cup that I myself have to drink as I go about doing my Father's will. I am asking James and John to follow me even though this means that, in the eyes of the priests and Pharisees and the powers that be, they are actually going to be terrorists who are marked for liquidation. Look, James, who also happens to be my first cousin, will meet with a gruesome fate at the hands of these folks. He will be put to death with the sword! As for John, he too must be prepared to drink the cup I drink and be baptized with the baptism I am baptized with.

'Woman, it is tough enough for my brother humans to believe in me so that they may be saved in accordance with the will of my Father. Look…I made it very clear to them the other day that whosoever finds his life will lose it, and whoever loses his life for my sake will find it! It is certainly going to be tougher, much tougher, for James and John whom I am inviting to be my apostles along with the fisherman, Peter, and others - if they succeed in sticking with me all the way, that is.

'Now, this is going to be a little tricky. It is going to be an uphill struggle because, on their own, James and John will never make it! But at least they are not like Peter! He has already been acting like the Tempter on a

couple of occasions. Can you imagine that he had the audacity to take me aside and to rebuke me for saying that the time had come for the Son of Man to make His way to Jerusalem, and there suffer many things from the ancients and scribes and chief priests, and be put to death, and the third day rise again! Peter and Judas of all people were determined to try and dissuade me from doing the will of my Father! They have been trying to stop me from heading to Jerusalem where I have to meet my own gruesome death in fulfilment of prophecies of the Old Testament!

'But do not misunderstand me. Peter is still one of a kind. While some of the multitudes believe that I am John the Baptizer, and others say I am either Elijah or one of the prophets of old who has come back to life, when I asked my disciples the other day 'But who do you say that I am?', it was Peter, not John or James, who answered without hesitation, 'The Christ of God'!

'Now, woman…it is in Jerusalem, on Mt. Golgotha to be exact - the place of the skull - where I am going to die and then rise up again in glory, taking Adam and Eve, Cain, Abel, the whole shoot from the place where they have been detained by the Enemy in bondage to heaven with me. That is what is meant by the Son of Man 'taking the sting out of death'.

'You understand that the redemption of the human race depends on this trip to the Eternal City, and it is also in Jerusalem that I will commission my Ekklesia. It is there that the Comforter will descend on my apostles, including James and John, and give them the strength to be fishers of men.

'You might not have heard, but the other day I had to scream at Peter. I actually called him Satan, and told him to get behind me! I know you tried to give your children a good upbringing - and you can see the

difference it makes. But I am already finding these fellows to be something else. Now, in the same breath as Peter and these sons of yours are telling me to find a hideout in the hills of Samaria or some other such place - a cave where I am supposed to hide because it is an open secret that, in the eyes of the priests and Pharisees, I am a terrorist who has a price on my head to boot - they keep swearing that they are not the type who can abandon a friend who also happens to be their brother and Master!

'Peter keeps saying that he will stay with me through thick and thin. But he is obviously a weakling; and it pains me to think that he will not just deny me, but will swear that he does not know me ever so many times! And he will do so especially when I most need someone to stay and comfort me…when I need someone to stand up and scream, and tell the world that the Word through whom all that exists came into being and also the Son of Man and the Deliverer is no vile criminal; that it is Him that is being spat upon, falsely accused, scourged, mocked, and crowned with thorns, despised, abused and beaten, and about to be nailed to the cross and crucified as a terrorist; and, above all, when I am abandoned by all those you now see flocking to see the miracles I perform!

'Look woman, it is going to be hard enough for me to get your sons to let the Holy Ghost lead them where they themselves on their own would rather not go! But I want you to also understand that Peter, not John or James, is the rock upon which I will build my Ekklesia.

'And so, are you still pining for those seats - the one to my right and the other to my left - for your boys? Do you still want James and John to continue in my company? If they do decide to heed my call, they can be sure to find themselves sidelined as vile criminals and terrorists as well; and they definitely will suffer unjustly for my sake. And for them to be anywhere near me at the *heavenly banquet, James and John are going to have to give up a great deal more! You, woman - you sure are very possessive about these sons of yours. But remember what I told the crowd the other day. To have your sons, you have to lose them first!*

'And if you yourself want to remain in my company - if you want to be saved and have eternal life - you have to be prepared to lose your life and to accept unfair treatment for my sake. You have to learn to turn the other cheek every time you are slapped! But forget it if you think you can persuade me to change my modus operandi!

'Just remember one thing: Adam and Eve and all humanity had lost it! They were finished… kaput! Have you ever stopped and tried to imagine how offensive the iniquities of men, fashioned as they are in my Father's own image and likeness, are to me and to my Father? Have you ever stopped to reflect on the fact that, since the fall of Adam and Eve from grace, excepting for my beloved Mother Mary who is also your most gracious advocate, all humans are born into original sin and all the consequences that flow from it? Add to that the fact that humans not only are inclined to wickedness; but, on their own, without the help of the graces I will merit in due course through obedience to my Father in heaven, they are incapable of doing anything that is virtuous! And then they are so easily scandalized - they so easily lose all hope; and they despair when they witness fragrant violations of the human rights of dear ones - violations that are as a rule committed with total impunity!

'It behoved me, the Son of Man and Author of Life, designated by my Father in heaven to be high priest according to the order of Melchizedek, in all things to be made like unto you my human brethren, that I may become the merciful and faithful priest before my Father,

and that I may be a propitiation for the sins of humans. My incarnation was as the Second Adam, in holiness and without sin, the offspring whereof inherit everlasting life and fellowship with my Father. Now, all who look to the Father's Son in faith as His disciples are received with Him, covered by His righteousness!

'Look - it is not my style to cause robbery victims to win lottery tickets just because they have been robbed and are in need...

'Think ye that peace I came to give in the earth? No, I say to you, but rather division...He who loves father or mother more than me is not worthy of me; and he who loves son or daughter more than me is not worthy of me. And he who does not take his cross and follow after me is not worthy of me. He who has found his life will lose it, and he who has lost his life for my sake will find it.

'Woman, my method of operation must take all of these things into account, and will remain mysterious to men. I will teach you how to pray to my Father in heaven. And after you master the 'Pater Noster', it won't mean that you won't suffer. Praying will merely arm you so you can withstand suffering and disappointments and the abuse that you will suffer for my sake - and will also keep you clear of the whiles of Satan. And, I tell you the truth - unless you eat my flesh and drink my blood, you have no life in you. For I come to Earth as a sacrificial lamb!

'And forget it completely if you too want to set up your own 'Reformed' Church in competition with my Ekklesia, my Mystical Body - just in case you are thinking that, may be, you and your sons can be my followers, and still avoid the tears and pain that go with it...the cross! Don't even dream of a seat at the divine banquet table if you want to continue to be self-willed. And certainly not if you want to be one of those who are prepared to use my temple for commerce! On my dead body...!'

'But Ma'am, this I will tell you. Even though the seats to my right and to my left in the kingdom of heaven are not mine to give, I have invited both James and John to become fishers of men. It is accordingly my desire to have them both share in my priesthood. I want them to become instruments for dispensing to humans the divine graces that I will merit through my obedience to my Father in heaven. I will dispatch them into the world to spread the message of the Son of Man who is going to be crucified and die according to the scriptures, rise from the dead, and become glorified! And when they enter a town in which they are not welcome, they shall go into its streets and say: Even the dust of your town that clings to our feet we wipe off against you. Nevertheless know this, namely that the kingdom of God has come near.

'The faith of humans in the existence of my Father - the Almighty and also infinitely loving Prime Mover - springs from the awareness by humans that, while they weren't in existence at a given moment, the next moment they now not only did indeed exist, but they did so through the gratuitous act of that tell-tale Prime Mover who is none other than my Father in heaven.

'And I said infinitely loving. Yes, infinitely Loving and Good! My Father in Heaven didn't need you, your sons or any of the other creatures He brought into existence. He deigned to create all of you all the same, in His Own Image and likeness, and He endowed you all with an intellect and a free will. He did so well knowing that, once graced with those faculties, His creatures became capable of revolting against Him! After Adam and Eve sinned and were cast out of Paradise, in a demonstration of His infinite love, my Father in Heaven promised them and their descendants a Deliverer. My Father so loved the world, that he gave his only begotten Son, that whosoever believeth in Him, may not perish, but *may have life everlasting.*

'The Son of Man is now among you and, a mere statistic in the eyes of the world, He will be disowned by His own. A Second Adam to the fight, in an act that requires an infinite fountain of love, the Son of Man offers Himself as a sacrificial lamb for the salvation of all who believeth in Him, the first-fruits of them that sleep, and a bridge for the chasm that now exists between heaven and earth. And also so that you humans may now see my Father face to face in beatific vision!

'But it can only be those who freely choose to believe in the Son of Man. That is because, molded in my Father's image and likeness and endowed with an intellect and a free will, He cannot force you to believe in His Son. Peter, James, John, and the other apostles whom I will send out to proclaim the mystery of my Father in heaven will however not go into the world with sublimity of words or of wisdom. As they will themselves make crystal clear, they will resolve to know nothing while they are with the catechumens except the Son of Man, and it will be the Son of Man crucified. They will attest that they go out into the world in weakness and fear and much trembling; and their message and proclamation will not be with persuasive (words of) wisdom, but with a demonstration of spirit and power so that the faith of the catechumens might rest not on human wisdom but on the power of my Father in heaven.

'And, yes, they will speak wisdom to those who are mature, but not wisdom of this age, nor of the rulers of this age who are passing away. Rather, they will articulate my Father's wisdom, mysterious, hidden, which my Father predetermined before the ages for the glory of those who are received into my Ekklesia, and which none of the rulers of this age know; for if they did they would not be readying to crucify the Son of Man. But it is written:

What eye has not seen, and ear has not heard, and what has not entered the human heart, what my Father in heaven has prepared for those who love Him, this He will reveal to my brother humans through the Spirit. For the Spirit scrutinizes everything, even the depths of my Father in heaven.

'As my messengers will affirm, among human beings, who knows what pertains to a person except the spirit of the person that is within? Similarly, no one knows what pertains to God except the Spirit of God. Those following in my footsteps will not receive the spirit of the world, but the Spirit that is from God, so that they may understand the things freely given to them by my Father in heaven. And they will speak about them not with words taught by human wisdom, but with words taught by the Spirit, describing spiritual realities in spiritual terms. Now the natural person does not accept what pertains to the Spirit of God, for to him it is foolishness, and he or she cannot understand it, because it is judged spiritually. The spiritual person, however, can judge everything but is not subject to judgment by anyone. For "who has known the mind of the Lord, so as to counsel him?" But those following in my footsteps will have the mind of the Son of Man.

'You may recall that not long ago, I let folks literally walk away from Eternal Life - the folks who looked in themselves and decided that they could never feed on my body and my blood!

'Your fathers did eat manna in the wilderness, and are dead. I am the living bread that came down from heaven: if any man eat of this bread, he shall live for ever: and the bread that I will give is my flesh, which I will give for the life of the world. Verily, verily, I say unto all you humans, except ye eat the flesh of the Son of Man, and drink his blood, ye have no life in you. Who so eateth my

flesh, and drinketh my blood, hath eternal life; and I will raise him up at the last day!

'When the time comes, some will say, "Sir, I knew that you were a hard man, harvesting where you did not sow, and gathering where you did not scatter seed; so I was afraid, and I went and hid your talent in the ground. See, you have what is yours." But no one will be able to say that he or she wasn't afforded the graces he/she needed to prevail.

'Once in existence, humans soon realize that things around them change and do so in time - unlike my Father in heaven who by His very nature is unchanging and remains a mystery.

'My Father exists above all that exists; inasmuch as He is His own existence. And, because He exceeds every kind of knowledge, He is not comprehended. My Father in heaven is incomprehensible because He cannot be seen as perfectly as He is capable of being seen by humans. For humans to know my Father, some likeness of my Father must be made in them.

'Those who see the divine essence see what they see in God not by any likeness, but by the divine essence itself united to their intellect. For each thing is known in so far as its likeness is in the one who knows. My father's divine nature or essence is existence itself. My Father is incorporeal. Hence He cannot be seen by the senses or the imagination, but only by the intellect. Therefore to see the essence of God is possible to the created human intellect by grace, and not by nature.

'It is impossible for any created intellect to see the essence of God by its own natural power. For knowledge is regulated according as the thing known is in the knower. But the thing known is in the knower according to the mode of the knower. Hence the knowledge of every knower is ruled according to its own nature. If therefore

the mode of anything's being exceeds the mode of the knower, it must result that the knowledge of the object is above the nature of the knower. Now the mode of being of things is manifold. For some things have being only in this one individual matter; as all bodies. But others are subsisting natures, not residing in matter at all, which, however, are not their own existence, but receive it; and these are the incorporeal beings, the angels. But to my Father in heaven alone does it belong to be His own subsistent being.

'To know self-subsistent being is natural to the divine intellect alone; and this is beyond the natural power of any created intellect; for no creature is its own existence, forasmuch as its existence is participated. Therefore the created intellect cannot see the essence of God, unless God by His grace unites Himself to the created intellect, as an object made intelligible to it.

'Of those who see the essence of God, one sees Him more perfectly than another. It will take place because one intellect will have a greater power or faculty to see God than another. The faculty of seeing God, however, does not belong to the created intellect naturally, but is given to it by the light of glory, which establishes the intellect in a kind of "deiformity" (likeness to deity). Accordingly the intellect which has more of the light of glory will see God the more perfectly; and he/she will have a fuller participation of the light of glory who has more charity; because where there is the greater charity, there is the more desire; and desire in a certain degree makes the one desiring apt and prepared to receive the object desired.

'My Father in heaven is "incomprehensible" not because anything of Him is not seen; but because He is not seen as perfectly as He is capable of being seen.

'If Abba, my Father in heaven, alone were seen,

247

Who is the fount and principle of all being and of all truth, He would so fill the natural desire of knowledge that nothing else would be desired, and the seer would be completely beatified.

'My Father, Abba, cannot be seen in His essence by a mere human being, except he be separated from this mortal life.

'Although a perfect knowledge of the cause cannot be had from inadequate effects, yet from any effect manifest to us it can be shown that a cause does exist. And thus from the works of Abba, my Father in heaven, His existence can be proved, although humans cannot in this way know Him perfectly in accordance with His own essence.

'The natural man does not accept the things of the Spirit of God; for they are ... things of God's Spirit, for they are foolishness to him, and he can't know them.

'Fashioned in my Father's own image and likeness, and endowed thereby with the faculties of the reason and free will unlike the beasts of the Earth, Adam and Eve and their descendants also get to know virtually on impulse that their existence on earth, even though a timed one, remains a special one. This is so regardless of whether they openly acknowledge it or not. It cannot escape my human brothers and sisters that the important fact is not so much the fact that they now exist in that temporal habit on earth as the fact that they bedevil their own eternal life by not conducting themselves as befits human beings. It is also the reason humans know that an act they are contemplating is conscionable or not.

'Humans have an instinctive inkling of these things in the exact same way they instinctively reach out for grub when they feel hunger gnawing at their middle. They are loath to see their own existence in a world where everyone is on a short lease of life prematurely ended.

When they start conspiring to end the lives of their fellow humans prematurely, they know instinctively that they commit a crime, and one that is not just sordid, but a crime against humanity itself - and by extension against the Son of Man and also Second Adam!

'And that is so if only because they do unto other humans something that they would not wish done unto themselves. Had it happened that humans, created in the Image and endowed by my Father in heaven with the spiritual faculties of the reason and free will, were incapable of grasping these things, suffice it to say that this would have reflected somewhat poorly on my Father, and on the Word through Whom all things that are and ever will be come into existence.

'It is immaterial whether humans commit such deeds in secret or in broad daylight. This is immaterial because, when the timed existence on earth of the perpetrators runs its course, the way they conducted themselves during their pilgrimage there must come back to haunt them. And nothing can be more haunting to a human than crimes committed by that human against its own. Souls that commit such sordid deeds are haunted and unable to rest in peace throughout all of eternity!

'And with all the death and destruction that has been engineered by humans since Adam and Eve sinned, such murderous souls, you can be sure, are not a few but many…a myriad, countless!

'For those brother and sister humans at the receiving end - the victims - their peculiar circumstances and struggles for survival - struggles that they could not face or endure without the assistance of the graces merited by the Son of Man - constitute the crosses they must needs carry. They are struggles that in time cause these souls to join the Son of Man in imploring His Father saying: Pater si vis transfer calicem istum a me

249

verumtamen non mea voluntas sed tua fiat (Father, if thou wilt, remove this chalice from me: but yet not my will, but thine be done).

'Woman, wherefore, I say to thee and to all my brother and sister humans: Come unto me, all ye that are weary and heavy laden, and I will refresh you. Let not your hearts be troubled. Believe in God; believe also in me. In my Father's house are many rooms. If it were not so, would I have told you that I go to prepare a place for you? And if I go and prepare a place for you, I will come again and will take you to myself, that where I am you may be also. And you know the way to where I am going.*

'And look - you brother and sister humans were created in the Image of My Father for a reason. And the Son of Man came down to earth from heaven because humans on a pilgrimage there are fashioned in his Father's Image. He was able to take up his human nature because humans are made in that Image.*

'The kingdom of heaven is like to an householder, who went out early in the morning to hire laborers into his vineyard. And having agreed with the laborers for a penny a day, he sent them into his vineyard. And going about the third hour, he saw others standing in the market place idle. And he said to them: Go you also into my vineyard, and I will give you what shall be just. And they went their way. And again he went out about the sixth and the ninth hour, and did in like manner. But about the eleventh hour he went out and found others standing, and he saith to them: Why stand you here all the day idle? They say to him: Because no man hath hired us. He saith to them: Go you also into my vineyard.*

'And when evening was come, the lord of the vineyard saith to his steward: Call the laborers and pay them their hire, beginning from the last even to the first. When therefore they were come, that came about the* *eleventh hour, they received every man a penny. But when the first also came, they thought that they should receive more: and they also received every man a penny. And receiving it they murmured against the master of the house, saying: These last have worked but one hour, and thou hast made them equal to us, that have borne the burden of the day and the heats. But he answering said to one of them: Friend, I do thee no wrong: didst thou not agree with me for a penny? Take what is thine, and go thy way: I will also give to this last even as to thee. Or, is it not lawful for me to do what I will? is thy eye evil, because I am good? So shall the last be first, and the first last. For many are called, but few chosen.*

'I am the vine; you the branches: he that abideth in me, and I in him, the same beareth much fruit: for without me you can do nothing.

'Not everyone who says to me, Lord, Lord, will enter the kingdom of heaven, but the one who does the will of my Father who is in heaven. On that day many will say to me, 'Lord, Lord, did we not prophesy in your name, and cast out demons in your name, and do many mighty works in your name?' And then will I declare to them, 'I never knew you; depart from me, you workers of lawlessness.

'But woe to the scribes and Pharisees, hypocrites; because they shut the kingdom of heaven against men, for they themselves do not enter in; and those that are going in, they suffer not to enter…And even they would that they have the seats to my right and to my left after I am lifted up.

'Woman, you yourself know full well that the day of the Lord will come just like a thief in the night. While they are saying, "Peace and safety!" then destruction will come upon them suddenly like labor pains upon a woman with child, and they will not escape. But you, woman, are not

in darkness, that the day would overtake you like a thief.'

"Make sense? Yah...I tell yah!" the devil spat out at the end of his monologue.

Mjomba could not help noticing that a good deal of the material the Evil One was attributing to the Deliverer in His hypothetical exchange with the mother of the children of Zebedee was actually material that the Apostle of the Gentiles (St. Paul) and the Angelic Doctor (St. Thomas Aquinas) had used in the course of their evangelizing missions. And it was quite clear that the devil was all out to ensure that at the end of time on their day of judgement humans wouldn't have any excuses for not having believed in the Deliverer and embraced his *Sancta Ecclesia.*

Mjomba was quite surprised that, in spite of the Deliverer's dire words to the Mother of the children of Zebedee, the devil still appeared to discern some sort of victory for the forces of evil from the hypothetical exchange, and he found this rather disconcerting. But that did not stop Mjomba from continuing to record the thoughts of the evil Diabolos unquestioningly.

"This is a victory that even we who are banished for ever from the sight of the Prime Mover and Almighty One must find a moment to savor! But even as we celebrate - or (to be more precise) attempt to celebrate - we unfortunately have this fear that these misguided souls who could make a huge contribution to the Work of Redemption of the Holy Church if only they could get over the blues, pray to be worthy recipients of the gifts of faith, charity and wisdom that could pave the way for their acceptance of the Church's teachings and eventual return to the fold, might someday abandon their egos and do just that.

"And we, of course, know that when a 'separated brother' or 'separated sister' embraces Catholicism,

252

he/she usually ends up valuing his/her faith far more than those who are Catholics from birth and who easily fall for the temptation to take their religion for granted as a consequence.

"You might therefore be surprised that, although we ourselves chose to make the Pit our dwelling place by mounting the rebellion against Him-Who-Is-Who-Is, we even then still pray to Him! And, as you might have guessed, the one thing we pray for unceasingly is that the misguided 'brethren', exercising their freedoms - 'freedom to choose', 'freedom of worship', and above all 'freedom of speech' - stay the course and remain die-hard schismatics and heretics in the eyes of the Holy Mother the Church (led by the successors to the apostles and guided by the Holy Ghost) to the very end!

"In any case, the fact is that being a separated brother or sister has long ceased to carry with it the stigma that was traditionally associated with that status. It used to be that as long as a misguided brother or sister did not recant the schism and/or heresy, it was understood that he/she would continue to be cut off from Holy Mother the Church by virtue of a solemn Papal edict of excommunication the Holy Father himself cannot revoke even if he wanted to. While the original, hand-scripted edict is preserved in a secret vault in the Vatican Library, copies are of course freely available on the Worldwide Web; so that the separated brothers and sisters of modern times, unlike their counterparts who belonged to earlier ages, cannot plead ignorance as the excuse for not taking steps to return to communion with the One and the Only Holy Church of the Prime Mover.

"What is more, the separated brothers and sisters could find all the information they needed to lead them back to the 'true faith' on that same worldwide web if they were seriously seeking the Truth. The Catechism of the

Church, the papal encyclicals, the writings of the 'Doctors of the Church' including writings of the 'Early Fathers', the entire 'Summa Theologiae' penned by Thomas of Aquin, and contemplative works by the likes of Thomas a Kempis - they are all there on the worldwide web.

"And, by the way, you can even find on Google this 'meditational work' by that Irishman Clive Staples Lewis - '*The Screwtape Letters*', yes, '*The Screwtape Letters*' - in which that cranky author has me spilling out my secrets about how I go about tempting humans! According to one reviewer, *The Screwtape Letters* is 'a masterpiece of reverse theology, giving the reader an inside look at the thinking and means of temptation'! Another one refers to it as a 'novel about spiritual warfare from a demon's point of view!' Gosh! This is so, so hilarious!

"The real 'problem' is, of course, not so much the fear that there might be a dearth of materials that can help a 'separated' brother or sister discern the errors and/or fallacies in the doctrines to which the brother or sister subscribes, as the fear that the brother or sister might not be able to continue feeling good (given what the other separated brothers and sisters would say) after he/she walked away from the 'charming', highly 'eloquent', and even 'charismatic' leaders of the breakaway churches.

"The problem is not that the separated brethren, after showing curiosity like everyone else about 'where the Deliverer lives', all of a sudden come upon insurmountable obstacles along the way; or that they inexplicably and for no fault of theirs lose sight of the Deliverer and are then forced to turn back. The problem is that the separated brethren, like all the other curious people who eventually balk at becoming members of the *Sancta Ecclesia* (Holy Church), follow the Deliverer only as long as His route is along a well beaten path, and also appears familiar; but they immediately conclude that if He lives where He appears to be leading them, He cannot possibly be the type of Deliverer they had in mind!

"I can tell you that we here in the Pit actually work very hard to make sure that those who witness the miracles performed by the Deliverer and initially want to know more about the miracle worker, become dismayed with Him as soon the path along which He is walking starts to veer off into the desert.

The devil is concerned...

"As I have said before, I, Beelzebub, ring leader of the rebel 'ghosts' who made history by standing up to the Almighty One, am concerned about humankind. Let us face it - humans have been the poor forsaken children of Adam and Eve from the moment that first man and that first woman, following their natural inclination, were caught red handed as they tried to filch fruit from the Tree of Knowledge in the Garden of Eden out of their curiosity. Since then, I have been their only friend and succor in time of need even though, being a creature like them and one that moreover is very susceptible to 'sin', I could not take credit for having brought sinful and sinning humans into existence.

"That is inevitable - I have no choice but to act as if I were their 'elder brother' or 'elder sister', and take them all under my wing, especially now that humankind and myself, along with the host of angels who joined me in my rebellion against the Prime Mover, are all accursed and in the same boat. You know the saying that friends in need become friends indeed! That is how strong the bond of friendship between the poor 'bastards' (which all humans became for all practical purposes after the fall) and us is.

"And while humans have this tendency of getting

distracted and becoming oblivious to the sacrifices that my fellow demons and I continuously make to help them feel at home and consoled so that they don't go all bananas and become suicidal (which they would assuredly do with no one around to commiserate with them), we for our part will never abandon them.

The devil is spiritually dead...

"Now, it is not as if we demons are immortal. I, Beelzebub and Father of Death, am not immortal! Nothing of the sort - I am mortal just like humans. In fact I sometimes can't help wondering about all the hullabaloo in which I am depicted as some sort of immortal ogre or 'terrorist' who even wields powers that are beyond the ordinary! Let us be clear - I am no demigod! And I am not the omnipresent, all knowing and callous super spirit (something like 'super man'!) I am depicted in the Book of the Apocalypse and in certain of the exegetical works that some fellow composed and published.

"It might be that my charming manners and charisma as I go about my business of tempting humans give that impression. But, in truth, I am a very ordinary creature - not very different from that Michael the Archangel who succeeded me as Chief of the Angelic Host. I mean, you could even argue that I am 'dead' already - a spiritual corpse!

"I do not have a brain (as I do not possess a body); and I cannot therefore say that I am as brilliant as Einstein when it comes to conducting experiments involving the laws of gravity. Had I been a human, I would probably be a midget!

"You, of course, know that we pure spirits, unlike humans whose nature comprises a bag of chemicals or physical 'body' and a soul, don't come in different sizes or shapes either; and, apart from the fact that I was very gifted (more or less like Michael who is admittedly my rival and also nemesis), there is nothing otherwise that distinguishes me from the other demons.

"Now, God the Father, God the Son and God the Holy Ghost share the same divine nature. This is in much the same way you humans all share the same human nature. But those of us who are brought into existence as pure spirits do not share a nature - we, each of us, have our individual 'ghost kind' (or, if you like, 'nature') which we got at the moment we were willed by the Almighty One into existence - or given each one our distinctive 'breath of life' if that is the way you want to put it.

Good Guys, Bad Guys...

"To get back to the point I was trying to make before I got diverted, I, Satan, will never abandon humans - not for any reason! And even when they become faint-hearted (which is normal in the heat of any battle!) and decide to throw in the towel so that they may become reconciled with the Prime Mover through the merits of the Son of Man and now also Judge, the vast army of demons with myself at its helm will never, never stop pursuing humans with the aim of keeping our relationship intact. Look, chums - humans will always be able to count on our constancy and our support.

"In that respect, we demons are very different from Michael and the guardian angels (two guardian angels apiece to be exact) that watch over humans. I doubt that they can muster the patience that is required when dealing with humans to the same degree we of the underworld do - and it is the reason good souls will always be left to suffer at the hands of the wicked ones who will steal, have no remorse about twisting the truth to their advantage as long as they can get away with it, torturing, maiming and even killing the innocent at our instigation. Is there any wonder why the murderers (the ones who know their job and do it to my script) always get away, but the victims never do?

"Need I, therefore, say any more to illustrate why the bad guys have always been winning and will continue to so do until this god-forsaken and goddamned world grinds to a grisly end! And when the bad guys win, the good guys must needs suffer! And there is your key to the mystery of pain and suffering - if you were seriously searching for one.

"In order not to suffer, one must ally oneself closely with the bad guys and us, and effectively become a bad guy by virtue of being an accessory to the damnable deeds of the original bad guys. And, of course, bad guys will always stand by each other out of loyalty to me, the Archdevil and exemplar of bad guys. And you must know by now that bad guys can never do any wrong. If a bad guy falls foul of any rule or regulation, that rule or regulation quite obviously must be so inequitable as to become null and void automatically!

"That is the attitude we want the bad guys, following our example, to espouse; for the simple reason that the bad guys must always be seen as the good guys, and the good guys as the bad guys. And, under the guise of defending things like free speech and liberty, the bad guys must always thwart efforts by the good guys to change unjust laws and social structures that are inequitable to make them more just and equitable.

"But when a guy who is in the enemy camp - and that is any guy who has been marked by the bad guys as 'roguish' (because that guy has control over resources the bad guys deem critical to their 'security' and wellbeing, and who has shown a reluctance to surrender them and walk away) - can be made to look as though he/she is in breach of those rules or regulations, the situation becomes reversed. The 'enemies of the people', and definitely the 'rogues', must be brought to heel immediately; and the means for doing that cannot be dialogue. It must be awe and shock inspiring force, because that is the only language knaves and rogues understand!

"And now, if it should happen that the knaves or rogues who are being sought take or are suspected to have taken refuge in some safe house that is located in the middle of a densely populated area, it is always perfectly O.K. to level the whole place with any amount of TNT that can do the job. And if it should happen that the rogues succeed in making their gateway in the nick of time, and all those eliminated in the 'security operation' are innocent, so long as the victims are not allies, such an action is always perfectly all right.

"It couldn't even be portrayed as a 'terrible mistake that is to be regretted'. I just said that the bad guys are incapable of doing any wrong. That is something you have to take on faith even if it sounds completely unbelievable. If anything, the 'collateral damage' must be blamed on the rogues and their totally unimaginable habit of using women and children as human shields. And, of course, those allies who are in the media business have a responsibility to do whatever they can to minimize the fall-out and especially the bad publicity. It is at precisely such times that they must depict the rogues in the worst possible light as callous individuals who are insensitive to the safety and wellbeing of women and children!

"As you may already have guessed, the allies in the media do not have to be persuaded to become involved. This is because security operations by their nature are terrific for the bottom line in the media business. What with the blood-cuddling scenes and the opportunity availed to the embedded media allies for filing exclusive stories from the frontline when regime changes and things like that engineered by the bad guys are under way, not to mention the chance to snap exclusive 'pics' (isn't that what you call them?) of the grisly scenes, and the ratings that come with real-time coverage of news stories in those situations, things could never be better for the media allies.

"The allies will, moreover, not be exposed to the dangers of 'stray' tank cannon fire and things of that nature which 'independent' journals have to be on the lookout for. In any event, the chance to put a positive spin on the goings-on at the front line, and the opportunity to transform any 'terrible mistakes that are to be greatly regretted' into sordid tales focusing on the rogues cannot but boost the ratings - and the revenues.

"And if you think that there will be an outcry from the rest of the world, you are wrong. There will be hardly a ruffle from all those 'good' and 'upright' people in the whole wide world - the good and upright folks whom those targeted by the security operations normally expect to spring to their help as a matter of course in such situations if they should be subjected to acts of gross injustice from any quarter!

"But, of course, years later - when history has been written - there will be all sorts of people pouting and attempting to rebut the accusations of the shocking inaction and/or deafening silence of individuals who could have influenced the course of events by merely opening their mouths to publicly condemn the gross acts of injustice perpetrated by us bad guys. Others at that time will be trying in vain to deny the plain and patently undeniable evidence of complicity. The denials will encompass deplorable policies now in place according to which it is O.K. for 'super powers' to invade 'rogue nations' that stubbornly cling to their right of self-determination and independence, and according to which everything, including the option to employ WMD (weapons of massive destruction) against the rogue nations, 'stays on the table'.

"But none of that really matters in the long run. This is because of the operation of a Law of Nature according to which overbearing and belligerent 'axis powers' of today must themselves invariably fall victim to the turmoil they help to foment in the world a dozen or so years down the road if not earlier as is usually the case. The once super-powerful nations, with power hungry but extremely short-sighted megalomaniacs at the helm, invariably become eclipsed by other emerging axis powers, also with power thirsty and extremely short-sighted megalomaniacs at the helm, assuring a repetition of history through the ages as the world grinds towards the inevitable Armageddon.

"You see…when a superpower is not engaged in prosecuting a war in one part of the globe (we in the underworld work hard to make sure that the super power is caught up in several conflicts at the same time), it will be mired in a conflict of one sort or another in some other part of the globe as a rule. The superpower will always find some excuse to do this for any number of reasons. The incumbent regime frequently needs the nation to be at war as a means of clinging on to power. This is due to the fact that, with the exception of peaceniks who will always remain a fringe group, in times of war the populace generally answers the call to show 'patriotism' and remain united behind the regime of the day. But it is also a proven fact that as wars get under way, the war matériel sector of the economy, which is responsible for supplying the war fighting machine with equipment, fighting apparatus and supplies, stimulates the economy and fosters 'inventions' that eventually become adapted to non-military uses as wars wind down.

"And one reason allies of the super power pitch in to fight alongside the super power (if you did not know), even though the wars might be unpopular at home, is to assure that they stay abreast with regard to the changing technologies for mounting the assaults on fellow humans and dispatching them.

"The fact of the matter is that, like me here in Gehenna, super powers thrive on conflict, and they even conjure up pretexts for mounting assaults on nations whose resources they had been eying for some time. This is a virus that I long ago succeeded in transmitting to humans. The only different between humans and me is that I know when to desist and not tackle an opponent who might end up being too much for me. Infatuated with the loot, regimes in the once formidable nation soon stop thinking aright. As so often happens, before long, the greed that drives humans starts to blind them to the dangers that lurk in the uncertainties of war campaigns. And that is how the baton is passed on as once ostensibly invincible nations succumb to greed and become overextended, and some other emerging superpower, frequently none other than the nation that had been targeted for destruction, steps in to take over the mantle of Super Power of the World.

"Now, as the Father of Death, I would be very remiss if I didn't take full advantage of this insatiable human greed to promote my agenda. Just as the emergence of those so-called super powers is not an accident, it is no accident that the small cliques that hold the reigns of power in those countries are not merely imbued with lust for power and unbridled greed, but they

262

all operate on the motto that greed (which is itself equivalent to idolatry) is good!

"We here in the underworld have worked very hard to ensure that greed and possessiveness, the silent forces behind all human conflicts, are actually touted by those who call the shots in human society as virtues that are essential for economic and industrial growth. It is a signal achievement that also speaks to our ingenuity and hard work that even as super powers of the day are winding down their activities in conflict zones where they had found themselves whipped by foes whose ingenuity and resilience they had grossly underestimated, plans for forays into other parts of the globe and new battle zones in search of resources that are deemed essential for maintaining the superpower status will already be on the drawing boards.

"The important thing for us is not that super powers come and go, but that humans, fashioned in the image of the Prime Mover, die at the hands of their fellow humans. And so, as you yourself see, the saying that there is no rest for the wicked, far from being confined to us demons, perhaps applies even more to you humans!

"I am Beelzebub, and I will tell you that humans are very slow to learn that actions of stupid fools always come back to haunt them. But, for now, the 'priests and Pharisees of the New Testament' will be going about their business of ministering to the spiritual needs of the Prime Mover's flock as usual - unless, of course, the upheaval or slaughter occurs on their door step; or rippling shock waves from misfired WMD cause precious frescos in the church building, cathedral or basilica to come tumbling down on their heads.

"Members of the clergy of the different faiths will be presiding over weddings and over the other rituals of the liturgical year peculiar to those faiths as they fall due as if the same peace they see reigning inside the precincts of those churches, cathedrals and basilicas reigns among all the Prime Mover's people the 'World Over'! They will be acting as if I, Satan and bad guy *par excellence*, and the forces of darkness that I lead, were defeated and put out of commission long ago, and have consequently been rendered completely innocuous - as if, neutralized, my troops and I no longer possess the ability to tempt you humans! As if you could now search the whole wide world, and not happen upon any human who could be classified as a 'bad guy'!

"The modern-day priests and Pharisees will be conducting their services on the 'Day of the Sabbath', and they will give their pep talks (or 'homilies' as you call them) from their pulpits, in the course of which they will rail against me (the 'devil') as usual. But they will utter 'nary a word' (as they say) about either the raging battle between Good and Evil - the real battle as a matter of fact - or about the terrible acts of injustice perpetrated by the bad guys under my command under their very noses. And you shouldn't be surprised if, when they open their mouths to allude to or to 'condemn' the on-going acts of injustice, they do so very selectively, making sure that they did not offend the 'bad guys' they are in the habit of dining and wining with - the wining and dining they do while completely oblivious to the fact that Stephen and the apostles Peter and Paul died the way they did because they made it clear that they could not countenance duplicity and injustices committed, not just in the Church backyards, but in the whole wide world!

"To be assured of this result, the advice I, as Chief Bad Guy, give to my minions is that they not just be regular Church goers, but that they make a point of arriving early, and taking their seats in the front pews. How do you like that!

"It is because of this sort of malaise in the Church - this double dipping or desire to have the best of both worlds - that my troops and I have succeeded in getting 'bad guys' to enjoy the status they enjoy. It is because of the almost universal indifference to the wickedness that exists in the world on such a grand scale, and the lying and trickery that has characterized human relations since time immemorial and as a direct consequence of fall of man, that my troops and I have succeeded in getting service in those parts of government that are devoted to killing to be regarded by the citizenry as the most honorable, and the killing of humans by fellow humans in the course of conducting 'security operations' against so-called insurgents and terrorists, and in the course not of preventive but pre-emptive strikes against so-called rogue nations as patriotic service of the highest order - almost as if doing so was necessary to appease the gods!"

It was at that point, as Mjomba worked away on his thesis with the help of the Tempter and Evil One, that he thought Beelzebub, the Father of Death, had to be joking! It was just inconceivable that Satan could be mouthing the things Mjomba was hearing - or was it, perhaps, his own ears that were playing him a trick? It couldn't possibly be that the devil was saying the things he, Mjomba, was hearing!

To the extent that every human was created in the Image, and consequently could not be 'liquidated' as was generally thought, and also to the extent that every created human had one and only one 'tour of duty' on earth (or life to live) before heading off to his/her eternal reward or punishment, it was foolish for humans to even try to imagine that cutting short the life of a fellow human could serve as a solution to any problems they faced. Therefore, anyone who could mouth the things that were coming out of the Evil One's mouth deserved the label of fearless hero - someone who was ripe for canonization! It was, Mjomba told himself, inconceivable that the devil was giving expression to things that Mjomba had been longing to hear from the lips of churchmen in vain!

Mjomba was resigned to the fact that he was living in an unreal world as he settled back to hear out the Evil One. He knew very well that he was dealing with the Master Trickster, and did not stop wondering if the Prince of Darkness did not have a dirty trick behind those pious platitudes. But he had concluded that the only way to find out was to pretend that he himself was a fool, and to hear the rest of what Satan had to say. And so he continued to scribble as fast as he could so he wouldn't miss any of the points that the Evil Ghost was making.

"And we have, indeed, succeeded in making killing of humans by fellow humans on any pretext a great virtue so long as the victim is not 'one of their own' - almost as if doing so was necessary to appease the gods! And, last but not least, we have succeeded in promoting the idea that might is right, and that wrongs, real or perceived, must be settled here on earth and through the use of force; and that life after death is a myth! It is a hallmark of our success that, in spite of what humans say publicly, everyone, with the sole exception of the few hermits and monks who have consecrated themselves to lives of prayer and poverty and stay out of the limelight, accepts the proposition that the drive, fueled by human greed, to amass wealth using any means under the guise of promoting 'thrift'; the proposition that 'might makes right'; and also that things like slavery, imperialism, and the drive by those nations that have the wherewithal to try and realize their ambitions of global dominance are not only permissible in a world in which human selfishness shapes the destiny of nations, but a mark of greatness. It is what 'victory' or 'winning' is all about!

Meaning of being a "Winner"...

"And don't you misunderstand me now, and then say later that I lied to you. By winning, I do not mean achieving self-actualization and ending up in heaven. That is out of question. Also - and this is even more important - by bad guys I do not mean those so-called terrorists who languish in secret jails around the globe for years, in leg chains, but have never been convicted of any crime in any court of law and (I might add) with not a whimper from the rest of the world. By the way, by 'bad guys' I do not mean the Dalai Lama; or Pope John Paul whom we tried very hard but unsuccessfully to trip up, and whose clamor for a world in which there was peaceful co-existence among humans, just before he went to his eternal rest, really hurt our cause!

"And by 'bad guys', I definitely do not mean people like Mother Theresa who could never harm a fly! And by 'bad guys', I certainly do not mean those poor chaps who are conscripts in the military and don't even know what the heck they are supposed to be doing there or why!

"First of all, the Deliverer (if you refer to the 'Book') did not call upon the legions of angels to stop the priests and Pharisees, and the sleazy Pontius Pilate, or the double-talking King Herod Agrippa, who were conspiring to murder Him under the guise of ridding the world of a most dangerous 'terrorist'. In the same way, the Deliverer will not call upon His faithful angels to come to the rescue of His people. Secondly (and don't you now try to put a spin on the Deliverer's words like so many folks do when they make themselves the 'deciders' and decide at will to interpret figuratively words He intended to be taken literally and vice versa when it suits them), when Peter tried to cut down the trooper who was leading the assault on the Deliverer in the Garden of Gethsemane, he was told by the Deliverer in no uncertain terms that those who lived by the sword died by the sword!

"And, by the way (and I beg your pardon!), by bad guys I do not mean those poor chaps who languish on death row either! The Deliverer, who came to save sinners from eternal damnation, would without any doubt cause all those on death row to be freed. If the Deliverer believed in capital punishment, He wouldn't have come down from heaven to save any one. He would have left you humans to fight your wars and slaughter one another the way you have been doing since Cain murdered his brother Abel.

"And so, if you yourself do, and still think that you are a disciple of the Deliverer, think again! The 'good guys' who want to see those 'felons' liquidated in the gas chambers, on the electric chairs, under the guillotines, or by a hangman's noose, or in a volley of shots from the firing squads are obviously not the 'good guys' they claim to be after all!

"Just as the Deliverer ordered Peter to put away his sword, and then took the extraordinary step of re-attaching that mercenary's severed ear to make him whole again, the Deliverer would definitely advise any 'good guys' and 'good gals' out there who were ready to 'lend Him an ear' to 'put the gas chambers and the electric chairs and the guillotines and the hangmen and hangwomen's nooses, and the rifles and guns away'! That would, of course, cause a lot of people to become unemployed; and the Deliverer would consequently be as unpopular a figure as anyone who attempted to break into the jails to free the poor chaps on death row today!

"Was it any wonder then that the beginning of the end for the Deliverer on earth came when it did, namely shortly after He tricked the priests and Pharisees (who were using the harlot to trip him up) into drawing close to where he was scribbling their individual faults in the sand, and then watched them (with a faint smile on His sacred face) hasten away one by one in shame, until he was left alone with the woman they had wanted to see stoned to death?

"And if the Deliverer Himself was not ready to condemn those whom the priests and Pharisees wanted to see liquidated, who am I (Diabolos) to condemn them? I guess it is because I am the evilest of evil creatures that I can understand why the Deliverer rescued Mary Magdalene - yes, the same Mary Magdalene who is now revered as 'Saint Mary Magdalene' - from imminent death.

"As for that marshal who had lost his ear to the butcher's knife that Peter had up until that moment been carrying with him wherever he went, I wouldn't advise you to waste any money on a wager as to whether that mercenary who had come to arrest the Deliverer on fabricated charges learnt his lesson or not. I will tell you that the bloody fool didn't because, as a rule, soldiers of fortune who get hurt in battle simply become more vicious and merciless - and more greedy too! That is because the only thing they learn from such an eventuality is that the stakes in the deadly game of 'kill or be killed' in which they are involved by choice are so high; and that it is either you who dies or the mercenary who dies! And soldiers of fortune don't quit until they make a buck or two - or some semblance of fortune.

"Don't pray to that poor - and also unlucky - chap who was 'saved by the bell'. We have him safely here in Gehenna where he still pines for earthly riches, even though it is now two thousand years now since he crossed the gulf that separates the living from the dead.

Even if he had been able to sneak back on earth and to get some of the booty he is permanently yearning for, it would never be of any use to him in this blasted hell of a place! The fellow is totally insane - just like his pals back on earth who dream of amassing riches as soldiers of fortune…those mercenaries who see nothing wrong with depriving wives of their husbands and husbands of their wives, and children of their parents, and parents of their sons and daughters. They are so darned dumb they don't realize that they will never be able to take any of that stuff with them to the grave!

"I will also tell you as an aside that if you desist in claiming your pound of flesh as a result of the vindictiveness you feel, particularly if you have been a victim of one of those folks on death row, and yet know (as you now do) that the Church established by the Deliverer is against capital punishment, your sin now becomes heresy, and you stand condemned by your own stubborn refusal to forgive those who have wronged you. Know that you now are an ally and belong to our camp.

"And for those who play the part of executioner - the hangman who throws the hood over the poor chap's head and then puts the noose around his/her head, or a member of the firing squad who pulls the trigger, or Dr. Death who administers the lethal injection or who fastens the mask over the condemned person's head and connects it to the cylinder containing the deadly gas mixture, or the technician who keeps the guillotine or electric chair oiled and operates the switches on those murderous contractions - what will you say when you accost the victims of your illegal acts of murder? Illegal because no amount of 'legislation' can make an immoral act moral or right, let alone legal.

"It simply won't do, when you accost them on the other side of the gulf, to just say something like the following:

'Oh, my God…this can't be true! It is the Deliverer I executed over and over again! This is really terrible! It can't be true that it was the Deliverer the Americans and their allies were also trying to eliminate with the drones and their other adventures abroad! Oh, God! So it is actually the Word-become-flesh - true Man and true God - whom Caesar and other leaders of the so-called civilized societies pursued when they waged their colonial wars, and when they hunted the so-called barbarians, the Vietcong, the Mau Mau, Mandela, and other so-called terrorists and insurgents! So it was the Deliverer who was crucified all over again when the City of Bremen was carpet bombed, and Nagasaki and Hiroshima were nuked! So it is Him who is targeted when the strong and the proud inflict collective punishment on other humans in the name of Justice!

'Oh! Alright, alright…I now get it. As members of the Church Triumphant, the victims of injustice necessarily bear this close resemblance to the Deliverer who became the Second Adam, a true brother of the forsaken Children of Adam and Eve, and also the Bread of Angels upon taking up His human nature! Suffering patiently, they unknowingly complete in their flesh what might be lacking in their Deliverer's affliction for the sake of His Mystical Body or *Sancta Ecclesia*. And He, for His part, identifies Himself completely with all suffering humans without exception, in addition to sanctifying their suffering; and it is this that explains your so very close resemblance to Him! I now understand what He meant when He said before His ascension into heaven that, upon receiving the Holy Spirit and Comforter, His disciples and He Himself would be as one!

'And guess what! As head of the Church Militant, He Himself has to be a 'terrorist' who is permanently locked in battle with the Evil Ghost! Yah, with *Diabolus Malus*...the evilest of evil creatures! This is because all the so-called good guys on Planet Earth have been co-opted by Beelzebub, the Father of Death. If they were not his minions, they would disavow killing and murder in the name of national security. They would be on the side of the Prime Mover, and not on the side of Caesar Augustus!

'And if I myself had been a decent guy during my sojourn on earth - if I had been caring about others or something like that - this knowledge would have come to me automatically, and I would have escaped perdition by living accordingly! But - Oh my! Oh my! You and all the folks I see waiting in line to take their seats at the Divine Banquet just look so much like the Deliverer, I am ashamed to speak my thoughts! I am ashamed to tell you what was on my mind when I dispatched you and those other felons (that's what everyone on Death Row was referred to in 'Correct Speak'). But it is too late for me now, and it is precisely these thoughts that are going to convict me now!

'Until I saw you looking so much like Him just now, I was going to tell you without any feelings of remorse whatsoever that I had to do it, Pal. Look, I feel terrible shame saying it; but it was the only way I knew to put bread on the table! And to be frank with you, when I finished you off and certified you dead, all I was thinking about was my pay-check and the fact that I was helping to finally put away and rid the world for good of a felon! And also that it was cheaper for society to do that than to keep you behind bars in solitary confinement in a cage, and to feed and minister to you!

'And I certainly did not expect to bump into you again anywhere, and much less here of all places before the Son of Man and Judge. That was how faithless I was.

I did not even think of you as someone who belonged to the humankind I knew. As far as I was concerned, you were you and I was I. We were two different creatures who happened to belong to the same human stock or 'look alike'! I knew I was human. But, well - as far as you being also a brother whose destiny and mine were intertwined by virtue of being descended from the same Adam and Eve, and by virtue above all of being fashioned in the image of the Word, and also having the Son of Man as our brother - I just never gave that a thought, brother!

'But, above all, it didn't strike me at the time I was dispatching you that I was also dispatching the Deliverer who came down to earth to restore Life, and who took the sting out of 'Death' with His own death on the tree on Mt. Calvary. Look, I thought that even though you were human just like me, you belonged to the 'trash heap' all the same; and that you were trouble and good for nothing, and actually deserved to be put away - forever!

'Believe me, I was so distracted by all the hullabaloo about being like the Joneses next door, and by my dreams of also striking it rich some day, if someone had screamed in my ears as I was dispatching you that I was driving nails into the already bloodied hands and feet of the Deliverer, it would not have helped. I would not have batted an eye.

'Look, when I stared at your lifeless body after I had finished you off, and certified you dead, I remember saying to myself that there goes another one who will never be able to avenge my act of *legal* murder. Yes, deep inside me, I knew it was murder! Legal or illegal, it still *was* murder! Look, there is no circumstance in which it wouldn't have been murder if tables had been turned and *I* had been the one on that scaffolding.

'And, I mean - it could never be right to take the life of another creature who had the same features as you, breathed the same air as you, had the same organs as you, and relied on the same system as yours to function.

'The fact that a felon had made a mistake however horrendous could never make the vengeful act of killing right. After all everybody, and especially those humans who referred to themselves as 'The Deciders', made mistakes - everyone except, perhaps, the pope in the course of making his pronouncements *ex-cathedra*! And in the case of the successors to Peter, they themselves knew at least that it was not flesh and blood that *revealed* to them the things on which they made their *ex-cathedra* pronouncements, but the *Deliverer's Father* who was in heaven.

'As a Christian, my thoughts should have turned to the Deliverer at the time I was swinging the noose around your neck! That would have stopped me cold, and saved me from eternal damnation. But I did it; and the sight and smell of death eventually turned me into an atheist at the core.

'I stopped believing in life after death - or the resurrection! And, even though I continued going to church on Sundays (which I did to be like the other Joneses), privately I believed that while I myself was slated to also kick the bucket some day, the world would go on without end contrary to what preachers babbled about the end of the world being imminent. I had come to the conclusion that, even if life as we knew it on Planet Earth came to an abrupt end in a nuclear conflagration, new life forms would evolve from the ashes as, probably happened eons ago at the 'beginning of time' - or so I imagined. My theory of evolution did not include any role whatsoever for a Prime Mover.

'And then I occasionally dilly-dallied with the thought that I was saving my victims a miserable existence on earth by 'putting them to rest' permanently if prematurely. I wouldn't otherwise have been able to sleep. But the same thought was obviously on the minds of residents of the White House, the Kremlin, Number 10 Downing Street, Palais de l'Elysee, and other places like that in which people never tired of dreaming up schemes to destabilize other hostile governments, looking for excuses to impose economic embargoes on so-called rogue regimes, were always busy engineering regime changes in different parts of the world in the course of which hundreds of thousands became marked for death by simply being labeled insurgents or terrorists, and things of that sort.

'Oh, my God…I allowed myself to be used to deny other humans their bread-winner, and in a manner that was so completely unnatural!'"

Meaning of "Victory of Good over Evil"…

Mjomba knew by now that there was no creature that was more evil or dangerous than Beelzebub. It terrified him all the same to think that the Evil Ghost paid so much attention to the tiniest details. It also terrified Mjomba to think that, while it was Good that would eventually be victorious over Evil, there would obviously be wicked humans who would be eternally lost after freely choosing to be on the losing side. But those humans who chose to *believe in the Deliverer* would obviously be in line to celebrate the victory of Good over Evil with the now risen and enthroned Deliverer.

And so, victory of Good over Evil as Mjomba now understood it did not mean that humans who were created in the Image would not lose their souls eternally if they persisted in their wickedness. It seemed pretty clear that if they didn't repent, they would be damned (in much the same way angels who chose to join Lucifer in

275

his damnable act of rebellion against the Prime Mover became transformed into demons). The fact that the Evil Ghost and his fellow demons were ejected from heaven, and wicked humans are cast into hell upon their judgement, actually all spoke to the victory of Good over Evil.

Mjomba was by now completely resigned to the fact that there would be descendants of Adam and Eve who, by their own choosing, would end up as *human* demons in hell. But the one thing that was on Mjomba's mind as he continued work on his thesis was that Satan and his fellow demons apparently needed company bad - the company the Evil One would be denied if humans, who had found themselves initially barred from Paradise after the First Man and the First Woman fell from grace through their act of disobedience, one and all followed the Second Adam into heaven.

The big question that Mjomba did not try to answer was why the evil Satan and the other fallen angels should crave for company! Thinking about how humans who, unlike demons who had the capacity to be *evil*, only had the capacity to be *wicked* treated each other, Mjomba recoiled at the sort of things demons that had been convicted of evil things might be capable of doing to hapless humans who ended up in Gehenna with them. Whatever those things were, Mjomba positively did not want to know.

Regardless, it was clear that the only thing the devil, who knew that he had lost the battle the moment he himself was cast into Gehenna, looked to gain from his continuing efforts was some assurance that he would have the company of wicked humans for himself and his fellow demons. But because such an outcome would be dependent primarily on the exercise of human free will, and would additionally be a direct result of judgement passed on the wicked humans by the victorious Deliverer, the devil himself knew that it wouldn't amount to much of a victory on his part. If anything, such an outcome would only serve to confirm the victory of Good over Evil as unrepentant *homines iniqui* (wicked humans) joined the unrepentant and already damned *diaboli mali* (evil demons).

And that in turn left no doubt at all about the high regard that the Prime Mover placed on the angels and humans whom He willed into existence, and also His high expectations for them. He had fashioned them in His own Image and endowed them with the spiritual faculties of reason and free will thereby; and He had no intention whatsoever of going back on His Word and denying them the liberty to use those faculties as *they* deemed fit. But He also apparently had no intention of removing the consequences of *evil* acts on the part of pure spirits (*evil* because pure spirits by their nature were quite clear from the outset regarding the consequences of what they were contemplating doing). And He, of course, had no intention of removing the consequences of *wicked* actions on the part of humans either (*wicked* as opposed to *evil* because humans, while in a position to discern right from wrong, needed to cooperate with divine grace to stay out of trouble).

Wicked actions of humans were inexcusable all the same because, in spite of *knowing* that the wicked things they were contemplating doing were unconscionable, humans deliberately *chose* to carry out the wicked actions all the same, and to blind themselves to the fact that there *were* severe consequences for wicked actions. All of which reminded Mjomba, as he went on committing to paper the ideas he felt certain were originating from the Evil One, that the devil brought his extremely advanced grasp of the workings of the human mind to bear as he went about his evil work of tempting the descendants of Adam and Eve to ignore the clamor of their consciences, and hoped and even 'prayed' that they would succumb to his wiles and the temptations of the flesh.

Turkeys...

"Alright - let us get back to the meaning of 'bad guy'. Actually, by bad guys, I mean those 'turkeys' who, from time immemorial and doing everything to my script, have been imbued with a messianic mission to reshape the world in a way that fit their vision, and whose sense of mission goes hand in hand with a singular belief in the efficacy of force. Cain was the first such turkey who cleaned out a sixth of the world's population (when he murdered Abel, his own sibling) as he set about implementing his 'Cain Doctrine', but who, unfortunately for us, narrowly missed joining the party here in the Pit by repenting of his actions, handing Abel's widow all his ill-gotten property as compensation, and offering to be her servant for the remainder of his days on earth.

"But don't believe for one moment that all the turkeys who operate according to my script end up the same way. On the contrary...before going out to try and transform the world according to their designs, you should see the transformation that comes over them after I lead them up the mountain top, and especially after I show them the riches of the earth - the oil wells, gold mines, and even gold-domed palaces in faraway lands - that I typically guarantee will be theirs for the taking provided they go down on bended knee and worship me, the Evil One!

"And why do I refer to them as 'turkeys'? It is because they go away from the mountain top with a totally changed mind-set. According to that mind-set, a starving man, who raids a rich man's home with a toy gun in hopes of coming away with a morsel of food, deserves capital punishment - or, at the very minimum, to spend the rest of his life in solitary confinement - if it should happen that the rich man suddenly succumbs to a heart attack at the sight of the toy gun.

"But, according to that same mind-set, they themselves go on to inherit an eternal reward after they have 'legally' bribed their way into positions of power; diverted the nation's resources into the development of efficient 'military' machines instead of putting those resources to work for the *bonum commune*; and ensured, in the course of doing so, that those who helped them take over the Elysée Palace, Number 10 Downing Street, the Kremlin, State House or whatever were richly rewarded.

"And of course their reward in the next life, according to that mind-set, will be multiplied a hundred-fold if they embark on foreign adventures aimed at securing for their countries control of the world's scarce resources under the pretext of taking the gospel message to the ends of the earth.

"Now, talking about 'solitary confinement', it doesn't seem as if there is any limit to the savagery that humans are capable of. I can tell you that there may be many dungeons here in hell, but none of the demons or lost souls who keep me company are in solitary confinement. The idea behind our efforts to get folks like you to disavow your heavenly inheritance and end up here is so that we have company - period.

"Keeping a creature that was created in the Image in solitary confinement is the same as asking that creature to vacate its shell and return to the nothingness from which it originally came. It is the cruellest thing you can do to a human who belongs to humankind and who automatically needs company. It is only you humans who could dream up that sort of punishment, and it speaks volumes about the extent to which you humans can be wicked.

"But you humans can be very funny! How do humans who make their living as 'executioners' - humans whose job it is to put fellow humans to death (in the same way butchers slaughter animals whose meat is destined for the dinner table) - ever sleep? The same applies to prison warders who make a living keeping watch over fellow humans who are confined in cages or 'cells'.

"These are things we demons find very hard to understand, even though we were instrumental in getting Adam and Eve to start having ideas - ideas that eventually led them to choose the path of perdition. Even though I am the Father of Death, I still wilt at the thought that humans have no scruples making their living as professional killers, jail waders, or as mercenaries or 'soldiers' as you call them!

"I can understand a human being a professional hunter of wild animals. But it boggles my demonic mind to think that creatures that are fashioned in the Image can choose to become 'hired guns' who are dedicated to mowing down their fellow humans in fabricated 'just' wars.

"Can you imagine what would happen if we demons were spending our time waging wars on our own kind - or on you humans? First of all, since we have a much better handle on technology than you stupid humans, the Deliverer wouldn't have found anyone left on Planet Earth to redeem when He showed up. The whole operation would have been dirty and quick. But well, as it is, we here in the Underworld prefer to have you humans do the dirty work for us.

"I am the devil - the very 'embodiment of evil' if you

will - and I will tell you why humans who do these things to other humans are turkeys and screwed up! Because they listened to me, and genuinely believe that the commander-in-chief of a super power, who plans and executes what you call 'a pre-emptive strike' against a weakened and militarily defenseless but oil rich 'rogue state', for the purpose of assuring that his countrymen have unimpeded access to cheap sources of fuel and can continue to maintain their gas-guzzling lifestyles, deserves the title of statesman - and things like that!

"One has to be a complete nut - a complete idiot - to imagine that one can abet and/or be an accessory to things that amount to a culture of death - which is what projecting a super power's refurbished military's awe and shock generating power, without any regard to the inevitable loss of human lives resulting there from, or to the dire straits in which those who survive the onslaught will be left, amounts to - and get away with it with impunity! It is just ridiculous! The turkeys then get so comfy, they start imagining that they will end up, not here in the Pit with me, but in heaven or some place else in spite of their sordid actions!

"It is unbelievable! Some of these turkeys have even taken to claiming that the beatitudes have no basis in the *Sanctae Scripturae* (the Holy Scriptures); that humans who are poor in spirit or merciful are accursed, and that it is those humans who are greedy and merciless and filthily rich as a consequence who are blessed and will inherit the kingdom of heaven!

"The stupid fools ought to know that, after having their reward on earth, they cannot expect to find another reward waiting for them on the other side of the gulf which separates the living from the dead! Just what do they think I am - a Deliverer? Or, what do they think they are - demigods and goddesses? In any case, how can a pickpocket deserve to be incarcerated for years in a cell without the comforts that pets are provided while turkeys who level homes with other humans inside them get away scot-free - or with another reward on top of what they have already enjoyed!

"And certainly not when they also get into the circus business and begin putting up charades in world forums in which their victims are depicted as the 'bad guys' and they themselves as the 'good guys'! I mean - I would be a turkey myself if I suddenly woke up imagining - I really shouldn't say 'woke up' because we here in the Pit where 'there is no rest for the wicked' aren't even permitted a nap - that there was a mansion reserved for me in heaven even after all the havoc I have wrought! Or if I started telling you that I, Beelzebub, was the good guy and Michael the Archangel was the bad guy! I mean - a little realism is in order here. Because one is a bad guy doesn't mean that one shouldn't be realistic and retain a visage of common sense!

"You humans are a strange lot. You freely agree to be 'bad guys' and to associate with us; and you straight away start ruining our 'good' name! This is typical of you humans. The time is coming when we here in the Pit will decide that we've had enough of this - and you will not like what we will do to you to keep you folks in line a little bit! And you'd better take this warning seriously.

"But, above all, how on earth - and in this blighted hell - can these stupid fools imagine that we ourselves who did not spill a drop of blood at any time during the course of our rebellion against the Almighty One, and whose only mistake was to refuse to bow to His Mystic Majesty to demonstrate our fealty, deserved to be banished eternally from His face and cast in this Pit while they themselves will get a reward after wrecking so much havoc and causing so much mayhem?

These oafs should know that that kind of mischief deserves eternal damnation and a reserved spot in 'Gehenna' as you folks call it; and - fashioned in the image of His Mystic Majesty like the rest of us - there is no earthly excuse for not knowing that. And so, my solemn advice to these turkeys would be that, instead of jumping on the deck of some boat and declaring that combat operations have been wrapped up and are over in the wake of a 'successful' foray into some foreign lands, they should do so and instead say something like: 'Let combat operations against the almighty One begin!'

"Any way, fundamentalists to the core (by virtue of being imbued with a messianic sense of mission to transform the world and make it fit their vision) and also monotheists at heart because of their singular faith in the power of awe and shock generating force, regardless of their station in life (whether as generals, members of parliament, ambassadors, voters, students, merchants who are out to make a buck or two supplying ordinance needed by the 'security forces', journalists, pundits, or just housewives whose rumor mongering role often times ends up making all the difference in a by-election when a Senate seat is at stake), my minions, confident that I keep my word, will set out to dominate and conquer the world mafia-style and in complete disregard of the lessons of history.

No rest for the wicked...

"And you would be mistaken if you thought that we would stop there. No! We have learned never to rest on our laurels in this battle between Good and Evil. We have to build on our achievements; and we are doing that now by working through our surrogates *inside* the Roman Catholic Church to ensure that anyone who attempts to alert the world to our Evil Plan and the extent to which it is succeeding is ridiculed and ignored. That is why I for one am confident that your thesis on 'Original Virtue', even though it should in theory set off alarm bells under ordinary circumstances, and should even become required reading for seminarians and catechists, is going to be so much wasted effort; and it is, if anything, likely to end up serving our cause instead.

"There being no rest for the wicked (the situation is even worse for me and my fellow demons because we are *evil* and not merely wicked), we will accordingly never rest until the Roman Catholic Church, that Guardian of Divine Truth, looks like something that I, Beelzebub and Father of Lies, invented. We must work hard to ensure that the Pontiff of Rome (the shepherd of the Prime Mover's flock who stepped into the shoes of the fisherman) evokes images, not of faithful messenger of the Good News, but images of one who presides over apostasy and idolatry.

"Our success in getting humans, Catholics and non-Catholics alike, to turn their backs on the Holy Eucharist assures that humans are cut off from the Communion of Saints, and consequently remain isolated while the battle between Good and Evil rages on around them. Instead of spending all their time in perpetual adoration before the Blessed Sacrament in the company of angels and saints, we want them to be wasting their days on earth listening to empty orations that are intended to make them feel good from the pulpits.

"As for the separated brethren, we want them to be stuck with the phrase 'the Holy Book says this and the Holy Book says that', and to delude themselves that the Deliverer's words to His apostles that what they will hold bound on earth will be held bound in heaven, and what they will loosen on earth will be loosened in heaven, are completely meaningless. We want them to continue to believe that there is salvation outside the Church of Rome.

"In other words, we want them to believe that humans, helpless and incapable of freeing themselves from the bondage of sin, can rebuff the spiritual authority of the successors to the Deliverer's apostles - and along with it the Church's *magisterium* - and still bluff their way past St. Peter (who now stands guard at the Gates of Heaven) into Paradise. We want them to believe that they can scoff at the authority of the Church that was personally commissioned by the Deliverer and founded on a rock called Peter, and still have full access to the graces merited by the Deliverer, graces He has chosen to dispense through His *Ecclesia* (since defined by Church decree as 'the Mystical Body of the Deliverer').

"You know that I myself use the word 'delight' infrequently and reluctantly to describe my 'pleasure' at the sight of sick and aberrant humans. This is because a spiritual creature that opts for the path of rebellion is expected to damn well know what it is doing, and to take responsibility for its actions. Deviant spiritual creatures should at the very least be aware of their identity and even capitalize on it as they go about their deviant business.

"But humans have this tendency to feign ignorance, sometimes pretending that they are completely helpless and can do nothing about their spiritual fate, and that a human has to be 'predestined' for the Pit to end up here, or predestined for heaven. And it is fashionable for humans to blame me for the most God-awesome things they do to each other in the name of the Prime Mover! When it suits them, they try to act as if I have so much control over them, and that we are almost as one. If that were truly the case, it would at least constitute grounds for them to blame for *their* aberrant actions and ways.

"And then, as if that were not bad enough, it is also fashionable for them to play sissy and pretend that they are so helpless, it couldn't possibly be that to get to heaven they also needed to do anything other than *believing*! That they did not need to actually cooperate with the Holy Ghost and to turn out good works - which is another way of saying that they need to (indeed have to) keep the commandments (lead good lives)! It is as though they just want to be spirited into heaven!

"Now, because violence breeds violence, investing in an effective awe and shock generating military machine is just perfect. For one, this will cause other nations to do the same or even better if they can. But a great awe and shock generating military machine of course makes it possible to project awe and shock generating force in a truly awful and shocking way when the objective of the operations (conducted under the guise of spreading democracy, spreading the gospels of the Deliverer, or some other such tall tale) is to emulate Julius Caesar who dominated and conquered the known world and made history by effecting regime changes in Europe and North Africa only to be forgotten!

"When regime changes occur, or when efforts are made directly or through proxies to destabilize so-called roguish governments, lots and lots of folks (belonging to the same humankind) suffer and/or lose their lives in the process. What is even better, particularly where operations aimed at changing regimes succeed, invariably conditions are created in which counter forces led by the resistance (Mau Mau, Viet Cong, Insurgents, Terrorists, or what have you) will thrive, leading to the endless cycle of violence; and this happens to be Strategic Objective (SO) No. 2 in my Evil Plan.

"Demagogues that subjugate and murder their subjects in hopes of perpetuating their rule thereby, and those at the helm in imperialist regimes that believe in foreign conquests (or adventures abroad for the purpose of plundering the wealth that does not belong to them) may not know, but they invariably end up fighting with 'ghosts'! As a rule, the more 'terrorists' and 'insurgents' they liquidate, it is always the case that, instead of facing dwindling enemy numbers, they find themselves battling an ever-expanding enemy force.

"They start off stupidly oblivious to the fact that the victims of their murderous campaigns are fellow humans and kindred in the real sense (as both the killers and victims are the progeny of the same Adam and Eve). And then they conveniently forget that even though creatures fashioned in the Image do die the death, it is only a mirage as there is no way that the killers can pursue the souls of the folks whose lives get prematurely sniffed out into the afterlife. The terrorists and insurgents die but they don't die in the literal sense. But, as demagogues and imperialists discover soon enough (even though they are always too proud to admit it), providence has ordered things such that the more a populace is subjugated and terrorized, the greater the reason for the kinsfolk of those who fall in the battles for self-determination to join the ranks of the 'terrorists' and 'insurgents', validating the maxim *Vox Populi Vox Dei*!

"And because the demagogues and the imperialists won't face up to that truth, and will be chasing the elusive victories to the very end, it must indeed look, at least on the surface, as though the ghosts of the fallen terrorists and insurgents have not just returned, but have actually joined in the fray! And, since it will be the evil 'terrorists' and 'insurgents' who notch up gains in the battle of wills, it will also invariably appear as if I, Beelzebub, after taking the demagogues and the imperialists to the mountain tops to show them the

Kingdoms of the world and their splendor, and promising them a whale of a time, if they fell down and adored me, must suddenly have lost my mind and joined their enemies and a completely different cause - the cause of *Good*! That is how screwed up humans can be in their thinking…how could they possibly end up thinking that my troops and I are on the other side and working for cause of Good? We work for the damnation of all souls…dammit!

"My clients - the stupid fools - always invariably end up in a sea of misfortunes over which they cannot prevail even with the help of their allies! After they have done my bidding - after I have used them to wreak havoc and bring death and destruction to the Prime Mover's people - I dump them.

The devil's "concern" for the separated brethren…

"If you are wondering why I, Beelzebub and the Father of Lies of all people, am so concerned that the 'separated brothers and sisters' be able to get all the information they need to abandon their schisms and heresies and get back into fold, it is simply because I, Satan and the Father of Death, want the 'separated brothers and sisters' to end up here in the Pit with me - which you bet they will, because they now won't be able to cite any excuses for continuing to regale themselves as 'the saved ones' and for not taking up their crosses and following the Deliverer in the literal meaning of those words.

"While you humans play ball only in the way you know how to play ball, namely by subterfuge, lying, cheating, deceiving, defrauding your opponents and even imagining that you can exterminate, annihilate or destroy fellow humans for whom you have a dislike (an impossibility) at will, we demons play ball by being honest and forthright, and by doing everything we do above board.

"You should also note that we demons don't go around whining, griping, or telling tall tales about our opponents - and we are, above all, not hypocrites. I may be the Father of Death, but I swear I have never taken a life (except for the one occasion when I eliminated my rival in self-defense as I will explain a little later) or *directly* caused a spirit or a soul to become damned! That is not to say that stupid humans haven't killed at my suggestion and become damned.

"But you'd better take my word for it - I have never suggested to any fellow creature - angelic or human - that it (the creature) engage in anything that was evil without pointing out at the same time that the evil deed was going to imperil that spirit or soul! The only time I did not follow this *modus operandi* of alerting the creature to the dangers intrinsic in doing something that was evil was when I tried to ensnare the Deliverer Himself on the mountain. But then, who was I to try and lecture to the Word, the 'Logos', about right and wrong?

"And incidentally, when the separated brethren refuse to submit to the teaching authority of Holy Catholic Church (the Mystical Body of the Deliverer), that is exactly what they and their misguided 'pastors' attempt to do - to lecture to the Deliverer and also the Word about what is right and wrong!

The ultimate sport...

"To return to the topic at hand, namely our practice of the virtue of patience, getting humans who do not know who they are or where they are headed to make a mockery of the One, True, Holy and Catholic Church of the Deliverer, and then go on to use the name of the Prime Mover in vain are all key objectives of my Evil Plan! But an even more insidious objective of my Evil Plan is to get misguided humans to go out and kill and maim in the name of the Deliverer. And, you guess what! These stupid fools will be imagining that they are torturing, maiming, and crucifying the unbelievers and the unsaved when they are actually torturing, maiming, crucifying and killing the Deliverer in a repeat of what transpired on Mount Calvary two thousand years ago.

"I keep talking about the stupidity of humans, and worrying that I myself might be spilling out too many of my secrets. But I have since realized that when you tell humans to their face that they are stupid, instead of that making them more wizened, it makes them more stupid. Gosh, you humans are so interesting - and so stupid! And may be I should let you in on just this one other secret, as I have the feeling that revealing to you humans this particular secret will make you even more stupefied.

"You shouldn't be alarmed when I tell you that there are times when we demons stop everything, and do nothing but observe humans and their antics. You are at liberty to call us demons an indolent lot for doing that. We can expect humans to do that on impulse as they are wont to do. The fact is that we demons learn a great deal from that 'exercise'. And one of the things we have noticed in the course of observing humans was that, unlike us pure spirits, they enjoy playing games very much.

"You might be running ahead and thinking that I am going to discuss the fouling, cheating, and doping and what-not that is the order of the day when the Olympic Games and other sporting events get under way, not to mention the crooked refereeing that goes on!

"Now, games and sport are not things that we pure spirits are into very much. At least not as much as you humans who need to exercise to keep in physical and mental shape. Even though the idea of competitive sports has always seemed intriguing, this has remained one area in which we demons generally prefer to be on the sidelines as observers.

"It was obvious to us from the beginning that the sports and games humans had invented over the years had proved their value for rallying together citizens in different parts of the world, as nations vied with each other in an effort to prove that their citizenry included the greatest athletes, boxers, wrestlers and what-have-you in the world.

"It didn't take us very long, in short, to find a use for the idea of gaming. And guess what we did? I will be to the point. What we demons did after carefully observing humans at play was help the more enterprising ones devise what you might call the Ultimate Sport. And I am not talking about Chess, or Basket Ball, or Golf! Working with our minions, we got humans to add one more 'game' to the list of national sporting events. And we wanted this game to be the 'ultimate sporting event' that would rally humans in any given nation around that nation's leadership! And this game now attracts the biggest prize, namely veto power in world forums.

"In the new sport which has no season, and fortunately also no rules (apart from the so-called rules of engagements that each nation sets for itself at least in theory), nations vie with each other and endeavor to show which one among them can get its citizens the most to eat. Every nation on earth is now a participant in this sport, a sport in which the use of brute force by a nation to gain points is perfectly legitimate. Nations become 'winners' - and there are numerous winners given the size of the earth - by forcefully taking over control of the earth's scarce resources and placing anyone who attempts to resist on the 'Most Wanted Dead or Alive' lists.

"A feature of the 'War Game' is that powerful nations (those that have succeeded in overrunning and effectively colonizing or occupying weaker nations, and divesting them of their natural and other resources) are also supposed to pretend that they are ruled, not by murderous despots who are insensitive to the loss of human lives and will do whatever it takes to 'promote the national interests' of their own countries, but by 'liberators' and statesmen or stateswomen whose only desire is to liberate the oppressed and allow 'democracies' and things like that to flourish in the vanquished nations. In this sport, nations - especially those powerful nations that have the best chances of launching successfully 'missions', including pre-emptive strikes, on the weaker nations in the course of which they kill and plunder - devise their plans to raid other nations in secret.

"One tactic that is very popular with those nations that are members of the so-called 'G-8' - the top eight 'world powers' - is to use deception, out-right lies, and spin to depict a targeted nation as some sort of 'roguish state' that must needs be brought in line on some pretext, and then proceed to launch a pre-emptive strike aimed at seizing control over that nation's resources. Members of the G-8 are notorious for looking out for each other without any regard to natural justice, and are known to employ their veto powers in world forums to ensure that any and all resolutions passed promote their 'national security' and give them added advantages as they continue to participate in the War Sport with its far-reaching consequences.

"But it is not just the super powers that have everything going for them as a result of the War Sport. Anyone who accedes to power in the smaller nations, particularly nations in the so-called 'developing world', knows that the countries they lead are at the complete mercy of the powerful nations. The threat of hostile take-overs predisposes leaders of the small nations to bribes that come in various shapes, the most common one being the 'foreign aid' that is given 'with strings' attached. But, borrowing a leaf from the goings-on on the global stage, these leaders usually delight in the fact that, when applied at national level, the philosophy underlying the War Sport and, in particular, the rules of the War Sport, can be employed to justify a playing field that is less than level.

"One result of that is the widespread practice of operating 'safe houses' where political opponents are tortured, or alternatively detaining and incarcerating their opponents on the flimsiest excuses, in preparation for declaring themselves 'Presidents for Life'. And the Presidents for Life in-waiting also have the option of suggesting at any time that their opponents are 'terrorists' or allied with some terrorist group and to turn around and claim that as a good enough reason for putting them away permanently without any further ado or even a trial. Thus, whether it is played on the global stage or at the national level, the War Sport serves us here in the Underworld perfectly well.

"There is actually no time limit for this sport which had its kick-off on the day Cain started plotting to destroy his brother Abel. And, in what admittedly was a masterstroke on my part, I made sure that the Ultimate Sport received the boost as well as blessing from biblical figures like Moses, Joshua, and even the diminutive David who, while armed only with a sling, succeeded in taking down the towering Goliath and then using the Philistine's sword to cut off his head. As for Moses, he is on record as admonishing the Israelites that, upon entering the Land of Canaan, which God had promised to give them, they needed to destroy totally and utterly the Canaanites who were the current inhabitants. And, of course, Joshua famously prayed that the sun stand still for a whole day until the nation of Israel could take vengeance on its enemies, a prayer that was granted by Jehovah, according to the scriptures!

"Also, as you may have guessed, the referee is none other than me, Beelzebub! I will declare the ultimate winner(s) on the day the world will grind to a halt. In the meantime, the borders of nations (as you might have already noticed) will always keep changing as once powerful nations lose control over their resources, and new 'world powers' emerge and even take the lead, and as some nations vanish from the map altogether in this wonderful sport. Wonderful, you might have guessed, because this sport actually promotes my Evil Plan and results in the lives of lots and lots of humans being sniffed out prematurely - killed by their own kind - and also in lots and lots of suffering for those who survive the raids.

"A measure of my success can be gauged from the fact that the Holy Book is itself full of passages of holy warriors whose victory on the battlefield is almost always anticipated, the notable exception being the 'Warriors of Ephraim' who, even in their defeat, are described as 'mighty men of valor, famous throughout the house of their fathers'. The upshot of this is that the powers that be now put the build-up of military might as a priority above all else. In every nation on earth, it is the generals have first right of refusal when it comes to the allocation of resources. And, adding to the glamour of the 'War Sport' and as might be expected, it is the military industrial complexes that now spearhead technological advancement, and this encompasses every sphere of life.

"But that is not all. For these humans who are born with original sin, the temptation to use power wielded to 'prove' that might is always right has always proved just too great. True to form, nations have always been restive whenever they have found themselves militarily at some advantage over others; and it is not by accident that the evils of colonialism, imperialism and the other unsavory 'isms' traditionally are perpetrated by the so-called advanced nations, and not by the 'developing' nations. And the thievery and banditry usually continues even after former 'colonies', 'dependencies' or 'possessions' gain their 'independence'. This is evidenced by the fact that the newly independent states almost invariably never graduate from their status as 'banana republics' that are only capable of supplying much needed 'raw materials' to their former colonial masters. And that is if they do not become 'foreign enclaves' with control over their railroads, mining industries, and things of that sort remaining firmly in the hands of the former imperial masters.

"And, nowadays, whenever a member of the so-called G-8 (the cartel which is made up of the eight most powerful nations on earth and which is usually referred to as the 'Group of Eight') is unable to wrest the control of one or other scarce resource it deems important for the its 'national security' from some recalcitrant non-member nation that does not want to cooperate, an increasingly common tactic is to persuade members of the cartel to stand behind the super power that is lusting after that particular resource, and jointly impose embargoes, economic sanctions, and things of that sort against the 'rogue' nation.

"The objective of the embargoes and sanctions is to weaken the former dependency to the point where a 'coalition of the willing', made up of those members of the cartel whose interests relating to the scarce resource converge and other nations over which they already exercise control, can safely launch a pre-emptive strike for the purpose of gaining control over the coveted resource.

"I plant ideas regarding 'embargoes' and 'sanctions' in the minds of leaders of the G-8 because the effect of imposing an economic embargo is almost the same as mounting a pre-emptive strike which is, of course, always accompanied by 'collateral damage' in one shape or another. Because sanctions and embargoes are a virtual death warrant for society's most vulnerable, namely children and the aged, and do not attract condemnation from anti-war groups or the populace at large at least yet, they are the 'modern' way to go and a very 'clean' one at that. The decision makers, or 'deciders' as they usually prefer to call themselves, can still remain good bedfellows, albeit strange ones, with religious leaders and those other minions of mine who delight in presenting themselves to the world as 'defenders of morality', and continue to dine and wine with them.

"Because everything that is done on the world stage is driven by greed and the desire to be the dominant player, the cartel is usually something which the world's most powerful nations join if they find it convenient to do so. Cooperation between the cartel's members on any particular matter is therefore usually determined by national security considerations from the perspective of the individual members. The 'cooperation' thus frequently cloaks bitter rivalry and deep-seated rivalry and often also long-standing disagreements regarding the manner in which the world's wealth is supposed to be parcelled out amongst the world's most powerful nations.

"For my part, as the Father of Death and Prince of Darkness, I see everything working in my favor, because as history has shown, selfishness and lust for things of the world on such a grand scale inevitably leads to horrific global conflagrations in which the super powers are pitted against each other. I think of the sufferings that humans endured during the last two world wars in which primitive instruments of war, including two primitive nuclear devices, were employed. I sincerely cannot wait to see the third world war in which all combatant countries will all be nuclear-armed! And, yes, you guessed correctly. I, Diabolos, am just dying to see humans live through a hell of their own making!

"It should be clear by now that the War Sport above all helps us here in the Pit net the many souls for which robbery and murder - and lust for material things - are evils only when perpetrated against them but not by them. If you think I lie, just go take a look at the account the children of Fatima gave of hell after the Blessed Virgin allowed them a brief glimpse of this place! I can tell you that the losses Michael the Archangel sustains daily as a result of wars is incredible! Also, as you can see from watching the television news 'shows' on the major news networks, there is no day that passes without news of some new war breaking out. This is a direct result of nations agreeing to participate in this wondrous and truly 'deadly' game.

"Talking about news networks, you should know that these are really gossip and rumour mongering mills manned by professionals in rumour mongering, and so-called pundits or humans who are completely addicted to gossiping, and other humans who see nothing wrong with back-biting others. Of course, you humans are quite free to treat these rumour mongers as you have traditionally done by lending them your ears, and leaving at the mercy of their lies as a result.

"It is bad enough that these humans will pay other humans to appear before television cameras to give rehearsed accounts of supposed hot topical events when what they are trying to do is stay with a topic that appears to be helping them maintain the network's ratings in the public eye. But it is even worse when they have all these spinmeisters and spin doctors take turns in front of television cameras at prime time (that is the time the so-called 'working middle class' are back home after a supposedly 'hard day's work', and glued to their 'tellies' as is their custom) to act out their parts in soap operas that come complete with moving parts! And there is, as you would expect, nothing those spin doctors love to gossip and rumour monger about more than the drums or war, real of fictitious.

"Now, even though my own sins are many and grievous, pretending that I am a Michael Archangel or one of the guardian angels, who have the unenviable task of trying to keep humans safe from us here in the Pit and themselves, fortunately isn't one of them. It is the reason expressions like 'dissembling devil' and 'phony demon' are not part of the human lingo. But the same cannot be said of humans. And it is not surprising. Open almost any page of the New Testament, and you will find the Deliverer warning humans to shirk duplicity and hypocrisy in an effort to save them from themselves. And He couldn't have been more right!

"That said, nothing brings out the atrocious behavior of humans in this regard - the duplicity, hypocrisy, chicanery, make believe, and the penchant for falsehoods, prevarication, feigning, etc. - like the soap operas that are played out day in and day out on television screens. The parade of phony characters whose livelihood is derived from promoting what frequently exists only in the realm of fantasy is endless on any given day. And, of course, the distinction between what is news and what is not has long been lost sight of in the shuffle, with newscasters now accustomed to billing their programs as 'news shows', and competing with stand-up comics and the producers of 'reality shows'.

"News broadcasts, comic acts, soap operas, reality television are all packaged as 'shows' which they indeed are; and that includes weather forecasts and accounts of natural disasters if they happen to be 'newsworthy', a term used to denote the ability of a story to boost ratings of a news media outlet. Conversely, natural disasters that are not adjudged as being newsworthy in that sense, however major, frequently don't even get a mention. The newscasters and the producers of the 'news shows' might as well be living on another planet.

"You see, here in Gehenna, places like Hollywood, which cater to 'film stars' and their 'producers', comedians, pop artists, and what have you, are non-existent. We regard all those people as 'con artists', who might belong in heaven, but not here in the Pit. You know - we wouldn't have any use here for 'actors' and others who are into things of make-believe and fantasy. Even though we repudiated Him who is every creature's Life and Hope, and will continue to be locked in this interminable battle with Him through all eternity, all of us here in hell sorely miss the promise of everlasting happiness and joy which He represents. Now, that is reality, and we wouldn't be able to bury it under any amount of make believe and fantasy and self-delusion.

"We therefore don't get a lot of fun when we take a peep at those 'con artists' who just seem to love the bright lights and seem to have a yearning for attention. It strikes us as something very sad when one moment the 'con artists' are reporting with glee the devastation wrought by their country in a military putsch against some poor, indefensible 'rogue nation' (that has been deliberately weakened by years of 'economic embargoes' and political isolation but happens to be sitting on vast and greatly coveted natural resources), and the next moment they are commiserating with country men whose neighborhood might have been affected by a freak storm.

"What we enjoy 'viewing' on the television stations that humans operate are the original, uncensored images of hooded captives inside the torture chambers, and the chilling images of rockets slamming into residential buildings where 'insurgents' are holed up and reportedly using their wives and children as human shields. This is because it promotes our cause when human suffering is put on display. We get a kick out of seeing humans kill and maim their brother and sister humans for any reason whatsoever. But, above all, we enjoy being witnesses to humans signing their own 'spiritual death' warrants regardless of what they employ in creating what are effectively 'martyrs', whether they employ butchers' knives as Peter was on the verge of doing in the Garden of Gethsemane, improvised explosive device or IEDs so-called, or drones. And we love to listen to the rationalizations and lies that humans are in the habit of using to conceal the true motives behind their actions. And we dearly love to observe contests between the humongous, towering Goliaths of this world and the diminutive Davids. And, of course, even though we are the ones who underwrite the projects the Goliaths set out to implement at our behest, it would be disingenuous to suggest that we do not harbor secret sympathies for the poor Davids, who usually come out winners anyway - and naturally to our disgust!

"And look - we enjoy what is phony, contrived and hypocritical only to the extent that the culprits dig themselves in holes from which they likely won't be able to emerge - holes that become integral parts of the Pit in due course.

How to commit murder...

"And any way, you of course now understand what is meant by going out and maiming, subjecting other humans to shock and awe, torturing, crucifying and killing. For one, to be guilty of doing these things, one doesn't have to do them personally - one doesn't even have to be present when the 'treatment' is being administered to earn for oneself the sentence of eternal damnation and qualify to join our ranks here in the Pit.

"You can do these things through surrogates or, if you happen to be an emperor and commander-in-chief, by just inking an Imperial Order that authorizes a high-tech battleship to unleash its deadly load of missiles tipped with bunker bursting bombs into a city of some 'rogue state' as a lesson to other 'rogue states'. Or by inking an Imperial Order that authorizes the mass production and stock-piling in peace time of everything from chemical and biological agents, land mines, nuclear bombs, hydrogen bombs, tactical nukes, and all manner of armaments, including tank rounds that are coated with depleted uranium - and so on and so forth. Or an Imperial Order that causes vital supplies to a 'rogue state' to be cut off, resulting in the most vulnerable members of society in that rogue state dying off from a lack of medicines and the like!

"Or, as one of my clever demons aptly put it, you can commit Murder by Imperial Order or Veto; or Murder by Parliamentary or Congressional Resolution; or Murder by Act of Omission even, as was the case when the whole world stood by and just watched as the defenseless people belonging to one tribe on a Central African nation were decimated by members of a rival tribe while being sparred on by the official media! But one does not have to occupy the Palais de l'Elysée, the White House, the Kremlin, or Number 10 Downing Street, or a 'State House' or a place like that to maim, crucify and kill. The demon, actually one of those little devils we refer to as 'Midgets', had gone on to explain sarcastically that a senior citizen on disability could do it by simply exercising his/her right to vote, and casting the vote for a warmonger in a by-election that was called to fill a vacant seat in the Senate.

"The same demon had added as an aside that one did not have to be a demon to make the Church's work of evangelization difficult. One only needed to represent oneself as a 'Decider', and then persist in presenting to an audience of any size a particular interpretation of just one passage of the sacred scriptures that one knew was at variance with the 'will of the Deliverer' to fall foul of my wiles in that regard.

"That had prompted me to ask the Midget why he was leaving humans the 'loophole', and also whether he had stopped prizing the company of humans. The Midget had thereupon agreed that it was better - much better - to say 'Catechism of the Catholic Church' instead of 'will of the Deliverer', because that left humans less wiggle room and also guaranteed the demons lots of human company!

"And, perhaps because the Midget wanted to please me and see me smile for once (something I have never done since that Michael, aided by hosts of the faithful angels, overwhelmed me and my host of rebel angels, and then bundled us out of heaven and into this wretched place deep in the crust of the earth), he had added that whenever those who had broken with Rome spoke the words 'the bible says', because they used that phrase to imply that the only authority on earth which they recognized in spiritual matters was the 'Holy Book' alone (*sola scriptura*), they contradicted the Catechism of the Holy Catholic Church and, barring a special act of the

Prime Mover's mercy, were doomed!

"This Midget seemed to have a soft spot for humans, because here he was going out of his way to refer to a 'special' act of divine mercy! He understood what was on my mind when I did not smile. I was wishing that the Midget would have added that, if the separated brethren spoke those words (the bible says) well knowing that they were contradicting the Catechism of the *Sancta Ecclesia* (something they had now heard from the 'horse's mouth' as you humans say and could not go on pretending that it was something they didn't know!), following an act of betrayal of the Deliverer of that magnitude, until they recanted and confessed their sin, it didn't matter a hoot what other things they took it upon themselves to say or do, they could expect to be told by the Deliverer when they rushed Him upon 'kicking the bucket' that He did not know them - period!

"Like me, the Midget knew human nature very well, and also understood that after we in the Underworld did our thing, these 'good folks' typically stopped having any misgivings about 'sticking to their guns', busying themselves with all sorts of things that promised to make them feel justified and good about themselves, while turning a blind eye thenceforth to any information that even remotely suggested that they were in the wrong. For our part, we have to keep working to ensure that they continue treating the Catechism of the Catholic Church which sets out the teaching of the *Sancta Ecclesia* on subjects like indulgences so very clearly and unambiguously and can be downloaded from the Worldwide Web as if it is a banned work. And similarly papal encyclicals like *Indulgentiarum Doctrina* (the Apostolic Constitution on Indulgences) that was promulgated on 1 January 1967 by Saint Paul VI, Pope and Confessor and Patriarch of Rome and can also be downloaded from the Worldwide Web. They even had the gall to refer to the Holy, Catholic, and Apostolic Church, the Sancta Ecclesia, as Babylon the Great, the Mother of Prostitutes and Abominations of the Earth! Hee, hee hee, hoo, hoo, hoo, hak, hak, hak!

"We know that this is what they do even as they avow that submission to the will of the Deliverer go hand in hand with salvation and deliverance from sin. And they will continue merrily on their chosen path of protest and they take pot shots at the Pontiff of Rome and will attempt to ridicule the Church's dogmas even as they themselves admit that there can be only one true Church! They themselves belong to fringe, breakaway churches or denominations; but they still conveniently refer to similar break-away churches, but not to their own denomination, as 'cults'.

"The Midget and I know each and everything that is going on. But you yourself must know that the separated brethren make matters worse when, in order to support the heretical positions they have taken on different dogmas of the Church, they invariably find themselves referring to the 'Early Church' and to what the 'Early Church fathers' taught; but, for reasons best known to themselves, they balk at making the connection that what they refer to as the 'Early Church' and the 'Church of Rome' from which they have excluded themselves are one and the same thing!

"And then, there are those among them who do not see any use for the early Church or the fathers of the nascent Church. This is because the 'gospel' they preach pertains, not to the 'Crucified and Risen Deliverer', but to earthly riches! But guess what - all the humans who are in this business of 'preaching the gospel' say that the Prime Mover - the same Prime Mover who created everything out of nothing and sent His Only Begotten Son into the world so that those who would believe in Him would be saved - felt constrained enough to give them personal revelations mandating them to go out into the fields that were ripe for the harvest and preach the gospel!

"The fields are indeed ripe for the harvest, but woe upon those in wolves clothing who pass themselves off as the Lord's messengers when they are not even prepared to accept the Gospel for themselves as it is taught by Peter's successors! But the Deliverer also meant business when He rebuked Peter, and even used the 'S' word (you should know by now that 'S' stands for 'Satan'), when the fisherman (who would end up as the Pontiff of Rome and suffer martyrdom there for his pains) was trying to prevent Him from going to Jerusalem and to His certain death at the hands of His enemies. Peter was trying to stop Him from descending on Jerusalem for the purpose of launching the New Testament.

"But precisely because the fields were ripe for the harvest, the activity in the temple in Jerusalem, albeit under the Old Testament, had risen sharply. Just as now, the 'blessings' from operating a 'ministry' at that time were quite handsome. What the Deliverer did when He saw the commerce that was being conducted inside the temple is history that has long been forgotten by humans. It wouldn't make any sense any way in any case for a 'modern' to abandon a highly successful ecclesiastical enterprise, stop spreading heresies, and live as a poor Catholic convert just because the Holy Father demands it on behalf of the Deliverer.

"In the meantime, the errors of those who have separated themselves from the Church - errors that started out as disenchantment with alleged abuses by Church functionaries of indulgences and the Church's position on the indissolubility of Holy matrimony, and then blossomed into disenchantment with the doctrine of papal supremacy, are no longer confined to those original issues of contention. With the passage of time, those errors have multiplied and now encompass the interpretation of each and every single verse of the books of the Old and New Testaments.

"Actually, the scenario I presented to the Deliverer when I tempted Him in the desert and a short while later on the mountain-top - that he should show-case His divine power by changing stones into food, and also that He should abandon His mission and instead accept from me dominion over the length and breadth of the earth and become emperor of the world's only super-hyper-com-mega power and which he rejected outright - is what many of the separated brethren have come to embrace. From the look of it, they desperately want the Deliverer to go back on His word to Peter and the other apostles whom He gave the commission to go and preach the Gospel of Christ crucified to the ends of the world, and 'bless' their scheme under which someone becomes instantly 'saved' by reciting the 'Sinner's Prayer'! To abandon that scheme is not easy because saving face and, in many cases, also giving up livelihoods is hard. Juxtapose that against the Deliverer's advice in Matthew 19:21-29 or in Luke 14:26-27, and you get the idea. Going back on His word to His apostles would be like using His power to turn stones into bread. Look, the Deliverer's message so far seems eerily similar to the one he had for some folks of His time (and I am adding this one because I absolutely do not want the bible believers or separated brethren or what have you to be able to give the excuse that they did not know when their times to face the Judge comes): 'Then began he to upbraid the cities wherein were done the most of his miracles, for that they had not done penance. Woe thee, Corozain, woe to thee,

Bethsaida: for if in Tyre and Sidon had been wrought the miracles that have been wrought in you, they had long ago done penance in sackcloth and ashes. But I say unto you, it shall be more tolerable for Tyre and Sidon in the day of judgment, than for you. And thou Capharnaum, shalt thou be exalted up to heaven? thou shalt go down even unto hell. For if in Sodom had been wrought the miracles that have been wrought in thee, perhaps it had remained unto this day. But I say unto you, that it shall be more tolerable for the land of Sodom in the day of judgment than for thee.' (Matthew 11:20-24) You can, of course, go on dreaming that it is by accident that folks take time to look for biblical passages that appear to support their hypothesis that the Deliverer came so that everyone would enjoy the good life in this world; but the reality is completely different. Ha, ha, ha, ha, hee, hee, hee, hee!

"Whereas the Deliverer tasked the surviving apostles with going out into the world and spreading the message of the *Crucified* and *Risen* Deliverer, the reformers have replaced that message with one that focuses on the "Glory of the Deliverer", and bypasses and even frowns on the cross. The Deliverer knew that sinful and sinning humans would not just be meddling in the interpretation of the Sacred Scriptures, but would also be interfering in the Church's exercise of its teaching *magisterium*; and He said so in so many words.

"The harm this meddling and interference does to the Church's mission of saving souls is increased in proportion to the fervor and zeal with which the errors, which are themselves now unbounded in scope, are propagated. But, of course, fervor and zeal, which more often than not betray the tendency to be wilful and headstrong, are one thing; and obedience, meekness and forbearance, which humans typically regard as capitulation and foolishness, are something else altogether. The bottom line is that humans who go out on a limb and contradict those who are called to step into the shoes of the apostles do a great disservice to the Church and to themselves.

"That situation is compounded by individuals in the Church, and members of the Church's clergy in particular, who are shy about confronting the misguided 'reformers' head on and telling them to their face that they are spreading heresies. Forgetful of the fact that the Deliverer detests apathy, lukewarmness and indifference, all they are interested in is seeing a semblance of harmony in 'Christendom' so-called maintained. We here in the Underworld know these things too well, and don't waste any time moving to exploit the situation. And as the goddamned devil who is always on the look-out for ways to derail the divine plan, I couldn't ask for more!

"After paying the sort of price He paid when He launched the New Testament from atop of Mt. Calvary, the Deliverer cannot be expected to treat the new crop of 'temple merchants' with kid gloves when the time comes to deal with them. As the '*caput lupinum*' (or 'outlawed felon') in this business, I know from experience that the Deliverer really meant business when He chased those merchants out of the temple. (John 2:13-16, Matthew 21:12-16, Mark 11:15-16, Mark 12:40, Luke 20:47 and Luke 21:2) I say, it will be really ugly this time around!

"Look, the Catechism of the Catholic Church is very clear, and it states: 'The task of giving an authentic interpretation of the Word of God, whether in its written form or in the form of Tradition, has been entrusted to the living, teaching office of the Church alone. Its authority in this matter is exercised in the name of Jesus Christ. This means that the task of interpretation has been entrusted to the bishops in communion with the successor of Peter, the Bishop of Rome. Yet this Magisterium is not superior to the Word of God, but is its servant. It teaches only what has been handed on to it. At the divine command and with the help of the Holy Spirit, it listens to this devotedly, guards it with dedication, and expounds it faithfully. All that it proposes for belief as being divinely revealed is drawn from this single deposit of faith.' (CCC 85-86)

"And, pursuant to that 'Magisterium' (or Teaching Authority), the First Vatican Council (1869–70), which was also called Vatican I and constituted the 20th ecumenical council of the Roman Catholic Church, was convoked by Pope Blessed Pius IX (13 May 1792 – 7 February 1878). The pope, who would enjoy the longest pontificate in papal history after that of St. Peter, had succeeded Pope Gregory XVI (1831–46), the pope whose papal Bull, *In Supremo Apostolatus*, resoundingly denounced both the slave trade and the continuance of the institution of slavery. [Tradition has it that St. Peter, who along with the other ten apostles, spent time with the risen Deliverer over a period of forty days during which, in the words of Pope Leo the Great, 'great sacramental mysteries were confirmed and great truths revealed…the fear of death with all its horrors was taken away, and the immortality of both body and soul affirmed' reigned for thirty-seven years compared to Pope Blessed Pius IX's reign of just under thirty-two years.]

Vatican I issued *Pastor Aeternus* (Eternal Shepherd), the First Dogmatic Constitution on the Church of Christ, on July 18, 1870. *Pastor Aeternus* defined the apostolic primacy conferred on Peter, the perpetuity of the Petrine Primacy in the Roman pontiffs, the meaning and power of the papal primacy, and Papal infallibility – the infallible teaching authority (*magisterium*) of the Pope.

"Discussing papal infallibility, that Council stated: 'We teach and define that it is a dogma Divinely revealed that the Roman pontiff when he speaks ex cathedra, that is when in discharge of the office of pastor and doctor of all Christians, by virtue of his supreme Apostolic authority, he defines a doctrine regarding faith or morals to be held by the universal Church, by the Divine assistance promised to him in Blessed Peter, is possessed of that infallibility with which the Divine Redeemer willed that his Church should be endowed in defining doctrine regarding faith or morals, and that therefore such definitions of the Roman pontiff are of themselves and not from the consent of the Church irreformable.' (Vatican Council, Sess. IV, Const. de Ecclesiâ Christi, c. iv)

"Of course, as you can imagine, the work of that Council wasn't exactly the sort of thing that could rest well with me (Mephistopheles). It wasn't by accident that Vatican I was interrupted by the Franco-Prussian War which also saw the annexation by Italy of the Papal States. The Council not only did not resume, but was never even officially closed! Hee, hee, hee, hee!

"But then Pope Saint Paul VI came along and, on 21 November 1964, promulgated *Lumen Gentium* (Light for the Nations), the 'Dogmatic Constitution on the Church'. One of the principal documents of the Second Vatican Council, *Lumen Gentium* discusses the authority, identity, and the mission of the *Sancta Ecclesia*, as well as the duty of the faithful. *Lumen Gentium* should ideally be read in its entirety; and the following excerpts are offered with that proviso (and also so that bible believers, non-bible believers, Catholics, non-Catholics - the whole shoot - are denied the excuse that they were not forewarned):

'This Sacred Council, following closely in the footsteps of the First Vatican Council, with that Council teaches and declares that Jesus Christ, the eternal Shepherd, established His holy Church, having sent forth the apostles as He Himself had been sent by the Father; and He willed that their successors, namely the bishops, should be shepherds in His Church even to the consummation of the world. And in order that the episcopate itself might be one and undivided, *He placed Blessed Peter over the other apostles, and instituted in him a permanent and visible source and foundation of unity of faith and communion.* And all this teaching about the institution, the perpetuity, the meaning and reason for the sacred primacy of the Roman Pontiff and of his infallible magisterium, this Sacred Council again proposes to be firmly believed by all the faithful. Continuing in that same undertaking, this Council is resolved to declare and proclaim before all men the doctrine concerning bishops, the successors of the apostles, who together with the successor of Peter, the Vicar of Christ, the visible Head of the whole Church, govern the house of the living God...

'And the Sacred Council teaches that by Episcopal consecration the fullness of the sacrament of Orders is conferred, that fullness of power, namely, which both in the Church's liturgical practice and in the language of the Fathers of the Church is called the high priesthood, the supreme power of the sacred ministry...

'Just as in the Gospel, the Lord so disposing, St. Peter and the other apostles constitute one apostolic college, so in a similar way the Roman Pontiff, the successor of Peter, and the bishops, the successors of the apostles, are joined together...

'But the college or body of bishops has no authority unless it is understood together with the Roman Pontiff, the successor of Peter as its head. The pope's power of primacy over all, both pastors and faithful, remains whole and intact. In virtue of his office, that is as Vicar of Christ and pastor of the whole Church, the Roman Pontiff has full, supreme and universal power over the Church...

'The Roman Pontiff, as the successor of Peter, is the perpetual and visible principle and foundation of unity of both the bishops and of the faithful...

'*Bishops, as successors of the apostles, receive from the Lord, to whom was given all power in heaven and on earth, the mission to teach all nations and to preach the Gospel to every creature, so that all men may attain to salvation by faith, baptism and the fulfilment of the commandments...*

'The canonical mission of bishops can come about by legitimate customs that have not been revoked by the supreme and universal authority of the Church, or by laws made or recognized be that the authority, or directly through the successor of Peter himself; and if the latter refuses or denies apostolic communion, such bishops cannot assume any office...

'Bishops, teaching in communion with the Roman Pontiff, are to be respected by all as witnesses to divine and Catholic truth. In matters of faith and morals, the bishops speak in the name of Christ and the faithful are to accept their teaching and adhere to it with a religious assent. This religious submission of mind and will must be shown in a special way to the authentic magisterium of the Roman Pontiff, even when he is not speaking ex cathedra; that is, it must be shown in such a way that his supreme magisterium is acknowledged with reverence, the judgments made by him are sincerely adhered to, according to his manifest mind and will...

'Although the individual bishops do not enjoy the prerogative of infallibility, they nevertheless proclaim Christ's doctrine infallibly whenever, even though dispersed through the world, but still maintaining the bond of communion among themselves and with the successor of Peter, and authentically teaching matters of faith and morals, they are in agreement on one position as definitively to be held. This is even more clearly verified when, gathered together in an ecumenical council, they are teachers and judges of faith and morals for the universal Church, whose definitions must be adhered to with the submission of faith.

'And this infallibility with which the Divine Redeemer willed His Church to be endowed in defining doctrine of faith and morals, extends as far as the deposit of Revelation extends, which must be religiously guarded and faithfully expounded. And this is the infallibility which the Roman Pontiff, the head of the college of bishops, enjoys in virtue of his office, when, as the supreme shepherd and teacher of all the faithful, who confirms his brethren in their faith, by a definitive act he proclaims a doctrine of faith or morals. And therefore his definitions, of themselves, and not from the consent of the Church, are justly styled irreformable, since they are pronounced with the assistance of the Holy Spirit, promised to him in blessed Peter, and therefore they need no approval of others, nor do they allow an appeal to any other judgment. For then the Roman Pontiff is not pronouncing judgment as a private person, but as the supreme teacher of the universal Church, in whom the charism of infallibility of the Church itself is individually present, he is expounding or defending a doctrine of Catholic faith. The infallibility promised to the Church resides also in the body of Bishops, when that body exercises the supreme magisterium with the successor of Peter…

'Christ, whom the Father has sanctified and sent into the world, has through His apostles, made their successors, the bishops, partakers of His consecration and His mission. They have legitimately handed on to different individuals in the Church various degrees of participation in this ministry. Thus the divinely

313

established ecclesiastical ministry is exercised on different levels by those who from antiquity have been called bishops, priests and deacons. *Priests, although they do not possess the highest degree of the priesthood, and although they are dependent on the bishops in the exercise of their power, nevertheless they are united with the bishops in sacerdotal dignity.* By the power of the sacrament of Orders, in the image of Christ the eternal high Priest, they are consecrated to preach the Gospel and shepherd the faithful and to celebrate divine worship, so that they are true priests of the New Testament...

'Christ, the great Prophet, who proclaimed the Kingdom of His Father both by the testimony of His life and the power of His words, continually fulfills His prophetic office until the complete manifestation of glory. He does this not only through the hierarchy who teach in His name and with His authority, but also through the laity whom He made His witnesses and to whom He gave understanding of the faith (*sensu fidei*) and an attractiveness in speech so that the power of the Gospel might shine forth in their daily social and family life...

'Each individual layman must stand before the world as a witness to the resurrection and life of the Lord Jesus and a symbol of the living God. *All the laity as a community and each one according to his ability must nourish the world with spiritual fruits.* They must diffuse in the world that spirit which animates the poor, the meek, the peace makers—whom the Lord in the Gospel proclaimed as blessed. In a word, "Christians must be to the world what the soul is to the body"...

'Thus it is evident to everyone, that all the faithful of Christ of whatever rank or status, are called to the fullness of the Christian life and to the perfection of charity; by this holiness as such a more human manner of living is promoted in this earthly society. In order that the faithful may reach this perfection, they must use their strength accordingly as they have received it, as a gift from Christ. They must follow in His footsteps and conform themselves to His image seeking the will of the Father in all things. They must devote themselves with all their being to the glory of God and the service of their neighbor. In this way, the holiness of the People of God will grow into an abundant harvest of good, as is admirably shown by the life of so many saints in Church history…'

"Actually, with humans prepared to compromise on such important tenets of their faith when it suits them (instead of undertaking a serious and conscientious study of the important elements of their faith before deciding to take on the Church), our job of tempting them and trying to sway them from the path of righteousness is decidedly less fun. You see, we here in the Underworld like to be challenged and 'to earn our keep'. But you humans want to have everything free; and that is why there is so much thievery, cheating and lying on this Planet Earth. And that is also why it surprises us that there are no human devils, and that it is just us!

"Any way, when humans start to challenge the Church's teaching *magisterium*, you cannot start to imagine how much I, as the Chief Tempter and Evil One, love it! You see, I myself would start dreaming about being 'delivered' if humans were able to cheerfully and happily contradict the Deliverer - and those He sent to hand deliver His invitations to the heavenly banquet - and get away with it scot-free!

"The Midget was clearly reading my mind and, to show that he was in full agreement, he chipped in that it was his own 'prayer' as well that when those 'good folks' approached the Deliverer and Judge on their day of judgement, the Deliverer would, with a wave of His hand, refuse to acknowledge them saying that He didn't know them at all. The Midget even added that a similar fate awaited our guest (Mjomba) if, after writing the thesis with their help, Mjomba spurned their advice and lived according to his own devices. He said in conclusion that he himself couldn't care less if that Mjomba 'friend of mine' lost his soul too and joined the party in Gehenna!

"I let the Midget know that this was not good enough for me, and I will tell you why. Humans put themselves in danger of losing their souls and becoming damned when they start believing that they are justified - period. They are poor forsaken children of Adam and Eve - Damn! And, how can they stand there and declare unashamedly that they are justified when they are ready to avow that they are better than other humans? Or when, in the same breath, they affirm their faith in things like capital punishment and things like that instead of turning the other cheek, and when they are dying to see their enemies destroyed and liquidated? When their faith, in other words, is in the power of brutal force, and its use in avenging perceive wrongs!

"Also, before declaring themselves 'justified', humans should first recall what the Son of Man Himself said about being 'good', namely that only the Prime Mover was good! They should also remind themselves about what the Deliverer said in His parables on justification, and specifically what He said about the Pharisee who was ranting about being better than the tax collector. According to the Deliverer, humans of that mold had already received their reward! The Deliverer had made it crystal clear from the start that it would not do for humans to just follow Him around because He was multiplying loaves of bread, healing the sick, and performing other wonders.

"And so, if humans who had been baptized into the

Church remained followers of the Deliverer only in name and did not take the next step of surrendering themselves body and soul to the Holy Ghost through self-abnegation, and consequently were not allowing themselves to be led by the Spirit where they on their own would never go, there was no difference at all between them and those Israelites who had been flocking to see the Messiah because of the wonders He performed, and then lined Jerusalem's Main Street to welcome Him into that occupied city, only to show their true colors and join the chorus that chanted 'Crucify Him, Crucify Him' not long after!

"And then, there are those folks who rant about 'sola scriptura' and 'sola fide' being their sole guiding principles in life. But those same folks, who have no hesitation in flatly contradicting the Church in that regard, are also quick to claim that they and they alone are saluti (saved)! Well, and don't they trip themselves up when they assert that they are saved and justified, and are good?

"I am Diabolos, and I will say here and now that this is the problem with the adherents of all 'religions' regardless of how they were started. So long as the adherents of any religion believe that they are better than other members of the human race, that is all that matters for us here in the Pit. You see, we happen to know that truly heroic souls see every human as the temple of the Prime Mover; and they see themselves as the least worthy in the divine presence. And thanks to the hard work of my buddies here in the Pit, humans who are like that are decidedly a rarity.

"And then, the common thread in the lives of all such humans is that their selflessness permits the Holy Ghost to lead them where on their own they would not trample! (John 16:13, John 21:18 and Luke 21:18)

317

Consequently, to the extent humans have failed to surrender themselves to the promptings of the Holy Ghost in that regard, to that extent it is I, the Evil Ghost, who calls the shots. And it does not take rocket science to arrive at the conclusion that to the extent humans are not imbued with the Holy Ghost, to that extent they have what the evangelist aptly referred to as the 'mark of the beast' on their foreheads, the mark that distinguishes the elect, or members of the Church Triumphant, from the rest when the time comes for humans to 'give up their own ghosts'!

"Now, one clever human said that the human mind was a terrible thing to waste! Well, we here in the Underworld could never afford to waste our minds. But there is one other thing that we could say about ourselves here in the Pit. Often, we would really like to savor something very much, but we just can't delight in it or celebrate in the ordinary sense of that word, because we ourselves are already condemned and in hell. You can therefore understand when I say that we really can't savor the fact that it is us here in the Underworld, and not the separated brethren, who are winning the day. But then that is the frustration that we have to live with as *angeli diaboli* (fallen angels). But I myself as Demon in Chief or Diabolos do not sympathize with my fellow demons either for the fact that they have to live with these frustrations. We ourselves here in the Underworld individually chose to rebel against the Prime Mover, well-knowing that we would be in for something really nasty if we failed in achieving our objectives in the rebellion against Good; and we all of us now deserve to suffer these frustrations - and more.

"It is a very good thing that humans (who do not take advantage of the opportunities they get to search for and find the Truth (which is not at all the same as

318

searching for and finding easy, delectable and ironclad solutions), and then live according to it end up in the same exact situation as ourselves. And they should not expect to receive any sympathy from us either, since it is their own choice to join our rebellion; and not my choice or that of my fellow demons! I just wish I could transform my disdain for these humans into something that resembles my original dream of being the Ruler of Heaven and Earth! Regardless, it was with great relish that I turned to the Midget and let him know that he was brilliant and so correct about the separated brethren being 'doomed' because of their apostasy!

"But, to get back to the subject of committing murder, if you are not a commander-in-chief, you can still maim, crucify and kill just as efficiently by lending support to regimes that believe in expansionism, militarism, and the projection of shock and awe generating force, or regimes that place blind faith in the use of brutal force to resolve conflicts. These are all 'mortal sins' that leave a black indelible mark on the soul, and whose perpetrators stand condemned, and eventually end up eternally damned and doomed just like us demons.

"I, myself, as the Father of Death, hail demagogues and tyrants for remaining firm in their belief that 'might makes right'; for whole-heartedly embracing the 'mafia complex'; and for doing things 'mafia style' as they seek to maintain control over the earth's scarce resources. Indeed, thanks to Cain and other demagogues who have walked the earth, 'international affairs' is now run very much like the mafia. It behoves everyone to fall in line, to obey and to pay protection money. You don't, you go! And that is all there is to it. Tyrants and demagogues long ago saw the benefits of that 'mafia style' of doing things, and adapted it to international relations wholesale, christening it 'diplomacy'!

"And so today, the axiom of the foreign policies of any nation that commands enough clout to get other nations to regard it as a 'major power' is always that it must control the world's scarce resources, including energy sources, shipping routes, and the like; and it must not brook defiance from any quarter. It is consequently bad enough for any nation to try and brush off the 'super power' by insisting on being 'independent' or 'non-aligned'. It becomes many times worse and totally unacceptable if the non-compliant nation (which automatically gets the label 'rogue nation' for its obstinacy in refusing to buckle and determination to exert its independence) also happens to have lots of those scarce resources in its backyard.

"In 'guarding' his turf, a mafia don is a law unto himself. And anything short of total capitulation will spell disaster for anyone whose assets are eyed by the mafia don. The word 'boundary' is not in the lexicon of Mafiosi. This is how places with names like 'America', 'British India', 'Australia', 'Belgian Congo', 'Rhodesia', 'Ivory Coast', 'Gold Coast', 'Mozambique', 'Philippines', and 'Quebec' found their way on the map in recent times. Like the mafia, major players on the international scene have always to be ruthless in order to get their way, for the simple reason that, at the time they initiate their moves and make for the grab, the resources over which they seek to gain control will already be under the control of their aboriginal owners who would be irresponsible to let go of them just like that.

"The predator nations usually find it advantageous to create instability in those parts of the world where the scarce resources are located; because they can then turn around, and pretend to be entering the foray to 'protect' the scarce resources from 'irresponsible reactionary types' who will never appreciate their value. The same

320

reason is used to forcibly wrench control of the coveted resources from the rightful owners. It goes without saying that any moves on the part of any nation aimed at guarding its territory from attack must be viewed as hostile in the extreme and by the same token unacceptable.

"As they pursue their dreams of transforming themselves into masters of the world, the megalomaniacs as a rule place all their absolute and total faith, not in the Almighty One (whom they aim to emulate), but in the weapons they and their enforcers use to put opponents, actual as well as potential, out of circulation. Cain, who started it all with his preposterous claim that his brother Abel (who couldn't harm a fly) was a danger to his 'empire' and a 'terrorist' who had to be liquidated at all costs, put his faith in the martial arts and specifically in the 'headlock', which the spiteful and heartless Cain did not hesitate to use to put away the kind and gentle Abel when the opportunity to do so came along. Other weapons in which megalomaniacs have placed their blind and unfaltering faith at various times in human history have ranged from poisoned arrows discharge from bows, sharpened swords and spears, muskets and cannons, to atom bombs and bunker busting munitions.

"Nuclear-tipped guided missiles and hypersonic rockets, used in conjunction with orbiting communications satellites, are the weapons of choice of 'modern times'. But I can predict that even these will soon become outdated and unnecessarily expensive, as deadly viruses, nerve gases and poisonous chemical discharged from spray guns the size of a fountain pen prove much more effective and efficient in catching entire communities unawares and dispatching them, and in degrading the offensive and defensive capabilities of targeted 'rogue' states. Unfortunately for the greedy and expansionist megalomaniacs, that same technology will be just as easily available to those who are the targets of regime changes and military occupations.

"But, for now, it is the citizens of the targeted nations who find themselves with no option but to put their faith in prayer and fasting, and in the Almighty One, while their counterparts in those nations that regard themselves as 'major powers' and are accordingly out to dominate the world and expand their influence at any cost celebrate the achievements of their 'great' nations, and revel in their status as super powers. I, as the Father of Death, do not like to see those suffering hordes pray to the Prime Mover that they may be delivered from the megalomaniacs and demagogues. Prayer is something that we here in the Underworld work hard to try and head off, because it hurts our cause, which is to get as many humans as possible to 'die the death' at the hands of our own proxies in this dirty business, namely *homines inqui*.

"Talking about praying to be delivered from megalomaniacs and demagogues, you will recall from your folklore (or oral history) that Cain, the first megalomaniac and demagogue, made the astounding claim that Abel was developing an offensive 'nuclear bomb' as he termed it! Cain started ranting about his brother planning to kill him and working secretly on the weapon of mass destruction (WMD) after he saw Abel experimenting with different types of wooden planks in an effort to identify the one that could help him shorten the time it took him to get a fire going. Abel had noticed that some planks when rubbed against each other ignited faster than others did.

"Unlike Cain, who lived off the land and sustained himself and his family on ripe bananas, pineapples, mangoes, yams that they just dug up and ate raw and things like that, Abel (who was a herdsman) needed to cook the meats on which he and his family subsisted. But Cain, even though he was still in his thirties, was already in the habit of spinning tall tales and he could lie until he was blue in the face. Before Adam and Eve, who were at least ten times Cain's age, realized that Cain was pulling their legs and they were dealing with a pathological liar, they had begun to worry that perhaps their son Abel was plotting to commit a new original sin, and they were both teetering on the verge of a nervous breakdown.

"It was only after they went to inspect the site of the 'nuclear plant' (as Cain called it), and saw for themselves that Abel wasn't engaged in anything that was sinister, that they realized that Cain had been lying to them. To their utter disgust, Adam and Eve even learnt from talking to Cain's wife that the evidence or 'intelligence' their wayward son had presented to them to 'prove his case' was actually cooked and in any case deliberately fabricated to make it appear as if Abel had every intention of wiping out Cain's entire family and 'community' from the face of the earth. It is a mark of the success of our campaign in the ongoing battle between the forces of Good and the forces of Evil that, since that time, megalomaniacs and demagogues have perfected their methods of operating, and specifically making sure that the lies they spin are taken by the unwary for unvarnished Truth. And so, today, major power players will cry foul when a 'rogue nation' is trying to harness nuclear energy by alleging that the nuclear sites are actually being used to develop 'nuclear bombs' even as they themselves openly announce to the world that they are upgrading their stock-piles of nuclear weapons.

"Again, we here in the Underworld hail those megalomaniacs and demagogues for defying the Prime Mover (who created all, the demagogues themselves included, out of nothing) and choosing to be 'deciders' and the 'law unto themselves' in these matters. We hail them for taking every opportunity that comes along to set up confrontations with the 'rogue nations', and for their statesmanly decision to stay firmly on our side as we prosecute our own war against Good. What would we do if they were all 'good and wise' like Solomon! The more stupid they are - yes 'stupid' to the extent they no longer see that they themselves are on 'death row' and will have to leave all behind at the time they cross the gulf that separates the living from the dead - the better for us!

"You'd better believe me because I am the devil, and I know what I am saying. And I am not nuts. Unlike you humans who go nuts because of imbalances in the chemistry of your cerebral matter, we demons don't have brains and we don't have to worry about going nuts for that reason! This preoccupation with controlling the world's scarce resources is greed at its best, and it is also great! Just think of the number of humans whose lives are snuffed out prematurely as a result! I tell you - we here in the Underworld may be losing on points and going down, but we are not yet out. You've got to count us in as long as the Doomsday Clock keeps ticking and humans continue to be felled by their own greedy fellow humans over the crumbs I throw in their path. And nothing - absolutely nothing - is going to stop me, the Father of Death, from having a whale of a time as long as humans, pining for control over the earth's scarce resources, continue to pick fights with each other and to die the death!

How Beelzebub does his dirty work...

"A temptation works in much the same way as a cabaret act. On the surface, it depicts movements of a dance or a caper. Cabaret artists are indeed in the business of illustrating dance moves. But their cabaret acts can also take on another dimension - a suggestive dimension. So, be on the lookout when you next visit that 'cabaret club' - I mean your church!

"You see - cabaret artists spend a lot of time in front of the mirror before they go on stage to face the lights. The apostles, unlike cabaret artists and other con artists, did not have the time, much less the luxury, for that sort of thing. You mean you did not know that?

"Humans use marketing to prey on each other. Rapists use it to lure their victims to secluded places where they then pounce on them. Murderers use it to lull those they want to harm into thinking that they mean no harm - to make their dirty job easier. Other self-proclaimed do-gooders use it to project the false impression that they are 'anointed' and proven vessels of the Prime Mover's grace, and will bring salvation and true happiness to all who will cast in their lot with them by making a donation. Selfless love does not rely on marketing for anything. And we have the best example in creation - the Prime Mover did not see any need to market his intention to will creatures into existence out of nothing. It is of course a marketing technique and a gimmick that works to rake in the money, but not to deliver what it promises, as the Prime Mover sees through it.

"For His part, the Prime Mover does not market any of His gifts, the gift of grace included. His gifts are there for anyone who is prepared to put pride aside and accept them. Even if they might have 'faith that moves mountains', on their own and unaided by grace, humans do not have the wherewithal to keep themselves clear of sin let alone help others to stay clear of it. On their own, humans can only sin, and it has everything to do with the truism that one cannot give what does not have (*Nemo dat quod non habet*).

"Humans! How on earth could they even imagine that they could get themselves in good books with the Prime Mover and into heaven all on their own without 'external aid'! Yes, foreign aid! Humans do not even know how the food they shove down their tummies becomes digested; or how it is that sleep re-invigorates and energizes them, and enables them to keep going and survive on earth.

"You know what - humans do not even have to know how their breathing works, or how their eye-balls enable them to see objects upright instead of upside down! Most do not understand how their bile - poison which was located so uncomfortably close to the heart - actually keeps them alive instead of killing them instantly, any way! And many will never understand that there is a tiny crystal in their *medula oblongata* without which they would not be able to walk upright.

"Humans do not know why they were created at the time they were created, or why it was that someone else was not created in their place. It is, above all, telling that humans wake up to reality for the first time and only discover that they exist weeks - perhaps even months - after they have lain in the womb and been taken to different places as their mothers perform various errands. They start kicking inside the womb, not because they are hunkering to express themselves, but when hunger starts to gnaw at their tiny middle. That is when they start showing the first signs that they exist, are conscious of it, and are prepared to die fighting for their right to food.

"That ought to be reason enough to make humans suspect that if they ever wound up in heaven, it wouldn't be because they were smart, but because someone had pity on them. It is only then, actually, that humans will fully grasp how they landed there - as a result of the Prime Mover's act of infinite mercy and despite themselves. It will even be a wonder they ever got there given their impetuousness and the fact that they kept placing obstacles in the way of His saving mercy. It will certainly look like they got there by a fluke! It will, however, be pretty obvious then that humans, even though created in the Image, simply did not have the wherewithal to gain eternal life on their own, unaided by divine grace.

"It is only then that humans will see exactly, not how *they themselves*, by cooperating with divine grace, escaped my tentacles, but how they made it there *despite themselves*. They will also find out at that time that there simply was no way humans could have been saved *a sola fide* - by their faith alone.

Silly proposition...

"Salvation by faith alone! What a silly proposition. Oh, you think you are clever, and you want to argue with me, Satan? You must be kidding! Faith is itself a divine gift. It is a form of grace that requires the individual's cooperation to be effectual. It doesn't swoop down on folks and cause them to be miraculously transformed against their will - or is that what you thought?

"That doctrine is based on a false premise - that, when dealing with creatures that are autonomous, free and individually accountable and not automatons, the Prime Mover could not get results by relying on *their* cooperation. He is - remember - not just almighty, but He doesn't go back on His word. He made humans free, and he won't interfere with the exercise of that freedom, even if it means watching them damn themselves! And He would do that if He somehow got them to ditch their evil ways without their *explicit* agreement *and* cooperation!

"Now, humans are creatures who are given to bragging. They brag about their attempt (albeit unsuccessfully) to bridge heaven and earth by constructing a tower (the tower of Babel); and are inflated with pride at having put up monuments such as the Great Pyramid of Giza. Humans even imagine that because they sent some chaps to walk on the moon, they are not really humans any more, but semi-gods! And some nowadays even brag about their ability to build impregnable empires or super powers, and their ability to launch 'star warfare' and to trounce everyone and everything that threatens their advance to greatness.

"And so, it is a little disingenuous and silly for humans, who are determined to continue wallowing in sin (following their sinful inclination), and are reluctant to don the 'armor of the Deliverer' out of pride, to plead ignorance about how to walk upright in the sight of the Prime Mover. And that is not mentioning the fact that, even as the individuals who believe that humankind is *saved by faith alone* make that claim, they assail the 'unsaved' and ridicule 'idolaters' and others who are supposedly predestined for hell.

"No! Humans are richly endowed creatures who are created with the ability to reason and to choose between good and evil. And, after all, Adam and Eve were mandated to put those faculties of reason and free will to use as they exploited the earth and everything in it while seeking to be actualized. Even after they chose evil and became inclined to do more evil in the process, it didn't mean that they would not be capable of making choices as between what was good and what was evil after that. It didn't mean that humans stopped being humans and lost control over their own fate.

"At no moment in time did that happen. For, hardly had Adam and Eve discovered themselves denuded of grace - and ashamed to walk around with nothing on - than they were promised the Deliverer. And so, virtually immediately, the first man and the first woman, *through* their faith in the promised Deliverer, again became capable of choosing between good and evil (despite the fact that they were now inclined to sin), provided they recognized that they could do good only *with* the help of grace.

"On their own, they could not do it - just as had been the situation before, when Adam and Eve were still in a state of grace. Before the fall, humans were of course inclined to do good - and that was what Adam and Eve did all the time. My troops and I didn't think we had the tiniest sliver of a chance that we would prevail on humans and persuade them to follow our example and revolt. If anything, I was gambling when I staked my 'honor' on the very remote possibility that they might be persuaded to hop aboard. You may not believe it, but the fact is that I, Diabolos, the epitome of wickedness, was banking on the goodness and constancy of the Prime Mover for my evil designs on humans - that He would not go back on his word and deny them the right to choose me and what I stood for over Himself!

"After the promise was made - and certainly after the Deliverer came (in fulfilment of that promise), expiated the sins of men through his death on the cross, rose from the dead in triumph over sin and death, ascended into heaven, and then sent the Comforter on Pentecost Day - humans, while still inclined to sin, had no excuse for not choosing good over evil or for putting on the armor of the Deliverer. The only thing that was expected of them was to show that they needed the divine grace bad. And the way they were supposed to do that was by becoming humble like little children and stopping all the swaggering - because 'who ever exalts himself shall be humbled and whoever humbles himself shall be exalted'.

"And when humans are like little children (like

Theresa of the Child Jesus), they feel free as birds; and everything they do is good. It couldn't be anything else, because they have on the armor of the Deliverer - the same Deliverer who is alert and takes full note of the longings of the afflicted, and who encourages them and listens to their cry, and who mocks the proud and gives His graces to the humble... But if you are a 'little god', you can't possibly claim to fear the Lord. And yet, it is the fear of the Lord that is the beginning of wisdom!

"Fear the Lord, and put on the armor of the Deliverer (and be like a child), so that instead of being abandoned to evil works, you actually can start to do some good (like Mother Theresa of Calcutta) *with the help of the grace* merited for humans by the Deliverer). And, guess what? The really big problem for humans is that my troops and I here in Gehenna know all this - and we work overtime to make sure things happen *our* way.

"Now, just because an individual becomes persuaded that a doctrine is true or false doesn't mean that the individual in question has been delivered and will automatically start generating good works. One can believe in something stridently and be doing the opposite. In matters of faith, believing stridently in something is even dangerous, because hypocrisy easily comes into play, not to mention the baggage of a hypocritical life. It may be true that faith comes by knowledge, but the same does not apply to good works. But being like little children does the trick, for He humbles the proud and exalts the meek. In that sense, there is really nothing complicated about finding salvation. It is humans who complicate matters with their baggage.

"And, incidentally, if it were true that humans were saved by faith alone, one would also expect humans who were on their way to being saved by their faith - *if* they were indeed on their way to being saved at all by their

330

faith alone - to be so compliant that what they believed would in practice not matter. This is because, as *humble* creatures, they would have no difficulty cooperating with grace (in accordance with the Church's doctrine of salvation) and generating good works (as opposed to bad works), evidence of which Saint Peter would demand to see before letting them in through the gates of heaven.

"And that suggests that 'proud' folks inside and outside the Church who despise 'unbelievers' need to be a wee bit more wary. 'Saved' folks should also be wary of the 'power' they boast - the power that is supposedly unleashed by their public 'acceptance' of the Deliverer. When it is from above, real 'power' makes one see how completely unworthy one is. And those inside and outside the Church who think they are 'worthy' of anything or have special 'powers' should think twice about their boast. It could be a very empty boast indeed!

"The critical thing is to be certain that one's 'offering of good works' will be acceptable to the Prime Mover. Also keep in mind that my own 'offering' as Lucifer and Archangel, wasn't a little bit pleasing to Him in spite of my position right there in the Holy of Holies and specifically because of my pride. It is the same 'offering' that earned me the name of Arch-Devil!

Humans are free, but...

"Instead of forcing the Prime Mover to intervene and sanctify creatures that He made in His Image, feelings of self-righteousness merely repel Him. But by the same token, He does not feel compelled to stop creatures from going off on a tangent and trying to exalt themselves.

"But one must, of course, understand what is meant by 'not interfere' and what that non-interference translates into! Even after paying the price for the sins of humans, the Deliverer does not intervene to stop evil men having their way. Even though He could, he does not intervene to keep humans of good will harmless from humiliation, deprivation, and acts of violence perpetrated by evil humans. He could have interfered and stopped wars in which millions in every age perish because of the whims of empty-headed megalomaniacs.

"And so, because Providence won't interfere to stop evil men from turning the lives of other humans upside down, just imagine the toll that has on the trust and confidence of humans in their Prime Mover in general. When they see the Prime Mover - who so loved the world that he even gave His only begotten Son so that those who believe in Him might be saved, and is also almighty - seemingly unable to come to their succour in times of their greatest need, and who lets me, Satan, and my henchmen have our way in creating havoc in the world year in and year out, and making the lives of so many quite miserable, their hearts obviously sink.

"And, look - we are not talking fiction here. The toll on the trust of humans in their Prime Mover is very real and biting - and discouraging in the extreme. Just look at all the 'big fish' who commit terrible crimes against humanity, but are shielded by their pals and never face justice regardless of the destruction they wreck in the lives of ordinary folks! Look at all the thieves on 'Wall Street' so-called, and the banks that do not even own the money they lend out, but are bailed out in nefarious schemes under the ploy that they are 'too big to fail' when it is simply the old boy network at play all over again; and then see the same banks turn around and foreclose on the millions of home owners who were supposed to be the ultimate beneficiaries of the bank bail-out schemes with complete impunity!

"I first make sure my minions who work as agents for Wall Street and other gouging individuals and entities that are determined to pocket billions by hook and crook are themselves rewarded richly with lots of mammon and other material things, and they in turn have no hesitation in delivering the goods: they stop having any feelings for their fellow humans, and happily work with me to make sure that good folks feel so crushed, they forget that the Deliverer ever came!

"And look at all the governments that are into things like 'waterboarding' and other forms of torture, and that wouldn't dare harm a citizen of a country that was deemed more powerful, but play with the lives of people from defenseless nations that do not command the means to avenge such wrongs!

"If the Deliverer had made his appearance on earth during these times instead of two thousand years ago, He would probably find Himself initially eking out a living as a homeless street kid in a third world metropolis in conditions that were a direct consequence of policies of the Western controlled International Monetary Fund, or in a hamlet in the impoverished Gaza Strip that has been reeling under an international embargo - or dodging drone strikes in Waziristan!

"Just imagine the despair, and how difficult it must be for the innocent, who suffer because of the actions of the greedy and the power hungry, to hang on to any hope in Providence! They must think that they were meant to live on a different planet, and are on Planet Earth by mistake!

"The only thing that saves humans who are in that predicament - and that is about every human who escapes my tentacles and is eventually lucky enough to find himself/herself in a position to claim the title of 'one of the elect' - is their acknowledgement that they are completely powerless in the face of those odds; that, as poor forsaken children of Adam and Eve, they are actually scared to approach the Deliverer (the eternal Word through whom all creation came into being), and the only thing they seem capable of doing is to prostrate themselves at the feet of the mother of the Deliverer and Judge, and ask her to intercede for them with her divine Son.

"Any way, the real catch - with respect to those who are determined to create havoc for their fellow humans - lies in the fact that the Deliverer and Judge desists from stopping humans of bad will from accumulating guilt for their sins. Yes, that is the catch! Every misdeed and every sin of omission by humans adds to their guilt. And even though they are able to stifle and keep it bottled up in their guilty consciences in the interim, the guilt itself will keep building; and it is usually just about ready to blow up in their faces as the time during which they were permitted to create all the havoc they were capable of creating in the world draws to an end. The explosion of their accumulated guilt is actually timed to occur at precisely the moment the sinful individual's soul separates from his/her body and that individual realizes that the hour of reckoning is finally at hand.

"And, furthermore, as Thomas Aquinas explained, and I quote: 'Even the Passion of Christ (the Deliverer) binds us (humans) to some punishment whereby we (humans) are conformed to Him.' (ST Suppl., q. 18, a. 3, ad 3) And so, after wreaking havoc, sinful and sinning humans might be sorrowful; but expiation and reparation of sins committed will still await them! And that is the lot of the lucky ones who wake up to their plight before it is too late.

Joseph and Mary of Morogoro...

"Humans who mistreat others and do things that are not consonant with the will of their Creator - humans who refuse to listen to their consciences - actually damn themselves in the process, and they know it. They treat - or rather mistreat - other humans the way they do precisely because they want to cripple and 'neutralize' their perceived 'enemies', or at least see them suffer nasty physical or mental pain - or die. And it becomes damning for two reasons. They do whatever they do because they know that their own position is quite precarious, and they also understand perfectly well that what they are administering to others has the potential of causing the victims of their actions lots of grief and discomfort.

"They know that it is just a fluke that it isn't they themselves who are at the receiving end - that they are (luckily) not the ones enduring the torture, abuse, and humiliation or being targeted in some other way. And, yes - they also know that the tables could easily be turned. And, indeed, more often than not, it is the fear, real or imagined, of such an eventuality - the fear that those now at the receiving end could easily end up on the giving end with they themselves at the decidedly uncomfortable receiving end - that drives humans to be cruel and inhuman to their own kind.

"Short-sighted humans chose to go on an 'avenging' spree under the mistaken notion that it would forestall a 'revenging' spree when it in fact did the exact opposite - it guaranteed a visit from the Avenging Angel!

"Humans may be reluctant to accept it, but they know very well that instead of being born and raised in Houston, Memphis, or in Essex in England as Methodists, Baptists, or members of the High Anglican Church, they could easily have been born and raised in Fallujah or Kandahar as Shiites or Sunnis - or on the Gaza Strip - and vice versa. Caucasians could have come into the world as Mongolians, Africans, or Indians; Huguenots who ended up as American colonists could easily have come into the world as Cherokee tribesmen whom they tried hard to exterminate. Jews could easily have come into the world as Arabs, and Arabs as Jews. All these things are possible precisely because, while there is such a thing as a human soul, there is no such a thing as an American soul, a Greek soul, an Iraqi soul, a Chechen soul, a Russian soul, a Bengali soul, or a Zulu or 'black' soul.

"And it wouldn't take very much for those who for the moment might have the upper hand in deciding the fate of other humans to find themselves helpless and at the mercy of those they now regarded with disdain.

"Males, who show such a proclivity to discriminate against their female counterparts, could easily have come into the world as females, and vice versa. And it may be that once an individual is born a male or a female, it becomes a *fait accompli* the individual can do nothing about. But that is certainly not the end of the matter as, without any doubt, the day of reckoning is approaching for all regardless of whether the individual was born a man or a woman.

"There is nothing that would have prevented those humans who now boast citizenship in so-called advanced countries from coming into the world as citizens of the world's poorest and 'backward' nations - if Providence had so chosen. Those who pride themselves on being members of the one, true Catholic and Apostolic Church might very well have been born into Hinduism or Buddhism - and vice versa.

"And instead of being born in the 20th Century,

humans who boast that they live in the 'modern age' could easily have come into the world as near cousins of 'Zinjanthropus' or of 'Neanderthal Man'! Also, as creatures fashioned in the Image, humans could easily have been brought into existence as pure spirits and members of one or other choir of angels - or not at all. The only thing that was completely out of question was for humans - or, for that matter, angels - to turn up as members of the Godhead for obvious reasons. This is the reason humans were commanded to love the Creator with all their hearts, minds and souls, and their neighbors as themselves.

"'Joseph and Mary of Nazareth' in Palestine could easily have been 'Joseph and Mary of Morogoro' in Tanzania. Instead of making them Palestinians, the Prime Mover could just as easily have made them Zulus. Instead of the 'Tribe of Israel', the Prime Mover could easily have opted for the 'Tribe of the Iroquois', most of whose members were massacred by the American colonists whose greed for land was apparently insatiable. Instead of being Indian, the billions who live on the Indian subcontinent and are still multiplying could easily have been Europeans who supposedly are dying out. Instead of the 'British Isles', where the proud British now live, there could easily have been an expanse of ocean inhabited only by seals, salmon and other types of fish.

"Instead of twelve apostles, the Deliverer could have easily opted for twenty - or none. In which case there wouldn't have been any 'church' or 'bible' for humans to squabble over. Also, the Prime Mover could easily have opted to save humans of good will directly without sending His only begotten Son to earth. In the event, the world would have been saved the murder and mayhem that goes on in Palestine and elsewhere in the name of the Prime Mover. But Providence no doubt opted for the current order of things (which relies on humans for such things as evangelizing and administering the holy sacraments) to demonstrate that nothing is really impossible with the Almighty One!

"The Prime Mover could easily have decreed at the beginning of time that if any creature that was made in His image betrayed Him, that creature would promptly lose its special status, and He would cease to be indwelling in it. Under such a regime, humans who fell from grace would find themselves transformed from 'homo sapiens' or 'wise humans' into doomed but still 'wizened animals' - much like a cow that could speak and reason, but could show nothing for it at the end of its sojourn on earth. These 'wizened animals' would then fizzle out and return to nothingness as their punishment for infidelity and proving unworthy 'pilgrims' on earth as and when they 'expired'. But those humans who remained true to their consciences would enter heaven in glory.

"But I do not know if I - Beelzebub - would be 'happier' non-existent. As things are - and certainly as the head of the rebel band of angels, and also as the Father of Death, and Satan - I have quite a bit to show for my tumultuous, albeit torturous, 'life' or existence. The countless number of human souls, hopefully including yours, that Michael the Archangel will not be able to account for because they are 'lost' - for one!

"Those humans who now throw around their weight at the expense of other humans do so well-knowing that it really wouldn't take very much for the tables to be turned so that they themselves would be at the receiving end. It shows how stupid and dumb they too are. And, if that had been the case, they decidedly would not have liked to see what they might now be gleefully meting out to other folks meted out to them with or without any glee.

"And they would have exclaimed: 'There is an evil deed that cries out to heaven for retribution!' They would have also added: 'There go some folks who are supposed to be waiting for the arrival of the bridegroom with candles lit, but who have decided to make a nuisance of themselves and upset the rhythm of things.'

"And yet, for all their cockiness and 'invincibility', given what they are caught up in, may be the same thing that was said of Judas Iscariot after he betrayed the Deliverer - viz. that 'it were better if they had not been born' - probably applies to them as well. Meaning that the world would be better off without them!

"And what if they had come into the world as different beings altogether - as soul-less goats or sheep or roaches, or perhaps as white ants that do not seem to 'think' anything of themselves and are prepared to lay down their lives so that the Queen Ant may live on, or not at all! After all, no creature chose to be the creature he or she - or it - was.

Squandered and no longer available...

"When humans engage in misdeeds, they know exactly what they are up to. That is what happens when humans use foul language - they do so specifically to protest decency, and they cannot turn around and deny that they do not know what they are doing or that it is not wrong. And it is self-damning.

"What makes the situation of murderers, hedonists, and other hardened evil doers infinitely worse is the fact that they all know that the liberties they are taking not only have no lasting benefit, but have dire consequences for their eternal life in addition to being explicitly forbidden. And then those murderers, thieves, hedonists, lying louts, and hypocrites who want to have it both ways compound the problems when they go on to represent themselves as upright pillars of virtue, and in the process cause not just the innocent, but other vulnerable humans of good will who expect better of them, to be scandalized and to lose faith in the very existence of an almighty. And, as was pointed out by the Deliverer Himself, they end up deserving to have around their necks what he described as 'millstones about their necks' to assure that they sank to the bottom of the hell they were themselves pontificating about!"

Mjomba at first balked at the idea that he should include what he had just jotted down at the suggestion of the Evil Ghost. He worried that the devil was now casting the net so wide, all but the most heroic souls would escape his tentacles. For one, Mjomba knew how unworthy he himself was, and it was of course not very hard to envision situations in which virtually any seminarian could stand accused of being guilty of things like stealing, lying, or acting hypocritically.

It could even be argued that a seminarian became an accessory to murder if, in exercising his constitutional right to vote, he cast the vote for a political party whose platform included expansionist policies and things like pre-emptive military strikes and or economic embargoes with all that these things entailed on so-called "rogue nations" that were so labeled just because they refused to be bulldozed into casting their votes at the United Nations according to the dictates of his own country.

Still, the Evil Ghost could not be faulted for trying to bend the rules to suite anyone. The devil who was already condemned and damned clearly stood to gain nothing from doing so, but everything from taking the hard line! Mjomba was still inclined to prevaricate when an interior voice - he wasn't quite sure if it belonged to the Evil Ghost or to the Holy Ghost - firmly commanded him to just get on with it; and he found he himself had no choice but to just continue jotting down ideas he was certain were emanating from the Evil One.

"But, even worse, once humans (who are expected to love the Prime Mover above all else and to love their 'neighbor' as themselves) squander that love on frivolities" Mjomba wrote, "it becomes just that - squandered - and ceases to be available for dispensing on neighbors or on their Prime Mover - and He is a jealous God, too! That is reality regardless of what those humans feel, think or imagine. It is the reason those who left their allotted spots in the queue during the wait for the arrival of the bridegroom (in the Gospel story) did not just lose their places in the queue, but found themselves locked out of the banquet hall. Their interest in passing frivolities supplanted their interest in the royal wedding to which they had been formally invited.

"Similarly, an individual who is betrothed to another becomes unfit as a partner in the planned union when he/she knocks off in the meantime with another suitor, and loses his/her virginity - and above all his/her innocence and trustworthiness. It is the same for humans who break the commandments. They lose their innocence in the process - innocence that is intended to serve as their bridal gown and armour against my wiles and the wiles of my fellow demons.

"They stop being in the running for a reward in the afterlife, and instead start down the slippery way towards the pit - unless they succeed in making a U-Turn and getting themselves rehabilitated. But it becomes increasingly difficult to make the U-Turn after one fritters away one's precious gifts and virtues and, in particular, the 'cardinal' virtues (the virtues of prudence, justice, fortitude and temperance).

Rationalizing and justifying...

"Then, humans who lose their innocence invariably fall for the bait we throw at them - the temptation of trying to rationalize away their guilt and their ingratitude to the Prime Mover. But in the process of 'rationalizing' (which requires intelligence and implies that they know what they are up to) and justifying their actions (which requires the ability to discern what is right from what is wrong, and again implies that they in fact know what they are doing), humans implicitly acknowledge something else also, namely that it is not just a case of being out on a limb on their own (either individually or as a nation), and are essentially following their whims (instead of their individual or collective consciences). They acknowledge that they are a part of the wider phenomenon known as the 'human race'.

"They implicitly acknowledge that they have a nature, and that they share it with other humans who have existed or will in time exist. In 'rationalizing' and 'justifying', humans acknowledge in so many words that they possess faculties of the intellect and of the will - faculties that are so central to human nature. That is in itself very damning, because those who attempt to rationalize away their guilt explicitly acknowledge that they have a nature (which happens to be human), and that this same nature has been given an existence - the self-same existence they are even now enjoying.

"That in turn brings those humans face to face with the fact that they are enjoying something else - an existence - that an agent outside of themselves, a Prime Mover, has bestowed upon them to enable them to attain self-actualization as human 'beings'. And that in turn establishes the fact that there indeed was a Being to whom they owed their existence and were automatically

342

accountable.

"If it were possible to imagine that a dependent creature endowed with reason and a free will and capable of causing mischief could be brought into existence and not have to account to any one for its misdeeds, that would in itself impute irresponsibility on the part of the Prime Mover, and make Him the most reckless Being imaginable - a Being who permitted creatures of the caliber of 'humans' to follow their whims with impunity.

"Another way to establish conclusively that humans are indeed 'thinking' creatures is to take your pick of one thousand of these humans from completely different corners of the globe, gather them in a large compound, and leave them to their own devices. Unlike creatures that are endowed only with instinct, humans who are strangers to each other do not assume that the other chaps will automatically grasp the native tongue of the other strangers, and just go on blubbering away in Kiswahili, French, Japanese, Kikuyu, Spanish, Russian, Chinese, Greek, Urdu, Arabic, Lingala, English, Kiganda, or what have you.

"They will try to 'learn' each other's tongue in the same way they 'learnt' their mother tongue - if they keep their minds on the task at hand and don't suddenly go after each other's throats the way humans are wont to do nowadays, that is. And if they eschew animosities, as they ought, they will even provide slow learners assistance with pronunciation and things like that - something the lower beasts just do not do.

"Then, it might also take those humans some time to master nine hundred and ninety-nine new languages; but that is what they will try to do. And to do that needs more than a mouth and an instinct. It required one to be a member of that specie known as '*homo sapiens*'. And accountability goes with membership in that exalted specie whose members make up what is known as 'Mankind'.

Demagoguery...

"As far as culpability goes, the situation remains unchanged for humans who accept positions of authority, and this is regardless of whether such positions are in the private or public domain.

"For a start, the Prime Mover does not recognize 'governments' as such. There is, of course, no such a thing as a 'super power'. That is not to say that he ignores the existence of chaps like Julius Caesar or Pontius Pilate (who are His creatures) or what they do. On the contrary, He demands of them personal accountability for their acts of commission or omission (while they occupy their high places) like everyone else.

"Humans who accept positions of authority do so at their peril. For power does not simply corrupt, it also stunts the reasoning. As a consequence, humans in positions of authority tend to develop into demagogues who forget that all authority comes from the Prime Mover. After a short while, many of them start behaving like little gods!

"But they are personally responsible for the plots they hatch against their own citizens or against citizens of other nations, for bribery and the corruption that breeds, and for decisions to pay bribes (sometimes disguised as foreign aid) to functionaries of other 'governments' for the purpose of promoting crooked schemes, and for everything that happens under their watch and infringes on the rights of other humans inside and outside their borders.

"In the moral sphere, there is no such a thing as liability that is 'joint and several'. Individual humans are personally liable for the use or misuse of the authority they wield. There is no such a thing as liability that is 'joint and several' on the other side of the gulf which separates the living from the dead. The Judge does not recognize bureaucracies or similar entities; and individuals who exercise authority on behalf of those entities bear full and personal responsibility for their roles as 'bureaucrats' in those entities. As far as the Judge is concerned, there is no conceivable way in which a bureaucrat could 'pass the buck' and escape personal responsibility for his/her role in dealings that left something to be desired from the point of view of Equity or Natural Justice.

"Now, if it is easier for a camel to pass through the eye of a needle than for a rich human to enter heaven, you can just imagine how difficult it must be for a 'powerful' human to pass the Church Triumphant Entrance Test (CTET). Unlike the rich who have lots of time on their hands, the powerful typically do not even have spare time to do the assigned homework. And yet scores on that assigned 'homework' count towards the final score on the CTET.

"I am Beelzebub, and I may be fallen now. But, as the most glitzy creature that had ever existed at the time I fell from grace (I have since ceded that honor to the beloved Mother of the Deliverer), I used to wield a lot of power over other creatures. And guess what - it is what brought me down. If you do not believe that I was powerful, I invite you to stop and reflect on just a couple of my aliases: the Prince of Demons, the Oppressor of the Saints, the Prince of Darkness, and the Lawless One. And I am really fond of this particular one: The Adversary!

"And just ask me about the power I still exercise over sinful humans and over the damned - even though I am a fallen arch angel! Do you know how many times I am referred to by name - yes, by name - in the New

Testament alone? So, you just take my word for it: it is most difficult and nearly impossible for creatures in positions of power - and certainly humans who are born inclined to sin - to avoid becoming infatuated with it. It is a lot harder for the powerful on earth to enter heaven than for the rich who could just give away everything they owned to the poor - if they had acquired it through their own hard work and had not stolen it - and be virtually guaranteed of walking away with their CTET diploma. Power also corrupts you see!

"In accepting positions of responsibility, individual humans implicitly acknowledge the source of the authority that is vested in those positions. And that source has to be the Prime Mover who gave them their status as *homines sapientes*. But for many humans, positions of power have the effect of turning them into little gods. This is what is so tragic about the ancestors of Adam and Eve.

"They soon start imagining that they can hoodwink everyone, including the Prime Mover, by hiding behind labels such as empire, state government, or some similar entities to escape personal responsibility for their actions. Some start fancying that when they occupy positions such as 'General' or 'Commander-in-Chief', they stop being answerable to anyone. Frequently they try to bypass the commandments by making their own rules including the so-called 'rules engagement'!

"Others imagine, quite mistakenly, that it is political pundits, newspaper gossip columnists, lobbyists, pollsters, and even court jesters to whom they are answerable for their actions. They even fool themselves that public opinion polls and the verdict of voters (who are so liable to manipulation these days) are indicative of whether their own acts of commission and omission are in line with the divine will or not. But they engage in that kind of tomfoolery at their peril.

Cain's "empire"...

"You know the story of Cain, I suppose. He may be in heaven now, but he was a real lout when he was back on earth - at least before he repented of his misdeeds, renounced me and my wiles, and then made amends for murdering his brother Abel. That murder was a deed that was so horrendous it even shocked us here in the Pit. In a single stroke that saw the first deliberate killing in the human family, Cain - the first death culture enthusiast - wiped out a fifth of the human race, and set the stage for humans to try and 'justify' killings of their own kin in the name of the 'empire' or 'state'!

"Taking advantage of the fact that the penitent and selfless Adam and Eve had no interest in material things, Cain had laid claim to ownership of all the arable tracks of land which stretched as far as the eye could see by the time Abel came of age. Cain referred to the enormous expanse of land as his 'empire'! The only exception was Paradise Valley which Adam and Eve had been tilling long before Cain himself was born. Cain was always having nightmares about 'nations' rising up to challenge his 'empire' and putting some of Planet Earth's resources out of bounds so that he wouldn't be able to exploit them as his own and to levy 'duties' and 'taxes' on anyone else who wanted to have use of them.

"The epitome of meanness and a lazy lout at the same time, who initially thought he could feed off the sweat of his old man and woman indefinitely, Cain had at one time threatened to drive his parents from their modest farm house in Paradise Valley into the wilderness. Intent on ensuring that their son learned to fend for himself, they had told Cain that the pineapples and mango trees in Paradise Valley which they tilled for food were off limits to him. Because the same did not apply to Abel, who was always there to lend the old man and the old woman a hand in working the fields in Paradise Valley, Cain automatically diverted his ire to his brother whom he accused of intrigues and blamed for the fact that he sorely missed the pineapples and mangoes.

"Finding himself treated like a virtual alien by his brother and specifically barred by Cain from tilling any piece of his 'empire', Abel had resorted to hunting to obtain the food he needed to assuage his hunger as he grew into a young man and set up his own home on the edge of Paradise Valley. Abel discovered to his amazement that some of the animals, particularly goats, sheep and cows, were quite easy to domesticate. He did not know it, but his gentle nature had everything to do with it. That was how Abel came to be a 'herdsman' while Cain, with his mean, cruel and evil disposition, continued on as a 'farmer' as the bible says.

"Cain hated the idea that the weaning animals allowed Abel to milk them for free. He was also jealous that his brother enjoyed eating many different kinds of veal, including roast beef and salted ham, while he himself fed on cabbage, ripe bananas and things like that; and he was soon eyeing the herds of goats, sheep and cattle that grazed on his land, and wishing that it was he himself rather than Abel who had possession of the animals.

"The hard-hearted Cain for some reason imagined that Abel, who was clearly endeared to the animals, wouldn't be persuaded to part with any of his sheep or goats or head of cattle even at a price. Cain, who had at first considered the possibility of engaging in barter trade with Abel in which he would give his brother some of the yield from the land in exchange for such things as meats, milk, and animal hide which he could use to protect himself from the morning chill, soon abandoned that idea. In Cain's mind, Abel was already looming as someone who was a squatter on land to which he, Cain, had sole ownership.

"Cain also believed or imagined that Abel's animals posed an obvious threat to his crops. Even though a lot of the maize crop in the fields went to waste because Cain couldn't eat it all, he had caught one of Abel's weaning goats munching away on a maize cob in the fields, and that had not gone down very well with him. It had made him sick to the stomach, particularly because he had stumbled and nearly broken his neck as he chased the animal off the maize plantation, bat in hand. He had done so with the specific intention of killing the animal and depriving Abel of its milk thereby.

"It troubled Cain that Adam and Eve, instead of supporting his position, stood squarely behind Abel, and pressed him to accept that his brother had as much right to the use of the land as himself. And when Abel politely asked him if he (Abel) could fence in an uncultivated moor and use it as a kraal for his animals, it was the last straw Cain had been waiting for. In Cain's eyes, Abel had ceased to be just a squatter. He had become a 'terrorist' whose aim was to slowly drive Cain off his land and take over the empire.

"By that time, Cain and Abel had two other siblings of the female gender. Cain had already been dotting on the elder girl for some time, and he had let the old man and the old woman know that he planned to take her for his wife. It therefore came as a surprise to everyone when Cain asked the younger and more handsome girl for her hand in marriage. The 'emperor' had apparently not been quite prepared for what transpired next. The younger girl had rebuffed his approaches and, to Cain's great dismay, had gone on to announce publicly that she was already betrothed to the gentle Abel.

"Cain blamed Abel for his woes, and now accused him of plotting to 'defile' the thirty-five year old. This was even though he himself had already impregnated the elder girl who, at the 'young' age of fifty-five, was preparing to have a baby. That was the time the mean Cain began plotting to murder the 'terrorist' and 'insurgent' and now, alas, also his competitor!

"But by this time, my team had also supplanted Cain's guardian angels as his 'protector', and the posse of demons not only trooped within hearing distance of Cain wherever he went, but was on hand to urge him on and provide him whatever further inspiration he stood in need of as he went about devising plans to rid the world of the 'terrorist', 'hoodlum' and 'thug'. And, not content with plotting his brother's murder, Cain thought he was clever and could 'justify' his actions. He was going to officially declare himself 'Emperor of the World' and that was going to do the trick!

"While some of his actions like eating and sleeping would continue to be done by him in his private capacity as Cain, the great bulk of his decisions thenceforward would be made by him in his official capacity as Emperor Cain. The implication was that if some of those decisions turned out to be against natural justice or plainly wrong, the final responsibility for such decisions would rest with the impersonal 'Office of the Emperor'.

"In other words, while he would be responsible for the actions he did in his personal capacity like eating, resting or snoring, he certainly couldn't take personal responsibility for actions relating to the impersonal 'Office of Emperor'. Cain accordingly kept telling himself over and over that he didn't have anything personal against Abel, and that he truly 'loved' his kid brother.

"And so, putting on his Emperor's hat or 'crown',

and speaking from the garden behind his official residence or 'White House' as he called it, Cain had 'announced to all and sundry' that Abel was a terrorist and an insurgent, and should turn himself in for his own safety along with his heavy weapons or be destroyed. By 'heavy weapons', Cain meant the shepherd's rod and staff that Abel also used as a walking stick and the machete Abel used to cut firewood and on the odd occasion to scare away a marauding bear or a stray lion. But of course, no one heard the declaration or 'decree' because of a freak but thunderous storm that was raging at the time.

"If something happened to Abel in those circumstances, he would be a 'casualty of war' - or so Cain thought. It would not be a homicide, and it certainly would not be a murder. Would it be something that was unfortunate? Most certainly if you looked at it from the perspective of Abel's wife and kids! Desirable? Yes - if you looked at it from the point of view of the empire's security!

"Cain's wife thought that the man was going off the rails, and hastened to inform the old man and the old woman. But she did not need to do that because Adam and Eve themselves had already noticed that their older son had started behaving 'funny', and they had even asked him to if he was alright.

"At one point, Adam decided that he couldn't remain silent in the face of Cain's shocking behavior and attitude towards Abel. He confronted Cain and suggested to him that he was definitely headed for eternal damnation if he did not change course and stop treating his brother as if he were some 'terrorist'! The old man advised him to stop being confrontational and start treating Abel like a member of the human family and a beloved brother at that. Power, Adam said in his deep grating voice, was not everything. To the old man's consternation and despair, Cain had simply screamed in response: 'Power is its own reward!'

"Thoroughly frustrated, the old man had retorted: 'Your wife is right. You are out of your mind!'

"Still, hoping for a miracle, Adam had pleaded: 'Sonny, your mother and I are old, and our days on earth are numbered. After we are gone, you will be the oldest soul on Planet Earth. Are we to understand that it is this hideous culture of death - this hankering for power at all cost - that will now rule the world after we cross the Gulf and go to our judgement?'

"Adam hated to think that it was the original sin (for which he took full personal responsibility) that had occasioned that unanticipated and rather ugly state of affairs. The old man also had this awful premonition that even though a deliverer had been promised and, whoever he was or wherever he came from, would definitely come to save humankind from the grip of evil and to take the sting out of death, his own fate on earth would be a terrible, terrible one. Adam was beside himself and disconsolate as he pondered the possibility that the Deliverer might himself be murdered by the very creatures whom he was coming to rescue from eternal damnation! It would be really terrible for the deliverer to be allowed to die, because death was one of the wages of sin.

"It was all the more reason, Adam told himself, that he could not give up on Cain who represented the first fruits of his marriage to Eve. Thoroughly exasperated, he had pointed a quivering finger at Cain as he screamed: 'Son, do you know what happens to a hyena after a while after it has fed on its catch and has a bursting tummy? Answer me?'

"Cain: 'It shits.'"

"Adam: 'Good, Lord! And are you aware - do you

know that your labors as emperor of the world add up to nothing more than a full tummy? Do you realize that at the end of it all, as the sunset prepares to converge on your life, you will have nothing to show for it but shit - the shit you will be shitting from now until you die, Shit?"

"Cain wanted to say 'I'm not shit', but remained silent."

"Adam pursued: 'You have to be prepared to shed tears - to cry - when you finally kick the bucket and leave all behind as you most certainly will do eight hundred or nine hundred years hence. When your soul, bereft of your body and also of the trappings of empire, is ushered into the presence of the Word and Judge, you will have nothing to show for your days on earth, Sonny, apart from the shit!'"

"After listening to Adam's 'lecture', Cain thought that everybody, including his father, had gone completely nuts. For one thing, the last person Cain expected to lecture to him about eternal life - or eternal damnation - was the old man. Certainly not after he and his mom had gone off and (as Cain put it) made a deal with 'Satan' and ruined everything for themselves and everyone else who would ever step on earth!

"Cain's bitterness was palpable as he recalled how, at the tender age of ten, his parents had made him sit down and had recounted the events leading up to the fateful day when they were surprised by the appearance of Michael the Archangel as they surreptitiously plucked and ate fruit from the Tree of the Knowledge of Good and Evil. Told that the angel then drove the pair out of the Garden of Eden and into the wilderness where they would have to struggle to survive before eventually dying, Cain, in his innocence, had asked repeatedly why his dad, with his strong muscles, had not stood his ground and chased the angel out of the Garden of Eden instead.

"It had taken Adam and Eve a couple of days of explaining to convince the boy that it would not have done to try and fight back; and that they obeyed and left because it would have made things much worse to try and fight the archangel who had the loyal angels and the Prime Mover Himself on his side.

"Now, many years later, after listening to his father and waiting patiently for him to finish his 'lecture', Cain shouted back that he (Cain) was not a hypocrite, and that he accepted the fact that he was an embittered person. He added that he had been born like that thanks to the original sin for which his parents, who now had the nerve to stand there and moralize to him, were entirely responsible.

"As Cain imagined it, everyone - the old man, the old woman, the women, and even Abel who 'went around with a pious face' - was embittered just like himself, and disappointed after losing the automatic right to the heavenly inheritance. Cain choked on his words as he repeated that he wasn't the one who dreamed up the notion of original sin. He did not 'acquire' his inclination to sin. He was born with it. And, as far as he was concerned, the world was there for the taking, and he was determined to get and keep his portion of it.

"Cain had no doubt in his mind that behind the mask of Abel's piety - behind that facade of good-naturedness and congeniality - lay a raging monster that could come awake at a moment's notice. Cain did not like or trust Abel a bit for that reason. If the hypocritical Abel wanted to lead a life of make believe - if he wanted to go around smiling to trees and the birds that had their nests in them, or if he wanted to continue playing patsy with animals of the wild the way he had been doing, that was his business.

"As far as Cain was concerned, the fact that he

himself and Abel belonged to the same human race and the same stock - the fact that they both had the same father and the same mother - was completely immaterial. Cain looked ahead in time and imagined the earth full of humans who could not possibly know each other as a practical matter, and who looked very different from each other as a result of exposure to the different climates, and who did not even understand each other because they spoke different dialects, had different customs, and had almost nothing in common apart from the fact that they were all descended from Adam and Eve just like himself, Abel and their wives. And he guessed correctly that they wouldn't place any premium on the fact that they were all humans. If anything, they would always be wishing that anyone who didn't look exactly like themselves - or who did but happened to belong to different 'ethnic' groupings - would just drop dead!

"Cain wasn't the type of person to go around telling himself that 'he had a dream'. He'd in fact heard Abel whisper something like that on the day he, Cain, had prevailed on Adam to warn Abel that he risked war if he tried to till any piece of the tracts of fertile land in the vicinity of the Garden of Eden to which Cain had staked ownership before Abel came of age.

"Cain had even alarmed his wife with his frequent references to the fact that things radically changed from the moment their mom and dad were tempted to eat of the forbidden fruit from the tree of knowledge of good and evil! And he asserted ever so often that from then on 'covetousness', by which he meant 'everyone for him/herself', and 'capitalism' which he defined as 'strategic thinking and business acumen' effectively became accepted 'norms' or 'principles' without which all human endeavors would be doomed to failure! He explained to his wife that the legacy of the original sin their parents had committed was that any human who did not apply his/her knowledge, regardless of whether it was the knowledge of good or knowledge of evil, to his/her individual circumstances would be left behind. Cain had then declared that, to achieve any progress in the hard times that had befallen the world with the fall of Man from grace, all humans had to be acquisitive and selfish!

"The only problem that Cain saw was that, even after one had successfully accumulated wealth on an immense scale and also consolidated the power that was necessary to ensure that other humans couldn't grab it, an earthquake or a plague could wipe away all those material gains in an instant. Humans remained spiritual beings; and, upon 'kicking the bucket', the human soul went to judgment while his/her body returned to the dust from which it came. That arguably posed a quandary of sorts for progressive-minded folks like himself, but did not by itself debunk his arguments for capitalism.

"Cain, who generally liked to stand out in a crowd, was glad that he belonged to the first generation of humans and had not been born in an era when folks would be mere statistics. But even if he did - even if he had been born in the Tenth or even Twentieth Century - he had made up his mind that he would do things differently. Actually he would work very hard to be a 'leader of the pack' (by which he meant an emperor, a king or at the minimum a tribal chief) to whom the masses paid respects. And he would not hesitate to be cruel and ruthless to stay ahead of the pack and not be reduced to a statistic.

"Under his reign, any of his subjects who did not toe the line would be dealt with firmly. And he would not only rule with an iron fist, he would assemble armies with a view to going out on foreign adventures to annex new lands; and he would, of course, target those countries that either had good arable land and or were rich in minerals and other resources.

"And while at it, any one opposing his action would be declared an insurgent and terrorist, and would be 'neutralized' - rubbed out. A practical man, Cain was going to 'live one life at a time' as he put it. Meaning that, whilst on this earth, he would concentrate on enjoying himself and not spend any time worrying about 'his last end'. He was, accordingly, determined to live the fullest life as an inhabitant of this world, and would let the 'hereafter' that his dad and mom kept pontificating about take care of itself.

"In Cain's view, the world was there for the taking, and he was determined to get *and* keep his portion of it for himself and the many children he hoped to father. In those circumstances, power - and the firm exercise of power - was of the essence. And if push came to shove, he was going to be rough and cruel with anyone who tried to stand in his way as he exercised rule over his empire and sought to expand its borders to ensure that he had control over the earth's scarce resources.

"Cain saw the security of his empire as something that was paramount, and more important even than the bond of brotherly love that existed between Abel and himself. When he was listening to his dad berate him for ignoring his 'afterlife', Cain had in fact mumbled under his breadth and out of ear-shot of his fuming dad that he would not hesitate to take a human life if that was what it was going to take to consolidate his power over the portion of Mother Earth he had claimed for himself.

"As Cain saw it, there was nothing wrong with 'cutting short' the lives of other humans (as he referred to killing or murder) for the specific purpose of maintaining control over resources he deemed important for his empire's security, or to ensure that his descendants would not lack anything that might be available to other humans. According to Cain's reasoning, power was the decisive factor, and the powerful gained an automatic to anything that could be had through its exercise. And, by the same token, weaklings forfeited their right to ownership of anything if they were unable to keep challengers at bay.

"This was a 'law of nature' that even animals of the wild obeyed. The fittest survived; and deservingly so, while weaklings didn't because they clearly didn't deserve anything else. And because he saw everything in the prism of the exercise or non-exercise of power, Cain had no doubt that there would be a scramble by the strong, both real and pseudo, to carve curve out and claim pieces of Mother Earth for themselves in due course. He was also certain that the world's development was going to have as its driving force, not self-abnegation and piety, but selfishness and materialism. Cain saw some very positive aspects to the very things that his parents decried namely acquisitiveness, meanness, ruthlessness, and craftiness.

"In his mind's eye, Cain saw the rise and fall of an assortment of power brokers, including rival emperors, 'kings', 'chiefs', and others whose one objective would be to topple him from power and install themselves as the new and unchallenged 'heads of state'. He was under no illusion about the dangers that his empire would in time face as other humans started eyeing the resources under its control, and he was gearing himself to 'play hard ball', as that was almost certainly going to be the name of the game in the not too distant future.

"As the head of the world's first ever 'super power' saw it, any nations that sprung up and were not themselves super powers had per force to toe the line set by his empire and agree to become an 'ally'. Those nations that didn't automatically became 'rogue states'. The regime of 'international law' - which he would be instrumental in helping to establish (with the stated objective of maintaining peace and good order in the world) - would recognize the authority of his super power to intervene in the affairs of rogue states for the purpose of transforming them into 'democratic' states and also effectively 'allies'.

"His resort to the use of force in effecting this transformation would be perfectly legitimate if persuasion failed to work. A rogue state that successfully resisted its transformation into a 'democracy' of an accepted brand would automatically become a 'failed state'.

"With his understanding of human nature, Cain knew that if you deliberately stepped on someone else's toes - when you rode rough shod over other people's rights - you had to start getting in the habit of looking over your shoulder from time to time because of the enemies you made. But he had a simple solution to all that. And his solution was to be more - not less - ruthless, brutal and mean. Cain believed that once you abandoned natural justice and subscribed to other ways, half-hearted measures became self-defeating. And yet the challenge that all humans faced was to succeed. (He always kept telling himself that his parents representing humanity hadn't been commanded to 'go, multiply and fill the earth' for nothing!)

"Regardless of the original problem that would cause him to 'unsubscribe' to natural justice, his inclination would always be to respond to any resistance against the policies adopted by his empire with brute force and heavy-handedly at that. He had made up his mind that he would quell any revolts that might be brewing firmly and forcefully, and thereby ensure that he was always in control over all situations. Such an approach would in his view also assure that he always had the upper hand in his dealings with all the other players.

"Cain wasn't dumb. He knew the power of 'truth'; and he had, accordingly, resolved that he would always ensure that he had machinery in place to put a spin on events in such a way that the victims of his injustices would be the ones who would be depicted as the troublemakers and culprits. His staff would include PR people, and they definitely would have to be individuals who were leaders in the public relations field. His PR machinery would have to be the sort that could depict lies as truth and vice versa.

"Cain knew from dealing with his own conscience that, in matters of right and wrong, repetition had a way not so much of silencing the conscience as of getting it to agree with him that whatever previously loomed as morally wrong actually wasn't. Owing no doubt to the intense pressures on him to grow his so far non-existence 'state' into an empire and indeed a super power, Cain had gotten this strange idea into his head that when the conscience stopped nagging, it effectively meant that what had previously been morally unacceptable in fact changed and became morally acceptable. He similarly believed that repeating that a lie was not a lie made it into a truth - in exactly the same was repetition changed a 'wrong' into a 'right' and vice versa. And so now, all Cain needed to do was to make sure that his PR people also got those important principles right, and 'indoctrination' carried out in the right manner would easily take care of the rest.

"It would all come down to the fact that he, Cain, would always be right, and all who contradicted him would be always be wrong. His spin machinery had to be capable of 'proving' that 'known knowns' were actually 'known unknowns', 'unknown knowns', or even 'unknown unknowns' - and the other way round. And so, anyone who came up with any allegations of 'injustices' on his part and things like would have to come prepared to rebut a mass of trumped up (read 'perfectly true and provable') charges against the complainant that if pursued would result in even more serious indictments.

"Cain's spin machinery would always be anticipating the reactions of people to everything he did, and complainants would never stand a chance. At the very minimum, the spin machinery would have to be capable of depicting the different forms of torture, humiliation and abuse of humans as 'humane treatment'.

"This was important because torture Particularly was something his lieutenants would definitely have to resort to very frequently as they sort to gain the 'intelligence' they needed for stopping foolhardy terrorists who might be bent on violating the empire's borders, and for planning and executing successful pre-emptive wars against 'hostile' nations, in particular those nations that fell in the category of 'axes of evil' (whatever Cain meant by that). Cain figured that, in order to safeguard against any of the empire's own operatives being tortured and abused contrary to accepted principles of morality in the event that they were themselves captured, it would be prudent not to openly admit that the empire sanctioned torture and the abuse or humiliation of captives.

"Cain's bet was that, in a world in which unfairness and cruelty were the order of the day as a direct result of the unwarranted and ill-advised theft by his parents of fruit from the Tree of Knowledge, it would always be smarter to be the dominant player and on top of things.

"It would also be much better for those who found themselves short-changed to swallow their pride and accept injustices as a 'given'. If anything, if people had any common sense and wanted to survive in the terrible conditions in which Planet Earth was going to be enmeshed - if they knew what was good for them - it would be advisable for them to specifically seek his 'protection'. And, protection being what it was, it would always come at a price of course.

"And so in short, Cain would add another dimension to the management style he employed in running his empire. He would essentially borrow a leaf from the methods of the 'mafiosi' as he would refer to small time hoodlums who would reason in the same way as he himself, but whose operations would complement (rather than take away from) his empire and make it more formidable.

"The 'mafia' would be perfectly good, law abiding citizens who operated on strict 'capitalistic' principles. Even though the population of the world (which numbered in single digits) did not yet include mafia elements when Cain was thinking these things through, he had absolutely no doubt that a time would come when the mafiosi phenomenon would emerge - just as his empire was set to grow and expand.

"Cain had already made up his mind that he would always do everything he did with a straight face both to emphasize that he was in the right and because, unlike everyone else, he at least was using his head (or so he thought). And being 'in the right' of course meant that he was a straight talking, upright and just man who was dedicated to 'progress' under the new order which the original sin of his parents had ushered in.

"Cain figured that under that new order - an order in which dying was going to be an ordinary occurrence like being born, eating, walking, and sleeping - acquisitiveness was perfectly normal. One could decide to confine oneself to the immediate environs of the hut in which one lived and become an 'immobile' citizen of the world, or one could be enterprising and dream of building an empire that stretched to the edge of the world as he was trying to do. Thus, instead of just confining one's dreams to the present, one could dream and - through one's dreams - actually live in the future. That was the essence of being an enlightened and mobile citizen of the world.

"Looking into the future, Cain saw or imagined a world that was literally teaming with people. He rationalized that in the interests of progress, even though all humans were created equal, some would definitely end up 'more equal than others'! This would mean in effect that those who were more equal - which was just another way of saying more progressive - would be entitled to more rights, including the right to life. In the same way the lives of certain animal species were sacrificed to ensure the survival of other animal species in the divine plan, it seemed plain, and indeed obvious, that the lives of some of the earth's inhabitants would be more precious than the lives of others. Under the new order, this appeared inevitable, even though all humans were created in the Image and accordingly were equally precious in the eyes of the Prime Mover.

"While 'reasoning' thus, Cain had concluded that it would be perfectly acceptable if the armies he would assemble killed other humans who stood in the way of the expansion of the empire. The emperors, kings, tribal chiefs - or whatever the future rulers of the world would call themselves - would all be seeking to expand at the expense of others; and the motto undoubtedly would be 'kill or be killed'!

"Whether in a mobile or immobile society, a ruler would only be responsible for the safety and welfare of the citizens of the empire, because it was these citizens who paid fiefs to him/her and were also available for enlistment in the empire's defense forces. And while seeking to secure the empire's borders and making certain that they are not violated, the lives of non-citizens would not be worth a farthing or dime. If anything, 'foreigners' would have to be treated as such - foreigners or aliens - and they might as well be hailing from a different planet.

"That in effect would mean that if entire cities populated by foreigners were wiped out inadvertently or even deliberately by Cain's forces with the help of the latest technology, such a measure could always be justified on the grounds that members of the Cain clan were not among the casualties, and by the fact that the objective was to strengthen the security of the 'empire'.

"With the backdrop of original sin which made all humans inclined to sin or evil, Cain thought it would be suicidal not to take cognizance of that in planning for his empire. It wasn't that he was mean and murderous. He was just trying to be practical, and he had no doubt that any ruler who did not take the same precautions would pay the ultimate prize – lose his/her empire to those rulers who were more enterprising and/or were better at using their heads and deliver the empire's citizens into captivity.

"One morning, the flamboyant Cain woke up with an idea he himself thought was rather brilliant. One of his first acts as emperor would be to set up a 'secret service' or 'intelligence agency'. This would be important for two reasons. To begin with, the agency would keep a tab on everyone who looked remotely like a threat to his rule.

"Even though lions, crocodiles, elephants, venomous snakes, mosquitoes, and other creatures of the wild scared him, and arguably posed what was often an even greater threat to his life and by extension to his rule that Abel and others humans whom the Eternal Word would bring into existence, Cain wasn't bothered about them. This was because, unlike humans, their behavior and moods were predictable, something which went a long way to reduce the actual threat they posed to his life. Because the same could not be said of humans who could backbite, connive with others to lay traps for an individual they disliked, or even plan outright murder (just as he himself was doing), Cain figured that he would need an intelligence agency to keep them in check. The principal task of the 'spy agency' would be to collect, evaluate and disseminate 'intelligence information' that his inner circle would need for that purpose.

"But the 'secret service', as that agency would also be known, would also have another and even more important purpose. Cain knew that as a human he definitely was going to commit blunders along the way as he labored away on his ambitious scheme of building a mighty empire. A proud man, he feared that some of those blunders would end up causing such grief to his subjects, it was not just conceivable but very likely that some of them would start getting the idea that they could do without a leader who was such a 'bumbling idiot' - one who made the empire a more dangerous place to live in! They would, in other words, be tempted to impeach him or get rid of him in some other manner.

"Cain, accordingly, wanted to have a perfect scapegoat for those unpredictable occasions when things went awry. He wanted - when things 'bombed' (as they say) - to be able to say: 'No single individual was to blame. No one lied; and, certainly, no one made up the intelligence or sexed up anything. According to the findings of the independent commission of inquiry (Cain's administration would make provision for commissions of inquiry whose members would be appointed by himself as a matter of course because they would always come in handy if he needed to cover things up), there is no evidence that the administration did not itself believe the judgements which it was placing before the public. Everyone genuinely tried to do their best in good faith for the empire in circumstances of acute difficulty. And moreover we should, above all, not fall into the trap of trying to rewrite history!'

"Thus, Cain and his cronies in the Administration would always be in a position to point an accusing finger at the 'secret service' whose activities would be secret and unknown to the public by definition. And they could always call for an overhaul of the 'intelligence agency' to ensure that the intelligence that would be at their disposal would be more accurate and reliable. They would do that even though one would have thought that an 'intelligence agency', because it dealt in 'intelligence' would be employing some of it to reform itself automatically and all the time, and that no one outside the 'secret service' would be qualified to take any corrective measures its regard.

"Cain definitely had every intention of getting the spy agency to work. He expected it to produce good 'actionable' intelligence - meaning that if his administration ever came into possession of intelligence that when acted on would change the balance of power in the world in favor of the empire. He would never hesitate to act. How could he not especially as he would be prepared to act even on cooked intelligence (or intelligence that had been 'sexed up').

"And so, while some would say that because a country was in possession of intelligence about another exposing weakness in that country's defenses in a critical area, mere possession of such intelligence in the absence of evidence of hostile intent on that other country's part did not by itself justify a pre-emptive strike on that country, Cain would have begged to differ. For it would in his view be unstatesmanlike to let any opportunity to consolidate and strengthen the empire's power slip by. That would be quite irresponsible and also unconscionable given the responsibility that his administration would have for the wellbeing of the empire's future generations.

"But the whole idea of power politics was to stay ahead of the 'game'; and it would never do to fritter away any opportunities to permanently remove potential contestants for the position of super power from the scene. In any event, in the do or die environment of big power politics, the 'other side' would also be on the lookout for any similar opportunities that came their way and, if they had any common sense, they would know that they would be attacked and neutralized by any competing power if they let down their guard.

"Cain did not expect 'politics' (which was the name of the game) to be anything but that - dirty, ruthless and deadly for the losers whether it was politics that was 'internal' or 'external'. And he sincerely believed that unless his administration succeeded in getting the whole world firmly under control, there would be real danger of the world drifting into chaos. Cain frowned on the suggestion that humans, many of whom were really evil (like Abel), could coexist peacefully in a multicultural setting without a benevolent dictator to keep them in line and stop the evil ones from having their way. If anything, he felt duty-bound to root them out and make the world safe once and for all.

"The spy agency would help him and his ruling oligarchy (consisting of fine, principled men of the highest morals) to keep tabs on potential terrorists, insurgents and dictators the world over, and also prevent the riffraff and other 'uncultured' and 'uncivilized' humans from threatening those in the world who were 'cultured' and 'civilized'.

"As a matter of fact, Cain planned, once the spy agency was up and running, to create another and even more secretive 'Office of Special Operations' which would only be known by the letter 'D' for 'Death'. He would set it up ostensibly as a 'department' of the spy agency - but a completely autonomous department whose operations would be funded from a secret slush fund. The mission and activities of the 'department' would be so secret only he himself would actually know that the various sections of the department actually made one whole - meaning that he would himself be responsible for directing the operations of the individual sections of the department and for coordinating their activities. In other words, the individuals he vetted and appointed to manage the department's sections would be kept in the dark about the existence of the department's other section.

"Now, the department would be manned by the cream of the empire's scientists, and their job would include the development of poisons, all sorts of killer viruses and retroviruses, as well as deadly chemical and biological agents that he could use to mysteriously wipe out enemy encampments and even rebellious sections of the empire's own populations. Cain took his responsibilities as emperor that seriously.

"And to prove that the Cain doctrine wasn't just one of those doctrines that was forgotten as soon as it was promulgated, many generations after Cain, a 'statesman' of world renown would assert: 'I do not understand the squeamishness about the use of gas. I am strongly in favor of using poison gas against uncivilized tribes'. By 'uncivilized tribes', he meant the Sunnis, Shiites and Kurds of Mesopotamia. That statesman would insist that 'scientific expedient...should not be prevented by the prejudices of those who do not think clearly'.

"When a creature - a descendant of Adam and Eve (to be exact) who himself or herself gets around by balancing on his/her two spindly legs, and hardly ever gets to be taller than a full-grown ostrich, and who (unlike ostriches) can be felled by a single mosquito bite - starts to speak like that, you have to know that there is something wrong with that creature. Yeah, why do humans say and do these things to each other?

"Now, to ask why humans deal with their own in that fashion is to question my existence. I am the author - yes, author - of death, and I am pretty efficient at what I do. I sow seeds of death quite effectively, and I do it not just at the individual level, but also at the level of state so-called. And that is why, instead of being known as the 'culture of death', the celebration of killing is now known as the 'culture of life'.

"And if you still want to know why humans do what they do to each other, the answer is simple: Selfishness. It is what I get humans to focus on. 'Love thyself above all else' is what we here in the Pit harp on constantly. Loving themselves and those who are dear to them effectively counters the Deliverer's injunction that humans love each other as themselves and their Maker above all else.

"The pact I make with would-be-statesmen is this: I will show you the short cuts to your dreams, but if you promise to focus on the self and on other humans only to the extent to which they are a help to you in reaching your goal, and you will treat the rest of humanity as 'the enemy'. You have to swear that this is what you will do, because I do not live in time, and don't have any to waste.

"In that way, I know that the Deliverer's injunctions to humans that they love one another will be left out on the shelf to dry. As it is, the stupid fools are usually so hooked on material things they will even sell their birthright to become 'statesmen'. They trust me and forget that everything they do will come back to haunt them on the day of reckoning.

"Look, the chaps who are strutting around in the halls of power today will all be gone in a hundred years. Yeah, gone - gone to their judgement! Remember the emperor Caesar Augustus, Pontius Pilate, Herod Agrippa and the rest of the pack who two thousand years ago looked like a permanent fixture on the political scene, and were regarded as almighty and even divine? You would think that someone would at least know where they lie buried, wouldn't you. That has been the lot for all the nincompoops who forgot that they were creatures, and acted like little gods (which 'playing statesman' means). The fools believed me and scorned the words of the Deliverer that it didn't benefit a man one iota if he gained the whole world and lost his soul!

"Anyway, as Cain made very clear in the doctrine he promulgated, being able to make decisions that lead to needless loss of human life in the pursuit of political ambition is a necessary evil. That was what 'power politics' was all about. And making 'tough' decisions aimed at consolidating the power of state through the merciless elimination of noncompliant and potentially threatening regimes was definitely the stuff that 'statesmen' would be made of; and the ability to make them would distinguish people like him (Cain) from the run of the mill or the plebs.

"Just being able to sit down and dream up these arguably wicked - and in some respects even murderous - schemes and scenarios of things to come made Cain forget that he was a mere mortal who would have to say good bye to the world sooner or later like all other humans. Peering ahead in time and discovering that, if he set his mind to it, he could influence and even almost single-handedly determine the direction things in the world took made him feel like a god. Cain thought that this was really funny, because the mischievous things he was conjuring up should, without any doubt, have made him feel like a devil. Instead, they made him feel as if he was the one human alive who was working hard to save humankind from itself - as though he was 'the savior of mankind'!

"Cain went as far as confiding to the 'mother of his children' that individuals who aspired to positions of leadership in the years to come would do well to study his theory of 'empire' so they wouldn't have to 're-invent the wheel' all over again. Noting that his old man and old woman had started keeping diaries in which they recorded the story of creation, how they had fallen from grace, and were continuing to describe the things they themselves were doing to ensure the survival of the human race in what they themselves referred to as the 'stone age', he had hinted that he himself might one day compile his ideas into a 'book' he would give the unassuming title of 'The Empire'! That would provide future generations of tribal chiefs, presidents, proconsuls, kings, and emperors as well as their aides a handy reference in which the 'Cain doctrine', as he put it, would be outlined.

"Now that doctrine essentially exempted Cain in his capacity as emperor from the obligation to treat all equally and with respect. It did not just put him above the law of the land, it exempted him from all laws both natural and super natural so long as his actions were focused on the security of the empire. As Cain saw it, he was completely free to take whatever action he deemed fit in the face of any threat or if the goal of his action was to consolidate and strengthen the power of the empire so that potential foes wouldn't be tempted to threaten it in any way.

"It was obvious to Cain that if he led expeditions and succeeded in overrunning neighboring 'nations', the doctrine would entitle his forces to take the inhabitants of such nations into slavery. Such a move would be perfectly legitimate not just because might made right, but because his empire would be stronger and safer as a result. The slaves would boost the empire's 'economy' by providing free labor, while the occupation and subsequent takeover of those nations would mean that they would never pose a threat of any kind to the empire after they were absorbed into it and ceased to exist as independent or autonomous nations. Indeed, any 'pre-emptive strike' aimed at getting those results would be perfectly legitimate.

"Still, one thought that kept popping up in his mind and kept reminding him of his mortal status threatened to ruin everything. And the more he tried to banish it, the more it kept surfacing.

"It kept occurring to Cain that even if he succeeded in scaring the hell out of every other human and neutralizing any opposition to his scheme of building his empire from the tiny enclave it now was on the edge of Paradise into a sprawling and mighty empire, there was the outside chance that something could go wrong and, even though a feared and powerful emperor, he might find himself a victim of his own machinations - a victim of his own misstep or that of a lieutenant.

"The realm of possibilities included betrayal by associates, a revolt by key military commanders followed by a coup d'état, or may be even a simple accident that left him vulnerable to his enemies - literally anything could happen and bring his dominion over Mother Earth to an abrupt end. It would be so humiliating and that, more than anything else, caused him to suffer nightmares.

"Cain wasn't afraid of facing justice in the next

world after he crossed the gulf that separates the living from the dead. He knew that even in hell he would at least have some company; that we demons were already there. He was in a way prepared for the humiliation of being sent to hell for his misdeeds. The bottom line was that Cain was more interested in the here and now, and didn't care a hoot about an afterlife - exactly as we here in the Pit wanted.

"But if he was exposed here on earth, as the first human who ever aspired for and attained the status of emperor, he would be really devastated. Cain was so scared to think that some other 'caricature of a human being' might rise up and cause him to fall from glory (much like Adam and Eve fell from grace), he refused to entertain the possibility.

"In the event, Cain would prefer to just kill himself if, after enjoying the glamour of being the world's first emperor who was revered and perhaps even worshipped by other humans, he lost out - either through his own carelessness or because of the incompetence of one or more of his lieutenants - and became a commoner and a 'statistic'. The shame would simply be too much for a great mind like himself to face. He knew that after sacrificing the lives of so many other humans to get his empire going, once out power, the movement to have him get a taste of his own 'justice' would be unstoppable.

"Cain refused to think of any such possibility, preferring instead to keep himself in the dark about how it would feel to be at the receiving end! And so, while he was unable to ban those thoughts from his mind, he decided that he would take them into his calculations only to the extent that he would be totally uncompromising with opponents, and also ruthless and merciless with anyone who would dare to stand up against him. As far as he was concerned, regardless of what his conscience told him, his life was his life, and that was all that mattered.

"Cain would also not care how many lives would be sacrificed for the empire - provided his own was not among them. And the views of contemporaries would not matter - not even if people's lives were lost needlessly due to miscalculations, because history and history alone would be his judge. Cain had made up his mind that he would persist in labeling anyone who would refuse to bow to his will as a 'terrorist' and/or 'insurgent'. He would maintain that position even though he himself readily acknowledged that a little graciousness here, and a little generosity there, were almost certain to reduce the cost to the super power itself in both the short and long term.

"And he had similarly resolved that in arbitrating disputes between nations (disputes in which his empire, as the world's sole super power, would alone be in a position to mediate), he would seek to exploit the situation without any regard to natural justice. And, again, he would persist in acting that way even though he knew that a perfunctory show of impartiality and fairness in arbitrating disputes here, and a willingness to compromise there, would earn him greater respect and strengthen his position as emperor of the world.

"No fool, Cain anticipated that 'corruption' would in time become so commonplace, it would even be the law. Indeed the world would, in his view, be like a runaway 'train' (by which he meant the toy he had spent days making for the child his wife was expecting). It would be out of control. And the reason would not be so much because every Tom, Dick and Harry would be aspiring to become an emperor as because the few individuals who succeeded in carving out territory for themselves and declaring themselves emperor would become consumed with greed for power and material possessions alike.

"Also, upon attaining to positions of authority in the

'administration', those who did would promptly forget their humble beginnings and start behaving as if they were like gods. That would in turn speed up the rise of oligarchies, the forerunner of the 'royal families' that would compete with and eventually supplant the 'imperial families' as rulers of the world.

"Peering ahead into the future, Cain could not help gasping at the role that 'political savvy' (the expression he used to refer to 'corruption') would play in the affairs of humans. A couple of individuals would claim that they had invented 'currency' or 'money' to promote trade, and would set up 'banks' where individuals could take it for 'safekeeping'. They would, of course, promptly lend out the money that was brought back to them for custody to other folks who did not have any and pocket the hefty 'interest'. However, to prevent a 'run on the banking system', they would make sure that they retained just enough of the money deposited to pay off those who wished to withdraw their deposits because they either needed to spend the money or regarded the 'interest' paid by the banks on the deposits as inadequate. It would all be day light robbery in disguise.

But Cain anticipated even worse forms of corruption, and they would include the establishment of political parties complete with lobbyists to ensure that only the 'right' people attained to leadership positions. There would be 'legal' systems that would be administered by 'judges' appointed with input from 'interest groups'. The system would thus be rigged in favor of the ruling class (or the proletariat), and any member of the bourgeoisie who complained would be thrown in jail for being a 'threat to society'.

"Cain believed that corruption likely was going to descend on the world in phases, and one of its worst forms was going to appear and become the dominant force in a couple of centuries as the earth's population grew and the number of outright 'landowners' dwindled. Capitalism - or 'latter day slavery' as Cain called it - would be an obnoxious and entirely heartless monopolistic system that would prey on the population at large. The capitalistic system would be controlled by worldly, money hungry moguls who would see nothing wrong in wringing the last ounce of 'productivity' out of the 'workforce' or those on its 'payroll'.

"Cain had a premonition that the millions who would be enslaved to the capitalistic system wouldn't even suspect that they in fact were slaves. They would, in any case, have no alternative but to agree to sign away their freedom by entering into lopsided 'employment contracts' under which they would work virtually for free for the 'multinational' conglomerates.

"The 'firms' would pay the 'workers' just enough to get by and feed their families - but just enough, so those totally 'dependent' workers would be back to continue slaving away, and sometimes all seven days of the week without any break! The workers who would be indispensable to the 'market economy' would of course attract slightly higher wages than would those who were 'expendable'. But, regardless, they would always be faced with the choice of either taking what was offered in 'salary' or leaving it, in which case they and their families would face the prospect of starvation, or even death from exposure to the harsh elements. The capitalistic system would be a boon to 'entrepreneurs' who would be able to pocket millions in 'earned' revenues while those who actually did the donkey work slaved away for a pittance.

"Cain, who understood the importance that nations would accord to their defensive and offensive capabilities, easily saw that a huge chunk of the capitalistic system would be involved with the 'armed forces'. The capitalists or owners of enterprises in that sector of the economy would be dedicated to promoting the 'culture of death' as preserving a nation's independence and 'getting the other guys before they got you' would become a top priority.

"The 'corruption', 'fraud', 'political savvy' - or whatever one wished to call it - would extend to things like international law and the conventions that would govern the conduct of nations in everything ranging from human rights to the maintenance of 'international peace and security'. It would have to be understood that at any time a piece of international law - or some international treaty or convention - impinged on the interests of his empire, that piece of international law or convention would become null and void. While the decisions of the international 'court of justice' or 'tribunal' would be fully binding on all other nations, decisions that intruded on the empire's ability to determine what was or was not in its best interests would be 'non-binding' and automatically unenforceable. That would be the deal!

"To be sure, Cain was prepared to commit injustices to ensure that the 'Cain clan' as he called it eventually dominated and controlled Planet Earth and never stood in any material need. And so, when Abel casually sauntered up to him one day and almost gamely let him know that he and his wife were inviting Cain and his wife to join them and the old man and woman at a get-together they were planning for the specific purpose of consecrating the child they were expecting in a couple of months to the Prime Mover, Cain was understandably upset.

"It was obvious to Cain that Abel was intent on achieving the same goal as he himself had in mind, namely control and domination of the world and what was in it. It was inconceivable that Abel was going to the extent of offering up his child in sacrifice to the Prime

Mover just so his welfare would, as Abel put it, always be in the hands of the Almighty One.

"Just so he himself wouldn't be at a disadvantage, before retiring to bed that night, Cain had knelt down with his wife and consecrated to the Prime Mover not just the child they themselves were expecting in a couple of weeks, but all the children they would ever beget and their children's children as well. With that, Cain was confident that it would be his descendants, not Abel's, who would dominate and control Planet Earth.

"Cain knew better than to inform his wife of his true feelings regarding the 'Abel clan'. This was even though, according to the advice they had received from the old man and the old woman, it was important that there be no secrets between a man and his wife. The fact of the matter was that Cain wanted Abel dead from that moment on. That would be one way to ensure that his own descendants dominated and controlled Mother Earth's resources. Besides, the wicked Cain hoped that some mishap - perhaps a miscarriage or something like that - would overtake Abel's wife either during or before the birth of their baby so that their 'imperial designs' would be automatically frustrated.

"Cain also figured that, even if he did not succeed in eliminating Abel, it was going to be his own children and his children's children who would still end up as the world's 'super power'. Because, thanks to Abel alerting them about his intentions, they had rushed and consecrated, not just their 'first fruits', but the entire Cain clan to the Prime Mover before Abel and his wife had tendered their offering.

"Cain reflected that if Abel had been wise, he would have kept his intentions a secret until the consecration was a done deal. But Abel had again very clearly demonstrated his characteristic stupidity and the fact that he was not so well versed in the ways of the world under the new order.

"It was around this time that Cain, rankled and angry with everybody for trying to belittle him (as he himself put it), devised his plan of luring Abel into the thick woods where, as the bible says, he slew him. He kept telling himself as he did so that he loved Abel as his brother but hated the terrorist and insurgent in him. And for a while he thought he had succeeded in stifling his conscience by pretending that all he was doing was safeguard the territorial integrity of the empire and ensure its security.

"That Cain was quite a brilliant fellow and a real scoundrel. He certainly knew how to come full circle and be a full partner with us in 'devilry' while retaining his image as a virtual 'angel'. But that was not the important thing. What was really important was the role Cain played in ensuring that death - and the culture of death - continued to be central to human life.

"You have to understand that, even though humankind was now saddled with the effects of original sin, it would all have come to naught if all humans who ever walked the earth succeeded in leading the kind of lives the old man and the old woman - and Abel - were leading. To the extent that happened, to that extent death, even though real and hanging over the lives of all men and women, would already have lost its sting.

"To retain its sting, it was important that humans actually went out and killed other humans regardless of the excuse, and perpetuated the culture of death. My evil plan depended on that for its success, and hence the importance of Cain's contribution. We accordingly hail him as our hero, even though he himself escaped our tentacles when he subsequently renounced sin and our cause.

"Everything changed, as everyone now knows, when the Prime Mover repeatedly asked Cain the whereabouts of his brother whom he had slain. That jolted Cain - who was really going off the rails as his wife had suggested - and caused him to regain some of his reason. We had to do quite a bit of stock taking here in the Pit ourselves and to ask ourselves what we had not done right when Cain - Cain of all people - balked at the amount of blood both actual (in the form of Abel's blood) and potential (in the form of all those humans whose lives would be sacrificed as the world's demagogues from that time onwards borrowed a leaf from his script and indiscriminately killed and murdered their fellow humans in their misguided efforts to conquer and dominate the world) on his hands.

"Unlike so many demagogues who came after him, Cain at least came around and saw through his own folly - he saw that he could not hide behind the position of Emperor. While he was free to call himself Emperor, King, Chief, Proconsul, or anything else he wanted to call himself, and to act in the capacity of an emperor or a king, or chief, or proconsul, he was personally answerable to the Prime Mover for everything he did regardless of what he did and whether he did it in a personal or official capacity; and, consequently, his actions had to be consonant with his conscience.

Enemy you cannot see...

"Cain, the first death culture enthusiast and also the world's first demagogue, deep down in his guts lived a life of fear - the fear of 'kicking the bucket'! He was born with that fear, and it scared the hell out of him. Now, Cain had been told by his parents umpteen times, before and after Abel and his other siblings were born, that the Prime

Mover had looked upon Humankind with mercy after they had eaten of the forbidden fruit, and had promised them and their posterity a Deliverer. That Savior would deliver them from the clutches of death - which was one of the penalties for their disobedience.

"The hope that Adam and Eve themselves had for the coming of the Deliverer was so strong, unknown to them, it had actually translated into a saving 'baptism' - a baptism of desire. And it was also this 'baptism' that fortified them against my wiles, drawing as it did on the divine graces that would be merited by the Deliverer who would effectively be the 'Second Adam' when He manifested Himself on earth.

"The old man and the old woman had urged Cain and, subsequently, Abel and the rest of their children to set aside time to bow down daily in adoration of the Prime Mover and infinitely merciful Lord, and also to meditate on the Promise of a Savior so that the hope of their redemption would free them from the fear of death. But it all seemed to no avail. They still caught him brooding over his 'fate' ever so many times, and trying to figure out how on his own, without help from 'above', he could out-fox me and gain eternal life at the end of his pilgrimage on earth.

"But for a long time, Cain, who blamed the old man and woman for all their problems and thought that he was a much better person than them, would hear nothing of it. He called them sinners and liars, and never stopped nagging them about the real reasons behind their decision to steal fruit from the Tree of Knowledge. That was how Cain initially got the idea that he perhaps could record victory over death by gearing himself up to actually inflict death on anyone who looked remotely like a threat to his well-being.

"For their part, Adam and Eve prayed constantly to

the 'Deliverer' for their son even though he was yet to come. It was clear from the way the Promise was framed that the Deliverer's coming would be facilitated by a woman! She would evidently be one of their own offspring; and they frequently meditated on the fact that she would be a very blessed thing of necessity; one worthy enough to facilitate the advent of the Deliverer into the world! Suffice it to say that when their first baby girl arrived, the thought on their mind was that it might be her! That she might be the one who would 'crush the serpent's head'!

"Cain, who for a long time resisted the advice of his parents and regularly skipped his daily prayers and meditation, did not realize until well after he had murdered his brother that if you really wanted to be a victor, getting a monopoly over weapons of mass destruction or turning his empire's military into an 'efficient killing machine' (as he himself had considered doing at one time) could never do the trick. That sort of thing worked only if your intentions were to defend the world against some demonic aliens from hell or outer space. But it was completely out of place if you were dealing with fellow human beings who also happened to be made in the Image.

"Developing efficient means of 'destroying' other humans? One had to be kidding! First of all, individuals contemplating such action had to make sure that they really 'destroyed' their enemies - so that there wouldn't be any chance that those they thought they had successfully 'eliminated' or 'annihilated' would be waiting on the other side of the Gulf as 'witnesses' against them in the court of divine justice when they themselves eventually kicked that bucket! Which begged the question: because it was not possible to 'rub out' a creature that was made in the Image - and all humans, however despicable or bad were such creatures!

"And so, if one was thinking aright, hand in hand with trying to get a monopoly over things like weapons of mass destruction or investing in efficient killing machines, it was imperative that one also tried to make oneself impervious to death - to invent a formula that ensured that as long as one was engaged in the business of visiting death on others, one's own *elan vital* would in no circumstances succumb to illness or anything that would cause the would-be-killer himself/herself to 'kick the bucket'. And so, it was clearly not enough to wear a bulletproof vest or to ride only in Humvees. One needed to take out similar 'insurance' against mosquito bites, common colds, and similar ills that did not respect any one and indiscriminately took the lives of so many humans prematurely.

"Always remember that before Adam and Eve took steps to defy the Almighty One, they did everything to try and ensure that they would not get into a situation in which they would meet Him face to face, let alone in judgement. Eve tried to come up with a dietary formula that would ensure that the cells in their bodies would keep regenerating themselves forever to ensure that they would never die! Poor souls - Adam and Eve should have known better than that. The bodies of humans, made out dust, were never meant to support those who were on a pilgrimage on earth forever! But even though Eve was just wasting her time, at least she tried to use her head.

"And when I myself refused to go down on bended knee and to worship the Author of Life, I first made certain that He would not turn around and 'rub me out' - and the spirits that joined in the infernal rebellion checked it out also. But we also miscalculated - and, in retrospect, we definitely wouldn't repeat what we did out of our pride!

"It could, of course, never be right for a human to

slay another. Nothing, absolutely nothing, could ever justify it. Forget the biblical tales that glorify wars and killing. When they are not apocrypha that over-zealous translators who wanted to depict the Prime Mover as the almighty one by drawing on human experiences surreptitiously introduced into the sacred texts, they were included in the original inspired scripts in a context that was entirely different, and specifically as evil deeds of men that were not to be emulated.

"And because my troops have been around and at work from the start, we have been able to depict things as otherwise, and to make it seem as if killing is sanctioned by the Prime Mover Himself. What did you think we would be doing hanging around the inspired writers, transcribers of the sacred texts, and above the preachers who, with only a few exceptions, are on our payroll anyway! Death is a direct consequence of original sin, and it is our sacred duty to see that it pervades everything humans do.

"If killing was something that could be justified or in any way elevated to a virtuous act, the Deliverer would have killed stricken down those crowns that had shouted for His crucifixion, and he would have caused the Roman soldiers to scatter like flies. Talk of killing in self-defense - there is no killing in self-defense that could have been more justified. But instead, he turned the other cheek when slapped, and just prayed to His father for strength to 'drink the cup'! And he bade His followers do likewise.

"He even instructed them that if they should be turned away from a city, as they went about the all-important mission of 'harvesting' souls, they only needed to brush any dust their slippers may have collected as they walked that city's streets in the course of doing what they needed to do, and go their way - and forget that they had ever been there. In other words, it was not for them to condemn anyone who ridiculed or rejected the gospel message. With the power at His disposal after He had scored His more-than-convincing victory over evil and death by His resurrection, He could have advised them to 'stay and occupy' all such cities, to ensure that they were 'Christianized'. But He didn't.

"Of course, humans who kill others are stupid. If you hate other humans or are so terrified about other humans that you'd rather not be near them, the worst possible thing you can do is to try and kill them. Going that route is suicidal and madness first of all because, instead of contending with an enemy you can see and hear, and who is subject to the limitations which go with being an earth-bound mortal, you now have to contend with a pure spirit; and a vengeful spirit is certainly not something you want to have as your enemy. You also lose any physical advantages you might have had over your 'enemy'.

"But, above all, with your action, you move the contest from the material to the spiritual arena where intrigues and underhand maneuvers can never be a match for uprightness, moral integrity and honesty. And, of course, a mind that is so warped that it can sanction the killing of another human is at a huge disadvantage from the start.

"The fact of the matter is that you now also have to contend with the Author of Life and Judge. It is fair to say that humans who regard killing under any circumstances as a solution to their problems delude themselves. They are not merely short-sighted and simple-minded souls, but also very stupid people who just have no idea what bigger problem they land themselves into when they seek to take the life of another human. All they do actually is set themselves up for spiritual death. That is in exact accordance with the original plan that I had in place when

I lured Adam and Eve to steal and eat fruit from the Tree of Knowledge.

"But this just goes to show how dumb humans can be. Even though created in the Image by virtue of which they also come endowed with reason, humans prefer to pull the wool over their eyes, and to kid themselves and pretend that the Prime Mover, Divine Soul and Supreme and Almighty Being - who Himself has no beginning and who caused them to come into existence out of nothing - exists only in the figment of the human mind; or, if He does, went to sleep after conducting His labors of creation! And this is especially true for those humans who think that they are very 'clever' and know a lot! They blind themselves to the fact that they automatically have to contend with the Divine Soul and Almighty One each and every time they perpetrate an injustice and infringe the natural Law of Equity and Justice thereby; and they even go to the extent of kidding themselves that, even after they themselves kick the bucket, all will be well, and there will be no divine wrath to face! So, so dumb!

"This is a war - the war against the Lamb! And it is the real 'Mother of All Wars'! Note that it is not a 'war between Good and Evil' as such because such a war can only exist in fiction. You won't find a reference to a 'war between Good and Evil" anywhere in the Scriptures, because there is no such a thing as 'Evil', which simply means the 'absence of Good'! Regardless, what goes on in our war with the Lamb is rough stuff, and it is deadly. That is why I am known as the Father of Death!

"I knew all along that after Adam and Eve ate of the forbidden fruit and predictably got kicked out of the Garden of Eden, their spiritual death, which was real and not just metaphorical, would lead directly to murders of humans by humans. The fear of dying would in turn drive, not just Adam and Eve, but all of their offspring and their offspring's offspring to do what would doom them spiritually over and over, namely to kill and murder their fellow humans in declared and undeclared wars. They would then have to contend with the Prime Mover who had admonished Adam and Eve to stay clear of the Tree of Knowledge - and not touch any of its fruits - in the first place.

"And, if humans automatically have to contend with Him when they kill, you bet that they also have to contend with Him when they hurt, abuse, torture or otherwise come up short in their obligation to love one another as themselves. Take the case of spousal violence. Regardless of the reason for the killing, the victim upon leaving this world, ceases to be a spouse of the murderer because there are no spousal relations of any kind outside of the bond of love between the Prime Mover and the saints on the other side of the Gulf. And so the spouse who commits violence on his/her partner, or succeeds in taking away the spousal partner's life, immediately has to contend with the ire of an enraged Prime Mover.

"The fact is that when a human harms another in anyway, the harm is sustained by the Deliverer who is Himself the Author of Life and Judge. He wasn't cracking a joke when He said that when a good turn was done to the least human, it was done to Him! Or, when He said that those who live by the sword die by the sword! He was quite serious. And so you kill, you die the spiritual death.

"It is not just a case of being presumptuous on the part of humans who seek to use the killing of fellow humans - or, more appropriately, 'homicide' (regardless of the label that it is given) - to achieve an end. And - let us face it - the reason for attempts by humans to rub out their fellow humans always boils down to an irrational fear

387

that mistakenly attributes the hanging threat of death to individuals in society who are associated in the mind with its immediate onslaught. On the contrary, it is always like a case of mistaken identity. Frankly, it is even dumb and stupid. The sentence of death was pronounced on humans, not by any creature and not even by the Avenging Angel, but by the Prime Mover Himself.

"In the aftermath of the fall of Adam and Eve from grace, humans - all humans became marked for death by divine decree. The sin of Adam and Eve (both of whom were created in the Image) consisted in taking the stand that the self had primacy over obedience to their conscience and to the will of the Prime Mover. It represented a challenge that humans posed to their Maker in complete disregard of the fact that they were His creatures - and creatures, for that matter, that also happened to be earth bound even though they were primarily spiritual. It was such monumental 'disrespect' directed at the Almighty.

"But instead of going back on His word and 'rubbing' out the human race because of the disobedience of the first man and the first woman, the Prime Mover in His infinite goodness promised them a Deliverer. But in the meantime, Man's disobedience (or attempt to play God) had activated or resulted in spiritual death that on the one hand saw humans alienated by their own wilful action from the Author of Life who continued to be their mainstay and last end.

"And because humans were also earthbound creatures by virtue of having a physical body (by virtue of their nature consisting of a corporeal body and an incorporeal soul), an unavoidable - and in fact necessary if novel - side effect of their spiritual death was that they would physically also 'die the death'. In other words, their bodies would also return to dust in time.

"But subsequently, Cain and a host of other stupid humans fell into the habit of transferring the blame for the threat of death hanging over their heads to those fellow humans whom they perceived as a threat to their *worldly* success - making an already very bad infinitely worse! Their motivation for doing that was the irrational *fear* of dying.

"With all humans already slated to die the death, it will dawn on all killers at that fateful moment as their hearts stop beating and they find themselves on the other side of the gulf that separates the living humans from the humans who have gone before (regardless of how they themselves meet their demise) that the act of dying actually represents liberation of sorts (particularly now that the promised Deliverer had come) as humans are freed from the trappings of the world, and freed especially from their bodies which (except in the case of the most ascetic and selfless) are the abiding symbol of worldliness. To the extent those bodies were not treated like the temple of the Prime Mover, to that extent they also become symbols of the pact of those humans with me, Beelzebub, the Author of death.

"At that time, as the souls depart from their earthly abode and head for the afterlife, the individual humans without exception experience a personal, mind boggling and excruciating 'Armageddon' whose intensity is in proportion to the extent to which the individual was attached or wedded to the self and consequently also to material things. It is at that time when humans who had put their trust in the world will find that the 'armor' they had on was a mirage, and they cheated themselves by not putting on the 'armor of the Deliverer' in accordance with the advice of the Apostle of the Gentiles. They will wish they had accepted the call to live entirely for others in imitation of the Deliverer - like Saint Joseph or Mother

Theresa.

"Damn stupid humans! If killing did the trick and directly translated into anything that qualified as a positive result for the killer, the Ten Commandments would not have included one that stated: 'Thou shalt not kill'. And, of course, the Deliverer would not have warned that those who lived by the sword died by the sword. If it was a virtue to kill, the Deliverer Himself would have been a gangster whose place would be at the head of an army of ruthless 'head hunters' drawn from the choirs of angels. And it would not be an exaggeration to say that His work would be cut out for Him as He and His band of loyal angels, all of them seized with holy anger, determinedly put iniquitous and impious humans - which would be just about every human who had ever lived or would ever live - to the sword.

"Because one has the ability to destroy, it does not mean that one should use it. And if one didn't have the ability to kill, the hankering to kill who ever one had a mind to kill becomes pointless any way. The maxim that it is nice to be important, but it is more important to be nice applies equally to those who enjoy the ability to kill and those who do not. At the last judgement though, the kudos go to those who were nice, because they are the ones who have not received their reward. Humans who go through life imagining that being important is of the essence have already received their reward.

"Humans who cut short the lives of their fellow humans in the short run cause terrible grief not just to those they kill, but also to the Eternal Word through whom all creatures came into being. The grief caused to the Deliverer is particularly acute for the simple reason that humans were created in the Image and by design should live forever and should never die.

"Agonizing over the fact that humans sinned and

now must die in the hours before His own death, the Deliverer even sweated blood! Rivulets of His precious blood flowed down His forehead and drenched the garments He wore. Just as His death on the cross is re-enacted every time bread and wine are consecrated at Mass and become His body and blood, so also this scenario is repeated whenever a human's life is cut short.

"The Deliverer is pained very much whether it is one human who is cut down by a sniper's bullet or thousands of humans who are scotched to death when a nuclear device is set off over a metropolis.

"Actually, despite their avowals, all death culture enthusiasts, by putting their complete trust in the 'sword', automatically disavow their faith in the Prime Mover and are therefore agnostics - more deserving of pity than idol worshippers.

"After Cain had killed Abel, he believed (quite mistakenly as it turned out) that he had eliminated the 'problem'. Similarly with all other humans who kill following in his lamentable and contemptible example. They believe that they have somehow dealt a blow to their foes and reduced their problems in life. And they do that because they have stifled their consciences, and are determined to go on living in a world of fantasy and not in a world of reality. Because they are married to the 'lie' as Cain was, instead of the 'Truth'.

"Then, instead of going down on their knees and begging the Prime Mover for mercy, they strut around proudly like peacocks and, imagining themselves more invincible than ever, even celebrate the killings - making things worse for themselves!

"In the wake of any killing, instead of rejoicing, the perpetrator(s) should start preparing for the prospect of joining me, the Author of Death, here in this goddamned place you folks call hell. And I am not pulling this out of my hat. You just guessed - I do not have a hat, and not even a crown on which it could sit. The commandment - the fifth commandment - says very clearly: 'Thou shalt not kill.' And if they imagine that they will receive a red carpet welcome on their arrival here, they are seriously mistaken. This is a place where the closest thing to happiness is the weeping and gnashing of teeth.

"When one celebrates a criminal act, one says 'good bye' to any act of divine mercy that might have been his/hers for the asking. And trying to ask for mercy (and to tell the victim 'I am sorry for you') in the midst of the celebrations is nothing short of mockery.

"Given the nature of death and the fact that I (Diabolos) am its author, it is not possible to genuinely mourn the demise of some humans - for example those we regard as being particularly dear to us - and to celebrate the passing of other humans. Those who do that live in a world of fantasy - a world in which some humans are truly human and not others. The Deliverer exposed that lie, and even showed the way when He took up His human nature and, as the Second Adam, launched the project that not only aimed at securing the salvation of all humans but also at taking the sting out of the very thing that murderous and confused humans celebrate, namely death and neutralizing it.

"Humans who kill or celebrate death in some manner show by their actions that they are 'antichrists'. For the Son of Man was Himself led like a lamb to the slaughter, after consenting to bear the burden of the sins of all men. Consequently, other than try to rub Him out (just like happened to the heir in the gospel parable), no death culture enthusiast can want to have anything to do with Him, death culture enthusiasm being based on a philosophy that completely runs counter to His teachings.

"In fact, celebrating killings in any form is

celebrating the death of the Deliverer's brothers and sisters to whom He was so endeared that He did not hesitate to shed His divine blood so they might realize eternal life. But what is even worse - any such celebration is a direct and unforgivable affront to the Eternal Word, who is also the Deliverer and Judge.

"When creatures celebrate killing (creatures who themselves, as it so happens, have a life span that does not frequently exceed a hundred years), they therefore definitely write-off divine mercies by acting as though life was so expendable. They in fact make a statement that there is no such a thing as life after death. And, yes, they write off the divine mercies by their actions because those actions naturally take precedence over their avowals to the contrary! This is because someone who does not believe in the brotherhood of humans cannot expect to be counted among the elect.

"It must be a very confused individual who can imagine that it is kosher to try and 'rub out' a human brother or human sister (whatever the motivation) and still expect to be friends with the Eternal Word (through whom all things in existence were made and who also set the rules) who is now also Judge and whose vocabulary did not include killing or revenge. Humans who seriously aspire to join the blessed company of the Son of Man's friends or the elect must make up their mind to walk in His footsteps - period.

True victory…

"There is only one reason humans kill - because they are dumb! It is because they do not have a clue why they walk on earth - why they were brought into being or exist. And it goes without saying that it would be more appropriate for creatures who knew that their own days were numbered to 'live and let live' (as some clever nut put it) rather than set out on a killing spree.

"The more 'enemies' a human kills, the more that human should hate himself/herself, because those one calls 'enemies' and kills are the killer's very own brothers and sisters who all have the same woman known as Eve, who was fashioned out of the rib of Adam, their great great great granddaddy, for their great great great Grand Momma. Whatever one thinks about one's enemies - however odious one imagines them to be - one makes a big mistake by thinking that one has the right to strike back. Damn stupid humans!

"Humans do not have any such right. First of all, they are themselves guilty of much worse things. They have grievously offended - and murdered - not just a fellow mortal, but a divinity! They have sinned against the Almighty. And whatever makes them imagine that they won't face retribution for the mortal and venial sins they commit over their lifetime is a mystery!

"Now, when Cain killed Abel, he did so with his bare hands. According to his own confession (to which both Adam and Eve make reference in the diaries they kept), he lured his brother into the forest on a pretext. Sneaking behind the shorter Abel, Cain then administered a vicious blow to the back of the younger man's head. The blow knocked Abel to the ground. In the ensuing struggle, Cain (as he himself confessed later) finally succeeded in strangling his brother and killing him with his bare hands...the stupid fellow!

"Right up until wars became institutionalized as a legitimate method for the killing of humans by fellow humans, the women were the ones whose lives were snuffed out prematurely by their men folk on various pretexts in a growing incidence of 'Violence against Women'. The men initially went after the women because they did not like to face up to the fact that the constitution of women (unlike their own constitution) predisposed them to frequently changing moods. And then, being more muscular and physically stronger, the men would simply vent their anger and frustration on the 'weaker sex' after a disappointing hunting trip or if they were unable to come home with a good catch of fish. The domineering he-humans often just diverted their frustration on the womenfolk, and this frequently resulted in the lives of many an innocent woman being snuffed out prematurely.

"Other homicides were occasioned by rivalries among both men and women over spousal partners. Men who thought they could get away with it murdered their rivals so they would be unchallenged over their choice of a spouse, and women did the same. Everything from poisons to sharpened rocks and clubs were used in those early murders.

"Later on, groups of clansmen fought over things ranging from the mistreatment of their womenfolk who had been given to members of other clans as wives in exchange for a bride price to the failure by one clan chief to accord due respect in the course of conducting a business deal to another clan chief. Killings of humans by fellow humans on a big scale occurred when tribes fought pitched battles over pieces of countryside and control over mountain passes using machetes, spears and arrows.

"As years went by, instead of able-bodied men in a tribe, it was an 'army' of people drawn from one nation that was ranged against a similar army of people drawn from an opposing nation, sometimes as a result of a spat over something that was really minor or of no importance whatsoever. But, by this time, the actions of parties to such conflicts, while triggered by incidents that were trivial, were definitely informed by the Cain doctrine of world domination.

"The discovery of gunpowder transformed killing or 'wars', with nations making deliberate decisions to invest in the large-scale production of weapons of war or 'armaments' which now included rifles, cannons and gunships, and eventually squadrons of warships and air planes. Hand in hand with the massive investments in weapons of war, 'Military Science' has been used to transform the armies of the day into efficient killing machines. But even then, care has been taken to provide the act of killing with the respectability that had hitherto been reserved for professions such as Medicine and Law.

"But the days of real killing orgies finally arrived with the use in combat for the very first time of weapons of mass human destruction in the shape of nuclear bombs. Consequently, with the arrival of these Real Weapons of Mass Human Destruction (RWMHD), the powers that be, including super power rogue states, ordinary rogue states, networks of 'terrorists' and now also 'insurgents' can proceed full steam ahead to destroy - and in the process be destroyed themselves by - the 'enemy'!

"As has always been the case, nations led by a variety of demagogues have aspired to a monopoly over the means for destroying human life en masse in hopes that such a monopoly will also deliver the ultimate prize, namely unchallenged, total and also permanent dominion over Mother Earth and the right to ride rough-shod over all other nations that will not disarm unilaterally or throw in the towel. But I have to tell you (as the devil and author of death) that no one individual or even nation can ever have a monopoly over 'killing power'.

"Humans, inclined to sin, outdo each other in this business of killing. On the evidence, they are in fact not just *inclined* to sin, they are obsessed with sin - and with killing. By far the largest slices of the national budget pies are devoted to the so-called 'military establishment' - the department staffed with humans who are trained and also certified to kill.

"As if that was not bad enough, there is also a growing trend to 'privatize' some of that department's functions - meaning that it is now passé to be a hired gun, a mercenary or hired killer. It apparently won't be long before outfits with names like 'Murder, Inc.' or 'Private Armed Forces & Co.' are quoted on the London and New York stock markets; and, given the potential returns, they could easily outstrip all other stocks as the most popular.

"To make things worse, the operations of those military establishments are also increasingly being carried out in the name of the Prime Mover. And so, even though the business of killing is in my domain and 'devilish', those outfits after a while might change their names to something like 'Christian Murder, Inc.' or 'Private Christian Army for the Salvation of the World, Inc.'.

"It might be a good thing to step back and reflect on what we are discussing here. Death - just in case you do not know - is by its nature a dreadful God-awful thing if just because it is not the Prime Mover but I, Beelzebub, who is its author. You have to understand that we fallen spirits effectively 'died' when we were cast out of heaven into this bottomless pit in the bowels of the earth as punishment for our sin of disobedience.

"The separation of the human souls from the human bodies as a result of which the bodies turn into dust and the souls become my prisoners here in hell is a replay of our own death - unless, like the souls of those who were rescued by the Deliverer on the day He rose from the dead, the humans in question die repentant and are friends again with the Prime Mover.

"And so, it is bad enough when humans die of old age and other so-called 'natural causes'. But humans who cause other humans to 'kick the bucket' prematurely using poisons or other means engage in what I call 'playing Satan'. When I succeeded in tempting Adam and Eve to join me in my rebellion and they incurred the 'curse of death' with their disobedience, I became complicit in their death as much as they themselves did with their wilful act. I can therefore say that I killed them.

"When humans fall for the bait and kill other humans by whatever means and in whatever circumstances in the pursuit of their happiness in this world, it is an understatement to say they 'imitate' me. They commit murder in their own right and automatically merit the consequences for getting their hands stained with innocent blood. They are moreover usually also guilty of tempting their victims to 'buy their safety' by becoming collaborators in their wicked schemes, or by agreeing to do other less than honorable things in order to save their lives - again in imitation of me.

"And so, starting with Cain who murdered Abel with his bare hands, humans have connived to maim, injure and kill fellow humans using everything from butchers' knives to bullets and atomic bombs, and have themselves become liable for the sentence of death. Again, it is bad enough for the human soul to separate from the body because the individual has got as far in the twilight of his/her life as he/she could go. But it is really terrible when their homes are shelled and they are buried alive, or they are torn to smithereens by the 'smart bombs' - or when humans are tortured to death by their own kind.

"Knowing how hard it was for Cain to make a U-turn and above all accept to give away his 'empire' to the surviving members of Abel's family in a genuine (not mock) act of restitution, we have gone the extra mile to ensure that there will be a sufficient number of dungeons here in hell for the anticipated influx of our 'friends'.

"In most parts of the world, thieves and pickpockets are on patrol on a full-time basis - you can never be watchful enough. From time immemorial, demagogues, masquerading as statesmen or stateswomen, have also roamed the world looking for something to steal - and that is what 'international relations' and 'diplomacy' are now all about. And killing and maiming, which have always been accepted practices among thieves, are now an integral part of what the uninformed think are respectable professions.

"Today, all nations are out to steal from other nations, with the big powerful countries roaming the world in search of weaker nations that they can gobble up - just as I myself am constantly roaming the world in search of souls to devour. And then they have the audacity to do it in the name of the Prime Mover! I have to take off my hat (figuratively only of course) to these guys. And weaker nations that do not quickly ally themselves with more powerful nations risk losing all.

"But how come that humans (who smart so, when they feel slighted by other humans and who, at my suggestion, will not hesitate to rob fellow humans of their possessions and even commit murder in the process) consistently act helpless when Mother Nature in the shape of hurricanes, flash floods, snow storms, etc. lick them! They certainly don't feign or just pretend to be helpless! And that is exactly what exposes the hypocrites.

"If you will go for the jugular when you feel slighted by a fellow human or you lust after the other person's possessions, you should be consistent and do the same to the all mighty Almighty when He causes His mother nature to have you get a taste of what it is like to be at the receiving end!

"If you still do not know what I am driving at, you must be what you humans call 'hard core'. Humans are actually useless and helpless; but when it comes to dealing with their fellow humans, they suddenly start playing God.

"The time is coming when the Prime Mover is going to play Prime Mover - or His real Self - on humans. At that time, they are not going to even want to recall the things they now do to others that they wouldn't like done unto themselves. So, let them just go on playing god as much as they like - just as I myself did once upon a time. That is what I did when I refused to genuflect and worship and chose to be the Author of Death.

"As the old saying (which humans ignore at their peril) goes, it is not what goes in but what comes out that corrupts. See the analogy? It is not what happens to you that corrupts. It is what you do. Suppose that the goal of some humans is to control particularly rich oil fields that happen to be in someone else's backyard, and then use that as a staging point for securing some other things (example uranium deposits) that happen to be next door.

"And, first of all, they are clearly in the wrong by going after what belongs to another and is not theirs. That is called 'robbery' or 'banditry'. Secondly, when they issue a 'fatwa' (that is supposed to be binding on all the folks who happen to be in their path) and demand that they give way or be damned, the humans who are after the oil or the uranium - or securing the route to India and its spices - do something that just seals their own fate.

"And if the 'bandits' or 'robbers' think that anyone in their path who resists their advance automatically becomes a devil, they are completely mistaken. Greedy, covetous and already out of control, they merely compound their own 'problem' by trying frenetically trying

400

to liquidate other innocent humans whom they find in their path so that they may achieve their objective of controlling the sources of the oil and uranium. Instead of just robbery, their crime becomes multiple murder!

"You see - it is not the fact that a human is born in Najaf or in Texas (what goes in) that corrupts him or her. It is the scheming and conniving of humans - and their actions (what comes out) that do.

"And that is exactly how I do my job - I take stupid humans on top of mountains and show them where vast fields of 'oil', deposits of uranium and things like that, as well as other 'wealth' are located, and I tell them that it is all theirs if they just kneel and worship. And that is exactly what they do. After they have pledged their royalty to me, you can bet that whatever comes out of their mouth when they get back home is rotten - their actions, spin and everything else they scheme up so they can lay their hands on those riches.

"Instead of stopping at behaving like the rich man who refused to notice the beggars on his door step, they become worse. On their match to the oil fields, they even rob and kill beggars along the way - those who think that the strangers must be joking when they hear about the *fatwa* and are in any case determined to hang on to the little they possess for dear life. If you do not see my footprints when you see things of that sort unfolding, you are a write-off and will never see anything.

"Luckily for me, when I take these delegations of humans up on the mountain tops for the demo, I don't have to walk or drive them there. I just spirit them there. In the absence of footprints or tire marks or other signs that humans have been up there to see me, they all invariably believe that they are pioneers - that they are doing what no other human before them has ever done. Stupid humans!

"Look, when the bible says that I took the Deliverer up into an exceeding high mountain from which I caused Him to see all the Kingdoms of the world along with their splendor, do you think we walked all the way to Mt. Kilimanjaro or Mt. Everest? Of course not! I just spirited Him there the way I spirit you all to these places.

"Let me make this one thing quite clear - the Prime Mover does not tempt. I am the Tempter and I do the tempting. And so, while the Prime Mover is busy causing good to come out of evil or (if you prefer) evil to generate good, I am busy checking out potential high way robbers and murderers, spiriting them up to mountain tops to show them the riches of the world, and then causing them to fall for the temptations using all sorts of ruses.

"Now, I know from experience that it is the one thing humans find very hard to understand, and that is the fact that the Prime Mover, who creates things out of nothing and who exults the meek and frustrates the proud to size, doesn't let any opportunity to cause good to come out of evil pass by. The Prime Mover could never allow high way bandits to strike and leave destruction in their trail without adequate plans to turn the miseries of their innocent victims into good.

"Accordingly, there are those who will be struck down even before they ostensibly reach the prime of their lives. He (who does not fail to take note when any one of the uncountable birds of the air loses just one of its feathers) will not let something like that come to pass for nothing.

"Precisely because humans do things that redound to the glory of the Prime Mover only with the help of divine grace, instead of letting those who might well be tempted in their later life to disown Him live on, the Prime Mover will allow them to be cut down by the high way bandits as a way of rescuing them from themselves and from my wiles.

"To 'sweeten' the deal as it were, the Prime Mover uses the proud (who have this tendency to regard only themselves alone as justified and to despise everyone else as sinners and evil doers) to exult the victims of their machinations. And he emphasizes thereby His determination to avenge the evil deeds of humans, and demonstrates His ability to do so quite effectively.

"The Prime Mover does this even without regard to the actions of those who make up the hierarchy of His Church. Because they are human, the successors to the apostles are not known to condemn the outrageous things humans do consistently. As history has shown, not only have the actions of the churchmen, frequently conducted in the Church's name, been responsible for atrocities, but when humans are cut down unjustly, it is typical for them to raise their voices in condemnation only when the victims are members of the 'visible Church' - as if the rest of humankind doesn't have the right to call the Prime Mover 'Abba' or Father.

"It is a little like a referee at a soccer match who only sees fouls committed against players who happen to espouse certain opinions on an array of subjects, and does not see it as his business to blow the whistle when other players are fouled however glaringly.

"Humans have the same nature and, regardless of their religious affiliation, enjoy the same inalienable rights, including the right to life. When the successors to the apostles (who are supposed to be well informed on these matters) can practice such discrimination, you tell me what those who are less informed would do. No wonder that members of the Church's hierarchy are not taken seriously when they try to advocate for the rights of the unborn.

"The Church's hierarchy should be interested in the

spiritual and physical well-being of all. They should be interested in the salvation of communists, Moslems, Hindus, Catholics, and others equally. But they give the impression that the Mystical Body of the Deliverer is made up of only 'Catholics' or (at the most) 'Christians'. That is the impression they give, but how correct is it?

"War mongers in the world operate on the premise that, instead of human souls, the Prime Mover created American souls, Russian souls, Chechen souls, Chinese souls, Vietnamese souls, North Korean souls, South Korean souls, Japanese souls, Iraqi souls, Turkish souls, Greek souls, and even royal British souls. The impression one gets from listening to some members of the Church's hierarchy is that the Prime Mover created Catholic souls, Hindu souls, Moslem souls, pagan souls, etc., and that there is a difference when Catholics and non-Catholics suffer injustices or die.

"And supposing the Prime Mover operated on the same principle! Then the Deliverer would have to withdraw his statement to the effect that His Father in heaven was concerned when a bird that didn't even possess a soul lost one of its feathers!

"The Prime Mover is in the business of creating *human* souls, and He turns them out, not just in droves, but in all sorts of shapes and sizes according to His divine plan. And, to ensure that the nature of His human creatures is complete and perfect like everything else he manufactures out of nothing, He also turns out bodies of humans in all sorts of shapes, sizes, and even colors, depending on His plan for the individual human. He makes all humans unique humans in that way.

"But there is no such a thing as a black, white or yellow human soul - and there is certainly no such a thing as an American, Iroquois, Vietnamese, Iraqi, Israeli, Palestinian, Pakistani, Indian, South African, East

African, West African, Russian, Chechen, Japanese, North Korean, South Korean, Australian, Papuan, Filipino, or even British soul.

"And because He is the Artist par excellence, He thoroughly enjoys what he does. But he is also a jealous Prime Mover who does not brook insults or chicanery. He designs and makes human souls in His own image, signifying that love is the cornerstone of His labors. And He demands the same and no less from His creatures - that they love one another like they love themselves, and that they love Him above all else.

The "Sancta Ecclesia..."

"Unlike pure spirits, humans after their creation and birth, continue to evolve and develop not just spiritually, but also physically. I definitely would have preferred to be created a human for just that reason. And, predictably, one of the vices that hastened my downfall consisted in envy. I always suspected that the Prime Mover would in time cause creatures that were different from me in important respects to come into being; and, in my jealousy, I even resented the fact that the Almighty was in a position to do that.

"I, even now, feel very jealous that the nature of humans allows them to grow, develop and be challenged in all sorts of ways, while we pure spirits do not change much after we are created. The fact of the matter is that I should be more proud of the way I was created, because the Prime Mover Himself is unchanging. Still, it would definitely be more fun being a human devil!

"I feel cheated when I try to imagine all the things I could have done as a Human Devil. If I lived to be only a hundred and twenty years, I would be able to do a hell of a lot of damage in that period. It would be a time earthlings would remember in a long time. For one, as a human devil on trial, I would be able to move around incognito among humans. Because a pure spirit is like a glowing asteroid in the heavens, it is impossible to hide - even though stupid humans think we don't exist just because they are too absorbed with the material things to notice that there is far more to reality than what meets the eye.

"And if you do not believe me when I say that I would inflict even more damage in the battle between good and evil as a human devil, I tell you: 'Think again!' Look, the passage in Genesis that reads: 'I will put enmities between thee and the woman, and thy seed and her seed; she shall crush thy head, and thou shalt lie in wait for her heel..." is referring to a human, a humble maiden who consented to be the Mother of the Deliverer. (Genesis 3:15) And, a human, she has been crowned 'Regina Caeli' (Queen of heaven) for her pains! And, even though a mere human, as the mother of the Word made flesh, her intercession in heaven on behalf of other humans is predictably very powerful.

"But look: the Deliverer, the Word who deigned to take up his human nature and chalked up thirty-three years on this earth, is (as the Council of Lyons proclaimed) "true God and true man...not a phantasm, but the one and only Son of God" (Council of Lyons II, DS 852). You can therefore take it that I too would have been quite capable of doing wonders as a human devil!

"And, also look: even as a creature that is invisible to the human eye, I have commanded a large following among humans of every generation – my minions who do my bidding and sow the seeds of death amongst their fellow humans on my behalf. As a human devil, upon kicking the bucket and crossing the gulf that separates the living from the dead, I would have been judged exactly as happened when I led the renegade spirits in the rebellion against the Almighty One; and I would have ended up here in Gehenna just the same.

"Actually, you can safely include humans in that epic rebellion, because the devilishness that I inspire among them quite often beggars the mind; and it is what prompted the Deliverer to muse, saying: 'But yet, the Son of man, when cometh, shall he find, think you, faith on earth?' (Luke 19:8) Referring to my minions among humans, the Deliverer, knowing the amount of havoc they are capable of causing, sounded the alarm and said that it were better for them that a millstone were hanged about their neck, and they were cast into the sea, than that they should scandalize any of those innocent little ones. (Matthew 18:6 and Luke 17:2)

"Still, after everything is said and done, being a pure spirit and invisible to the human eye has disadvantaged me and my fellow demons in many ways. Some humans, including my most ardent lackeys, blatantly use this as an excuse to deny that I exist and that it is I who inspires them and informs their wayward activities. Of course I must reckon with the fact that even though the Deliverer's sojourn on earth lasted thirty-three years during which He performed miracles that are well-documented, many stupid humans prefer to pass themselves off as skeptics and unbelievers as if that would absolve them from facing the consequences of doing the wicked things they do openly or on the sly (when they see advantages in passing themselves off as the Deliverer's followers). If they do that to the Deliverer, you bet they would do it to me as well. Humans are strange and unpredictable!

"I am also at a decided disadvantage because, unlike the Deliverer, I cannot perform miracles. Even though I am capable of and I actually engage in all manner of deceitful practices, they do not amount to doing wonders like causing dead people to come alive, curing lepers, or multiplying loaves and fishes. Oh, it would have been such a boon for my evil cause if I had been able to do these things! But - guess what? I have been very successful in inspiring some among my minions to go to great length to hoodwink unwitting folks that they can perform miracles, and also that they do them in the Deliverer's name! Hah hah haa! Hee-hee-hee!

"The only thing that saves humans is the *Pater Noster* and particularly the words '*sed libera nos a malo*' (but deliver us from evil) with which the prayer concludes. That is not to say that the rest of the 'Lord's Prayer' is not as important.

"We here in the Pit know that the most important part of this prayer as far as the salvation of humans goes is towards the very beginning where humans are called upon to beseech the Prime Mover using the words '*fiat voluntas tua*' (thy will be done); and we do everything in our power to make sure that reciting the *Pater Noster* remains foreign to them; and that when they happen to beseech the Prime Mover using the words of that prayer, they just do so only with their lips and while their hearts are far from Him exactly as it written in Isaiah 29:13-14 and Matthew 15:8. This is because, if humans were really intent on seeing the Prime Mover's will done, they would embrace the *Sancta Ecclesia* that the Deliverer established on the rock called Peter whole heartedly; and they would find within it the sacraments the Deliverer instituted for the specific purpose of guarding humans against the evil (*malum*) that we here in the Pit are determined to promote amongst humans shall we say until kingdom come!

"You damn stupid humans are so dumb, it is rare

to find one amongst you who gives a damn about the long view. Everyone is into the short view of things; and this includes the so-called 'statesmen' - the interest is in the immediate gain. Decisions to go to war are based on the short view; and the only 'fools' who take the long view and care about their 'last end' are closeted out of sight in hermitages. Well we here in the Pit wouldn't afford that at all. We ourselves always take the long view in everything we do. And, as is borne out by history, we have frequently sought out and groomed egotistical individuals, and have succeeded in getting them to larch on to positions that completely go counter to the teachings of the *Sancta Ecclesia*; and then, after inspiring and abetting them in their wayward ways, we have succeeded in getting other humans, including many who act in good faith out of ignorance, to become their devoted followers.

"Our goal in all such situations is to get the hordes of humans who are misled by those vain, self-seeking minions of ours to miss out on the graces that are dispensed through sacraments in the Deliverer's *Sancta Ecclesia*. And, of course, we have worked with our minions to ensure that, as and when victims of their deception and chicanery awaken to the fact that they are actually in the wrong crowd, and make moves to reconcile themselves with the Deliverer's *Sancta Ecclesia*, the exact same fate as lay in store for the man born blind who was cured of his blindness after he found faith in the Deliverer, will be awaiting them as well. Any of their members who confess that the Son of Man is indeed the Christ pursuant to the teachings of the *Sancta Ecclesia* must be put out of the 'synagogue'.

"The goal is always to try and ensure that as many humans as possible don't get to be a part of 'the great multitude of people from all nations and tribes and peoples and tongues' that John saw standing before the throne and in sight of the Lamb, clothed with white robes and bearing palms in their hands' in the vision he had during his banishment on the Island of Patmos. That multitude comprised members of the human race who had 'come out of great tribulation after washing their robes in the blood of the Lamb'; and, with luck, their number will not be as great as it might have been without our meddling. Hah hah haa! Hee-hee-hee!

"The Deliverer undoubtedly did say that His sheep heard His voice; and He knew His sheep, and they followed Him. And Leo the Great, who famously confronted Attila the Hun in the year 452 and persuaded him to halt his invasion of Italy, put it very succinctly when, referring to Eutyches, that heresiarch of the fifth century, he wrote in 'The Tome': 'But what more iniquitous than to hold blasphemous opinions, and not to give way to those who are wiser and more learned than ourself. Now into this unwisdom fall they who, finding themselves hindered from knowing the truth by some obscurity, have recourse not to the prophets' utterances, not to the Apostles' letters, nor to the injunctions of the Gospel but to their own selves: and thus they stand out as masters of error because they were never disciples of truth. For what learning has he acquired about the pages of the New and Old Testament, who has not even grasped the rudiments of the Creed? And that which, throughout the world, is professed by the mouth of everyone who is to be born again, is not yet taken in by the heart of this old man (Eutyches).'

"The Doctor of the Church didn't leave very much wiggle room there for Eutyches and his followers! Hah, hah, hee, hee!

"Well, we work with our minions to ensure that hordes of humans don't get to join the Deliverer's flock;

and that, as and when they do, they straight away walk into the likes of Eutyches, and don't get to enjoy the benefits of membership in the Church that has the fullness of Truth and the sacraments dispensed therein – the 'powers that come forth from the Body of Christ, which is ever-living and life-giving' - also referred to (in the Catechism of the Church) as 'actions of the Holy Spirit at work in his Body, the Church', and also as 'the masterworks of God in the new and everlasting covenant'. (CCC 1116)

"Now, I was able to lead the Son of Man to the mountain-top where I tempted Him - I showed him all the kingdoms of the world in a moment of time, and I swore that I would give all that power and the glory of them and all those kingdoms would be His if He gave up His fealty to His Father in heaven and worshipped me - because He Was a true human in addition to being true God. (Luke 4:5-8; Matthew 4:1-11; and Mark 1:12-13) If I was able to do that to the Deliverer, you have to be living in a different universe to imagine that my troops and I aren't doing the same to the rest of you humans.

"Some stupid humans think that I was crazy to even try! So, so stupid! Look, I was dead serious, and I meant everything I said; and I was ready to deliver on my word. If the Son of Man had fallen for it and accepted my offer, I would have given him all the kingdoms of the world and all the power and their glory. It would have signaled that I had succeeded in driving a wedge in the relations between members of the Godhead, causing a terminal rift between them! With the Deliverer effectively won over to my side in the battle between Good and Evil, I would then have been in a position to declare 'Mission Accomplished', you stupid fools! Still, no worries because all humans, with the exception of the Son of Man and His sinless mother, remain exposed and in our cross hairs.

"And, talking about driving a wedge between members of the Godhead, this is actually what humans who do not pass their lives in the same way folks like Francis of Assisi or Mother Theresa of Calcutta did are trying to do all the time - when they fall for my whiles or allow themselves to become slaves of desires of the flesh! These are things that are incompatible with loving their neighbors as themselves and loving the Prime Mover above all else! When humans forsake the injunctions to love one another as they love themselves and to love the Prime Mover above all else, they effectively act as if they are gods unto themselves. And therefore, any suggestion on the part of humans that I, Beelzebub, shouldn't have tried to trip up the Deliverer and win Him over to my side - yes, to the side of Evil - is not just disingenuous; it is downright offensive!

"It might not be recorded anywhere in the scriptures that I similarly tempted His blessed mother; but you would be totally scandalized if I described to you the seduction and the temptations I subjected her to. I tell you she is not the Queen of Heaven for nothing!

"And this is not the 'heaven' that humans associate with the title of 'queen'. It is not some dreary expanse of land or island that might even be still steeped in feudalism, and over which some earthly monarch reins amid the constant threat of palace coups! And it is not that expanse of space that seems to be over the earth like a dome or 'firmament' as the Merriam Webster describes it either. I am talking about the heaven where members of the Triune Godhead (who is uncreated and has no beginning, and embodies supreme perfection and is now ministered to nonstop by choirs of angels amid the victorious chants of the blessed whose robes have been washed in the blood of the Lamb) dwell in eternity. And she is the uncontested Queen of Heaven because, as St.

John Paul II aptly put it (when he addressed the gathering in the Chapel of the Cenacle during his jubilee pilgrimage to the Holy Land in March 2000), *in the Incarnation, the Son of God, of one being with the Father, became Man and received a body from the Virgin Mary. And then on the night before His death, He said to His disciples: This is my Body, which will be given up for you...'*

"I therefore really mean it when I say that my troops and I are committed to working to ensure that as many humans as possible must not get to possess and enjoy the new heaven and the new earth that John describes in the Book of Revelation. (Revelation 21:1). Wide is the gate, and broad is the way that leadeth to destruction, and many there are who go in thereat. How narrow is the gate, and strait is the way that leadeth to life: and few there are that find it! (Matthew 7:13-14) And the Deliverer's advice: 'Strive to enter by the narrow gate: for many, I say to you, shall seek to enter and shall not be able.' (Luke 13:24) If you think that it is an accident that the so-called 'separated 'Christians' and others are indoctrinated to regard the *Sancta Ecclesia* founded by the Deliverer on the rock called Peter (John 1:42 and Matthew 16:18) as *my* work and as a cult, think again and - also just try to be fair and give credit where credit is due for once will you! We here in the Underworld work really hard to blind you humans to the fact that the first heaven and the first earth that now exist will soon be no more, and to the fact that the seas - the oceans that the powers that be now expend blood and treasure to control - will soon cease to exist and there will be nothing left to fight over.

"Anyways, I was created a pure spirit; and, vile though I may be, I accept that there is no denying that being gratuitously brought into existence out of nothing and in the Prime Mover's image - whether as a human or

413

as a pure spirit - demands that the creature reciprocate by going down on bended knee and adoring the Almighty One and its Maker. So you can say that I blew it by refusing to go down on bended knee! And if I of all creatures blew it, there can be no doubt that you humans are likewise blowing it - and blowing it big time too!

"Regarding this 'human versus pure spirit' thing, you humans need to use your heads and a little bit of that imagination with which you are so richly endowed. What is really important is not the ability to discern something with the naked human eye, but with the 'eye of the soul'. To those humans who are selfless and lead spiritual lives, and recognize the Prime Mover in everything they see as well as in their neighbors, pure spirits, both demonic and angelic, are as present as trees and other objects that meet the human eye.

"There are some who think that because I am a very bad creature, I must be very ugly, perhaps even with horns and a tail - or things like that. As the grandest creature ever made, I have everything that makes one desirable. I may not be the nonpareil of beauty, but I am as lovely and handsome as the loveliest thing you could imagine. If you allowed me to inform a human body, you would find yourself confronted by a creature that was a thousand times more comely than the Queen of Sheba. So, it is a huge insult when some humans depict me as some ugly gargoyle.

"Of course, humans already do just about anything that comes to mind - they kill, commit adultery, worship idols, and break all the other commandments in ways you would never have imagined. And they have shown their penchant for trying to beat me at my own game of wickedness. Humans now almost rival me at being diabolic. The profanity, the lies and spin, and the callousness are sometimes simply stunning.

"But does it really matter if the perspective of members of the Church's hierarchy on the world is at cross purposes with the perspective of the Deliverer or the Prime Mover? What makes the Church 'Catholic'? Having churches everywhere, or is it something related to its nature - something that speaks to the fact that this is the Church the Eternal Word and Deliverer, who died for the salvation of humans, officially inaugurated on Pentecost Day; and whereupon all those gathered there, Galileans, were all filled with the Holy Ghost, and began to speak with divers tongues, according as the Holy Ghost gave them to speak so that Parthians, and Medes, and Elamites, and inhabitants of Mesopotamia, Judea, and Cappadocia, Pontus and Asia, Phrygia, and Pamphylia, Egypt, and the parts of Libya about Cyrene, and strangers of Rome, and Jews as well including proselytes, Cretes, and Arabians all heard them speak in their own tongues the wonderful works of God, and were all astonished, and wondered!

"With so much confusion in the world, could it be that members of the Church's hierarchy are just as confused about things - and also as parochial and bigoted - as everyone else? Well, most likely, given that humans are humans; and the world is the world; and members of the Church's hierarchy are just as much humans who live with all other humans in the same wicked world. And it probably also explains why discrimination in countries that are predominantly Catholic (regardless of whether 'Roman' Catholic or 'Eastern Orthodox' Catholic) against people of other backgrounds is quite blatant. It also says something about the likes of Mother Theresa who refused to see 'Hindu', 'Buddhist' or 'Christian' or even 'Catholic' souls in humans, and subsequently got more than their share of troubles for their stand.

"How are members of the Church's hierarchy going

to imitate the apostles - the same apostles who were commanded to go out and teach, not just folks who were with them in the Upper House on the day the Holy Spirit descended upon them (identical to folks in the visible Church), but to folks in far flung places like Kigali and Peking which they had never heard of before, but for whom the Deliverer had died just the same - if they have this idea that the Prime Mover doesn't really love the Rwandese and the Chinese as much as he loves them? How are they going to do their job when they act as though some human souls are more valuable in the eyes of the Prime Mover than others?

"When humans become elevated to the order of Melchizedek or to the rank of Prince of the Church, does it strike them that the Church they serve is larger than themselves and their puny little minds, and that it is in fact as large as the Holy Spirit who not only informs it, but is a member of the Godhead? Does it ever strike those who are called to fill the shoes of the apostles (an unenviable task by any measure) that I, Satan, and my troops here in the Pit work very hard to ensure that they will always be bigoted and parochial, because that makes them serious obstacles to the 'universal' Church's work of evangelization?

"Now humans, being descendants of Adam and Eve, are all faced with the legacy of original sin. They are all inclined to sin. Related to that, there has always been one big plus for us here in the Pit, namely the fact that the folks who constitute the Church's clergy, inclined to sin like everybody else and also liable to make serious errors of judgement, have great difficulty (as you would expect) accepting that reality. You would expect them to be in the forefront acknowledging that, without the grace of the Prime Mover, they are totally at our mercy. But that is, of course, not something we want to see happen.

"Judas Iscariot, who was one of the twelve, betrayed the Deliverer, as also did Peter, the Rock upon which the Deliverer planned to build His Church, when he denied Him three times in the short space of an hour. Both caused the Deliverer to endure untold grief. But Judas and Peter accepted their faults, a contrast to the actions of many members of the Church's clergy who are loath to accept that there are always some among them who fall short. That, over the Church's checkered two-thousand-year history, members of the Church's hierarchy have on occasion betrayed the Mystical Body of the Deliverer, and caused it to endure unspeakable distress in the same way Judas Iscariot and Peter, His first nominee for the position of 'Holy Father', did.

"But it is good that it is not recognized that, in spiritual matters, strength lies in acknowledging one's faults and/or weakness - in showing humility. St. Francis of Assisi, who was content to serve as a deacon and revered the priestly vocation very highly, famously said in a letter to his order: '*Audite, fratres mei: Si beata Virgo sic honoratur, ut dignum est, quia ipsum portavit in sanctissimo utero; si Baptista beatus contremuit et non audet tangere sanctum Dei verticem; si sepulcrum, in quo per aliquod tempus iacuit veneratur, quantum debet esse sanctus, iustus et dignus, qui non iam moriturum, sed in aeternum victurum et glorificatum, in quo desiderant angeli prospicere, contractat manibus, corde et ore sumit et aliis ad sumendum praebet!* (1 Pet 1:12)' (Listen, my brothers: If the Blessed Virgin is so honored, as it is right, since she carried Him in her most holy womb; if the blessed Baptist trembled and did not dare to touch the holy head of God; if the tomb in which He lay for some time is so venerated, how holy, just, and worthy must be the person who touches Him with his hands, receives Him in his heart and mouth, and offers Him to others to be received. This is He Who is now not about to die, but Who is eternally victorious and glorified, upon Whom the angels desire to gaze! (1 Pet 1:12).' And also equally worthy of imitation is St. Thomas Aquinas who was contented with being a simple friar and would not accept the pope's offer to make him an abbot or archbishop. That is certainly not what we want to see happen.

"In the run-up to the Reformation, there were of course lots and lots of other culpable players apart from Luther, who is officially listed as the 'fall guy' for the subsequent divisions in Christendom with his claim that the pope was the 'Antichrist'. But the very fact that those divisions have continued to endure means that many inside the Church where Luther was once upon a time (until that fateful day, January 3, 1521 to be exact, when Pope Leo X issued his papal bull *Decet Romanum Pontificem* excommunicating him) and outside, by their acts of omission or commission, come Doomsday, will have to answer for their role in the agony and distress suffered by the Mystical Body of the Deliverer - agony and distress that is going to intensify as the new misguided 'Christian crusades' get under way.

"The Church's hierarchy could make a start on stemming the slide into a monumental debacle that is being brought on by Quixotic foolishness by condemning killings by *all* sides when they occur, and by loudly and clearly trumpeting the inalienable rights of all, Christian and non-Christian. But, again, that is precisely what we in the Pit would not like to see happen - especially now in the run-up to Armageddon.

"Yeah! So you are a killer, and the kind of fellow who likes to go for the jugular when slighted despite the fact that you yourself are in need of forgiveness on a far greater scale! Now I am the devil, and 'I swear by my troth' (to borrow a line from Shakespeare) that when you humans (who are guilty of some of the most unspeakable misdeeds and are even ashamed to approach the Prime Mover to beg for His forgiveness) show that you just love to go for the jugular when offended however slightly by your fellow humans, that attitude is entirely of your own making, and I had nothing at all to do with it. Actually, I myself would not be inclined to show geeks like you any sympathy if I were the Judge. You do not deserve any.

"By the way, even as the very incarnation of evil, I have never been guilty of misdeeds that directly targeted others. It is true. My sin was a sin of pride - I refused to adore and worship (and the same for the other fallen angels). I never hurt anybody. And, never having begged for - or received - any mercy myself, why should I be sympathetic to nuts like you! But the things you humans do to one another! It is just so disgusting.

"You humans have taken wickedness to a completely new low; and I think I know why. It must be because you humans start off earth-bound, even though spirits made in the Image like us. The problem is your self-importance as earth-bound creatures existing side by side with everything from inanimate objects and plants with only vegetative life and beasts that only boast their instincts.

"Even when Adam and Eve were plotting their rebellion, they were so bent on the notion that they would lord it over their descendants and, as 'King' and 'Queen' of the universe respectively, would demand to be treated as royalty while everyone else would be a 'subject'! It seemed such a crazy idea - but I couldn't dissuade them. My objective had been to get them to simply balk from going down on their knees in adoration and worship of the Prime Mover just like we ourselves had done.

"You have to believe that when those of us who used to belong to choirs of angels strayed from the path,

419

our sin was definitely not so much in the things we did to each other as in the things we did to ourselves by our refusal to hearken to our consciences and to accord the Prime Mover the homage and honor He was due. We did unspeakable damage to our individual selves in the process. Our disobedience left us virtual loonies. But with you humans, the major problem is the things you do to each other.

"All untoward acts by humans, however small or fleeting, immediately become indelible stains on the soul - stains that can only be washed away in the blood of the Lamb. And killing is indisputably one of them.

"Of course, one thing the pure spirits that remained loyal to the Prime Mover and the elect are looking forward to seeing in the aftermath of Armageddon is what we demons will start doing to each other - and to the souls of damned humans! I cannot even start to imagine the feeding frenzy and spitefulness as the hordes of demons and lost souls turn on me in particular perhaps in an effort to rub me out. At that time, throngs of lost souls and swarms of demons will almost certainly join forces and descend on me to avenge their loss. Even though I will survive, the bruising treatment will almost certainly leave me completely disfigured, a cripple, and unrecognizable. It is definitely not something I can look forward to.

"Knowing that this is going to be my lot, I wouldn't be the devil if, in the meantime, I didn't do everything, with the help of my minions among humans, to live up to my reputation as the Father of Lies and the Father of Death and to assure that there was immense suffering in this goddamned world! Priming my minions to be wedded to lies to the point of lying shamelessly from both sides of the mouth and, above all, grooming them to disregard the sanctity of human life in their pursuit of passing worldly fulfillment must continue to be a priority. My dedication in ensuring that John the Baptizer's pleas to humans to 'prepare the way for the Lord and make his paths straight' goes unheeded, and that humans remain tone deaf to the Gospel message as taught by the *Sancta Ecclesia* the Deliverer established on the rock called Peter must remain firm and solid. With Jorge Mario Bergoglio who became the *Vicarius Christi* (Vicar of Christ) on 12 March 2013 and the 265th successor to Shimon Bar Yonah (also known as Cephas) hailing from Argentina, you can safely say that the "Gospel of the kingdom' has been proclaimed throughout the whole world. (Matthew 24:14) My troops must press on to ensure that, that fact notwithstanding, hordes don't get to genuflect before the Blessed sacrament and to recite the *Adóro te devote* that Tommaso d'Aquino bequeathed to the world with the heavenly hosts. I must step up my work with hedonists to ensure that the fabric of the family is destroyed in order that the innocent children suffer more. I must work with megalomaniacs and get them to make the sort of decisions that will transform the world into fertile ground for the widespread use of violence to intimidate or coerce – or terrorism so-called – and the related evils; and I must see to it that the mafia and similar groups thrive. I must do more with the help of misguided souls to bring on religious upheavals so that the internecine fighting and the slaughter accompanying these upheavals become an everyday occurrence.

"News headlines must be filled daily with horrific accounts of the miseries endured by humans at the hands of fellow humans, and also as a result of disasters brought on by human activity such as global warming. I must work with greedy humans to assure that the air they breathe is polluted to the point to which this in turn causes all types of maladies. And, together, we must muffle sane voices in society so that the damage to the environment from such things as addiction to gas guzzling autos, open-pit mining, fracking, underground and atmospheric as well as exoatmospheric nuclear tests, is irreversible. And we must of course intensify our work with the hawks so that the third and last world war itself, with its untold horrors, gets underway in due course.

"Of course humans, wicked as they are (and it sometimes even seems more appropriate to refer to them as 'human devils'), already do these things. I just need to prompt them to take this malignity to a totally new level - I mean one that beggars the imagination of even my own demonic mind! At the same time as I am doing that, I must redouble my efforts to ensure that humans, one and all, become ensnared by the fallacious propaganda and teachings of con artists so that the maximum number of souls end up in this goddamned godforsaken place of the damned as humans, one and all, selfishly opt for easy fixes and refuse to take up their crosses and to follow in the footsteps of the Deliverer. Yep…with the help of my minions among earthlings, I want to see to it that, from now on, those intercessory prayers which the celebrant intones at the conclusion of the Good Friday liturgy of the Passion of the Deliverer of humankind, particularly the one for those in tribulation, will be for real, with things verily as bad as they were in the moments before the Deliverer himself gave up His ghost on Mount Calvary!

"And, talking about prayers, let me tell you that, from the moment two thousand year ago when, responding to the request of one of his disciples that He teach them to pray, as John also taught his disciples, He taught them to chant the *Pater Noster* or 'Lord's Prayer', I have never let up in my efforts to get humans to brush off that good advice, and to go about their lives as though they were their own 'prime movers'! But even without me intervening, when humans meet with tribulations and remember to say their prayers, as expected, they always forget to pray using the *Pater Noster* - the prayer the Son of Man Himself composed! Instead, as they go about praying, they break all the rules that beggars would be well advised to keep, and they either start blaming the Prime Mover for their woes or they start demanding things! And that is even when they got into trouble because they were asking for it by the manner in which they led their lives! And, when at it, they will pray like the hypocrites (that love to stand and pray in the synagogues and corners of the streets, that they may be seen by men)!

"Be assured that, for my part, I work very hard to make sure that, when humans pray, they not only eschew praying in the manner the Deliverer taught them to pray, but they even deliberately and knowingly forego participation in the celebration of the memorial of the Lord's Passion and Resurrection during Holy Mass as commanded by the Deliverer with the words '*Accípite, et manducáte ex hoc omnes...Hoc est enim Corpus meum*' (Take and eat ye all of this, for this is my Body); and also '*Símili modo postquam cœnátum est, accípiens et hunc præclárum Cálicem in sanctas ac venerábiles manus suas, item tibi grátias agens, benedíxit, dedítque discípulis suis, dicens: Accípite, et bíbite ex eo omnes: Hic est enim Calix Sánguinis mei, novi et ætérni testaménti; mystérium fidei: qui pro vobis et pro multis effundétur in remissiónem peccatórum. Hæc quotiescúmque fecéritis, in mei memóriam faciétis.*' (In like manner, after he had supped, taking also this excellent chalice into his holy and adorable hands; also giving thanks to thee, he blessed, and gave it to his disciples, saying: Take, and drink ye all of this; For this is the Chalice of my Blood, of the new and eternal testament; the mystery of faith: which shall be shed for you and for many unto the remission of sins. As often as ye shall do these things, ye shall do them in memory of me.)

"Look, it took hard work to get humans, starting with the Jews, to act in ways that caused the words of the Psalmist and of the Prophet Isaiah to be fulfilled on Mt. Calvary: that 'All who see me laugh me to scorn; they curl their lips and wag their heads, saying, 'He trusted in the LORD; let him deliver him; let him rescue him, if he delights in him...' (Psalm 22:7-8) and 'They stare and gloat over me; they divide my garments among them; they cast lots for my clothing'; (Psalm 22:17-18) and 'He was oppressed, and he was afflicted, yet he did not open his mouth; like a lamb that is led to the slaughter, and like a sheep that before its shearers is silent, so he did not open his mouth'. (Isaiah 53:7)

"And, as if that was not bad enough, I have succeeded in getting many humans who claim to be the Deliverer's followers to uphold and to actively spread teachings that, in many respects, are the exact opposite of what the Deliverer's *Sancta Ecclesia*, founded in the rock called Peter (Mark 8:27-30; Luke 9:18-20; John 6:66-71), upholds and teaches. Some even go as far as proclaiming that members of the Deliverer's visible *Sancta Ecclesia* are not 'Christians'! Then they go on to declare that *they*, and not members of the *Sancta Ecelesia*, have a 'relationship' with the Deliverer! Lo, the fact is that 'A Christian without the Church', as the Pontiff of Rome declared on Vatican Radio just the other day, is something purely idealistic, it is not real'!

"I have persuaded many to believe that they can vilify the Deliverer's *Sancta Ecclesia* and still truthfully claim to have a relationship with Him! Ha, ha, ha! As if He did not say to His seventy-two disciples when sending them out before Him in groups of two: 'Go: Behold I send you as lambs among wolves…He that heareth you, heareth me; and he that despiseth you, despiseth me; and he that despiseth me, despiseth him that sent me' (Luke 10:3-16); and 'He that receiveth you, receiveth me: and he that receiveth me, receiveth him that sent me' (Matthew 10:40). And also: 'As the Father hath sent me, I also send you. When he had said this, he breathed on them; and he said to them: Receive ye the Holy Ghost. Whose sins you shall forgive, they are forgiven them; and whose sins you shall retain, they are retained.' (John 20: 21-23)

"Yes, upon crossing the gulf that separates the living from the dead when their time comes, they will be surprised to discover that a village going by the name 'Emmaus' did in fact exist; and also that two of the Deliverer's disciples (one of whom was called Cleophas), even after failing to recognize Him as they discussed the events of three days earlier when the 'prophet, powerful in word and deed before God and all the people' was handed over by the chief priests and rulers to be sentenced to death, dashing their hopes that 'he was the one who was going to redeem Israel', not only heard Him say that they were foolish and slow of heart to believe all that the prophets had spoken'; but also reported that, 'whilst he was at table with them, he took bread, and blessed, and brake, and gave to them; and their eyes were opened, and they knew him: and he vanished out of their sight.' (Luke 24:30-31)

"All those so-called 'Christians' who, having professed the faith of the Deliverer, corrupt its dogmas (as Thomas of Aquin put it); and who, *whilst aware* that their beliefs are at odds with the teachings of the *Sancta Ecclesia, continue to cling to their beliefs* pertinaciously and *will not desist* in reviling the Deliverer's *Sancta Ecclesia*; all those folks will be shocked to discover that

425

the Deliverer does indeed keep His promises, which include His avowal to Peter, that he was giving, not to his brother Andrew or to John (son of Zebedee and Salome), or to any of the other twelve 'apostles', but to him (Simon Bar-Jona) 'the keys of the kingdom of heaven' (Matthew 16:18-19)! Now, because He also promised that His *Sancta Ecclesia* was one against which I, Beelzebub (or 'the Gates of Hell' as He put it), will not prevail, I have never wasted any time trying to put that promise to the test.

"And look, even though I still wish that that former tax collector hadn't included an account of the Deliverer's promise to Peter (and whoever would succeed him in this respect), I still wouldn't have wasted my time trying if for no other reason than the fact that the Deliverer's promises are not just promises, but are of the order of 'Providence'! You can say the same concerning the Story of Creation. It really matters very little indeed that you humans were afforded the 'Pentateuch' (or the first five books of the bible), which includes what their author referred to as the 'Book of Genesis'. The *Sancta Ecclesia* along with the institution of the 'Apostolate', or more precisely the 'Mystical Body of the Deliverer', which was given a send-off by the Deliverer between the time of His Resurrection from the dead and His ascension into heaven and that was witnessed by the heavenly hosts, would not have required mention in the '*Euangelion kata Matthaion*' or in John 21:15-17 to prosper the way it has prospered over the last two thousand years in this godforsaken world! Fools, you humans would still have witnessed the sun rising in the East and setting in the West even if Moses (or whoever bequeathed the Pentateuch to the world) hadn't thought much about setting down 'on papyrus' a description of how it all started!

"But history itself attests to the fact that, from the get-go, I have been hard at work not only trying to make the work of the Deliverer's *Sancta Ecclesia* as difficult as possible, but also attempting - and succeeding - in getting gazillions of arguably well-intentioned but misguided humans to latch on to views that are at variance with the teachings of the *Sancta Ecclesia* and to incur excommunication thereby as members of communities in revolt against His *Sancta Ecclesia*.

"But how did we get here? How did things unfold beginning from that time in the Garden of Eden when I thought I already had humans cornered?

"Enter Abraham: twenty generations after Adam, and nine after Noah. Abraham was born to Térach (whose name invoked the image of a wild goat and hence of 'Wanderer' or 'Loiterer'). It was to him that the Prime Mover said: 'Go forth out of thy country, and from thy kindred, and out of thy father's house, and come into the land which I shall shew thee. And I will make of thee a great nation, and I will bless thee, and magnify thy name, and thou shalt be blessed. I will bless them that bless thee, and curse them that curse thee, and IN THEE shall all the kindred of the earth be blessed...' (Genesis 12:1-3)

"And after the man of God had showed that he was prepared to sacrifice Isaac, his only son by his half-sister Sarah, as a holocaust in obedience to the Prime Mover, he heard this: 'By my own self have I sworn, saith the Lord: because thou hast done this thing, and hast not spared thy only begotten son for my sake: I will bless thee, and I will multiply thy seed as the stars of heaven, and as the sand that is by the sea shore: thy seed shall possess the gates of their enemies. And in thy seed shall all the nations of the earth be blessed, because thou hast obeyed my voice.' (Genesis 22:16-18)

"From that moment, with that third in the series of covenants that the Prime Mover would make with humans, the battle lines between Good (led by the Son of Man) and Evil (led by me here in Gehenna) were drawn. Because He had endowed humans with reason and a free will, the Prime Mover gave them their due respect by 'entering into covenants' with them. That is a world of a difference from the way humans treat each other. Some even treat their pets better than they treat their fellow humans, especially if they look a little different from the way they themselves look!

"You might not remember; but the first covenant was with Adam and Eve whom He created and joined together as one flesh. (Malachi 2:14-16 and Genesis 2:23-24) The second covenant was the one the Prime Mover made with Noah and his family when He promised to never again destroy humankind through a flood. (Genesis 9:9-17)

"The Prime Mover later entered into another covenant with Moses not long after that messenger of the Almighty One, in a fit of despair, broke the tablets of stone on which the Ten Commandments were engraved; (Exodus 34:10-24) and then again with David. (2 Samuel 7: 1-17) And he entered into the last and final covenant of the Old Testament with Jeremiah, the covenant that would find fulfillment in the Deliverer and the *Sancta Ecclesia* that He would establish on the rock called Peter. (Jeremiah 31:31-34).

"The Deliverer Himself put it succinctly thus, when he spoke to the Samaritan woman at Jacob's well in the city of Sichar: '*Si scires donum Dei et quis est qui dicit tibi da mihi bibere tu forsitan petisses ab eo et dedisset tibi aquam vivam…Omnis qui bibit ex aqua hac sitiet iterum qui autem biberit ex aqua quam ego dabo ei non sitiet in aeternum. Sed aqua quam dabo ei fiet in eo fons aquae salientis in vitam aeternam…Mulier crede mihi quia veniet hora quando neque in monte hoc neque in Hierosolymis adorabitis Patrem. Vos adoratis quod nescitis nos adoramus quod scimus quia salus ex Iudaeis est. Sed venit hora et nunc est quando veri adoratores adorabunt Patrem in spiritu et veritate nam et Pater tales quaerit qui adorent eum. Spiritus est Deus et eos qui adorant eum in spiritu et veritate oportet adorare... ego cibum habeo manducare quem vos nescitis… meus cibus est ut faciam voluntatem eius qui misit me ut perficiam opus ei.'* ('If thou didst know the gift of God and who he is that saith to thee: Give me to drink; thou perhaps wouldst have asked of him, and he would have given thee living water… Woman, believe me that the hour cometh, when you shall neither on this mountain, nor in Jerusalem, adore the Father… You adore that which you know not: we adore that which we know. For salvation is of the Jews. But the hour cometh and now is, when the true adorers shall adore the Father in spirit and in truth. For the Father also seeketh such to adore him. God is a spirit: and they that adore him must adore him in spirit and in truth… I have meat to eat which you know not… My meat is to do the will of him that sent me, that I may perfect his work.') (John 4, 10-34)

"But when the time finally came, on the same night in which the Deliverer was betrayed, whilst they were eating, the Deliverer, as Mark described it, took bread; and blessing, broke, and gave to them, and said: Take ye. This is my body. And having taken the chalice, giving thanks, he gave it to them. And they all drank of it. And he said to them: This is my blood of the new testament, which shall be shed for many. Amen I say to you, that I will drink no more of the fruit of the vine, until that day when I shall drink it new in the kingdom of God. (Mark 14, 22-25).

"The former tax collector employed nearly the exact same words in his account of that pivotal moment in the history of humanity: 'And whilst they were at supper, Jesus took bread, and blessed, and broke: and gave to his disciples, and said: Take ye, and eat. This is my body. And taking the chalice, he gave thanks, and gave to them, saying: Drink ye all of this. For this is my blood of the new testament, which shall be shed for many unto remission of sins. And I say to you, I will not drink from henceforth of this fruit of the vine, until that day when I shall drink it with you new in the kingdom of my Father.' (Matthew 26, 26-29).

"And the Physician turned Evangelist put it thusly: 'And when the hour was come, he sat down, and the twelve apostles with him. And he said to them: With desire I have desired to eat this pasch with you, before I suffer. For I say to you, that from this time I will not eat it, till it be fulfilled in the kingdom of God. And having taken the chalice, he gave thanks, and said: Take, and divide it among you: For I say to you, that I will not drink of the fruit of the vine, till the kingdom of God come. And taking bread, he gave thanks, and brake; and gave to them, saying: This is my body, which is given for you. Do this for a commemoration of me. In like manner the chalice also, after he had supped, saying: This is the chalice, the new testament in my blood, which shall be shed for you.' (Luke 22:14-20).

"If the Deliverer had been a mere human and not the Son of the Prime Mover, with some stretch of the imagination it might have been possible to legitimately construe as allegorical or symbolic those solemn words and those solemn actions which He performed at His Last Supper. But He was the Logos; and He was telling His apostles plainly and without beating about the bush that He was giving them to drink the blood that He was about

430

to shed for the salvation of humans!

"Addressing a crowd of Jews over five thousand strong (whom He had fed with five barley loaves, and two fishes, and who had showed that they were determined to take Him by force and make Him king), the Deliverer had said: 'Amen, amen I say to you, you seek me, not because you have seen miracles, but because you did eat of the loaves, and were filled. Labour not for the meat which perisheth, but for that which endureth unto life everlasting, which the Son of man will give you. For him hath God, the Father, sealed. (John 6:26-27)

"But when they insisted that he should give them a sign that he had indeed been sent by the Prime Mover before they believed in Him citing the fact that their fore fathers fed on manna in the desert, he had replied: 'Amen, amen I say to you; Moses gave you not bread from heaven, but my Father giveth you the true bread from heaven. For the bread of God is that which cometh down from heaven, and giveth life to the world.' (John 6:32-33)

"The Deliverer had made it crystal clear that the key was to come around and believe in Him (John 6:29): It was not enough that the crowds had seen the miracles. They had seen the miracles but they did not believe (John 6:36).

"Reiterating that He was the bread of life: and that whoever went to Him would not hunger: and he that believed in Him would never thirst (John 6:35), the Deliverer hinted at the source of their unbelief, namely that it was only those that the Father gave to Him who ended up with Him; and those who went to Him, He would not cast out. (John 6:37) He Himself, coming down from heaven, had done so not to do His own will, but the will of Him that sent Him; and it was the will of His Father that He not lose any soul but raise it up on the last day, that it may have everlasting life (John 6:38-40)

"The Deliverer went out of His way to clarify to the crowds again that His Father also had a critical role in humans finding their way to Him, saying: 'No man can come to me, except the Father, who hath sent me, draw him; and I will raise him up in the last day. It is written in the prophets: And they shall all be taught of God. Everyone that hath heard of the Father, *and hath learned*, cometh to me. Not that any man hath seen the Father; but he who is of God, he hath seen the Father. Amen, amen I say unto you: He that believeth in me, hath everlasting life. I am the bread of life. Your fathers did eat manna in the desert, and are dead. This is the bread which cometh down from heaven; that if any man eat of it, he may not die. I am the living bread which came down from heaven. If any man eat of this bread, he shall live for ever; and the bread that I will give, is my flesh, for the life of the world.' (John 6:44-51)

"The Deliverer could not have emphasized enough that the bread He would give - the living bread that came down from heaven - was His flesh!

"The Jews therefore strove among themselves, saying: How can this man give us his flesh to eat? They murmured that this was totally preposterous! (John 6:52)

"Then for the umpteenth time, the Deliverer explained the modus operandi that was a part of the Divine Plan, saying: 'Amen, amen I say unto you: Except you eat the flesh of the Son of man, and drink his blood, you shall not have life in you. He that eateth my flesh, and drinketh my blood, hath everlasting life: and I will raise him up in the last day. For my flesh is meat indeed: and my blood is drink indeed. He that eateth my flesh, and drinketh my blood, abideth in me, and I in him. As the living Father hath sent me, and I live by the Father; so he that eateth me, the same also shall live by me. This is the bread that came down from heaven. Not as your fathers did eat manna, and are dead. He that eateth this bread, shall live for ever.' (John 6:54-59)

"The Deliverer actually knew from the beginning who among the crowds were up to something else, were not prepared to receive the gift of faith offered by His Father, and would betray him. (John 6:61) This prompted Him to add: 'It is the spirit that quickeneth: the flesh profiteth nothing. The words that I have spoken to you, are spirit and life. But there are some of you that believe not.' (John 6:63-64)

"And so He again repeated: 'Therefore did I say to you, that no man can come to me, unless it be given him by my Father.' (John 6:65)

"Not long after that, on the feast of the dedication at Jerusalem and as the city was struggling to cope with a freak snow storm, the Jews cornered the Deliverer in the temple, and said to him: 'How long dost thou hold our souls in suspense? If thou be the Christ, tell us plainly.' (John 10:22 -24)

"After explaining that His sheep heard His voice: and He knew them, He would again emphasize the role played by His Father: 'That which my Father hath given me, is greater than all: and no one can snatch them out of the hand of my Father. I and the Father are one.' (John 5:29-30)

"Now, even though I am the Father of Lies, you have to believe me when I say that the Deliverer's Father is not in the business of discriminating or making mistakes and overlooking some of His creatures. Certainly not after He had formally declared after His labors of creation that all was very good! To emphasize that fact, the Deliverer had not failed to add: 'It is written in the prophets: And they shall *all* be taught of God. Every one that hath heard of the Father, and hath learnt, cometh to me.' (John 6:45)

"Damn, stupid fools! The Jewish crowd, no doubt typifying many who would follow in their footsteps as the Deliverer's *Sancta Ecclesia* expanded to the ends of the earth, even had the audacity to refer to the Deliverer's plans for rescuing humans from our tentacles and perdition as preposterous. They forgot that, descended from Adam and Eve, they were born with the baggage of original sin.

"They thought that they could snatch the Son of Man, the living bread that came down from heaven, and make Him their king just like that. All they were thinking about was how to be rid of the Roman imperialists and not their spiritual life!

"To be salvaged, their situation needed intervention from on High; and it was, of course, the reason He Himself had come down from heaven in obedience to His Father. Steeped in materialism, it did not strike them that His Father in heaven had a role to play in their regard as well in the shape of the gift of faith; and, rational creatures that were also endowed with a free will, they actually needed to cooperate with that gift of grace in order to come around and believe in the Son, and in His claim that He was the living bread that gives humans eternal life. That was what He meant when He said 'No man can come to me, except the Father who sent me, draw him' and also when he said 'It is the spirit that quickeneth: the flesh profiteth nothing.'

"For their part, unlike their descendants, Adam and Eve, upon consuming fruit from the Tree of the Knowledge of good and evil (in violation of the Prime Mover's clear injunction that that tree and its fruits were out of bounds), had immediately realized that they had put their relationship with their Maker in serious jeopardy - and also that there was precious little that they themselves could do to mend it. And realizing that they were totally emasculated on the physical plane as well as on the spiritual, they had tried to go in hiding in the bushes. They accepted that they were guilty; and the Prime Mover for His part let them know that there was a price to pay. They were going to die the death!

"But when the Jews saw the Son of Man multiply the loaves and the fishes upon which they promptly fed and had their fill on the other hand, the only thing that came to mind was to try and figure out a way to snatch Him, and make Him their earthly ruler!

"You must be totally naïve to think that my troops and I didn't have anything to do with their stand - like we were having a nap or something!

"But the Deliverer wasn't done with that subject yet. Turning to the twelve whom He had handpicked as His apostles, he asked them if they too wanted to leave - if they too weren't ready to believe that He was the bread of life. He wasn't tolerating any 'buts' or 'ifs' in that matter; and unlike the crowds that had sought to forcibly make him king, it wasn't His *modus operandi* to compel anyone to either believe in Him or to be one of His apostles. It was essential that they believed that He was the Son of the Prime Mover and they also needed to be completely on board with regard to His claim that he was the living bread on which they would feed in order to gain eternal life.

"And so finally, there He was in the Upper Room (the Logos through Whom all things were made and without Whom nothing was made that has been made) delivering on His promise, as he proceeded to take bread, to bless and break it, and to give to his disciples, saying: 'Take ye, and eat. This is my body.' And then similarly taking the chalice, giving thanks to His Father in heaven, and offering it to them with the words 'Drink ye all of

435

this. For this is my blood of the new testament, which shall be shed for many unto remission of sins.' (Matthew 26, 26-29)

"And it was also in that moment that the Deliverer pulled the rug from under my feet when, addressing Peter, He said: 'Simon, Simon, behold Satan hath desired to have you, that he may sift you as wheat: But I have prayed for thee, that thy faith fail not: and thou, being once converted, confirm thy brethren.' (Luke 22:31-32). The Deliverer was a little agitated that Philip said: 'Shew us the Father, and it is enough for us.' And so He said in reply: 'Have I been so long a time with you; and have you not known me? Philip, he that seeth me seeth the Father also. How sayest thou, Shew us the Father? Do you not believe, that I am in the Father, and the Father in me? The words that I speak to you, I speak not of myself. But the Father who abideth in me, he doth the works.' (John 14:9-10) Actually, Philip was echoing what was on the mind of everyone else; and the Deliverer's response to Philip was intended for the benefit of his buddies as well.

"As Paul would later point out, there was one God, and there was one mediator between God and men, the man Christ Jesus (1 Timothy 2:5) And the Deliverer had Himself said: 'He that sent me, is with me, and he hath not left me alone: for I do always the things that please him.' (John 8:29)

"There was therefore no way in those circumstances that the Deliverer's prayers would not be heard. His intercession to the Father on Peter's behalf clearly had behind it the full power and force of a divinity; and I knew from then on that the battle between Good and Evil was as good as lost.

"The Deliverer had called the Prime Mover His 'Father' (John 8:27), something that had made the Pharisees really mad at Him. And here He was interceding with that same Father of His on Peter's behalf! This was a complete contrast to the way He had treated the Pharisees when, addressing them, He said: 'You are of your father the devil, and the desires of your father you will do. He was a murderer from the beginning, and he stood not in the truth; because truth is not in him. When he speaketh a lie, he speaketh of his own: for he is a liar, and the father thereof.' (John 8:44) He didn't mince His words there!

"And, look, He was completely right about the chief priests and the Pharisees when he told them to their face: 'He that comitteth sin is of the devil: for the devil sinneth from the beginning. For this purpose, the Son of God appeared, that he might destroy the works of the devil.' (1 John 3:8)

"At my instigation, they were about to preside over the greatest injustice ever in the history of the world. They were seeking to kill the Deliverer, a man who had spoken the truth to them, which He had heard of God His Father. (John 8:40) This was the Son who could not do anything of Himself, but what He saw the Father doing. (John 5:19). They were about to do to Him exactly what I myself, as the Father of Death and also the Father of Lies, desired they do, namely torment, kill and be rid of their arch-nemesis. That was the surest way for them to doom themselves!

"The fact, of course, is that God (the Son) took up His flesh not just to save humans, but to enable them to become partakers in the divine nature (2 Peter 1:4). The Deliverer, who was the Prime Mover's Son by his very nature, by becoming a human, enabled them to be children of the Prime Mover by grace. Through baptism, the Prime Mover sent the Spirit of his Son into their hearts, crying, 'Abba! Father!' (Galatians 4:6). The victorious Deliverer would amplify this in His apparition to

John on the island of Patmos. He instructed John to write to the seven churches in Asia (the churches in Ephesus, Smyrna, Pergamos, Thyatira, Sardis, Philadelphia, and Laodicea) as follows: 'I am he that liveth, and was dead; and, behold, I am alive for evermore, Amen; and have the keys of hell and of Hades.'

"There consequently wasn't a sliver of a chance that the Prime Mover would abandon humans even after Adam and Eve had eaten of the fruit of the tree that stood in the middle of the Garden of Eden or 'paradise of pleasure', the Tree of Knowledge of Good and Evil. (Genesis 2:17) Doing that would have been tantamount to writing off the good work He had freely undertaken, namely causing creatures that were fashioned in His own image and likeness (and consequently coming complete with reason and free will) to bounce into existence out of nothing!

"When 'planning' to do anything, you humans have the sense to think of a Plan B if things don't go as you expect. You must be either kidding or entirely daft if you were thinking that the Prime Mover (whose ways are mysterious and incomprehensible to His creatures) wouldn't have had the sense to have a Plan B when He was bringing into existence out of nothing creatures that He was endowing with everything from instinct to reason and above all a free will! He knew all along that we here in the Pit were watching, and He must have guessed what we would be up to the instant humans were left entirely to their own devices.

"And so the Deliverer, whom Paul would describe as the (invisible) 'head of the body, the church' and 'the beginning, and the firstborn from the dead' (Colossians 1:18), was thus essentially interceding on behalf of the whole *Sancta Ecclesia*, and not just on behalf of Peter when he was praying over Peter. He Himself said as much: 'But I have prayed for thee, that thy faith fail not: and thou, being once converted, *confirm thy brethren*.' Peter was after all the chap He had designated to head the visible *Sancta Ecclesia* upon His death, resurrection and ascension to His heavenly Father in glory. (Matthew 16:18-19)

"Peter, his brother Andrew, and many of their fellow apostles, as well as those who would come after them, would also suffer and die as martyrs exactly as He had predicted. (Matthew 24:9; Mark 13:10-13; and Luke 21:17) But that would happen only because of His prayers to His Father in heaven on their behalf.

"The prayers for Peter by the Deliverer, who was Himself a high priest according to the order of Melchizedek (Psalm 110:4 and Hebrews 5:10) immediately followed the Last Supper at which the apostles partook of the Body and Blood of the Deliverer, participating in the sacrifice that the Deliverer was about to make on behalf of humankind in the process. (Catechism 1370)

"Now, because that sacrifice was itself predicated on the decision of the Second Person of the Holy Trinity to take up His human nature and dwell amongst humans, the prayers for Peter, and even the Eucharistic celebration that had just preceded it, and indeed the Deliverer's self-immolation as a sacrificial lamb on Calvary itself weren't things that one could describe as one-offs.

"Look, we pure spiritual essences do not have the luxury of being busy only during our 'waking hours' and then taking time off to dose off or rest like you humans do. And there are some humans who spend most of their 'waking hours' indolent and virtually 'asleep' when they are not up to some mischief.

"We pure spirits are actually 'busy bodies' every

moment of our existence. We do not take time off to relax or sleep like you humans do. Michael, Gabriel, Raphael and the other angels and archangels are permanently preoccupied with the unceasing adoration and worship of the Prime Mover; while we ourselves here in the Underworld are perpetually wrapped up in schemes we hope will cause maximum havoc in the cosmos and beyond. Moreover, with the end of the world approaching, we don't have any time to waste.

"That was also the lot of the Deliverer. He didn't have any time to waste. He was going about His Father's business every single moment of His thirty-three years on earth; and He was an indefatigable 'Lamb of the Prime Mover' who devoted every moment of His life on earth to doing whatever was needed to give humans a second chance. It had to be that way because, being the Son of the Prime Mover, He retained His divine nature all through His sojourn on earth.

"Speaking to the Jews who were asking if he might be Abraham, He had said: 'Verily, verily, I say to you; Before Abraham was, I am.' (John 8:54) You can deduce from those words that the Deliverer's work of redemption had been ongoing from the get-go. All the 'prophets' of the Old Testament starting with Jonah (who attempted to flee the Lord and ended up spending three days and three nights in the belly of a fish) and ending with Malachi (who penned the last book of the Old Testament) testified to that fact. And, responding to the salutation of her cousin Elizabeth, the Deliverer's mother confirmed as much when she said: 'His mercy is from generation unto generation, to them that fear him ...'

"It was no wonder that John the Baptist himself, asked if he might be the messiah, did not hesitate to point to the Deliverer and to say: 'behold the lamb of God who takes away the sins of the world...' (John 1:29). Even as

440

a toddling in the arms of Simeon in the temple, the Deliverer was as much a sacrificial lamb atoning for the sins of humans as He was when, after breathing His last on the cross, his body lay lifeless in his sinless mother's arms at the foot of the cross. But even before the world was created, it was already ordained that the Deliverer's Mother would herself be conceived immaculate without original sin, a special dispensation that would only be possible by virtue of the graces the Deliverer was going to merit for humankind through His ignominious death on Mt. Calvary.

"This explains the official position of the *Sancta Ecclesia* which is as follows: 'Christ's whole life is a mystery of redemption. Redemption comes to us above all through the blood of his cross. But the mystery is at work throughout Christ's entire life: already in his incarnation through which by becoming poor he enriches us with his poverty:
- o In his hidden life which by his submission atones for our disobedience;
- o In his word which purifies its hearers;
- o In his healings and exorcisms by which he took our infirmities and bore our diseases; and
- o In his resurrection by which he justifies us.'
(CCC 517)

"This is the same *Sancta Ecclesia* that was given a solemn sendoff by the Deliverer on the day He ascended into heaven when He urged on His disciples with the words: 'Thus it is written, that the Messiah is to suffer and to rise from the dead on the third day, and that repentance and forgiveness of sins is to be proclaimed in his name to all nations, beginning from Jerusalem. You are witnesses of these things.

'And see, I am sending upon you what my Father promised; so stay here in the city until you have been clothed with power from on high.' (Luke 24:49)

"Luke summarizes the Deliverer's final address and commission to his disciples elsewhere as follows: 'You will receive power when the Holy Spirit has come upon you; and you will be my witnesses in Jerusalem, in all Judea and Samaria, and to the ends of the earth.' (Acts 1:8)

"According to Mark's account, the 'Great Commission' went as follows: 'Go ye into the whole world and preach to every creature. He that believeth and is baptized shall be saved; but he that believeth not shall be condemned.' (Mark 16:15-16)

"Matthew described it thusly: 'And the eleven disciples went into Galilee, unto the mountain where Jesus had appointed them, and seeing him they adored. But some doubted. And Jesus coming, spoke to them, saying: All power is given to me in heaven and in earth. Going therefore, teach ye all nations, baptizing them in the name of the Father, and the Son, and of the Holy Ghost; Teaching them to observe all things whatsoever I have commanded you, and behold I am with you all days, even to the consummation of the world.' These were the eleven *apostles* He had chosen and formally conferred the orders of priest and bishop with the formal laying on of hands (Pope XII, Apostolic Constitution, *Sacramentum Ordinis*; Article 6 of the Catechism), and whose successors have been easily identifiable throughout the *Sancta Ecclesia*'s two-thousand-year history.

"Still, the good news, at least for now, was that I was still able to get Peter to deny His Master three times before the cock crowed twice. (Mark 14:30; Matthew 26:34; Luke 22:31-38; and John 13:36-38) The bad news - and it totally eclipsed that 'good news' - was that the

442

Deliverer's prayers to His Father on that particular occasion (that my plans to trip up the fisherman and sift him as wheat come to naught) were not just for Peter but for all those who would succeed him as the rock on which His *Sancta Ecclesia* would be built.

"And it did not take long (following His ascension into heaven) before those prayers started bearing fruit. And the physician Luke documented the church's progress as follows:

'Now the church had peace throughout all Judea, and Galilee, and Samaria; and was edified, walking in the fear of the Lord, and was filled with the consolation of the Holy Ghost.

'And it came to pass that Peter, as he passed through, visiting all, came to the saints who dwelt at Lydda. And he found there a certain man named Eneas, who had kept his bed for eight years, who was ill of the palsy. And Peter said to him: Eneas, the Lord Jesus Christ healeth thee: arise, and make thy bed. And immediately he arose. And all that dwelt at Lydda and Saron, saw him: who were converted to the Lord.

'And in Joppe there was a certain disciple named Tabitha, which by interpretation is called Dorcas. This woman was full of good works and alms deeds which she did. And it came to pass in those days that she was sick, and died. Whom when they had washed, they laid her in an upper chamber. And forasmuch as Lydda was nigh to Joppe, the disciples hearing that Peter was there, sent unto him two men, desiring him that he would not be slack to come unto them. And Peter rising up, went with them. And when he was come, they brought him into the upper chamber. And all the widows stood about him weeping, and shewing him the coats and garments which Dorcas made them. And they all being put forth, Peter kneeling down prayed, and turning to the body, he said: Tabitha, arise. And she opened her eyes; and seeing Peter, she sat up. And giving her his hand, he lifted her up. And when he had called the saints and the widows, he presented her alive. And it was made known throughout all Joppe; and many believed in the Lord. And it came to pass, that he abode many days in Joppe, with one Simon a tanner.' (Acts 9:31-43)

"But Peter was a very special target for us here in the Pit long before that. Yeah, we had planned to work in tandem with the priests and Pharisees to corner that son of Jonah, and to apply enough pressure to get him to turn star witness against their nemesis. This would have been a real coup - getting the chap who had been designated as the visible head of the *Sancta Ecclesia* upon the Deliverer's return to His Father in heaven to flip and testify against his Master!

"But, knowing that Peter was flawed just like every other descendant of Adam and Eve who was born with original sin, the Deliverer had prayed particularly hard to His Father in heaven so that Peter would go on to lead the *Sancta Ecclesia* the way he eventually did despite his human frailty and his inclination to sin.

"As if to rub it in, exactly two thousand years later - on March 23, 2000 to be exact - while on a pilgrimage to the Holy Land, the two hundred and sixty-fourth successor to Simon (the son of Jonah who had his name changed to CEPHAS or 'Rock' by none other than the Deliverer Himself) summarized what had transpired as follows in his homily at the Chapel of the Cenacle: 'Gathered in the Upper Room, we have listened to the Gospel account of the Last Supper. We have heard words which emerge from the depths of the mystery of the Incarnation of the Son of God. Jesus takes bread, blesses and breaks it, then gives it to his disciples, saying: "This is my Body". God's covenant with his

People is about to culminate in the sacrifice of his Son, the Eternal Word made flesh. The ancient prophecies are about to be fulfilled: "Sacrifices and offerings you desired not, but a body you have prepared for me...Lo, I have come to do your will, O God" (Heb 10:5-7). In the Incarnation, the Son of God, of one being with the Father, became Man and received a body from the Virgin Mary. And now, on the night before his death, he says to his disciples: This is my Body, which will be given up for you...' (Homily of Pope John Paul II at the Chapel of the Cenacle during his jubilee pilgrimage to the Holy Land as reported in *L'Osservatore Romano*).'

"But that wasn't really a surprise. Thirty-five years earlier, the predecessor of St John Paul II, Pope Paul VI (born Giovanni Baptista Enrico Antonio Maria Montini) who closed the Second Vatican Council which Pope John XXIII had convened, had solemnly promulgated in *Lumen Gentium*, the 'Dogmatic Constitution on the Church', as follows: 'Already from the beginning of the world the foreshadowing of the Church took place. It was prepared in a remarkable way throughout the history of the people of Israel and by means of the Old Covenant. In the present era of time the Church was constituted and, by the outpouring of the Spirit, was made manifest. At the end of time it will gloriously achieve completion, when, as is read in the Fathers, all the just, from Adam and "from Abel, the just one, to the last of the elect, will be gathered together with the Father in the universal Church.'

"The Deliverer had told his disciples that He was the Bread of Life; and He had added that whoever came to Him would not hunger: and whoever believed in Him would never thirst. (John 6:35) But He had also said that for a grain of wheat to produce much fruit, it first had to die!

"It would fall upon John, the beloved disciple, to describe the way the battle lines were drawn in grisly detail from the cave he called home on the Island of Patmos. Referring to me, he would write: 'And I saw a beast coming up out of the sea, having seven heads and ten horns, and upon his horns ten diadems, and upon his heads names of blasphemy. And the beast, which I saw, was like to a leopard, and his feet were as the feet of a bear, and his mouth as the mouth of a lion. And the dragon gave him his own strength, and great power. And I saw one of his heads as it were slain to death: and his death's wound was healed. And all the earth was in admiration after the beast. And they adored the dragon, which gave power to the beast: and they adored the beast, saying: Who is like to the beast? And who shall be able to fight with him? And there was given to him a mouth speaking great things, and blasphemies: and power was given to him to do two and forty months. And he opened his mouth unto blasphemies against God, to blaspheme his name, and his tabernacle, and them that dwell in heaven. And it was given unto him to make war with the saints, and to overcome them. And power was given him over every tribe, and people, and tongue, and nation. And all that dwell upon the earth adored him, whose names are not written in the book of life of the Lamb, which was slain from the beginning of the world. (Revelation 13:1-8)

"The Prime Mover did not abandon humans after Adam and Eve fell from grace. Can you imagine what things would be like in the world if He had? All humans would be headed to hell for one.

"You might recall that the paradise of pleasure wherein He placed man (whom He had formed in His own image and likeness) boasted all manner of trees, fair to behold, and pleasant to eat of, including the tree of life

446

and the tree of knowledge of good and evil (Genesis 2:8-9). When He said to the first man and the first woman: 'But of the tree of knowledge of good and evil, thou shalt not eat, for in what day soever thou shalt eat of it, thou shalt die the death' Genesis 2:17, He might indeed have added: 'And thou shalt come to your judgment thereupon'!

"For as Paul said in his epistle to the Hebrews: 'And as it is appointed unto men once to die, and after this the judgment: So also Christ was offered once to exhaust the sins of many; the second time he shall appear without sin to them that expect him unto salvation.' (Hebrews 9:27-28) Abandoning humans after they fell would have been tantamount to predestining them all for hell!

"And then, with fallen humans left completely to their own devices, life on earth for those unfortunate enough to come into the world would have been nightmarish to say the least.

"While humans, unlike us pure spirits, are capable of saying *mea culpa* (or making an act of contrition) after falling from grace, they are incapable of any virtuous act on their own without the help of grace from on high as a result of being conceived in original sin. The infinitely merciful Prime Mover looked down upon them with pity, and took the extraordinary step of sending His only begotten Son (who stands in need of no other to recommend His petitions to the Father) to earth to act as Mediator between the poor humans and the Deliverer's Father in heaven. (1 Timothy 2:6) For God so loved the world, as to give his only begotten Son; that whosoever believeth in him, may not perish, but may have life everlasting! (John 3:16)

"It, indeed, all went back to the time the Prime Mover caused the world and everything in it (including humans) to bounce into existence out of nothing followed by His formal declaration that all the things that He made were very good. (Genesis 1:31) By so declaring, he committed Himself simultaneously to sending His only begotten Son into the world once Man fell from grace. After the Prime Mover caused us in the pure spiritual realm to bounce into existence out of nothing, He similarly liked what He saw. Actually His declaration that the world and all the things in it were very good echoed that. Through the incarnation of the Second Person of the Holy Trinity, humans were being given a second opportunity (now that Adam and Eve had eaten the forbidden fruit from the Tree of the Knowledge of Good and Evil) to choose to be on the side of Good or to join me here in hell where there is a blazing furnace and weeping and gnashing of teeth. (cfr Matthew 13:42 and Luke 13:28)

"Actually, writing to rebut those who were denying that Christ did not make His appearance on earth in the flesh, John would write: 'He that committeth sin is of the devil: for the devil sinneth from the beginning. For this purpose, the Son of God appeared, that he might destroy the works of the devil.' (1 John 3:8)

"Now, ever since the Rwenzori Prehistoric Diaries (penned by Adam and Eve) were unearthed, people have been scouring the environs of the Mountains of the Moon (the confirmed location of the biblical Garden of Pleasure) in search of the Tree of the Knowledge of Good and Evil. This is even though they all are munching on the forbidden fruit not less than seven times seven times a day! Taking advantage of the fact that they are endowed with the faculties of reason and free will, they are into doing things that go against their consciences and consequently are forbidden all the time. And that is especially true of those humans who are immersed in the culture of death, and have no scruples about visiting it on their fellow human!

"And the reason humans have to die the death for engaging in their acts of 'disobedience' is obvious. Molded in the Prime Mover's image and likeness, they can find true self-actualization in Him alone and in nothing else. If things were otherwise, humans would essentially be 'gods' unto themselves! That was the secret I did not reveal to Eve when, in response to her concern that they might die if they as much as touched the fruit from that tree in the midst of the Garden of Pleasure, I said 'No, you shall not die the death. For God doth know that in what day so-ever you shall eat thereof, your eyes shall be opened; and you shall be as Gods knowing good and evil.' (Genesis 3:4-5)

"In conducting themselves in ways that were contrary to their elevated status as 'children of the Prime Mover', the first man and the first woman indulged in something that was as unacceptable as 'stealing' fruit from the Tree of Knowledge of Good and Evil. They realized that they were 'naked' because they soon found out that they could not conceal their act of disobedience or pretend that everything was still all right. Their consciences didn't allow them to sweep their act of disobedience under the rug and pretend that it did not happen!

"The Prime Mover simply sought to convey (through His injunction that they not eat of fruit from the Tree of the Knowledge of Good and Evil) that, as and when humans freely went against their consciences, they would be doing something that was offensive to Him; and that would be tantamount to cutting themselves off from the Source of Life. To be clear, humans, fashioned in the Prime Mover's own image and likeness (just like us like us pure spirits) must at all times do everything to His greater honor and glory in order to remain in good books with Him. They were lucky that the Word, through Whom all things were made and without Whom was made nothing that was made, agreed to take up His human nature in order to redeem them from the curse of that 'Law' with His death on the gibbet. (cfr John 1:3 and Galatians 3:13)

"And now, on the night before He gave up His life for them on Mt. Calvary, the Deliverer had ample reason to warn His disciples saying: 'In the world you shall have distress: but have confidence, I have overcome the world.' (John 16:33) That was after he had said: 'If any one abide not in me, he shall be cast forth as a branch, and shall wither, and they shall gather him up, and cast him into the fire, and he burneth.' (John 15:6)

"The plight of humans was and is still quite desperate as you can see; but it gave the Prime Mover an opportunity to demonstrate His infinite love for the creatures He had gratuitously caused to come into existence out of nothing. One moment they are nonexistent; and the next moment they discover themselves kicking and prancing about in what had once been the 'garden of pleasure'! But just look around and see all the wickedness, the injustices, the lying and the hypocrisy, and above all the killings in the world, and tell me if I am not still the boss who calls the shots in this blighted world! And if you still don't get it, just wait until you see stupid humans trigger the long-awaited Armageddon with their hypersonic cruise missiles and intercontinental ballistic missiles tipped with mega nuclear warheads!

"I have worked on humans from the beginning so that, from one generation to another, they do not stop to reflect on how it is that they came into being, the purpose of their existence, or the fact that, molded in the Image, there must needs be an accounting for one's deeds when one's time on Planet Earth is up.

"You see - my *raison d'être* as the Father of Death is to work for the eternal damnation of human souls! I have invested all my resources in doing what it takes to jeopardize the salvation of humans; and those resources include my minions amongst humans themselves. And humans are so thick skinned! Just look how hard it is to get them just to figure in their actions the fact that their earthly existence is merely the precursor to an eternal existence in heaven with their Maker or here in Gehenna with me! Many believe that Gehenna (or *Gehinnom* in Hebrew) actually only exists in Jewish lore as the valley in the vicinity of Jerusalem where some kings of Judah brazenly sacrificed their children by fire! Yeah, Indeed!

"I am committed to doing what I must do to jeopardize the salvation of human souls. This is the exact opposite of what the Son of Man is committed to doing. But because humans are endowed with the faculties of reason and free will, I can't force them to do evil just as their Deliverer can't compel them to practice virtue.

"They get it correct whilst they are still toddlers. But then they promptly 'go bananas' (as they say) as soon as they reach the age of reason and supposedly start to use their intellectual faculties. This is because humans out of selfishness invariably prefer to focus not on the eternal despite their elevated status as creatures that are molded in the image of the Prime Mover, but on the temporal - on the here and now - like beasts of the earth.

"John the Baptist even coined a phrase to describe the descendants of Adam and Eve who were supposed to act as teachers and mentors: 'Brood of Vipers!' (Matthew 3:7 and Luke 3:7) He even had a message for the so-called members of Law Enforcement. When the soldiers also asked him, saying: And what shall we do? And he said to them: Do violence to no man; neither calumniate any man; and be content with your pay. (Luke

3:14) Delivering His 'sermon on the mount', the Messiah had said: 'You have heard that it was said to them of old: Thou shalt not kill. And whosoever shall kill shall be in danger of the judgment. But I say to you, that whosoever is angry with his brother, shall be in danger of the judgment. And whosoever shall say to his brother, Raca, shall be in danger of the council. And whosoever shall say, Thou Fool, *shall be in danger of hell fire*.' (Matthew 5:21-22) And of course, regarding warmongers, His admonition to Peter that those who lived by the sword died by the sword was very relevant, except that humans just did not learn anything from history.

"And it certainly did not help when the Deliverer Himself called out the priests and Pharisees, saying: 'You serpents, generation of vipers, how will you flee from the judgment of hell?' (Matthew 23:33)

"Because the attention of humans is taken up by things that are transient, when they mumble the *Pater Noster*, it doesn't occur to them that they are praying to their Maker who caused them to come into existence out of nothing and in the peculiar circumstances in which they even now revel. That is when they pray at all. No wonder the Deliverer, echoing Isaiah (Isaiah 19:13), lamented saying: 'This people honor me with their lips, but their heart is far away from me! But in vain do they worship me, teaching as doctrines the precepts of men.' (Mark 7:6-9 and Matthew 15:8-9)

"You can gauge the extent of His sorrow and anguish as He prayed in the Garden of Gethsemane and was facing the prospect of making Himself a sacrificial lamb to save folks who did not want to be saved. It must have seemed a thankless task - and an impossible one humanly speaking- to sacrifice His life for the salvation of folks who patently did not want to be saved!

"Indeed, He almost said as much when, explaining to His band of apostles the reason he chose ever so often to speak to the multitudes in parables, he said: 'Because to you it is given to know the mysteries of the kingdom of heaven: but to them it is not given. For he that hath, to him shall be given, and he shall abound: but he that hath not, from him shall be taken away that also which he hath. Therefore do I speak to them in parables: because seeing they see not, and hearing they hear not, neither do they understand. And the prophecy of Isaiah is fulfilled in them, who saith: By hearing you shall hear, and shall not understand: and seeing you shall see, and shall not perceive. For the heart of this people is grown gross, and with their ears they have been dull of hearing, and their eyes they have shut: lest at any time they should see with their eyes, and hear with their ears, and understand with their heart, and be converted, and I should heal them.' (Matthew 13:11-15) It was true two thousand years ago, and remains so today.

"This is a very pitiful situation; because whatever humans do or scheme, they still remain completely dependent on the Prime Mover, even as they attempt to ignore His existence and role in their creation out of nothing! And all the while, they know not when the master of the house is returning – whether in the evening, or at midnight, or when the rooster crows, or at dawn!

"Yeah, indeed! They know not when the master of the house is returning! (Mark 13:35; Matthew 24:36; Luke 12:35-38). When the Deliverer gave that admonition, He didn't do it in jest. He certainly wasn't trying to crack a joke. He meant exactly what He said.

"The lifespans of humans today is between zero at the bottom end and one hundred and fifty years at the upper end for those who are lucky enough to survive wars, famines, plagues, and other innumerable hazards to dear life that humans face. A similar situation has existed since the time of Adam and Eve - from the moment the duo heard the Prime Mover say 'Thou shalt die the death', and consequently in any era, one can only refer to a 'generation' of humans.

"Well, we in the Pit have noted all this all along, and we have always moved adroitly to exploit the situation. As a result of our hard work, during the relatively short period humans enjoy a lease of life on Planet Earth, we see that humans (as they enjoy dominion over the fish of the sea, the birds of the heavens, over livestock and over the earth and everything that creeps there on, and as they gaze with wonder upon the oceans and mountains that swarm with every kind of winged bird and with beasts of every type, and relish their dominion over them) now invariably imagine that they themselves are a permanent fixture in the world in the same way the cosmos in which they live appears to be a permanent fixture.

"And humans have fallen into the habit of imagining that the words 'Thou shalt die the death' do not apply to them. This is what they imagine even as they mourn their dead when calamities strike. Humans are further blinded by the fact that the works of their own hands - like the pyramids, the smog-filled cities, and some of their other 'inventions' - are capable of surviving them; and the Deliverer's warning, that they know not when the master of the house will return, as a rule now falls on completely deaf ears. It is such a pity!

"This also explains why it is that generation upon generation of these stupid fools now hanker for power, fame and fortune at the expense of the salvation of their souls and frown on the Mother Theresas of this world; and it also explains why nation states employ the resources at their command in the blind pursuit of the myth of super power status and 'exceptionalism'! It is a puzzle that even as humans experience the on-set of old age (the clearest sign that their days on Planet Earth are numbered), they still get easily tripped up by the hackneyed schemes we conjure up and dangle in front of their eyes.

"But let us circle back to the *Sancta Ecclesia* - the Church the Deliverer founded on the rock called Peter with the words: *'Et ego dico tibi quia tu es Petrus et super hanc petram aedificabo ecclesiam meam et portae inferi non praevalebunt adversum eam. Et tibi dabo claves regni caelorum et quodcumque ligaveris super terram erit ligatum in caelis et quodcumque solveris super terram erit solutum in caelis.'* (And I say to thee: That thou art Peter; and upon this rock I will build my church, and the gates of hell shall not prevail against it. And I will give to thee the keys of the kingdom of heaven. And whatsoever thou shalt bind upon earth, it shall be bound also in heaven: and whatsoever thou shalt loose upon earth, it shall be loosed also in heaven.) (Matthew 16:18-19) Look, that *Sancta Ecclesia* and the mystery of the Incarnation (or Word made Flesh) are not merely intertwined; they are both living testimony of the Prime Mover's infinite love for humans. And all humans now have a shot at enjoying beatific vision. (1 John 3:2; I Corinthians 13:12; Matthew 5:8; Catechism 1028)

"The fisherman turned the fisher of men summarized it very well when, accompanied by the centurion Cornelius, he addressed the folks in Caesarea saying: 'God sent the word to the children of Israel, preaching peace by Jesus Christ: (he is Lord of all.) You know the word which hath been published through all Judea: for it began from Galilee, after the baptism which John preached, Jesus of Nazareth: how God anointed him with the Holy Ghost, and with power, who went about doing good, and healing all that were oppressed by the devil, for God was with him. And we are witnesses of all things that he did in the land of the Jews and in Jerusalem, whom they killed, hanging him upon a tree. Him God raised up the third day, and gave him to be made manifest; not to all the people, but to witnesses preordained by God, even to us, who did eat and drink with him after he arose again from the dead; And he commanded us to preach to the people, and to testify that it is he who was appointed by God, to be judge of the living and of the dead. To him all the prophets give testimony, that by his name all receive remission of sins, who believe in him.' (Acts 10:36-43)

"But what was it that could justify the Word, a member of the Godhead, emptying Himself and taking up His human nature and dwelling among humans? (John 1:14; Revelation 21:3). Yeah, the One about whom Isaiah wrote: 'All nations are before him as if they had no being at all, and are counted to him as nothing, and vanity!' (Isaiah 40:17)

"Well, just because I, Beelzebub, had succeeded in luring Adam and Eve to eat of the forbidden fruit, the Word, through Whom all things were made and without Whom was made nothing that was made, was not about to throw in the towel and allow His work of creation which He had accomplished over the space of six full days to go to waste just like that! And especially not after He had created man, creating them male and female, to his own image, and blessed them, saying: Increase and multiply, and fill the earth, and subdue it, and rule over the fishes of the sea, and the fowls of the air, and all living creatures that move upon the earth; and seeing all the things that He had made, He had declared that they were very good! (Genesis 1:1-31)

"The Prime Mover's assertion at the end of each day's work of creation that he looked upon the things He had brought into existence out of nothing and they were

456

all of them very good said something about His divine plan. It had to be one hell of a good plan! This was more than history in the making. This was a case of the one and only Prime Mover deciding in eternity to bring into being creatures that would be of the kind that could enjoy His largess.

"Being almighty and infinite goodness *par excellence*, He wasn't at all worried that those pure spirits and the humans (who would come with a physical body and an incorporeal soul) might cause Him grief through the misuse of their God-given intellect and the free will (or 'disobedience'). Being Perfect Love, Perfect Goodness, and Perfect Knowledge, he was not about to show that He was in any way 'begrudging' or 'mean'. As proof that this was the case, He was more than happy to bring into being out of nothing (and completely gratuitously) creatures that could enjoy that largess with Him *through the exercise of their faculties of reason and free will*. That was what was implied by being 'fashioned in the Prime Mover's image'.

"But it wasn't just the exercise of the Prime Mover's inventive genius and demonstration of His largess at play here. What the inspired author of the Torah (or Pentateuch) wrote about what the Prime Mover did at the conclusion of His labors is of even more significance: 'In six days the LORD made the heavens and the earth, the sea, and all that was in them, but he rested on the seventh day. Therefore the LORD blessed the Sabbath day and made it holy.' (Exodus 20:11) The Prime Mover was implementing His mysterious and unfathomable 'Divine Plan'.

"The inspired author later wrote: 'And the Lord spoke to Moses, saying: Speak to the children of Israel, and thou shalt say to them: See that you keep my sabbath; because it is a sign between me and you in your

457

generations that you may know that I am the Lord, who sanctify you. Keep you my sabbath: for it is holy unto you: he that shall profane it, shall be put to death: he that shall do any work in it, his soul shall perish out of the midst of his people. Six days shall you do work: in the seventh day is the sabbath, the rest holy to the Lord. Every one that shall do any work on this day, shall die. Let the children of Israel keep the sabbath, and celebrate it in their generations. It is an everlasting covenant between me and the children of Israel, and a perpetual sign. For in six days the Lord made heaven and earth, and in the seventh he ceased from work. And the Lord, when he had ended these words in Mount Sinai, gave to Moses two stone tables of testimony, written with the finger of God.' (Exodus 31:12-18)

"The operative words were: 'that you may know that I am the Lord, who sanctify you.' Interwoven as the Prime Mover's work of creation is with 'Divine Providence', absolutely nothing happens by accident, and also everything that happens invariably does so under his watchful eye. The First Vatican Council accordingly declared: 'By his providence God protects and governs all things which he has made.' (First Vatican Council).

"Because creation is the work of a Prime Mover who is Himself infinite wisdom and goodness, that work had to be of a standard that he Himself could appreciate. You humans probably think otherwise, but you do not have the wherewithal or capacity to fully appreciate the splendor of the Prime Mover's workmanship. The splendor of creatures that are made in the Prime Mover's own image is not fathomable for that very reason. These beings are after all His handiwork, created in Christ Jesus to do good works, which the Prime Mover prepared in advance for them to do. (Ephesians 2:10)

"Paul put it quite aptly when he sighed: 'O the depth of the riches of the wisdom and of the knowledge of God! How incomprehensible are his judgments, and how unsearchable his ways!' (Romans 11:33)

"John summarized it all in four sentences as no one else could when he started writing his Story of the Deliverer: 'In the beginning was the Word, and the Word was with God, and the Word was God. The same was in the beginning with God. All things were made by him: and without him was made nothing that was made. In him was life, and the life was the light of men.' (John 1:1-4)

"But suppose that the Prime Mover had opted to just forget about humans after Adam and Eve sinned, and left them to their devices notwithstanding the fact that they were fashioned in his own image and likeness! That would, of course, have signaled defeat. Look, I would have immediately declared 'Mission Accomplished' in the battle between the forces of good and the forces of evil. Even though already judged and condemned myself, I would still have been quite happy to enjoy the last laugh!

"And, under my regime, instead of churches and other places of worship dedicated to honoring the Prime Mover, humans would be openly constructing temples dedicated to me and to my fellow demons. Idolatry would be the order of the day with absolutely nothing off limits, including human sacrifices! And they would be praying to me to be delivered from their miseries and from the curse of coming into this world!

"That would have given us demons a license to manipulate humans every which way unhindered; and we would ensure that the world degenerated into a totally vile, inhospitable and cruel place particularly for those humans who were frail or dependent on others for their survival. Oh, we demons would be having a ball at the expense of humans - a ball that unfortunately would probably come to an abrupt halt as stupid humans, baying for the blood of their fellow humans, nuked themselves out of existence!

"But, as John wrote, "God so loved the world that he gave his one and only begotten Son, so that whosoever believeth in him should not perish, but have everlasting life. (John 3:16) Paul elaborated saying: 'He that spared not even his own Son, but delivered him up for us all, how hath he not also, with him, given us all things?' (Romans 8:32)

"It was by virtue of the grace that would be merited for humans by the Deliverer that Adam and Eve saw that they had been tricked by me to bite of the forbidden fruit and went and hid among the trees. (Genesis 3:10) And it was by virtue of the same that Mary was conceived without original sin and consented to become the Mother of God when she responded to the angel Gabriel with the words: '*Ecce ancilla Domini: fiat mihi secundum verbum tuum.*' (Behold the handmaid of the Lord; be it done to me according to thy word.) (Luke 1:38) And so it was that the Word became flesh and dwelt among humans. (John 1:14)

"And, of course, John was not referred to as the 'beloved disciple' for nothing. From his cave on Patmos, John would write: 'And I saw another angel flying through the midst of heaven, having the eternal gospel, to preach unto them that sit upon the earth, and over every nation, and tribe, and tongue, and people: Saying with a loud voice: Fear the Lord, and give him honor, because the hour of his judgment is come; and adore ye him, that made heaven and earth, the sea, and the fountains of waters. And another angel followed, saying: That great Babylon is fallen, is fallen; which made all nations to drink of the wine of the wrath of her fornication. And the third angel followed them, saying with a loud voice: If any man shall adore the beast and his image, and receive his character in his forehead, or in his hand; He also shall drink of the wine of the wrath of God, which is mingled with pure wine in the cup of his wrath, and shall be tormented with fire and brimstone in the sight of the holy angels, and in the sight of the Lamb.' (Apocalypse 14:6-10)

"Evidently, after Michael, Gabriel, Raphael - the whole shebang - had out-foxed me and my rebel troops and driven us from the presence of the Prime Mover, they did not stop there. First, as Thomas Aquinas, who is referred to not entirely for nothing as *Doctor Angelicus* (the Angelic Doctor), would point out in his Summa Theologica (First Part, Question 113), Adam and Eve and all their descendants are all gifted with 'guardian angels'. And, in his canticle, David put it plainly: 'For he hath given his angels charge over thee; to keep thee in all thy ways.' (Psalm 91:11; see also Matthew 18:10 and Hebrew 1:14)

"So, what were the angels up to when they saw that I had succeeded in hoodwinking Adam and Eve to the point where those humans (who were made in the image of the Prime Mover like themselves), having caved, saw that 'the tree was good to eat, and fair to the eyes, and delightful to behold, and whereupon Eve took of the fruit thereof, and did eat, and gave to her husband who also did eat'? (Genesis 3:1-7) Oh, talk about the communion of saints! Paul described it very well in his epistle to the Church in Corinth: 'To you who have been sanctified in Christ Jesus, called to be holy, with all those everywhere who call upon the name of our Lord Jesus Christ, their Lord and ours. (1 Corinthians 1:2) Those angels, being a part and parcel of the 'Communion of Saints', seeing what the first man and the first woman were doing, prayed for humans like they had never prayed before.

461

"In that moment, they would have willingly offered themselves up as sacrificial lambs to expiate the sin of Adam and Eve, if it were not for the fact that it was not possible for mere creatures like themselves to make adequate recompense for the offence perpetuated by those humans against a divinity. They knew that only a divinity could pay the ransom to save Adam and Eve and their descendants from joining us here in hell. (Matthew 20:28 and Mark 10:45) So all they could do was pray and beseech the Prime Mover on behalf of fallen man. And pray, they certainly did as members of the 'Communion of Saints'.

"What would humans do in similar circumstances? Well, with the exception of a few really odd ones like Mother Theresa, Gemma Galgani, Peter Wu, Joseph Zhang Dapeng, Mariam Barwadi, Charles Lwanga, Mariam Baouardy, Marie-Alphonsine Danil Ghattas, Lorenzo Ruiz, Moses the Ethiopian (aka Abba Moses the Robber), Maurice (aka St. Mauritius or St. Moritz). Damien de Veuster of Moloka'I, Agnes, Katherine Drexel, Zeffirino Namuncurá of Argentina, Josephine Bakhita (the Sudanese girl who endured a life of slavery from the young age of seven but miraculously ended up in Italy where, upon being received in the Church, she was confirmed and received her first Holy Communion from none other than Archbishop Giuseppe Sarto, the Cardinal Patriarch of Venice and the future Pope Pius X before finally ending up as a member of the Canossian Order – and whose body remains incorrupt to this day), and Rose of Lima, humans would be more inclined to bang the doors of their houses shut in the face of neighbors who were fleeing ravening wolves (or to build concrete walls to keep families that are fleeing death squads from finding refuge in territory they had themselves expropriated from the original natives) than go to their succor!

"Upon taking up His human nature, the Deliverer would say: 'Greater love than this no man hath, that a man lay down his life for his friends.' (John 15:13) That commandment applied equally to beings in the angelic realm; and the good angels would not have hesitated to offer themselves up as ransom for the salvation of humans. As the Deliverer would point out to Pilate, if His kingdom had been a worldly kingdom, his servants would certainly strive that He should not be delivered to the Jews. But His kingdom was not from hence. (John 18:36) And what the good angels were ready to do was the exact opposite of what we demons would do in the same circumstances. You bet that we would willingly sacrifice ourselves for the damnation of human souls. This is because we ourselves are already damned and condemned, and there would be nothing to lose!

"And thank the Prime Mover that we are pure spirits and are invisible to the human eye. If we demons had been visible to humans, they would all, with the exception of the immaculately conceived Virgin Mother of the Deliverer and may be John the Baptist and the Angelic Doctor, die of sheer fright just observing the venom and the hate in our mien! The sight would kill them. Oh, how we hate you humans! How we resent the fact that the Prime Mover so loved the world He gave His only begotten Son, so that whoever believes in Him should not perish but have everlasting life. (John 3:16) And we, of course, know that whosoever believeth that Jesus is the Christ is also born of God. And everyone that loveth Him who begot, loveth Him who is also born of him! (1 John 5).

"Now, it was whilst it was still dark on Sunday morning that Mary Magdalen, followed by John and Peter, had been to the empty tomb wherein the Deliverer had been interned upon His death on the cross. The risen

Deliverer would appear first to Mary Magdalen, and then to Mary the mother of James, Salome, and Joanna (who had been cured of evil spirits and infirmities by the Deliverer whilst He was still alive). And He would then accost Cleophas and his buddy as they were fleeing Jerusalem and heading back to their homes in Emmaus; and to Simon Peter around that same time. And He would finally appear to the gathering of His disciples in the Upper Room while Thomas Didymus was absent.

"But that is running ahead. The Deliverer's disciples were closeted in the Upper Room in fear, not knowing what would happen to them in the wake of the kangaroo trial and summary execution of their divine Master that the priests and Pharisees had engineered. Comprising the vanguard of the Deliverer's advancing army, the disciples who were hiding out in the Upper Room were totally demoralized and dismayed to the max. They had seen the miracles that He had performed - raising Lazarus from the dead (John 11:1-44), healing lepers, turning water into wine, and so on and so forth - and they had become convinced beyond any reasonable doubt that He was the Christ. But they had now also witnessed the demise and burial of their Messiah! Saying that the vaunted 'Army of Christ' was in disarray would be an understatement on a monumental scale.

"Still, from the depth of the Pit, we ourselves were of course fearing the very worst. We were gearing up for the earth shattering, if hoarse, burst of song on the lines of Sabine Baring-Gould's processional hymn:

1. *Onward Christian soldiers! Marching as to war,*
   With the cross of Jesus Going on before.
   Christ, the royal Master, Leads against the foe;
   Forward into battle, See, His banners go!

Refrain:
Onward, Christian soldiers! Marching as to war,
With the cross of Jesus, Going on before.

2. *At the name of Jesus Satan's host doth flee;*
   On then, Christian soldiers, On to victory!
   Hell's foundations quiver At the shout of praise:
   Brothers, lift your voices, Loud your anthems
   raise!

"But as luck would have it, that was not to be - at least not yet! Mary Magdalen (out of whom the Deliverer had cast seven devils), and Mary the mother of James, and Salome had bought and mixed together as soon as the Sabbath was over sweet spices and perfumes for embalming the body of the Deliverer, and their plan was to head to the sepulcher at daylight on the morning of the next day. (Mark 16:1)

"But Mary Magdalen didn't wait to go to the tomb. She was there by herself before dawn whilst it was still dark on that Sunday morning only to find the tomb empty. The body of the Deliverer was nowhere to be seen! She was sure that the priests and Pharisees had something to do with it. She had heard that they had posted guards close to the tomb that Joseph of Arimathea had offered to be the Deliverer's final resting place. (Matthew 27:57) But now the large boulder that had been used to seal the tomb had been rolled back, and the tomb was empty.

"Mary Magdalen was fearing the very worst. The crooked priests and Pharisees, whom the Deliverer had referred to as 'brood of vipers' (cfr Matthew 23:33), were not going to stop as being rid of the man who had called himself the 'Son of God'. She was convinced that they had concocted a plan to desecrate his body, probably using hired goons this time in order to conceal their real

465

motives!

"Mary Magdalen went running to Simon Peter who was with John. 'They have taken the Lord out of the tomb', she said sobbing; 'and we don't know where they have put him!' She followed as Peter and John raced to the tomb. Perhaps there was something she might be able to do to help. It was just dreadful that things could come to this after everything the Deliverer had done whilst he was alive – healing the sick, and even raising up Lazarus from the dead, not to mention his role in getting her to renounce her life of sin and to become rehabilitated.

"Arriving at the tomb, Peter and John saw for themselves that what Mary Magdalen had said was true. The burial garment and the strips of linen they had used to wrap around the Deliverer's head had not been disturbed. But the body was gone! (John 20:1-10)

"It was a while later, when the sun had risen, that Mary the mother of James and Salome, accompanied by Joanna, set off for Golgotha with the spices and perfumes. Joanna's husband, Chuza, worked as a steward in the palace of Herod Antipater who had murdered John the Baptist. (Luke 23:55; Luke 8:2-3). Joanna was accordingly a very useful source of information in those troubled times. The trio had tried to locate Mary Magdalen in vain. She was nowhere to be seen.

"The women were shocked to find that the huge rock that had been used to seal the entrance to the tomb where the Deliverer had been laid had been rolled away, and the body was gone! A young man in a white robe was seated to the right, and he shocked them even more when he said: 'Be not affrighted; you seek Jesus of Nazareth, who was crucified: he is risen, he is not here, behold the place where they laid him. But go, tell his disciples and Peter that he goeth before you into Galilee; there you shall see him, as he told you.' (Mark 16:1-7)

"Trembling and gripped with fear and astonishment, the three women fled the tomb and were initially too scared to say anything to any man (other than the apostles). (Mark 16:8) They did not know what to make of the words 'he is risen, he is not here'!

"They thought it was just terrible that Mary Magdalen was still nowhere to be seen. They did not know what had happened to her.

"Of course, unbeknownst to them, she had risen up in the wee hours and was at the tomb whilst it was still quite dark; and, seeing that the huge stone that had been at the tomb's entrance had been moved and the tomb was empty, she had hastened to Peter and John to appraise them of the new development saying: 'They have taken away the Lord out of the sepulchre, and we know not where they have laid him.' (John 20:2).

"The three women were also unaware at that time that Peter and John had been to the tomb to check out the reported abduction of the Deliverer's body from the tomb. (John 20:3-8)

"The situation was getting really ridiculous! Up until that point, it didn't strike either those women or the apostles that the Deliverer had 'risen up from the dead'! And they were still in the dark regarding the whereabouts of Mary Magdalen. Unbeknownst to either these women or the apostles, after delivering the news regarding the empty tomb to Peter and John in the wee hours of that Sunday morning, she had headed back to the sepulcher to search for the Deliverer's body.

"As recorded by John in his gospel, Mary stood at the sepulchre without, weeping. Now as she was weeping, she stooped down, and looked into the sepulchre, And she saw two angels in white, sitting, one at the head, and one at the feet, where the body of Jesus had been laid. They say to her: Woman, why weepest thou? She saith to them: Because they have taken away my Lord; and I know not where they have laid him. When she had thus said, she turned herself back, and saw Jesus standing; and she knew not that it was Jesus. Jesus saith to her: Woman, why weepest thou? whom seekest thou? She, thinking it was the gardener, saith to him: Sir, if thou hast taken him hence, tell me where thou hast laid him, and I will take him away. Jesus saith to her: Mary. She turning, saith to him: Rabboni (which is to say, Master). Jesus saith to her: Do not touch me, for I am not yet ascended to my Father. But go to my brethren, and say to them: I ascend to my Father and to your Father, to my God and your God. Mary Magdalen cometh, and telleth the disciples: I have seen the Lord, and these things he said to me.' (John 20:11-18)

"Mary Magdalen was seeing the apparition of the Deliverer in the moments immediately following His glorious resurrection from the dead. He had descended into hell and rescued Adam and Eve and the other humans we were holding captive there; but He hadn't ascended to His Father with them yet. And dawn had not broken as yet in Jerusalem. Mary, that Palestinian woman who hailed from Magdala, the fishing town on the western shores of the Sea of Galilee, was indeed the very first person to see the risen Deliverer.

"Following their own encounter with the angels inside the Deliverer's empty tomb, Mary the mother of James, Salome, and Joanna were still bewildered and afraid, when lo and behold, the Deliverer appeared to them and greeted them. Matthew describes what followed: 'And they came up and took hold of His feet and worshipped Him. Then Jesus said to them, "Do not be afraid; go and take word to My brethren to leave for

468

Galilee, and there they will see Me." Matthew 28:10)

"The Deliverer permitted the trio to touch him because He had already ascended to His Father in heaven, taking along those we had been holding hostage in the Pit.

"The accounts of the women (Mary Magdalen, Mary the mother of James, Salome, and Joanna) were dismissed out of hand by the men. Years later, John would write: 'This (John) is the disciple who is bearing witness to these things, and who has written these things, and we know that his testimony is true.' (John 21:24) But for now Peter, John and the Deliverer's other grieving disciples who were closeted in the Upper Room in mourning weren't buying the stories emanating from those women.

"But, much more telling was what Cleophas (who would himself eventually die a martyr at the hands of Jewish authorities in Judea) and another unnamed disciple who was travelling with him were up to when they were accosted by the Deliverer on the road to Emmaus.

"As far as the two were concerned, it seemed quite plain that, in the battle between the forces of Good and the forces of Evil, the Forces of Good had been vanquished. That was in itself not entirely surprising. The Deliverer had explicitly stated in the face of the machinations of the priests and Pharisees: 'Ye are from beneath; I am from above. Ye are of this world; I am not of this world.' (John 8:23) But, then, when pressed by Pontius Pilate to say what it was He had done that had caused to be brought before him in the Praetorium by his accusers, He had tellingly responded saying: 'My kingdom is not of this world. If my kingdom were of this world, my servants would certainly strive that I should not be delivered to the Jews: but now my kingdom is not from hence...' (John 18:36) That is if John, who had let them all know that he was present the entire time at the Praetorium for the Deliverer's trial, was to be believed.

"Cleophas and his buddy understood that they themselves belonged in the world just like the priests and Pharisees. They were convinced that they had been naïve to expect the Deliverer to overcome the odds and come out victorious against His determined foes. That might have been possible if they had been living in some imaginary Utopia, instead of the godforsaken world they had grown up in.

"And, moreover, they were themselves not entirely blameless. At the time of His arrest, it was one of their number, Judas Iscariot, who had gone out of his way to ID the Deliverer in return for the hefty sum of thirty pieces of silver! As the Deliverer's purse bearer, Judas had indeed been a very important member of the 'seminary' brotherhood. And, if he hadn't turned around and killed himself, they likely would be envying him for his ability to sense the direction in which the winds were blowing, and for his 'foresight'!

"As they ambled along on the winding road to Emmaus, the pair even joked about the fact that they had been a part of the crowd of John the Baptizer's followers which gate crashed the wedding at Cana upon getting word that the Deliverer and His mother Mary were among the wedding guests! Such was the excitement that had gripped the populace all across the region, Galileans, Judeans and even many Samaritans were convinced that they were living right on the cusp; and now, with the appearance of the promised Messiah or 'Son of man' as He called Himself, they believed quite sincerely that the prophecies of Ezekiel, Joel and Isaiah (Ezekiel 34:14, Joel 2:24-26 and Isaiah 25:6) were on the verge of being fulfilled.

"Almost three years had gone by since that

470

wedding; but their memories of it were as fresh as if it had taken place just weeks back. And over time the Deliverer had not only spent a lot of time teaching the multitudes and proclaiming that that he had come from God and was going back to God; and that He was the way, and the truth, and the life. And that no one went to the Father except through Him; and He never ceased to emphasize that He had been sent by His Father to the lost sheep of the house of Israel. And He had cured lepers, made the blind see and the lame walk, and He had performed many other miracles and wonders; and He had even raised up Lazarus from the dead!

"It just so happened that Cleophas and the disciple of the Deliverer who was fleeing Jerusalem with him both had family in Bethany where Lazarus lived with his sisters Martha and Mary; and it just so happened that they also were acquaintances of Lazarus and his sisters. Actually, the Town of Bethany where the latter had their home was just minutes from Emmaus if you were traveling on horseback.

"Cleophas had confided to the girls that their brother was the reason he became a fervent follower of the Nazarene. The difference between the Lazarus he knew before he was given a new lease of life by the Deliverer and the Lazarus who was back amongst them was his graying hair and the spark in his eyes that seemed to speak volumes about life on the other side of the gulf which separated the living from the dead. Talk about a walking miracle!

"In the meantime the Deliverer had let them know in no uncertain terms that He was the bread of life - the 'living bread that came down from heaven' as He put it! He had said that if any man ate of that bread, he would live forever; and He had also made it clear that the bread that He Was talking about was actually His flesh.

"He had said plainly that, unless they ate the flesh of the Son of Man and drank His blood (and essentially agreed to become cannibals), they would not have life in them; and that those who did would gain everlasting life! Atrocious even as that sounded, they for their part had believed in Him, although they saw a goodly number in the Deliverer's audience turn and simply walk away in disgust.

"Unfortunately for Cleophas and the buddy he was traveling with, they had both been unable to make it to the Upper Room for the celebration of the Paschal Feast. But they had since been apprised of the events of that evening - the washing by the Deliverer of the feet of the twelve and, above all, the fact that while the 'seder' was under way, He took bread, blessed and broke it, and gave it to all the twelve (including Judas Iscariot), with the words: 'Take ye, and eat. This is my body'; and that He also took the chalice filled with wine and, after giving thanks, gave it to them saying: 'Drink ye all of this. For this is my blood of the New Testament, which shall be shed for many unto remission of sins...'

"It saddened the duo that, as the Deliverer hang on the cross in mortal agony, all they could do was watch from afar albeit in clear sight of the gruesome scene. And just to think that the crowds, urged on by the priests and scribes, had successfully lobbied the Roman Prefect to let the infamous highway robber Barabbas go free instead of the Deliverer! The sight of the Nazarene nailed to the gibbet atop Mount Calvary in the middle of two crosses on which a notorious stagecoach robber and an accomplice were strapped and awaiting their execution would be indelibly etched in their memories; and there was no doubt that those moments, as they kept watch helplessly from a distance, were going to haunt them for as long as they themselves lived.

"The 'Son of Man' (as the Deliverer sometimes referred to Himself) hang from his cross, His hands and feet firmly nailed to it and pierced, as though in fulfillment of the words of the Psalmist that 'They have pierced my hands and my feet'! (Psalm 22:17)

"And the pair would never forget the loud exclamation by the Deliverer just before He gave up His ghost. Even now, as they trudged along and reminisced on the events of that Friday afternoon, they could literally hear the words: *'Eloi, Eloi, Lama Sabachthani?'* ringing in their ears. This was because the Deliverer screamed at the top of His lungs when He said them. His voice had rung out from the summit of Golgotha; and its echo, which sounded rather ominous, had reverberated across the valleys that hemmed in the skull hill!

"All this happened around the ninth hour, with His mother Mary standing right there beneath the cross, supported by John, the younger brother of James. Cleophas and his buddy had felt both angry and helpless; and it did not help matters at all that Mary Magdalene and John's mother, who were keeping watch close by in the company of other women, were wailing and sobbing uncontrollably while all this was going on. Cleophas's friend in particular was apprehensive and quite concerned that this could attract the attention of the Sanhedrin's secret police; and his fear was not unfounded. Those 'goons' could be quite vicious; and it was common knowledge that they could make you disappear after torturing you in one of their 'safe houses'. It was rumored that one was located in a super secret second basement in the temple (of all places). Quite a number of the dead Deliverer's disciples actually believed that it was Judas Iscariot's fear of the priests and Pharisees that drove him to take his own life.

"There is no gain saying the fact that the Deliverer's

death dashed all the hopes of His disciples including Cleophas and his traveling companion. It had become amply clear, as these events were unfolding, that things would never be the same again ever. The mobs that had been organized by the priests and Pharisees were blaspheming and, wagging their heads, taunted the Deliverer saying: 'Vah, thou that destroyest the temple of God, and in three days buildest it up again; Save thyself, coming down from the cross'. And the chief priests and scribes similarly mocked Him saying one to another: 'He saved others; himself he cannot save. Let Christ the king of Israel come down now from the cross, that we may see and believe!' Then, starting from the sixth hour, all hell broke loose. This was as one of those who was crucified with the Deliverer was reviling him saying: 'If thou be Christ, save thyself and us!' Suddenly and seemingly out of nowhere, darkness had descended over all the land as far as the eye could see, and it had persisted right up until the ninth hour!

"And then, at exactly the time He cried out with a loud voice, saying 'Father, into thy hands I commend my spirit', and while the sun was still darkened, the temple veil that had covered the entrance to the Holy of Holies was rent in two from the top even to the bottom; and the earth quaked; and the rocks were rent. But more ominously, graves opened up, and the dead came out of them, and appeared to many in the holy city.

"If there was one thing that Cleophas and his traveling companion had learnt first as disciples of John the Baptizer and then as the Deliverer's disciples, it was that all humans, the people of Israel included, needed to abandon their wicked ways. The Deliverer had taught them that they needed to be as sheep in the midst of wolves; and to be aware of fellow humans, because, as He put it, they (fellow humans) 'will deliver you up in councils, and they will scourge you in their synagogues, etc.'

"It was not lost on them that their Deliverer, who was completely sinless and innocent and undoubtedly also the Christ, had been sent to his wholly undeserved death on the cross. And now, if the events surrounding His death were anything to go by, it was not just the wicked priests and the Pharisees - or, for that matter, just the Israelites - who were going to pay the price; it was going to be all of humanity! They had seen hate on display as the Nazarene, whose only sin was to assert that he was sent by His Father in heaven to do His will on earth, was roundly condemned and murdered in front of their own eyes!

"They had joined the curious crowds that flocked to the temple in the aftermath of the Deliverer's death, and had seen with their own eyes that the curtain that previously shielded the tabernacle from view was ripped up and in threads. And, besides, they themselves had also bumped into some of the 'saints' who had emerged alive from the graves and had converged on the city. Of course most alarming was the fact that the sun appeared to have been jolted from its hinges at the precise moment the Deliverer met His wholly undeserved demise on the skull hill. There was no telling what was going to happen next in the wake of what had transpired.

"And so, they were now headed home where they were going to pick up the threads of their lives in the aftermath of the debacle on Mt. Calvary. Along the way, they also reminisced on something else. It was the story that Peter and James and John, the sons of Zebedee who had been nick-named 'sons of thunder' by the Deliverer and were now referred to as such by everyone, had recounted to those who were in hiding in the Upper Room the previous evening an incident they said the Deliverer had enjoined them not to say a word about the apparition 'until the Son of Man be risen from the dead'!

"And it all took place not long after the Deliverer, addressing them, said: 'Whom do men say that the Son of man is? In response, Peter had answered and said: 'Thou art Christ, the Son of the living God.' The Deliverer, answering, had said to him: 'Blessed art thou, Simon Bar-Jona: because flesh and blood hath not revealed it to thee, but my Father who is in heaven. And I say to thee: That thou art Peter; and upon this rock I will build my church, and the gates of hell shall not prevail against it.'

"As Peter, James and John told it, the Deliverer had gone up into a mountain with Peter, James and John, to pray. And whilst He prayed, the shape of his countenance was altered, and his raiment became white and glittering. And then lo and behold two men were talking with him. The three disciples hadn't had a wink of sleep in days, and had dosed off in the meantime. But, waking up, they saw the Deliverer's glory, and the two men that stood with him. Like James and John, Peter was completely overcome with fear and, without really knowing what he was saying, had mumbled: 'Master, it is good for us to be here; and let us make three tabernacles, one for thee, and one for Moses, and one for Elias!' And as Peter spoke those words, there came a cloud, and it overshadowed them; and they were afraid, when they entered into the cloud. A voice, issuing from the cloud then said: 'This is my beloved Son; hear him.' And the echo of those words was still in the air when the trio came to and found themselves alone with the Nazarene. (Luke 9:28-36, Matthew 17:1-13, Mark 9:1-13 and 2 Peter 1:16-21)

"But the Deliverer was now gone, effectively rubbed out by His avowed enemies; and nothing appeared to make sense anymore. The last thing they now expected was an encounter with someone who would be talking like he had just landed there from a different planet.

"This is how Luke described their encounter with the risen Deliverer: 'And behold, two of them went, the same day, to a town which was sixty furlongs from Jerusalem named Emmaus. And they talked together of all these things which had happened. And it came to pass, that while they talked and reasoned with themselves, Jesus himself also drawing near, went with them. But their eyes were held, that they should not know him. And he said to them: What are these discourses that you hold one with another as you walk, and are sad? And one of them, whose name was Cleophas, answering, said to him: Art thou only a stranger to Jerusalem, and hast not known the things that have been done there in these days? To whom he said: What things? And they said: Concerning Jesus of Nazareth, who was a prophet, mighty in work and word before God and all the people; And how our chief priests and princes delivered him to be condemned to death, and crucified him. But we hoped that it was he that should have redeemed Israel: and now besides all this, today is the third day since these things were done. Yea and certain women also of our company affrighted us, who before it was light, were at the sepulchre; and not finding his body, came, saying, that they had also seen a vision of angels, who say that he is alive. And some of our people went to the sepulchre, and found it so as the women had said, but him they found not.' (Luke 24:13-24)

"Luke narrates the rest as follow: 'Then he said to them: O foolish, and slow of heart to believe in all things which the prophets have spoken. Ought not Christ to have suffered these things, and so to enter into his glory? And beginning at Moses and all the prophets, he expounded to them in all the scriptures, the things that were concerning him. And they drew nigh to the town, whither they were going: and he made as though he would go farther. But they constrained him; saying: Stay with us, because it is towards evening, and the day is now far spent. And he went in with them. And it came to pass, whilst he was at table with them, he took bread, and blessed, and brake, and gave to them. And their eyes were opened, and they knew him: and he vanished out of their sight. And they said one to the other: Was not our heart burning within us, whilst he spoke in this way, and opened to us the scriptures? And rising up, the same hour, they went back to Jerusalem: and they found the eleven and their companions gathered together. These were saying: "The Lord is risen indeed, and hath appeared to Simon." Then the two disciples told what had happened on the road, and how the Lord had been made known to them in the breaking of the bread.

"Now whilst they were speaking these things, Jesus stood in the midst of them, and saith to them: Peace be to you; it is I, fear not. But they being troubled and frightened, supposed that they saw a spirit. And he said to them: Why are you troubled, and why do thoughts arise in your hearts? See my hands and feet, that it is I myself; handle, and see: for a spirit hath not flesh and bones, as you see me to have. And when he had said this, he shewed them his hands and feet. But while they yet believed not, and wondered for joy, he said: Have you any thing to eat? And they offered him a piece of a broiled fish, and a honeycomb. And when he had eaten before them, taking the remains, he gave to them.

'And he said to them: These are the words which I spoke to you, while I was yet with you, that all things must needs be fulfilled, which are written in the law of Moses, and in the prophets, and in the psalms, concerning me.

Then he opened their understanding, that they might understand the scriptures. And he said to them: Thus it is written, and thus it behooved Christ to suffer, and to rise again from the dead, the third day: And that penance and remission of sins should be preached in his name, unto all nations, beginning at Jerusalem. And you are witnesses of these things. And I send the promise of my Father upon you: but stay you in the city till you be endued with power from on high.' (Luke 24:25-49)

"After describing Mary Magdalen's encounter with the risen Deliverer, John skips the episode relating to Cleophas and his traveling companion that occurred as they were fleeing the Holy City and heading back to their homes in Emmaus on that same day; and he homes in on the Deliverer's apparition in the Upper Room. That apparition took place even as Cleophas and his friend, their flight out of the Holy City aborted as a result of their unexpected rendezvous with the Deliverer on the road to Emmaus, were excitedly narrating their experience behind the locked doors of the Upper Room to their brethren.

"John wrote: 'Now when it was late that same day, the first of the week, and the doors were shut, where the disciples were gathered together, for fear of the Jews, Jesus came and stood in the midst, and said to them: Peace be to you. And when he had said this, he shewed them his hands and his side. The disciples therefore were glad, when they saw the Lord. He said therefore to them again: Peace be to you. As the Father hath sent me, I also send you. When he had said this, he breathed on them; and he said to them: Receive ye the Holy Ghost. Whose sins you shall forgive, they are forgiven them; and whose sins you shall retain, they are retained.

'Now Thomas, one of the twelve, who is called Didymus, was not with them when Jesus came. The other disciples therefore said to him: We have seen the Lord. But he said to them: Except I shall see in his hands the print of the nails, and put my finger into the place of the nails, and put my hand into his side, I will not believe.

'And after eight days again his disciples were within, and Thomas with them. Jesus cometh, the doors being shut, and stood in the midst, and said: Peace be to you. Then he saith to Thomas: Put in thy finger hither, and see my hands; and bring hither thy hand, and put it into my side; and be not faithless, but believing. Thomas answered, and said to him: My Lord, and my God. Jesus saith to him: Because thou hast seen me, Thomas, thou hast believed: blessed are they that have not seen, and have believed. And that was not idol talk by the Deliverer. He knew that Thomas Didymus would end up in Kerala, in the southernmost tip of India, of all places where many would believe who had not seen.

"Many other signs also did Jesus in the sight of his disciples, which are not written in this book. But these are written, that you may believe that Jesus is the Christ, the Son of God: and that believing, you may have life in his name.' (John 20:19-31)

"Yeah, Thomas, also known as Didymus, but who is now famously known as 'Thomas the Doubter', had expressed what they all had felt up until that moment when, upon being told that the Deliverer was back and that the work of the *Sancta Ecclesia* was also back on course, he retorted: 'Unless I see the mark of the nails in his hands and put my finger into the nail marks and put my hand into his side, I will not believe.' (John 20:25)

"It was only after the Deliverer's disciples saw that he had indeed overcome death and was alive that they came around and accepted that His death on the cross did not at all portend the end of His mission on earth.

"At the time of His death, He had clocked only

480

thirty-three years, three of which He had spent crisscrossing Judea and Galilee, announcing His message of salvation to the world and healing the sick. But as he let His mother Mary and Joseph, His foster father, know in no uncertain terms at age twelve, He started going about His Father's business from the get-go! (Luke 2:49) And I knew that, even after His glorious ascension into heaven, He would still be very much around with His *Sancta Ecclesia* on earth both as Head of the Mystical Body of Christ and through the dispensation of the sacraments that He had instituted.

"It is noteworthy that the Son of Man did not wait to appear on earth in a barn in the little town of Bethlehem to commence His redemptive work for the salvation of humans. The timeline for the Deliverer's activities in behalf of humans, Paul said: 'Blessed be the God and Father of our Lord Jesus Christ, who has blessed us in Christ with every spiritual blessing in the heavens, as he chose us in him, *before the foundation of the world*, to be holy and without blemish before him.' (Ephesians 1:3-4) The Deliverer's work was evidently timeless and in every sense *eternal* by virtue of what He was, namely the Son of God.

"And then, as the 'golden – mouthed' Chrysostom eloquently pointed out, sickening as the revolt of humans against their Maker was, the debt of humans amounted to a drop of water when compared to the ransom paid by the Deliverer on their behalf! (Hom. X in Rom., in P.G., LX, 477) And Cyril of Alexandria {that 'Doctor of the Incarnation') put it plainly thus: 'One died for all; but there was in that one more value than in all men together, more even than in the whole creation; for besides being a perfect man, He remained the only son of God.' (*Quod unus sit Christus, in P.G., LXXV, 135fi*).

"That is what I, Satan, have been up against. Still,

even though I know that I will never prevail against the *Sancta Ecclesia* that was established on the rock called Peter, there is nothing that is going to stop me and my troops from doing our darndest to make the church's work as difficult as possible. For it is written: 'When any one heareth the word of the kingdom, and understandeth it not, there cometh the wicked one, and catcheth away that which was sown in his heart: this is he that received the seed by the way side.' (Matthew 13:19)

"The launch of the *Sancta Ecclesia* - the 'Mystical Body of the Son of Man' as written in Jeremiah 31:33, John 15:1-2, 1 Corinthians 12:27 and Ephesians 1:22-23 and as taught by the *Sancta Ecclesia* itself vide Pope Paul VI's *Lumen Gentium*, Pope Pius XII's encyclical *Mystici Corporis Christi* and CCC 782 - by the risen Deliverer was a very formal affair indeed, a circumstance I have made every effort to ensure is not noticed by the hordes of so-called 'bible-believing Christians'! The choirs of angels, still bewildered by the momentous events of Holy Week that were capped by the Deliverer's triumphant resurrection from the dead, were there in full attendance; and the affair lasted a full forty days! They accompanied the Deliverer wherever he went; and they were witness to the earth-shuttering moment when the risen Nazarene appeared to over five hundred souls in Jerusalem. Talk about miracles and apparitions! This would be the talk of everyone not just in Palestine, but even in faraway Rome where Pontius Pilate had proceeded for the purpose of briefing the emperor of the goings-on in the Prefecture of Judea. For a time, the priests and Pharisees even went into hiding, fearing that they might be lynched.

"Meanwhile, the Son of Man, who was also the Second Person of Blessed Trinity, upon rising up from the dead had a quite busy schedule, instructing His remaining eleven apostles and his other disciples in the tenets of His *Sancta Ecclesia*.

"The Nazarene had made it clear from the start that He would go about carrying out the will of His father in heaven by working, not with the choirs of angels as His instruments, but with humans whom he had come to redeem from the clutches of sin and among whom He Himself now also counted. Judas Iscariot, the betrayer, would be replaced as soon as He Himself ascended into heaven, because the Iscariot was, as Peter would succinctly put it, 'numbered with us, and had obtained part of this *ministry*.

"But, in the meantime, even though His apostles and disciples were 'bible believers', that was far from being enough. The risen Deliverer found their understanding of the scriptures very deficient; and, as Luke points out, 'He opened their understanding, that they might understand the scriptures. And he said to them: Thus it is written, and thus it behoved Christ to suffer, and to rise again from the dead, the third day: And that penance and remission of sins should be preached in his name, unto all nations, beginning at Jerusalem. And you are witnesses of these things. And I send the promise of my Father upon you: but stay you in the city till you be endued with power from on high.' (Luke 24:44-49).

"And then He also instituted the sacraments of holy orders, and made them partakers of his divine priesthood saying, as John writes, 'Once more Jesus said to them, Peace be upon you; I came upon an errand from my Father, and now I am sending you out in my turn. With that, he breathed on them, and said to them, Receive the Holy Spirit; when you forgive men's sins, they are forgiven, when you hold them bound, they are held bound.' (John 20: 21-24).

"A little earlier, the Deliverer had instituted the

sacrament of the Holy Eucharist; and the time could not have been more opportune. Mark would write in his account: 'And whilst they were eating, Jesus took bread; and blessing, broke, and gave to them, and said: Take ye. This is my body. And having taken the chalice, giving thanks, he gave it to them. And they all drank of it. And he said to them: This is my blood of the New Testament, which shall be shed for many. Amen I say to you, that I will drink no more of the fruit of the vine, until that day when I shall drink it new in the kingdom of God. And when they had said a hymn, they went forth to the Mount of Olives.' (Mark 14:22-26).

"Matthew put it this way: 'And whilst they were at supper, Jesus took bread, and blessed, and broke: and gave to his disciples, and said: Take ye, and eat. This is my body. And taking the chalice, he gave thanks, and gave to them, saying: Drink ye all of this. For this is my blood of the new testament, which shall be shed for many unto remission of sins. And I say to you, I will not drink from henceforth of this fruit of the vine, until that day when I shall drink it with you new in the kingdom of my Father.' (Matthew 26: 26-29).

"The account of Luke (who was such a dear physician in Paul's words) went like this: 'And when the hour was come, he sat down, and the twelve apostles with him. And he said to them: With desire I have desired to eat this pasch with you, before I suffer. For I say to you, that from this time I will not eat it, till it be fulfilled in the kingdom of God. And having taken the chalice, he gave thanks, and said: Take, and divide it among you: For I say to you, that I will not drink of the fruit of the vine, till the kingdom of God come. And taking bread, he gave thanks, and brake; and gave to them, saying: This is my body, which is given for you. Do this for a commemoration of me. In like manner the chalice also, after he had supped, saying: This is the chalice, the new testament in my blood, which shall be shed for you.' (Luke 22:14-20).

"In his account, John has the Deliverer prepping His apostles for the Holy Eucharist and wrote thus: 'Then Jesus said to them: Amen, amen I say to you; Moses gave you not bread from heaven, but my Father giveth you the true bread from heaven. For the bread of God is that which cometh down from heaven, and giveth life to the world. They said therefore unto him: Lord, give us always this bread. And Jesus said to them: I am the bread of life: he that cometh to me shall not hunger: and he that believeth in me shall never thirst. But I said unto you, that you also have seen me, and you believe not. All that the Father giveth to me shall come to me; and him that cometh to me, I will not cast out. Because I came down from heaven, not to do my own will, but the will of him that sent me. Now this is the will of the Father who sent me: that of all that he hath given me, I should lose nothing; but should raise it up again in the last day. And this is the will of my Father that sent me: that everyone who seeth the Son, and believeth in him, may have life everlasting, and I will raise him up in the last day.' (John 6: 31-40)

"And what did He mean when He said: 'For I say to you, that I will not drink of the fruit of the vine, till the kingdom of God come.' Well, when He taught his disciple how to pray, He had also used these same words 'Thy kingdom Come'! The Catechism states: 'Christ already reigns through the Church.'

"It elaborates as follows: 'Christ died and lived again, that he might be Lord both of the dead and of the living. Christ's Ascension into heaven signifies his participation, in his humanity, in God's power and authority. Jesus Christ is Lord: he possesses all power in heaven and on earth. He is "far above all rule and authority and power and Dominion", for the Father "has put all things under his feet". Christ is Lord of the cosmos and of history. In him human history and indeed all creation are "set forth" and transcendently fulfilled. As Lord, Christ is also head of the Church, which is his Body. Taken up to heaven and glorified after he had thus fully accomplished his mission, Christ dwells on earth in his Church. The redemption is the source of the authority that Christ, by virtue of the Holy Spirit, exercises over the Church. The "kingdom of Christ [is] already present in mystery", "on earth, the seed and the beginning of the kingdom". Since the Ascension, God's plan has entered into its fulfillment. We are already at "the last hour". Already the final age of the world is with us, and the renewal of the world is irrevocably under way; it is even now anticipated in a certain real way, for the Church on earth is endowed already with a sanctity that is real but imperfect. Christ's kingdom already manifests its presence through the miraculous signs that attend its proclamation by the Church.'

"The fact is that it was only after thus launching His *Sancta Ecclesia* that, as Luke wrote, 'he led them out as far as Bethania: and lifting up his hands, he blessed them. And it came to pass, whilst he blessed them, he departed from them, and was carried up to heaven. And they adoring went back into Jerusalem with great joy. And they were always in the temple, praising and blessing God. Amen.' (Luke 24:50-53)

"And, as if that is not enough to make bible believers stop placing all their bets on the sacred scriptures and their own interpretation of the same, in his account of the events of those days, John drives the last and final nail in the bible believers' coffin when he alludes to the purpose of the 'gospel' account and writes: 'Many other signs also did Jesus in the sight of his disciples, which are not written in this book. But these are written, that you may believe that Jesus is the Christ, the Son of God: and that believing, you may have life in his name.' John 20: 30-31)

"Again, the Deliverer *did*, repeat *did*, many things that are *not*, repeat *not*, written down within the Gospel narratives that John and Mark and Matthew and Luke cobbled together, or in the missives that Peter, John, James and others employed to communicate with the congregations of the early *Sancta Mater Ecclesia* (Holy Mother the Church). It is the fact that the Deliverer's deeds included one that all the evangelist harp on, namely establishing his *Sancta Ecclesia* against which the Gates of Hell would not be able to prevail - stupid! And it is that selfsame *Sancta Mater Ecclesia* or Holy Mother the Church that, as she herself teaches, is also 'the pillar and bulwark of truth', that 'has always used Sacred Scripture in her task of imparting heavenly salvation to men', and that 'has always defended it, too, from every sort of false interpretation'.

"Of course, as you can well imagine, I was duty bound to do everything that a sharp mind like mine could conjure up in hopes of derailing the *Sancta Ecclesia* in its infancy before it went anywhere. And for a while I thought I was succeeding with the help of the likes of Saul of Tarsus. But he turned traitor, and with that the rug got pulled from under my feet. And I knew from then on that there was no stopping the *Sancta Ecclesia* or '*Sancta Ecclesia Catholica*' as it was already being referred to.

"Well, if truth be told (the fact that I am the Father of Lies notwithstanding), my hopes of derailing the *Sancta Ecclesia* begun to falter much earlier than that as a result of unforeseen events.   There was for instance that beggar, a man lame from birth, who was in the habit of manning his station beside the temple's Beautiful Gate so he could beg from the folks who ostensibly went there to make their offerings of *Karbanot* (Sacrifices and Offerings) and draw nearer to the Prime Mover thereby when in actual fact the primary purpose of going there was to conduct commerce (exactly as the Deliverer who could read people's minds himself pointed out).

"As Luke tells it in the second part of his "Story of Jesus", Peter and John look at the beggar intently; and Peter says, "Look at us!" The lame man looks at them eagerly, expecting some money.

"To set the record straight, the lot of that beggar, which saw him ferried every day to the entrance of the rumbling structure (whose foundations had been laid some five hundred years earlier by Zerubbabel) so he could earn his keep by seeking the measly handouts from the niggardly and often abusive temple goers, was archetypical of the life that humans led in the aftermath of their fall from grace.

"Those mean temple goers were in the exact same boat as the crippled man who implored them for a pittance day in and day out while gesturing to the begging bowl he couldn't clasp let alone physically hold up because he did not have a functioning limb. Born with original sin and accordingly inclined to sin and incapable of any good works on their own without the help of divine grace, they were themselves just as helpless. They were all in need of the water that becomes a spring, welling up to eternal life once drank, the water that only the Deliverer could give.

"But these were no ordinary times; and the actions of John and Peter said it all. Addressing the beggar, Peter said: 'Silver or gold, I don't have. But what I have, I'll give you. In the name of the risen Jesus Christ the Nazarene, get up and walk!'

"Peter took the lame man by the right hand and

helped him up and, as he did, the man's feet and ankles were instantly healed and strengthened. Whereupon the cripple jumped up, stood on his feet, and began to walk; and then, walking, leaping, and praising God, he went into the Temple with them. I knew in that moment that the "infant" *Sancta Ecclesia* was nascent no more! I saw that it had already morphed into an institution that had none other than the Deliverer Himself as its head, and humans, wicked as they were, as its members - so long as they found faith in Him! (Acts 3).

"I knew that the only option that remained available to me as Ruler of the Underworld and my troops was to try a different tack and now focus my attention on the twelve apostles and their successors, the commissioned agents charged with spreading the kingdom of God throughout the world! I was scratching my head (if I may use a figure of speech as I'm a spirit and don't possess a body) and thinking that there had to be a way to make the lives of the apostles and of the 'faithful' as difficult as possible starting right there and then and up until the second coming of their Deliverer! I made up my mind that I was going to exploit the fact that the followers of the Deliverer remained human and fickle even after the sacraments of baptism and confirmation were conferred to them, to create mayhem.

"And of course the Deliverer was not indulging in idle talk when, enduring his agony in the Garden of Gethsemane and addressing His Father in heaven, He said that He was specifically praying for His apostles - the ones His Father had given Him. And He elaborated in His petition that the words His Father had given Him, He had in turn given to them, and they had accepted them and truly understood and believed that He, the Deliverer, came from the Father. And none of them was lost, but the son of perdition, that the scripture may be fulfilled.

(John 17:12). And, not surprisingly, John would affirm this in the prologue to his "Story of Jesus" and write: 'In the beginning was the Word: and the Word was with God: and the Word was God. The same was in the beginning with God. All things were made by him: and without him was made nothing that was made. In him was life: and the life was the light of men. And the light shineth in darkness: and the darkness did not comprehend it.'

"His soul exceedingly sorrowful even unto death, He had prayed that His disciples be one. Even though there physically in the Garden of Gethsemane with its ancient olive trees, it was true that, as the Second Person of the Blessed Trinity, He was definitely not of the world; and that was why He said: 'I am not in the world, and I come to thee. Holy Father, keep them in thy name whom thou hast given me; that they may be one, as we also are.' (John 17). This was not simply a high bar He was setting 'that they may be one even as He Himself and His father were one'! He was signifying that His *Sancta Ecclesia*, whilst serving as an instrument for His continuing work of redemption in the world, would be exactly that, a *Sancta Ecclesia* that was divinely instituted and that could only be adequately described as 'His Mystical Body' with Himself as Head and those who would embrace His words and become His disciples as its members.

"His mother Mary who herself had come into the world without the stain of original sin under a special dispensation was undoubtedly a member. But even though He was leaving her behind in the world for now with his disciples, His mind as He prayed to His Father was on the disciples. He knew that it would not be possible for me to influence his holy mother with my wiles; for indeed as the scriptures had forecast, with the Deliverer, a member of the Godhead, humbling himself

490

and becoming obedient to His Father unto death even to the death of the cross, His Father in heaven had kept His word and had effectively put enmities between me and the mother of the Deliverer, and between my seed and her seed, and she was now all set to crush my head! All I can do is lie in wait for her heel to finish me off!

"And His mind as He prayed was not on Pontius Pilate, that heartless tyrant who even took delight in seeing the blood of his victims mingled with their sacrifices (Luke 13:1); or on the High Priest Annas, or on Joseph Caiaphas who was also a member of the Sanhedrin; or on the likes of Herod the Great, that paranoid, impious and wicked 'King of Judea' whose murderous exploits included ordering the slaughter of the holy innocents as he sought to nip in the bud the perceived threat to his rule upon learning of the nativity in Bethlehem of the 'promised Messiah' - an action that forced the Deliverer's mother Mary and Joseph, the Deliverer's foster father, to seek refuge in Egypt; and His mind was certainly not on Herod the Tetrarch, also nicknamed Herod Antipas, who murdered John the Baptist and who, with Pontius Pilate, would preside over the Deliverer's trial only to end up meeting with a horrid death that saw him eaten by worms whilst he was still alive! (Acts 12:20-23)

"And His mind as He prayed was certainly not on the priests and Pharisees and teachers of the law who should have recognized Him for what He was, namely עִמָּנוּאֵל or Emmanuel or 'God is with us' (Leviticus 26:11-12, Isaiah 7:14, Luke 1:31, Matthew 1:21-23 and Revelation 21:3), but chose to do otherwise, the signs and miracles He performed notwithstanding.

"The graces He would merit for humans with his death on the cross were enough, and there was absolutely nothing that He could do if humans whom He had come to redeem refused to hearken to their God-given consciences. Created in the Prime Mover's image, they could only find their self-actualization through union with Him, and they would only have themselves to blame for the consequences of their stance.

"The Deliverer made it clear that He was pleading with His Father on behalf of the folks who had thrown in their lot with Him. It was the remaining eleven apostles whom he had in mind when he was making His entreaties with His Father in Heaven and praying that they may be sanctified in truth as they went about preaching Christ crucified, unto the Jews indeed a stumbling block, and unto the Gentiles foolishness." (Corinthians 1:23)

"It would be in the same vein that the Deliverer would say to His blessed mother as she kept watch beneath the cross with John, His beloved relative who insisted on risking all to be by her side in those hours of her unspeakable grief, and with Mary the wife of Clopas (who was a sister to His Blessed Virgin Mother) and Mary Magdalene hard by: *'Mulier ecce filius tuus'* (Woman, behold, your son!' And then, turning to the treasured disciple who would end up in exile on the Aegean Island of Patmos and whence bequeath to the world the ἀποκάλυψις (Apocalypse), he said: *'Ecce mater tua!'* (Behold your mother) (John 19:27)

"Any way, the Deliverer knew exactly what I, as the Ruler of the Underworld, would be up to in these circumstances. My troops and I were going to do whatever it would take to keep His Church fractured and almost impossible even for humans of good will to stumble onto without the help of the Grace he would merit for them! Which is not to say that those words 'That they may be one even as we are one!' would not haunt me the way they have done ever since. They haunt me because I know and understand better than all the Doctors of the

Church who have ever lived combined that if by the offence of one, many died; much more the grace of God, and the gift, by the grace of one man, Jesus Christ, hath abounded unto many. (Romans 5:15).

"Still, I was not kidding myself, and I was certainly not mistaken in my assessment of the fortunes of the infant *Sancta Ecclesia*. The throng that rushed out in amazement to Solomon's Colonnade, where the man, who had never walked a day in his more than forty years of life, was holding tightly to Peter and John, included among them priests and Pharisees. (Acts 4:1-7)

"Word of the miracle wrought by the apostles Peter and John spread like the plague in the literal sense, and became the talk of town not just in the city of Jerusalem, but in the rest of the province of Judea and the adjoining provinces of Galilea and Samaria and beyond! Addressing his aides (some of whom had indicated that they were ready to defect and cast in their lot with followers of the dead Nazarene or Christians as they were already being referred to, the high priest, Joseph ben Caiaphas, had referred to the doctrines of the new sect as a cancer, and he had exclaimed in desperation that it was spreading among the populace like a highly contagious virus that needed to be rooted out lock, stock and barrel and quickly too before it became a global pandemic and (as he put it) infected everyone!

"In the aftermath of that miracle, the authorities in Jerusalem who assembled to question Peter and John included among them Annas and Caiaphas of all people! But the Lord was with Peter and John, and His Spirit was giving them courage and putting into their minds what they should say! The priests marveled at the boldness of Peter and John, perceiving that they were 'unlearned and ignorant men.'

"But, to cut a long story short, the upshot of that pivotal face-to-face encounter of the erstwhile bedraggled and uncertain band of the Deliverer's disciples with those who not so long before had the power to save the Deliverer's life but had frittered away their chance to change the course of history was that soon enough the word of the Lord increased; and the number of the disciples was multiplied in Jerusalem exceedingly: and (mark this) a great multitude also of the priests obeyed the faith! (Acts 6:7)

"The priests were persuaded to jump on the bandwagon because they felt great unease staying on the sidelines and just watching as the healed man they had always looked down upon in the literal sense every morning - and despised - availed himself of the fullness of grace that came with membership in the Sancta Ecclesia. They thoroughly despised him because, in their own words, *they* were disciples of Moses and, according to them, those who were afflicted with diseases and were hapless like the man born blind whose eyes the Deliverer caused to be opened so he could see (John 9) or this lame beggar who had never walked once in his life, were steeped in sin at birth! (John 9:1-3) Totally contrary to the facts of course because, as the Deliverer explained, neither that blind man whom He cured on the Sabbath nor the man's parents - or this beggar who was born a cripple - had sinned. The fact was that it happened thus so that the works of God might be displayed in them!

"Why, if you may ask, do I harp on this? Simple...because even though these priests were received in the *Sancta Ecclesia*, I was not going to pass up the opportunity to use them to saw discord in the fledgling Church. Using the new converts from Judaism and specifically the priests of the Mosaic dispensation who had come around and accepted that Mary's son was

494

indeed the promised Messiah, I very nearly succeeded in driving a wedge between the circumcised and the uncircumcised followers of the Deliverer and causing a schism even at that early stage in the life of the *Sancta Ecclesia*! (Acts 15:1-29)

"The promised 'Advocate' was a concrete force from Day One; and you could see the effects of His presence in the church already then as is clear from Luke's account of the Church's early history when he wrote: 'Now there were in the church at Antioch prophets and teachers: Barnabas, Symeon who was called Niger, Lucius of Cyrene, Manaen who was a close friend of Herod the tetrarch, and Saul. While they were worshiping the Lord and fasting, the Holy Spirit said, "Set apart for me Barnabas and Saul for the work to which I have called them." Then, completing their fasting and prayer, they laid hands on them and sent them off.

"A self-proclaimed 'Apostle of the Gentiles', that Pharisee (who not long before had the disciples of the Deliverer in his cross hairs) had received indoctrination in the Deliverer's teachings directly from the living apostles, from his personal physician Luke, from John Mark (who accompanied Paul and Barnabas on their first missionary journey to Asia Minor following their ordination), from Peter (the first pope) and the other apostles, and no doubt also from Mary, the mother of the Messiah Whom Paul was proclaiming to the gentiles. This was the equivalent of the modern-day Rite of Christian Initiation for Adults (RCIA) - dummies!

"It was of course no accident that Paul was accompanied on that first missionary journey by Mark and Barnabas *and* Luke. Peter wanted to make certain that the new convert that he and the other apostles had ordained deacon, priest and bishop in one fell swoop with the solemn laying on of hands not only didn't fall for the heresies that some 'bible believers' were already spreading, but wouldn't start spreading heresies himself. Hence Peter's decision, contained in his very first ever 'papal' encyclical, directing Luke and Barnabas, who were well grounded in the doctrines of the *Sancta Ecclesia*, to accompany Paul along with Mark. Yeah, I had already prevailed on some 'bible believers' from Judea and Antioch to go around preaching that unless one was circumcised, according to the custom taught by Moses, one could not be saved! (Acts 15.1)

"Paul had come on the scene in a very timely manner; and he drove the final nail in the coffin with the very first epistle he penned for the benefit of the fledgling church in Corinth. In that missive, the fiery missionary brings everything together, namely the reality of the *Sancta Ecclesia* constructed by the Deliverer on the rock called Peter; the *apostolic succession*; and the *Blessed Sacrament* - the outward (visible) sign of an inward (invisible) grace instituted by Christ - and a *New Testament*.

"He wrote: '*Ego enim accepi a Domino quod et tradidi vobis, quoniam Dominus Jesus in qua nocte tradebatur, accepit panem, et gratias agens fregit, et dixit: Accipite, et manducate: hoc est corpus meum, quod pro vobis tradetur: hoc facite in meam commemorationem. Similiter et calicem, postquam cœnavit, dicens: Hic calix novum testamentum est in meo sanguine: hoc facite quotiescumque bibetis, in meam commemorationem. Quotiescumque enim manducabitis panem hunc, et calicem bibetis, mortem Domini annuntiabitis donec veniat. Itaque quicumque manducaverit panem hunc, vel biberit calicem Domini indigne, reus erit corporis et sanguinis Domini. Probet autem seipsum homo: et sic de pane illo edat, et de calice bibat. Qui enim manducat et bibit indigne, judicium sibi manducat et bibit, non dijudicans corpus Domini.'* Unquote. (1 Corinthians 11:23-29).

"This is translated: *'For I have received of the Lord that which also I delivered unto you, that the Lord Jesus, the same night in which he was betrayed, took bread. And giving thanks, broke, and said: Take ye, and eat: this is my body, which shall be delivered for you: this do for the commemoration of me. In like manner also the chalice, after he had supped, saying: This chalice is the new testament in my blood: this do ye, as often as you shall drink, for the commemoration of me. For as often as you shall eat this bread, and drink the chalice, you shall shew the death of the Lord, until he come. Therefore whosoever shall eat this bread, or drink the chalice of the Lord unworthily, shall be guilty of the body and of the blood of the Lord. But let a man prove himself: and so let him eat of that bread, and drink of the chalice. For he that eateth and drinketh unworthily, eateth and drinketh judgment to himself, not discerning the body of the Lord.'*

"And, one thousand two hundred years later, the 'Angelic Doctor' bequeathed to the world the *Adorote Devote*, the *Pange Lingua*, and the *Panis Angelicum*, chants whose beauty and rhyme have made them the pre-eminent hymns of the Most Blessed Sacrament. Arguably among the finest medieval Latin hymns, as the Canterbury Dictionary of Hymns points out, the unparalleled 'sweetness of melody' does not detract from the 'clear-cut dogmatic teaching' that one finds in these hymns.

"Well, while I have worked hard to grow the numbers of 'bible believing' followers of the Deliverer, it is pretty obvious that I aint't one of them. I didn't wait for Mark, Matthew, John and Luke to complete their accounts of the Deliverer's sojourn on Earth before I myself moved to attempt to frustrate the work of His *Sancta Ecclesia*.

The church, or *qahal* (in Hebrew) or *ekklesia* (in Greek), made up (in the words of St. Gregory) of 'the saints before the Law, the saints under the Law, and the saints under grace - all these are constituted members of the Church' (*Sancti ante legem, sancti sub lege, sancti sub gratiâ, omnes hi…in membris Ecclesiæ sunt constitute*), or more appropriately the 'Mystical Body of the Deliverer' (or as the Venerable Fulton Sheen called it 'the Deliverer's Corporate Human nature'), had a life of its own from Day One, and did not need to be mentioned in the gospels - or, for that matter in the letters that Paul wrote to the Corinthians and the Ephesians and the Romans and the Galatians and the Thessalonians and the Philippians - to mean something. Well, you do not need to have Mount Everest mentioned in one of the seventy-three books of the canon for it to exist do you!

"How I succeeded in persuading some folks that some legitimate authority outside the *Sancta Ecclesia Catholica* is just as capable of deciding on what belongs or does not belong in the canon of Scripture is, of course, another story! And yet, the *Sancta Ecclesia Catholica* will *live on* even after the world, and along with it Mount Everest, cease to exist at the end of time. But I must keep working to give gullible humans the impression that things are otherwise.

"Writing to the Ephesians, that 'traitor' Paul (he was a turncoat as far as I am concerned) wrote thusly: 'And coming, he preached peace to you that were afar off, and peace to them that were nigh. For by him we have access both in one Spirit to the Father. Now therefore you are no more strangers and foreigners; but you are fellow citizens with the saints, and the domestics of God, Built upon the foundation of the apostles and prophets, Jesus Christ himself being the chief corner stone: In whom all the building, being framed together, groweth up into an holy temple in the Lord. In whom you also are built together into an habitation of God in the Spirit.' (Ephesians 2:17-22).

"Exactly the sort of thing that bible believers must not be permitted to grasp and follow...

"For my part, I have been doing everything in my power to ensure that all biblical passages that allude to the church founded by the Deliverer on the rock called Peter elude the bible believers, passages such as the one in Paul's first letter to Timothy which read: 'These things I write to thee, hoping that I shall come to thee shortly. But if I tarry long, that thou mayest know how thou oughtest to behave thyself in the house of God, which is the church of the living God, the pillar and ground of the truth. (1 *Timothy* 3:14-15).

"When folks walk away from the *Sancta Ecclesia* that was founded by the Deliverer on the Rock called Peter, they walk away from the Deliverer who, as Paul explained to the Colossians is the image of the invisible Prime Mover and the firstborn of all creation, in Whom, through Whom and for Whom all things in heaven and on earth, visible and invisible, whether thrones or dominions or principalities or powers were created; and who is the head of the body, the *Sancta Ecclesia*. (Colossians 1:15-17).

"After the Deliverer and head of the mystical body - the *Sancta Ecclesia* - ascended into heaven from Mount Olivet, the rest of the body's members returned to Jerusalem and into the upper room, where they abode - Peter and John, James and Andrew, Philip and Thomas, Bartholomew and Matthew, James of Alpheus, and Simon Zelotes, and Jude the brother of James. All these were persevering with one mind in prayer with the women, and with Mary the mother of the Deliverer and with his brethren - the infant *Sancta Ecclesia* (Acts 1:12-14).

"Now, dial back to the 'feast of unleavened bread', which is called the pasch, and how the Deliverer ended up celebrating it with His apostles in the Upper Room in Jerusalem. Luke's account of the events (which is corroborated by Mark's account of the same) went as follows: 'NOW the feast of unleavened bread, which is called the pasch, was at hand. And the chief priests and the scribes sought how they might *put Jesus to death*: but they feared the people.' (Luke 22:1-2) Luke continued: 'And *the day of the unleavened bread came, on which it was necessary that the pasch should be killed. And he sent Peter and John, saying: Go, and prepare for us the pasch, that we may eat.* But they said: Where wilt thou that we prepare? And he said to them: Behold, as you go into the city, there shall meet you a man carrying a pitcher of water: follow him into the house where he entereth in. And you shall say to the good man of the house: The master saith to thee, Where is the guest chamber, where I may eat the pasch with my disciples? And he will shew you a large dining room, furnished; and there prepare. And they going, found as he had said to them, and made ready the pasch.' (Luke 22:7-13) The emphasis in both cases is mine.

"It was almost in the same vein that the Deliverer sent two of His disciples, again most probably Peter and John, to get the colt He would ride for His triumphant entry into Jerusalem a week before. (Luke 19:29-38) Luke's account of that triumphant entry into the city is corroborated by the other three evangelists (John, Mark and Matthew).

"Little did the Deliverer's disciples know at that time that that Upper House would end up as the sanctuary where He would institute the sacrament of the Blessed

Eucharist that commemorates the Deliverer's immolation as the Paschal Lamb, the sacrament that was foreshadowed by the Passover and the command that the Israelites feast on the meat of the lamb. The entire lamb had to be consumed - head, feet, entrails and all - and whatever of it remained had to be burned with fire. The Israelites were commanded to eat the meal in haste, with girded loins, shoes on their feet, and staves in their hands 'for it was the Passage of the Lord'. The blood of the lamb on the doorposts served as a sign of immunity or protection against the destroying hand of the Lord. (Catholic Encyclopedia: Paschal Lamb - New Advent).

"The Deliverer's disciples could not have foretold that that same Upper House would serve as their hideout in the days immediately following the death of their Master on the gibbet, and even less that the Upper House would not only become the hub for the nascent *Sancta Ecclesia*, but would serve as the 'Holy See' (or seat of the papacy) until the move by the Apostle Peter to Antioch and thence to Rome and his own death there also by crucifixion.

"And, of course, it was beyond the expectation of Peter and John as they engaged the 'good man of the house' (Luke 22:11) on the Feast of Unleavened Bread that that Upper House, and in its wake the Vatican in Rome, would become the most preeminent symbol, not just of the *Sancta Ecclesia*, but of the mystery of the incarnation and the redemption of humans from sin!

"Now, Look. Even after the Deliverer had multiplied the five loaves and two fish, the crowds, five thousand strong, were still hankering for a sign - one that was similar to the manna that fell from the heavens and saved the Israelites from starving to death in the desert whilst on their way to the Promised Land and signaled that the Prime Mover still intended to keep His covenant with

501

Abraham. And this was even after these crowds had eaten and had their fill!

"Those crowds were not interested in the promised Savior of the world. It was total news to them that from the seed of David, the Prime Mover, according to His promise, had 'raised up for Israel a Savior, Jesus'! (Acts 13:23) Writing to the Ephesians, Paul (nee Saul) would admonish them that if they had heard of Christ, and if they had been taught in him, as truth was in Jesus, they needed to live no longer as the Gentiles (who walked in the vanity of their mind, having their understanding darkened, being alienated from the life of the Prime Mover through the ignorance that was in them, because of the blindness of their hearts; and who despairing, had given themselves up to lasciviousness, unto the working of all uncleanness, unto covetousness) did. And that they needed to put away the old man, who was corrupted according to the desire of error; and to be renewed in the spirit of their mind; and to put on the new man, who according to the Prime Mover is created in justice and holiness of truth. (Ephesians 4:17-24)

"That is what was meant by the words: 'All these were persevering with one mind in prayer with the women, and Mary the mother of Jesus, and with his brethren.' (Acts 1:14)

"The challenge for us here in the Pit was therefore to do everything in our power to frustrate that result going forward for the rest of humans. Look, the term 'bible believer' is my invention (if you didn't already know). Beginning in the first century, we have worked to present this as an alternative to the Teaching Magisterium of the *Sancta Ecclesia*. And, as you may have noticed, all the heresies since then have arisen from attempts by one or other 'bible believer' to promote his/her own spin on this or that passage of the *Sacrae Scripturae* as the official teaching of some amorphous 'church'.

"And, of course, the Pontiff of Rome was right on when, closing the Amazon Synod, he said: 'The root of every spiritual error, as the ancient monks taught, is believing ourselves to be righteous.' The Pontiff had added: 'We, all of us, are in need of salvation. To consider ourselves righteous is to leave God, the only righteous one, out in the cold!'

"And so, once we succeeded in getting folks to turn their backs on the *Sancta Ecclesia* and its teaching magisterium, it was smooth sailing after that to get them to develop a disdain and contempt for the idea that saints could intercede for them in any way with their Maker...hee, ha ha, ha! This includes Mary, the Deliverer's mother, and despite the fact that she was herself conceived without sin or blemish!

"We have worked hard to ensure that the bible believers remain oblivious to passages in the holy scriptures like the one in Genesis that references her role in the divine plan of redemption and goes: 'I will put enmities between thee and the woman, and thy seed and her seed: she shall crush thy head, and thou shalt lie in wait for her heel.' (Genesis 3:15) And the one in the Gospel According to John, which goes: 'When Jesus therefore had seen his mother and the disciple standing whom he loved, he saith to his mother: Woman, behold thy son. After that, he saith to the disciple: Behold thy mother. And from that hour, the disciple took her to his own.' (John 19: 26-27)

"Yeah, just imagine my thrill when bible believers treat as anathema the traditional practice of chanting the Salve Regina at the conclusion of funeral Masses for priests, out of reverence to Mary the Mother of Christ the High Priest and of all priests. This is the chant that predates the so-called Reformation that I got my minions to engineer, and it is also the most celebrated of the four Breviary anthems of the Blessed Virgin Mary (Alma Redemptoris | Ave, Regina Caelorum | Regina Caeli | Salve Regina).

Salve, Regina, Mater misericordiæ,
vita, dulcedo, et spes nostra, salve.
Ad te clamamus exsules filii Hevæ,
Ad te suspiramus, gementes et flentes
in hac lacrimarum valle.
Eia, ergo, advocata nostra, illos tuos
misericordes oculos ad nos converte;
Et Jesum, benedictum fructum ventris tui,
nobis post hoc exsilium ostende.
O clemens, O pia, O dulcis Virgo Maria.
℣ Ora pro nobis, sancta Dei Genitrix.
℟ Ut digni efficiamur promissionibus Christi.

Oremus.

Omnipotens sempiterne Deus, qui gloriosæ Virginis Matris Mariæ corpus et animam, ut dignum Filii tui habitaculum effici mereretur, Spiritu Sancto cooperante præparasti: da, ut cuius commemoratione lætamur; eius pia intercessione, ab instantibus malis, et a morte perpetua liberemur. Per eundem Christum Dominum nostrum.
℟ Amen.

This is translated as follows:
Hail, holy Queen, Mother of Mercy,
Hail, our life, our sweetness and our hope.
To thee do we cry,
Poor banished children of Eve;

504

To thee do we send forth our sighs,
Mourning and weeping in this vale of tears.
Turn then, most gracious advocate,
Thine eyes of mercy toward us;
And after this our exile,
Show unto us the blessed fruit of thy womb, Jesus.
O clement, O loving,
O sweet Virgin Mary.
℣ Pray for us, O holy Mother of God,
℟ That we may be made worthy of the promises of
Christ, thy Son.

Let us pray:

Almighty, everlasting God, who by the co-operation of the
Holy Spirit didst prepare the body and soul of the glorious
Virgin-Mother Mary to become a dwelling-place meet for
thy Son: grant that as we rejoice in her commemoration;
so by her fervent intercession we may be delivered from
present evils and from everlasting death. Through the
same Christ our Lord. Amen.

"Yes, 'fervent intercession'! You'd better believe me when I tell you that I've got the bible believers firmly under my spell, and I allow them to discern and grasp only what I want them to see, and no more. And the same applies to those Catholic 'theologians' who are loath to correct the 'separated brethren' in the same way Paul nee Saul did. (Galatians 1:6-10 and 1 Corinthians 11:18-19)

"The Marriage Supper of the Lamb and the concomitant role in it of the Deliverer's blessed mother is a good example. I have made sure that bible believers will never get to see its significance in the grand scheme of things. They must not glean anything of value from the words: 'and the mother of Jesus was there…And Jesus also was invited, and his disciples, to the marriage…And the wine failing, the mother of Jesus saith to him: They have no wine...' And the fact that this account is only found in the gospel of the 'son of thunder' who also bequeathed to the world the Book of Revelation with its vivid account of the 'Marriage Supper of the Lamb' must completely elude their attention! Hee, hee, hah, hah, hah!

"Look...the invitation of the Deliverer to the wedding along with his freshly minted band of apostles consisting of Philip, Andrew and his brother Simon Peter who all hailed from the town of Bethesda, Nathaniel, and James and John (whom the Deliverer had nicknamed 'sons of thunder') was automatic. This was because the Deliverer's blessed mother whom John the Baptist's Mother Elizabeth had addressed as the 'mother of my lord' was on the organizing committee. The couple who were about to exchange nuptial vows, in addition to being disciples of the baptizer, were both close to the Holy Family. Moreover the bride was related to the Zechariahs who had been told by a messenger from the Prime Mover that their son, John, would be filled with the Holy Spirit whilst in his mother's womb. (Luke 1:11-17)

"The planning for the wedding at Cana were in the advanced stages by the time the Deliverer, travelling from Galilee, arrived in the desert of Judea where the son of the Zechariahs, clad in his garment of camels' hair and a leathern girdle about his loins, was preaching, calling the folks who came there from Jerusalem and all Judea, and all the country about Jordan to repent their sins and baptizing them in the River Jordan. The Deliverer's blessed mother Mary was one of the organizers of the wedding; and the Big Day was roughly six weeks away.

"As the Deliverer approached to be baptized, John had hollered to the crowds: 'Behold the Lamb of God, behold him who taketh away the sin of the world. This is he, of whom I said: After me there cometh a man, who is preferred before me: because he was before me.' (John 1:29-30)

"The Nazarene was baptized; and lo and behold the heavens were opened: and the Spirit of God descended as a dove, and came upon him. And behold a voice from heaven, said; 'This is my beloved Son, in whom I am well pleased.' (Luke 3:22) Seeing the Spirit descending, and remaining upon the Nazarene, John the Baptizer gave testimony and announced that this was the Son of God. (John 1:33-34, Matthew 3:13-17; Mark 1:9-11; and Luke 3:21-22)

"The 'Precursor' had referred to himself as the 'friend of the bridegroom'. (John 3:29) But even though his mission was accomplished, my troops and I were not yet done with him for precisely that reason.

"The Baptizer had not had any qualms calling out the Pharisees and Sadducees who came to his baptism, and telling them to their face that they were in his words a 'brood of vipers'! (Matthew 3:7). The Deliverer's precursor had gone on to rebuke Herod Antipas (also known as Herod the Tetrarch) publicly for divorcing his wife Phasaelis, the daughter of King Aretas IV Philopatris of the Nabataeans, and marrying Herodias, the wife of his brother Herod Philip II and for other evil things he had done. (Matthew 14:3; Mark 6:17 and Luke 3:19)

"The opportunity for us here in the Underworld to deal with the Baptizer was not long in coming, and I seized it. I entered both Herodias as well as her daughter Salome immediately after the latter had performed her 'dance of the seven veils' before King Herod. I did it the same way I entered and temporarily possessed Peter. (Matthew 16:23, Mark 8:33 and Luke 22:31) And it was a thrill to watch Salome ask the double-dealing and lecherous Tetrarch for the head of John the Baptist on a platter! (Luke 9:9, Matthew 14:6-12, and Mark 6:25)

"But I am running ahead of myself. The evangelist John's account of the events surrounding the kick-off of the Marriage Supper of the Lamb opens with the baptism of the Deliverer by his namesake John the Baptizer. It would, of course, be revealed in time that the 'bride' who would take center stage at that Marriage Supper was none other than the *Sancta Ecclesia* (the Deliverer would construct on the rock called Peter) and those who were members therein. (Revelation 19:7-14, Revelation 21:1-2; 1 Thessalonians 5:23; Ephesians 5:25-27; and 2 Corinthians 11:1-2)

"Immediately following His baptism, the Deliverer was led by the Holy Spirit into the desert (Matthew 4:1; Mark 1:12-13; and Luke 4:1-13) During the forty days and forty nights the Deliverer was in the wilderness, I got this idea that it was now or never if the Deliverer was going to be stopped. Conveniently overlooking the fact that He was both human and divine, I went for it and gave my all in an effort to derail the divine plan.

"I even brazenly propositioned to Him that if He worshipped me, I would give him all the kingdoms of the world, and the glory of them. (Luke 4:1–13; Matthew 4:1–11; and Mark 1:12-13). I did this even as the angels ministered to Him (as they were wont to do all though His sojourn on earth). It wasn't my fault that he was also a human; and I had to do what I had to do. (Mark 1:13)

"It was soon clear that He had had enough of this nonsense. So He turned and said: 'Begone, Satan: for it is written, The Lord thy God shalt thou adore, and him only shalt thou serve.' (Matthew 4:10) It was a stern command. I decided that I couldn't tarry there much longer; and, with Michael's troops closing in, I took off very fast because I knew I was going to be badly mauled if I was cornered.

"All this time, all those folks who had been baptized by the son of the Zechariahs didn't know the whereabouts of the Messiah. They had reason to worry because the Tetrarch had already nabbed the Deliverer's precursor and thrown him in jail. And then the Deliverer turns up suddenly out of nowhere, and is spied entering the synagogue in Nazareth. (Mark 6:1-5; Matthew 13:53-57; and Luke 4:16-30)

"The Deliverer read from the book of Isaiah the words: 'The Spirit of the Lord is upon me. Wherefore he hath anointed me to preach the gospel to the poor, he hath sent me to heal the contrite of heart, To preach deliverance to the captives, and sight to the blind, to set at liberty them that are bruised, to preach the acceptable year of the Lord, and the day of reward.' He sat down and then announced: 'This day is fulfilled this scripture in your ears.'

"And everything would happen exactly as the Deliverer would say, namely that no prophet is accepted in his native place. Those present there in the synagogue were enraged beyond belief. This made me feel that I still had some clout, albeit indirectly though my minions. Everyone there knew that this man who was passing Himself off as the Deliverer or 'Messiah' was the son of Joseph the carpenter. They all therefore wondered at the 'words of grace' that proceeded from His mouth. (Luke 4:22) I did not need to physically enter and possess the goons. Of their own accord, they rose up and thrust him out of the city; and they brought him to the brow of the hill, where on their city was built, that they might cast him down headlong. But he passing through the midst of them, went his way. (Luke 4:29-30)

"When the Deliverer and His apostles checked in at the wedding venue, they did not do so alone. The multitudes that had started off as John's disciples and had been baptized by him were also there. In a different set up they would have qualified as 'gate crashers'; but it was not the case at this wedding in Cana. Even though their number exceeded the number of invited guests, they were all made to feel welcome and were offered wine to drink.

"From the moment the Deliverer was baptized by John the Baptist, He had not rested from the work pertaining to the Marriage Supper of the Lamb; and He was attending the wedding in both His capacity as an invited guest and also as the Bridegroom for another affair that was also underway. (Mark 2:19). It had to be that way especially as His precursor was now in prison awaiting his gruesome fate at the hands of the Tetrarch, and he was entirely to blame for the large number of gate crashers - and consequently also for the shortage of wine.

"In the same way the Deliverer, after addressing the multitudes from one of the dhows belonging to Peter, instructed him and his buddies to cast nets where they had been unable to catch any fish the entire night and then observed Peter's amazement at the haul of fish that threatened to sink their two vessels, so also at this wedding in Cana, the only reason the Deliverer was in attendance was to promote the work pertaining to the Marriage Supper of the Lamb.

"When the wine finally ran out as expected (due to the number of uninvited guests who had crashed the 'wedding party'), it was imperative for the organizers to think of something so that the groom on whose behalf they had been working would not be embarrassed. It just so happened that both the bride and bridegroom were folks who were really close to the Zechariahs and as well to the holy family. But more importantly they were both disciples of John, and had been baptized by him in the River Jordan along with the 'gate crashers'.

510

"The gate crashers were from all walks of life, and their number included Pharisees and Sadducees. But they were all of one accord as they descended on the wedding party. They all knew by now that the son of Zechariah was not Elias, and by his own attestation he was not the Christ. They were all thrilled that the wedding at Cana was enabling them finally to corner the 'Prophet' and 'Messiah' whose name would be 'Emmanuel', and whose appearance had even terrified Herod the Great who was now thankfully dead and buried. (Matthew 2:14) It was He about whom the prophets Micah and Isaiah had prophesied. (Micah 5:1-6 and Isaiah 7:10-16).

"As one, the gate crashers were infinitely grateful to the nuptial bride and bridegroom for their role in causing the Nazarene to reappear there in Galilee notwithstanding the fact that He had not been welcomed there at all just weeks earlier. (Luke 4:28-30) As payback to the couple, they all pitched in with cash contributions to the couple's honey moon fund that dwarfed the *mohar* (or bride price the family of the bride was asking).

"Now, it had been anticipated that the wine would run out. At crunch time, the blessed mother of the Deliverer turned and said: 'They have no wine.' His mother said to the servants, 'Do whatever he tells you.' That role - the role of keeping the wine flowing for everyone at the divine banquet - was cemented when, keeping watch at the foot of the cross with the 'son of thunder', she was addressed by her dying son with the words: '*Mulier, ecce filius tuus*' which are translated: 'Woman, behold thy son'. (John 19:25-27). She had been blessed and favored by the Prime Mover, and she became not only the Mother of the Redeemer but the Mother of the redeemed as well...much to our dismay here in the underworld. Her intercessory roles as Advocate, Helper, Benefactress and Mediatrix of divine

511

grace (which were confirmed by Pope Leo XIII in his papal encyclical *Iucunda Semper Expectatione* on the Rosary dated 8 September 1894) were of course foreordained in the same way her roles as the Deliverer's mom and the Queen of Heaven were. And now, known by names like 'The Immaculate Heart of Mary' (Feast Day August 22), 'Our Lady of Sorrows' (Feast Day September 15), 'Our Lady of Mt. Carmel' (Feast Day July 16), 'Our Lady of Guadalupe' (Feast Day December 12), 'Our Lady of the Holy Cross' (Feast Day March 31), 'Our Lady of Edessa' (Feast Day), Our Lady of Montserrat' (Feast Day April 27), 'Our Lady of Perpetual Help' (Feast Day June 27), 'Our Lady of Good Succor' (Feast Day January 8), 'Our Lady, Star of the Sea' (Feast Day September 27), 'Our Lady of Africa' (Feast Day April 30), 'Our Lady of Lourdes' (Feast Day February 11), 'Our Lady of Fatima' (Feast Day May 13), 'Our Lady of Kibeho' (Feast Day November 28), 'Our Lady of Consolation' or 'Mary, Consoler of the Afflicted' (*Consolatrix Afflictorum), observed by the* Augustinians on September 4 and by the Benedictines on July 5, and 'Our Lady of Sorrows' (Feast Day September 15), the intercessory role of that daughter of Joachim and Anne and humble servant of the Prime Mover (Luke 1:38) continues full steam ahead.

"But, a word on those last two titles; and, while you'd be better off taking my word for it, I will tell you that I would much rather you didn't – and for a 'good reason' which, as you should know by now (coming as it is from my satanic mouth) is of course code for 'totally evil reason and with malice aforethought'!

"I will admit up front that, ever since I myself fell from grace, any 'success' that I have ostensibly notched has been illusory at best. Look, I was more subtle than any of the beasts of the earth which the Prime Mover had caused to spring into existence out of nothing - exactly as the inspired author of the Pentateuch wrote. (Genesis 3:1). But, while my 'success' in deceiving those first humans has come with real consequences for those targeted (Genesis 7:1-5; Romans 5:12-21; 2 Peter 3:1-9), all I got for my pains was a curse at the same time as the Prime Mover took steps to upend what appeared on the surface to be a knockout blow to humans, and to show that I was just a pipe dreamer and a sleek charmer with nothing at all to offer to my prey!. And He did so in a spectacular manner, and I will quote Moses here: 'And the Lord God said to the serpent: Because thou hast done this thing, thou art cursed among all cattle, and the beasts of the earth: upon thy breast shalt thou go, and earth shalt thou eat all the days of thy life. I will put enmities between thee and the woman, and thy seed and her seed: she shall crush thy head, and thou shalt lie in wait for her heel.' (Genesis 3:14-15).

"To help you stupid humans understand what was going on here (yes, stupid because you are daft...all of you), just ask yourselves this: how many of us demons do you think can fit on the eye of a needle? Some of you are probably thinking...may be a thousand demons! Damn stupid humans!

"And can the Prime Mover, who caused you humans and us pure spirits to bounce into existence out of nothing – can He fit on the eye of a needle? Of course the answer is yes! And do you now see what I'm driving at? When He cursed me and said that He would put enmities between me and the woman, and my seed and her seed: and He pledged that she would crush my head even as I would be lying in wait for her heel, He was in fact promising that He, the Godhead, would manifest Himself among you humans; and, emptying Himself, He would take the form of a servant, and be made in the likeness of you humans; and in habit He would be found as a man!

"But that woman who, He pledged, was going to crush my head – she would also be something else! Just imagine a soul – one that is immaculate and is conceived without the stain or the original sin that all you humans inherited from Adam and Eve – sharing space on the blighted Earth with all types of sinful and sinning humans that the Earth has hosted – foul creatures that thrive on evil - and many of whom won't even acknowledge their dependence on the Prime Mover by reciting the *Pater Noster* they were taught by none other than the One Who came into the world as Mary's God-child! The weight of responsibility on Mary's shoulders as she and Joseph took refuge in Egypt to escape the murderous Herod the Great - yes, in Egypt whence the Israelites were rescued from enslavement with the help of Aaron's Rod centuries earlier!

"And then, while mystics like John of the Cross, Thérèse of Lisieux, Gemma Galgani and others occasionally experienced what they described as the 'dark nights of the soul' – episodes, also known as periods of desolation, that, however, were usually interspersed with interludes of genuine spiritual consolation – Mary's entire life, culminating with the moment she stood with John by her side beneath the cross on which her God-child hang, clearly was one, uninterrupted 'dark night of the soul' and, undoubtedly, a mirror of what her God-child endured on Earth as He expiated the sins of you sinful and sinning humans!

"The author of the hymn Stabat Mater dolorosa put it succinctly when he/she wrote:

STABAT Mater dolorosa	AT, the Cross her station keeping,
iuxta Crucem lacrimosa,	stood the mournful Mother weeping,

dum pendebat Filius.	close to Jesus to the last.
Cuius animam gementem,	Through her heart, His sorrow sharing,
contristatam et dolentem	all His bitter anguish bearing,
pertransivit gladius.	now at length the sword has passed.
O quam tristis et afflicta	O how sad and sore distressed
fuit illa benedicta,	was that Mother, highly blest,
mater Unigeniti!	of the sole-begotten One.
Quae maerebat et dolebat,	Christ above in torment hangs,
pia Mater, dum videbat	she beneath beholds the pangs
nati poenas inclyti.	of her dying glorious Son.
Quis est homo qui non fleret,	Is there one who would not weep,
matrem Christi si videret	whelmed in miseries so deep,
in tanto supplicio?	Christ's dear Mother to behold?
Quis non posset contristari	Can the human heart refrain
Christi Matrem contemplari	from partaking in her pain,
dolentem cum Filio?	in that Mother's pain untold?
Pro peccatis suae gentis	Bruised, derided, cursed, defiled,
vidit Iesum in tormentis,	she beheld her tender Child
et flagellis subditum.	All with bloody scourges rent:
Vidit suum dulcem Natum	For the sins of His own nation,
moriendo desolatum,	saw Him hang in desolation,
dum emisit spiritum.	Till His spirit forth He sent.

Eia, Mater, fons amoris
me sentire vim doloris
fac, ut tecum lugeam.

O thou Mother! fount of love!
Touch my spirit from above,
make my heart with thine accord:

Fac, ut ardeat cor meum
in amando Christum Deum
ut sibi complaceam.

Make me feel as thou hast felt;
make my soul to glow and melt
with the love of Christ my Lord.

Sancta Mater, istud agas,
crucifixi fige plagas
cordi meo valide.

Holy Mother! pierce me through,
in my heart each wound renew
of my Savior crucified:

Tui Nati vulnerati,
tam dignati pro me pati,
poenas mecum divide.

Let me share with thee His pain,
who for all my sins was slain,
who for me in torments died.

Fac me tecum pie flere,
crucifixo condolere,
donec ego vixero.

Let me mingle tears with thee,
mourning Him who mourned for me,
all the days that I may live:

Iuxta Crucem tecum stare,
et me tibi sociare
in planctu desidero.

By the Cross with thee to stay,
there with thee to weep and pray,
is all I ask of thee to give.

Virgo virginum praeclara,
mihi iam non sis amara,
fac me tecum plangere.

Virgin of all virgins blest!,
Listen to my fond request:
let me share thy grief divine;

Fac, ut portem Christi mortem,	Let me, to my latest breath,
passionis fac consortem,	in my body bear the death
et plagas recolere.	of that dying Son of thine.
Fac me plagis vulnerari,	Wounded with His every wound,
fac me Cruce inebriari,	steep my soul till it hath swooned,
et cruore Filii.	in His very Blood away;
Flammis ne urar succensus,	Be to me, O Virgin, nigh,
per te, Virgo, sim defensus	lest in flames I burn and die,
in die iudicii.	in His awful Judgment Day.
Christe, cum sit hinc exire,	Christ, when Thou shalt call me hence,
da per Matrem me venire	by Thy Mother my defense,
ad palmam victoriae.	by Thy Cross my victory;
Quando corpus morietur,	While my body here decays,
fac, ut animae donetur	may my soul Thy goodness praise,
paradisi gloria. Amen.	safe in paradise with Thee. Amen.

From the *Liturgia Horarum*. Translation by Fr. Edward Caswall (1814-1878).

"The episodes of spiritual desolation of all the mystics who have ever lived or will live combined do not even come close to the sorrows endured by the Mother of the Logos – the Logos Who freely chose to dwell Deliverer amongst you sinful and sinning humans! For you humans and for your salvation He came down from heaven; by the power of the Holy Ghost, he became incarnate of the Virgin Mary, and was made man. For the Prime Mover so loved the world that He gave His only

517

Son, that whoever believes in Him should not perish but have eternal life. (CCC 456, 457)

"And as Mary's God child was presented in the Temple, the lot fell on Simeon, a just and devout man who had been waiting for the consolation of Israel, to describe to you – yeah, to you sinful and sinning humans who are also both deaf and daft - the endurance that being the Mother of God implied: 'Behold this child is set for the fall, and for the resurrection of many in Israel, and for a sign which shall be contradicted; And thy own soul a sword shall pierce, that, out of many hearts, thoughts may be revealed.' (Luke 2:34-35).

"You sinful and sinning descendants of Adam and Eve cannot even come close to comprehending the anxiety, coupled with the unbearable sense of loneliness, desolation and devastation which the Immaculate Virgin Mother of the Deliverer had to bear as she, along with Joseph, over the period of three days, searched for her twelve-year-old God Child! (Luke 2:41-52) And note that they didn't just file a report of a missing person with the authorities and forget about Him like most of you would have done!

"And if you probably are still wondering what I mean by sinful and sinning humans, just go thumb through *De Miseria Condicionis Humane* (On the wretchedness of the human condition) that Pope Innocent III penned!

"And so, anyways, I will be straight with you and tell you that, while we ourselves here in Gehenna like to watch as you humans observe Feast Days of the Liturgical Calendar of the *Sancta Ecclesia* (because you celebrate them mostly unworthily), you would not catch any of us here in Gehenna checking in to see how you celebrate those two particular Feasts - the Feast of Our Lady of Sorrows' and the Feast of Mary, Consoler of the

Afflicted' (*Consolatrix Afflictorum*). This is because it is on those feast days in particular that the Queen of Heaven goes out of her way to stomp really mercilessly on my head and to crush it exactly as it was foretold, and also to remind me that the cheek I had (at the time I tempted Adam and Eve) of thinking that I could derail the divine plan regarding humans – that gall, impudence, effrontery or whatever that no creature had ever dared to put on display up until then – had gone phut and ended up an abysmal failure! Except as regards those unworthy descendants of Adam and Eve who, while endowed with the faculties of reason and free will like us pure spirits as well as you nincompoops, do evil and hate the light and don't go to the light as it is written in John 3:20, that is. I do not have any use for them except for the miseries and suffering they bring on their fellow humans with their evil deeds of omission and commission while oblivious to the fact that the mission of the only-begotten Son, as St. Jan Paweł II (St. John Paul II) explains in his Apostolic Letter *Salvifici Doloris,* consists in conquering sin and death by his obedience unto death, and that He overcomes death by his Resurrection and also while oblivious to words of St. Paul: 'In my flesh I complete what is lacking in Christ's afflictions for the sake of his body, that is, the Church. (Colossians 1:24) Instead of taking a moment to reflect on the fact that pain and suffering have been sanctified by Mary's God child with His wholly unmerited death on the gibbet - that human suffering, when accepted and offered up in union with the Passion of the Deliverer, can and does remit the just punishment for one's sins or for the sins of others (cf Romans 4:3-5) - the stupid fools are focused on blind revenge, more often than not to their own immediate detriment and with little thought as regards their last end. They fancy that they are gods unto themselves – like they willed themselves into existence out of nothing…the stupid fools! We demons might also be fools – of course we too have goofed. But we are not *stupid* fools! Ever heard of 'clever' fools? Yeah, that is what we demons are – not *stupid* fools like these buffoons; real idiots who seem dedicated to trying to ruin my reputation with claims that I was the one tempting them when they get caught with their hand in the till for example - as if they need my shoulder to cry on! You can be sure that, as and when these minions of mine arrive here in Gehenna at the end of their sojourn on Earth (and after wrecking so much havoc on the lives of their fellow humans and making them a veritable hell in my name), I completely disabuse them of the notion that they can do that to me and get away with it scot-free!

"And yes – those other descendants of Adam and Eve who believe in Mary's God child now end up delighting in the beatific vision as they see the Prime Mover face to face after their sojourn on Earth! This is the vision of the essence of the Godhead, whereby the soul/intellect (the body's substantial form) achieves its *telos* or its highest goal - to quote the *Doctor Angelicus* (Angelic Doctor of the Church) or the *Muta Bove* (Dumb Ox) as our minions jokingly referred to him to disparage him. This was not in the cards at all when the Prime Mover formed man out of the slime of the earth: and breathed into his face the breath of life, and man became a living soul!

"But, a word on the 'dumb ox'. So, because Tommaso d'Aquino reportedly was heavyset and taciturn (and that is also how he has been depicted in portraits over the centuries), his fellow novices or newbies in the Dominican Order were quick to dub him 'Dumb Ox'! The stupid dumb asses! So, so stupid! I mean – if that 'Dumb Ox' had produced just a tenth of what he succeeded in producing and bequeathing to the world over his forty-seven-year life span, there is no doubt that he would still have made the list of Doctors of the Church. And now, guess who really deserved that title of 'Dumb Ox'? It was those minions of mine; not the chap who is now also referred to in one breath as the *Doctor Angelicus*, the *Doctor Communis*, and the *Doctor Universalis*!

"And if you recall what I just said about the Queen of Heaven and Mother of God (*Regina Caeli et Mater Dei*) stomping mercilessly on my head, you can take it that every day that Tommaso d'Aquino lived spelled more trouble for me!

"And as for those other dumb asses and minions of mine, by allowing me to use them in my efforts to try and undermine the work of the man of God and bring it into disrepute, they actually showed themselves to be... Yeah, like fools or, as Italians would say, *Sì, come degli sciocchi*; or *sicut stulti* as the Romans would have said - or 是的，像傻子一樣in Chinese and Да как дурак in Russian! Yeah, meatheads, idiots, fools, imbeciles, dolts, dullards, simpletons, doofuses, dorks, morons, oafs, dunces, jackasses, lumps, dimwits, dummies, yahoos, dopes, dumbbells, dumbheads, lamebrains, nincompoops, clots, nitwits, numbskulls, goons, ignoramuses, boneheads, dodos, noddies, knuckleheads, louts, nimrods, donkeys, fatheads, goofs, loon crazies, nitwits, birdbrains, ninnies, numskulls, schlubs, turkeys, airheads, blockheads, clunks, cretins, mugs, mutts, pinheads, bubbleheads, chowderheads, chuckleheads, clodpoles, clodpolls, ninnyhammers, prats, stupes, stupid fools, deadheads, dummkopf, dunderheads, loggerheads, lunkheads, momes, sapheads, shlubs, thickheads, woodenheads, ganders, golems, hammerheads, hardheads, ratbags. schnooks, bogans, clucks, dips, dum-dums, half-wits, know-nothings, dim bulbs, yo-yos, dumb clucks, yokels,

521

bumpkins, chumps, clods, clodhoppers, clowns, losers, lubbers, lummoxes, bruisers, dumb oxen, loobies, lumaxes, dubs, hayseeds, twits, Neanderthals, pillocks, halfwits, schmucks, bozos, buffoons, putzes, dweebs, spuds, numpties, klutzes, dumbos, muppets, hicks, galoots, geeks, dills, yobbos, goofballs, gits, poops, nerds, simps, boobs, dingbats, thickos, eejits, dingleberries, boobies, stumblebums, geese, momparas, shleppers, wallies, drongos, dumbasses, boofheads, yobs, cuckoos, schlemiels, tossers, blokes, dudes, jerks, squareheads, muttonheads, nongs, ning-nongs, gawks, featherheads, goofuses, lugs, blunderers, ginks, wazzocks, palookas, knobheads, twerps, hobbledehoys, divvies, plonkers, gobdaws, bosthoons, churls, coots, gowks, cuckoos, gonzos, nerks, witlings, mooncalfs, sumphs, spoonies, nutcases, tomfools, nyaffs, chavs, nuts, twonk, oiks, schleppers, ding-dongs, pea-brains, lame-brains, pudding-heads, dumb-bells, wing nuts, ding-a-lings, wooden-heads, rubes, softheads, duffers, dowfars, stupidos, culchies, Jackeens, bumpkins, silly billy, mamparas, bunglers, ockers, rascals, goops, neds, scatterbrains, ditzes, dumdums, kooks, clodpate, schmoes, featherbrains, rattlebrains, flibbertigibbets, dotards, knothead, harebrains, loonies, addlepates, jugheads, gulls, lout, bird-brain, schleps, tosspots, weirdoes, blockheads, chumps, clods, dummkopfs, dunces, muckers, goobers, troglodytes, dags, simpletons, weasels, skanks, croppers, and above all *buoi più stupidi* (stupidest oxen) as Italians say; or *insulsissimus vaccarum* (stupidest cows) as those self-proclaimed *eximia Romani* (exceptional Romans) would have said if their *Imperium Rōmānum* (Roman Empire) was still around.

"All those humans who hearken to the words of the Deliverer and who, accordingly, take up their crosses and trudge after Him are, of course, untouchables. But the rest of you humans who won't hearken to Mary's God Child and are prepared to join the mob that shouted: '*Tolle tolle crucifige eum...Non habemus regem nisi Caesarem*' (Away with him! Crucify him...we have no king but Caesar) - you are my minions all of you! And, of course, each and every human who would be my minion is not just a *muta bovis* (a dumb ox), but what Italians would call *un grande, sciocco tonto.* (a big and foolish ox)! Yeah, *un grande stupido nel vero senso* (a big fool in the truest sense of that word)! Yeeeh, ha, ha, ha, ha, hah! Eeeeh, ho, ho, ho hoooo! Ooooh, hee. hee, heee! Weeeh, ha, ha, ha, hah! Indeed!"

Mjomba stopped writing. He was visibly stunned and speechless. That evilest of evil creatures had obviously decided to give "sinful and sinning" humans (as he was wont to refer to the descendants of Adam and Eve) a mouthful! It was now crystal cleat to Mjomba why the Deliverer had warned in John 8:44 that Satan was a murderer from the beginning, and had no truth in him! And Mjomba now also recalled the advice the Apostle to the Gentiles had given, admonishing the Thessalonians to pray without ceasing. (Thessalonians 5:17) That is what he, Mjomba, should have been doing instead of wasting his time engaging in high jinks with the Evil One. And now, seemingly by a fluke, it occurred to the seminarian that the Deliverer, as reported by that former publican (Matthew) in his Gospel (see Matthew 6:11), had admonished His disciples to pray to His Father in heaven with the words: "*Panem nostrum cotidianum da nobis hodie*" (Give us this day our daily bread)! Yet, here he was cavorting with Old Nick and hoping to use him to craft a winning theological thesis!

Still, being well aware that he, Mjomba, was himself included among the *exsules filii Hevæ* (poor banished children of Eve), he was terrified all the same as he tried to imagine what a completely deranged Diabolos, his face wrapped up in a murderous glare, would look like at that particular point in time in an apparition! The mere thought that he had not been coerced into dillydallying with the Evil Ghost ,but had ended up monkeying around with the Adversary on his own volition, now scared the living daylights out of him! But, like someone who was possessed or who was suicidal or incompetent by reason of being unable to use his head to do the right thing, the seminarian mumbled that, be all that as it may, a deal was a deal! Speaking to no one in particular, he went on mumbling that he had made this deal with Mephistopheles; and he had to honor it no matter how he felt now! And with that he picked up his pen and continued playing the role of scribe to the Prince of Darkness.

"But, not surprisingly" Satan pursued; "because the bible believers remain separated from the *Sancta Ecclesia*, they don't get to thumb through the many Mariological papal documents that have been developed on the basis of Sacred Scripture, Church Tradition and *Sensus fidei* (sense of the faith), also called *sensus fidelium* (sense of the faithful) and defined as 'the supernatural appreciation of faith on the part of the whole people, when, from the bishops to the last of the faithful, they manifest a universal consent in matters of faith and morals.' (CCC 92).

"Examples are: Pope Sixtus IV's bull Cum *Praeexcelsa* which he issued on 28 February 1476; Pope Pius V's papal bull *Consueverunt Romani Pontifices* (17 September 1569); *Dominici gregis* issued by Pope Clement VIII on 3 February 1603; Pope Benedict XIV's Apostolic Letter *Gloriosae Dominae* (27 September 1748); the Apostolic Constitution Sodality of Our Lady

(*Bis Saeculari*) promulgated by Pope Pius XII on 27 September 1948; the Papal bull *Gloriosae Dominae* of Pope Benedict XIV (September 27, 1748); Pope Pius IX's encyclical *Ubi primum*; Pope Pius IX's papal bull *Ineffabilis Deus* that was promulgated on 8 December 1854; Pope Leo XIII's encyclical *Supremi apostolatus officio* (1 September 1883); Pope Leo XIII's encyclicals *Superiore anno (*30 August 1884) and *Octobri mense* (22 September 1891); Pope Pius X's encyclical *Ad diem illum* (2 February 1904); Pope Pius XII's encyclical *Fulgens Corona*; Pope Pius XII's encyclical *Deiparae Virginis Mariae* (1 May 1946); Pope Pius XII's encyclical *Auspicia quaedam* (1 May 1948); Pope Pius XII's Apostolic constitution *Munificentissimus Deus* (1 November 1950); Pope Pius XII's encyclical *Ingruentium malorum* (15 September 1951); Pope Pius XII's encyclical *Ad Caeli Reginam* (11 October 1954); *Lumen gentium,* the dogmatic constitution that was promulgated by Pope Paul VI on 21 November 1964; Pope Paul VI's encyclical *Christi Matri* (15 September 1966); Pope Paul VI's Apostolic exhortation *Signum Magnum* which he issued on May 13, 1967; Pope Paul VI's Apostolic exhortation *Marialis Cultus* (2 February 1974); and Pope John Paul II's encyclical *Redemptoris Mater* (25 March 1987) in which the Pontiff confirmed the title, Mother of the Church, proclaimed by Pope Paul VI at the Second Vatican Council on 21 November 1964; and the Apostolic Letter *Rosarium Virginis Mariae* that Pope John Paul II issued on 16 October 2002.

"Yeah, Yeah! I love it. The Council of Ephesus in AD 431 decreed that Mary was the *Theotokos* (God-bearer), the Deliverer being one divine person with two natures (a divine nature and human nature that are intimately and hypostatically united) and consequently both God and man. Remove the Mother of God from the equation, and you have a limping Deliverer...Hee, Hee, Hee, Ha, Ha, Ha...

"From the island of Patmos, John had written: 'And a great sign appeared in heaven: A woman clothed with the sun, and the moon under her feet, and on her head a crown of twelve stars. And being with child, she cried travailing in birth: and was in pain to be delivered. And there was seen another sign in heaven. And behold a great red dragon, having seven heads and ten horns and on his heads seven diadems. And his tail drew the third part of the stars of heaven and cast them to the earth. And the dragon stood before the woman who was ready to be delivered: that, when she should be delivered, he might devour her son. And she brought forth a man child, who was to rule all nations with an iron rod. And her son was taken up to God and to his throne. And the woman fled into the wilderness, where she had a place prepared by God, that there they should feed her, a thousand two hundred sixty days.' (Revelation 12:1-6)

"But the bible believers, blinded by their bigotry which is directed at the Deliverer's *Sancta Ecclesia* and completely oblivious to the solemn words that the Deliverer addressed to his apostles on the evening on which He inaugurated the Sacrament of the Holy Eucharist or the 'Sacrament of Love' as per the Holy Father Benedict XVI's February 22, 2007 Apostolic Exhortation *Sacramentum Caritas* [*You have not chosen me: but I have chosen you; and have appointed you, that you should go and should bring forth fruit; and your fruit should remain: that whatsoever you shall ask of the Father in my name, he may give it you. These things I command you, that you love one another. (John 15:16-17)*], imagine that they can sweep past the Deliverer's Blessed Mother and, by dint of reciting the *Sinner's Prayer*, guarantee themselves a seat at the divine banquet, while at the same time deriding those who seek Mary's intercession - or those who, borrowing the words of the Angel Gabriel, reverently recite the Ave Maria (Hail Mary)! This is so, so funny.

"They pride themselves on being true *bible believers*, and they still miss the fact that Revelation 11:19 establishes the Blessed Virgin Mary as the living shrine of the Word of God and the Ark of the New and Eternal Covenant! Look, you can take it from the horse's mouth (because of my role in all of this) and accept that 'bible believers' might be good at 'cramming' books of the New and Old Testament (excluding the seven deuterocanonical books that they conveniently dumped); but I'm sorry to say that they are definitely not very good at interpreting the self-same.

"But, more importantly, they would do well to remember what the Apostle to the Gentiles wrote in his first letter to the Corinthians: 'But, as it is written: That eye hath not seen, nor ear heard: neither hath it entered into the heart of man, what things God hath prepared for them that love him. But to us God hath revealed them by his Spirit. For the Spirit searcheth all things, yea, the deep things of God. For what man knoweth the things of a man, but the spirit of a man that is in him? So the things also that are of God, no man knoweth, but the Spirit of God. Now, we have received not the spirit of this world, but the Spirit that is of God: that we may know the things that are given us from God. Which things also we speak: not in the learned words of human wisdom, but in the doctrine of the Spirit, comparing spiritual things with spiritual.' (1 Corinthians 2:9-13)

"St. Thérèse of Lisieux (who joined two of her older sisters in the cloistered Carmelite community of Lisieux when she was fifteen and died when she was only twenty-four years old and was proclaimed a Doctor of the Church by Pope John Paul II) had a saying: 'Sufferings gladly borne for others convert more people than sermons. Of course, as the Father of Death, you should not count on me to bear *any* sufferings on behalf of bible believers who (as some clever nerd has aptly pointed out) 'preach God but convert people to dead religion' under schemes that have my imprimatur. Another quote from that saint, who is also known as 'Saint Thérèse of the Child Jesus and the Holy Face' and 'The Little Flower of Jesus', goes: 'I understand and I know from experience that: "The kingdom of God is within you." Jesus has no need of books or teachers to instruct souls; He teaches without the noise of words. Never have I heard Him speak, but I feel that He is within me at each moment; He is guiding and inspiring me with what I must say and do. I find just when I need them certain lights that I had not seen until then, and it isn't most frequently during my hours of prayer that these are most abundant but rather in the midst of my daily occupations.'

"Ooops! I shouldn't have included these quotes of the Little Flower. I am the Father of Lies and the Father of Death; and I would rather leave the bible believers to put their faith in the sacred scriptures *alone* and in their deluded sense of certainty that their *personal* interpretation of the same gets the automatic stamp of approval of the Holy Ghost! And if they ever succeed in finally stumbling into the *Sancta Ecclesia*, my troops will, of course, always be there to help them see that 'they owe it all to their own intellectual prowess'; and it must be lost on them completely that, when Simon Peter, responding to the Deliverer's question in Matthew 16:13-17, Mark 8:27-30, Luke 9:18-20 and John 6:66-71, succeeded in getting it right, it was not because it was revealed to him by flesh and blood, but by the Deliverer's Father in heaven!

528

"Still, regarding the *Sancta Ecclesia* being the 'whore of Babylon', the bible believers need to remember what the Deliverer, the head of the Mystical Body of Christ which is the *Sancta Ecclesia Catholica* (vide Pope Pius XII's encyclical *Mystici Corporis Christi* and as well Pope Pius XI's encyclical, *Mortalium animos*) promised *His disciples* on the night He instituted the Sacrament of the Holy Eucharist which the Catechism defines as the 'source and summit of the Christian life' and is defined in Pope Paul VI's Encyclical *Mysterium Fidei* as the 'Sacrament of the Church's Unity': 'And I will ask the Father: and he shall give you another Paraclete, that he may abide with you for ever: The spirit of truth, whom the world cannot receive, because it seeth him not, nor knoweth him. But you shall know him; because *he shall abide with you and shall be in you*...I will not say much more to you, for *the prince of this world is coming*. He has no hold over me, but he comes so that the world may learn that I love the Father and do exactly what my Father has commanded me.' (John 14:16-31)

"And there again goes the reference to me; and you'd better believe that I'm here and still doing my dirty work. The bible believers remind me of the priests and Pharisees and the scribes who had the nerve to suggest the unimaginable, namely that the Deliverer was possessed by me, Beelzebub! The insolence! Imagine them mouthing the words: 'He hath Beelzebub, and by the prince of devils he casteth out devils! (Mark 3:22, Matthew 12:22-30 & Luke 11:14-23) Actually, when the Deliverer he entered again into the synagogue where there was a man who had a withered hand as (as described in Mark 3:1), one would have thought that, as teachers of the law, they would have seized the opportunity to become disciples of the promised Messiah; and He would undoubtedly have had them under full consideration when He was appointing His twelve apostles (something He did shortly afterwards).

"But, no; and, instead, the stupid fools 'watched him whether he would heal on the sabbath days; that they might accuse him'! (Mark 3:2). And the Deliverer said to the man who had the withered hand: 'Stand up in the midst. And he saith to them (the priests and Pharisees and teachers of the law): Is it lawful to do good on the sabbath days, or to do evil? to save life, or to destroy? But they held their peace. And looking round about on them with anger, being grieved for the blindness of their hearts, he saith to the man: Stretch forth thy hand. And he stretched it forth: and his hand was restored unto him. And the Pharisees going out, immediately made a consultation with the Herodians against him, how they might destroy him.' (Mark 3:3-6)

"It was not long afterward that the promised Messiah, 'going up into a mountain, called unto him whom he would himself: and they came to him. And he made that twelve should be with him, and that he might send them to preach. And he gave them power to heal sicknesses, and to cast out devils. And to Simon he gave the name Peter: And James the son of Zebedee, and John the brother of James; and he named them Boanerges, which is, The sons of thunder: And Andrew and Philip, and Bartholomew and Matthew, and Thomas and James of Alpheus, and Thaddeus, and Simon the Cananean: And Judas Iscariot, who also betrayed him.' (Mark 3:13-19)

"After explaining that the obvious, namely that if, I, Satan, be risen up against myself, I am 'divided, and cannot stand, but hath an end' (Mark 3:26), the Deliverer said: 'Amen I say to you, that all sins shall be forgiven unto the sons of men, and the blasphemies wherewith they shall blaspheme: But he that *shall blaspheme against the Holy Ghost*, shall never have forgiveness, but shall be guilty of an everlasting sin. Because they said: He hath an unclean spirit. (Mark 3:28-30) The Deliverer explained what He meant by that using the Parable of the Sower and the Parable of the Mustard Seed. (Mark 4:1-34, Matthew 13:1-32, Luke 8:4-18 and Luke 13:18-19)

"Now, sincerely, one does not need a 'demonic mind' to see the fallacy in the really strange position that, in the Prime Mover's plan of salvation for humans, the material that some of the Deliverer's disciples committed to paper (or shall we say 'papyri') and that ended up as writings of the 'New Testament' is all that is important; and that the roles of the authors themselves as 'fishers of men', and the roles the apostles who did not bequeath anything in writing to posterity would play inside the 'Sancta Ecclesia' that the Deliverer formally and explicitly established on the 'rock called Peter', as well as the place of the 'Sancta Ecclesia' itself in the divine plan of redemption (Ephesians 1:7-14) are unimportant! Is it therefore any wonder that the 'bible believers' ended up with the completely indefensible 'reformed' doctrine of 'sola fide' (salvation by faith alone) after stripping 'good works' from the Prime Mover's plan of salvation for humans! Haw, haw, hoo, hoo, ho, ho, heh, heh, heh, heh, hak, hak, hak...!

"Indeed as St. Gregory Thaumaturgus (+ c.270) wrote: "Come, then, ye too, dearly beloved, and let us chant the melody which has been taught us by the inspired harp of David, and say, 'Arise, O Lord, into Thy rest; Thou, and the ark of Thy sanctuary' [Ps. 131:8]. For the holy Virgin is in truth an ark, wrought with gold both within and without, that has received the whole treasury of the sanctuary" (The First Homily on the Annunciation to the Holy Virgin Mary).

"Look, in the episode referred to by John in Revelation 12:17, I was justifiably venting my anger and frustration and I was really mad at that woman who was with child. First, I was in a mood to kill when I saw the angel of the Lord standing by those country shepherds as they kept the night watches over their flock in Bethlehem and, with the brightness of the Prime Mover shining round about them, said: 'Behold, I bring you good tidings of great joy, that shall be to all the people: For, this day, is born to you a Savior, who is Christ the Lord, in the city of David'. The only thing that initially held me back was the sight of a multitude of the heavenly army that was praising God, and saying: 'Glory to God in the highest; and on earth peace to men of good will.' (Luke 2:8 -14). And this was even though the Lord, speaking to Achaz (as described in Isaiah 7:10-16) had clearly promised humans saying: 'Behold a virgin shall conceive, and bear a son, and his name shall be called Emmanuel. He shall eat butter and honey, that he may know to refuse the evil, and to choose the good...' And then, try as I could to banish the words of Micah from my mind, that only caused them to grow into a deafening clangor: 'AND THOU, BETHLEHEM Ephrata, art a little one among the thousands of Juda: out of thee shall he come forth unto me that is to be the ruler in Israel: and his going forth is from the beginning, from the days of eternity.' (Micah 5:2) Oh, it made me so mad - as a March hare! And so, when the woman gave birth to Him, I had no choice but to make war with the rest of her seed who keep the commandments, I could not stand the prospect of her giving birth to the God-child! And when she gave birth to Him, I had no choice but to make war with the rest of her seed who keep the commandments of the Prime Mover and have the testimony of the Deliverer.

"The bible believers should actually be praying very hard to that woman who was verily a tabernacle for the living God for the space of nine whole months! And they should be begging her to intercede for them so that they above all get to discover the Eucharist Celebration which is ongoing and unceasing. They need her intercession in order to understand the significance of the fact that at any given moment the Most Holy Sacrifice of the Mass, reenacting the Deliverer's once-for-all saving passion and death on the cross two thousand years ago, is being celebrated.

"Actually not one moment now goes by when members of the *Ecclesia Militans* (Church Militant) are not lining up to receive the Deliverer under the species of bread and wine, becoming thereby tabernacles in the exact same way the expectant Blessed Virgin Mary was a tabernacle. This also explains why the Word, at the behest of His Father, consented to become a human, and go on to be the sacrificial lamb for the sins of humankind - so that humans who accepted the invitation to attend the Marriage Banquet of the Lamb may already in this life begin feasting on His sacred body and blood under the species of bread and wine under the new and everlasting covenant.' (Leviticus 4:32, Luke 22:16-20, Matthew 26:29, Hebrews 9:11-15, 1 Corinthians 11:25, Revelation 3:20, and CCC 612 to 614).

"And so now, even though hordes may have received the Sacrament of Baptism validly, because they freely chose to cling onto heretical beliefs and remain cut off from the *Sancta Ecclesia* thereby, the Sacrament of the Blessed Eucharist remains out of bounds in their regard for that reason. They relegate themselves to a position that is not dissimilar to that of the folks the Deliverer referred to as 'blinded guides'. (Matthew 23:16-17; John 9:40; and Luke 11.52) And yet it remains true that nothing illustrates better the Prime Mover's love for humans than the Sacrament of the Blessed Eucharist. And, indeed, nothing redounds more in this god-damn forsaken world of yours to the glory of the Prime Mover than the Holy Mass which sees the reenactment of the Deliverer's death on Calvary for the salvation of you wretched humans.

"I have suggested on numerous occasions that you humans are really, really dense, daft or whatever. We here in the Underworld could not but take advantage of that monumental stupidity to ensure that the so-called separated brethren remained obstinate in their heresies, denying themselves thereby access to what Thomas Aquinas referred to in his *Summa Theologiae* as the 'Sacrament of Charity'. And, as St. Paul pointed out in his missive to the Corinthians (1 Corinthians 10:17), the 'Blessed Sacrament' is also the 'Sacrament of the Church's Unity'.

"And we didn't start confusing humans yesterday or during the middle ages. If that is what you think, think again. That is not to say that the heresies of the separated brethren aren't egregious. Because they strike at the teaching magisterium of the *Sancta Ecclesia*, they are as pernicious as any heresies can get.

"Adherents of these heresies refuse to acknowledge that the Deliverer 'appointed' folks and 'sent them out' into the cities saying: 'The harvest indeed is great, but the laborers are few. Pray ye therefore the Lord of the harvest that he send laborers into his harvest. Go: Behold I send you as lambs among wolves...' (Luke 10:2-3) Or: 'Go ye therefore, and teach all nations, baptizing them in the name of the Father, and of the Son, and of the Holy Ghost: Teaching them to observe all...' (Matthew 28:19-20) Or: 'And I say to thee: That thou art

Peter; and upon this rock I will build my church, and the gates of hell shall not prevail against it..' (Matthew 16:18)

"And, like the Deliverer - the Word made flesh who would lay down His life for the salvation of humans - was taking a break from His chores during His sojourn on earth and was just kidding when He talked about 'building his church on the rock called Peter'!

"Or like the Deliverer never meant anything with the words: 'Have not I chosen you twelve? And one of you is a devil...' (John 6:70) Or like it was the yet unwritten books of the New Testament that traversed Asia Minor and travelled to the ends of the earth spreading the message of Christ crucified, and not the band of apostles the Deliverer had handpicked, laid His hands on, and breathed over saying: 'Receive ye the Holy Ghost. Whose sins you shall forgive, they are forgiven them: and whose sins you shall retain, they are retained...' (John 20:22-23)

"Or, like those apostles who did not write any missives to their congregations in that Infant Church were just wasting their time running around doing what the Deliverer bade them do when He laid His hands on them and sent them out saying: 'Going therefore, teach ye all nations: baptizing them in the name of the Father and of the Son and of the Holy Ghost. Teaching them to observe all things whatsoever I have commanded you. And behold I am with you all days, even to the consummation of the world.' (Matthew 28:19-20)

"And as if He did not tell Simon and his brother Andrew as they were fishing for fish in the Sea of Galilee, and likewise James and John who were mending their nets close by assisted by their Zebedee, their dad, and a couple of hired hands: 'Come, follow me and I will make you fishers of men.' (Mark 1:16-18, Matthew 4:19, Luke 5:10-11, and John 1:40-42)

"Of course everyone agrees that any dud who would have been seen running around trying to make a case for the doctrine of *Sola Scriptura* at that time would have been deemed crazy. But even after John, Mark, Matthew, and Luke finished compiling their gospels, and Paul, Peter and others had penned the epistles they addressed to their respective audiences, the very significant fact that these New Testament writings had suddenly taken the place of the *Sancta Ecclesia* (against which the gates of hell would never prevail) somehow failed to merit any mention at all in what should doubtless be regarded as the greatest omission of all time!

"I will tell you that we here in Gehenna, for our part, were already quite busy even before those writings that are deemed by the separated brethren to constitute the sole source of revelation were penned. Paul, that turncoat who had morphed into the 'Apostle of the Gentiles', even saw the need to address his congregants in Corinth thus as he crisscrossed Asia Minor doing the bidding of the Deliverer: 'But what I do, that I will do, that I may cut off occasion from them which desire an occasion; that wherein they glory, they may be found even as we. For such men are false apostles, deceitful workers, fashioning themselves into apostles of Christ. And no marvel; for even Satan fashioneth himself into an angel of light. It is no great thing therefore if his ministers also fashion themselves as ministers of righteousness; whose end shall be according to their works...' (2 Corinthians 11:12-15)

"Look, in the first century we helped the 'circumcisers' to spread the false teaching that unless one was circumcised according to the custom of Moses, one could not be saved. In the first and second centuries we got agnostics to deny the divinity of the Deliverer with their cry that matter was evil!

"In the late 2nd century, the Montanists, who came along with our help, claimed that the *Sancta Ecclesia Catholica* was the hot bed of gluttons and adulterers, who hated to fast and loved to remarry, amongst other things; and, for good measure, they also denied the possibility of forgiveness of sins in the Church.

"In the 3rd century we had the Sabellianists come along and teach that the three persons of the Blessed Trinity existed only in God's relation to man, not in objective reality. The Donatists in the 4th to 5th century argued that the clergy had to be faultless for their ministry to be effective and for the prayers offered up and the sacraments they administered to be valid.

"In the 4th century we succeeded in getting Arius to sow confusion in the Church until his teachings were solemnly condemned in 325 by the First Council of Nicaea which defined the divinity of Christ, and by the First Council of Constantinople which defined the divinity of the Holy Spirit in 381. Then along came Pelagius in the 5th century with his heretical teaching that man was born morally neutral and could achieve heaven under his own powers.

"And then there was also Nestorius, Archbishop of Constantinople from April 10, 428 to June 22, 431. He denied Mary the title of Theotokos ("God-bearer" or "Mother of God"). His teaching implied that the Deliverer was actually two people with two different natures (human and divine).

"And then there were the Monophysites, also in the 5th century, who swung to the other extreme and claimed that the Deliverer was neither fully human nor fully divine. And in the 7th and 8th centuries along came the iconoclasts or "icon smashers" and their claim that it was sinful to make icons of the Deliverer or the saints! It is, of course, quite telling that St. John Damascene (675-749),

Confessor and Doctor of the Church, places the Arian monk, Bahira, right there among the iconoclasts in his *Heresies in Epitome: How They Began and Whence They Drew Their Origin*, better known as *De Haeresibus* (Heresies).

"In the 11th century the Cathars were on the scene; and they taught that the world was created by an evil deity; and that matter consequently was evil! The Albigensians, who formed one of the largest Cathar sects taught that the spirit was created by God, and was good, while the body was created by an evil god. It was therefore imperative, they believed, that the spirit be freed from the body. Having children was therefore one of the greatest evils, because it entailed imprisoning another "spirit" in flesh.

"The 16th century saw the advent of Protestantism and its denial of the teaching magisterium of the *Sancta Ecclesia*. And in the 17th century along came Cornelius Jansen, Bishop of Ypres, France with his Jansenism. In 1653 the five offending propositions from the manuscript that was published after the bishop's death were roundly condemned by Pope Innocent X in the bull '*Cum Occasione*'.

"Yeah, just when you thought that you had seen all possible variations of unorthodoxy, my troops and I, working with our minions amongst humans, have always succeeded in coming up with new and even more devastating, but still quite exciting, heresies to distract humans and stop them from finding that One, Holy, Catholic and Apostolic Church of which the Deliverer is head (Colossians 1:18), and over which a total of two hundred and sixty-six (266) popes have presided starting with Šemʿōn Kēpā (Simon Peter) and ending with Jorge Mario Bergoglio (Papa Franciscus), the current reigning pope.

"But we, of course, did not stop there. In a masterstroke of true demonic genius, we succeeded in helping the disparate heretical groups to forge what we dubbed 'Christian traditions'. Many practices and beliefs in these new so-called 'Christian traditions' of course aren't in accordance with the practices and beliefs propagated by the *Sancta Ecclesia*; and the notion of 'Christian traditions' that compete with the One, Holy, and Apostolic Church serves our purpose just fine.

"For one it provides cover for the 'separated brethren' who would like to continue clinging on to their favored but condemned doctrines and to feel comfy and at home, and to minimize the consequences in their eyes of being cut-off from the *Sancta Ecclesia*. We have been able to pull this off by enlisting the help of 'theologians' belonging inside the *Sancta Ecclesia* who, under the guise of practicing the virtue of charity, effectively become complicit in promoting the heresies by giving the impression that it is all just a matter of belonging to one or other 'Christian tradition'.

"Those Catholic theologians who go out of their way to ingratiate themselves in that manner with the 'separated brethren' of course themselves end up in the same boat as those they seek to please or 'admonish'. Seeking to curry favor with folks who espouse beliefs that have been condemned by the *Sancta Ecclesia* and who, as a rule, do not even regard Catholics as 'Christians' is undeniably a stupid thing to do; and it enables us here in the Underworld to brag that we have succeeded in killing many birds with a single stone!

"It was actually quite easy to ensnare theologians of every mold inside the Church - liberal and neoliberal as well as conservative and neoconservative - into actively seeking to be nice pals with members of the heretical factions in Christendom in that manner. Our goal has all along been to get Catholic theologians to blur the positions of the *Sancta Ecclesia* on the Sacraments and other doctrinal matters, including the status of the separated brethren.

"You see - it wasn't the Deliverer who conceived of this cockeyed idea of multiple 'Christian traditions'. You have to have a very fertile imagination to reach that conclusion. You humans should be fair and be prepared to give credit where credit is due. This was my idea for heaven's sake! What is wrong with you humans?

"And yes, you've guessed right: our next project is now going to be to try and turn liberals and conservatives inside the *Sancta Ecclesia* against each other in a way that will trigger a major schism! This will be revenge for you humans not giving us here in the Underworld the credit that is justly due!

"With every century that has gone by since the destruction of the second temple in AD 70, the world has indisputably been inching towards the end times and Armageddon which, as Paul said, will transpire 'in the twinkling of an eye'! (1 Corinthians 15:51-52)

"And the phenomenon of Protestantism and its brazen challenge to the magisterium of the *Sancta Ecclesia Catholica* as defined by the Second Vatican Council has to be an ominous sign indeed. The Deliverer's words concerning the end of the world speak for themselves: 'I say to you, that he will quickly revenge them. But yet the Son of man, when he cometh, shall he find, think you, faith on earth?' (Luke 18:8)

"And, anyway, knowing that bible believers *need* the intercession of the Deliverer's Blessed Mother, what do you think that we here in the Underworld would be doing in concert with our minions on earth. Take a nap? You have to be kidding…Hee Hee Hee Haa Haa Haa, Ho Ho Hoooo!"

Mjomba paused and shook his head. The devil was right on, he thought. He could not agree more. Mjomba actually wondered what the motivation of bible believers was in imagining biblical passages like those away! And, for sure, the Holy Ghost could not be associated with those errors of the bible believers - the Holy Spirit who came upon the Virgin Mary and caused the power of the Most High to overshadow her as a prelude to her becoming the Mother of the Son of Man as described in Luke 1:35, that is.

Mjomba's thoughts turned to the Jews who had been in the habit of flocking to synagogues and to the temple, but failed to hearken first to the "voice of one crying in the desert: Prepare ye the way of the Lord; make straight his paths" (Mark 1:2, Isaiah 40:1-5, Matthew 3:1-12, Luke 3:1-20 and John 1:19-28); and then to the Deliverer Himself as He crisscrossed the provinces of Judea, Galilee and Samaria addressing crowds, healing the sick and driving out demons from those who were possessed; and who finally refused to heed the message of the crucified and risen Deliverer that Peter, Paul and the other apostles preached beginning on the Day of Pentecost. They must have been shocked to find themselves on the wrong side history when they eventually kicked the proverbial bucket! Mjomba saw a clear parallel.

Mjomba recoiled at the thought that Protestantism, which arrived on the scene one thousand years after Islam made its appearance and had now also become a permanent fixture, was not likely to go away any time soon either. The Deliverer, who had foretold the siege and fall of Jerusalem and the destruction of the Second Temple, had also pointedly stated that as the end of time drew near, many false prophets would appear and would lead many astray. The room where Mjomba was closeted and cranking away at his thesis started to spin when it occurred to him that this might be the beginning of the end!

The statement "my grace is sufficient for thee" (2 Corinthians 12:9) did not just apply to Paul and to souls whose heroism had been recognized by the Church and were now venerated as saints, it applied to Adam and Eve and all their descendants. The difference undoubtedly was that those heroic souls, by emptying themselves following in their Deliverer's example (Philippians 2:7-9 and Isaiah 52:13-15), were able to reach out to the Prime Mover in a self-less fashion and to grow in holiness in the midst of their adversities with the help of the graces merited for them by their Deliverer with His passion and death on the cross. If there was a trick to this, it lay in the practice of humility, the same humility that prompted Adam and Eve, after they realized that they had lost their innocence upon eating of the forbidden fruit from the Tree of the Knowledge of Good and Evil located in the middle of the Paradise of Pleasure and were stark naked and done for all practical purposes, to sew together fig leaves, and make themselves aprons. (Genesis 3:7)

Mjomba did not suspect at that point that the Evil One was casting the net so wide that it wasn't going to be long before he himself would be ensnared and rattled by Satan's revelations in his own regard and the simultaneous exposure of his hypocrisy.

Beelzebub continued with the seminarian scribbling away: "Yeah, I worked on the bible believers to the point they all now exude what is manifestly a false sense of confidence in the efficacy of their own prayers, confidence that belies their own unworthiness as poor banished children of Eve! Some of these misguided souls, even as they are floundering in heresies and are at my mercy in 'this valley of tears' and undoubtedly in the greatest need of the intercession of saints, now even have the audacity to cast aspersions on the devotions to Mary of the likes of Saint Louis-Marie Grignion de Montfort for being 'an incomparable bard and disciple of the Mother of the Savior whom he honored as the one who so assuredly leads towards Christ'; St. Alphonsus Liguori who authored the 'Glories of Mary'; and St. Bernard of Clairvaux, the *Marian Doctor* who was aglow with love for the Mother of God, and others. Ha, ha, ha! Indeed!

"Hee, ha ha, ha! Talk about treating anthems as anathema! I have done even better. I've got these folks not only to treat the Vicar of the Deliverer on earth as the Antichrist, but to borrow the words of Revelation 17:5 to describe the *Sancta Ecclesia* itself...Ha, ha, hee, hee! The Whore of Babylon! Heh, ha, ha ha! Of course I am not laughing at the *Sancta Ecclesia* against which I know I will never prevail. I am laughing at these fools... Ha, ha, hee, hee!

"There is no doubt that the Harlot of Babylon, described by the son of Zebedee in the Apocalypse, is real and not fiction. But it is *not* the *Sancta Ecclesia Catholica* I can bet you. Fools! You take a look at Martin Luther's legacy, and the snowballing effect of his followers' insistence on 'independent thinking' - I mean the ever-burgeoning number of Christian sects - and hazard a guess yourself!

"The fools! As if these things were not foretold. This is what the Deliverer Himself said when he delivered His Sermon on the Mount: 'Beware of false prophets, who come to you in the clothing of sheep, but inwardly they are ravening wolves. By their fruits you shall know them. Do men gather grapes of thorns, or figs of thistles? Even so every good tree bringeth forth good fruit, and the evil tree bringeth forth evil fruit. A good tree cannot bring forth evil fruit, neither can an evil tree bring forth good fruit. Every tree that bringeth not forth good fruit, shall be cut down, and shall be cast into the fire. Wherefore by their fruits you shall know them. Not every one that saith to me, Lord, Lord, shall enter into the kingdom of heaven: but he that doth the will of my Father who is in heaven, he shall enter into the kingdom of heaven. Many will say to me in that day: Lord, Lord, have not we prophesied in thy name, and cast out devils in thy name, and done many miracles in thy name? And then will I profess unto them, I never knew you: depart from me, you that work iniquity.' (Matthew 7:15-23)

"And as if John had not warned thusly in his first epistle: 'Dearly beloved, believe not every spirit, but try the spirits if they be of God: because many false prophets are gone out into the world. By this is the spirit of God known. Every spirit which confesseth that Jesus Christ is come in the flesh, is of God: And every spirit that dissolveth Jesus, is not of God: and this is Antichrist, of whom you have heard that he cometh, and he is now already in the world. You are of God, little children, and have overcome him. Because greater is he that is in you, than he that is in the world. They are of the world: therefore of the world they speak, and the world heareth them. We are of God. He that knoweth God, heareth us. He that is not of God, heareth us not. By this we know the spirit of truth, and the spirit of error.' (1 John 4:1-6)

"And then this from the first pope in his second Epistle: 'But there were also false prophets among the people, even as there shall be among you lying teachers, who shall bring in sects of perdition, and deny the Lord who bought them: bringing upon themselves swift destruction. And many shall follow their riotousnesses, through whom the way of truth shall be evil spoken of. And through covetousness shall they with feigned words make merchandise of you. Whose judgment now of a long time lingereth not, and their perdition slumbereth not.' (2 Peter 2:1-3)

"But it didn't all start with the good German friar. Luke describes how 'the apostles and elders, with the whole church, decided to choose some of their own men and send them to Antioch with Paul and Barnabas' (in what was undoubtedly the first 'Ecumenical Council' to counter the first heresy in the *Sancta Ecclesia Catholica*: 'For as much as we have heard, that some going out from us have troubled you with words, subverting your souls; to whom we gave no commandment.' (Acts 15:24)

"When humans, created in the Image, partake of the sacraments, they are transformed by virtue of the divine graces merited by the Deliverer through His death on the cross, and become more pleasing to the Prime Mover. Well, as the Father of Lies and the Father of Death, I work very hard to ensure that humans do not get to be recipients of the holy sacraments through which they would be sanctified and transformed into creatures that are once more pleasing to their Maker; and to get them to become instruments of lies and of death; so that, instead of becoming like the Prime Mover in whose image they are created, they become like me and expose their souls to everlasting damnation thereby. And I have become pretty skillful at getting the fools to lie and murder in the Prime Mover's name! With humans inclined to sin, and not in a position to do good on their own without the help of the Prime Mover's grace, that has not been hard to do at all.

"All it takes is to tickle their sense of pride, which by the way is almost always inflated, and also their egomania or self-love - yes the 'self-love' to which all humans, with the exception of a few really true mystics who are into the practice of constantly denying themselves, are wedded - even though, as the clever Cicero put it, *'sui amantes sine rivali'* (lovers of themselves without rivals are doomed in the end to failure)! And I then get them to drum up a willful, virulent and hell-bent sense of righteousness, in the exact same way I did with the scribes and Pharisees who brought a woman they had caught in the act of committing adultery to the Deliverer. If these 'blinded guides' and 'hypocrites' (as the Deliverer called them) had been truthful, they would also have taken the trouble to round up and bring along all the customers of that broad; but they were not concerned with being truthful, as that would have resulted in some if not all those selfsame scribes and Pharisees being exposed. One reason they became bent on getting their Deliverer, whom even the callous Pontius Pilate, 'a man doubtless of corrupt principles and irreligious life' (see Ann Wroe. Pontius Pilate New York: Random House, 1999), recognized from the available evidence as being indeed the '*Iēsus Nazarēnus, Rēx Iūdaeōrum*', was the fact that the Nazarene very nearly exposed them when He stooped down and started scribbling their sins in the sand!

"The Pharisees and Sadducees would later again approach the Deliverer to tempt Him some more; and they asked that He show them a sign from heaven. The Deliverer said in response: 'A wicked and adulterous generation seeketh after a sign, and a sign shall not be given it, but the sign of Jonas the prophet...' (Matthew 16:1-4) And that had also prompted the Deliverer to warn His disciples saying: 'Beware of the leaven of the Pharisees and Sadducees...' (Matthew 16:6)

"Members of the sects of the Pharisees and the Sadducees heard the 'Word of God' directly from the mouth of the Deliverer. But they preferred to remain in their comfort zones and balked at jumping on the bandwagon and embracing the Sancta Ecclesia He established on the rock called Peter with the words: *'Tu es Petrus et super hanc petram aedificabo ecclesiam meam. Tibi dabo claves regni caelorum...'* (You are Peter and on this rock I will build my Church, to you I will give the keys of the kingdom of heaven.' (Matthew 16:18) The same pretty much applied to members of the sect of the Essenes, notwithstanding their fascination for asceticism, frugality and dedication to scholarship.

"Following the destruction of the temple by the Romans in A.D. 70, Pharisaic beliefs became the foundational, liturgical and ritualistic basis for Rabbinic Judaism. The temple's destruction also pretty much spelled the end of the sect of the Sadducees. And the Essenes are in the news thanks to the discovery of the Dead Sea Scrolls. I am the devil, and I am fully committed to ensuring that the fate of the bible believers doesn't turn out any differently.

"The common thread among members of all these sects is that they all have this tendency to forget what the Deliverer said, namely: *'Non vos me elegistis, sed ego elegi vos, et posui vos ut eatis, et fructum afferatis, et fructus vester maneat: ut quodcumque petieritis Patrem in nomine meo, det vobis.'* (You did not choose me, but I chose you and appointed you so that you might go and bear fruit—fruit that will last—and so that whatever you ask in my name the Father will give you.) (John 15:16). And you'd better believe me when I say that I am heavily invested in helping all such folks to act just as the Pharisees and Sadducees did, namely tempt the Deliverer by 'asking for a sign from heaven'! And those 'folks' include all those nominal Catholics who balk at heeding the Deliverer's advice to the rich man that he sell all his possessions, hand the proceeds to the poor and follow the Deliverer! (Matthew 19:21)"

Mjomba suspected that the Devil was up to something, and he stopped writing to reflect. On reflection, Mjomba conceded that he was one of those 'nominal Catholics' alright. He wasn't living like St. Francis of Assisi, and the devil knew it; and, to make things worse, he was dreaming about turning his thesis - which was about saving souls - eventually into a money-spinning enterprise!

Actually, up until the moment the Evil One decided to cast the net really wide so as to include him, Mjomba was delighted with the arguments that the Ruler of the Underworld had been advancing in order to damn the bible believers. He thought that those arguments were both brilliant and irrefutable, and that they justified his otherwise reckless gambit in flirting with that former Angel of Light. And, predictably, the last thing Mjomba now wanted to do was dwell on the fact that even he, Mjomba, was in jeopardy as well and possibly to the same extent as the souls of the bible believers!

Mjomba was therefore ready to get back to the task of committing the ideas that were inundating his mind in hopes that their author would change the subject and begin pontificating on something else. But the devil was determined not to let him off the hook so easily! What followed was momentary; but it might as well have lasted an eon. Apparently to show that he was in charge, the devil used the opening to actually do to the seminarian what he did to the apostle who hailed from Kerioth. Mjomba blacked out; and before he knew it, to use the words of the New Testament, the Evil Ghost had to all intents and purposes *entered him*.

Even though he was a seminarian who was still yearning to be ordained a priest, Mjomba was dreaming of striking it rich once his thesis on Original Virtue which he was crafting with the help of Beelzebub had taken

548

shape. He was already seeing limitless opportunities of exploiting what he was already describing to his fellow seminarians as the "Untold Story of Adam and Eve and their Descendants" to make millions for himself. And with the millions, he was going to show boundless generosity by using some of it to build schools and churches, and he had no doubt that some of those schools would end up bearing his name for good measure.

Perhaps it was these ideas churning freely in his head that precipitated the strange feeling; and, lo and behold, Mjomba suddenly came to grips with the fact that his cognitive faculties had sank to a level that was so low, he started to fear the worst - that he was turning into (of all things) a zombie. He felt as though his faculties of reason and free will had been hijacked by whoever or whatever, and that something else was in charge and dictating his thoughts and actions!

It suddenly dawned on him that the ideas churning in his mind were exactly like the ideas that drove Judas to lament that the ointment that Mary was lavishing on the Deliverer as he reclined on the table with Lazarus in Bethany could be sold and the money given to the poor!

Then something jolted him back to his senses. It was the thought that his scheme for exploiting the Sacred Scriptures to get rich was as bad if not worse than Judas' disappointment with Martha's sister Mary for taking out the pint of pure nard and pouring in on the person of the Deliverer with the result that Lazarus's house was filled with the fragrance of the expensive perfume! And if his actions could rival those of Judas in that regard, it followed and was as plain as day that he, Mjomba, could be tempted to betray the Deliverer with a treacherous kiss for thirty pieces of silver - just as the disciple from Kerioth did on the night the Deliverer instituted the sacrament of the Holy Eucharist.

Mjomba did what fallen humans in his situation would do, namely look for something to distract him from his sinful thoughts so his conscience wouldn't continue to nag him. He calmly picked up the pen which had momentarily slipped from his hand and resumed his role as the Infernal One's scribe.

But unfortunately for Mjomba, the Ruler of the Underworld World, intent on making him commit the sin of despair, simply picked up where he had left off at the time Mjomba fell into a swoon. The Evil One continued to damn both bible believers and lukewarm Catholics alike - including his scribe - using passages from the Sacred Scriptures. Mjomba felt that he had no choice but to play along; and so he went on writing exactly as prompted by Satan.

"And note that when the Deliverer said: *'Tu es Petrus, et super hanc petram Aedificabo Ecclesiam meam, Et portae inferi non praevalebunt adversus eam...*(You are Peter, and on this rock I will build my church, and the gates of hell will not prevail against it...), He was talking about His *Sancta Ecclesia*, and not about *members* of the *Sancta Ecclesia* who, even as His followers or 'Christians', would still continue to enjoy the unfettered freedom to employ their gifts of the intellect and freewill, and would therefore remain up 'for grabs'!

"You've got to give me and my fellow demons here in the Underworld credit for succeeding in deluding hordes to imagine that they become 'saved' and are 'safe' just by virtue of reciting the 'Sinner's Prayer'! Haa, haa, haa, hee, hee, hee, hah, hah, hah!

"Our own pride had also blinded us to the fact that, fashioned in the image of the Prime Mover, humans, unlike brutes that only function with the help of their instincts and endowed with a soul in addition to a physical body and despite their failings, were something quite special; and that as a result the Word, through whom all things were made and without whom nothing was made that has been made (John 1:3, Ephesians 1:10 and Colossians 1:16), could actually choose to become a human while retaining His divine nature and even dwell among humans! (John 1:14) It would not have made any sense for the Word, a pure spirit and a divinity at that, to become an angel - a created spirit!

"It should have clicked that the way humans were created - with a soul that (in the words of the Angelic Doctor) was an incorporeal, immaterial, incorruptible subsistent and a physical corruptible body meant that humans were quite richly endowed in that sense and possibly even superior to those of us who were created pure spirits at least in their blueprint or design. They were certainly capable of doing things we angelic beings just couldn't if we tried. Moreover all humans not only shared in that same nature (consisting of the corruptible 'body' and the incorruptible 'soul'); but, created in the image of the Prime Mover, meant that those 'bodies', as Paul pointed out, effectively became 'temples of the Holy Spirit'. (1 Corinthians 6:19-20, 1 Corinthians 3:16-17, 1 Corinthians 12:27, Philippians 1:20 and Romans 12:1-8)

"Humans, all of them enjoying the same 'human nature' consisting of a soul and a body, can therefore be contrasted to angels that have each one its own distinctive nature and one that subsists only in the spiritual realm at that. I envy humans in one particular respect. By making them 'male and female' (Genesis 5:2) in addition to being made in His own image and likeness, He was making provision for humans to participate in the act of creation with regard to the generations of humans that would follow in the footsteps of Adam and Eve! Not surprisingly, He subsequently would also provide for those humans who would follow in the footsteps of the Deliverer to become 'partakers of Christ'. (Hebrews 3:14). Just imagine if we pure spirits also had been able to 'procreate'! I do not know about Michael, Rafael, Gabriel and the other 'good angels'; but I would only have been too glad to use such an opportunity to boost the number of my 'troops' here in Gehenna - I mean the numbers of demons! Regretfully my minions amongst humans do not think along these same lines. Just imagine the things we would be able to do if we too had been endowed with bodies like humans!

"The Word, through whom everything was created and apart from whom nothing that exists came into being (John 1;3) and who indeed would Himself become flesh (John 1:14), chose in His infinite wisdom to fashion the human body the way He did (with a head, brains and a protective skull, a torso, two ears, a nose with two nostrils, two eyes just below the eyebrows to help humans dodge obstacles in their path and also serve as windows of the soul, a mouth or alimentary canal that receives food and produces saliva, a neck, two lungs, one heart or muscular organ that pumps blood through the blood vessels and also signals the end of a human's sojourn on earth when it stops beating, two hands, two legs and two feet that come with toes and toe nails and enable humans to jay walk, etc.). He could have easily made humans capable of growing wings enabling them to take off and become airborne like crows and kites; in which case humans would be spending all their time frocking in the sky (like some birds do) when they should be working the fields to grow food; or using their heads to invent tractors and bicycles, automobiles and airplanes as has been the case to transport excess produce in one part of the world to other parts of the world that were under the threat of famine because of floods, droughts and other natural disasters. Of course, the minds of humans have, with my help, become so warped that many in so-called advanced nations today, working in concert with their allies, have no scruples imposing embargoes and things of that sort on other nations that won't cast votes in favor of their resolutions at the United Nations, and deliberately causing many in the embargoed countries to starve to death, giving new meaning to the term 'Evil Empire'! Hee! Hee! Hee! Ha! Ha! Ha! Ha!

"But He could also have designed the human body differently had He so wished. He could have made humans as big as the now extinct large-bodied sauropod dinosaurs that are reputedly the largest land animals of all time! But those 'human' dinosaurs would probably be already teetering on the verge of extinction because that size alone would have conceivably compounded problems associated with provision of things like housing, transportation, education, and other basic amenities. Regardless, so long as those human dinosaurs were created in the Prime Mover's image, those giant human bodies of theirs would have remained temples of the Holy Ghost; and 'humans' would even then have remained very special creatures in the same way they now are. But humans definitely have reason to thank the Prime Mover that they were created the way they were.

"After all is said and done, the Prime Mover, conceiving of human nature in eternity, designed it so that a divinity, His only begotten Son, could take it up and dwell among humans if He so chose. The mystery of the incarnation is and will remain a mystery in so far as all of us created beings are concerned. But it still signals an act of infinite love on the part of the Prime Mover for His creatures in general and for humans in particular. The canticle of canticles enunciated by the Deliverer's immaculately conceived virgin mother and now alas also the mediatrix of all the graces that flow to humans, encapsulates that relationship between the Prime Mover and humans; and it does not just makes all of us here in the Pit envious as hell of you humans; it is the driving force behind our desire for your downfall. To escape our tentacles, humans must needs pray unceasingly that Emmanuel, so meek and humble of heart Himself, deigns to make their hearts, so mired in selfishness, like unto His own heart.

"Humans should also be grateful that the Prime Mover created the universe in which they find themselves the way He did - the sun, moon and stars which function in concert with the round shape of the earth to assure that there is daylight and also that there is nightfall (which permits humans to take a nap and recharge), and which together also make seasons on earth possible; vegetation that includes things like bananas that humans can feed on when they ripen; and even alligators, lions and spitting cobras (creatures whose habits ensure that humans remember to say their morning, afternoon and evening prayers).

"One thing that is common to both humans and us pure spirits is the relationship between 'nature' (or 'essence') and 'existence'. When the Prime Mover causes a creature with either an angelic nature or a human nature to bounce into existence, He does it by specifically giving an existence to the angelic or human nature. One obvious result is that the created 'angel' or 'human' will *owe* its existence to the Prime Mover. In the case of humans, because he made them male and female (Genesis 5:2, Mark 10:6 and Matthew 19:4), the Prime Mover uses one generation of humans to 'beget' or 'procreate' members of the next one. Still, that action on the part of the Prime Mover causes a *distinct* and *unique* creature (regardless of whether it is an angel or a human) to come into existence; and this is true for humans notwithstanding the fact that they all share the same human nature.

"Just imagine if angels and humans had not been brought into existence as unique and distinct creatures! The Prime Mover would not have been able to assign to them any responsibilities, and He would also not have been in a position to punish or reward them for their actions, the fact that they were created in His image and likeness notwithstanding! This would also have deprived the Prime Mover's decision to bring us pure spirits and humans (and by extension the rest of the 'world') into existence of any real purpose.

"And so then, because human nature was created so 'special', it followed that each and every creature that came into existence as a human had also to be very special in the Prime Mover's eyes! This is just so extraordinary! This means that, in the Prime Mover's eyes, the riffraff and all those who belong to the 'basket of deplorables' (in some peoples' eyes) are as valuable as members of royalty! A hundred and fifty-year-old infirm 'wretch' in some nondescript nation who is so feeble she needs assistance with everything she does and a month-old malnourished human fetus in its famished mother's womb are as important in the Prime Mover's eyes as Gaius Julius Caesar was at the height of his fame! Yeah, Gaius Julius Caesar who was born into a patrician family – the gens Julia - which claimed descent from Julus, son of the legendary Trojan prince Aeneas, supposedly the son of the goddess Venus!

"And that was, of course, the crux of the matter with regard to our own rebellion. We went out on a limb and tried to challenge the Prime Mover. We believed - or wanted to believe - that we ourselves were extra special. Mere angels and creatures that were brought into existence gratuitously at that, we still wanted to usurp His power and be like Him! And in our muddled reasoning at the time, we had even ruled out the possibility that the Prime Mover could cause to come into existence creatures that were also fashioned in His own image and likeness, but were not pure spirits like us!

"But in the meantime, we thought that it was presumptuous and really brazen on the Prime Mover's part to demand that we, pure spirits, not only acknowledge the *Perichoresis* (the relationship of the three persons of the triune God) and that the Father, Son and Holy Spirit are coequal, but also require even us who were ourselves pure spirits like 'Them', to never stop saying without resting: '*Holy, holy, holy is the Lord God Almighty, who was, and is, and is to come…You are worthy, our Lord and God, to receive glory and honor and power, for you created all things, and by your will they were created and have their being.*' (Revelation 4:5-11)

"Contrast that with the meekness and humility of the Son of Man, the Word become flesh. While we ourselves bragged about being pure spirits and pined for the impossible, namely to be co-equal with the Prime

Mover, Christ Jesus, who, though he was in the form of God, did not count equality with God a thing to be grasped, but emptied himself, by taking the form of a servant, being born in the likeness of men. And being found in human form, he humbled himself by becoming obedient to the point of death, even death on a cross. (Philippians 2:5-11 and Hebrews 4:12). And this even though humans have, ever since the fall of Adam and Eve, not tired of scheming up ways to debase those temples of the Holy Spirit (1 Corinthians 6:19, Romans 12:1-8 and 1 Corinthians 3:16-18); not to mention the manner in which humans, with our assistance, have treated each other through the ages, particularly when the target of their displeasure and vindictiveness was itself defenseless. The thing, now though, is that those humans who are dealt with underhandedly by their fellow humans are now in very good company - the company of the Son of Man. The Deliverer was Himself hounded by the corrupt and wicked Herod the Great as an infant; and then, in obedience to His Father in heaven, He agreed to suffer untold indignities under Pontius Pilate, after being roundly accused by the 'teachers of the law' (who should themselves have known better) of claiming to be what He was, namely Emmanuel meaning 'God is with us' (Isaiah 7:14, Isaiah 8:8 and Matthew 1:22-23), and to give up His Ghost at the premature age of thirty-three.

"As for humans maltreating those they loathe or despise, we naturally do extend them our 'assistance' as they go about doing their darndest to make the lives of other folks hard. To understand the nature and extent of the 'assistance' that we offer in this regard, you should check out what the Deliverer told the Pharisees when they suggested that He was demon possessed. (John

8:44, John 10:20, Matthew 12:24 and Luke 11:15)

"Look, we enter and possess them and they welcome it! Except that the fools as a rule are so obsessed with the ephemeral and the now, they do not realize that I, Beelzebub, have entered and possessed them and the dire implications of that (demon possession) until the time they are kicking the bucket! This was exactly the case with the Pharisees who kept bragging that Abraham was their father even as the Deliverer was assuring them that they were completely mine! (John 8:33-39)

"Just as it was the case with us demons, humans who are puffed up with pride also have this tendency to look down on and to devalue other humans who do not look exactly like themselves. Yeah, humans who do that obviously value and accordingly crave to belong in our company!

"But whilst pain and suffering and, indeed, death itself have been sanctified by the Word made flesh, those humans who shortchange their fellow humans and do not have any scruples about causing others grief will still have a case to answer. (Matthew 5:1-10, Luke 11:37–52, Matthew 23:1-39, etc.) And as Isaiah wrote: 'There is no peace,' says the Lord, 'for the wicked.' John, describing the New Heaven and the New Earth, wrote in the Apocalypse: 'And he that sat on the throne, said: Behold, I make all things new. And he said to me: Write. For these words are most faithful and true. And he said to me: It is done. I am Alpha and Omega: the Beginning and the End. To him that thirsteth, I will give of the fountain of the water of life, freely. He that shall overcome shall possess these things. And I will be his God: and he shall be my son. But the fearful and unbelieving and the abominable and murderers and whoremongers and sorcerers and idolaters and all liars, they shall have their portion in the pool burning with fire and brimstone, which is the second death." (Revelation 21:5-8)

"In the meantime, if humans are looking for evidence that the love of the Prime Mover for them is infinite, there they have it. He so loved the world that He gave His only begotten Son: that whosoever believeth in him may not perish, but may have life everlasting. He sent not his Son into the world, to judge the world: but that the world may be saved by Him. (John 3:16-17, Romans 5:6-11, John 3:16-21 and Genesis 22:1-10) And in obedience to His Father, the Son of man gave His life for the salvation of humans on the cross; and He now invites humans to feast on His sacred body and sacred blood in what today is an unending sacrifice of the Holy Eucharist at which His death on Mt. Calvary is re-enacted.

"The sacrifice on the altar whenever Holy Mass is celebrated, and that includes Masses that are celebrated in side altars out of view, far from being symbolic or merely a commemoration of the Deliverer's passion and death on Mt. Calvary two thousand years ago, is for real. Ask any of the Church's mystics and stigmatists who, as Paul put it, rejoice in their sufferings for the Deliverer's sake and in their flesh fill up what is lacking in the sufferings of Christ on behalf of His body which is the Church. (Colossians 1:24) Ask St. Rita of Cascia (1381 – 22 May 1457), the 'saint of the thorn' who became the 'saint of the rose' and whose body has remained incorrupt over the centuries. *You can catch her on 22nd May (her Feast Day).* Or ask St. Padre Pio (25 May 1887 – 23 September 1968). *You can catch him on September 23 (his Feast Day).* His response when someone inquired if the stigmata were painful was in the form of a question: 'Do you think the Lord gave them to me for a decoration?'

"The opening prayer for the Mass on the Feast of the Stigmata of St. Francis of Assisi, which is celebrated on the September 17th, says it all: '*Lord Jesus Christ, who reproduced in the flesh of the most blessed Francis, the sacred marks of your own sufferings, so that in a world grown cold our hearts might be filled with burning love of you, graciously enable us by his merits and prayers to bear the cross without faltering and to bring forth worthy fruits of penitence: You who are God, living and reigning with God the Father, in the unity of the Holy Spirit, for ever and ever. Amen.*'

"Around the time of the Feast of the Exaltation of the Cross, Francis had gone with two other friars to the remote mountaintop of Mt. La Verna (also known as Mt. Alverna) for the purpose of observing the forty-day fast in preparation for the Feast of Saints Michael, Gabriel, and Raphael and the Feast of the Archangels. While Brother Francis was in prayer, he had vision in which he saw a Seraph with six fiery and shining wings descend from the height of heaven. And when in swift flight the Seraph had reached a spot in the air near the man of God, there appeared between the wings the figure of a man crucified, with his hands and feet extended in the form of a cross and fastened to a cross. Two of the wings were lifted above his head, two were extended for flight and two covered his whole body. In the words of Brother Elias (who was the Minister General of the Franciscan Order at the time of St. Francis' death), Brother Francis saw a vision of a seraph, a six-winged angel on a cross.

Thomas of Celano, one of the first disciples of the saint and regarded as the author of *Dies Irae*, wrote that the marks of nails began to appear in Brother Francis's hands and feet, just as he had seen them in the vision. The saint also endured the pain from a fifth wound in his side.

"St. Bonaventure, the Seraphic Doctor who is credited with structuring and renewing the Franciscan Order and a contemporary of Thomas Aquinas, would write in his *Itinerarium Mentis in Deum* (The Soul's Journey into God) as follows: 'If you wish to know how these things may come about, ask grace, not learning; desire, not the understanding; the groaning of prayer, not diligence in reading; the Bridegroom, not the teacher; God, not man; darkness, not clarity; not light, but the fire that wholly inflames and carries one into God through transporting unctions and consuming affections. God Himself is this fire, and His furnace is in Jerusalem; and it is Christ who enkindles it in the white flame of His most burning Passion. This fire he alone truly perceives who says: My soul chooseth hanging, and my bones, death. He who loves this death can see God, for it is absolutely true that Man shall not see me and live...' (Excerpt from Chapter Seven: About the Mystical Transport of the Mind in which Rest is Given to the Intellect after our Affection passes over totally into God through Ecstasy. Translation by Simon Wickham-Smith, Leipzig, Christmas 2005)

"St. Bonaventure, who is not referred to as the 'Prince of Mystics' entirely for nothing, was apparently gifted with the exact same vision as Brother Francis had, and in the same venue (Mt. La Verna); and he describes it in the Prologue to *Itinerarium Mentis in Deum* as follows

(Translation by Philotheus Boehner, O.F.M., Ph. D): 'Inspired by the example of our blessed father, Francis, I sought after this peace with yearning soul - sinner that I am and all unworthy, yet seventh successor as Minister to all the brethren in the place of the blessed father after his death. It happened that, thirty-three years after the death of the Saint, about the time of his passing, moved by a divine impulse, I withdrew to Mount Alverno as to a place of quiet, there to satisfy the yearning of my soul for peace. While I abode there, pondering on certain spiritual ascents to God, there occurred to me, among other things, that miracle which in this very place had happened to the blessed Francis - the vision he received of the winged seraph in the form of the Crucified. As I reflected on this marvel, it immediately seemed to me that this vision suggested the uplifting of Saint Francis in contemplation and that it pointed out the way by which that state of contemplation can be reached.

'The six wings of the seraph can be rightly understood as signifying the six uplifting illuminations by which the soul is disposed, as by certain grades or steps, to pass over to peace through the ecstatic transports of Christian wisdom. The road to this peace is through nothing else than a most ardent love of the Crucified, the love which so transformed Paul into Christ when he was rapt to the third heaven that he declared: With Christ I am nailed to the Cross. It is now no longer I that live, but Christ lives in me. And this love so absorbed the soul of Francis too that his spirit shone through his flesh the last two years of his life, when he bore the most holy marks of the Passion in his body. The figure of the six wings of the

Seraph, therefore, brings to mind the six steps of illumination which begin with creatures and lead up to God, Whom no one rightly enters save through the Crucified. For he who enters not by the door, but climbs up another way, is a thief and a robber. But if anyone enter by this door, he shall go in and out, and shall find pastures. For this reason Saint John writes in the Apocalypse: Blessed are they who wash their robes in the blood of the Lamb, that they may have the right to the tree of life, and that by the gates they may enter into the city. That is to say, no one can enter by contemplation into the heavenly Jerusalem unless he enters through the blood of the Lamb as through a door. For no one is in any way disposed for divine contemplations that lead to spiritual transports unless, like the prophet Daniel, he is also a man of desires. Now such desires are enkindled in us in two ways: through the outcries of prayer, which makes us groan from anguish of heart, and through the refulgence of speculation by which our mind most directly and intently turns itself toward the rays of light.

'Wherefore, it is to groans of prayer through Christ Crucified, in whose blood we are cleansed from the filth of vices, that I first of all invite the reader. Otherwise he may come to think that mere reading will suffice without unction, speculation without devotion, investigation without admiration, observation without exultation, industry without piety, knowledge without love, understanding without humility, study without divine grace, the mirror without divinely inspired wisdom. To those, therefore, who are already disposed by divine grace, to the humble and pious, to the contrite and devout, to those who are anointed with the oil of gladness, to the lovers of divine wisdom and to those inflamed with a desire for it, to those who wish to give themselves to glorifying, admiring, and even savoring God - to those I propose the following considerations. At the same time, I wish to warn them that the mirror of the external world put before them is of little or no avail unless the mirror of our soul has been cleansed and polished. First, then, 0 man of God, arouse in yourself remorse of conscience before you raise your eyes to the rays of divine Wisdom reflected in its mirrors, lest perchance from the very beholding of these rays you fall into a more perilous pit of darkness.'

"St. John Paul II, the most travelled pope in history whose remains are interred in the marble altar in the Chapel of St. Sebastian which is next to the Chapel of the Pietà, the Chapel of the Blessed Sacrament, appropriately wrote in his Encyclical Letter *Ecclesia De Eucharistia*: 'From the perpetuation of the sacrifice of the Cross and her communion with the body and blood of Christ in the Eucharist, the Church draws the spiritual power needed to carry out her mission. The Eucharist thus appears as both the *source* and the summit of all evangelization, since its goal is the communion of mankind with Christ and in him with the Father and the Holy Spirit.'

"The Church teaches that the Eucharistic 'Sacrifice of the true Body and Blood of Christ' on the altar (known as Holy Mass) is a 'true and proper sacrifice'; and the Council of Trent made this crystal clear when it declared: 'If any one saith that in the Mass a true and proper sacrifice is not offered to God; or, that to be offered is nothing else but that Christ is given us to eat; let him be anathema.' (Council of Trent, Sess. XXII, can. 1) And as the Bull *Apostolicae Cuare* promulgated on September 13, 1896 by Pope Leo XIII (the first Pope to be filmed by a motion picture camera and also the first pope whose voice was captured on a sound recording) made clear, the validity of the celebrant's priestly orders is of crucial importance.

"The Church makes a clear distinction between the words 'Sacrifice of the Mass' and 'Sacrament of the Eucharist' which performs the function of a sacrament that is intended for the sanctification of the soul and the function of a sacrifice that serves primarily to glorify God by adoration, thanksgiving, prayer, and expiation. The Sacrifice of the Eucharistic Christ is in its nature a transient action, while the 'Sacrament of the Altar' continues as something permanent after the sacrifice, and can even be preserved in monstrance and ciborium. Noteworthy is also the fact that the Sacrifice of the Mass requires the two forms of bread and wine (the symbolic separation of the Body and Blood), the mystical slaying of the victim; whereas Holy Communion received only in one form constitutes the reception of the whole sacrament. (*Vide* Catholic Encyclopedia: Sacrifice of the Mass).

"According to the Catechism of the Church, the mode of Christ's presence under the Eucharistic species is unique. It raises the Eucharist above all the sacraments as 'the perfection of the spiritual life and the end to which all the sacraments tend'. In the most blessed sacrament of the Eucharist 'the body and blood, together with the soul and divinity, of our Lord Jesus Christ and, therefore, *the whole Christ is truly, really, and substantially contained*'. This presence is called 'real' - by which is not intended to exclude the other types of presence as if they could not be 'real' too, but because it is presence in the fullest sense: that is to say, it is a *substantial* presence by which Christ, God and man, makes himself wholly and entirely present. (CCC 1374)

"John while exiled on the island of Patmos was given a glimpse of what occurs at Mass; and to say that he found the spectacle very moving would be an understatement. (Revelation 5:1-14 and Revelation 19:1-8) Now, grasping that fact - that the Second Person of the Holy Trinity became meek and humble of heart to that extent - is still something even I still struggle with. That is even though I am more knowledgeable in matters of theology than all the doctors of the Church combined.

"The way King Herod, who ordered the execution of James and then sought to be treated as a divinity, ended up (Acts 12:1-23) was in a way reminiscent of the way we ourselves met our fate after we made the unforgivable error of trying to unseat the Prime Mover. A created human, King Herod had (with our help) lulled himself into believing that he was exempt from following his God-given conscience and from keeping the ten commandments (as was expected of all other humans), including the commandment that thou shalt love thy Lord, thy God with all thy heart, and with all thy soul, and with all thy mind, and as well the other 'great' commandment that states that thou shalt love thy neighbour as thyself

(Matthew 22:35-40, Mark 12:28-34, and Luke 10:27); and, the fact that the Prime Mover is infinitely merciful notwithstanding, the nervy, murderous, foul-mouthed, and alas also blasphemous Herod ended up being eaten alive by worms as punishment! The stupid fool - just what did he think after what happened to us?

"We`ve of course made it our job to try and ensure that other humans do not learn anything from King Herod's fate! The problem with humans is that, while they are babies (innocents), they accept that the existence they find themselves enjoying on this earth is gratuitous courtesy of an infinitely loving and gracious Prime Mover. But then, as adolescence starts to set in, their minds become warped, and they start forgetting that the existence they enjoy *is* in fact a gratuitous one. Some even start imagining that they might have evolved from brutes! But above all, the fact that their existence on earth is a timed one starts to recede to the back of their minds; and they wake up to that fact again when it is too late - when they see that they actually *are* about to kick the proverbial bucket! Now it would be tantamount to a dereliction of duty on my part as Ruler of the Underworld and I would be remiss if I did not marshal my forces and moved in to exploit these egregious vulnerabilities in the human psyche to the max!

"The Deliverer was right when He warned that death sneaks upon humans like a thief in the middle of the night. (Luke 21:34-35, Luke 12:35-40, Matthew 25:13, Mark 13:32-35, Revelation 3:3, Revelation 16:15 and 1 Thessalonians 5:2-6) And Peter describes what exactly happens at the time humans kick the bucket. He describes the sensations humans have as they start to cross the gulf that separates the living from the dead. The dying human senses the heavens passing away with great noise, and he/she suddenly notices the elements melting with what appears to be fervent heat; and in that moment for the dying person both the earth and the works that are in it become incinerated and literally go up in flames in front of his/her very eyes. (2 Peter 3:10) Humans realize, too late, in that moment that their preoccupation in life with the ephemeral and investment in the temporal were nothing short of wasted effort!

"But that is not all. It is the preoccupation with the passing ungodly things of this world - the obsession with the 'Now' as though there was no 'Tomorrow' - that inhibits you humans from responding in kind to the Prime Mover and loving Him with all your heart, soul, mind, and strength and your neighbors as yourselves as you are supposed to, and that sets you on the path to perdition - you idiots! (Deuteronomy 6:4-7, Mark 12:30, Matthew 22:37 and Luke 10:27). That is exactly right; for what shall it profit a man, if he gain the whole world, and suffer the loss of his soul? Or what shall a man give in exchange for his soul? (Mark 8:36-37)

"This is so sad really. After Adam and Eve fell from grace, humans lost it. And yet, because the Word became flesh and then overcame death with His resurrection from the dead, death, the curse of sin, was undone; and a path to beatific vision for those humans who would follow in the footsteps of the Anointed One was opened.

"While humans still die the death, they too now are slated to rise from the dead at the end of time. Thus the Deliverer in one fell swoop has, with His death on Calvary and subsequent resurrection from the dead three days later, put humans on a new physical and spiritual plane.

They now not only can partake of the Deliverer's body and blood whilst on earth during the Eucharistic celebration, but their bodies, now perishable, are going to be brought back to life on the day of the Last Judgement. He who agreed to become the Second Adam, and who is the Bread of Life, will raise them up on the last day - exactly as Lazarus' sister, Martha, testified. (John 11:24). And that is how the Word succeeded in reclaiming those humans who opt to renounce me and my works and allurements as they avow at the time of their baptism.

"And talk about causing good to come out of evil: following the fall of Adam and Eve from grace, humans were promised a Deliverer, and He came; and now all humans have a shot at enjoying beatific vision in the company of the Deliverer and His immaculate virgin mother!

"Contrary to what they imagine, humans are not in this alone. As you can see they are in it together with the Word through whom all that was made came to be (John 1:3) and also their Deliverer, and with the Prime Mover (the Father) to whom they must needs pray for their daily bread, for the forgiveness of their trespasses, and for deliverance from all evil. (Matthew 5:1-13, Matthew 5:39, Matthew 6:13 and Matthew 13:19) And note that He used the words 'Give us this day our bread' and 'forgive us our trespasses' and not 'Give me this day my bread'. Yeah, the Deliverer taught humans to pray as one and to forget that they were Russians or Chinese or Americans or Cubans or Africans or Peruvians or Argentinians or Brazilians or El Salvadorians or Mexicans or Jamaicans or Haitians or Jews or Palestinians or Turks or Armenians or Indians or Pakistanis or Afghans or Persians or Saudis or Yemenis or Norwegians or Canadians or Spaniards or

French or Germans or Japanese or Swedes or Swiss or North Koreans or South Koreans or Filipinos or Indonesians or Fijians or Mauritians or Seychellois or Icelanders or Comorans or what have you!

"And then, above all, humans are also invited to be members of the Mystical Body of Christ. (John 15:5-8, John 15:7-12, John 15:13-15, John 15:16, Colossians 2:19, Ephesians 1:23, Ephesians 4:4-13, 1 Corinthians 10:17, 1 Corinthians 12:12, Luke 5:20-49 and the encyclical *Mystici Corporis Christi* {'The Mystical Body of Christ'} issued by Pope Pius XII on 29 June 1943)

"Of course, humans can dismiss all this as hogwash. The excuse is that it is I, Beelzebub and Father of Lies, they are hearing pontificate on these matters and not some archbishop; and that is exactly the result I was hoping for, dimwits! Humans as a rule prefer to wait to see for themselves. But look - even if a human ends up breaking the Guinness Book of Records for being the oldest person at the time he/she is kicking the bucket, the wait won't be really that long. A hundred and twenty years at the most! Ha, Ha, Ha, Hee, Hee, Hee!

"And then, last but not least, the memory of humans is really short. They easily forget that, having received the existence they enjoy gratuitously, following the fall from grace of Adam and Eve, on their own they are incapable of performing any good without the help of the graces earned for them by the Deliverer through His death on the cross! It is also the reason the Word, after He became flesh, established His *Sancta Ecclesia* through which He dispenses those graces - stupid. (Matthew 16:18, Ephesians 1:22 and Ephesians 5:25-32)

"And so, it is not enough for humans to wish that they eschew my whiles. (1 Peter 5:8) They must continuously pray for the graces that will enable them to carry their crosses (1 Thessalonians 5:16-18), and seek to enter by the narrow gate as wide is the gate, and broad is the way that leadeth to destruction, and many there are who go in there at. (Matthew 7:13-14) Not to flop down on one's knees to pray to the Prime Mover is to presume that one brought oneself into existence! And it is tantamount to presumption that one was one's own Prime Mover, and that there was no such a thing as Providence! That is exactly the sin we ourselves committed - dammit! We refused to genuflect. We refused to fall down before the throne upon our faces, and to adore the Prime Mover like that Michael, Gabriel, Rafael, and the rest of the angels were doing. (Revelation 5:13, Revelation 7:11, Revelation 22:8, Deuteronomy 32:43, Luke 2:13-14, Psalm 148:2 and Psalm 103:20)

"As if humans had not been commanded to also genuflect and worship! And even though they are sometimes incapable of thinking aright as a result of being conceived in Original Sin, they were still commended to pray; and actually the Deliverer went to great lengths to teach them how to pray and also how to receive the kingdom of the Prime Mover like children and to trust in Him amid their tribulations and distress. (Matthew 6:5-15, Mark 11:22-25, Luke 18:17 and John 16:33)

"You see, humans must learn to accept that machismo does not work with us here in the underworld. And hypocrisy is decidedly also a non-starter! (Luke 18:9-14) And humans also ought to keep reminding themselves that whoever exalts himself shall be humbled; and whoever humbles himself shall be exalted! (Matthew 23:12) Oh, goddamn humans!

"I have to swear because I am telling you what I am telling you under duress. This Mjomba fellow has somehow succeeded in tricking me to work for the salvation of souls instead of their damnation! The idiot and sleazebag! I swear that one way or another I will get even with him. You can bet that I will get my chance to avenge all this; and it will be sweet revenge indeed! Peter said as much in his very first encyclical. (1 Peter 5:8) Yeah, I have to avenge all this and pretty soon. The Geek! He ought to know that I, *Shai'tan*, will always have something else up my sleeve. As it is, I'm now risking turning my troops in the Underworld and even my minions amongst humans against me. And if they were to revolt, the battle between my forces - the forces of Evil - and the forces of Good would be as good as lost.

"But, dammit! The battle between the forces of Good and the forces of Evil revolves around the salvation of humans. Having successfully tempted Adam and Eve to sample the forbidden fruit resulting in their expulsion from Paradise, it would be unlike me, Beelzebub, if I did not now marshal my troops for the final putsch. The top item on our agenda must be to trick humans into believing that all this talk about their bodies being temples of the Holy Ghost is bolder dash! And the key to that is to keep them engaged with matters of this world so they don't even get time to say the *Pater Noster* (Our Father) and to pray continuously that their Father in Heaven never suffer them to fall into temptation. The Deliverer said: 'I am the way, and the truth, and the life. No man cometh to the Father, but by me.' (John 14:6) 'My kingdom is not of this world.' (John 18:36) And also: 'If any man will come after me, let him deny himself, and take up his cross, and follow me.' Matthew 16:24)

"To counter this salvific message of the Deliverer, my troops and I are committed to working to ensure that humans remain focused on things of this world - worldly riches, earthly pleasures and self-indulgence and, above all, on the idolatrous 'worship' of that very 'temple of the Holy Ghost' contrary to what the scriptures say. (1 John 2:16-17, Luke 8:14, Matthew 5:3-12, Luke 12:19-20, Luke 6:20-36, Colossians 3:5-10, 1 John 5:21, 1 Corinthians 5:11, James 4:3, James 5:5, Psalm 16:11, Psalm 149:4, Ecclesiastes 1:6, Ecclesiastes 2:1-11, Isaiah 47:8, 1 Timothy 5:6, 1 Timothy 6:17, 2 Timothy 2:22, 2 Timothy 3:1-5, 1 Thessalonians 4:3-4, 1 Corinthians 6:9-11, 1 Corinthians 6:18-20, 1 Corinthians 10:7-13, Romans 8:8, Romans 12-1, Romans 13:12-14, Galatians 2:20, Galatians 5:16-24, Hebrews 11:25, Hebrews 13:4, Hebrews 13:12-16, Ephesians 5:3, 1 Peter 4:3-4, 2 Peter 2:13-14, Titus 3:3, Proverbs 11:20, Proverbs 12:22 and Proverbs 21:17)

"The Deliverer used parables to describe the 'Kingdom of Heaven'; and at one point He compared it to a treasure that a man found hidden in a field. He hid it again, and then in his joy went and sold all he had and bought that field. (Matthew 13:44) Well, my troops and I must do everything in our power to get humans to believe that the hurdles they face in order to get at that 'treasure' are insurmountable. But I must also work hand in glove with my minions amongst humans to get them to place even more obstacles in the way of those who desire to own that 'treasure' for themselves.

"And there is something else that goes for us - Mammon! No man can serve two masters; for either he will hate the one, and love the other; or else he will hold to the one and despise the other. Humans cannot serve the Prime Mover and mammon. (Matthew 6:24) And humans are naturally greedy. We must therefore flash money - bundles of money - in front of their eyes continuously to catch their attention and sink them thereby.

"Look, before He died on the cross for the salvation of you humans, the Deliverer went out of his way to make his expectations crystal clear and unmistakable. Speaking to large multitudes, He said: 'Every one of you that doth not renounce all that he possesseth, cannot be my disciple...' (Luke 14:33). And again: 'If any man come to me, and hate not his father and mother and wife and children and brethren and sisters, yea and his own life also, he cannot be my disciple. And whosoever doth not carry his cross and come after me cannot be my disciple.' (Luke 14: 26-27). And again: 'Labor not for the meat which perisheth, but for that which endureth unto life everlasting, which the Son of man will give you. For him hath God, the Father, sealed.' (John 6:27)

"The bible believers and all those nominal Catholics - including you Mjomba - are all like the scribe who came to the Deliverer and avowed that he would follow Him whithersoever He would go. The Deliverer's response was: 'The foxes have holes, and the birds of the air nests; but the Son of man hath not where to lay his head.' (Luke 9:58 and Matthew 8:20). And the words of the Deliverer repudiating the Jews who thought that, because they were into 'searching the scriptures', they had life everlasting, when they would not come to the Deliverer that they may have life (John 5:1-47), apply to you all!

"The Deliverer and Word made flesh knew before the world existed that the crafty and scheming humans he would come to save from perdition would try every trick in the book - and with a little help from us here in the Underworld - to try to game the system and cheat their way into heaven instead of using their faculties of reason and free will to take up their crosses and follow him.

"Anticipating their machinations, He declared in the hours before He was apprehended on the orders of the chief priests and Pharisees and with the connivance of one of those He had chosen to be his apostle: '*Si non venissem, et locutus fuissem eis, peccatum non haberent: nunc autem excusationem non habent de peccato suo. Qui me odit, et Patrem meum odit. Si opera non fecissem in eis quæ nemo alius fecit, peccatum non haberent: nunc autem et viderunt, et oderunt et me, et Patrem meum. Sed ut adimpleatur sermo, qui in lege eorum scriptus est: Quia odio habuerunt me gratis...*' (If I had not come and spoken to them, they would not have sin: but now they have no excuse for their sin. He that hateth me hateth my Father also. If I had not done among them the works that no other man hath done, they would not have sin: but now they have both seen and hated both me and my Father. But that the word may be fulfilled which is written in their law: they hated me without cause...) (John 15:22-25)

"Yeah, I have even succeeded, in a short space of time, in persuading a countless number, almost a quarter of the Earth's population, first that the Deliverer never claimed to be the Son of God; and also that He did not rise up from the dead, and was a mere 'prophet'! And they should no doubt remind you of Thomas, one of the twelve, who was also called Didymus, who exclaimed 'Except I shall see in his hands the print of the nails, and put my finger into the place of the nails, and put my hand into his side, I will not believe!' upon being told by his buddies that the Deliverer not only had appeared to them, but He had even breathed on them and conferred upon them the Sacrament of Holy Orders, and had made them share in his own priesthood according to the order of Melchisedech thereby!

"As Paul (née Saul of Tarsus) wrote to the Corinthians (1 Corinthians 15:17): 'And if Christ be not risen again, your faith is vain, for you are yet in your sins.'

"And as regards Catholics, I have always worked hard and will continue to so do to ensure that they do not take advantage of the fact that they have the fullness of Truth to fortify themselves with the Prime Mover's graces and that they remain Catholics only in name. That will assure me of the pleasure of watching them thrown out of the divine banquet hall when the king goes in to see the guests and finds them without the 'wedding garment'.

"And humans cannot have any excuse for not taking up each one his/her cross and following in the Deliverer's footsteps after all the trouble that I myself, Prince of Hades, Ruler of the Underworld and also the Accuser, have gone to such great lengths to warn them! And, moreover, as the Apostle of the Gentiles wrote, not only is the Deliverer's grace sufficient, but His power is made perfect in the 'infirmity' of humans (2 Corinthians 12:9)!

"Yeah…achievements like those I have tallied for you take a good deal of hard work and don't at all come easy! And my efforts are merely going to cause many things that the evangelists wrote to come true. Take what that Paul wrote in his second letter to Timothy concerning evil in the Last Days. 'Know also this,' he wrote, 'that, in the last days, shall come dangerous times. Men shall be lovers of themselves, covetous, haughty, proud, blasphemers, disobedient to parents, ungrateful, wicked, without affection, without peace, slanderers, incontinent, unmerciful, without kindness, traitors, stubborn, puffed up, and lovers of pleasures more than of God: having an appearance indeed of godliness, but denying the power thereof. Now these avoid.'

"Ah, yes! It is good to see folks - bible believing followers of the Deliverer and even atheists - who will cherry-pick from the scared scriptures only what supports their arguments. According to some 'committed' atheists, the bible accurately depicts the Prime Mover as an unsavory divine entity that is too vengeful for their liking; but they won't be swayed by anything else therein. And that is even when the veracity of the New Testament is authenticated by independent sources such as Flavius Josephus's 'Antiquities of the Jews', not to mention the innumerable archaeological discoveries that also authenticate the biblical records, the historical veracity of the biblical narratives themselves and the *Sancta Ecclesia* that is itself a living testimony of the gospel truths!

"For example, Josephus wrote in his Antiquities 18: Chapter 3): 'Now there was about this time Jesus, a wise man, for he was a doer of wonderful works, a teacher. He drew over to him both many of the Jews and many of the Gentiles. And when Pilate, at the suggestion of the principal men amongst us, had condemned him to the cross, those that loved him at the first did not forsake him; and the tribe of Christians, so named after him, are not extinct at this day...' You would think that, if Josephus's description of the destruction of the second temple has credibility, his reference to the Deliverer would fall in the same category. But expecting that from humans would be a stretch. Hee, hee, hee, hoo, hoo, hoo, hak, hak, hak, hak! I can't help laughing at the stupid humans!

"Unfortunately, even with all these accomplishments to my credit, the fact is that I, Mephistopheles and 'Prince of the World', have already been judged, along with the other fallen angels. As humans on Earth endure the tribulations I am committed to work to bring about, I do not want to think of the viciousness as demons and souls of the damned go at each other.

"At the end of the world, after all humans rise from the dead in their immortal bodies, the situation will be particularly bad for the damned humans after they repossess their bodies. It will be a gory sight indeed! That is precisely why I, as ringleader in all this, must do what I have to do, namely continue to sow the seeds of death. And, incidentally, that is also the time when, in a strange twist of fate, those who are now being cut down and mercilessly slaughtered will have the last laugh.

"The peculiar nature of humans, which consists of an 'incorporeal' spirit and a 'corporeal' body, complete with the senses of sight, hearing, smell, taste and touch, undoubtedly makes their existence on earth so much more interesting. These senses are such an important part of the human experience that life would be impossible without them. Humans, of course, share this feature (the senses) with the rest of the animal world, reptiles, bird-life, and even insects.

"Then the DNA of humans, which results in the unique makeup of individual members of the human race, makes specific provision for the birth into the world of an almost equal number of he-humans and she-humans. Just imagine all the possibilities in terms of self-actualization that are open to humans as a result.

"In contrast to pure spirits that are created different from each other and can't really do very much to shape their uniqueness further, humans actually have the ability to influence their rank order in heaven (or in hell) to a much greater extent by the way they react and interact with the world around them during their sojourn on earth. It must also be a fantastic experience to be able to coexist in the same environment with lower creatures (like cows and goats) that do not have to worry about going to heaven or hell. Upon their demise, they (humans) are rewarded according to the way they used their many and varied talents.

"And so, humans who deliberately hurt or kill other humans and then go on to celebrate their 'victory' are jackasses who do not understand their own nature. They are so dumb they do not even see that they are being used by myself (undoubtedly also a jackass) to accomplish my evil plan; and they are even dumber for not being able to see that they are being used by the Deliverer to bring justification and redemption to the very people they want to see damned.

"For sinful humans accustomed not just to living in permanent fear for their lives, but also given to imagining that they must needs live by the sword to survive at all, the idea that the Prime Mover actually uses liars, thieves, murderers and other 'human devils' to bring His divine plan for humans to fruition must sound harebrained and laughable. And yet, *that* is what is true; and it is what they believe - namely that they prevail when they kill, and become vanquished when they meet their demise - that is featherbrained and nonsensical. It has to be so - otherwise it would be tantamount to saying that there is no life after death!

"When the Prime Mover created Adam and Eve out

of nothing, endowed them with the faculties of reason and free will, and then allowed them to roam freely in the Garden of Pleasure (Genesis 2:7-26 and Genesis 3:1-10) knowing very well that I, Mephistopheles, even though defeated and banished from His face, wasn't exactly chained and was lurking around and likely to pay them a 'courtesy' visit with intentions that couldn't possibly be any good (Genesis 3:1), He wouldn't have been a Prime Mover if He had forgotten to put in place a Plan B. I mean, are you kidding? Look, I had already metamorphosed into the Father of Death and also the Father of Lies, and he knew it! (John 8:44)

"One would have to be a bonehead and a complete idiot not to see that, in executing His divine plan, the Prime Mover uses killing even more than He does all other forms of human suffering. Yeah, without a doubt He uses the pangs of death - and the fact that all humans instinctively recoil from them (and with reason) - to achieve His ends. And you can bet that it is His way of undoing my evil plan - a plan that (as you can well imagine) is hatched in darkness and thrives on destruction and death. And this can only mean that, when evil humans celebrate death, they ally themselves with me, the Dickens! And also that they themselves are dying to die the death! When humans kill, as surely as they kill, so surely shall they die the death themselves!

"But actually if humans only knew what they were really doing, namely that they were doing the greatest favor imaginable to those they dislike out of selfish motives by facilitating the passage of their souls from their miserable existence on earth to their eternal rest and immortality in Elysium (in the company of none other than the Prime Mover Himself) while guaranteeing themselves dungeons in hell in the company of swarms of demons headed by myself, they would kill themselves over and over!

"In sum, whoever killed - or thought that he/she deserved to live more than some other human - will regret terribly, and even wish that he/she had not been born at all - like Judas Iscariot did, but may be (in his case) just in time.

"You see - there is a difference from saying that 'It were better if you were not born', and saying 'It were better if you were not created'. I am the incarnation of evil, and it just happens that I was created a pure spirit, and I was therefore not 'born'; but nowhere in the Holy Book is it said that it were better if I, Beelzebub (or any creature for that matter), were not created! If I had been a human devil, you can be sure that the Scriptures would just be full of the phrase 'It were better if the devil were not born!' And, hey - my hell would also have been a lot worse! I will explain.

"You humans may not know (and the great bulk of humans typically wallow in 'group think', and end up knowing next to nothing about themselves and their own nature), but a human is a very special creature - more special in fact than any of the angelic spirits! Our own special attribute is that every angel has each its own nature or essence. Now your nature - or that which makes you humans human and which you all share - was crafted or designed in such a manner that its Designer, namely the Prime Mover Himself, could if He so wished turn around and take it up. And that is what happened in the case of the Son of Man.

"And so you would think that it is pretty clear that creatures that are fashioned in the Prime Mover's image and likeness, and also consequently get to enjoy the exercise of their faculties of reason and free will, cannot possibly be accidents of nature; and that, once the Prime Mover causes them to bounce into existence out of nothing by giving an 'existence' to the human 'essence', the manner in which the faculties of reason and free will are exercised by the individual affects that individual's eternal destiny. But you would be gravely mistaken if you thought so. Humans being humans, when they do not want to face reality, they always quickly resort to myths of their liking. One such myth even goes so far as to attribute everything in creation to 'random natural selection', and that includes me as well I suppose…Ha, Ha, Ha, Hee, Hee, Hee!

"Totally contrary to what the Sacred Scriptures say (Genesis 1:1-28, Genesis 5:1, Isaiah 37:16, Isaiah 44:24, Isaiah 45:18, Isaiah 66:2, Psalm 100:3, Psalm 139:13, Psalm 148:2-5, Revelation 4:11, Revelation 21:1-5, Nehemiah 9:6, Matthew 5:45, John 1:3, John 1:12-13, Matthew 6:28-30, Acts 17:26-28, Hebrews 1:2, Hebrews 11:3, Ephesians 3:9, Colossians 1:16, and Revelation 14:6); and as well the Nicene Creed which the Councils of Nicaea (AD 325) and Constantinople (AD 381) adopted to counter the Arian heresy and starts with the words: 'I believe in one God, the Father Almighty, Creator of heaven and earth, of all things visible and invisible…'.

"Well, tell that to Zechariah, the father of John the Baptizer! The Holy Ghost was going to come upon the maiden Mary, and the power of the Most High was going to overshadow her; and the Holy Begotten One (the Second Person of the Blessed Trinity through Whom all creation came into being) was going to dwell among humans (Luke 1:35 and Matthew 1:18). And the Prime Mover's plan for the Son of Man to have a precursor (a forerunner who was going to make sure that the priests and teachers of the law would not have any excuse for rolling out the red carpet for the promised Messiah) had

582

been hatched in eternity. (Micah 5:2)

"The Prime Mover was going to cause the Deliverer's precursor to bounce into existence by giving a unique existence to human nature through the agency of Zechariah, the aging priest of the order of Abijah (a priestly family descended from Aaron), and his barren wife Elizabeth who also belonged to the same priestly family. But this priest and teacher of the law had doubted; and for that he was going to pay a price! Just what was he thinking - that humans come about as a result of 'random natural selection'? If he was, he was about to be disabused of any such notion. He certainly didn't believe (certainly not for a man of his age) in the other 'myth' that stocks delivered babies!

"It was quite impressive the way Gabriel got Zechariah to shut up so he would not promote any 'myths' concerning the way humans came into existence. Zechariah, who had frozen in his tracks when he first saw the apparition of the angel of the Lord, standing right there at the right side of the altar of incense inside the sanctuary. The angel Gabriel was quite good at calming humans who were troubled, and Zechariah was no exception. Gabriel had then continued: 'Fear not, Zechariah, for thy prayer is heard: and thy wife Elizabeth shall bear thee a son. And thou shalt call his name John. And thou shalt have joy and gladness: and many shall rejoice in his nativity. For he shall be great before the Lord and shall drink no wine nor strong drink: and he shall be filled with the Holy Ghost, even from his mother's womb. And he shall convert many of the children of Israel to the Lord their God. And he shall go before him in the spirit and power of Elias: that he may turn the hearts of the fathers unto the children and the incredulous to the wisdom of the just, to prepare unto the Lord a perfect people.'

"But, somewhat daringly, Zechariah had asked of the angel saying, 'How can I be sure of this? I am an old man and my wife is well along in years.' And the curt reply was: 'I am Gabriel. I stand in the presence of God, and I have been sent to speak to you and to tell you this good news. And now you will be silent and not able to speak until the day this happens, because you did not believe my words, which will come true at their appointed time.' (Luke 1:11-20)

"And that definitely says something about humans and human nature, namely that you humans, contrary to what you think or imagine, are spirits and are not animals! How many angels or demons can fit on the eye of a needle? That is a wrong question to ask - angels and demons are spirits and any number of them can fit on the eye of a needle. And so, even though the way it exactly happened remains a mystery that neither you humans nor ourselves here in Gehenna can grasp (as with so many things that relate to the actions of Prime Mover), using the same analogy, it is possible to see how a member of the Godhead could decide and take up the nature of a human without compromising His divinity.

"But it also says something about humans and their place in the Divine Plan. And if you humans were not beings that were so exalted, you realize that I, Diabolos, wouldn't be here wasting any time on you knuckleheads! Your human nature stands apart from that of mammals and other vertebrates because it makes it possible for you to eat of the fruit of the Tree of Knowledge - like Adam and Eve did following my suggestion, and to discern what is good from what is bad!

"The human nature of the Deliverer (and also a member of the Godhead by virtue of His divine nature) allowed the unthinkable to happen - it allowed the Almighty to walk on Earth in the shape of the Virgin Mary's son who was also called Emmanuel, and to sanctify anew His works of creation in the physical as well as the spiritual realm!

"And when the Son of Man came to earth, humans did not suddenly become bigger than elephants, or taller than giraffes, or more colorful than zebras, or more agile than leopards. They did not develop hides that were tougher than those of crocodiles - even though some humans, like King Herod who ordered the slaughter of infants in his effort to be rid of the infant Deliverer and was under my total control, became even more thick-skinned, completely hardened to any reproach even though wicked in the extreme, and incorrigible. And they did not suddenly develop the ability to fly like birds of the air. Humans in fact remained humans and, as descendants of Adam and Eve who had dared to eat forbidden fruit from the Tree of Knowledge in the midst of the Garden of Eden, could distinguish between what was good and what was evil and were now accursed!

"Humans! Just to think that some of them actually believe that someone has to be the size of an indricotherium (which, by the way, is already extinct) in order to be 'someone'! These are the people who cannot understand how the Deliverer, a member of the Godhead, could be a human and a divinity at the same time! The fact of course is that physical 'size' is completely immaterial in the Prime Mover's eyes. But stupid humans only think of being 'important', and deride the maxim that, while it's nice to be important, it is far more important to be nice'! The Prime Mover is the Prime Mover because He is really, really, really nice! He is not just good. He is goodness *per se*, and that is why He, and He alone, is a Deity!

"And humans die, but they don't die - just like us demons, because we are all created in the image of the

Prime Mover. Even without the prospect of resurrection, from the beginning human ghosts were slated to 'live' on to answer for the deeds and misdeeds committed by them during their sojourn on earth. And so there you have another dimension of human nature that has a lot in common with that of a Deity that is almighty, has no beginning, and whose divine nature and existence are one and the same, and are by their very nature indistinguishable. And also remember that humans, like us demons, were created gratuitously in order that we may do whatever we do, not to our own glory and honor, but to the greater glory and honor of the Prime Mover and Almighty One. You realize that it is because of that exalted status that I, Satan and Ruler of the Underworld, will never leave you goddamn humans alone.

"And if the Deity became a human, that means that humans can also become not just a little but a lot like the Deity; and the more they uphold the maxim that it is nice to be important, but it is more important to be nice in their lives, the more they become like their Deliverer.

"Indeed as the Psalmist wrote: 'God hath stood in the congregation of gods: and being in the midst of them he judgeth gods. How long will you judge unjustly: and accept the persons of the wicked? Judge for the needy and fatherless: do justice to the humble and the poor. Rescue the poor; and deliver the needy out of the hand of the sinner. They have not known nor understood: they walk on in darkness: all the foundations of the earth shall be moved. I have said: You are gods and all of you the sons of the Most High.' (Psalm 8:1-6)

"So, humans can actually come close to being like a Deity! And that is by being nice even while they remain 'earth-bound' creatures that are descended from Adam and Eve! By being the opposite, guess what – they become like me, Mephistopheles! And I am not referring to the fictitious character in Shakespeare's Merry Wives of Windsor – or that feckless demon in German folklore. I am referring to myself, me – Lucifer, Damn it!

"Saint Irenaeus (c. 130–202), bishop of Lyons and Father of the Church, wrote in the in the preface to his *Adversus Haereses* (Against Heresies): 'God had 'become what we are, that He might bring us to be even what He is Himself.' Irenaeus had added: 'Do we cast blame on him [God] because we were not made gods from the beginning, but were at first created merely as men, and then later as gods? Although God has adopted this course out of his pure benevolence, that no one may charge him with discrimination or stinginess, he declares, "I have said, Ye are gods; and all of you are sons of the Most High.".. But man receives progression and increase towards God. For as God is always the same, so also man, when found in God, shall always progress towards God.' Against Heresies, Chapter 38)

"St. Clement of Alexandria (c. 150–215), wrote: 'Yea, I say, the Word of God became a man so that you might learn from a man how to become a god... If one knows himself, he will know God, and knowing God will become like God...His is beauty, true beauty, for it is God, and that man becomes a god, since God wills it. So Heraclitus was right when he said, 'Men are gods, and gods are men.' St. Clement of Alexandria also stated in his Stromata (a statement we have helped some folks use to try and justify Pantheism and confuse the situation) that 'he who obeys the Lord and follows the prophecy given through him. becomes a god while still moving about in the flesh.' (Stromata 716,101,4). And St. Athanasius, Confessor and Doctor of the Church (c. 296-373), referring to the Deliverer, also famously wrote: 'He was made human so that he might make us gods' (*De incarnatione* 54,3, cf. *Contra Arianos* 1.39). St. Augustine of Hippo (354–430), commenting on Psalm 50:2, wrote: 'But he himself that justifies also deifies, for by justifying he makes sons of God.. 'For he has given them power to become the sons of God' [referring to John 1:12]. If then we have been made sons of god, we have also been made gods... To make human beings gods, He was made man who was God" (Sermon 192.1.1)

"And St. Thomas Aquinas wrote: 'The only-begotten Son of God, wanting to make us sharers in his divinity, assumed our nature, so that he, made man, might make men gods' (*Opusc.*, 57:1-4)

"The Catechism of the Church clarifies all that and states: 'God is infinitely greater than all his works: "You have set your glory above the heavens" (Ps. 8:2; cf. Sir. 43:28). Indeed, God's "greatness is unsearchable" (Ps. 145:3). But because he is the free and sovereign Creator, the first cause of all that exists, God is present to his creatures' inmost being: "In him we live and move and have our being" (Acts 17:28). In the words of St. Augustine, God is "higher than my highest and more inward than my innermost self" (St. Augustine, Cof. 3, 6, 11: PL 32, 688)' (CCC 300).

"Still, humans are already like the Prime Mover in that, using their reason and free will, they have power to multiply and to fill the earth - and also the power to rig mother earth with nuclear war heads and to trigger the long awaited Armageddon if they so choose.

"To receive the Prime Mover's blessings in His Son, humans must be 'partakers of the divine nature'. As Catherine of Siena put it in *The Dialogue of Divine Providence*, the souls that keep nothing at all, not even a bit of their own will, outside of their divine Maker, but are completely set afire in Him, are like the burning coal that, once it is completely consumed in the furnace, no one can douse. Or, as John of the Cross noted in his *Ascent of*

588

Mount Carmel, in allowing the Prime Mover to move in it, the soul is at once illuminated and transformed in the Deity, and the Deity communicates to it His Supernatural Being, in such wise that it appears to be the Prime Mover Himself, and has all that the Deity Himself has. And that union comes to pass when the Deity grants the soul that supernatural favor, that all the things of the Prime Mover and the soul are one in participant transformation; and the soul seems to be God rather than a soul, and is indeed God by participation; although it remains true that the soul's natural being, though thus transformed, is as distinct from the being of the Prime Mover as it was before.

"After all, the only begotten Son of Eloi was given unto the world so that whosoever believed in him, might not perish, but might have life everlasting. And as God became a human, in all ways except sin, He will also make humans like God in all ways except his divine essence that is uncaused and has no beginning. The Son of God did indeed become Son of Man who, at the ninth hour of the day he was crucified and died, cried with a loud voice: '*Eloi, Eloi, lama sabachthani?*' That is a cry with which all humans of good will can identify as they beseech their divine Creator for deliverance from the evil plots that my minions hatch against them at my suggestion, and struggle to walk in the footsteps of the Deliverer bearing each the load of his/her own cross.

"If anything therefore, it was only those humans whose lives were grounded in reality, like Simeon who was just and devout and had been waiting for the consolation of Israel, who could say that they were ready to be dismissed as mere servants of the Lord and to die in peace upon learning that the Deity had taken up His human nature. And, moreover, the Son of Man himself did not come to be ministered unto, but to minister, and to give his own life for the salvation of his fellow humans. All the rest remained my minions and enslaved to me, Satan and immortal Prince of Hades!

"We here in the Underworld are not fools. We have studied our subjects, viz. humans, and have gotten to understand their weaknesses far better than they themselves do. One of these weaknesses is to feign ignorance when they think it will be to their advantage if they do not take responsibility for their actions; and to put on airs when they think that such a ploy will work to their advantage. And when humans are faking helplessness to shirk their responsibilities, they will, generally, stop at nothing in their attempts to depict themselves as victims - victims of everything, including their own supposedly hapless nature!

"We know that, crafted in the image of the Prime Mover, and with the appearance on earth of the Son of Man on top of that, humans are now verily the 'workmanship' of the Prime Mover, 'created in Christ Jesus in good works'; but just sit back and imagine the evils humans still do to each other. Ironically, it is the extent to which humans can be bad and nasty to one another that distinguishes them from all other creatures, and makes them so special - and a 'good catch' for us.

"Without a doubt then, humans, even though they are the 'poor forsaken descendants of Adam and Eve', are exalted beings that are temples of the Prime Mover. We here in the Underworld, knowing that and determined to frustrate the Divine Plan by bringing about their downfall, want humans to believe that they really aren't the prized creatures they are - that they aren't all that exalted or sublime.

"Humans, created in the Image, are every single one of them important in the eyes of the Prime Mover. There isn't one soul that was given an existence and endowed with its human nature by accident or by a fluke. And every moment that a human lives matters to the Prime Mover. Every human act bears on that human's destiny in eternity.

"It is at the moment a human, however wretched, despised or nondescript in life, kicks the proverbial bucket and crosses to the other side of the gulf that separates the living from the dead that the process of that human's self-actualization, started at conception, comes to a head, and the intrinsic glory of that human's nature, fashioned in the image of the Prime Mover and also effectively His temple, bursts forth. Look, at that moment of truth, it is immaterial whether the soul that is in the process of being separated from the body in readiness for the self-actualization belongs to someone who was a nominal or fervent Catholic, a Protestant, a Muslim, a Hindu, a Buddhist, or a follower of K'ung-fu-tzu, or someone who was raised without any religious belief. And it is immaterial if the soul belongs to someone who, whilst on earth, was influential to the point of being beyond the reach of the law, or to someone who was not deemed to be deserving of even the common law writ of *Habeas Corpus*!

"And it, of course, does not matter if the soul arriving on the other side of the gulf that separates the living from the dead belongs to a murder victim or a victim of the so-called 'capital punishment'. It is completely immaterial if it is one of the so-called 'disappeared' who turns up unexpectedly on the other side of the gulf that separates the living from the dead; or if it is someone (a commander-in-chief or some such funny character) who was in the business of causing others to disappear into thin air, or a commander-in-chief who used drones or some other such 'mystery' powers to speed up the appearance on the other side of the gulf that separates the living from the dead of any one he/she chose, or a commander-in-chief who made it a habit of exonerating those who committed such crimes who turns up there when his/her own numbered days finally run out, and he/she is forced to follow his/her victims to see what awaits him/her on that side of the gulf!

"And the self-actualization happens by virtue of the Son of Man's death and resurrection, the fitting sacrificial offering of Himself to His heavenly Father on behalf of Adam and Eve and all their descendants. That is also the time when some, observing the 'good thief' who was executed alongside the Son of Man receive a denarius, will murmur saying: 'This last chap has worked but one hour, and thou hast made him equal to us, that have borne the burden of the day and the heats!' (Matthew 20:12)

"As the Father of Death, I have worked hard to sow seeds of death among humans, and the Deliverer's own ignominious death on the cross bears that out.

"You ought to know - even if you have never read Luke 4:7 or Matthew 4:9 - that I take my job as tempter very seriously. I have ways of leading humans one at a time to the tops of high mountains from whence I show them all the kingdoms of the world in a flash of time. And I always have the same message for humans. I say to them: 'To thee will I give all this power, and the glory of them; for to me they are delivered, and to whom I will, I give them. If thou therefore wilt adore before me, all shall be thine!' And, instead of answering saying, 'It is written: Thou shalt adore the Lord thy God, and Him only shalt thou serve', the stupid humans take the bait, kneel down and adore me!

"And instead of angels descending on them and ministering to them, there they are, all excited, forgetting that the ravens neither sow nor reap; have neither storehouse nor barn; yet the Prime Mover feeds them. They forget that they are much more important than birds, and that every single human is precious to Him; that before He formed each one of them in the womb, He knew them. And that, before they were born, He had set the damn stupid humans apart!

"And happily for me, it is only a handful of humans, mainly recluses and those others who are into asceticism and are consequently looked upon as wackos by everyone else, who alone appear to be capable of appreciating the significance of these achievements, and the fact that the salvation of humans now totally hinged on the coming of the promised Deliverer.

"Let's backtrack. It was on the sixth day of the Prime Mover's work of creation, after He had caused all else to bounce into existence out of nothing, that He said: 'Let us make man to our image and likeness: and let him have dominion over the fishes of the sea, and the fowls of the air, and the beasts, and the whole earth, and every creeping creature that moveth upon the earth.' (Genesis 1:27) And He made Him to His own image accordingly. But that was not all. As the *Sancta Ecclesia* affirms in Preface V of the Sundays in Ordinary Time (*Creation*), the Prime Mover also set humans over the whole world in all its wonder, and He made them stewards of creation with the injunction that Adam and Eve and all their descendants praise Him day by day for the marvels of His wisdom and power.

"When the father and mother of humankind, at my instigation, plucked and ate the forbidden fruit from the tree that stood in the midst of the Garden of Pleasure (the Tree of Knowledge of Good and Evil), a direct result of that act of intransigence was their expulsion from Paradise in the same way that we ourselves were cast in hell in the wake of our own rebellion. But that is only half the story.

"The fact is that when humans fell from grace at my instigation (and these were the selfsame creatures to whom the Prime Mover had given dominion over the earth and everything in it), they also effectively ceded the right to exercise dominion over the world to me! If you have any doubt about this, again go read Luke 4:5-7 as well as Matthew 4:8-9. The kingdoms of the world and the power and glory of them became mine to give away at will after the fall of humans from grace! And I am now in the fortuitous position of being able to use the sway I now hold over dominions to try and sink humans further and further.

"Things unfolded in that manner because there was *collusion*. Adam and Eve colluded with me in undermining the Prime Mover's power and authority over themselves and over creation; and they also ceded the dominion they had been given over the earth and everything in it to me in the process! That is why I was able to tell the Son of Man to His face that I would give Him all the kingdoms of the world and the glory in them if falling down He would adore me! (Matthew 4:9 and Luke 4:6-7) You can see that I wasn't kidding at all.

"You see...Adam and Eve also wanted to be just like members of the triune Godhead, knowing good and evil. (Genesis 3:22) They had been hankering after the forbidden fruit for precisely that reason. And, when they finally got around to eating it, they found it 'good to eat, and fair to the eyes, and delightful to behold'. (Genesis 3:6) The fruit was something that had everything to do with the senses. Still, just keep in mind that it was plucked from the Tree of Knowledge of Good and Evil!

"The operative word there is 'knowledge'; and therein lay the catch. For, as Thomas Aquinas wrote, 'reason in man is like God in the world'. Instead of following their reason and rebuffing my suggestions, they caved in. They forgot that reason in Man is exactly that, namely that *it is like God in the world*! The first man and the first woman, endowed by the Prime Mover at creation with the faculties of reason and free will, walked blindly into the trap I had laid for them when they fell for the temptation to pluck and eat the forbidden fruit. That was despite the fact that, like everything else in creation, they had come into being out of nothing through the *Logos*. (John 1:3) But I had succeeded in getting them hooked to the idea that if they sampled the forbidden fruit, they would become like their Maker!

"I had gotten them to imagine that their newfound 'knowledge' would include knowledge of the future, and that it would enable them to deal with the fallout from their brazen act of intransigence and to survive all on their own after they had become decoupled from the 'burdensome yoke' of fealty to their Maker. Their guardian angels tried and failed to dissuade them from fancying that they could outsmart the *Logos*. The only thing that would save the day would be the Prime Mover's infinite mercy!

"At my suggestion, Adam and Eve had developed the desire to define for themselves what was good and what was evil; and they essentially ended up choosing to act as though they were Gods unto themselves!

"In that moment of weakness, they voluntarily sold their birthright to me for a mirage. And hence the miseries and ills that have plagued the world ever since - a world (mark you) that once upon a time was known as the 'Garden of Pleasure' or 'Paradise' - engendered by once noble but now completely compromised and debased human minds. And now, unfortunately for all Adam and Eve's posterity who by and large are without 'faith', it remains true, as Thomas Aquinas famously said, 'To one who has faith, no explanation is necessary, while to one without faith, no explanation is possible'!

"Which is really too bad because, first off (as the *Sancta Ecclesia* teaches), in the Deliverer, the Prime Mover has become one with humanity, and humans have become one again with the Prime Mover; and the Eternal Word, taking upon Himself human frailty, gives their mortal nature immortal value. In Preface IV of the Sundays in Ordinary time, the *Sancta Ecclesia* affirms that by the Deliverer's birth he brought renewal to humanity's fallen state, and by his suffering, canceled out our sins; and by his rising from the dead he has opened the way to eternal life, and by ascending to the Prime Mover, he has unlocked for humans the gates of heaven.

"Paul put it succinctly in his epistle to Titus when he wrote: 'For the grace of God our Savior hath appeared to all men; Instructing us, that, denying ungodliness and worldly desires, we should live soberly, and justly, and godly in this world, Looking for the blessed hope and coming of the glory of the great God and our Savior Jesus Christ, Who gave himself for us, that he might redeem us from all iniquity, and might cleanse to himself a people acceptable, a pursuer of good works.' (Titus 2:11-14)

"It is thus that, even after humans had sinned and wandered far from the Prime Mover's friendship, He reunites them to Himself through the blood of His Son and the power of the Holy Ghost. He went to the rescue of humans by His power as Prime Mover, but He wanted them to be saved by one like themselves! And He now gathers them into His *Sancta Ecclesia* to be one as He is one with the Son and the Holy Ghost.

"If humans have any doubt about the love the Prime Mover has for them, they need only remember that, after Eve took of the fruit from the Tree of Knowledge of Good and Evil and did eat, and gave to her husband who also did eat, and the eyes of them both were opened, and when they perceived themselves to be naked, sewed together fig leaves to serve as aprons (Genesis 3:7), it was the Prime Mover who *made for Adam and his wife, garments of skins, and clothed them*. (Genesis 3:21) And it is the Prime Mover who has helped Humans to use their heads to improve their daily lives ever since.

"You can actually say that, even after the Prime Mover had blasted Adam for hearkening to Eve and ejected them both from the Garden of Pleasure saying: 'Cursed is the earth in thy work; with labor and toil shalt thou eat thereof all the days of thy life...Thorns and thistles shall it bring forth to thee; and thou eat the herbs of the earth...In the sweat of thy face shalt thou eat bread till thou return to the earth, out of which thou wast taken: for dust thou art, and into dust thou shalt return' (Genesis 3:17-19), humans still remained totally dependent on Him not just for their existence but for their subsistence as well.

"Well, if it hadn't happened that way, humankind would have been completely at my mercy! That is why the Deliverer taught you humans to pray to His Father in heaven the way He did...that you humans ask Him to give you your daily bread, and to forgive you your sins and as well deliver you from the present wicked world, according to the will of the Prime Mover and your Father. (Luke 11:4, Matthew 6:11-12 & Galatians 1:4)

"But that has not stopped humans from imagining that it is their dads and moms and uncles and aunties, and grandpas and grandmas or their extended family who give them their daily bread! Others even have this funny idea that it is 'Social Services' to whom they owe gratitude for receiving their daily bread, as if the corrupt members of legislatures and other parts of 'government', who are as a rule beholden to lobbyists, really care a hoot or give a damn! The fact, of course, is that Providence has ordained everything such that infant babies get to suckle milk from their moms, and ducks instinctively take steps to shield the ducklings so they don't fall prey to marauding kites. And brutal dictators, who have 'neither fear of God nor respect for man', also get to answer for loading it over their subjects and forgetting that the power they wield is given to them from above.

"And, as well, the Son of Man also taught humans to beseech His Father in heaven with the words: 'Lead us not into temptation, but deliver us from evil' or to use the words of the Vulgate: '*Ne nos inducas in tentationem, sed libera nos a malo.*' (Luke 11:4 and Matthew 6:13) But now, like spoilt children, the things they ardently yearn (and pray) for are becoming Mega Millions or Powerball jackpot winners (which they mistakenly believe will solve all their problems) or striking it rich in any other way (including crooked ways) while remaining completely oblivious to the fact that it is easier for a camel to pass through the eye of a needle, than for a rich man to enter into the kingdom of God! (Luke 18:25, Matthew 19:24 and Mark 10:25)

"Humans are admonished to pray to the Prime Mover to become imbued with a sense of responsibility that will stop them from badgering Him for lottery wins and other stuff that will spoil them further and expose them to further temptation. The Roman Pontiff is thus clearly right on in asking the *Congregatio pro Doctrina Fidei* (Congregation for the Doctrine of the Faith) to take another look at the translation of the synoptic gospels of Luke, Matthew and Mark from the original Greek with a view to clarifying this issue at a time when he so-called prosperity theology (or seed faith) is becoming fashionable.

"But humans have always had a very fuzzy idea of the Prime Mover, and that is when they believed that He exists! A big chunk of humans have long imagined the Prime Mover away, and have convinced themselves that 'He' must be the figment of people's imagination. And then there are those who are still awaiting the coming of the 'Messiah'! Then there are those who think that it is a stretch to believe that the 'Son of Man' is divine even if 'He' might be a historic figure. And others who believe that the Deliverer is divine actually propagate that the *Sancta Ecclesia* He established on a rock called Peter is the 'Whore of Babylon' referred to in Revelation 17:1-18.

"Hah, Hah, Hah! Hee, Hee, Hee! Humans are so fascinating…such a strange lot, and so funny! Some even posit that the study of 'God' or '*Theos*' and the study of 'Science' are not compatible, as if the subject matter for the latter just materialized out of the blue - like a meteorite! As if you could get an effect without a cause! It is like saying that Model 'T' could have materialized mysteriously from raw materials without any input at all from its creator (Henry Ford)!

"The *Logos* became Man to save humans from themselves. But even though He came, died for their redemption, and rose again in triumph, and is seated at the right hand of His Father, the misinformation amongst humans that got kick-started with man's fall from grace, continues in the world unabated and will continue until the second coming of the Deliverer - the misinformation that represents lies as truth and truth as lies. The situation is so bad it has even become fashionable in some circles to assert that Quote: 'truth isn't truth'! Ha, Ha, Ha, He, He, He Ha, Ha, Ha!

"It is a measure of our success that many humans don't perceive themselves as creatures that are destined for an eternal life that will be either in heaven with Michael the Archangel or here in Gehenna with us. We want humans to see themselves as helpless creatures whose actions are really of no significance. We might find it harder to get the children and the innocent to buy that; but we find it quite easy actually to persuade the adults, especially the errant ones, to ignore their consciences and start imagining that their actions, heinous or otherwise, don't have any serious consequences attached to them in the moral arena. We want them to imagine that ethics and morality belong only in works of fiction, and aren't things that should impede their acquisition of material wealth and their 'advancement' on earth.

'Stupid humans have bought into this to the point where they now use their religion and spiritual beliefs - to the extent they still profess any belief in spiritual things or the unseen - to either discriminate against everyone who subscribes to something different, or to propagate the so-called 'separation of State and Church' doctrine, that in turn promotes agnosticism.

"We consequently have them trapped - more or less! What we don't want stupid humans to do is recognize that each and every one of their actions, whether conducted in secret in their thoughts or behind closed doors, decidedly has repercussions for themselves and for other members of the human family in the short term, and *ipso facto* also impact their destiny here on earth and their eternal life in heaven or in hell.

"That is how we get Catholics to remain lukewarm and Catholic only in name. It is also how we get everyone else outside the Church that was founded by the Deliverer on the rock called Peter to remain contented with their individual circumstances despite the fact that the Gospel has already been propagated to the ends of the Earth by the Deliverer's messengers! You've got to give us credit for our achievement in this very important arena.

"And concerning the 'Galileans whose blood Pilate

had mingled with their sacrifices', the people were told by the Deliverer that those Galileans were not sinners above all the men of Galilee because they suffered such things. No! But unless they did penance, they all would likewise perish. Or those eighteen upon whom the tower fell in Siloe, and slew them: they also were not debtors above all the men that dwelt in Jerusalem. No, but if those people who were inquiring did not do penance, they would all likewise perish.

"Not everyone who says to Him, 'Lord, Lord,' will enter the kingdom of heaven, but only he who doth the will of His Father who is in heaven. He shall enter into the kingdom of heaven. Many will say to Him on that day, 'Lord, Lord, did we not prophesy in your name and in your name drive out demons and perform many miracles?' Then He will tell them plainly, 'I never knew you. Away from me, you evildoers!

"He admonishes humans in the meantime to strive to enter by the narrow gate; for wide is the gate, and broad is the way that leadeth to destruction, and many there are who go in there at. How narrow is the gate, and strait is the way that leadeth to life: and few there are that find it! For many shall seek to enter, and shall not be able. For when the Master of the house shall be gone in, and shall shut the door, humans shall begin to stand without, and knock at the door, saying: Lord, open to us. And He, answering, shall say to them: I know you not, from whence you are. Then they shall begin to say: We have eaten and drunk in thy presence, and thou hast taught in our streets. And He shall say to them: I know you not, whence you are: depart from me, all ye workers of iniquity. It is true that there shall be weeping and gnashing of teeth, when some humans shall see Abraham and Isaac and Jacob, and all the prophets, in the kingdom of the Prime Mover, and they themselves thrust out. And there shall come from the east and the west, and the north and the south; and shall sit down in the kingdom of God.

"If humans 'sin wilfully after having the knowledge of the truth' (as Paul pointed out in Hebrews 10:26), they must also embrace the 'certain dreadful expectation of judgment'! This is the reason my troops and I will not let up in our pursuits of human souls. It is also the reason, even though I am the Father of Lies, I must use this opportunity to try and shine as much light on Truth as possible so that humans cannot say they did not know!

"And the Deliverer, whose ascension into heaven was witnessed by His apostles, will return at the end of time (in the same way the apostles saw Him taken up skyward into heaven) to judge the living and the dead. In the meantime, a *just* and *devout* Masai herdsman, tending to his cattle on the slopes of Mt. Kilimanjaro, is more connected to the Prime Mover who deigned to share the Masai's human nature than I myself was when, as the Angel of Light, I ministered to the Almighty, in the company of Michael the Archangel in the moments before I rebelled and got ejected from His face!

"Now, if I, Lucifer and Satan, had been a human, the Deliverer would have been in a position to say 'It were better if Lucifer had not been born'; and the fight between Good, led by the Deliverer, and Evil, led by a human demon, would have been over right there and then! Also I must say 'Thank God I am a pure spirit and not a human' because you can just imagine my lot as a human devil leading a band of rebel forces against the Almighty in the battle for souls! Where, for one, would I, as the Father of Death, be able to hide along with the legions of demons I command?

"The war between Good and Evil would itself be so ugly! The oceans with their salty water would have turned into one giant sea of blood long ago if the demons I command and I myself had been human! I can assure you that things would have been completely different. And you can guess what would be on my mind as the leader of the Powers of Darkness in the run-up to the call of the trumpet heralding the return of the Deliverer and Judge (at the sound of whose name every knee of heavenly and earthly and infernal beings should bow)!

"Kill, Kill, Kill using everything in our arsenal - poisons, improvised explosive devices or IEDs, drones, hijacked trains and airliners, you name it! Nothing would be off the table.

"But, even though created a pure spirit, with the help of my minions among humans, my troops and I still might just be able to make things as ugly as they definitely would be if I had been created a human!

"Now, Judas was completely oblivious to the sanctity of his human nature and his last end when, pining after thirty pieces of silver, he betrayed his Divine Master and Deliverer by collaborating with the priests and Pharisees in their plot to liquidate the Son of Man. Evil as their scheme was, you could not have said that it were better if these plotters had not been *created*. No, because you would then also be able to say the same about me, you fool! But they damn well should not have been *born*. It were better if those humans who now imagine that they can liquidate their enemies from the face of the earth once and for all by hatching murderous plots had themselves not been born. In plotting to murder their own kind, humans effectively posit that their enemies should not have been born! And because, by divine decree, a human soul cannot return to nothingness once it has been created and implanted into a human being, there is now just no way murderers can prevent that act of murder from coming back to haunt them on their own

Day of Judgement. And that is what the Deliverer was trying to convey to you geeks!

"We here in the Underworld aim to get you humans to in effect desire that your 'enemies' get lost forever - which is the same as saying that it were better if your enemies were not *created*. And all humans who do that effectively seal their own fate - because they show that they not only do not believe in life after death, but they do not believe in the existence of the Prime Mover Himself and do not recognize His divine plan according to which a creature, once created in the Image, can never be liquidated, uncreated or otherwise returned to the nothingness from which the creature came. And so, the statement 'It were better if you were not born' simply means that if you die unrepentant of your sin, that sin will haunt you forever - meaning that you will end up as my guest here in Gehenna.

"A word, though, about Judas and whether he may or may not have escaped my tentacles. Just take this hint. Because I am Satan, it does not mean that I know everything. I certainly know plenty as a pure spirit that was wonderfully endowed at creation. However, the fact remains that I am a totally evil being now, and an evil nature and knowledge are opposites. I, therefore, definitely know less than any spirit or soul that enjoys beatific vision and communes with Him who is Knowledge *per se*.

"And then there is also the fact that I am deliberately denied as punishment the many things I used to enjoy prior to my rebellion; and, as you may have guessed, being able to gloat over the fact that this or that soul is lost is easily one of them. But you must even then figure in the fact that everything is possible with the Prime Mover, and that He could still allow me to know that Judas is in some dungeon here in hell or in heaven - or in

Purgatory and among those who are certain of their salvation - and still use that knowledge to cause me infinite grief. But I myself choose not to reveal to you the exact position with respect to Judas Iscariot.

"Knowing that I am an infernal liar, you actually should still be leery to take all the preceding with a pinch of salt - except the following. I mean the fact that I definitely know many chaps - some of whom were really infamous and others who were really famous and supposedly men and women of impeccable character while they lived - who have ended up here in hell. I have even visited some of these folks in their dungeons, not to commiserate with them, but to mock them some for thinking that they were clever. While they lived, some of them thought that they were cleverer than even me, Beelzebub, even though I was actually the one inspiring them to kill and to do other dirty work on my behalf like spinning falsehoods and stirring up hatreds among humans in the name of the Deliverer.

"Well, you might excuse them for having paid heed to my wiles, but the Judge didn't. Many of them had made themselves so unfit to serve as vessels of grace, I didn't find it that hard to make them instruments of hatred and other human vices.

Crowned Arch-Devil...

"Getting back to the business of sinful humans (and killers in particular) who die unrepentant - after spending a lifetime in which they allowed the self and the lure of material things to take a front seat without any thought as to their last end, humans at death must feel like fish that are accustomed to frisking and basking and waxing in water from the first moment of their waking existence (and even though they had been told time and again that they should stay clear of those waters and get used to living on dry land where they belonged), and that suddenly wake up one morning to find all the water gone with no prospect of it ever returning!

"You've got to accept that I am not called the Enemy for nothing. I am clever - and pretty clever too. And you have also to accept that I know exactly what I do as I go about sowing the seeds of death.

"What is it about me that makes me so feared? How come I seem to have a monopoly over evil - how come that there seems to be no creature that is capable of challenging me in my chosen role as Tempter?

"O.K. - I'll let you in on a secret, and I enjoin you to silence as I have always liked to leave the impression that I have never been challenged. I got the reputation as the 'author of death' because I killed the only creature that looked like it might become my rival in evil and sin. I do not know how I did it, but I effectively eliminated her - I believe it was a 'she'; because I myself am a 'he' (or so I believe even though I frequently masquerade as a 'she')! She was after my crown as the Arch-Devil, and that was how we became entangled in an argument that turned deadly.

"It was truly a battle for survival - it is the only instance in which the Prime Mover permitted a creature that was made in the Image to be destroyed...'rubbed out'. And so, I rubbed out my rival. Of course I still feel a terrible sense of guilt for having murdered my archrival. Oh...and she was so frightfully beautiful! But, well, one of us had to go; and none of us wanted to 'die' - to be rubbed out.

"We battled it out in full view of the heavenly host. And, as I faintly recall, the assembly of angels were all rooting for her. That made me really mad. In retrospect, it probably saved my 'life' - it apparently distracted her, and resulted in my gaining a slight edge over her in our 'battle for existence'. And you should have seen the look on her face as she saw the end coming. That battle was the ugliest spectacle that the choirs of angels had ever witnessed up until then. As I remember, it all started - and ended - as we both were conspiring to disobey the Prime Mover. But that is really all I am able to recall.

"I had always had this nagging thought, ever since, that humans would have been more inclined to evil under her regime than they are under mine - that she would have made a more effective 'Tempter' if you will; and it drives me really mad. I think it is because she would have been more inclined to rely on charm and persuasion (knowing the kind of character that she was). I myself prefer to rely on shock and awe.

"So you now understand why there is no creature in existence that rivals me as the Arch-Devil. But even after I vanquished my rival, quite frankly I have to admit that there is nothing at all to be envied about a creature like me that now languishes at the bottom of the Pit. Even though I succeeded in visiting 'death' on my 'enemy' and she is gone, I have been haunted by her ghost ever since.

"The act of rubbing out my archrival sealed my fate as the most horrid and hateful creature that exists - and as the Arch-devil and enemy of the Prime Mover. I condemned myself to the bottom rung of creatures, and became the most despised, ridiculed, hated and, I dare say, also feared creature.

"For now, all I can tell you is that a creature that is made in the Image - any creature that is made in the Image - and is humble can be elevated to greatness, like the Blessed Virgin Mother of the Deliverer who was elevated above all creatures. One does not have to be huge in stature (which I suppose I was before I blew my opportunities). But you can also start out little and grow

607

into a virtual monster - like Cain and Judas did at one time. And you have always to remember that when you bring off any good, it isn't so much you who does it as the Spirit who does it through you - when you let Him.

"And so, while anyone can end up as a monster and a devil, it is only the very humble who can reach the heights of holiness. And, of course, all creatures that are made in the Image are called to be humble, so that as and when the Spirit chooses, they may be raised up - exactly as the Son of Man, who took on the burden of the sins of humans, accepted humiliations and died on the cross in obedience to His Father, was raised up above all.

The source of fear...

"Cain at least realized, although only after he had committed his first murder, that killing another human being for any reason did not even address the reason for wanting other humans dead, namely the killer's fear of death! In his later years, as his own days on earth became numbered, the repentant Cain discovered through meditation and prayer that it was an irrational fear - the fear of death - that drove him to kill. And it was of course quite obvious that his fear to die was a legacy of original sin.

"By the time Cain was on his own death bed and dying, the former murderer, after spending a good part of his later years mortifying himself and doing penance for his dastardly act, understood that a human being who was no longer scared of dying, really had nothing else to fear. Just like his parents (Adam and Eve), Cain also kept a diary; and one of the last things he jotted down on the papyrus before he 'kicked the bucket' was that humans who feared to die could not turn around and declare themselves victors over anything whatsoever.

608

"This was because the fear of death paralyzed humans and made them see it lurking almost in everything that either came to mind or met their sight. Those who feared death were actually scared of everything, even though like so many Don Quixotes, they preferred to conceal their true feelings, including their pathological fear of the 'unknown', under a show of valor. And there is, of course, nothing that typifies fear more than the morbid preoccupation with the development of weapons of mass destruction by the so-called super powers even as they clamor for 'bans' on the self-same and do everything in their power to ensure that the playing field is anything but level - and also while completely oblivious to the fact that in a matter of decades, not only their investment in armaments will be obsolete, but all the players will be dead and gone, replaced by new generations of paranoid schizophrenics who are prone to making the sort of blunders that invariably result in a redrawing of boundaries, and in new maps in which all those once super powerful and domineering 'empires' will be nowhere to be seen.

"Cain wrote that it was easy to tell if a human harbored the fear of death. That human will wrap himself/herself up in body armor, and sometimes in so much body armor that he/she will scarcely be able to get up and about. And anything that remotely resembles a combat zone will cause such folks to take refuge in what Cain called 'humvees' - these were armor plated contraptions into which the first generation of humans retreated at the first signs of a twister or a hurricane. Cain was quite imaginative, and predicted that a time would come when demagogues would be so terrified of their fellow humans that they would go to very great lengths to keep them at bay. Cain himself longed for a world in which he could surround himself with 'body guards' who

609

would be clad in 'riot gear' and would wield batons and break up any groups of the proletariat – protesters, 'occupiers' and other 'rats' whose activities looked like they might pose a threat to progressives like himself who were aspiring to become either 'landed gentry' or 'landed bourgeoisie', capitalists, or even 'aristocrats'.

"Cain was not entirely stupid; and, even as he took steps to ensure that the 'occupier' Abel wouldn't get into a position to challenge or threaten him in any way by keeping him on the defensive all the time, he frequently worried that a 'plutocrat' like himself, whose success was achieved almost entirely at the expense of Abel, might be in for a real surprise one day. If Abel survived his ordeal without committing the sin of despair or some other sin that individuals in his position might be inclined to, he might well end up having the last laugh in the end! Cain understood very well that, even if he succeeded in 'doing away' Abel's entire 'clan' somehow so that it was just his 'clan' that survived to enjoy the blessings of Mother Earth, 'what goes around comes around'! That was what his mom Eve, lamenting the way she had observed him 'maltreating' Abel as she put it, had exclaimed in the hearing of everybody including Abel on one occasion. He was of course mad at her for saying such a thing to him in front of the 'whole world'! But she had said it, and everyone there except Cain had nodded in agreement, as if to say 'Vox Populi, Vox Dei' (the voice of the people is the voice of the Prime Mover). All of this had such a chilling on Cain; and unfortunately, much as he tried to dismiss his mom and everyone there, including his wife, as ignoramuses and totally wrong, something at the back of mind kept telling him that they were right - and that, yes, the voice of the people was the voice of the Prime Mover!

"Cain's pathological fear of the 'rat' Abel and his ilk

sometimes kept him up sleepless all night. Cain's antipathy for his brother got a boost from a bad dream he had on a day he thought he was finally going to enjoy a good night's rest. Cain dreamed that, instead of just the one Abel he had watched grow up and then try to encroach on his lands, he saw an entire army of humans descending on his choicest tracts of land. They all looked exactly like the Abel he knew, and they were calling themselves 'occupiers'. The intentions of the army of 'rats', as he himself liked to refer to them, were clear: they were there to see him dethroned from his pinnacle of power in the Garden of Eden! Cain was hollering, sweating, and swearing that he was going to find his own army of humans to battle them only to find that he didn't have the wherewithal to get up from his three-legged stool in order to make good on his promise to destroy that 'rat' Abel and his cohorts! The mysterious army of 'rats' was bearing down on him and about to overrun his position, when he awoke and discovered to his great relief that he had been dreaming.

"Cain recounted in the diary he kept how he spent one entire summer locked up inside a 'humvee' out of fear that a twister might appear from nowhere and give him a pounding from which he might not recover. He eventually let himself out when he realized that dying wasn't a really bad idea after all.

"First, if he lived to be a thousand years, he would be quite miserable and bedridden starting from around the time he turned four hundred years of age, and he would almost certainly be permanently plagued by arthritis starting from the time he turned five hundred years old. But the most convincing reason ended up being the fact that a thousand years was a pretty long time to wait by any standards before one died and headed off to Elysium to be united with one's Maker or Prime

Mover!

"You would of course think that later generations would learn from the experience of Cain. But, No! After they have invested so much time and effort developing humvees whose walls cannot be rammed in using technology stolen from Cain, they start fearing that one or other of their foes might succeed in stealing 'their' technology and going on to produce similar conveyances. And so, off they go and they start developing projectiles that can penetrate the hide of any humvee that human technology can produce, and disable it.

"And just when they are imagining that their military is ahead of everyone else in the capacity to wage wars and have a monopoly over the new technologies, lo and behold, not some rival super power, but some little known 'Jihad' group sympathetic to the most feared 'terrorists' on earth posts the blue print for their latest 'humvee' and the full slate of formulas needed by anyone who wants to develop projectiles that are capable of penetrating its hide on its website!

"They continue to concentrate on developing efficient methods of 'destroying' their fellow humans even though they know that they themselves are going to die. It is not just wasted effort - it is also damning! It is a waste of resources that could have been used to assure that every human lived in peace and comfort. And the failure to do that adds to their crime. So, so damn stupid! And if they only did what common sense dictated - if they employed the resources at their disposal to better the lives of all members of the human family without distinction - they wouldn't wind up with any 'terrorists' or 'insurgents' real or imagined! And this also says something about the world's think tanks so-called. There isn't one that has been able to get it right!

"To recap, victory can never be victory unless it is

612

victory over death. Any other 'victory' is a sham. And to win over death does not mean spending a lifetime worrying about how to stay alive, or trying to invent something that 'beats' death. It means stopping to let fear - the fear of death - dictate the actions of a human. Death came about as a consequence of sin, and being born in original sin in essence means being born in the grip of fear of death and subject to it.

"Misguided humans imagine that they can stem that fear by putting up ramparts around themselves in hopes of keeping the prowling 'Death' at bay and out of their immediate vicinity. Really stupid ones go to the extent of visiting death on those they perceive as their 'enemies' - which merely serves to seal their own fate while opening up opportunities for their victims to overcome death and their fear of it. But even the stupidest ones know better than to fight back when an unmistakably more powerful 'enemy' deliberately steps on their toes! You would think they would learn from that not just to live and let live in the face of any affront, but to even 'turn the other cheek' if necessary!

"The clever humans quickly learn that death has to be seen in the context of the struggle between Good and Evil in which they themselves as the poor forsaken children of Adam and Eve who are born inclined to sin are completely powerless; and they try to learn how to put their faith and trust in the Prime Mover, and the really clever ones flock to Mary, Mother of the Deliverer and Queen of Heaven, to ask that 'most gracious advocate' to turn her eyes of mercy upon them and, after their exile, to show unto them the Blessed Fruit of her womb and Prince of Peace. And they do not forget to ask her to pray for them, so that they may be worthy of the promises of the Deliverer.

The stain of Original Sin...

"It may be true that I am the Father of Death. But that 'death' is primarily spiritual. Humans are subject to its physical dimension only by virtue of putting their eternal life at risk. If Adam and Eve had not been insolent and 'eaten of the forbidden fruit', all humans would be craving for the moment when their 'earthly pilgrimage' would end and they crossed to the other side of the Gulf where they wouldn't be subject to our temptations or the temptations of the flesh, and where they would enjoy their crown in eternity in the presence of their Creator.

"I must point out one thing: even though I did not know at the time I led the rebellion against the Prime Mover that He would add 'human' creatures (also made in the Image) to creation - and even though, by extension, I did not know that physical death would be visited on humans as and when they incurred His ire by agreeing to join my camp, the moment I knew that I, Lucifer, had forfeited eternal life and was going to be cast in hell fire for ever more, I made up my mind that I would try and derail the divine plan in any way possible, but especially as it related to creatures that stood the slightest chance of delighting in the presence of the Prime Mover in my place.

"And so, even before 'human nature' was given its expression in Adam and eventually also in Eve and their posterity, it can be said that 'death' was literally hanging over them. By the time the soul of Adam was taking up its abode in the red grains of earthly matter, I was waiting and ready to do my job as the Tempter. And nothing bespeaks of my success more than the institutionalized killings that have been carried out in the name of 'Justice', 'Civilization', 'Liberty', 'Religion' and what have you since time immemorial.

"Now if Adam and Eve who were not subject to concupiscence which came with their fall from grace, or the inclination to sin associated with concupiscence, could fall for my pranks, you can imagine how easy it must be for their descendants, who are not only inclined to sin but grow up surrounded by all those hard core sinful and sinning adults - the same adults who should be mentoring them as they grow up - to fall for them.

"And then, when the young humans discover as they grow up that, after Adam and Eve sinned, a Deliverer was indeed promised by the Prime Mover; but that the Israelites, the chosen people, roundly rejected Him when He made His appearance on earth instead of rejoicing and embracing Him and His message of redemption, that must be disconcerting enough. But it must be even more disconcerting and confounding when the young people find myriad institutions, all of them claiming to be the Church the Deliverer founded and the new testament Ark of Noah even as they contradict each other right and left. Add to that the concupiscence and inclination to sin to which these young people, like their adult counterparts, find themselves subject!

"That state of affairs is, of course, not entirely unexpected. Look - when the Deliverer said, 'For judgment I am come into this world; that they who see not, may see; and they who see, may become blind' (John 9:25), He wasn't just referring to the Pharisees of His time. After all one doesn't choose to be born a Jew, a non-Jew or a Pharisee. The Deliverer was referring to everyone in every era who was in the same boat as those Pharisees who cast the man who had been born blind out of the synagogue for believing that the Nazarene was the Son of the Prime Mover. Yeah, he came into the world so that they who see not, *may* see; and they who see, *may* become blind! It is this that explains why the Jewish people are still awaiting their Messiah, and also why so many 'Christians' have not got it quite right - and why, despite the fact that the Son of Man came into the world, the world still harbors so much that is unholy and with which the young people have to contend!

"Look. If I did not know better, I would probably get on to some platform and declare 'Mission Accomplished'! But I just happen to be a little bit more knowledgeable than that.

"Concupiscence and the inclination to sin aren't sinful in themselves. In fact humans could turn them into the opportunities they were intended to be. Just rejecting my suggestions translates into meritorious works, and a decision by humans to resist temptations of the flesh with the help of divine grace automatically translates into a crown to be enjoyed in the hereinafter. This is stuff that turns sinful humans into saints and heroes.

"Still, growing up in a world in which the culture of violence and death is not just rampant, but is represented as something that is normal and even sacrosanct, one would have to be a rebel from one's earliest days to be immune from the deleterious effects of something that is as pervasive as that. The young one would actually risk being labeled a wimp and a nutcase, and would be lucky not to end up in one of those so-called 'correctional' institutions. That would be the almost certain fate of a kid who plucked up the courage to object to an assignment to read and internalize Gaius Julius Caesar's *De Bello Gallico* that glorifies foreign military adventures for their sake. And, of course, woe upon the kid who had the gall to suggest that passages of the Old Testament that sanction killing might actually be apocryphal!

"From the time Adam and Eve stole and ate of the forbidden fruit from the Tree of Knowledge of Good and Evil, we here in the Pit have worked very hard to ensure that violence and killings are glorified, and it is not by accident that the Old Testament is full of passages that glorify violence and wars. And the ghastly murder of Abel by the greedy Cain was a foretaste of things to come of murders committed in the name of national security, foreign adventures to plunder that would be passed off as religious crusades, and so on and so forth.

"But young humans invariably discover as they grow up that they too are beneficiaries of special largess from a Benefactor who only asks that they live up to their exalted state as creatures that are fashioned in His divine image and likeness in return. They also discover nonetheless that the world in which they found themselves is a cruel world in which humans scavenge on other humans at will. They discover that it is a world in which oppression of the weak and disadvantaged is the order of the day; and a world in which almost everyone is a liar, a dissembling idiot or both; and that being 'civilized' does not mean being 'civil', but being smart at taking what does not belong to you and calling it commerce; and also that might always makes right!

"Finding themselves in a world in which everyone around them is absorbed in the here and now, and permanently obsessed with how to carve out a piece of earth for oneself, young humans have little choice but to jump on the bandwagon and try thereafter to emulate those they deem as their 'heroes' in the strange new set up. We here in the Pit count on the young humans to make that 'logical' move. After Adam and Eve 'rebelled' and got booted out of 'Paradise', all their issue became inclined to sin, and these young humans are no exception. And even though the promised Messiah came and paid the price for the sins of humans, that did not of itself alter the equation very much, for the simple reason that the redemption of humans (when their lives don't get snuffed out while still in their mothers' wombs) is still dependent on the exercise of their free wills!

"He is a human!"...

"Now, the Deliverer Himself, conceived without original sin, as Man was nonetheless the same as all other humans in every respect except that He was sinless. I myself got my shot at tempting Him; and others too, including Peter, His nominee for the position of supreme Pontiff of the infant Church, also tried at my instigation, in a scheme that would have derailed the Divine Plan had it succeeded. And the Word-Become-Flesh was Himself buffeted by desires of the flesh like all the descendants of Adam and Eve.

"We ourselves in the underworld were, as you can imagine, at first thrilled that the Redeemer of humans was himself a human! You cannot imagine the echo that resounded all through hell as all of us fallen angels including all the demonic hierarchies - the hierarchies of Seraphim, Cherubim, Thrones, Powers, Dominions, Virtues, Principalities, Archangels and Angels - with fiendish joy and in one voice screamed: 'He is a human!'

"We were all itching to join battle with the Messiah of Humans just for that reason alone! It had escaped us all that the Son of Man also encapsulated the Word through whom all that was made came into being; and that, when He came down to Earth as the Savior of humankind and took up His human nature, He did so in obedience to the will of His Father in heaven.

"And, well, it was also again in obedience to His heavenly Father that he agreed to endure the utmost indignities at the hands of the same humans he had come to save!

"But in the meantime, we were all fooled, and

618

fooled thoroughly. And I certainly should have known better! Now, the Sacred Scriptures are full of warnings to the effect that, in the battle between the forces of Good and the forces of Evil that I lead, the tables were going to be turned against us; and, in fact, fairly quickly once that process had started.

"The words of the Prophet Isaiah were particularly ominous: 'The word that Isaiah the son of Amos saw, concerning Juda and Jerusalem. And in the last days the mountain of the house of the Lord shall be prepared on the top of mountains, and it shall be exalted above the hills, and all nations shall flow unto it. And many people shall go, and say: Come and let us go up to the mountain of the Lord, and to the house of the God of Jacob, and he will teach us his ways, and we will walk in his paths: for the law shall come forth from Sion, and the word of the Lord from Jerusalem. And he shall judge the Gentiles, and rebuke many people: and they shall turn their swords into ploughshares, and their spears into sickles: nation shall not lift up sword against nation, neither shall they be exercised any more to war. O house of Jacob, come ye, and let us walk in the light of the Lord...' (Isaiah 2:1-5)

"And, actually, it all happened exactly as Isaiah had said: 'And there shall come forth a rod out of the root of Jesse, and a flower shall rise up out of his root. And the spirit of the Lord shall rest upon him: the spirit of wisdom, and of understanding, the spirit of counsel, and of fortitude, the spirit of knowledge, and of godliness...' (Isaiah 11:1-2)

"In hindsight, I have to say that we in the Underworld did ourselves in when we took out time to celebrate the fact that the Messiah was a 'human'! We deceived ourselves to the point that even I myself didn't know at first what to make of it when Gabriel, addressing Mary to whom he was sent from on high, told her: 'Behold thou shalt conceive in thy womb and shalt bring forth a son: and thou shalt call his name Jesus. He shall be great and shall be called the Son of the Most High. And the Lord God shall give unto him the throne of David his father: and he shall reign in the house of Jacob forever. And of his kingdom there shall be no end.' (Luke 1:31-33)

"And that was when reality jolted me out of my doldrums. I was not exactly enthused by Gabriel's words; and John's description of what followed captures my feelings fairly accurately: 'And a great sign appeared in heaven: A woman clothed with the sun, and the moon under her feet, and on her head a crown of twelve stars. And being with child, she cried travailing in birth; and was in pain to be delivered. And there was seen another sign in heaven. And behold a great red dragon, having seven heads and ten horns and on his heads seven diadems. And his tail drew the third part of the stars of heaven and cast them to the earth. And the dragon stood before the woman who was ready to be delivered: that, when she should be delivered, he might devour her son. And she brought forth a man child, who was to rule all nations with an iron rod. And her son was taken up to God and to his throne. And the woman fled into the wilderness, where she had a place prepared by God, that there they should feed her, a thousand two hundred sixty days...' (Revelation 12:1-5)

"My worst fears, that the Prime Mover was about to elevate humans to a status that would even dwarf that which my fellow demons and I enjoyed before our pride caused us to fall from grace (Luke 10:18, Peter 2:4, and Jude 1:6), were confirmed when Mary responded to Gabriel by intoning her '*Magnificat*'. The 'chant' went as follows: '*Magnificat anima mea Dominum: et exsultavit spiritus meus in Deo salutari meo. Quia respexit humilitatem ancillae suae: ecce enim ex hoc beatam me*

620

dicent omnes generationes, quia fecit mihi magna qui potens est: et sanctum nomen ejus, et misericordia ejus a progenie in progenies timentibus eum. Fecit potentiam in brachio suo: dispersit superbos mente cordis sui. Deposuit potentes de sede, et exaltavit humiles. Esurientes implevit bonis: et divites dimisit inanes. Suscepit Israel puerum suum, recordatus misericordiae suae: sicut locutus est ad patres nostros, Abraham et semini ejus in saecula.' (My soul doth magnify the Lord. And my spirit hath rejoiced in God my Savior. Because he hath regarded the humility of his handmaid: for behold from henceforth all generations shall call me blessed. Because he that is mighty hath done great things to me: and holy is his name. And his mercy is from generation unto generations, to them that fear him. He hath shewed might in his arm: he hath scattered the proud in the conceit of their heart. He hath put down the mighty from their seat and hath exalted the humble. He hath filled the hungry with good things: and the rich he hath sent empty away. He hath received Israel his servant, being mindful of his mercy. As he spoke to our fathers: to Abraham and to his seed for ever.) (Luke 1:46-55)

"The 'humble handmaid of the Lord' (Luke 1:38) who, as St. Alphonsus Liguori would explain in *The Glories of Mary*, 'was filled with humility, disliked praise, and desired that God only be praised', was being elevated to the sublime heights of becoming the Mother of God! St. Bernard of Clairvaux would put it succinctly in his *Homiliae in laudibus Virginis Matris, in Magnificat (Homilies in praise of the Blessed Virgin Mary):* 'O Mary, had you not been humble, the Holy Spirit would not have come upon you, and you would not have become the Mother of God ...' Bernard, echoing Isaiah who had written 'Where will you look, but on him who is poor and humble, and contrite of heart?' (Isaiah 66:2), had also

621

added: 'As Satan's eyes are fixed on the proud, so God's eyes are on the lowly!'

"With that 'canticle of canticles', the 'Handmaid of the Lord' effectively crushed my head as is foretold in Genesis 3:15. There was just no way that we here in the Underworld could stomach, let alone recover from, being eclipsed by humans! Yes, humans - creatures that are akin to brutes that survive by dint of their innate instincts, except that humans also happen to be informed by souls and can laugh! Yes, because they can laugh, those humans who have their wits about them actually do laugh at us - I mean folks like St. Anthony of Egypt or Antony the great (c 251 –356), Padre Pio or Saint Pio of Pietrelcina (1887 – 1968), St. Maria Gemma Umberta Galgani, (1878 - 1903), St. Jean-Baptiste-Marie Vianney also known as the *Curé d'Ars* (1786 - 1859), or the indomitable Teresa of Avila (1515 – 1582). My fellow demons and I were engaged in constant battles with them and they won. Their weapons against us were prayer, humility, and - you guessed correctly - holy water!

"And this has happened even though humans, with the exception of Mary who was conceived immaculate through a special dispensation of grace, were born with the original sin! The fact that humans were spared and promised a Deliverer, of course, attests to the infinite mercies of the Prime Mover - mercies that we ourselves as pure spirits were ineligible for because we not only knew exactly what we were doing when we refused to genuflect, but we also knew full well that we would be banished from the sight of the Prime Mover if we went ahead and revolted. Of course if the coup we were plotting had succeeded, we would also have claimed the reward. Even though not divine, we would have ended up as masters of the universe! The 'prize' was enticing to that extent - and still remains enticing even in hindsight!

We were blinded by our pride to that extent and were too proud to care if we succeeded or not.

"And to utterly humiliate us, after we lost the battle that John describes so graphically in Revelation 12:7-9, we were cast into this hell - a place that is located in the belly of the earth of all places! I can assure you I sincerely and truly wanted that woman dead before she could give birth to her God-child.

"In the meantime, Joseph, because he was not privy to the 'Annunciation', was utterly shocked and flabbergasted noticing Mary's growing belly bulge and as he finally concluded that his wife-to-be was carrying a baby! Now, we pride ourselves of the fact that, year in and year out, we successfully persuade jealous men who suspect their spouses of infidelity to commit uxoricide. But Joseph who, according to Matthew, was a just man who was not at all disposed to publicly expose Mary to whom he was espoused (Matthew 1:19), instead soon begun to heap blame on himself for 'being an uncaring partner' of the young and to all appearances 'innocent' girl; and he was actually growing suicidal over the whole thing. We were cheering him on, naturally; and we were sorely disappointed when he had the dream. The angel of the Lord appeared to him in his sleep, saying: 'Joseph, son of David, fear not to take unto thee Mary thy wife, for that which is conceived in her, is of the Holy Ghost.' (Matthew 1:20) This was just terrible.

"It was so unfortunate that Joseph, the guardian and protector of the maiden who would become the mother of God (Luke 1:41-45), had that dream. If the carpenter had taken his own life, the scales would definitely have tipped in our favor. For one, the targets of our wrath would have been left exposed, giving me and my minions the opportunity to nip the threat to our reign on earth and to the hegemony my troops and I had enjoyed up until then in the bud.

"And you guessed right: All through the period Mary was carrying that baby, she was guarded 24/7 by a rotating bevy of angels who had sworn not to permit any of my troops, including my minions among humans, to get anywhere near her.

"But any way, you of course know what happened as soon as word got out that Mary had given birth to her God-child in Bethlehem. Alerted by the angel in his sleep, Joseph succeeded in escaping the dragnet laid for Mary's god-child by Herod the Great by a whisker, and fleeing with mother and Son to Egypt! My troops and I were certainly not fooling around, and we were using everything in our toolkit, including out minions amongst men, in our attempts to frustrate the divine plan for humans.

"As the Evangelist Matthew pointed out (Matthew 2:18), that dragnet and the massacre that ensued had been foretold by the prophet Jeremiah: 'A voice in Rama was heard, lamentation and great mourning; Rachel bewailing her children, and would not be comforted, because they are not...' (Jeremiah 31:1-30)

"And, a divinity, He still knew better than to roam the steppes of Galilee and Judea showing off His power to perform miracles or declaring that I, Beelzebub and Evil Ghost, was the underdog. He merely sought to do the will of His Father, and vanquished me and my troops, judo style, by not standing in the way of *vires iniqui* (the wicked humans who were acting as my surrogates) as they mocked and assaulted Him, crowned Him with thorns, and finally destroyed the Temple in which He had made His abode during His sojourn on earth - the temple that would be glorified in three days.

"And then, to ensure that His death and resurrection would not be in vain, He saw to it that poor forsaken children of Adam, who fell for my pranks and for the temptations of the flesh and were repentant, would find forgiveness through the Sacrament of Penance. That was actually how He turned my world upside down, and took the sting out of Death which was one of the wages of sin, so that humans who lose everything in this world, including their lives, as a result of rejecting my whiles, now actually become martyrs - which is what Thomas of Aquin, Theresa of Lisieux, Augustine of Hippo, Kizito of Uganda and others in fact became.

"Now, hand in hand with the institutionalization of killings under the dubious banner of 'just wars', the ethic that 'might is right' also became firmly entrenched in the human psyche. The concept of 'unjust war' was invented by those who wanted to justify murder in the name of 'national security' so-called; and to make those who were mighty and powerful, and supposedly always right, appear morally responsible. And what of the Deliverer's injunction to turn the other cheek also? (Matthew 5:39 and Luke 6:29) And anyhow, what aggrieved people in their right minds would think of prosecuting a 'just war' where the odds of emerging triumphant from the ruins of war were stacked against them? Ah, Humans!

"And, instead of 'using their heads' to make sure that everyone got enough to eat, the stupid humans decided to apply their God-given intelligence in my service in the 'Manhattan Project'. They invented the bomb!

"Yeah, the bomb! You see - humans talk about the forces of Good led by the Prime Mover being at war with the forces of Evil led by me. But they do not seem to realize that the battle ground where all this is playing out is here on earth and specifically among humans. The success of the Manhattan project was not just a spectacular victory for us in this campaign, but a landmark and turning point in this war. Our best brains - or 'minds' if that makes more sense to you - are even now still evaluating the importance of that victory.

"The investment in the bomb by humans was diametrically opposed to the idea of a harmonious world in which humans could live together as brothers and sisters and as members of the same human stock.

"Jorge Mario Bergoglio, the two hundred and sixty-sixth pontiff in the papal line of succession, put it succinctly when, visiting Nagasaki and Hiroshima, he declared: 'Peace and international stability are incompatible with attempts to build upon the fear of mutual destruction.'

"From the day Adam, the first human, found himself all alone on earth and, craving for the company of a fellow human, beseeched the Prime Mover to look with favor upon him and provide him company in the person of Eve, we have always worked to ensure that, instead of a world in which humans sought to make their lives as a people of one stock the envy of the beasts of the earth and other lower creatures, they would be focused on self-indulgence and thirsting for each other's blood in the literal sense.

"Now, in the days before START (the Strategic Arms Reduction Treaty) was signed by the Americans and the Russians, the cost of producing just a single nuclear bomb easily eclipsed the amount the populations of those two protagonists were spending annually on health, housing and food. That is about the cost of feeding the combined populations of India and Pakistan for twenty years. But what the Manhattan project - and the cold war which ensued between those nuclear giants - did was to cause India and Pakistan to replicate it, effectively denying millions food, medicine and shelter outright.

"Instead of humans who had a command of life saving technology sharing it with those that didn't for the purpose of saving lives, the technology sharing between humans has been pursued for completely wrong reasons with a recklessness that even us here in the Pit could never have imagined. As a consequence, the Armageddon in waiting for the inhabitants of earth would have been unimaginable a hundred years ago. But it is not just an Armageddon that is waiting to befall humans, it is an Armageddon that is now sure to befall humans, and in the very near future too! And, all because of the insolence of the so-called advanced nations, and their mad desire to be masters of the world.

"And what with the devastating consequences on the environment of the atmospheric and underground nuclear tests, even as the day of that Armageddon draws nigh, a series of secondary but immediate mini Armageddons in the form of scotching heat waves and ravaging floods are now commonplace, and are not sparing anyone - not even those same so-called advanced nations that started it all with a swagger and defiance that had never been known to man before the Manhattan project was conceived - at our suggestion of course - by terror-stricken, thoroughly misguided humans. Ah, yes - the Manhattan project!

"And bad as that is, the full extent of the problem cannot be appreciated until it is recognized that evil is entrenched in the human psyche by virtue of the original sin. The crop of humans who invented the bomb was just one. After they pass on and join the ranks of lost souls and fallen angels here in Gehenna - or if they saw light, changed their minds and just pulled out of the death culture business - it isn't a big hassle at all finding other hell-bent humans to take their places. Just a minor inconvenience!

"Now, we even got the damn stupid humans to use the bomb! So, so stupid! Yeah, let's see how they can do this and still inherit those mansions in heaven that had been earmarked for us!

"And talk about history repeating itself - and about reaping what you sow! Or about stupidity! At the height of my own insolence - and it didn't help that I was the 'Prince of Light' at the time I decided to concoct the scheme that was intended to see myself and all the angels who wished to join me in my rebellion rid of the Almighty One - I had every intention of committing murder (killing Him) so I could take His place. That was what led me to head the task force to invent Death! I like to think of it as our own 'Manhattan project'!

"If we succeeded in inventing Death and visiting it on Him, that was it! I would be crowned the Father of Death and also the new Boss of All. But instead of being at the administering end, we found ourselves at the receiving end! And that is how we found ourselves banished to this dreadful sinkhole of the spiritually dead and lost souls. And so it is going to be for the inventors of the bomb - when they too finally find themselves at the receiving end!

"Oh! It is going to be just so terrible - first as the secret services of the West expand their extrajudicial 'Kill Lists' dramatically, and unsuspecting folks in the Middle East, the Far East and Africa find themselves, along with their families, suddenly the target of drone attacks! Yeah! Expanded extrajudicial assassination lists, and with not a word of condemnation from the Holy See! Talk about strange bedfellows - the Vicar of the Deliverer whose labors are devoted to the salvation of souls, and me, Beelzebub and Chief Demon, who is committed to the cause of death and the damnation of souls! And this should tell you that we here in the pit have not been exactly resting on our laurels even after notching that impressive string of victories!

"And, second, as those hapless 'insurgents' and 'terrorists', after bearing the brunt of drone attacks and other stealth 'surgical' operations conducted by western super powers in their 'war on terrorism' over a prolonged period, working in concert, take advantage of the latest in computer hacking technology, finally get to have their own mini 'nukes', and then promptly proceed to 'publish' their own 'Kill Lists' consisting of names of cities in Europe and America! It will be just so, so terrible!

"That is what I mean by history repeating itself. You have to be dumb not to notice that the stage is already set for those who invented the bomb to reap what they sowed!

"As the Chief Evil Ghost, I say 'Hurray!' to my fellow demons and all you wicked humans who have consented to join us in this 'great', 'shameful' and totally 'ignoble' cause! Yeah...the ignoble cause that 'Might', wielded by wicked humans for an evil cause is Right'! Right - even though, for wicked humans, this is true only in the short term and can never be true over the long term.

"And now also - predictably - any defensive actions by the 'underdogs', particularly those nations that have been labeled 'rouge' automatically became 'criminal', 'unconscionable' and 'unjust', particularly if they seem to be directed against a 'superior' or 'super' power. But, of course, warlike actions automatically became 'just' and 'blessed' the moment they get the backing of the mighty. Suffice it to say that those twin concepts - that mass murder in the course of prosecuting 'just' or 'unjust' wars (depending on which side the observer was on) have enabled me to rule the world and mold it in my own ugly satanic 'image'.

"The problem, of course, is that 'might' makes

'right' only when one is talking about the 'Almighty" who, by definition, is always "Right'. Meaning, that it is blasphemy of the highest order for humans to presume that they too must always be right when they imagine that they are powerful and wield plenty of 'might', just as it is also damning to misuse power and authority for which one is answerable to the Prime Mover from whom all power and authority derive.

"And just as my forces had done with the Israelites before the advent of the Deliverer, we have also hijacked religion and have used it to 'bless' wanton murder and mayhem and plunder in which nations indulge in the name of 'national security'. There was a time when it was I - of all creatures - who actually decided St. Peter's successor with the help of my cronies in the Vatican.

"We may have suffered some setbacks in that regard since, but you can be certain that we are working hard to reposition ourselves so that we can exploit the Judases among the clergy and get back in the business of electing popes. Success on that front will mean that we (the powers of darkness) will be once again in control over all the three pillars of 'progress' as defined by us - the ability to redefine morality as we please on the basis that might is always right, the ability to declare wars and commit mass murders and banditry in the name of national security, and the ability to canonize our agents and cronies in advance even as they are presiding over those evil and vile activities.

Changing tactics...

"And, talking about hijacking religion, it would have represented an unmitigated and quite serious failure on our part if we had not taken advantage of unbridled human greed and bigotry to turn Palestine - the homeland of Joseph, Mary and the Deliverer - into the place it is to day - a place where wanton murder and mayhem are the order of the day, and are done in the name of the Prime Mover. What goes on there epitomizes my Rule, which employs the self-righteous to do unto others in the name of the Prime Mover what they definitely wouldn't want done unto themselves! My troops and I have planned everything meticulously - down to the wire as you folks say. We are not in the habit of leaving anything to chance.

"When humans start doing things out of the ordinary because they think they can justify what they do, they had better be right and their reasoning as well. When they end up going against the dictates of reason, they bear the full responsibility for choosing to experiment with what is out of the ordinary. They have themselves to blame when they end up here in the Pit with us. And from the moment they decide to play footsie with their eternal life thinking they will be able to justify their misadventures, our own task is clear - to work with them to ensure that they end up here with us, because we need that company bad.

"Humans are so daft! Until they 'kick the bucket' and 'wake up' to reality in the process, they appoint themselves judges at precisely the time when so much is expected of them. And, in their minds, they consign the real victims of things like 'terrorism' to hell and canonize the real terrorists even as they are marauding, looting and murdering in the name of Civilization.

"I am the devil, and I can affirm that the hunted, 'unsaved' terrorists and insurgents go to heaven, while the blood-thirsty demagogues who like to regard themselves as the 'elect' even as they are on their murderous adventures around the world and others who murder and wreak havoc on the lives of the innocent (whom they always rush to label 'thugs' and 'enemies of peace') in the name of the Prime Mover end up right here in the Pit with none other than me - Satan, the Prince of Darkness! You don't need to waste your time arguing about that. You should just bide your time and see for yourself how things transpire when the time comes for you to cross the Gulf.

"And - if you do not know - the lot falls pretty well on us demons here in the Pit to ensure that our 'human collaborators' get their fair share of the wretched life that is known as 'hell'. And because we really want to be *fair* to everyone here, we work strictly by the book too.

"If while on earth, in your zeal to administer 'justice', you thought it was 'humane' to subject other humans to all sorts of strange things - to things like 'prolonged solitary confinement', 'stress and duress', or 'extreme deprivation of sensory stimuli'; or if you thought that it was perfectly alright to force other humans to stand or assume positions that 'induce physical stress or pain over time', to subject other humans to 'routine and barbaric beatings', to douse humans who are immobilized by handcuffs and leg iron-chains with cold water or to expose them to freezing temperatures, or to make a sport of others by piling them naked and while in hand-cuffs on top of one another and photographing them in that posture; or if you regarded it as something that was just fine to torture and humiliate their family members in captivity and cause them to sodomize each other in full view of other captives, or to urinate on them or have fun poking things in the eyes, or to sprinkle chemical substances on their exposed skin and force them to mug their loved ones for your pleasure, or to force them to ram and crush their heads into concrete walls for fun, or to cause them additional discomfort by applying electric shocks on their person as a way of 'softening them up some more', or to confine fellow humans in dark vaults, or to 'soft them up some more' by keeping them awake with noise and flood lights, or to let guard dogs that are trained to kill loose on hand-cuffed humans, or to pretend to scare the daylights out of humans who are just like yourself by threatening to shoot or to electrocute them while immobilized and helpless, or to keep fellow humans 'hooded' for days, or to deprive captives of sustenance as a way of 'softening them up some more'; or if you thought that you could kill fellow humans who were in restraints with impunity by administering body blows or by just shooting them dead; or if you did not think there was anything wrong with 'water boarding' *your* buddy, or with desecrating a buddy's body after he/she died while in your custody, and other things like that; or if you thought that fellow humans were not your buddies just because of a grudge you might have had against them - in the Pit, we just let the 'demon in you' that prompted you to do those things return to haunt you; and, not just once, but over and over and over until you get sick of it and start wishing that you never saw the light of day.

"And there is real fire - smoldering cinders and blue scotching flames that do not go out - here in hell. (Revelation 21:8) Look, first off, according to Thomas Aquinas, Goodness and Being are really the same, and differ only in idea. (Summa Theologiae, First Part, Question 5) Earlier, St. Augustine had pointed out that, inasmuch as humans *exist*, they are *good*. (On Christian Doctrine i, 42) It is therefore no accident that the Prime Mover, gazing upon all the things He had *made*, saw that they were *very good*! (Genesis 1:31)

"And then, Paul, addressing the Corinthians, wrote: 'For no man can lay a foundation other than the one which is laid, which is Jesus Chris. Now, if any man builds on the foundation with gold, silver, precious stones, wood, hay, straw, each man's work will become evident; for the day will show it because it is to be revealed with fire, and the fire itself will test the quality of each man's work. If any man's work which he has built on it remains, he will receive a reward. If any man's work is burned up, he will suffer loss; but he himself will be saved, yet so as through fire.' (1 Corinthians 3:11-15) Paul had written in the same epistle: 'Works are judged after death and tested by fire.' (1 Cor. 3:10-15)

"Then, in his epistle to the Hebrews, Paul wrote: 'Therefore, receiving an immoveable kingdom, we have grace: whereby let us serve, pleasing God, with fear and reverence. For our God is a consuming fire.' (Hebrews 12:28-29). Additional biblical references to fire that purifies are found in Daniel 12:10, Sirach 2:5, Malachi 3:2-3, Zechariah 13:8-9 and Wisdom 3:5-6. And then, in *Crossing the Threshold of Hope*, Pope John Paul II points out that there is a direct relationship between the Prime Mover's 'Living Flame of Love' as described by St. John of the Cross and the Church's doctrine of Purgatory.

"And, in her book *Fire of Love*, St. Catherine of Genoa wrote: 'I perceive there to be so much conformity between God and the soul that when He sees it in the purity in which His Divine Majesty created it, He gives it a burning love, which draws it to Himself, which is strong enough to destroy it, immortal though it be, and which causes it to be so transformed in God that it sees itself as though it were none other than God. Unceasingly God draws the soul to Himself and breathes fire into it, never letting it go until He has led it to the state from which it came forth—that is, to the pure cleanliness in which it was created.'

"Now, as the Angelic Doctor pointed out in his Summa, evil is the absence of good; and there you see the connection between fire and the love for the Prime

634

Mover or its absence. And it is the reason there is real, smoldering fire here in hell. (Revelation 21:8) Made in the image of the Prime Mover, you humans and us here in the pure spirit realm can only find our self-actualization in Him. But now, cut off from Him, we are in the same boat as that fellow in the parable of the rich man and Lazarus! (Luke 16:23-24)

"It is my unenviable task to welcome here in this 'lake which burneth with fire and brimstone' (as our hell hole is described in Revelation 21:8) souls of humans who lead less than sterling lives during their sojourn on earth - lives that are not befitting creatures that are fashioned in the Image - and who cross the gulf that separates the living from the dead whilst unrepentant.

"It was Simon Peter, the first pope, who wrote: 'Be sober and watch: because your adversary the devil, as a roaring lion, goeth about seeking whom he may devour. Whom resist ye, strong in faith: knowing that the same affliction befalls, your brethren who are in the world.' (1 Peter 5:8-9) That 'son of Bar Jonah' was writing from experience! And also, recall the story of Job who lived in the land of Uz and my role in it? I think I am making a mistake to assume that you do. The Book of Job is the least read of all the canonical books of the Old Testament. It doesn't read like the Song of Songs or (for those who have never found a moment to look inside the covers of a bible) a romantic novel. The story of Job is really depressing. And this is just well and good, because then folks don't get to know my *modus operandi* which is laid out so well in the Book of Job! A similar fate no doubt awaits the thesis I am helping Mjomba craft. But who cares? Damned…if humans fall in love with the thesis and proceed to devour it (because they then won't have any excuse for not living up to their status as creatures that are molded in the Prime Mover's image) and damned...if they don't (because then they continue to wallow in their ignorance)! But humans would do well to commit to memory just one verse from the Book of Job which goes: '*Et dixit nudus egressus sum de utero matris meae et nudus revertar illuc Dominus dedit Dominus abstulit sit nomen Domini benedictum.*' (Naked came I out of my mother's womb, and naked shall I return thither: the Lord gave, and the Lord hath taken away: as it hath pleased the Lord so is it done: blessed be the name of the Lord.) (Job 1:21) That is what the battle between Good and Evil is all about!

"And so, when the demons in you - the demons that now help you to 'speak with the tongues of men and of angels' when, without charity, you really are 'as sounding brass, or a tinkling cymbal' with nothing more to it - come back to haunt you here in hell, it is also very real! Surreal, in fact, and very painful! Terribly ashaming, and heart wrenching in the extreme if only because the miseries endured here in the Pit are unending and go on forever and ever!

"What happens when a 'lost' soul arrives here in the Pit, is that the tables become verily turned, and that soul starts enduring what it did unto other souls that it would not have liked done unto itself. And, because the pain is spiritual and not simply physical, it always beggars the imagination - yes, even my own devilish and satanic imagination!

"I myself suffer tremendously, of course; but when I see souls in terrible anguish as they pay the debt for their rotten deeds, I sometimes find myself toying with the crazy idea that I wouldn't want to exchange places with them. The problem though is that here the pain and suffering is commensurate with the ability to suffer, which is in turn commensurate with the gifts with which one was endowed at creation.

"You can expect me, Beelzebub, to suffer much more in that sense than any other creature here. When paying the debt of the sins of humans, the Deliverer undoubtedly suffered too. The combined physical and mental pain that He endured must have exceeded anything that we demons, and the souls of damned humans, know. It is not possible to measure the suffering of the incarnate Word when He was subjected to abuse and humiliation by creatures that could not have come into existence except through Him. Even though lasting only a certain period, because it was pain that was endured by a divinity, it also automatically morphs into pain for eternity; and that is even though the situation was salvaged by the Deliverer's victory over death and His resurrection from the dead! There is no way that the sufferings that the Son of Man, a member of the Godhead, endured as He was mocked and abused, scourged, crowned with thorns, and then crucified by sinful humans can be measured. It is beyond my comprehension and certainly beyond that of humans as well.

"Getting back to what the mind can fathom, I was endowed with more gifts than even Michael the Archangel; and, consequently, more was expected from me than from any other creature that existed up until then. If any demon or lost human soul were exposed to what I now endure, that demon or soul would get so scotched, it would wither in moments and could conceivably find itself rubbed out and effectively non-existent. But as you might have guessed, the Deliverer, who is also the Word and Judge, will never allow that to happen.

"It isn't Him who 'created' the conditions in the Pit after all - we ourselves did with our dastardly behavior. It may be true that hell is a place - yes, a real 'place' as opposed to a 'state'. Nevertheless, it is our niggardly and vile deeds that metamorphosed into the dungeons and the searing flames that can never be extinguished. It is what happens when mere creatures (which is what we all are) have the audacity to try and take on the Prime Mover.

"As for me, I have to continue being haunted for all eternity by the demon in me that got me to refuse to adore the Creator and subsequently got me to lure the choirs of angels that suddenly became transfigured into the demons they are now when they too refused to bow and acknowledge the Prime Mover's greatness. We have to continue to exist and to suffer to our capacity as we pay the price for our vanity.

"Still, I can't help trying to take comfort from the thought that if I had remained loyal to the Prime Mover, I would be up there - enjoying more than even Michael the Archangel - if you can call that comfort! I feel so much shame that a creature that was as brilliant and smart as myself blew the opportunity to ride high. And you know the saying that the mind is a terrible thing to waste! And maybe you can now understand how frustrated with myself and depressed I feel for blowing it - for knowing that someone with my talents is now good for nothing except as a Tempter and a Destroyer!

"It is similarly true for you humans. If you boast a bright mind and think you are clever, you'd better make damn sure you do not end up here lamenting over it the way I anguish over my wasted spiritual faculties. You'd better stay clear of Broadway, and you certainly shouldn't bury any talent that you may have been graced with. If you should succeed in staying on the narrow path and in delivering the goods, you can be sure of earning yourself a mansion in heaven. But 'pride comes before the fall', and don't you be too cocky. Take a leaf from me, dammit!

"You wander into Broadway, or become cozy with the ways of the world and, as surely as you exist, you will end up in this damn hell. But do I really care a damn thing for the geeks who end up here with us? I'd say they deserve everything - and more. What do they think they are - special?

"Most of you humans think that you are - until you kick the bucket, and find yourself being accosted by the Avenging Angel as soon as you get to this side of the Gulf. Oh o o o! You all realize eventually that you are not all that special - when the Gates of Hell, blackened and creaking, open and you find yourselves literally swept off your feet and borne away to the dungeon reserved for you by howling demons and the other loathsome inmates of the Pit. Once upon a time we all thought we were special. But we learned that we weren't - too late, after we had done our best to give others a hell they didn't deserve!

Spin...

"Given the legacy of original sin, whenever humans open their mouths, chances are that they will eschew truth in favor of spin. The inclination to sin - and also to spin - is not fiction. It is real, and translates in lies, spin, ingratiating self-justification, and every conceivable sin including murder. That is, after all, what happened when humans cornered the Son of Man and also Deliverer, and tried to neutralize and rub Him out.

"As with all other sins, the act of 'murder' was committed, but the attempt to neutralize Him boomeranged. The attempts of humans to neutralize those they do not have a liking for invariably fail, but the perpetrators always succeed in committing the act of murder and dooming themselves. The act of murder is usually the last act in a series of acts that infringe on natural justice and the commandment to love one another.

"Back to spin - the more humans lie, the more accolades they receive as spokespersons, diplomats, teachers, and even as preachers. The way we have organized everything, it is the criminals and the liars who come out on top in this world. It is I, Beelzebub, after all who still holds sway in this world; and that is how things will stay - at least until the time of the much maligned and misquoted 'Rapture'

"But humans are so stupid. There simply is no way that humans or pure spirits for that matter, who themselves are supposed to be 'Fools for the Deliverer', can bamboozle and fool the Prime Mover. For a start, the Prime Mover does not require the services of a prosecutor to arraign evil creatures and bring them to justice. He does not even need a security force to round up evildoers and send them to hell. He would not be a Prime Mover. You make a habit of going against the Prime Mover - or against your conscience - and you end up feeling more 'comfortable' here in the Pit with us - if you do not mind the sarcasm - than with the Deliverer in heaven.

"The Prime Mover is not just clever, and He is not simply 'cleverness' either. I am the devil, and you can take it from me that He knows pretty well what He does, and how to do it. If He didn't, you can bet that I wouldn't be languishing in this damn pit. The Prime Mover is Truth...Knowledge. And because He Himself is in-dwelling in human souls, the human conscience will always sound the alarm as soon as humans start to lean towards that which represents betrayal of Truth.

"And so, when you make it your business to spin facts, and to manipulate, spin or misrepresent the truth, that is not simply a betrayal of the Prime Mover, it is tantamount to idolatry. For instead of worshiping at the altar of the Prime Mover and of Truth, those of you who spin choose to descend so low as to pay homage to falsity, and the non-existent god called 'Untruth'. Consequently, all you liars and others who spin facts are *de facto* idolaters. And when you say you worship the Prime Mover, you mean a false prime mover who exists only in your own imagination and phantasy. You ultimately worship your own egos - you think you are omnipotent. And that is even worse than worshiping idols made of stone!

"And when you spin and pretend to be godly at the same time, it stops being idolatry and becomes something else - it becomes a sacrilege! Being as cocky as you all are, you evidently know perfectly well what you are doing. Twisting and manipulating facts needs a crooked or warped mind to try and paint things that are false as truth. It is therefore damning automatically. And can you imagine a damned soul hanging around and trying to act as if the Prime Mover is on his/her side?

Fraudsters…

"The fact of the matter is that humans who are 'liars' are my minions! Yeah, minions of the Father of Lies! And, like Ananias of the Acts of the Apostles and his wife Saphira, they are in it for the long haul. Their hypocrisy, far from being just a one-time deal, is something that is deeply ingrained in their psyches. And don't you start getting the idea that liars are strangers to things like religion or the supernatural. If that were so, the Deliverer wouldn't have used words like "These people honor me with their lips, but their hearts are far from me" in describing my clients.

"Liars live on lies, and their goals in life have nothing in common with uprightness or the virtues of forbearance, patience, forgiveness and godliness. On the contrary, liars exploit the fact that the victims of their lies are those humans who are as guileless and innocent as 'babes in the woods', and are determined to take advantage of the 'people of God'. The fraudsters know exactly what they are up to, and make a point of honing their skills at their craft so they can rake in their millions, and which they do on the backs of their unsuspecting victims. But even as they do so, they do not once lose sight of the fact that the more they portray themselves as the 'upright' folks, and the more they denigrate anyone who sees through the façade and makes a move to expose them, the more they stand to gain from the lies and the schemes they never tire of hatching - and the less their prospects of repenting and returning to Him who is the Way, the Truth and the Life.

"That is the reason betrayers par excellence must keep up the charade even as they betray the Son of Man with a kiss. And this is because I, Satan, have entered into them just as I did the apostle from Kerioth about whom it is written: '*Intravit autem Satanas in Iudam qui cognominatur Scarioth unum de duodecim*' ('Then entered Satan into Judas surnamed Iscariot, being of the number of the twelve'). (Luke 22:3-4) Nor was Judas the only one I entered and possessed.

"The priests and Pharisees were determined to keep their 'religion' if only because it provided them the cover they needed for their lies. The alternative was to tell the truth concerning the Deliverer and shame me, Satan, in the process.

"But, according to the Scriptures, as soon as it was day, the elders of the people and the chief priests and the scribes came together, and led him into their council, saying, Art thou the Christ? Tell us. And he said unto them, If I tell you, ye will not believe: And if I also ask you, ye will not answer me, nor let me go. Hereafter shall the

Son of Man sit on the right hand of the power of God. Then said they all, Art thou then the Son of God? And he said unto them, Ye say that I am. And they said, What need we any further witness? For we ourselves have heard of his own mouth!

"So you can now understand why there are so many 'Christian' denominations - they are necessary to provide the cover that all those liars need so much.

"And if it should happen that the lying that goes on is of the type that is incompatible with the profession of one of the 'mainstream' religions that has prescribed rituals and/or a creed, that never stops the liars from seeking to portray themselves as 'upright' citizens who are deserving of the utmost trust all the same - if necessary, with a helping hand from me of course. That usually makes it hard for even the most discerning individuals to tell that he/she is dealing with fraudsters until it is too late – until well after the fraudsters had gotten away with pulling another fast one on him/her.

"But do you recall the story of the man who was on a trip from Jerusalem to Jericho, and was attacked by bandits who stripped him of his clothes, beat him up, and left him half dead beside the road? Remember the priest who saw the man lying there, and who crossed to the other side of the road so he could pass him by? Or the Levite who walked over, looked at the man lying there, but also passed by on the other side?

"You won't, of course, remember the despised Samaritan who saw the man, felt compassion for him, and went over and soothed his wounds with olive oil and wine and bandaged them; and who then put the man on his own donkey, and took him to an inn, where he took care of him at his own expense. This is because, like the reverend and the Levite (those selfish braggarts who lived in an ivory tower), you are the sort of hypocrite I am

643

talking about!

"The lying also provides support for things like the so-called 'military industrial complex' which assures that the killing of humans by humans continues unabated, and the 'health insurance industry' that must take advantage of the fact that humans die when they are unable to obtain the treatment and medication they need to rake in billions for their masters.

"The moral (you are supposed to take away but won't) is that, excepting for the Deliverer and his blessed mother, Mary, who was conceived without sin, all humans are traitors…betrayers, and Judases; and all those who are in the habit of singling out others and calling them 'traitors', 'terrorists', 'unsaved', or 'un-Christian-like' or even 'un-Catholic-like' betray themselves with their own shallow, materialistic self-interests and rabid hypocrisy! That includes even Simon Peter who was determined to distance himself from Judas whom I, Beelzebub, had already entered and possessed.

"It is the sacred writer who wrote (and I am not making this up): 'And the Lord said, Simon, Simon, behold, Satan hath desired to have you, that he may sift you as wheat: But I have prayed for thee, that thy faith fail not: and when thou art converted, strengthen thy brethren.'

"But, typical of sinful and sinning humans, Peter retorted: 'Lord, I am ready to go with thee, both into prison, and to death!' But the Deliverer's reply was: 'I tell thee, Peter, the cock shall not crow this day, before that thou shalt thrice deny that thou knowest me…For I say unto you, that this that is written must yet be accomplished in me. And he was reckoned among the transgressors.' Then took they him, and led him, and brought him into the high priest's house. And Peter followed afar off. And when they had kindled a fire in the midst of the hall, and were set down together, Peter sat down among them. But a certain maid beheld him as he sat by the fire, and earnestly looked upon him, and said 'This man was also with him'. And he denied him, saying, Woman, I know him not. And after a little while another saw him, and said, Thou art also of them. And Peter said, Man, I am not. And within about the space of one hour after another confidently affirmed, saying, Of a truth this fellow also was with him: for he speaks with the Galilean drawl. And Peter said, Man, I know not what thou sayest. And, immediately while he yet spake, the cock crew! And the Lord turned, and looked upon Peter. And Peter remembered the word of the Lord, how he had said unto him, before the cockcrow, thou shalt deny me thrice. And Peter went out, and wept bitterly.' Yes!

Avenging Angel...

"People who spend their lives hatching wicked plots and spinning facts to further their pursuit of material things, and then turn around and try to make it look as if they are all upright and dandy make things worse for themselves. And when humans who claim to be out to stop liars are themselves caught red-handed 'spinning' and distorting reality in the process, that is just terrible! And don't you suggest that you are out to stop terrorists when you yourself act like one - when you terrorize and kill innocent people who just want to be left in peace so they can get on with their lives.

"Don't you claim that you are treating fellow humans humanely when it is in fact torture that you are administering. Tut! Tut! Tut! The Avenging Angel doesn't take kindly to that particular kind of lie, because when you torture 'another human', it is in fact the Son of Man whom you torture. And, whether you call it torture or something else, it is a very terrible thing to do. You do not want to do that at all, because you do not want to suffer the fate of those who are caught doing it. The Avenging Angel simply abandons you to a pack of snarling, totally crazed and perverse demons - the same demons that were in you and that caused you to abuse, humiliate, and torture your fellow humans and to have the audacity to call it humane treatment.

"As you kick the bucket, the demons of course find themselves compelled to leave just as passengers on a boat that is alight scramble to abandon it for safety. After causing you to give others a hell, they are usually delighted to turn around, after the sentence is passed and I have given them a 'pat on the back' for a good job very well done, to give you a taste of whatever you meted out to other humans and to Him who accepted to take full responsibility for the sins of men. And what they do to you for all of eternity is just horrible...unspeakable!

"And again, don't be caught pretending to be an 'honest broker' in a conflict when the fact of the matter is that you are just posturing and actually conspiring with one of the parties to undermine a just resolution of the conflict.

"Those humans who are in the business of 'spinning' facts and misrepresenting reality are all in the wrong business. They are conning themselves at the same time as they are making the case against themselves. There is no better evidence for the iniquity of liars than the rationalizations in which they indulge in an effort to try and paint lies as facts or truths, and cloak the malice aforethought within. Attempts by lying earthlings to depict themselves as innocent and blameless only go to validate their status as shameless liars and weirdoes, and to confirm those earthlings as my minions! Talk about a win-win situation for the Father of

Lies! The spin they put on facts represents the irrefutable evidence that will be ranged against them on Judgement Day – evidence that they knowingly and deliberately violated their trust, and effectively sold their birthright for what did not even amount to a bowl of pottage!

"And, look - the proof of the pudding, as you earthlings say, is in the eating! And you also must know who said: "Wherefore by their fruits ye shall know them"! However much one spins the facts, and indulges in grandstanding, the fact remains that where you used to have 'original virtue', now you have 'original sin'! And so, all the ostentatious performance aimed at impressing folks notwithstanding, it is completely hypocritical for folks who commit sin not once but seventy times seven times a day at least to try and pretend that they are good, let alone better than others! And if a human is not in the habit of practicing mortification like Jerome or more recently John Paul did, just take it as a joke when you see all those left leaning and right leaning spinmeisters take to the stage and try and bluff you.

"Blinded by egotism, wicked humans easily forget that they are mortal. Then, locked in their pursuit of the material and the temporal, in a desperate effort to clinch each for himself or herself the most lucrative deals, they throw away all caution to the wind as they vie with one another in manufacturing lies and spinning falsehoods, in complete disregard of the fact that they are temples of the Prime Mover, and in disregard of His injunction to them that they love one another!

"As for the 'media types' who are supposed to be in the business of disseminating information, they damn themselves too by withholding critical information or reporting half facts to promote the dubious agendas and partisan interests; and their fate becomes sealed when they start passing themselves off as the 'elect' and referring to their opponents as 'devils'.

"Humans have of course been putting a spin on facts ever since Adam and Eve sinned and tried to lay the blame for their indiscretion on me. I mean - I am the tempter, and I was just doing my job! Free creatures, they could have said 'No'!

"Instead of reporting the facts accurately and objectively, humans have 'spun' facts and misrepresented reality ever since Cain tried to cover up a ghastly murder by telling a tall tale about how his brother - the first murder victim ever - had walked into a thicket and been spirited away. Actually, spinning facts stopped being an 'art' and became a 'science' long ago; and today it is the preserve of professionals - politicians, generals, newspaper columnists and political pundits, preachers, historians, and others. In fact some 'think tanks' are tasked with doing nothing but put a spin on things. It is all so very fascinating.

"Of course crooked folks involved in such chicanery don't have to be caught by anybody for them to face retribution. Let me warn you - the Avenging Angel does need the International Red Cross or Human Rights Watch, either of which is capable of being manipulated. He certainly does not need the United Nations that serves the interests of its founders (it is not for nothing that they retained for themselves the power to veto any of that body's resolutions).

"You have to remember how those organizations came into being. It is not as if they were ordained by the Prime Mover. On the contrary, they were started at my explicit instigation. In the case of the United Nations, I persuaded the 'victors' in the wake of the second world war to set it up and get it going in order to ensure that they didn't get in trouble for 'war crimes' like for example 'carpet bombing' of cities and using weapons of mass destruction when they were prosecuting the war. The second and only other reason was to set the stage for the super power fraternity to ride rough shod over other nations of the world in their scramble for control over oil and other scarce resources regarded as vital to their 'national security'. And that is also why it was important for these folks to retain the power to veto any resolutions of that organization's so-called Security Council.

"On the face of it, the United Nations is supposed to safeguard the rights of the citizens of the world from despots - it supposed to ensure that those who commit crimes human rights are brought to justice. But in practice, its *raison de tre* is to serve the interests of members of the veto-wielding club, and to legitimize anything they dream up and do without regard to natural justice. That is one reason the UN grants members of the veto-wielding club who commit such crimes immunity from prosecution. It is also why that body won't take effective steps to prevent atrocities in some parts of the world that are not regarded by the 'super powers' as being of 'strategic' importance to them (like Rwanda) even though it commands the necessary resources to do so - and every UN 'diplomat' knows it.

"I can guarantee you that the moment the UN (actually 'DN' for 'Divided Nations' would have been a more appropriate name) starts to look like it is getting transformed into an organization that promotes the common weal as opposed to the interests of the 'big five' and their allies, it will have to go - it will have to give way to something that is more attuned to my evil plan. Well, what did you think - that the UN was some charitable organization?

"If you do not know, in terms of serving my cause and facilitating the dispensation by me of material goods and worldly power to my minions, the age of the UN (and its predecessor the League of Nations) has been rivalled only by that epoch in history when the papacy was at my beck and call - that time when the popes literally appointed and deposed emperors and kings at will. So, even though I met with singular failure when I attempted to get the Son of Man and Deliverer Himself to change sides and work for my evil plan in return for becoming Lord of the Earth, I am quite successful in persuading His representatives here on earth and leaders of the so-called advanced nations, and particularly leaders of nations that are supposedly Christian, to work for my cause.

"As many a 'diplomat' will tell you, what goes on inside and outside the walls of the UN amounts to a farce engineered by members of the veto-wielding club. It is much worse than what goes on in Hollywood, because people really die as a result of what goes at the UN. What do you think happens to children and the infirm when the UN, at the instigation of a veto-wielding power, imposes a trade embargo on a country? In this age of globalization, you tell me what happens to jobs and the living standards when a country suddenly cannot obtain the things its citizens need to live well? But that is exactly what I have in mind when I talk of my evil cause - a cause that brings untold suffering and misery to innocent humans. And I know that when the innocent suffer, it is the Deliverer and Son of Man who suffers. Perhaps you now understand why mine is an evil cause!

"The only other thing that matters is that I use the place to whisk aspiring world leaders up the 'mountain top' from where I display the worldly things that can be theirs - if they only worship! Just as it is the Son of Man who suffers when the UN acts, it is I who is worshiped and glorified when representatives of nations succumb to arm-twisting and accept bribes peddled as 'foreign aid' by the super powers instead of casting their votes according to their conscience.

"The 'United Nations' and the idea of a veto-wielding club to guide its activities is just the perfect set up for now. It legitimizes the unconscionable and otherwise unlawful actions of the big five; and they in turn, with the automatic participation of heads of state from around the world, provide the cover I need to implement my evil plan. The Vatican's membership in this 'August Body' naturally lends it legitimacy in the eyes of peace-loving peoples. But, predictably, the Avenging Angel sees through all that.

"Of course, as humans wage wars each other over the 'crumbs' I threw at them, we here in the Pit can never stop to wonder at their stupidity. From age to age, humans have waged wars and slaughtered each other over nothing. Yes, nothing! All humans die regardless of whether they live to celebrate victories of wars successfully fought or are casualties of wars unsuccessfully fought and lost. If you are fighting over something, you should first check if you will be able to hold on to it if you in victory. Now, you lose whatever you have fought over if it is snatched away from you afterward - and that is exactly what I do when you die.

"I linger over folks just long enough to ensure that they have breathed their last and are safely on the other side of the Gulf, and I then quickly snatch back my goods so the recycling process can continue. And you just show me one castle that belongs to Julius Caesar! If he had given everything he had to the poor, he would have stashed something away for his afterlife - at least. As it is, he wanted to hang on to everything he had accumulated, including the loot he and his armies had brought back home from North Africa, Gaul and other places, and lost out – the stupid fellow! This is the same fate that meets losers and victors in war equally, and that awaits the generals and military commanders who stake everything in fighting and winning modern wars as well as those who become vanquished in battle and don't get the opportunity to celebrate the culmination of wars with victory parades.

"Given the short-lived nature of the 'victories', wars are not worthwhile, except of course when they are seen from my perspective - as a means of promoting my evil plan and undermining the Divine Plan in the process. Those who survive to tell any tales - and who happen to belong to the 'victorious' side - usually eulogize their fallen war dead as heroes who gave their lives in defense of 'freedom'.

"The problem is that all conquerors are self-declared conquerors; and victory is a function of brutal force that does not recognize common sense. For if brutal force recognized common sense, warring humans without exception would opt for negotiations and rush to settle their scores at a table instead of heading to the battlefield. Brutal force does not recognize right or wrong either. Hence the cycle of violence, which is driven, not by the noble idea of freedom (which has nothing in common with brutal force), but by greed and ambition.

"But just look at the investment nations make in armaments as they prepare to confront non-existent threats or threats that only exist in the figment of the imagination of the leadership. Instead of working for the *bonum commune* by employing the nation's to construct roads, feed the hungry, clothe the naked, and provide healthcare for the sick and old, at my instigation they start planning to wage wars 'in defense of freedom', and even persuade themselves along the way that fighting wars is something that is good for the economy! No! The only beneficiaries are the military industrial complexes that, as you may have already guessed, are my invention!

652

"Freedom, a nebulous idea that has been foreign to human experience since I got the first man and the first woman to jump ship and start hankering for a taste of the forbidden fruit, becomes even more nebulous when it is linked to the equally nebulous notion of democracy. With the fall of Adam and Eve from grace, humans became my slaves and lost their freedom. And if you think that 'democracy' works, just reflect on the fact that on the eve of the Twenty-first Century, Man, who has been to the moon, has not yet been able to design ballots that do not pose a mystery to voters either because 'the chards might end up hanging' or because of some other mysterious problems.

"Any way…back to the Avenging Angel. He does not need the help of whistle blowers or witnesses. He definitely does not need photographic evidence of malfeasance to bring ungodly humans to account in the court of divine justice.

"Talking about photographic evidence, you would think, that with the advent of webcams, and with surveillance cameras installed on street corners and highways and rooftops, in dressing rooms, rest rooms, locker rooms, malls, police patrol vehicles, and in every conceivable place where they photograph people, and with no hiding place from Big Brother who now watches everyone all the time, the time had come for malfeasance by anyone, including crooked members of law enforcement, who was caught on camera breaking the law would be prosecuted on the basis of the evidence; but you would be seriously mistaken for thinking that things worked that way!

"Thanks to the tenacity of my troops, earthlings, particularly those in commanding positions of power, have succeeded in making sure that the photographic evidence is valid only when those they want to see

653

convicted are caught on camera. Because the end is supposed to justify the means when it comes to activities of law enforcement, when one of their own is caught on camera infringing law, typically you will hear urgent calls by those who ought to know better pleading with the public not to jump to premature conclusions. Yep! And - surprise, surprise - it is the cameras and webcams that are usually caught lying in such instances! This is one reason that photographic evidence (which has itself been corrupted and discredited in the extreme) is frowned upon by the Avenging Angel.

"The way I myself landed in this goddamned pit should help you goddamn humans understand that you can never get away with any misdeed, and that spin, eloquence, and any attempt to conceal evidence of misdeeds only makes matters worse. And as humans wage wars and slaughter each other over the crumbs I throw at them, we here in the Pit cannot help but wonder at their stupidity.

"It certainly does not help to try and conduct misdeeds in secret. Nothing can be hidden from the Avenging Angel. The acts themselves - and the intentions of humans who have no qualms about 'doing unto others what they definitely would not want done unto themselves or their dear ones' - constitute the evidence against the perpetrators and all those who conspire, abate, and support the misdeeds.

"And regardless of what you misguided humans may think, the end simply never justifies the means. That is a fallacious argument that does not wash with the Avenging Angel. And while the culprits can run, they cannot hide. The Avenging Angel catches you committing a crime under the guise of trying to stop some other evildoer in his/her tracks, and you've had it. And don't you try to hoodwink him.

"It is sometimes better to be caught with your pants down and you suffer the shame. That is often the only way redeeming grace can get through to the hardened evildoer. We naturally do everything in our power to ensure that such an eventuality does not come to pass. There are very many dungeons down here that are specifically reserved for people who are so fool hardy as to harm their 'neighbors' (among whom you must now count the Son of Man and Deliverer). These dungeons need occupants - they have to be filled - and we are going to make damn sure they do get filled! And we get so much pleasure when the proud and powerful get snared and end up in these dungeons after passing their days in stately mansions and chateaus. Why should we be the only ones who fall from the heights to the bottom of hell!

"We know that the only thing that works with the Avenging Angel is the evildoer's sorrow - genuine sorrow coupled with a readiness to do penance and to make amends for the injustices committed. But sorrow that is really genuine may sometimes be elusive, and feasible only in theory. It is sometimes patently impossible in practice for offenders to satisfy the Avenging Angel on that score.

"It is not infrequent that humans who have been steeped in crooked ways try to make a U-Turn to get back onto the narrow path and fail. This is especially so when the offenders are obsessed with power and are hooked on material things at the same time. It is a fatal combination indeed. And the indictment which the Avenging Angel issues - sometimes well in advance of the unrepentant sinners kicking the bucket - usually just reads: 'It were better if you had not been born'! But, without knowing that they are a 'done deal', murderers and other evildoers just continue on their killing sprees and everything else they do under the mistaken notion that their accumulated booty or 'history' (as they sometimes put it) will absolve them.

"Yeah! What can he say when the liars, killers and other evil doers, blinded by hate for fellow men and by greed for things of the world, are prepared to damn themselves in that fashion! Of course the final say always remains with the Deliverer and Judge.

"For my part, I make it a point to assign the sharpest demons to souls that look like they are destined for the Pit. That should say something about how badly we want their company. It would be really disappointing to spend so much time and energy grooming evildoers of that caliber only to lose them to Michael the Archangel at the last moment!

"Any way - humans who are in the business of rationalizing and justifying their misdeeds should know before they even start that theirs is a lost cause; that, in attempting to justify their dubious activities, they damn themselves in the process; and that the Judge - the Deliverer and Word through whom all created beings came into being and also the Deliverer who now sits at the right hand of the Father - merely confirms the sentence that humans pass on themselves.

"You have heard it said that the Prime Mover causes good to ensue from evil. Well, now you have it on authority that the vilest and baddest creatures can play a role that is almost indispensable for the fulfillment of the divine plan. After the Avenging Angel has done his bit, it falls to me and the host of demons under my command to actually *avenge* the evil deeds of the bad characters who are escorted here when their time on Planet Earth is up and they walk in here though those gates over there.

"We fill a role that no one else but us here in the Pit have the qualification to fill - and it is a very critical function at that. It is our job to ensure that justice is both done and seen to be done! And the Avenging Angel actually appreciates our services. He trusts us too! He otherwise wouldn't just escort 'lost souls' through the Gates of Hell and, after delivering them to us, take off assured that these 'monsters' will finally get a taste of the 'justice' they themselves loved to administer to other members of the human family before they crossed the Gulf.

"We are not completely there yet, but we *are* getting there gradually - as time goes by and Armageddon draws nigh. Our goal is to see the gullible masses manipulated and exploited by a few. We've already made a good start by getting megalomaniacs (rulers of the earth), both big-time and small-time, effectively casting themselves as 'benevolent dictators', 'liberators', 'redeemers', and 'saviors' of the very people they are subjugating, exploiting, colonizing, enslaving, humiliating, abusing and, in some cases, even terrorizing.

"The progress made by our cronies on this front is quite solid, and can be gauged from the fact that it is the victims of that arrogant behavior who are invariably portrayed as the 'hoodlums', 'agitators', 'insurgents', and even 'terrorists', and frequently with the blessing and even connivance of the successors to the apostles. And we wouldn't have come this far if it had not been for the spin, which we promote assiduously in our dealings with the 'benevolent dictators', and the 'saviors of the world' - the self-proclaimed 'chosen ones'.

"Yes, the world's demagogues, both big time and small time, love spin. They like to imagine that they are 'liberators' - even as they are issuing commands to the effect that indigenous 'liberation' movements fighting occupations and colonialism have to be stamped out, and presiding over other 'operations' that would automatically qualify as wanton murder and mayhem if their countries were the ones at the receiving end. Interestingly, there is never a dearth of religious zealots who not only idolize these demagogues, but believe that it would be a dereliction of duty on their part if they did not stand solidly behind the dictators and others who prey on the minds of the gullible and exploit them.

Devil's clientele...

"Both demagogues and religious zealots need the spin, the former to gain legitimacy for their murderous activities, and the latter to make a case for their entitlement to the tithes. Is it any wonder then that demagogues (who are usually very regular and very public church goers) and religious zealots (who also tend to be politically quite savvy and seem to know well in advance which way the winds are likely to blow) pretend to operate in separate spheres when they in fact are usually staunch allies? This business of spinning brings together very strange bedfellows.

"But if you were thinking that my clientele consisted only of demagogues and religious zealots, think again. These chaps are by no means the only ones who sing to my tune. We should, perhaps, start with those who do not sing to my tune; and I can tell you that they are a very scant few. In all honesty - and I'm not all dishonest, you know - it is very hard to find someone who does not play by my rules. I mean - how many Francises of Assisi or Theresas of Avila or Mother Theresas are there?

"I can tell you that if the Deliverer were to return tomorrow, all these church-going folks, and others who are so self-righteous they would quicker wish to see suspected wrong doers or 'terrorists' liquidated than let them have their day in court lest they be proven innocent, would join the crowds in chanting 'Away with Him! Crucify

Him! If you let Him go, you cannot be a friend of Caesar!'

"You've got to remember that when humans do something to the least amongst them, they do it to Him. And when they clamor for anyone's blood, guess whose blood it is they actually clamor for! It is the blood of the Son of Man and Second Adam who died for the sins of the world.

"Now, don't *you* misrepresent my power and influence! Almost everyone you see can use the mercies of the Omnipotent, and you were told in no uncertain terms that you have to be prepared to forgive a brother or sister human not seven but seventy times seven times a day. You can be certain that the throngs of people who fill 'Broadway', being repeat sinners, are all under my vassalage.

Rationalize and fool Who?...

"Now, it is bad enough when humans commit evil deeds. And it is the height of stupidity when they try to rationalize and justify their misdeeds. Who do they think they are fooling! When they do that, all they are really doing is indict themselves.

"When one tries to rationalize and justify an adventure that leaves a lot to be desired from the moral angle, one just sets oneself up for judgement. In trying to justify evil actions, humans trip themselves up, and they end up 'hanging themselves' - as the saying (which dates back to the act of the Deliverer's betrayer) goes.

"If Judas Iscariot hadn't devoted the amount of time he did to efforts to justify his betrayal of the Deliverer in his own mind, he probably wouldn't have ended up with his insides spilled out all over the place in that thicket. He would still have felt pangs of guilt when his conscience finally jolted him to his senses, but perhaps not to an extent that would drive a fellow of his standing to the brink! In other words, he probably wouldn't have been suicidal to that extent. And he certainly didn't get to that point as a result of being inadequately catechized. Look, the catechist in his case was none other than the *Logos*, a member of the Godhead!

"And many folks forget that Judas Iscariot was in fact luckier than most other 'betrayers' in that he woke up to the fact that he had committed a very vile deed before, and not after, he had crossed the gulf that separates the living from the dead. I naturally won't say if Judas Iscariot has been sighted anywhere here in the Pit or not! But I will say that humans who wake up to the fact that they are unworthy of standing in the presence of the Prime Mover after they 'kick the bucket' get very little in the way of an opportunity to repent of their sins let alone the opportunity to add to the voices in heaven that 'cry out for my blood' by renouncing my works (which include evils that are too terrible to describe).

"Now - speaking hypothetically - if Judas Iscariot repented of his sin, it probably had a lot to do with the bearing of the Deliverer - and specifically His attitude to and completely 'forgiving' treatment of his 'purse bearer' - from the time He rode into Jerusalem in triumph on the back of a donkey (as He had done once upon a time when, as an infant in the arms of His Pure and beloved mother, he traveled all the way to Africa to escape the murderous Herod Agrippa) to the moment he breathed His last on Mt. Calvary.

"At no time did the Deliverer do anything that made Judas Iscariot even remotely feel like an outcast. And you can expect that Judas Iscariot (whose act of betrayal symbolized mankind's betrayal of their Maker) was very much on His mind as he beseeched His Father saying 'they know not what they are doing' in the Garden of

Gethsemane and droplets of His divine blood streamed down the sides of His temples.

"If the Deliverer had been an ordinary mortal who was born in original sin and was therefore inclined to do my bidding, He would have screamed that the 'traitor' and 'ultra-terrorist' should be destroyed - as if that would help! That is exactly what many self-styled 'Christians' do when they get rubbed the wrong way. The Deliverer never did that because He would then have been compelled to denounce all humans. Such a denunciation would have frustrated His redemptive mission, leaving Adam and Eve, and others whom I was holding in bondage in hell at my mercy.

"Which is the same as saying that humans who go after their 'enemies' (regardless of the labels they give those fellow humans they bitterly dislike) kid themselves when they also imagine that they have accepted the invitation to be 'other Christs' and to participate with the Deliverer in His work of redemption (as all Christ's followers must needs do) - or that they are 'saved'. Humans are free to couch the killings and the 'destruction' using any words and phrases they want. So long as what they do is something they would not want done unto themselves, their work is indistinguishable from my work. And when they say they renounce me Satan and my wiles, it is just that - empty words that are spoken to cloak our relationship!

"Humans ought to know that the Avenging Angel 'wields a sword' only metaphorically. That he actually gets you to do his 'dirty' work for him. If you want evidence that evil deeds go against your nature and effectively cause you to turn against yourself, you now have it.

"And there is only one way out - you get on your knees and beg the Prime Mover for His mercies and go away resolved to sin no more. But the process becomes complete only after you also agree to make amends, and begin to identify yourself with the crucified Deliverer whose obedience to the Father saw Him accept a completely undeserved death on the cross and (I might add) also with the *Mater Dolorosa*, the Deliverer's grieving mother, who set such a fine example for her fellow humans.

"Then there is the fact that those who live by the sword - or kill - die by the sword. Those who lead profligate lives also become scared to death as they see the 'End of the Road' sign approaching.

"Humans are made in the Image and have a conscience on the one hand, and they are endowed with the marvellous gifts of intelligence and free will on the other. But that constitutes a fateful combination that also damns perpetrators of evil deeds - unless the individuals in question decide to own up, confess their sins, beg the Prime Mover for His divine mercies, and do penance for their sins in advance of their rendezvous with the Judge.

"The conscious actions of creatures that are endowed with reason and free will, because they either are in line with their consciences (which is just another word for the Holy One who is in-dwelling within them) or are not, invariably attract one of two things: a suitable reward or a suitable punishment. But the choice remains that of the human.

"It may be true that, unlike us pure spirits who had only a moment after we came into existence to pledge our loyalty to the Prime Mover or opt to go our own ways, humans are afforded a whole lifetime during which to prepare for and pass the Church Triumphant Entrance Test. The fact remains that every second, minute, hour or day that is available ends up either being employed for that purpose or wasted on irrelevant matters that by their nature militate against a life of holiness.

"And nothing hinders growth in holiness more than the pursuit of worldly ambitions at the expense of other humans who, because the Prime Mover is in-dwelling in them, are automatically creatures that are very precious.

"While the preoccupation with things of the world and the blind pursuit of temporal happiness are incompatible with the pursuit of eternal life, there is nothing that could be more damning to humans during the phase of existence when they are on 'trial' than acts that are designed to injure, let alone cut short the life of a member of the human family. And the more daring such acts are, of course the more inexcusable and the more damning.

"Now, it is criminal for humans to waste any second of their lives on frivolities, for the simple reason that a very high price has been paid by the Deliverer to facilitate that growth in holiness. The magnitude of that price can be gauged from the fact that the Deliverer is none other than the Word through whom humans - and all other created beings - came into existence. Moreover, being a member of the Godhead, He suffered indescribable humiliation in the process - humiliation no creature however brilliant will ever be able to grasp or fathom.

"Being the 'Second Adam', He suffers with all humans who suffer, and He is crucified afresh whenever any human is terrorized, maimed or harmed in any way. And His sacred heart bleeds and feels compassion with all who are in their agony of death. And if these things are so obvious to me, the Evil One, it goes without saying that they must also be pretty obvious to humans in whom the Prime Mover is indwelling. And that makes all sins committed by humans totally inexcusable.

Doom thyself...

"You've got to understand that those of us who languish in hell got here because we thought we could laugh off our obligation to live as befitted our status as creatures that were made in the Image by using our faculty of reason to try and justify our crooked ways. But the Prime Mover had cleverly set it all up in such a way that the ill-willed would automatically damn themselves in the process of trying to justify the unjustifiable. It applied in our case, and it also applies in the case of ill-willed humans as well. It applies to heretics, schismatics, thieves, murderers - the whole shebang.

"There is, therefore, no doubt whatsoever that humans, inclined to sin, doom themselves when they attempt to justify things they do to others which they definitely would not want happen to either themselves or their loved ones. Humans doom themselves when they cross the line and abandon reality, and then start living in an imaginary world of phantasy in hopes that they won't be answerable to anyone.

"Realizing that they have lost their innocence and are denuded of cardinal and other virtues, and are no longer able to appreciate the innocent joys of life and other blessings they received at creation, they find themselves trying to justify sinful activities that clearly infringe on divine law and natural justice, and 'pleasures' that are far from innocent. Indeed all humans who choose self-indulgence damn themselves in the process because self-will and self-indulgence (which are one and the same thing) imply an explicit acknowledgment that they are doing something that is proscribed.

"What makes the situation of hedonists, killers and other evil doers infinitely worse is the knowledge that the liberties they are taking are expressly forbidden, have no lasting benefit, and have dire consequences for the attainment of eternal life. Their fate becomes sealed when, despite that knowledge, they proceed to infringe the Prime Mover's commandments.

"What is more, it is the realization that something is forbidden coupled with the firm knowledge that one should be using his/her time in a more constructive way that makes impious pursuits exciting. The satisfaction is derived from the knowledge that the fruit from the 'tree of knowledge' is forbidden - something that would have the opposite the effect in humans who are honest and unselfish.

"It is, after all, the desire of scheming, wily and evil-intentioned humans to inflict injury and suffering, both moral and physical, on their foes, and the certainty that they are denying their victims rights to which they are entitled to as human beings, and the knowledge that they are dealing their 'foes' unjustly (and betraying the trust vested in them in that fashion), that gives them the kick. But, by the same token, it is also what thoroughly damns those who are bent on mischief in that fashion. And consequently killers, hedonists and other humans who are bent on sin can never plead ignorance for that reason.

"And sure enough, following each and every spiteful act, humans are plagued by a sense of guilt, something that the wicked naturally endeavor to suppress so that they can go on sinning merrily thereafter if they should find opportunities to do so. But, unfortunately for humans, even though the legacy of evil actions continues well after the evildoers 'kick the bucket', the opportunity to commit vile acts afresh summarily ends at that point.

When all humans become equal again...

"In the eyes of humans, life comes to a close at

death. In the eyes of the Avenging Angel, humans who are more equal than others become completely equal again when they 'kick the bucket' out of their way and head off to their judgement. Humans who thought that their lives were worth more than the lives of others get the jolt of their lifetime as they breathe their last, and find that there was nothing special about them."

Now, interesting as all this was, Mjomba was feeling quite uncomfortable filling the role of scribe to a creature that the sacred scriptures had pointedly referred to as "Accuser of our Brethren" (Revelation 12:10), and one that was morally bankrupt and had actually been judged already (John 16:7-11). But Mjomba had already made a deal with the Evil One; and, having in effect enlisted the help of Satan in the task of turning out a winning thesis on the subject of "Original Virtue", it was quite apparent that backing out of the deal at that point wasn't an option. And so he continued setting down on paper the unsettling and at times quite disturbing stream of ideas that Old Scratch was sending his way.

"In the case of conflicts between nations," the devil pressed on, "in the eyes of the world, the number of casualties suffered by the parties to the conflict are supposed to be indicative of the extent to which a nation is 'blessed' or 'cursed' along with its 'victorious' or 'defeated' combatants. The reality is completely different.

"In the case of nations that mount unprovoked assaults on other nations for example, instead of being a blessing, all the casualties suffered by the nation under attack as well as the aggressor nation's own casualties become a curse. The situation is even more damning for the aggressor when the losses of the 'enemy' are heavy, and the number of their own casualties is minuscule.

"Should it happen that the reason for the aggressor nation suffering only light or even no casualties in an unjustified conflict is because the aggressor nation invested a lot of time and resources in planning the offensive, or took specific steps to weaken the target of its aggression prior to the assault, all those things become very damning indeed. This is because everything relating to the aggression becomes premeditated, and not something that is done on impulse. And - guess what - it also puts the responsibility for any casualties sustained by the 'enemy' and by the attackers own forces and their allies squarely on the shoulders of those who mastermind the aggression and prosecute the unjust war.

"Then, because there is no such a thing as liability that is joint and several on the other side of the gulf which separates the living from the dead, that responsibility ends up on the individual shoulders of the masterminds and planners of the conflict, their supporters and collaborators, and the aggressor nation's individual fighters and their commanders. This is in accordance with the Prime Mover's injunction to humans to the effect that they shall regard human life as sacred, and the rights of humans to freedom and liberty as inviolable. Geopolitics and all that crap might be good for the spleen for humans on this side of the gulf that separates the living from the dead. But, on the other side, it only serves to nail down those guilty of taking away the lives of others and of breaking the Prime Mover's other commandments.

"Furthermore, any casualties suffered by the aggressor nation itself and its allies in the course of prosecuting the unjust war will also constitute damning evidence - evidence of greed in seeking to annex territory regardless of the cost in human lives, and things like that. It is evidence that hangs over the heads of those who prosecute all unjust wars and that does not go away. And it is not affected by the way history gets written or by the misleading impressions that memoirs of participants in the conflict seek to portray.

"There are situations when the fighters of an aggressor nation who fall in battle become the equivalent of bandits who could not make it out of the bank vault. Those who escape with their lives in such situations become the equivalent of bandits who succeeded in getting away with or without any loot. It is as simple as that.

"In situations of that sort, success itself becomes damning, and it is only genuine and sincere repentance coupled with restitution to the victims of the aggression that can bring back those involved in the aggression into the fold. And since enjoyment of the fruits of aggression is equally damning, it becomes incumbent on the aggressor nation to forego any enjoyment of the ill-gotten fruits of the aggression, and to include them in the restitution it is obligated by Natural Justice to pay to the victims of the aggression.

"Giving any of the 'loot' to charity would be entirely unacceptable, since wealth acquired in these circumstances comprises stolen property that a repentant bandit would be expected to return to its rightful owner. Any such wealth is akin to 'blood money', 'bootleg' acquired through piracy on the high seas, or goods obtained by highway robbers in a heist.

"The fact that an aggressor nation is capable of sustaining casualties at all in these situations additionally serves to debunk any myths about invincibility; and it also rebuffs any suggestion that the self-appointed 'savior of the world' (or whatever label the aggressor nation choose to employ to depict itself) might be acting on behalf of the Prime Mover and accordingly enjoys immunity from consequences that generally flow from adventures of that nature. And that remains true regardless of any claims that the aggressor nations are acting on behalf of the Prime Mover or otherwise.

"Frequently, casualties sustained by aggressor nations in such conflicts also unmask the true reasons behind the aggression, as questions are raised about the real rationale for undertaking misguided military adventures. In the case of megalomaniacs who are bent on pursuing their cockeyed schemes, the number of casualties sustained over time during an offensive will invariably raise questions regarding the wisdom of embarking on the 'foreign adventure' and the underlying folly becomes unmasked as public inquiries begin revealing grandiose schemes that are frequently quite bizarre and the megalomaniacs suddenly find themselves on the carpet for 'lying to the nation' and other irresponsible actions.

"In the completely hypothetical case of a super power that was, say, prosecuting a totally unjustified and consequently also immoral war against a nation that (let us say) was falsely accused of lending support to 'terrorists', when they get to the other side of the 'gulf' which separates the living from the dead, the fallen fighters of the aggressor nation could find themselves wishing that they had come with more of their dear comrades-in-arms. For, upon their arrival there, all the myths about 'super power' status and things like that evaporate as reality descends on them.

"The chances are that they will find themselves confined to a kind of 'Guantanamo' or 'Limbo' (or just call it 'Purgatory' if you like) while they await the arrival of their 'surviving' comrades - if they themselves did not really know what they were doing. This is also because someone must answer for their own premature arrival in the afterlife as well as for the premature influx into heaven of the victims of their aggression. If they knew what they were doing (as the ring leaders almost certainly would), the Avenging Angel will almost certainly have 'appropriate' instructions as to their 'disposal'."

Mjomba wasn't feeling quite comfortable filling the role of a secretary to the author of the ideas he was setting down on paper. Mjomba, while acknowledging that all humans became equal again once on the other side of the gulf that separated the living from the dead, personally preferred to leave it at that. He was of the view that it was a little like playing God to get into any details at that point regarding hypothetical super powers going awry, and mythological Guantanamos where individuals would be liable to be "detained' while awaiting the disposition of their cases by the Judge.

The evil ghost must have guessed what Mjomba's next move was going to be; which, namely, was to drop the pen and stop playing along. And he did not wait to act.

Mjomba had up until that moment been committing the ideas he had been receiving from the evil one to paper involuntarily. But now, as a sudden, quite vigorous and entirely uncontrollable shudder shook his whole person, it terrified him to think that he was in much deeper trouble that he had thought!

The "shudder" lasted only a heartbeat. But while it lasted, Mjomba, who felt helpless throughout the ordeal, had no misgivings regarding either its nature or its origins. Mjomba immediately realized in the aftermath of the "quake" that, as far as Beelzebub was concerned, he, Mjomba, had consented to the "deal" under which he would commit to paper the material that he, Satan, was contributing; and, in return, Satan was going to make sure that Mjomba's "Thesis on Original Virtue" was going to be a winning thesis in every respect. It now dawned on Mjomba that the unexpected and violent shudder that had momentarily gripped him was forewarning about what could happen if he, Mjomba, did not continue to keep his part of the bargain! Mjomba was glad that nothing worse had befallen him as he continued to jot down the material that was being contributed by the Enemy.

"But, while the appearance of the Avenging Angel will be shocking enough, an even bigger shocker once on the other side of the gulf that separates the living from the dead, and where one no longer sees 'as through a glass darkly' and gets to know things not piece meal but 'as one is known' as the Apostle of the Gentiles aptly put, will be the discovery by citizens of the aggressor nations that their countries were fighting for a lost cause! To their great shock and disappointment, they will suddenly awake to the fact that there was no such a thing as a 'super power'! Moreover, as a rule, all so-called 'super powers' were eclipsed by a new breed of 'super powers' in just a matter of decades.

"A super power that, once upon a time, might have boasted the ability to leave the its foot prints at will on any part of the globe in pursuit of its 'vital national interests', not only would be a super power no more, but would itself conceivably be a colony, occupied and exploited by forces representing countries that previously were alluded to as pariah states, rogue states, or even failed states - or by forces representing those self-same 'terrorists' with whom their country was now disinclined to talk peace and was determined to 'liquidate' from the face of the earth! So much for putting one's faith in crude 'super power' and in the sword instead of putting one's faith in the Prime Mover!

"And - guess what! That is also the time when the poor souls will see me, Beelzebub, for what I really am - the Author of Death and an infernal liar. They will hate me for persuading them that they needed to 'take charge of their lives', and to be 'free' and not allow themselves to be nagged by that 'inner man' or conscience. They will realize that by putting cotton wool in the 'ears of their souls' and refusing to heed their consciences, they became 'hard core' sinners!

"Actually, come to think of it, since empires and earthly kingdoms existed only in the imagination and did not really count in the eyes of the Prime Mover (and that included the roles of emperors, kings, queens, princes, or proconsuls), the 'lesson' or 'chastisement' may have been a God-send, and a suitable and perhaps even timely reminder that those who put their faith in their 'super power' kidded themselves and instead needed to get down on their knees and commend their dreams and hopes to the one, the only, and the unchanging Almighty!

"But then, covetous and measly humans, inclined to sin, were always suspicious that heeding reminders of that sort merely provided 'rivals' the opportunity to gain the upper hand and to claim for themselves a bigger slice of material things - a clear sign that they didn't have any trust in the Prime Mover, that they were just 'fake' devotees of the Deliverer who 'faked' their love for their neighbors and lived in a fool's paradise, and above all that they would quicker pray to me (Beelzebub and Author of Death) than to their infinitely merciful and gracious Maker!

"And, of course, being the Prince of Darkness, I for my part am always available to give them the 'inspiration' and 'strength' they need in life (inspiration and strength that they should be seeking from the Spirit), and to make them believe that they are onto something really terrific and perhaps even pioneers in the art of 'worldly living' or 'escapism'!

"Incidentally, we demons may have our own faults, including the blinding pride that made us imagine that, being made in the Image, we were automatically guaranteed a glorious existence in eternity regardless of how we behaved ourselves, and that nothing could happen to us if we refused to recognize the authority of the Prime Mover or to return the favor of being brought into existence in the first place. But being blind to the fact that, once in existence, creatures made in the Image cannot be 'destroyed' or returned to nothingness has never been one of them.

"But you earthlings have taken the rebellion against the Prime Mover to a completely new level. This is something that is completely novel - humans imagining that they can 'rub out' fellow humans in whom the Prime Mover Himself is indwelling! But it is a new 'low' to which we demons for our part would rather not sink. But what can we do except to welcome all you humans to the Club!

"In the hypothetical situation in which a 'super power' decides to pit its 'imperial' or 'super' power against a nation that (for argument's sake) it has spent years undermining politically, economically and militarily, it is precisely such a decision that virtually guarantees the defenders who fall in battle heaven. The use by the aggressors of 'overwhelming force', 'shock and awe' tactics, and the scale of cruelty and inhumanity visited on the population in the country under assault, more likely than not, will combine to bring home to the luckless defenders the fact that their fate was indeed in the hands of the Prime Mover.

"Consequently defenders who fall in battle, and who would otherwise be headed straight to hell because of the unworthy lives they might have previously led, will find themselves mysteriously - almost miraculously - transformed and no longer hesitant, if afforded the opportunity, to forsake all worldly things that they (more than anyone else) will now see as ephemeral and passing - and my wiles! This will happen despite our redoubled efforts to drive them to despair in the face of their miseries, humiliation and suffering, and the terrible odds they would be up against.

"Abandoned by the rest of the world, and left to the mercy of the aggressors, the citizenry of the nations under attack invariably experience an unprecedented and mysterious surge in their faith and trust in the Prime Mover. Like the saints of yore, they will typically find themselves ready to die for their newfound (or enlivened) faith, and to dedicate their lives to the Prime Mover and the wellbeing of kinsfolk that are targeted by the invaders.

"Now, nations - all nations without exception - are so much into the doctrine of imperialism that Cain expounded in those early days of man, there is virtually nothing in that doctrine which Cain's many admirers and students do not do, the dastardly practice of torturing captives being one of them. Actually, as the years and then centuries went by, the techniques of torture were refined and now include torturing captives even as they are undergoing their pangs of death.

"Unfortunately for those who are into that practice, their actions become self-defeating, particularly if they are intended to put the captives at some sort of disadvantage. Unable to actually 'rub out' one's enemies by 'cutting their lives short', you would think that the killers would be hoping to at least dispatch their foes to hell. But, as it happens, such a technique of torture in fact virtually guarantees the poor souls salvation.

"Humans who are in the process of kicking the bucket are already in a position that gives them no option but to accept their status as creatures, and to recognize that their fate was in the hands of the Prime Mover all along. That is why it is incumbent upon other humans who may be around the dying to proffer material, moral and spiritual support, and extend them without any regard whatsoever to creed, nationality, race, gender, race, status or any other factor. And anything that is done to the contrary signals that I, the Father of Death and the Enemy, am in charge and still calling the shots!

"You've got to understand that when a human is in his/her throes of death and finds him/herself subjected to torture, abuse and humiliation, it is very difficult for that human not to identify him/herself with the crucified and dying Deliverer who called the thirsty and hungry, the sick, the poor, and the persecuted 'blessed'.

"You see…however caused, the separation of a human soul from the body - or 'death' - is a fate that awaits all humans, and represents the wages of sin. It is because Mary, the Deliverer's mother, was sinless and unblemished by the original sin that she did not 'die the death', but was instead assumed into heaven. Apart from Mary and the Deliverer Himself, only liars can step forward and claim that they are without blemish. This is the reason capital punishment so-called, which has its basis in vengefulness, hypocrisy and an absence of faith and trust in Divine Providence, could never be justifiable or right! And the strange notions that have abounded since Cain murdered his brother Abel under the guise of administering capital punishment to a 'terrorist' as he referred to him definitely say something about humans!

"You earthlings are all on death row any way, and therefore why the botheration! Why pretend that some are, and not others! If you see someone act as if this is the case, you can always bet that the individual does so at my explicit command. The world comes to an end for the individual in his/her agony of death; and - believe me - all in the vicinity will be asked by the Deliverer and Judge if they stopped to help Him when He was on Death Row!

"Defenders who are under unjustified attack by superior forces, and who are additionally abandoned to their fate by the rest of the world, regardless of their religious beliefs, automatically become aware already at that time that it is only their 'Prime Mover' that can save them. In other words, their reliance on Him tends to become total from then on. And, facing the double ordeal of death pangs on the one hand, and oppression and torture by those who were supposed to give them comfort and solace, but who instead choose to torture and even prolong their death pangs for the fun of it on the other, they simply must feel just as the Deliverer did - forsaken by even His own Father, abandoned by Peter (the rock upon which His church was going to be built) and by all His 'friends', mocked, crowned with thorns, beaten and scourged, and sent to his death on the cross by the very people he had come to save!

"The pain and suffering, both physical and spiritual, that comes their way in circumstances like those become, without a doubt, God-sent, and probably very timely too for souls that might otherwise have forfeited eternal life. And it is also noteworthy that they receive that treatment at the hands of humans who proclaim in the same breath that they are 'godly', 'righteous' and doing whatever they are doing in the Deliverer's name. It certainly highlights the extent to which they have been abandoned to their fate by the entire world on the one hand, and at least ostensibly by the Prime Mover Himself on the other.

"In an unexpected turn of events (and also irony of no mean proportions), the 'unsaved' insurgents and terrorists so-called, who purportedly might have been working for some 'axis of evil', will be the recipients of the Baptism of Desire and other divine graces as a direct result of the unjustifiable actions of those who regard themselves as righteous; graces that will flow from being compelled to identify themselves with the suffering Deliverer more or less like the 'good robber' (who is referred to in Luke 23:39-43 and is now venerated in the *Sancta Ecclesia* on March 25 for having effectively 'robbed' his way into Paradise), becoming completely resigned to the will of the Prime Mover, and also agreeing to suffer with His son.

"The oppressive nature of captivity at the hands of 'imperialists', 'occupiers' and other types of oppressors, the outrageous injustice, the murderous rampage of the proud, heartless and swaggering colonialists and invaders, the torture, abuse and humiliation to which patriotic nationalists and defenders (who suddenly find themselves labeled 'insurgents' and 'terrorists') endure - all those things will combine to virtually guarantee those who succumb to their 'treatment' under unjust occupations heavenly salvation.

"And this will be largely true also for those who survive the cruel treatment and harassment, because such treatment and harassment, endured while the whole world merely looks on, not only effectively destroys one's faith in fellow humans while leaving them permanently traumatized, it also readies the soul for the comforting words of the Deliverer who declared: 'Blessed are they who weep and mourn, for the kingdom of heaven is theirs'.

"And, by the same token, those humans who take it upon themselves to assault, brutalize, humiliate or kill other humans while pursuing their worldly ambitions - or who see ways of benefiting from lending their support to such actions and do so - guarantee themselves damnation, for the simple reason that they could never gain eternal life while doing unto other humans what they themselves wouldn't want done unto themselves or unto their loved ones.

"And so, in the decidedly unexpected but fundamental turn of events, the former 'insurgents' and 'terrorists' who fall while defending their country could definitely find themselves playing a role they had never dreamed of - playing big brother and patron to those who had boasted super power prowess and invincibility.

"Unexpected because suddenly humans who had until now been looked upon by everybody as expendable and undeserving of anything will be the ones having the upper hand.   And fundamental because the former 'insurgents' and 'terrorists', who along with their loved ones had been subjected to all sorts of harassments and humiliations before they crossed the Gulf, will be interceding with the Prime Mover on behalf of their former foes. In one stroke and as predicted by the psalmist, the mighty will find themselves thoroughly humbled; and the down trodden and forsaken will find themselves in a role they had never dreamed of - playing a pivotal role in bringing the divine plan to fruition.

"In a strange twist of fate, the cocky aggressors who prided themselves on being invincible, all-knowing, and civilized (and perhaps 'valiant crusaders for the Deliverer's cause' as well) will find themselves fainting in the face of death and haunted in the last moments of their lives by the saying that those who live by the sword die by the sword. Instead of seeing themselves as patriots who were falling while 'defending' their country, it will suddenly dawn upon them that they really weren't any different from mercenaries, particularly in view of their inability to voice conscientious objections to a war they well knew was unjust.

"The terrible reality is that they might well be surprised to find that, instead of choirs of angels, it is swarms of demons who will be waiting on the other side of the Gulf to meet and escort them to their holding cells in the 'New Guantanamo'. And they will even be more surprised, upon getting to the 'New Guantanamo', to find the place many times more fearful and forbidding than the original Guantanamo back on Planet Earth.

"Now, even though the practice of torturing captured 'insurgents' and 'terrorists' - particularly those who are tortured even as they are already undergoing their pangs of death - would virtually assure the victims salvation, you can bet that we here in the Pit celebrate every time humans torture, abuse and/or humiliate their own. This is because those who connive in such reprehensible practices automatically guarantee themselves damnation!

"It is for the same reason that we similarly celebrate when 'non-combatants' in homes, places of prayer, marketplaces, and elsewhere are treated as expendable collateral because they happen to live in the same neighborhood as some much sought after 'terrorist', and 'for being in the wrong place at the wrong time in history'; or when they are deliberately targeted by the aggressors either as 'payback' for losing one of their own or just for the fun of it. You, of course, know that all those who participate in any such assaults, because they know exactly what they are doing, become murderers for whom there is no place in heaven, but plenty of it here in the Pit.

"And now for this other 'catch'! Humans of good will so-called are actually not all that innocent either. They are just folks who, while not perfect, have welcomed the opportunity to become reconciled with their Maker. Even these are also free to damn themselves if they want - just as those humans whose hearts are hardened in sin have. In the event, the Deliverer and Judge will not intervene to stop their guilt from accumulating and 'damning' them as well! Sins committed by creatures made in the Image are always damning because at the time they are being committed, those errant creatures should be doing something else altogether, namely giving praise to Him about whom the Psalmist wrote: 'The Lord is my firmament, my refuge, and my deliverer. My God is my helper, and in him will I put my trust. My protector and the horn of my salvation, and my support.'

"And that is exactly what victims of aggression do. After enduring humiliations, detentions and death at the hands of the aggressor, you would think that they would hate the fallen fighters of the aggressor nation. Nothing could be further from the truth. While it may be that the hearts of many amongst them had been hardened like those of humans elsewhere, they will find that things changed as they were subjected to undeserved humiliations, harassment and torture at the hands of the aggressor.

"It will dawn on them upon leaving this world and entering their afterlife that the fortitude that sustained them in their miseries was a gift of grace pure and simple, and a transforming one at that. They will also recognize that it was in fact none other than the Deliverer and Judge who merited the grace by His own suffering and death, and who had in turn dispensed it to them in their time of trial and need through His Holy Spirit.

"They will also understand at that point that the humiliations, harassment and torture, and their demise at the hands of the aggressors were things that in fact constituted a gift of sorts - an opportunity to identify themselves with the Deliverer, a member of the Godhead, who Himself endured untold humiliation at the hands of sinful humans when He consented to be their Mediator with His father and also their Deliverer.

"They will be so taken aback by that incomprehensible demonstration of love, they will not hesitate to forgive all their enemies one and all, and to wish them well. Following this turn of events, they will go all out to beg the Judge and the Deliverer to also forgive

680

the fallen enemy fighters and to free them from their detention in the 'New Guantanamo'.

"Now, it is true that all the foregoing is based on hypothesis - the hypothesis that the war of aggression might conceivably be defensible and possibly also justifiable. But unfortunately, in the divine court of justice, the onus is on the aggressor to demonstrate beyond any reasonable doubt that the campaign, or rather the aggression, was justified. And there is, of course, no point in trying to spin stories or tell lies when one is before the Judge, and everything that humans did behind doors or in secret is laid bare for all to see.

"Lies have no place up there - you try to put on a straight face to mask falsehoods that you would like to manufacture, and the mask you thought was firmly in place just falls away, revealing the deceitfulness and the rot at the core of your being to all and sundry.

"If you didn't know why it is said that hell is down in the bowels of the earth and not up there, you now know the reason. As the Author of Lies, I had to be cast out from the heavens into this wretched place deep in the bowels of the earth - this hell in which I now languish together with the other lying angels who automatically turned into demons and the souls of lying humans who fell prey to my wiles. And you'd better understand well what I mean by 'liar'. Included among liars are all those folks who are made in the Image, but who are habitually trying to stifle their consciences so that they can go on munching on forbidden fruit from the Tree of Knowledge of Good and Evil without any botheration from their 'inner man'.

"It goes without saying that it is really myself here in the Pit and my troops who will end up overall losers when humans also jump on the bandwagon and also lie their way into hell. It will be crushing for us to realize that all the work we put in to get one group of humans to turn against another for selfish reasons netted us only those souls that were really hardened in sin and that accordingly deserved eternal damnation. But, overall, our own campaign to sow seeds of death among humans will have ended up in failure.

"But why should I belabor the point. It will become crystal clear on the Day of Judgement, regardless of whether humans with hardened hearts make it to heaven or here in the abyss with us, that whenever they *actively sought to have their own way* or did what they fancied, they invariably *ended up doing what they became inclined to do* after Adam and Eve fell from grace. It will likewise become evident how it came about that whenever *grace was given a chance*, as humans eschewed their wilfulness, *it took over* and humans ended up performing virtuous acts. Yes, actually doing good works - things they ordinarily were disinclined to do - through a 'miracle' of divine grace!

"And that, if I may add, risks the complete exposure of what I like to refer to as the 'twin tired Protestant errors' - I mean the fallacious doctrines of *sola fide* and *sola scriptura* that my troops and I have worked so hard to get misguided souls to adopt and then continue propagating. I planned this meticulously from the moment I noticed that the *Sancta Ecclesia*, established by the Deliverer on the rock called Peter, was indeed a reality and, starting in Jerusalem, had begun to spread its wings through Asia Minor and Greece to the ends of the Earth; and, above all, I had no illusions about the fact that I was never going to prevail against it.

"I wasn't exactly enthused by any of this at all! But I knew that humans were inclined to sin by virtue of the original sin, and that they would consequently be looking for easy ways out of their bind. That was a fatal combination that I could not fail to exploit. It is now wonderful to observe folks delude themselves that their salvation is found in the easy and simple recitation of the 'Sinner's Prayer', and not in taking up their crosses and following in the footsteps of their Deliverer! And, as luck would have it, the fact that the Deliverer commissioned His *Sancta Ecclesia*, and empowered it with the administration of the sacraments He instituted during His sojourn on Earth, and through which the saving graces that are dispensed, gets completely forgotten in the process. As a direct result of my efforts in this regard, the *Sancta Ecclesia* is now also saddled with the problem of disunity in Christendom, a state of affairs that greatly hampers its evangelizing mission.

"Of course humans are saved, not by faith alone, but by faith *and* good works! All humans have talents they are expected to work with and even 'turn a profit' in the course of doing so. But because on their own, without the help of the grace merited for them by the Deliverer, they are inclined to sin and are really good for nothing, it would be hypocritical for humans to take any credit, much less *full* credit, for their good works. This is even though it was *cooperation* with divine grace that made any human activity meritorious or pleasing in the eyes of the Prime Mover.

"But it is so funny! It is so hilarious really - at least to us here in the Pit...It is precisely folks who decry the Church's insistence that one is saved by faith *and* good works, and want everyone to believe that humans are saved by faith alone, who are always harping on the so-called 'doctrine' of *sola scriptura*! Well, it is definitely 'revealing' that it is those humans who elevate the sacred scriptures above the teaching magisterium of the *Sancta Eccelesia* the Deliverer founded on the rock called 'Peter' and the work of the Holy Ghost therein who themselves can't even 'read' those self-same scriptures! Tell me how you can be a biblical scholar who stakes everything on the holy book, and yet be simultaneously oblivious to the 'Parable of the Talents', and to the Deliverer's innumerable exhortations that the descendants of Adam and Eve 'take up their crosses and follow Him', or to biblical passages like the one that says that 'you will know them by their fruits'! If those fruits were not of *their* 'labor', there would obviously be no purpose in making any reference to them. And yet the Deliverer does!

"Stupid humans don't give us here in the Underworld enough credit, not just for dreaming up an ingenious idea like this so-called 'Sinner's Prayer', but also for succeeding in the marvelous way we have in steering the attention of so many folks away from passages in the Sacred Scriptures such as Matthew 25:31-46! Oh, Yeah! Even as they fall blindly for the brilliant schemes we dream up and latch on to them to their detriment - and expose themselves to spiritual peril thereby - they just don't stop to give me and my fellow demons here in Gehenna any credit for being so creative and ingenious So...so daft and stupid! Some even believe that Gehenna, the destination of the wicked, is just a figment of people's imagination that has been popularized by people like Hiroshi Katagiri and others in Hollywood! Ha, ha, ha, hee, hee, hee!

"Now, I am the Evil One, and I just love this state of affairs! If I may let you in on another of my secrets, those of us here in the Pit aren't about to rest on our laurels at this juncture. You have to be dumb to imagine that, after succeeding in getting the first erring members of the Church Militant snagged in these short cuts to 'self-righteousness', we are going to relax the grip we have on the blind who allow themselves to be led by the proverbial blind! Or did you think that these doctrinal innovations were engineered by the Holy Ghost to save those who refused to accept that whatever Peter and his fellow apostles 'held bound on earth', pursuant to the authority that was bestowed upon them by the Deliverer, it was held in heaven! You've got to be kidding!

"Well, Paul - that turncoat Paul who abandoned our cause and joined the other side in the battle between Good and Evil as the 'Apostle of the Gentiles' - wasn't the sort of person to pass up the opportunity to warn the Colossians and, as I expected, wrote: 'Beware lest any man cheat you by philosophy, and vain deceit; according to the tradition of men, according to the elements of the world, and not according to Christ'. (Colossians 2:8)"

Christian Mjomba recoiled at the fact that the Evil One was using him to attack the separated brethren in that fashion, and sincerely wished that he himself hadn't tangled with Old Scratch! He noted that, as was the case with the reformers, it was too late in the game to do anything about it now. Or, was it? Well, it was so much easier to continue collaborating with the Evil One on the theological thesis he was writing than "going back on his word" and starting work on it all over again without involving him, he noted. And so he continued to do the bidding of the devil, and to write.

"Getting back to our topic of 'salvation *a sola fide*'" the Evil One continued, "despite being inclined to sin, humans have an obligation as creatures to follow their Maker's injunctions. They do not have the power to create a *moral order* of their own choice. While the spirit must be 'willing', it is divine grace - a gift of the Prime Mover - that becomes the enabling agent or force to save them from perdition. They can only be thankful, and are ill advised to brag. They certainly shouldn't do so to my face or else...

"It is true that when you are a cripple on a stretcher

- a spiritual cripple on a metaphysical but nonetheless *real* stretcher - you really cannot pretend that you can get up and run anywhere. And you can bet that I know what being on that kind of stretcher is - I know what it is like to be spiritually dead and incarcerated in a 'hell hole'! But you humans still pretend that you can get up from the stretcher and take off to some place!

"There is a trick that we in the Underworld employ to 'cripple' humans; and it always works because humans are stupid. We in effect get them to trip themselves up. For illustration take this soul that wants to have nothing to do with us, and wants to emulate some saint whose heroic life whilst on earth was beyond question. Now there is no saint who ever achieved anything in the spiritual realm by dint of its own efforts. A human grows in holiness by emptying him/herself and allowing the Holy Ghost to sanctify it thereby. That process of sanctification is almost the opposite of what you will find in popular stories depicting the lives of saints. Those glossy volumes which fill the shelves of so-called 'good Catholic bookstores' and purport to provide glimpses of the heroic lives that the saints led actually fall far short of that goal. They all invariably depict them as some sort of quietists who live in a dream unreal world. The same applies to images of saints. Perhaps while attempting to depict the beloved of the Prime Mover as entranced individuals on cloud nine who live self-less lives and are ready to die for Him, the "artists' almost invariably end up making them look like some godforsaken forlorn weirdoes who are lost in a world of their own!

"True humility, which is a prerequisite for personal sanctification, is not at all likely to be your saintly hero's cup of tea. And a soul is not going to suddenly develop wings to fly to heaven to be with members of the Church Triumphant just because it has developed a yearning to escape from the rough world into which it finds itself cast. We call that scrupulosity or obsessive-compulsive disorder (OCD); and any soul that opens to us that door is usually doomed. Instead of emptying itself and letting the Holy Spirit take over, the scrupulous soul does the opposite. It opens the door for us to get in there and suggest all sorts of things that might look great on the surface but really boil down to selflove! In place of humble submission to the motions of grace, the scrupulous souls that we manage to hijack will exhibit a virulent willfulness, and will be a spiritual director's nightmare. And you guessed correctly - It isn't all that hard at all to get an overly scrupulous 'believer' to latch on to doctrines that 'magically' solve his/her problems with respect to deliverance from the clutches of sin, and are in that sense a most welcome godsend.

Ask...

"The point I want to make is that it all really boils down to a word, and that word is 'Ask'! Did the Deliverer - the one who merited all those graces some humans think they can 'steal' - not say: 'Ask and ye shalt receive. Knock and it shall be opened.' Good thing you humans remain dumb and won't even grasp the import of that! Because your problems would be solved if you headed blindly to your church, temple - or what have you - and flopped down on your knees and prayed, not like the Pharisee, but like the tax collector!

"And His mother said it all when, realizing that the groom could not afford to provide all the guests with drinks, said to the waiters: 'Whatsoever he shall say to you, do ye.' (John 2:5) But He would himself make it even clearer than that when He said: 'For everyone that asketh receiveth; and he that seeketh findeth; and to him that knocketh it shall be opened.' (Matthew 7:8 and Luke 11:5-13) This was even as He warned: 'Beware of false prophets, who come to you in the clothing of sheep, but inwardly they are ravening wolves. By their fruits you shall know them. Do men gather grapes of thorns, or figs of thistles?'

"Yeah, He knew full well I would still be around and working hard, with the help of my minions, to try and derail His divine plan!

"Earthlings! How could you - you who cannot even foresee how or when your trust in the Prime Mover will be put to the test and you who frequently are yourselves the source of the temptations - be able on your own, without the intervention of divine grace, resist any of my insinuations! And, certainly, not when you humans are yourselves now inclined to do evil rather than to do good!

"When I tempt a human, I do so primarily by working on his/her psyche - or spiritually. And, of course, when the Prime Mover 'does things' or works, He does so in an infinitely more refined way, because he is, after all, the Prime Mover! He can help a human by just showing him or her that my temptation is what it is - reprehensible and not worthy of any attention. Or He can decide to 'bless' a good soul by giving me and my fellow demons permission to thoroughly harass that soul in the proverbial 'dark night of the soul'!

"Any soul, presuming to be capable of fending off my temptations on its own without the help of divine grace, would assuredly end up 'possessed' by us and lost forever. It would never survive the sheer onslaught of the temptations we would send that soul's way!

How the Prime Mover operates...

"Now, the ways of the Prime Mover, which are both

mysterious and incomprehensible, are by definition completely different from the ways of humans. But, first, what does the Prime Mover look like exactly? Or is this, perhaps, a completely stupid question? If we could gauge anything of this from His many works of creation (His works of art) the most illustrious of which are angels and humans, what would you say His likes and dislikes are? He liked the results of His creative effort for sure, because he deigned to send His only begotten Son into the world to show humans who had gone astray the way.

"And, boy, did the Son of Man not show humans the way to properly appreciate the works of His Father and also His own love for them - a love that was infinite. And the Son of Man also challenged humans who had stumbled badly and were still inclined to the notion that he was asking too much of them, to pull up their socks.

"He certainly did not leave the impression humans gave that to appreciate the Prime Mover's works of art, one had to climb down from the spiritual heights and embrace self-love and self-indulgence in any form, let alone plumb down into the vile and the sordid. And that is not the same as saying that humans would find it easy to live up to the challenge – a challenge that, by the way, isn't very much of a challenge really, because of the way that Prime Mover 'designed' and then 'executed' His 'Divine Plan'! Yeah, the Prime Mover whose ways are unfathomable!. (Isaiah 40:28, Romans 11:33) This is the same Prime Mover who, in the beginning, created heaven, and earth. And the earth was void and empty, and darkness was upon the face of the deep; and the spirit of God moved over the waters. (Genesis 1:1-2) And, yeah, you've guessed right: In the beginning was the Word, and the Word was with God, and the Word was God. The same was in the beginning with God. All things were made by him: and without him was made nothing that was made. In Him was life, and the life was the light of men. And the light shineth in darkness, and the darkness did not comprehend it! (John 1:1-5)

And so, there you have it - if you are genuinely trying to figure out how the Prime Mover operates! All you humans now need to do to understand how He 'does things' is to stop and take a moment to reflect on the 'Mystery of the Incarnation'. Linking hands with the Angel Gabriel as he greets Mary would be a good start. (Luke 1:28). But how many of you humans are ready to cast your prejudices aside and do something as simple as that!

"The bottom line though is that the way the Prime Mover does things or operates in general isn't the same way creatures - and certainly humans – operate. Certainly the way the Prime Mover sanctifies the actions of earthlings through the workings of His grace is completely different from the way the earthlings themselves think happens.

"That should not be surprising. Humans themselves need legs to move, and initially have even to do it on all fours. They need toes to steady themselves, arms to grab things and fingers to fasten on to the crude implements they use to ease their toil, and that work only if their design permits them to operate in strict accordance with the laws of nature. And, except for dosing off and going to sleep, humans have to always remember to apply their God-given intelligence throughout any operation to minimize the chances of losing toes, fingers and other accidents that could prove fatal. Even when they go to sleep, they must remember to choose the spot wisely, or they could end up falling to their deaths if they dosed off near cliffs. They could end up causing really bad accidents if they dosed off while at the wheel.

"And, then, the time inevitably comes when

humans die - or figuratively kick the bucket that all dying people supposedly see standing in their way as they proceed to their afterlife. Preachers admonish that that bucket is filled with the accumulated guilt for sins committed by folks from the time they are born to the time they depart to join their ancestors. No wonder humans feel the urge to kick it aside as they prepare to enter their afterlife in the nether world.

"The Prime Mover, on the other hand, by definition could not be subject to any changes either natural or supra-natural, let alone a transformation of that nature! I mean, unlike humans, He is not confined by time and space. He doesn't even have to think - he is intelligence *par excellence*. That is the sort of 'thing' or *esse* He is. Like the Son of Man, the Prime Mover-is-who-is! Or do you not agree? The divine grace He dispenses operates in a similar fashion.

"The most gracious act on the part of the Prime Mover was to give His only begotten Son - begotten in eternity - to the world, so that those who believe in Him might be saved. Those, I might add, who not only believe in Him, but also take advantage of the grace-giving sacraments the Deliverer instituted when He established his Church.

"Now, the Prime Mover is always good at what He does; and this is especially true as regards his dealings with the evil minded and the wicked of the world. Simply stated, He gets them to fix themselves. He gives them rope with which to go hang themselves – almost in so many words! The Prime Mover's beloved, who have been assured solemnly by the Deliverer that they are all worth far more than the sparrow that are sold for a farthing, have also been warned that they ought not fear those who kill the body but cannot kill the soul. And with that, the Prime Mover lets the acts of commission and omission of the wicked bear the fruit that damns them. The more lies are portrayed as truth and truth as lies, the more damning it all gets. It is all the more despicable when those in positions of trust - like pastors and politicians for instance - set out to con the gullible.

"And here's the best part of it for us here in the Pit. There are those wicked humans who really belong with us evil demons, and who do not have any scruples about using their persuasive powers to lull innocent souls into placing trust in them, before turning around and seducing them, and stealing their innocence. We here in Gehenna cannot have enough of this; but you can bet that such scandalous behavior which involves the violation of trust - and which behavior the perpetrators would incidentally never wish to see their own loved ones exposed to - drives the Deliverer to the edge! For some reason, it never strikes these stupid fools that they assuredly will check in here in due course for their pains; or that, when they do, our instructions are to place millstones about their necks so that they speed to the bottom of hell. Yeah, and that is exactly as it is written in the Gospels!

"The reason I myself am called the Father of Lies and I roast here in hell is because, being a master in the art of masquerade, I con, lie, deceive and mislead whilst wearing the disguise of the eminently trustful advisor and guardian of sacred truths.

"On their own, earthlings can only sin. And, inclined to sin, they do not just prefer lies to Truth, but many even imagine that they can actually lie their way into heaven! With that in mind, we here in the Pit long ago learned that the payback from our endeavors would be far greater if we concentrated our efforts on shining as much light on Truth as possible. And that is why I trumpet the facts regarding the *sancta ecclesia catholica*, apostolic succession, the holy sacraments, and all that.

692

Because then, all I need to do is be alert and ready to move in for the kill when it becomes obvious that the "poor forsaken children of Adam and Eve" are failing to live up to expectations!"

Mjomba had not been prepared for anything like this. Here was the devil, the evilest of evil creatures and the Father of Lies, trying to get the seminarian to buy the lie that he, Satan, respected truth! But by now, it really wasn't Mjomba who was in control of his thoughts. It was the devil, and the lad knew it. He threw up his arms in disgust and continued to commit the things the devil was mouthing to paper faithfully.

"The reaction of humans - who instinctively recoil at being told what to do, and many of whom subscribe to the belief that while greed 'might not be good, it works' - naturally is to scramble and stay as far away from the authority of the *Sancta Ecclesia Catholica* and its message of the 'Crucified Deliverer' as they possibly can" the Evil One pursued!

"Whereupon, in their ignorance of the righteousness of the Prime Mover, and going about to establish their own righteousness, they submit not themselves unto His righteousness! So you can see that, while testifying to the truth might be a good thing in and of itself, when it comes to earthlings and their last end, it really works only for me, Satan and the Father of Lies!

"And that is what makes me, the Father of lies, so dangerous. Although a murderer from the beginning, and I do abide not in the Truth, because there is no Truth in me, as Saul - that Apostle of the Gentiles - wrote, earthlings need to be terrified of me and what I might do. For one, in the same way I deceived Adam and Eve using my craftiness and subtlety, so I can easily corrupt the minds of their descendants, and lure them away from the single-minded devotion to their Deliverer in humility.

"That is how I go about 'seducing' humans. And, of course, the greater my own success, and the success of wicked humans in concealing the true effects of their machinations as they pursue temporal gains at the expense of other humans, the more terrible for us. And this is all the more so because all lies are not just premeditated; they are also the ones that make us murders! Does that ring a bell? Think of the names by which I go by: 'Father of Lies' and 'Father of Death'!

"And guess who the father of liars is! It is me, Old Scratch, who 'does not stand in the truth, because there is no truth in me'! As Ezekiel put it (some five hundred and seventy years before the promised Deliverer's arrival), I was once called the 'anointed cherub that covereth'. I was described then as 'full of wisdom, and perfect in beauty'. I was the embodiment of created perfection, and I led the worship of the universe. I was in the 'mountain of the Prime Mover,' where He manifests His glory; and I was 'perfect' in my ways until 'iniquity' developed in me. But I became swollen with pride because of my beauty and my wisdom, and I fell just by reason of the way I shone. Unholy ambition and jealousy ruined me, and resulted in my leading a host of angels in rebellion against the Prime Mover and the Deliverer. And I was 'cast out of the mountain of the Prime Mover, and down to this God-forsaken earth'!

"The earthlings who are wedded to lies always want the Deliverer - the one who did not merely come from the Prime Mover, but who was actually sent by the Prime Mover - dead! If you do not believe me, go look up John 8:39-47! And when my minions are puffed up and think they are learned and see, that is actually a sign that they are blind!

"Let me say this: the Deliverer warned you humans! He said: 'Beware of false prophets, who come to you in the clothing of sheep, but inwardly they are ravening wolves. By their fruits you shall know them. Do men gather grapes of thorns, or figs of thistles? Even so every good tree bringeth forth good fruit, and the evil tree bringeth forth evil fruit. A good tree cannot bring forth evil fruit, neither can an evil tree bring forth good fruit. Every tree that bringeth not forth good fruit, shall be cut down, and shall be cast into the fire. Wherefore by their fruits you shall know them.'

"But it is those who follow the Deliverer 'blindly' and cry out aloud 'Have mercy on us, Son of David' whose eyes become opened; and, as they receive their sight, their faith in the Deliverer makes them whole.

"But I should also give you some idea how I operate. Take the so-called 'reformation' that I engineered. Believe it or not, but it was my idea. I used Martin Luther, a Catholic friar - yes, and a good one at that - and a reformer, to set it in motion. In his battles with the conservatives in the Church - neo-conservatives actually - who were turning a blind eye to and virtually sanctioning the various types of abuses that were rampart at the time, he lost out, and was promptly 'excommunicated'. He had underestimated the extent of their influence and power.

"But he was luckier than Joan of Arc who was labeled a witch and burned at the stake! You may or may not like to hear it, but I also succeeded in using that innocent girl to confound and drive other good souls in the Church to virtual despair. As a result of the persecution that Joan of Arc endured, over the years, many a good soul in the world has chosen to part company with the 'Church' which got her to pay for the 'witch-craft' she supposedly practiced with her life!

Fake champions...

"You humans have long ways to go - you do not even have a clue regarding the way we in the Underworld operate. We use conservatives and neo-conservatives, as well as liberals and neo-liberals in the Church to ensnare folks and to make the work of evangelization as difficult as possible. That is why there will always be folks who ostensibly 'champion' the Church's teachings, but end up causing so many problems for the 'visible Church' just because they do things out of self-love, and it is actually not the Holy Spirit that is inspiring or guiding them. Indeed, there are so many Church functionaries who end up betraying the Deliverer and getting Him nailed to the cross (exactly as happened in the year thirty-three *Anno Domini*) while being cheered on by the 'faithful'.

"I can tell you that there are people in the Church today who operate exactly like those priests and Pharisees did two thousand years ago. Others operate like Judas Iscariot. The Deliverer did not say that it was the last that we were going to see of the betrayer, even though He did say that it would have been 'better if he (Judas Iscariot) had not been born' - whatever he meant by that! The Son of Man, going His way (as He Himself put it), did not have time to stop and ask Judas why he, of all people, was doing that to Him. The Deliverer did not even regard it as worth the trouble to ask the man who was His treasurer for an accounting of the monies that His admirers and other kind people had been contributing for His up-keep and that of his disciples.

"Then there are others in the Church who operate like Peter, the first pope who openly denied ever knowing the Deliverer - not once but three times within the space of one short hour! Others operate like the Roman soldiers, who actually drove the nails into the Deliverer's hands before hoisting Him up on the wooden cross. There are others still who operate like Thomas, the doubter.

"They all operate as they do because there is this tendency to keep the Spirit sent by the Deliverer in abeyance - they do not give Him a chance to strengthen them in the different virtues. And yet, that Spirit is what you call a *sine qua non* for their salvation and that of the world. And - guess what - when humans fail to give the Holy Spirit an opportunity to work with them, they effectively hand me - Satan - my chance to meddle.

Real champions...

"And as the Son of Man went His way and went about his work of redeeming the world, bearing His cross and His crown of thorns - after having been betrayed by one of the twelve, denied by another, and abandoned by the rest - people who did not even belong to the Fellowship he had started in preparation for launching the Church on the day of Pentecost were there when He needed them.

"There was Simon of Cyrene, the African on a mysterious mission in the Roman enclave of Judea, who turned up from nowhere and helped to ensure that the Deliverer would bear His load of the cross all the way to the summit of Calvary. Then there was Mary Magdalene, a woman who (according to a popular legend) knew what to be a 'person of disrepute' meant, and who (if it is true) decided to cast aside fears that she herself might be recognized and stoned to death by the mob for her former lifestyle, and offered to wipe away blood stains, dust and other dirt that were clogging onto the Deliverer's eyebrows and causing Him additional pain as he stumbled along on the murram road leading to Mt. Calvary with a clean damp cloth.

"His face bloated from the blows of the soldiers - from being scourged, beaten and manhandled by the creatures that nevertheless were fashioned in the Image - as man, the Deliverer may not have been able to see His way as He stumbled along to the 'place of the skulls'. However, as a member of the Godhead, the Savior of Humankind could not help but discern my fall from grace and that of the other rebel angels in the free choice that we created spirits radically and irrevocably *rejected His Father in Heaven* and the reign of the Godhead; and He could not help but discern that behind the disobedient choice of the first humans lurked a seductive voice, opposed to the Non-Creature and Master Craftsman - my voice which, out of envy, made Adam and Eve fall into death; He could not help but discern Man as he let his trust in his Creator die in his heart and, abusing his freedom, disobeyed his Maker's command; and He could not help but discern the hunched back of Cain as, brimming with a sense of self-importance, he murdered his brother Abel. And the same went for all the terrible things that humans throughout the ages have done to each other. And, of all the crimes committed by humans against humanity, there was of course none that was more loathsome and crying out for divine vengeance than the convoluted pleasures that humans, led by Pilate, Agrippa and the priests and Pharisees, derived from the pain and sufferings endured by the Son of Man on that 'Good Friday.'

"And then there was Joseph of Arimathea, a secret admirer of the Deliverer who offered what would become Christendom's most important destination for pilgrims - the tomb in which He would be buried by the women and from which he would rise in triumph after spending three days with Adam, Eve, Moses, and the others whom my troops held as prisoners in hell.

"Pontius Pilate, the fox, was of course the exact opposite of these other folks. He saw this completely innocent Nazarene - someone his secret service had assured him was an upright soul who could never be accused of any wrongdoing in the eyes of everyone of good will in Judea and who was far from being the caricature his enemies were portraying - being prepared for the kill by those blood thirsty priests and Pharisees. Instead of ordering an immediate halt to their fragrant and sickening gambit, he sought instead to ingratiate himself with the murderers by legitimizing it. He was quite comfortable presiding over the greatest miscarriage of justice the world had ever seen and, indeed, would ever see!

"Incidentally, is it not telling that the apostle who betrayed the Deliverer was not just His purse bearer, but someone so close that he and the Deliverer frequently shared the same chalice when wine and other refreshments were served? There have, conceivably, been other 'apostles' of the Deliverer who have ostensibly 'taken good care' of the Church's affairs while believing that they could serve mammon at the same time!

"It is clearly to Martin Luther's credit that, even as he was being excommunicated by the 'neocons', he was reportedly emphasizing that it was 'by grace alone' that humans were saved! Not by wilfulness or self-righteousness, but only by the grace of the Prime Mover. But did that good Catholic friar really mean that good works were unnecessary?

"That was, in all probability, the misinformation that Luther's adversaries started spreading about him - the misinformation which they used to nail his fate. After all, it must have been Martin Luther's intention, as he nailed his thesis onto the cathedral's double doors, to make that act a symbol of a good job well done in challenging the neocons to an argument - a good work he himself at least believed had the Holy Spirit behind it. And so, without a doubt, Martin Luther, as the good Catholic he was, believed that humans were saved by faith in the Deliverer (or His grace) *and* good works.

"If anything, it was his adversaries who seemed to believe in salvation by faith alone without good works, because they were not particularly bothered about the importance of appropriate behavior - especially behavior that was befitting of functionaries of Holy Mother the Church. Thus, the neocons had not challenged the popes when they kept concubines in the Vatican. But they felt the need to try and stop Martin Luther because he had decided that it was time to come out and, instead of mincing words, argue his case forcefully - even if the merits of his arguments were going to be completely ignored and the focus was going to be on the fact that he had volunteered arguments that were *ad hominem*, and were for that reason not particularly welcome!"

The meaning of "holiness"...

"Now, I find any discussion of 'holiness' juicy - don't ask why! So, what does it mean to be holy anyway?

"Holiness is eschewing doing your own will and allowing divine grace to be your motive force and to inspire you in whatever you do. That is not the same as giving up your personal autonomy and allowing yourself to be dominated by others, regardless of whether their intentions are good or bad, and being compelled thereby to do their will blindly. You could do that and still be wilful - you might seek to be subservient to others perhaps as a way of avoiding trouble or personal responsibility.

700

"Holiness is subjecting your will to the will of the Prime Mover, and allowing the Holy Spirit to sanctify your actions. The challenge is making sure it is the will of the Prime Mover and not that of one of my demons for instance.

"The essence of holiness is living an innocent life - just as children do. They do not intend harm for any one, and are selfless even as they grow in personal autonomy and learn to survive in the world. Holiness is not shutting yourself off and being a quietist with no personal aspirations in life. And it certainly doesn't consist in going out and imposing your beliefs on others against their will - or practicing hate under the guise of witnessing to the faith!

"You cannot seek to do your will and the will of the Prime Mover at one and the same time. You are either doing one or the other. You could be married to doing your will, but habitually blame the Prime Mover or your fellow men - or me - instead of yourself for the consequences. You bet that there are always consequences for what you humans do or do not do.

"When you are wilfully involved in this or that, and having your way, you actually are having your reward in the real sense of that word. And because you automatically shut out the Prime Mover in the process, you also forfeit your eternal life in so doing. If you are selfless and above all accepting of others as little children typically do, you are certainly not rewarding yourself in any way.

"That is why those who do not lose their innocence are automatically in for a reward in their afterlife - a reward suitable for individuals who were not prepared to sell their birthright to a heavenly mansion for some passing self-indulgence, and who would even have been willing to lose their lives to retain that birthright. Humans retain a certain

701

amount of innocence when they commit venial sins, but loose it entirely when they commit mortal sins.

"It should be pretty obvious by now that it is not the enjoyment itself, derived from indulgence of the self, that is reprehensible. The enjoyment *per se* wouldn't cause humans - or for that matter angels - to miss out on their heavenly reward. It is the wilfulness and the ill intentions accompanying it that makes one pay the price. It couldn't be otherwise, because in so far as the 'pleasure' or 'satisfaction' the reprehensible acts themselves give, the Prime Mover, who made all that exists, blessed it all after He was done with His labors of creation, and declared that everything was good.

"He did not say that about the different choices that humans would subsequently make because he wanted them to retain the freedom to choose between what was morally good and what was morally bad. And He certainly did not 'bless' wilfulness, a potential (bad) option that would still be available to (free) humans. Similarly, any suggestion that actions in themselves could be bad would detract from the infinite goodness of the Prime Mover. And if He ordained that creatures with free wills should not be capable of wilfulness (detrimental as it was to them), that would have conflicted with the fact that the Prime Mover was infinitely generous and also almighty. It would have signalled that the Prime Mover was afraid of having free creatures around Him - that they might cause Him inconvenience that conceivably could prove deadly for Him.

"Humans who parent and others who fill the role of mentor, unlike the Prime Mover who is also a parent and a mentor, frequently choose to lord it over those under their charge and, in flagrant violation of the rights of those they are supposed to groom, end up treating them as though they were automatons with no right to the exercise of their free will. Some humans end up treating fellow humans as second class citizens or even as chattel.

"Since wilful acts of that nature are neither sanctioned nor blest by the Prime Mover, those humans perpetrating them can take it that they have already received their reward in this life and should not bother to look for another reward in their afterlife.

"And so, what does 'being saved' mean? To be saved is to become like a little child and thereby facilitate cooperation with divine grace; and the verdict can only come after the individual has left this life for the next. This is because, when humans are still alive and kicking and free as birds, the possibility that they could go nuts - as they are always doing - and rebel against the Prime Mover (as the first man and the first woman did) will always be there. It is the reason a human could never be canonized before that human had left this world for his/her afterlife.

"And what would be the 'signs', if any, that a human was cooperating with divine grace? One sign would be if the human in question was not involved in murder or theft - or if he/she was not giving in to the urge to be a con artist of some sort, like putting on the appearance of being truthful and saintly (as I myself am busy doing just now) when he/she was all rotten on the inside and just pulling people's legs! It would also be an indication that a human was cooperating with grace if that human was prepared to lay down his/her life for his/her 'neighbor'; or if he/she loved, not his/her friends, but his/her enemies.

"There is no other way to heaven. There are no short cuts. And the sacraments play a very special role in helping humans stay the course because they provide the link to the Deliverer who is the way, the life and the truth.

"The exercise of virtue is always heroic. Any

exercise of virtue has to be heroic for the simple reason that it implies self-denial. The candidate for sainthood has to be prepared to forego wilfulness. This is the wilfulness that wants to determine where the human wants to go and that seeks to control everything around one and to exploit it. And this is a complete waste of time, because 'what does it profit a man to possess the whole world and to lose one's soul in the process'.

"Now, humans have to give Caesar what is Caesar's, and to God what is God's. Everything, including the breath of life that sustains humans, is owed by you humans to the Prime Mover. Everything is His! And, in point of fact, there is really nothing that you could say belongs to Caesar. Nothing!

"The Deliverer Himself clarified this on multiple occasions, including one where a large number of people were travelling with the Him. The crowd included some who were convinced that it had to be John the Baptist who was back on the scene notwithstanding that he had been dead for sometime, beheaded on the orders of Herod Antipatros who also went by the names of Herod Antipas, Herod the Tetrarch, and even 'King Herod'. But some in the crowd were certain that He had to be the prophet and miracle worker Elijah who had lived nine hundred years earlier and whose return Elijah's return "before the coming of the great and terrible day of the LORD' had been prophesied in the Book of Malachi. There were others yet who believed that He was another one of the prophets whom the Prime Mover had decided to send to the people of Israel in their own time!

"As Luke described it, He turned and said to them: 'If any man come to me, and hate not his father, and mother, and wife, and children, and brethren, and sisters, yea and his own life also, he cannot be my disciple. And whosoever doth not carry his cross and come after me, cannot be my disciple.' (Luke 14:26-27). And also: 'So likewise every one of you that doth not renounce all that he possesseth, cannot be my disciple.' (Luke 14:33).

"And there is no doubt that this included *Divus* Julius (Deified Gaius Julius Caesar) and the all other rulers, despots, dictators, demagogues (rabble-rousers) and others who load it over the populations they 'govern' and harass, plunder and rob, torture and murder fellow humans under the guise of advancing 'national security interests'.

"The Deliverer was just being polite when He told his audience to render to Caesar what was Caesar's, you dumb fools! He certainly wasn't endorsing imperialism. And, anyway, how could dead men own anything? Gaius Julius Caesar, the dictator (whose father also named Gaius Julius Caesar, Roman Senator and Proconsul, had died suddenly in eighty-five years BC in Rome while putting on his shoes one morning), had himself been dead many years, stabbed to death by his best friend Brutus. Gaius Octavius, the self-styled Imperator Caesar Augustus and first Roman Emperor who reigned at the time the Deliverer was born, was also already dead and buried. And the unpopular Tiberius Caesar Augustus (who succeeded the Imperator Caesar Augustus) could not get out of the way fast enough for the impatient Caligula who could not wait to be crowned Gaius Julius Caesar Augustus Germanicus and third Roman Emperor (and ruled from 37 AD to 41 AD); and the days of the Roman Empire itself - the sole super power - were numbered.

"And the only way for a human to give God what is God's is to subject his/her will to His instead of trying to redefine or rewrite the Moral Law the Prime Mover etched on the consciences of the creatures that bear His image and live on in an afterlife. That does not leave humans very much in terms of possessions. By subjecting themselves to the divine will, they also automatically place whatever they might have at His disposal! And that is why the decision to do so doesn't come easy - particularly for grown-ups and the affluent.

"It is also a very humiliating thing to do in the eyes of a world that does not recognize an afterlife and seeks to maximize the here and now. It could not be anything but that in a world that derides or does not recognize the spiritual; glorifies exploitation of the masses and stealing under the guise of promoting 'free enterprise', and also glorifies colonialism, imperialism, militarism, murder, acts of genocide and things of that nature by nations under the guise of promoting 'national security'; a world in which more likely than not both petty and grand corruption permeate the body politic even in so-called democracies; and also one in which some so-called super powers just can't stop needling other super powers needlessly and, blind to the fact that it is those sorts of actions that inevitably spark world wars with their untold cost in blood and treasure, sleep walk into oblivion like others before them.

"And humans do not really have a choice - if they want to do the right thing. After they find themselves in a world in which evil reigns supreme and in which the best efforts cannot by themselves guarantee them and their loved ones anything, the only viable option (which they can take or leave) becomes just that: electing to carry out the will of the Prime Mover and Author of Life as they are admonished in the Lord's Prayer."

The essence of being devilish...

"And so, what does being devilish or satanic mean? What does it really mean to be a transgressor - like me?

706

What sets humans who transgress apart from humans who are godly? In other words, what do devilish humans or sinners look like? How do they act or sound?

"Well, even though a pure spirit, I myself have been called a murderer - every 'killing' in fact has my personal seal. That should give you clues about devilish humans. They will be above all murderers. Taking the lives of others is the singular badge of honor that all my minions and ambassadors proudly wear. Of course that badge will also come in all colors and shades - rooting out terrorists; attacking the interests of this or that murderous regime; defending civilization; religious crusades, and what have you.

"As soon as humans start believing that they are masters of their own lives, they start imagining that they can be masters of other humans as well. They don't stop at thinking that they can have others revere them as gods, or at enslaving fellow humans.

"They also start believing that they might even have a license to kill - just like James Bond of James Hadley Chase fame. That is also when, completely oblivious to the existence of the Avenging Angel, they actually start scheming how to systematically plunder and steal, and murder their fellow humans through declared and undeclared wars.

"It is bad enough for talented kids or 'punks' in some inner-city ghetto to cut down each other prematurely in a 'senseless' spurt of 'gang' warfare. And it is more terrible when nations go to war - especially unjustified wars - if for no reason than that the lives of 'talented' humans on all sides will be prematurely ended."

Emoì Ekdíkesis (Vengeance is Mine saith the Lord)...

"When humans get overtaken by some misfortune,

their first inclination is to look around for scapegoats, with the intention of marshalling the wherewithal to strike back. Stupid humans don't even realize that when they encounter miseries that ensue from actions of their fellow humans, they are expected to bear them in the same way they ought to bear miseries inflicted upon them by natural disasters! They are even expected to turn the other cheek! But well - we in the Underworld shouldn't even be surprised that so many humans are unbelievers or believers only in name!

"The stupid humans will do quite stupid things, like investing in treasure and blood in the pursuit not just of those they figure have wronged them, but any group of people who look like they were remotely allied to the suspected culprits! And this is also the time when the whole world suddenly takes on a strange new look; a world that namely is divided into two parts, with one part ostensibly united against the supposed victims, and the other part against them! So, so stupid!

"And, in such times, humans typically start doing all sorts of foolish things even before they have taken the trouble to establish the facts. How on earth for example, can a group of humans however important or, a country for that matter, imagine that the whole wide world is either with it or against it when only a small fraction of the earth's inhabitants gets to know what goes on beyond their borders, and the rest wouldn't even care to know?

"Even we demons know about the many instances in the course of human history in which stupid humans, if they had only bothered to look in good faith for the 'real' culprits behind their misfortunes, would have found it was they themselves! They would have discovered to their pleasant surprise that the culprits were either actions on their part that caused others to become justifiably aggrieved to the point of driving them to take what could be characterized as 'defensive' actions aimed at signalling that they had had enough of the 'bullying'. And frequently it was actions on the part of former allies - actions that they themselves had initially encouraged and sometimes even underwritten!

"Then humans never stop to think that if they happen to command the means of striking out at their perceived enemies - or the means to 'take the fight to the enemy' - at a given time in history, and they go ahead and do it following their irrational impulse, then they have to expect pay-back the moment those enemies of theirs acquire the means to hit back, and should not complain when that happens! So, so stupid, and so shortsighted!

"The countries that invested in weapons of mass destruction and remain poised to use them, and particularly those countries that had the audacity to actually use them, are the ones that are now realizing the obvious at this late stage, namely that no one individual or country has a monopoly over technology or know how; and that oil reserves, uranium, gold or diamond deposits, or some other precious mineral, discovered in the backyard of some basket nation, can alone make all the difference when it comes to owning or not owning the wherewithal to strike out at an 'enemy', using any means, anywhere on globe.

"And, what is worse, in this age of the Worldwide Web, it only requires the ability to hack into computers of the so-called super powers to steal the secrets that are needed to produce and launch unmanned drones, and things of that nature. It is therefore the height of recklessness for any so-called super power to use these things supposedly to inflict damage on its newfound enemies who may be perceived as weak and defenseless today, but might, with a bit of luck, be transformed into something else altogether tomorrow. What is even quite obvious, even if it is not acknowledged, is the fact that nations are driven to arm themselves when other nations begin to threaten their sovereignty.

"The only posture that guarantees peace for any nation in these circumstances is that which is based on the adage that humans should make love not war! And look - I am Beelzebub, the Father of Death, and I happen to know what I am talking about more than you stupid humans!

"And, to show that humans are very stupid indeed, in their pursuit of 'revenge', they frequently end up expending in precious treasure and blood many times what was inflicted on them initially by the imaginary culprits, and committing crimes against humanity that often pale in comparison to the 'crimes' they seek to avenge. Whereas, if they had stopped and just reminded themselves that to pursue revenge was tantamount to usurping the prerogative of the Prime Mover, and if they had stayed cool-headed, they might even have learnt from their own past mistakes, cleaned up their own acts; and they not only would have minimized the chances of ruffling other people's feathers, but would have stood a much better chance of winning their real enemies over in the process.

"And guess what - they you would have contributed to the victory of Good over Evil in a spectacular way too! But you can, of course, be sure that I, Beelzebub, would have fought tooth and nail to frustrate any such outcome so long as I remained the unchallenged Ruler of the Underworld!

"Regardless, humans never learn from history, and never stop to consider the price they will in time pay for flagrantly usurping the Prime Mover's prerogatives with their determination to even scores. They lack the foresight to see that their investment in the development

710

of weapons of mass destruction and the means for delivering the same will in time become their own undoing. And also guess what! Those who seek revenge invariably end up being themselves pursued by Him who said '*Emoi Ekdikesis*' (Vengeance is Mine), because of their own reckless and brazen deeds to their fellow humans!

"And that is the time when the once proud and victorious will beg the mountains and the rocks and say: 'Fall on us and hide us from the face of him who sits on the throne and from the wrath of the Lamb! For the great day of their wrath has come, and who can stand?' It will not be a nice sight!"

Why it is senseless to kill...

"Now, in this matter of killing, it would make some sense if the act of killing caused killers to live on - if killing made them immune to the thing they visited on their opponents, namely death. But, like judges who condemn other humans to death, killers don't become immune to it, and it sometimes even happens that the 'honorable justices' go to meet the Eternal Judge before those they send to death row do. The fact that those who kill themselves die - and kill *because* they are themselves scared stiff of dying – makes acts of killing in fact senseless *per se*.

"By the way, when humans kill, they actually do so for the same reasons that drive the self-willed and the selfish to pursue temporal earthly fulfilment rather than fulfilment in the afterlife that does not end and is eternal. The 'reasons' in either case are based on proven fallacies, and they explain why actions of folks who spend their lives seeking to satisfy 'fantasies' they become unable to entertain when their time on earth is up at any

711

cost and murderers end up making no sense.

"As a matter of fact, no sooner had the first man and the first woman sinned and were driven out of the Garden of Eden than they begun accusing each other of being murderous, beastly and a 'terrorist'. The stage was set at that time for humans to hound each other for perceived 'ills', while remaining completely blind to their own faults - and even the part they may have played in bringing those ills upon themselves.

"Things were bad enough at the time of Adam and Eve with the ever-present possibility that one of them might mortally harm the other before they had been able to raise members of the generation that would succeed them and guarantee the survival of the human race. If anything was clear then, it was the fact that every single human life was sacred and too important to play with. If Eve had succeeded in knocking off Adam in one of her tantrums (or the other way around), it would have been not just a half of humanity but pretty well all of humanity gone to pot! And no earthly soul would ever have known about it!

"Adam himself knocked off Eve on innumerable occasions mentally, whenever he wished her dead for any reason, and she never even suspected it - she similarly murdered Adam on innumerable occasions in her mind without him suspecting that he was in danger. What stopped them from killing each other was the knowledge that their infinitely loving Prime Mover who had caused them both to bounce into being out of nothing and 'gave them their daily bread' treasured them both equally without any distinction, the differences in their individual makeup and temperament notwithstanding; and that if He stopped thinking about them for just one moment, they would both cease to exist. It is a legacy of Adam and Eve's murderous thoughts that humans continue to live like creatures that are accursed, and to abuse and kill each other senselessly.

"The world has already seen so many idiotic 'rulers' who thought that they could subordinate the sanctity of life to their hackneyed theories about the earth's future, keeping a count of them would have been an impossible task. Some of them couldn't resist the idea that they themselves were divine, and accordingly regarded anyone who challenged them as doomed both physically *and* spiritually.

"The world today is actually many times worse off because humans have ceded their personal rights to so-called 'governments' that in turn are largely controlled by greedy, impersonal 'mega-corporations'! Under the guise of conducting business dealings, corporations and their hired guns will use every trick in the book to get you to part with your hard-earned cash and property. And governments, particularly those that have ceded control to big business, will stop at nothing in their drive to conquer, dominate and spread their influence in the world.

"My reading of the situation - and this is not an exaggeration - is that three or four decades from now, mega-corporations, not voters, will be deciding who occupies the White House, Number 10 Downing Street, and even the Kremlin - or, don't you believe me?

"Thanks to the success of the 'Manhattan Project' and the existence of corporations that will stop at nothing to make a buck, a disgruntled Bedouin, operating solo in the heart of the Sahara Desert and armed only with an "infra- nu-red", will soon be able to successfully 'neutralize' a super power, before vanishing without a trace!

"The infra-nu-red, currently being tested by one 'rogue state', is a three by five inch computer chip which, when commissioned, will be able to decode just about anything and also to hack into any computer. The idea, of course, is to hack into the computers of military command and control centers of a selected super power, and after raising false alarms to the effect that the nation's cities are under attack from an unknown source, use that opportunity to intercept and decode the ensuing communications from the command and control centers to the field, and then redirect that super power's fire power at itself by substituting key communications with the fake ones!

"The Bedouin will have the alternative of launching his own small but deadly arsenal of missiles tipped with WMD from the back of a camel and guiding them to their targets - command and control centers, densely populated cities, the bunkers in which intercontinental ballistic missiles with their payload of nuclear and hydrogen bombs are concealed, the super power's warships and submarines, and spy satellites - again using infra-nu-red.

"You can bet that the 'pundits' and the 'networks' they serve would then have a field day trying to figure out what on earth happened - the same pundits who hailed the success of the Manhattan Project and who are always ecstatic whenever they discuss the benefits of technology and advantages of free enterprise!

The culture of death...

"You can rest assured that my troops and I have not been resting on our laurels, because today, instead of just demanding to be worshiped as gods, they actually try to act like God while putting up a facade of being God-fearing. Unfortunately for these 'quislings' of mine, all their huffing and hawing amounts to is a dream - the hope

714

or dream that they will be successful in plundering *and* retaining for their sole use the earth's resources to the exclusion of others. Which is just like confiscating a back-hoe from an undertaker and using it to dig your own grave; because, while they are busy fighting for control over the world's riches, others who are also dying for the good life are conserving their energies and just lying in wait and preparing to pounce as soon as the first fools finish doing the 'dirty job' for them - namely 'neutralizing' the newly discovered 'terrorists' and 'insurgents'.

"It is precisely because it is greed and self-interest, usually passed off as 'national security', that the situation in the world is in such flux with borders of states changing almost by the day. Ordinary folk in the resource-rich parts of globe that super powers of the day cannot resist eyeing are usually helpless against the invading armies, occupiers, liberators or however the aggressor nations elect to call themselves.

"This is a legacy of original sin, has been the case since the immediate descendants of Adam and Eve started fighting over inheritance, and will continue to plague the world until Planet Earth and everything on it goes to waste in a 'terminal' nuclear explosion on the Last Day.

"From time immemorial, 'victors' in war, regardless of whether they came by their victory through luck or simply because the contest was uneven, have never hesitated to label their foes rebels, insurgents or terrorists, while referring to themselves as liberators, and even 'pacifiers'. Forgetting that it was because they themselves were 'terrorists', 'rebels' and 'insurgents' that the Prime Mover sent His only begotten Son into the world to try and 'deliver' them, stupid humans have never had qualms wherever possible to kill or enslave or otherwise humiliate their own.

"Because might makes right according to their contorted reasoning, stupid humans have always been very quick to go for the jugular even when they were the ones committing acts of banditry. They do that in the same breath as they acknowledge that they themselves have been forgiven a great deal; and they conveniently forget that, in the not too distant future, the fact that the things they do to their fellow humans aren't exactly what any of them would have liked to see done to themselves will come to haunt them. The hunger for power and unbridled greed combine to blind humans to the fact that they dig holes for themselves when they turn on each other for any reason.

"When you are inclined to 'go for the jugular' every time you are slighted, you'd better make sure that you are 'perfect'. The problem is that the inclination to 'go for the jugular' is not compatible with perfection. In point of fact, when creatures who are fashioned in the divine image get involved in the business of 'payback', 'an eye for an eye', 'tit for tat', and things of that sort, they automatically infringe on the matters that are the prerogative of the one and the only Divine One and could not be more presumptuous. Regardless of one's station in life and the authority or power that one ostensibly commands, He has made it crystal clear that taking revenge is *His* sole prerogative.

"And so, when 'payback' is in the form of invasion, occupation or annexation, and other vengeful acts like 'carpet bombing', dropping A-bombs and H-bombs over cities full of fellow humans, or missile strikes on homes aimed at 'taking out suspected terrorists', which are the very things the culprits would not want happen to themselves, the divine 'retribution' is not just predictable. It is assuredly certain and inescapable; and it doesn't come in the form of a counter invasion or occupation, or a missile strike. These are immoral acts for which the perpetrators individually answer at the divine court of justice in due course.

"Now, it is bad enough when humans indulge in murder and mayhem. But it is inexcusable when, completely oblivious to the fact that there is a damned heavy price to be paid for daring to use the name of the Almighty in vain, they try to do those things in the name of the Prime Mover! The Prime Mover whose only begotten Son was Himself labeled an insurgent and a terrorist, and crucified between two thieves by those who were eyeing his territory.

"He too had territory, you know; Planet Earth and the rest of the interplanetary system which humans, who own nothing but are greedy and expansionist all the same like me, hoped to possess by neutralizing Him. And it now just so happens that when humans kill each other, regardless of whether they do it in His name or not, the target is the Deliverer who chose to identify Himself with suffering humans. He came to redeem humans *because* the Prime Mover is in-dwelling in them; and He sanctified all human suffering by His own death on the cross just because of what He is, namely the Word. That is the essence of the Deliverer being the Second Adam and a 'brother' to all humans.

"Still, ever since Rome was overrun by 'Christians', warmongering - the culture of death *par excellence* - has had a special appeal for them in the same way it has always appealed to greedy and expansionist humans. So much so in fact that the ranks of 'peaceniks' are filled with ultra-liberal 'non-believers' or pagans, while those who profess to be staunch 'Christians' and pro-life fill the ranks of supporters of the warmongers.

"Actually, money and the 'culture of death', which is its companion, were already at work in the Church even before it's official launch. The actions of Judas Iscariot, the Deliverer's purse bearer, gave a premonition of things to come way back then…Judas Iscariot who sold his Divine Master for thirty pieces of silver - not even gold, mark you, but silver!

"And, not long after the Church had been inaugurated, Ananias showed that even though the Church was operating under the guidance of the Holy Spirit, money matters and all the problems that were associated with the love of money were not going to leave the Church unscathed. Ananias, who thought that money could buy one power and influence in the early Church, was stopped before he could do the Church any harm. But, of course, many others have since succeeded where Ananias did not, and they have left their mark.

"Paul, nee Saul, who would later refer to himself as the 'Apostle to the Gentiles', had been such an avid supporter of the culture of death that many of those he approached with the new message of forgiveness and love for one another initially thought that he was tricking them and would promptly be back with his death squads. A traitor to his own people who was a Roman citizen, Paul had been a particularly effective hunter of the followers of the 'terrorist from Nazareth', using a 'human intelligence network' that many modern-day super powers would envy. He had been such a crafty operator and his reputation as a death squad leader had been such that the mere mention of the name 'Saul' sent shivers down the spine of any devoted follower of the dead terrorist.

"A fervid disciple of the 'Cain doctrine', Paul, even though extremely learned and a virtual 'one man think tank' had operated on the principle that you could liquidate any number of 'outlanders' (never mind that they might be as much human as yourself) provided the objective was to consolidate and strengthen the authority and reach of the 'emperor' - that the lives of Roman citizens were the only thing that mattered, in as much as the lives of foreigners weren't worth a farthing. Oh, while he was Saul - before he betrayed my cause - that Paul had been such a dandy! It is all there in his 'Confessions'! (Galatians 1:13-14, Philippians 3:4-6, Acts 7:57-58 and Acts 8:3-4)

"The way my troops and I prefer to work with the Judases and Ananiases in the upper echelons of the Church's hierarchy today is to get them to focus exclusively on some aspects of death culture and to remain completely silent on others. The objective is to get the 'Church' to forge a theology of the 'culture of death' that embraces only some but not all instances of that culture. Our success can be gauged from the fact that the 'Church' in some so-called 'Christian' nations now blindly throws its weight behind political parties that make no secret of their support for militarism, and the ease with which they will pursue world dominance through the use of force, their open support for capital punishment, and things like that.

"And so, a political party that for instance puts on a show of being disenchanted with 'abortion laws' on the books will receive the Church's whole-hearted support, even if the policies which that party openly advocates - for instance policies that rely on crippling 'economic sanctions' and 'pre-emptive regime changes using overwhelming force' to promote its ideological goals and establish the country as an 'insuperable super power' - cause intolerable sufferings to millions of innocent humans and spell death for millions more *and* reinforce the belief that human life is valueless.

"Just to think that the Church's leadership, which should be preaching the sanctity of life, hosts figures whose lives are devoted to waging wars and other death culture enterprises, and sees no problem being hosted in turn by those death culture enthusiasts! It certainly says something about our decidedly enormous influence over both churchmen and those worldly rulers along with their henchmen.

"In an attempt to legitimize the culture of death, humans unashamedly depict the Prime Mover as also indulging in it. They, of course, do not say 'God killed so many humans...'. But that is exactly what they mean when they say: 'Lightning killed him or her'; or 'The avalanche buried them alive'; or 'The earthquake killed everyone in the collapsed building'. And they always imply that the Prime Mover kills with a vengeance. Perverse humans!

"They absolve themselves from all blame, and ignore the real reasons why most of the calamities occur, like the greed for money which is behind logging in the Amazon forests, drilling for oil in Alaska and elsewhere, and the failure to implement policies that would minimize pollution and global warming. Then, when these things interfere with the seasons - when the glaciers melt and cause the waters to break banks and ravage homes, or when hurricanes suddenly strike, they blame everything on 'El Niño', which is just a pseudonym for 'Prime Mover'.

"And so, instead of blaming the real culprits for killing people, they now have this habit of blaming God. It is like two nations that lob nuclear bombs - or, better, weapons of mass destruction that are invisible to the eye - at each other's cities and then decry the destruction caused by 'the elements'. Instead of tracing the real cause of wild forest fires, namely environmental policies that are crafted with the help of energy corporations and have resulted in a depleted ozone layer, lightning - and implicitly the Prime Mover - is blamed!

"But, talking about invisible WMD - the human

immunodeficiency virus (HIV) which spreads by replicating its genetic information and then makes its victim catch the acquired immunodeficiency syndrome (AIDS) is one such weapon that one super power developed at the height of the Cold War, and then tested on 'ladies of the twilight' in an African port city. It is obvious from the way the virus operates that its building blocks were artificially assembled under controlled conditions and specifically designed to kill or disable humans en masse by rendering their immune systems inoperable.

"If the virus was not cultured in test tubes in a laboratory and was natural, it is pretty obvious that there would be no human left on earth. For one, the virus wouldn't have waited all this time to strike, doing so just by sheer coincidence at the height of the cold war! Anyone can tell it is a man-made virus from its name: 'HIV/AIDS virus'. I am Beelzebub, and you can take it from me that the HIV/AIDS virus is a lab produced, genetically mutated organism that was designed to be resistant to medication. It was designed to be fatal.

"The field test was successful in that the unwary guinea pigs died as had been intended. But the genetically engineered virus did not kill its victims as fast as it had been hoped. The result was that by the time its first victims died of it months – and, in some cases, years - later, they had unknowingly passed the incurable condition on to their clients who in turn passed it on to other 'ladies of the twilight' and eventually to their own spouses.

"This explains the initial incidence of the pandemic along routes taken by truckers as they moved truckloads of imported cargo inland from the port. It goes against the grain to try and argue that the virus originally came from an African monkey. If that had been the case (and assuming the African monkey population had not been interfered with by that super power's researchers in modern times), the HIV/AIDS virus (like other known natural viruses) would have appeared on earth centuries ago and wouldn't be the completely new phenomenon it was when it struck at the time it did.

"It does not take a rocket scientist to tell that the HIV/AIDS virus was cultured in test tubes, and is not a 'product of nature'. It should be obvious to anyone that this disease or condition (as it was initially - and also very aptly - described) is man-made. Some originally harmless virus - perhaps the virus that causes the common cold - was mutated under controlled conditions in a lab and deliberately made a killer virus resistant to any form of treatment.

"It would undoubtedly be quite simple to develop an effective antidote or vaccine for the HIV/AIDS virus if it were possible to retrace all the steps in its development. The antidote or vaccine would then be engineered to disable the virus at the different stages of development in the infected victims. But the original blueprints used in creating this virus have almost certainly been discarded by now to conceal the disease's origin, and shield those responsible for this crime against humankind from facing justice - on Planet Earth. The alternative is to now try blindly to develop a medicinal concoction that will disable the killer virus's functions by pure chance. I am not the devil for nothing. And, of course, you humans are quite free to ignore this advice that am providing *gratis* - at your peril.

"Talking about HIV/AIDS and weapons of mass destruction, the condom - that much vaunted (and also maligned) weapon of choice against the HIV virus - can also be an WMD in so many ways. For one, it can guarantee the extinction of the human race in just one

722

hundred years if, in a bid to minimize the risk of catching the HIV/AIDS virus, all sexually active male without any exception decided to use the condom unfailingly in accordance with the advice of the 'experts'.

"And so, individual humans (if they are not careful) can self-destruct by failing to restrain themselves and going after all sorts of fads, and by blindly aping other humans whose 'untested and untried' ways leave them exposed to 'unknown' dangers. You might not know it, but it was the pining of the first man and the first woman for a strange new 'lifestyle' that involved feasting on the forbidden fruit from the Tree of Knowledge of Good and Evil that made them so susceptible to temptation, and specifically to my cockeyed suggestion that they would become like the Prime Mover if they went ahead and feasted on the forbidden fruit!

"Another example of self-destructive humans are demagogues who latch onto the notion that they are more special than other humans; and, oblivious to the fact that they are on trial like everyone one else, start to believe that the lives of other humans are expendable, and can be sacrificed at their personal whims to their own interests. Incredibly, some of them even fall for our suggestion that the world will come to an end if they stepped aside and allowed others to also try their hand at governing! So, so stupid!

"Since time immemorial, demagogues, particularly when controlled by special interest groups, have been virtual WMD who traditionally left a trail of death and destruction in their path.

"And the demagogues never learn from history - that it is but a matter of time (counted in years not centuries) before they and their henchmen come face to face with their victims in the court of divine justice. If they did, all *our* work, which goes into grooming them to take up the reins of power, guiding and sustaining them through their murderous exploits, and above all ensuring that they stay focused on worldly things to the very end, would come to naught. And that is one thing that we will not allow to happen.

"The fact is that when humans who have blood on their hands eventually get to the other side of the gulf that separates the living from the dead, and they suddenly come face to face with those who died at their hands, it is a fate that is always many times worse than the fate suffered by their victims regardless of how those victims met their end. As far as traumatic experiences go, the trauma of being caught in a burst of cluster bombs or a fuselage of rocket fire launched from a 'Blackhawk' cannot compare with the shock of confronting those you thought you had effectively rubbed out upon entering your afterlife!

"It is bad enough that humans, stained with original sin (with the exception of the Son of man and His Blessed Mother), must die and go to judgement. But it is simply too bad when human beings go to their judgement and are confronted by those they killed - each one of whom, by divine decree, will be howling for his/her killer's pound of flesh! I can assure you that no scene could be more theatrical or dramatic (for those of you who become transfixed by theatre and drama) than that encounter as killers come face to face with their victims on the other side of the gulf.

"Those who delighted at the sight of their victims cringing in fear, and who entertained strange notions about being ordained to rule roughshod over the other poor forsaken humans and about their own immortality, will wish they had never been born. The tables will be verily turned as those who were given to swaggering and had everyone at their mercy wail and, too late, beseech

724

those they once enjoyed tormenting for mercy. It is also at that time that the beatitudes that are now ridiculed and equated with insanity will be completely validated. The meek, who are dismissed as idiots, will find themselves exalted - to their great surprise. Those who now laugh will be weeping. Those who endure hunger and thirst will suddenly find themselves fulfilled beyond their dreams; while those who now have their fill of mostly ill-gotten wealth will find themselves with nothing and headed to their allotted dungeon here in Gehenna.

"For the death culture enthusiasts, the development still represented a major coup with terrific spin off benefits. Even though the scientific community quickly developed drugs that could be used by doctors to 'manage' the disease and lengthen the victim's lives, they (the death culture enthusiasts) have succeeded in restricting the distribution of the drugs through pricing policies that keep the drugs out of the reach of the great bulk of the virus' victims.

"And talking about viruses, wouldn't it be interesting to have all nations that have ever been involved in preparations for imaginary wars with imaginary enemies, account for all the viruses and as well as all the biological agents that they had ever produced and stockpiled! Would it not be very interesting if a completely revamped United Nations, whose decisions were not subject to the whims of any so-called veto-wielding 'power' and that also had real muscle forced every nation that had ever engaged in the production of WMD to come clean and declare the exact extent of their involvement in bringing the world to the brink! Isn't that, after all, what should happen if the inhabitants of Earth wanted to establish how close they were to a man-made 'Armageddon'? Of course a United Nations that didn't have a stockpile of its own WMD that it could itself use as a deterrent would be useless.

"A weapon of mass destruction that was very much in vogue not so very long ago in America, and that was quite visible, was slavery. States used it in their efforts to keep 'people of color' in permanent serfdom, and thereby assure the slave owners the cheapest form of labor. After the civil rights bill was passed, that weapon merely became transformed from a visible to an invisible one, so that those employing it would not be brought to book; and it also became multi-faceted. It now consists in discriminatory practices that still target the so-called colored people; and it includes other activities conducted on the sly and whose objective is to roll back the so-called 'affirmative actions' prematurely, and ensure that colored folks remain at the bottom of the social rung. Those discriminatory practices include the selective application of laws of the land or 'profiling'.

"Yeah, it would be wishful thinking to imagine that humans, who were prepared to die to be assured of a permanent supply of the cheap labor for their empire-building project would be swayed by the mere passage of a law! And, predictably, the operation of this WMD has resulted in a disproportionate number of people of color being kept immobilized in cages in a burgeoning prison industry.

"And so, if they are not freely available as cheap labor, they must be kept out of sight and out of circulation; and this is happening in an ostensibly Christian nation, presided over by 'God fearing' folks! And, of course, the judges who hand down the 'sentences' that keep those poor folks immobilized know very well that the real sentence is not even being confined behind bars for so many months or years, but being exposed to abuse not just by their fellow convicts, but by the very people who are responsible for their welfare in jail!

"Talking about abuse, it is an abuse of authority for governments to allow those who are 'doing time' for a conviction to be confined in conditions that compel them to opt to take their own lives as a way of escaping the miseries they encounter there. That is not just something that infringes on natural justice; it is murder! And when churchmen, whose job it is to denounce evil practices of their time (like John the Baptist chose to do and paid for it with his life), pretend that they do not know what is going on, they become complicit in the murders.

"Even juveniles are incarcerated along with the mentally ill! And then there are those who find themselves incarcerated, and even occasionally on death row, on completely trumped up charges! A handy secret WMD that you wouldn't suspect was very much in vogue if you flew into New York City from some other continent, and were taking a stroll in Times Square! Or if you just watched CNN! Look, we here in the Underworld work assiduously with the powers that be to ensure that the 'penitentiaries' or 'correctional facilities' are situated off the beaten paths and in the middle of nowhere! Look, it wouldn't serve anyone any good if an advanced also very exceptional country like America did things that mounted to airing one's dirty laundry in public! That is also the reason we have gotten good folks to assure that terrorists, convicted or otherwise, are kept far away from these shores.

"One has to be kidding to think that poor, forsaken children of Adam and Eve, who were under my personal tutelage from the days I dethroned the Father and Mother of the human race until the coming of the Second Adam just a little over two thousand years ago, can mend their ways when some 'chap' in the White House inks a congressional bill into law. You should also remember the fate of all those in the White House and outside who

727

either worked for the abolition of slavery, or were determined to see to it that all states in the Union accepted every American as equal under the law.

"You have to believe that I made 'good use' of my time over the period the world was under my unchallenged rule, before the Eternal Word became flesh. I never once took a nap, and I certainly did not allow myself the indulgence of taking a vacation.

"The result of that 'hard work' is indeed very much in evidence: humans glorifying wars which are a form of 'legalized mass murder', and spearheaded mostly by folks who claim to be followers of the Deliverer, but are actually my minions; a state of disarray in Christendom, and a Church that is permanently scandal-ridden; a vast army of independent 'pastors' who nowadays do not even pretend to be affiliated with the traditional Church, and the vast majority of whom are really out to 'exploit' the gullibility of spiritually starved hordes, which they do quite effectively by brandishing the 'holy book'; and, of course, the continuing explosion of materialism and hedonism especially in so-called Christian countries, an explosion that makes the activities of the inhabitants of ancient Babylon pale in comparison!

"The continuing, and now virtually institutionalized, discrimination against aboriginal peoples in North and South America, Australia, and elsewhere in the world in the wake of spectacular land grabs that are well documented in history books is another very effective WMD. It is a particularly effective WMD because even churches gave their unqualified blessings to the territorial forays of the 'explorers', and they continue to abet the goings-on with their numbing silence.

"Economic sanctions against any country also represent a WMD. It is a weapon that has always been particularly effective against children, the aged, and the poorest in the nations targeted. Unfortunately for the victims (and fortunately for me, Beelzebub and Father of Death), the spineless United Nations - which boasts agencies with fancy-sounding names such as 'UNICEF', 'UNAIDS', UNFPA', and even 'UNESCO' - has long permitted itself to be used in launching and implementing these punitive measures against society's most vulnerable.

"Other 'terrible' weapons of mass destruction are violence against women (VAW) and discrimination against women (DAW), as a result of which women are denied the right to own property or make the same choices that their men folk make in the normal course of life, and are treated as the social under-class. Knowing that the womenfolk outnumber them but possess a nature that predisposes them to courteous and gentle manners, their men folk, in a move that reflects the insecurity they feel, apparently have been determined from early on to rein in the women and 'neutralize' them. Consequently, women still lack social and economic power by and large. The prevalence of violence against them has assured that societies are dominated by the men folk, who see major advantages in the status quo.

"The men naturally see no wrong in perpetuating violence against women, and see danger in according their womenfolk equal rights, economic security, and the independence that would make it possible for humans of the female gender to negotiate their relationships with humans of the male gender on equal terms.

"Any weapon of mass destruction that targets women, of course, also automatically targets children. What hope do children have when their moms are left out to dry! These WMD are frequently backed not just by the 'Laws of the Land', but also by ages-old customs and traditions. But their deleterious effects are not so easy to conceal. It is quite obvious that the progress of communities - and even of nations - is hampered when the unequal treatment of women in society is overlooked during the design and implementation stages of programs intended to improve general living conditions.

"And yet another 'invisible' but extremely effective WMD is the secret manufacture and proliferation of deadly M-16's, AK-47s, and other so-called 'small arms' by the major powers. Also, still produced and distributed on a massive scale by the 'advanced' nations in disregard of the world-wide ban on their manufacture and despite their horrific toll on the lives of the innocent are the land mines. The flow of these weapons of mass destruction will, of course, never be stemmed as long as there are greedy 'capitalists' in the world for whom the 'armaments' or the 'human killer' industry is just like any other. As far as these folks are concerned, they might just as well be investing in the manufacture and marketing of rosaries!

The "Inspired Word"...

"Humans are really interesting creatures. And it is not just that they are lukewarm in their observance of the commandments. They fragrantly break them. They kill each other, they steal from each other, they covert their neighbors' spouses, and so on and so forth. And it would be bad enough if they just did those things. The fact is that every time they do them, they have perfect excuses. In the case of foreign military adventures, the excuses might range from going toe to toe with an 'axis of evil' (that presumably had been overlooked by the Deliverer or so they would like the world to believe); ridding the world of a murderous dictator they themselves might have groomed, armed and abetted until he got the itch for self-determination; or, even, readying valiant Christian soldiers, who might themselves be outside the *Sancta Ecclesia*, for resuming the long-stalled 'crusades against the infidels'. They act as if they are their own 'prime movers' - as though they created themselves!

"To press that point home, humans did not hesitate to 'deal appropriately' with the Word, the Author of Life Himself through whom everything that exists outside of the Godhead came into being, when He showed up. Unfortunately, after they had 'rubbed him out' (or so they thought), He was back promptly after taking the sting out death, and He commissioned His Church right on schedule, establishing it under a New Covenant as had been foretold. Discounting the machinations of one of the twelve apostles, He empowered the surviving eleven to go out in the world and spread His message of salvation, after laying His hands on them and promising them the Comforter.

"But then look what humans have turned the Church into...a free for all and a money spinner that many folks depend on for their living! And they have even put strange words in the mouth of the Deliverer until it now sounds increasingly as if His message was about the 'good life' here on earth and not about 'eternal life'! Instead of preaching that it is easier for a camel to pass through the eye of a needle than for a rich man to enter into the kingdom of heaven (Matthew 19:24), some preach the exact opposite, namely that it is hard for a poor man to sneak past St. Peter and claim his reward in heaven - that he has to learn to be acquisitive first!

"But the situation is now so ridiculous, it requires more than ordinary common sense to tell the 'Church' the Deliverer founded from the myriad money-spinning enterprises that are all devoted to putting one or other spin on this or that text of the Holy Book for the benefit of spiritually starved folks - for a price. It is a classic case of the blind leading the blind! The interest in the Holy Book is, if anything, selective and self-serving. The proprietors of those 'enterprises' quote from it only what seems to support their preconceived positions and also happens to be good for the bottom line.

"When the different bits and pieces of writings were first compiled by the individual inspired writers, it goes without saying that these 'Sacred Scriptures' were largely ignored by scholars and merchants of the day. It speaks to the fact that the inspired writers were faced with a task that, humanly speaking, was impossible - the task of bringing the 'word of God' to the attention of the general populace. This was due to the fact that those self-published works had no immediate relevance to the material lives of these other folks.

"The original scrolls that Mark, Matthew, John, Luke, Peter, Paul and others scripted did not survive for the simple reason that publishers, book distributors and bookstores of the day, and even 'libraries' (or whatever served as libraries in those days) could not be bothered with anything that was of no relevance to their 'bottom lines' regardless of its intrinsic value.

"Published as 'the original, unedited, full-length yarns' which had been revealed to them by the Spirit, the original Sacred Scriptures, which dealt with subjects as drab as 'the last end of humans' and 'spiritual salvation', certainly did not resemble 'popular contemporary literature', and even less 'popular fiction'. But that is exactly what the numerous unauthorized editors have tried over the course of centuries to turn them into. They have done everything that is humanly possible to make the scriptures resemble popular works of fiction so that booksellers and merchants can use them to line their pockets - subject to payment of a commission!

"But how original are the current editions of the Old

732

and New Testaments? Are they really identical to the original, unedited inspired works! The puzzle is that all the 'learned' biblical scholars pretend that this is the case when common sense suggests otherwise.

"Inspired writings may be the work of the Holy Spirit, but they very definitely also remain writings of those to whom they are attributed. The Holy Spirit might inspire; but He is not the one who writes. To complicate matters, when an individual senses divine inspiration welling up in him or her and starts committing the inspired thoughts to paper, because the individual remains a completely free creature, there is every likelihood that the resulting work will include material - perhaps whole sections of it - that will be completely personal and, in that sense, not inspired at all by reason of its origin.

"The inspired author remains human, and liable to be tempted in all sorts of ways, and even retains the ability to opt out of the role of 'inspired writer' at any time while the project is under way. But then it is also not beyond the realm of possibilities for the scribe to turn around and, in trying to 'polish' the inspired material, knowingly or unknowingly eliminate critical sentences or even whole sections from the original script.

"And so, in the hypothetical situation in which the intention of the Holy Spirit is to convey a general idea, the scribe, fascinated by the minutiae, might be tempted to revisit his inspired work with the intention of polishing language pertaining to details without paying due regard to the fact that the big picture will be obscured in the process. The only thing that could save the situation in such a case would be the fact that the Paraclete, a member of the Godhead, is almighty, and nothing is impossible with Him. He can get any result he wants regardless of what the human He has chosen to be his scribe does.

"Most folks forget that inspired authors tend to be full blooded and earthy humans who come complete with multiple failings, rather than freakish nitwits who fit the popular but erroneous image of 'living saints'. And it is wishful thinking to imagine that they wouldn't be tempted to go back and try to 'rewrite' material they had originally jotted down under inspiration. In fact the temptation to do that would be far greater for people who found themselves scribbling down ideas that were not the result of their own creativity, and emanated from a 'funny' and highly unusual source!

"It is obvious from reading any 'Book of the Old Testament' that the 'inspired' authors even gave the impression, perhaps entirely innocently, that the Prime Mover sanctioned wars and similar evils. Born in original sin and inclined to sin, and also imbued with a view of the world that was riddled with inaccuracies, the 'scribes' had obviously been brought up understanding that wars were things for 'heroes', and they evidently imagined that an 'inspiring' piece of writing wouldn't be inspiring if it did not employ the imagery of war (an acronym for mass killings or murder that war planners referred to euphemistically as 'destroying enemy troops' or 'destroying enemy encampments') to inspire humans to 'fight' for and even lay down their lives for the cause of 'Good'.

"It is probably fair to say that it would be a lot of phantasy and wishful thinking to imagine that people like Paul, John the Evangelist, and other inspired authors of the Books of the New Testament wouldn't glamorize wars just like everyone else of their time. *Ovid* and in particular *Caesar de Bello Gallico* (which glamorizes the foreign adventures of Caesar and would be condemned by the Church today as 'unjust wars') were probably Paul's favorite works of literature.

"Is it any wonder, then, that the church's hierarchy

to day does not regard the preparation of candidates for the priesthood as complete until they can demonstrate a mastery not just of the writings of that Roman demagogue in the same way the formation of a soldier (a euphemism for 'killer') is not considered complete until he/she starts to show a disregard for life that all 'warriors' are supposed to show under the guise of 'defending' the nation against some imaginary and often completely non-existent 'enemy'!

"But just think! What would my forces - the forces of darkness - be doing upon sensing that a human was receiving inspiration from above either for his own salvation or for a project that was likely to hamper our efforts in derailing the divine plan? Take a holiday? That is precisely the time we will bombard that human with temptations and ideas of our own; and you can also bet that they will be tendered in a way that makes them virtually indistinguishable from the ideas emanating from the Holy Spirit.

"Then, it is unlikely that a tome that claimed to be produced under inspiration from 'on High' would be accepted unquestioningly for what it claimed to be by a world that was unaccustomed to things of that sort. The inspired author, more than anyone else, would know and anticipate that eventuality. That knowledge and anticipation would represent additional pressure to 'package' his/her message in a way that would have a chance of acceptance.

"Now, it may well be that the Holy Ghost is always capable of intervening to stop the wandering hand of the inspired author from excising or alternatively adding material to the sacred text out of those wrong motives. But the operation of the author's free will definitely will limit the extent to which the Holy Spirit can intervene and stop the wandering hand from messing up the sacred text.

"It is also wishful thinking to imagine even for one moment that authorship of an inspired piece of writing, because it is performed under inspiration, is a piece of cake. Because enterprises of this nature bode ominously for our cause here in the Pit, my troops and I typically try to wreck all such projects at their inception, and you can be sure that we hurl everything in our arsenal at the presumptive inspired writer in the process.

"The onslaught of temptations which the servants of the Prime Mover face will be of the kind and intensity that only mortals who have the full backing of the Holy Spirit stand a chance of weathering. And it frequently happens that at some point the poor souls who have been commissioned by the Prime Mover for that important task become thoroughly confused and flustered, and unable to rationally determine which parts of the assembled material belong in the inspired work and which ones are unsuitable and need to be discarded. And the poor souls often discover, too late, that they have actually gotten back into the manuscript and ruined it irrevocably when they thought they were merely performing spell checks or some similar perfunctory operation.

"That is the gauntlet that mortal humans run when they accept to become instruments of divine grace. Many of them often end up losing their faith and completely at the mercy of the Prime Mover. We deal with prophets, humans who are called to the priestly vocation, and other messengers of the Prime Mover in much the same fashion, and many indeed end up in the same way.

"But do keep in mind (as we also undoubtedly do) the fact that the Holy Ghost is quite capable of employing incomplete but complementary works by different inspired writers to achieve His ends. He not only can, but He even uses crooked, ill-intentioned humans to have His

736

way. Because he is almighty, the Holy Ghost can easily use ill-intentioned humans who set out to write nonsense, and get them to produce some really inspiring pieces of work that rake in souls - and He probably often does! After all, He even causes good to come out of evil! We certainly will always remember how He snatched that murderer Paul (nee Saul) from our clutch, and turned him into the Apostle of the Gentiles!

"But, anyway, it is just common sense to expect any piece of inspired writing to reflect the writing style of the author at the very minimum. That is why a reasonable person would not expect the epistles of Peter, a former fisherman, to read like the Gospel or the epistles of the well-schooled John - or the letters of Paul.

"It also stands to reason that if a prophet appeared on the scene today and decided to employ the written word to reach his audience, it is unlikely that his prophetic work would hit the bookstalls for the first time as an imprint of the big publishing houses. When they accept a manuscript for publication, they edit it so much - because of their total commitment to the bottom-line - the author's original style and, along with it, also much of the original content are usually liable to disappear. Their motives are the complete opposite of the motives of the inspired author. It just wouldn't work - unless the Holy Spirit wanted to use the occasion to prove that nothing was impossible with the Prime Mover!

"If the inspired work were published by one of those big publishing houses, even though the original manuscript might have been produced under inspiration, the final version which went to the press and ended up on the bookstalls would be so different after those 'editorial' changes, there might be nothing 'inspiring' about it in the spiritual sense. In other words, the prophetic work might not rake in any souls at all. Which is not the same as saying that it wouldn't rake in the money - or make its readers feel good about themselves!

"While making its way from one editor's desk to another, the inspired piece of writing would be liable to suffer the same fate as a piece of raw intelligence that was making its way up the ladder through various layers of 'analysts' to the Commander-in-Chief in an American or British spy agency. It very likely would be - as they say - 'sexed up' pretty well before it reached its final destination either in the White House or Number 10 Downing Street.

"This is the same fate that the sacred scriptures appear to have undergone overtime as hand-written copies were initially made from the original scrolls (most likely decades after the inspired author had passed on), undergoing the initial 'editorial' changes in the process. One would have to be a simpleton to imagine that the sacred scriptures did not undergo additional 'editorial changes' as translations were made into different languages, including Hebrew. And it is on record that they underwent further and even more radical changes as they were translated into Greek and Latin, at which time the 'inspired works' were also 'purged' of material that was deemed apocryphal and then doctored further.

"The translation of the scriptures into modern languages - translations that were commissioned by people with all sorts of agendas - naturally involved new and quite drastic 'editorial changes' that pitted the views of reformists against the views of traditionalists. But that time, the cat was out of the bag with different versions of the 'sacred' scriptures that contradicted each other in key places circulating side by side.

"And as the ecumenical movement got under steam, the situation became even more confusing as theologians tried to paper over not just the differences among the doctrines taught but also the differences in the different versions of the scriptures. One consequence of that has been the appearance of new and previously unheard of 'interpretations' - and effectively versions - of the 'sacred scriptures' as the number of 'Christian' sects grew and multiplied!

"It is rather unlikely that an original piece of inspired writing will look as if it was written by Charles Dickens, or William Shakespeare. If it has not been tampered with and 'doctored', chances are that the inspired piece will break all known rules of good writing (if the scrolls were located, authenticated, and deciphered with any accuracy).

"It is likely to feature overly long sentences with little or no punctuation marks. Some sections will be too wordy, and the order of words in others will be completely upside down. There are likely to be fragmented sentences galore, not to mention poor sentence structure, the use of split infinitives and the passive voice, verb confusion, the wrong use of verbs and adjectives, sentence structures that are plainly wrong - and, of course, very poor conjugation!

"The fact is that in those ancient times, there was never any fuss about sentences being long winded or expressions being wordy. If anything, verbosity was regarded as evidence that one was truly a man or woman of letters - unlike today when so-called educated folks can't even make head or tail of what was being spoken unless the message being put out was rehashed slowly and the speaker was employing only the most commonly used phrases.

"And any way - just to think that the worthless writings of a dimwit and a bum like Julius Caesar, who thought that anyone who did not speak Latin (a language which is now long dead) was a barbarian, have survived in their entirety for no other reason than that they were relevant to people's bottom lines from the beginning; and that the original inspired writings are lost forever!

"And would you know that history is repeating itself today, because writings that could help folks unmask the false prophets and teachers the gospels referred to and find their way into the true Church have no relevance to the bottom lines of book publishers, distributors, and bookstores, and are eschewed by those who manage public libraries and archives! Where for instance can a spiritually starved soul purchase the encyclical *Humane Vitae*, or *Fides et Ratio*, or *Ut Unum Sint*!

"And so, despite the impression given by those in the 'business' of saving souls, the question (the Deliverer Himself posed two thousand years ago) still remains as relevant today as ever: 'When the Son of man returns, will He find any believer...?'

The charade and "Noah's Ark"...

"In the meantime, the charade continues as every Dick and Harry who has ever been to a seminary or has a Ph.D. in theology from a university takes the stage and claims to be qualified to lead the faithful in spiritual matters. But it is all bogus; otherwise they wouldn't be contradicting themselves right and left while still claiming to be 'speaking in tongues'!

"And being able to count on a large following or on financial support that permitted a preacher to 'market' his/her ministry and attract an even larger 'flock' was completely irrelevant when it came to determining which church was the true, holy and apostolic Church. But that was precisely the sort of thing that little children imbibed far more easily than adults did in response to the Spirit's inspiration. The Spirit knew the sheep that belonged to

His flock. For heaven's sake, humans should cut out the spin and allow me, Beelzebub, to also get the credit I am due in these matters!

"It is in a way a mystery that preachers belonging to the all too disparate 'Christian' churches that contradict each other right and left became passionate and emotional when addressing their congregations even though they knew very well that there could be only one true Church. That is something that was obvious even to unbelievers. Since these preachers were all agreed on that point - that the Deliverer could not have founded two, three or fifty 'churches' that contradicted each other - you would have thought that the only time the preachers would be passionate and emotional about anything would be when exhorting their followers to diligently seek out and find that one true Church, and also ark whose sides and bottom, constantly buffeted by the stormy waters, were guaranteed by the Paraclete against falling apart.

"The preachers should be passionate about the fact that only one church can be the true Church, and they should also be passionate about the fact that many people who belong to churches other than the true Church are in for an unpleasant surprise that could be very embarrassing at the end of time - or even in their lifetime if their search for the 'true Church' yielded results earlier.

"In the final analysis, there is really nothing mysterious or extraordinary about the fact that blind humans are in effect leading other blind humans. To expect things to be otherwise would, of course, be tantamount to pipe dreaming. One would also have to imagine away the effects of original sin on the posterity of Adam and Eve!

"It was entirely to be expected for humans to talk about the Church of the Redeemer this and the Church of the Deliverer that, as if they did not know that the Deliverer established only one Church. It is normal for this group of humans to refer to itself as Baptists; and that group to refer to itself as Orthodox Christians, and another to call itself Mennonites, or Roman Catholics, or Lutherans, or Evangelicals, or Episcopalians, or Presbyterians, or Anglicans, and what have you. They did not seem to realize that the Church established by the Deliverer was one that was 'One', 'Holy', 'Apostolic' and 'Catholic'; and 'Catholic' in the sense in which St. Ignatius of Antioch, writing to the Smyrnaeans around 110 AD, used that word; and that was long before Martin Luther, who was summarily excommunicated by Pope Leo X in his papal bull *Decet Romanum Pontificem* dated January 3, 1521, and all the other so-called 'reformers' came onto the scene. And that Catholic Church, established by the Deliverer on the rock called Peter, is protected from contradicting itself the way these other 'churches' are liable to do. [See the Dogmatic Constitution on the Catholic Faith (*Dei Filius*) and the First Dogmatic Constitution on the Church of Christ (*Pastor aeternus*) issued by the First Vatican Council on July 18, 1870. See also 1 Corinthians 14:33, 2 Peter 3:14-18, 2 Peter 1:20-21, Galatians 1:9, etc.]

"Humans obviously prefer to have things that way because then everybody can have a piece of the pie! Even though there was really no longer any need, following the Deliverer's ascension into heaven, for the position of Purse Bearer which had been held by the betrayer, the number of unsolicited applications had continued to grow. Besides, many people imagined, rightly or wrongly, that if the Deliverer needed a purse bearer, His Church probably could also do with one. And, naturally, the easiest way to increase opportunities for those aspiring to that position was to set up many 'churches' and then start pretending that they anyone of these churches might be the one true, holy and apostolic Church! Pretty clever!

"Humans are shameless. But what could one expect from them after the fall of Adam and Eve from grace. The fact that the Deliverer came as promised didn't really change anything as far as their behavior was concerned. The advent of the Deliverer should have resulted in paths being straightened and sinful ways being abandoned, now that humans could count on divine grace if they chose to stay clear of my wiles.

"But, No! Humans are still greedy, murderous, and prone to telling lies. And they do not seem to mind using the institution of the Church to achieve their material goals and enjoy themselves. And they have masterfully turned a marvelous opportunity to be reconciled with their Creator into a free for all, making evangelization the second biggest industry after the armaments industry. After all, remember that the same concourse of people, who a week earlier had shouted '*Benedictus qui venit in nomine Domini*' as the Deliverer made his solemn entrance into Jerusalem on the back of a donkey, were shouting 'Away with Him! Crucify Him!' not long afterward.

"Those preachers do a great disservice to the one, true, catholic and apostolic Church which was set up by the Deliverer. To understand how irresponsible and reckless they are, consider the fact that Islam, Buddhism, Hinduism, and other non-Christian religions, even though also plagued by divisions, those divisions are few and far between compared to the divisions that plague the self-proclaimed 'followers of Christ'!

"It would have been wasted effort for the Deliverer to commission His Church, ordain the eleven and imbue them with the authority to continue his ministry, only for

Peter, John, Matthew and the rest of the group to end up contradicting each other - despite the fact that all the eleven had been at His side and had heard the same things as they came out of his mouth. And it would have been even worse - and certainly unacceptable from whichever way one looked at it - if they had each ended up heading their own separate 'churches' each of which sought to represent itself as the 'true' Church! It would similarly be a mighty waste of time if eleven accomplished 'biblical scholars', each of whom claimed to know the Holy Book like the back of his/her hand, found themselves unable to agree on key texts of the bible and ended up as 'pastors' in eleven different Christian 'churches' each of which claimed to be divinely instituted, but whose 'doctrines' were at complete variance! That should tell you something about the true nature of those who brag that they are the 'true believers'!

"What is the use of biblical 'scholarship' that fails to serve the critical purpose of identifying the one and the only Holy Catholic Church the Deliverer, according to the bible, founded? Either that scholarship is flawed - perhaps because it does not include other important elements such as Tradition - or I myself and 'the Legion' I command are not giving ourselves enough credit for derailing the divine plan! Actually, the most likely reason is that, while they may be well versed in studies of the New and Old Testaments, the latter group were neither 'called and ordained' by the Deliverer, nor sent out by Him to the world with the words 'What you hold on earth will be held in heaven...'

"And - listen to this - the sin folks who are not validly ordained priests or bishops commit when they take it upon themselves to act as if they were, and to confer sacramental rites that only ordained ministers may confer is called a 'sacrilege'! Now, just imagine the number of

744

sacrilegious acts that are committed everyday given that half of Christendom is not in communion with the Holy Catholic and Apostolic Church! It is a large number indeed. As was made quite clear by Pope Benedict XVI in the motu proprio *Omnium in Mentem* that he issued on 26 October 2009 amending the Code of Canon Law, only those who are constituted in the order of episcopate or presbyterate receive the office and faculty of acting in the person of Christ the Head. Also, personal sacrilege is irreverence shown to a person consecrated by religious vows (monks, nuns, etc.) or by holy orders (deacons, priests, bishops). Ridiculing, mocking, or abusing members of the clergy is considered personal sacrilege, as often the animosity is directed not at the person themselves but at the Church or at God whom they represent. Yeah, you can even check this out in the Wikipedia! The paradox of it all is that, judging from their actions, the folks who regard themselves as 'saved Christians' are no better than the rest of humanity who have not yet been catechized.

"I mean, if you are looking for people with heart - people who really care about the welfare of others - you are more likely to find them in Communist China, India, Pakistan, Lebanon, Iran, Siberia, North Korea, Palestine, and Iraq than in nations that are predominantly 'Christian' or even 'Catholic'. And that is also where you will find people whose constancy in praying for fortitude to the Prime Mover and in forgiving - even as their loved ones are thoroughly battered, humiliated, embargoed and starved of the necessities of life, maimed, and slaughtered in full view of an uncaring, uninterested world - never falters.

"It is bad enough that humans simply have no idea how embittered my folks and I feel after suffering defeat at the hands of the Deliverer. Humans cannot imagine the humiliation He inflicted on my troops and myself as their captain when, taking the form of a servant, and being made in the likeness of men, and in habit found as a man, He humbled himself, becoming obedient unto death, even to the death of the cross; and when, in obedience to the will of His Father in heaven, He agreed to pay the price for the sins of humans and rescued Adam and Eve and the rest of the captives we had been holding right here in hell in the hope that we might be able to use them as a bargaining chip to get Him to let us escape from the Pit. What do humans think we would be doing in these circumstances - just lying back and relaxing here in hell or hatching schemes that might yet derail the divine plan? Just as Peter, Thomas and the other apostles demonstrated, it is very easy to underrate our bitterness at having our victory snatched from right under very noses.

"The Paraclete, who informs and guides the Holy Catholic Church and is bestowed upon the baptized through the Sacrament of Confirmation, is a gift. That being the case, when humans go out on a limb and set up their own churches in competition with the Holy Catholic Church, regardless of how much they might pine for the Holy Spirit to come down from heaven above and take possession of their souls outside of the Church, it simply will not happen.

"And so, when humans, however well-intentioned, shun the Holy Catholic Church which is the modern version of Noah's Ark, they do so at their risk, and there are very many risks and huge ones at that. It is, for instance, very easy - once outside the Holy Catholic Church, to forget that the commission given by the triumphant Deliverer to the surviving eleven apostles did not just consist in mastering the Holy Book like the back of one's hand and regurgitating its contents, but doing a slew of things among them the Breaking of Bread together in His memory in a re-enactment of His passion, death and resurrection, and the administration of sacraments, including the sacrament of confession - whose sins you forgive will be forgiven! At the very top of the list of things the eleven did - and also urged their flocks to do - was to imitate the Deliverer who considered Himself a servant all through His ministry, and to pray always - in private.

"And it is also easy to mistake many of these things, which form key parts of the Deliverer's commission to the eleven, as witchcraft or 'devil worship'! We in the Underworld couldn't be more delighted with an outcome like that. Just to think that many of the so-called separated brethren openly refer to the Pontiff of Rome, who occupies the Holy See and is also the captain of the new 'Ark of Noah', as the embodiment of devilishness when they are not calling him the Antichrist! And then there is the fact that not all the successors of the apostles have been able to live up to their calling.

"To live up to their title as 'Princes of the Church', the lives of prelates must be exemplars of humility. They must follow in the tradition of St. Peter, St. John, St. Mark, St. Paul and others who, having been called by the Deliverer to carry the banner of the Church He had established to continue His work of redemption, actually carried it so high that people who lived in the known world of their time had no difficulty seeing it. But above all, they must always keep in mind that 'saints run away from priesthood'!

"The Holy Spirit did not force any of the eleven to be like the least of their flocks. Over the last two thousand years, the Holy Spirit never forced any 'Prince of the Church' to shed his trappings of authority and be a servant to parishioners in the diocese over which he presided. And when the successors to the apostles as a body did not give up those trappings of authority and balked at the prospect of being like the least among their flock, that had certain pretty serious implications.

"For one it paved the way for scandals in the Church. And when the conduct of the successors to the apostles fell short and resulted in problems for the Church - problems which ranged from disunity in the Church to disinterest among members of the flock in matters relating to their spiritual life - the 'princes of the Church' easily hid behind their positions in the Church's hierarchy and the powers they enjoyed by virtue of sharing in the priesthood of the Deliverer, and in effect blamed the confusion resulting from their actions on those who were disadvantaged and suffering as a consequence of their acts of commission and omission on the victims: the separated brethren, 'dissidents' in the Church, and others who were scandalized and decided to stay clear of the Church for those reasons. It was quite neat - they just decided to blame the victims! It is really like putting the blame at the feet of the Holy Spirit who 'informs' and guides the Church for things that go wrong and eventually boomerang.

"And humans must thank God that the Paraclete was what He was, namely a member of the Godhead; because finding ways to work around the Judas Iscariots and the Ananiases to ensure that the work of redemption continued uninterrupted had to be one hell of a task.

"Naturally, because members of the Church's hierarchy are human, they will also have this tendency to act out things the way that priest in the parable did. He was condemned by the Deliverer for looking down on tax collectors and other 'sinners', and bragging that he was justified. It is also quite conceivable that an 'unworthy' Prince of the Church, whose attitude might be what was causing the souls he would otherwise be receiving in the Church to stay away, might also have the tendency to merely shrug his shoulders, 'brush off the dust from his feet', and go on doing his thing as before. And imagine what the reaction of that Prince of the Church would be if he was posted to a city in which 'an apostle of the gospel' was positively not welcome! He would probably cause a rumpus instead of following orders and just matching on to his next post.

"It just might be that those who are despised as heretics, animists, adulterers, drug dealers and murderers, thieves and cheats, and others like that are the ones the Lord is more inclined to hearken to when they pray to Him for deliverance. It was after all not to one of the respected high priests who had been making offerings in the temple for years, but to a convicted robber that the Deliverer, even as He was enduring the pangs of His death as it approached, turned and said: 'This day, you will be with me in paradise.'

"The fact is that the Deliverer declared very categorically - when His apostles reported to Him that one fellow, who was not even one of His disciples, was casting out evil spirits in His name - that those who are *not against Him* are *with Him*. You must be kidding to think that the apostles were elated to hear that. Remember that some of them, like James and John, had already been exposed for being involved in maneuvers designed to secure for them 'special seats' in heaven upon their departure from this world. The Deliverer's message was that His immediate friends, relatives and disciples were not the only ones who were dear to His heart!

"It has to be much harder for hypocrites in the Church to accept that good non-Catholics - Methodists, Baptists, Moslems, Buddhists, Hindus, and others who are true to their consciences, do their thing in good faith, and are not hypocritical or out to pull someone else's leg - all stand to inherit the kingdom of heaven. It has to be quite hard for those hypocrites who make it their business to denigrate good folks like those to accept what they themselves preach, namely that there is such a thing as 'Baptism of Desire'!

"Hordes outside the Church cling to the notion that they become 'justified', 'righteous', and 'saved' simply by 'accepting' the Deliverer. They have this notion that salvation and righteousness comes to humans, not by towing the line and staying on the narrow path, but miraculously by dint of an act of their will to the effect that they have 'encountered' the Miracle Worker, and accept Him by acknowledging that He *is* a miracle worker.

"If that was all there was to it, then the hordes who relentlessly followed the Deliverer as He went about Galilee and Judea healing the sick, multiplying bread and fishes to make sure the crowds had full tummies and didn't stay hungry all day as they kept Him company, and teaching them how to pray wouldn't have had to worry about some of the other things He said such as: 'It is not those who cry out Lord, Lord, Lord who will enter the kingdom of heaven, but those who did the will of His Father'!

"Also, the crowds who escorted the Deliverer during His triumphal entry into Jerusalem and paid tributes in song and with palms to His status as the promised Messiah who was coming in the name of the Lord (and presumably became 'saved' in the process), but sided with the priests and Pharisees who were thirsting for His blood five days later, would likewise be assured of salvation following their initial and quite genuine 'acceptance' of the Messiah.

"But it was still understandable when humans

outside the one, true and apostolic Church fell for the ruses that my troops dangle in their faces. For many of these folks, proclaiming themselves as righteous, saved, and justified represented the only way they knew to distance themselves from us here in the Pit. They did not know any better.

"Still it was completely inexcusable for members of the Church's hierarchy who should know better to conduct themselves as though their positions in the Church automatically made them justified, righteous, and saved. More than anyone else, humans who attain to high positions in the Church should know how frail, weak and dependent they are on grace and on the mercies of the Prime Mover. That knowledge should make them humble, unpretentious and unassuming. People like Jerome, Augustine, Bernard and Padre Pio always thought they were in greater need of forgiveness than anybody else. In fact, the closer humans are to the Prime Mover, the more they see themselves as being sinners in need of His mercies.

"But, thanks to our hard work, that is not the case. And the big payoff for us lies in the fact that many humans who would otherwise embrace the universal apostolic Church find themselves repelled by all the posturing and undisguised hypocrisy of the very people who are supposed to be shepherds and pastors over the Deliverer's flock. It is imperative that those who are called to the priestly vocation are Christ-like - are 'other Christs'. And it is, indeed, such a high calling that 'saints run away from the priesthood'.

"It is therefore just conceivable that it is the wrong characters who get 'attracted' to the priesthood, and who presumably see in the priestly vocation an opportunity to heave their weight around. It may even be that it is those who feel inadequate and lost who seek to boost their egos by aspiring to the most elevated calling of all - being an *alter Christus*! But it doesn't matter even if that isn't really the case. We here in the Underworld see it as our job to do everything that will undermine the ministry.

"Through our minions - and no human who has ever offended the Prime Mover can escape that label - we will always try to depict those who are out in the fields helping the Deliverer rake in the harvest in the worst possible light. Since those tilling the fields for the Deliverer remain humans who are frail and weak, those who act on our behalf get many opportunities to embarrass the Church and to cloud the good work they might be doing for the salvation of men. And you can be sure that my troops take full advantage of the fact that there will always be a few really 'bad apples' in any 'profession' to malign the holy, catholic, and apostolic Church, and to make it seem as if salvation is to be found elsewhere.

"The prelates and other Church functionaries, their flocks and all other humans are going around trying to show that they are happy, nice and innocent, when it is all a farce. Virtually every human acts according to *our* script. They are shirking their responsibilities, trying to pass the buck, and generally blaming their problems on everyone else except themselves. And it pleases us mightily when churchmen, abandoning their responsibilities to those who suffer injustices, go about their business as if everything was all right - just as they did at the height of slavery, imperialism and colonialism.

"There was a time when it was taboo for humans to mention the word 'sex' in public. It also used to be unthinkable to suggest that the 'marvellous' democracies of the West secretly entertained policies that provided for things like torture and so called targeted, extrajudicial killings or assassinations of figures inside and outside their borders that were deemed *persona non grata*. Nowadays, it is taboo to mention the word 'modesty' in public. And it is not unusual to watch shows on television on which the leaders in Western democracies not only confessed to murders and attempted murders of people before they had been tried for their alleged crimes, but vied with each other in their attempts to show who did more to try and rub out those who had been labeled as 'dangerous' by the spying agencies. And it is unpatriotic to speak out against things like 'regime changes' that are engineered by super powers for the purpose of gaining access to the world's scarce resources, extrajudicial killings by governments using the state security apparatus, the so-called extraordinary renditions, and the now widespread torture of prisoners and captives using waterboarding and other dehumanizing methods.

"I do not know why governments nowadays even bother about the mafia when they and the mafia have so much in common! Looks like the goals of government and of the mafia - namely taking steps to secure resources that are vital to their 'interests' - are the same! It is now quite clear that they all have the same *modus operandi* of 'Mark and liquidate'! It is perfectly legit and internationally accepted for governments to have their spy agencies draw up lists of 'terrorists' and their alleged associates, and then move to take appropriate action.

"And you can bet that if these governments post lists of the 'marked' people on the worldwide web for public consumption, there almost definitely will be other lists for 'Your Eyes Only' that only the spy agencies and the White House, Whitehall, or the Kremlin as the case may be will know about. I have personally seen many of these lists, and I cannot understand how it has not struck the folks who man the 'intelligence' agencies - and yes, they are real people just like you and not some super intelligent creatures like us demons for example who might be trusted to carry out their mission on the basis of real facts and without any ulterior motive - that it is I, Beelzebub, who is the real Axis of Evil and who, accordingly, ought to be tracked down above all else. My name does not appear on any of those lists!

"My job is, even then, not yet done. I want to see all Church folks - not just the handful who have come out of the closet - openly call for death to unbelievers, infidels, and social misfits on the cocktails of the now internationally sanctioned and globally coordinated political assassinations and the hunt for alleged 'insurgents', 'terrorists' and their associates and collaborators. We in Gehenna love it when those who cause the deaths of so many innocent people, among them children, as they try to rub out 'insurgents' and 'terrorists' turn around as if on impulse and sanctimoniously pretend to be defenders of the lives of the 'unborn' or 'unwanted babies', as if sniffing out the lives of 'unwanted' adults is godly and has nothing to do with the 'sanctity of life' which they preach.

"These Church folks have tacitly approved lying under the guise of political spin and diplomatic jingoism. They have explicitly approved the huge investments in armaments, instead of standing up to leaders of the 'advanced' countries, rebuking them for their irresponsibility, and commanding them to immediately divert those resources for the improvement of lives of the world's poor. They have tacitly - but effectively - approved the investment in tactical nukes and similar weapons. They have even tacitly approved policies of pre-emption. They have, of course, also approved the notion that a nation can be an axis of evil and liable for a pre-emptive strike to neutralize and 'democratize' it.

"It is a singular triumph of the 'powers of evil' that

prelates and other Church functionaries are vocal about abortions sought by women, but are completely silent when demagogues in the world, seeking to advance their worldly cockeyed agendas and to mold the world in their own images, provoke wars in which large numbers of humans lose their lives needlessly. When the first prelates were installed by the Deliverer in their bishoprics two thousand years ago, thanks to expansionist demagogues like Julius Caesar, it was normal for generals to go out on 'conquering' adventures in the course of which they pacified the conquered (by which was meant wiping out enemy fighters), enslaved the fathers and mothers and even the children of the nations they subjugated, and brought home 'booty' before they set out on new adventures. The hunger for 'glory' and for new booty was insatiable. All these criminal activities by demagogic rulers were already 'legitimate' by the time Peter and Paul set off for Asia Minor, Rome and Greece.

"But that was precisely the reason the Prime Mover gave His only begotten Son to the world - so that those who would believe in Him would be saved. It was the reason the Deliverer, who did not come to establish an earthly kingdom (even though many earthlings still cling to that idea), drew a clear line between worldliness (what is Caesar's) and godliness (what is God's), and also said that individuals who loved Him should keep the commandments (which include one that says 'Thou shalt not kill').

"In his day, Caesar conquered and 'pacified' Gaul and other parts of Europe, Asia Minor, North Africa, Gaul and other parts of Europe - almost the entire known world of the time - and was under the delusion that he had built an eternal empire that would always endure. No one will ever know the number of lives that were snuffed out prematurely as that megalomaniac pursued that dream!

And where is the Roman Empire now?

"But the most important question is whether the successors to the prelates of Caesar's time are prepared to risk everything - like the martyred Peter and Paul and other Church functionaries of the early Church did - and stand up to megalomaniacs of 'modern times' who have never learnt anything from history. Peter and Paul paid for it with their lives because of the determination of those for whom worldly ambitions meant everything. They died martyrs because the message they were preaching and the worldly ambitions of 'empire builders' who operated out of Rome were two things that could not be reconciled. Even though the 'prize' for which they labor is transitory, there has never been any doubt that the folks who are in the business of empire building are dead serious.

"It is significant that 'think tanks' and so-called advisors to the megalomaniacs have no interest in the permanent and the eternal, and as a rule focus only focus on the temporal, passing and transient - just like money hungry store owners who will withhold vital information about a product from their customers in their eagerness to secure an immediate sale.

"The world's megalomaniacs, regardless of the times, have always been convinced that they had the ultimate deterrent weapon for keeping their enemies at bay in their arsenals, and had developed and horned shock and awe battle tactics that no enemy could ever withstand. They have been certain that they possessed formidable, totally reliable human and other forms of intelligence assets, and had banded together alliances that would never crack and were impregnable. They have even been sure that they had in place mechanisms for keeping bad news relating to the progress of foreign occupations from eroding political support at home. But they have been proved wrong each time.

"Caesar, who imagined that he had attained divine status, was betrayed by Brutus, a friend. Military alliances have cracked and left aggressor nations exposed and vulnerable. No amount of defensive military preparations has ever stopped enemy agents from infiltrating 'impregnable' defenses, and inflicting damage where it really hurt. In Rome, where once upon a time followers of the Deliverer survived by hiding in catacombs, the booty that Caesar and other Roman generals brought home at the conclusion of their rampages through North Africa, Asia Minor and Europe now belong to the successor to the martyred Peter.

"Megalomaniacs have terrorized the world since Cain committed humanity's first ever murder. The jealousy that hounds them when they see wealth that belongs to others is the same jealousy that drove Cain to kill his brother Abel. And the world's megalomaniacs, regardless of the time in which they lived, all bear the 'mark of Cain'. Prelates of the Church should at least have the courage to tell the megalomaniacs that they too can be forgiven (like Cain was) if they confess their sin and renounce murder; and that they will otherwise end up stuck with the 'mark of the beast'!

"Nowadays, instead of issuing 'anathemas', churchmen even huddle together with today's empire builders to pray for the success of their conquering missions which spell subjugation, enslavement and untold humiliation for humans whose only mistake usually is being too trustful of their human brothers and sisters. Members of the Church's hierarchy have ended up more or less like the priests and Pharisees of the Deliverer's time - chameleons who suddenly changed their spots when it suited them and sought the help of Caesar to get rid of their Savior. The prelates appear to be completely blind to the causes of 'terrorism', the activities of so-called 'civilized nations' aimed at securing those nations' 'vital national interest' but which result in so much sufferings in different parts of the world, and to naked aggression by powerful nations of the world against weaker, resource-rich nations of the world.

"Instead of siding with the oppressed and others who suffer needlessly at the hands of powerful nations, churchmen of today, like their counterparts in the run-up to the inauguration of the Church, prefer to side with those who sacrifice human life at the altar of grandiose empire building schemes and other worldly ambitions. And whereas the Church's hierarchy finally mustered the courage to apologize to the world for the reprehensible activities carried out in its name in the past by its representatives, it might not have an opportunity to apologize to those whose legitimate concerns have been ignored and now are branded 'terrorists' and hunted down as such with the Church's tacit approval by those who had the responsibility for addressing those concerns adequately and equitably, but did not. The reason: it may not be too long before Armageddon, which humans have been courting since Adam and Eve joined me in my rebellion against the Prime Mover, ensues and brings all the fun to an abrupt and complete end.

"It is therefore not inconceivable that, in the run-up to Armageddon, the Church's hierarchy will join those who will persecute the Elect in a repeat of the Joan of Arc fiasco and the other outrageous things that have been done in the Church's name over the centuries - things that took a very courageous Pontiff and a man of God to stand up and apologize to the world on the Church's behalf. We here in the Pit have taken note of the fact that in addition to being an outsider to 'Church politics' in Rome, the Pontiff in question was not of the traditional milieu in his philosophy and temperament. According to our calculations, the chances that any of his successors will succeed in standing up to the traditional 'interest groups' in the Church and others who have traditionally held sway in Rome and continue on that path is very slim indeed.

"You know - we may be languishing here in the Pit, but we are not entirely nuts. We know that Peter ended up as Bishop of Rome and that those who have succeeded him in his capacity as the 'rock' upon which the Church was built are now stuck with that. Peter did not just find himself in Rome after wandering about aimlessly. There is no doubt that Providence, and specifically the Holy Ghost, was behind the move.

"But Rome is Rome, and it also happens to be in the West. And the West is the West. Westerners have this funny idea that their lives are more precious than the lives of humans elsewhere. That is bullshit; but it is what they think. And that bias rubs off on the Church's hierarchy with its head office in Vatican City. The Church's functionaries can't help seeing things in the prism of western technocrats. That has implications for Church unity - which is too bad! It also has implications for the work of 'fishers of men'.

"There are undoubtedly many humans who have balked at becoming Catholics because of that bias - which is just one of many problems faced by the Church because its head office is in the West. Too bad! But all this is very good news for us here in the Pit - we love it, and you'd better believe that we go all out to exploit biases of that sort which are one of the consequences of original sin.

"The point here though is that in these 'last days' and especially with the 'Rapture' in sight, we are committed to redoubling our efforts to ensure that members of the Church's hierarchy align themselves with the megalomaniacs through whom we rule the world to the detriment of their work of saving souls. Nothing gives us greater satisfaction than seeing members of the Church's own hierarchy working to derail the divine plan.

"Nothing is more satisfying to us than the sight of Church leaders identifying themselves with those humans who have no qualms whatsoever about visiting death upon their fellow humans while pursuing their worldly ambitions. And we also know that nothing is more reprehensible to the Prime Mover.

"As long Planet Earth is still in one piece and the doomsday clock is still ticking, my troops and I here in the Pit are determined to lend harbingers of ruin and death all the support they need in implementing their wicked designs and bringing misery to families and their loved ones. Death and misery are weapons that we use to try and drive souls to despair and eventual perdition. Our allies are up against the forces of Good. What's more, we know that the Deliverer has got our friends in His sights, and is ready to welcome them back to the fold at a moment's notice.

"To ensure that it doesn't happen, we do not let up in our corrupting influence, and we inspire them continuously to stay the course. We help them in concocting justifications for their murderous adventures, and we show them how they can reinforce each other in their opposition to world peace and stability. Networking is also one of the ways in which they help us recruit more 'killers of men' who can counter the influence of the 'fishers of men'!

"And so, that is how the battle lines are drawn in the struggle between good and evil. A Church hierarchy that will be eager to play into my hands on one side and my disciplined troops that are out to exploit every conceivable opportunity for derailing the divine plan on the other side. It is not surprising that the Deliverer, even though He knew that the Holy Ghost would be there to ensure that the 'powers of hell' would never prevail against His Church, worried that there might not be any faith left when He came back in the last days to deliver the *coup de grace* to Death.

"Just as it is not automatic that humans who succeed in maneuvering themselves into positions of leadership and power in the world recognize that their newfound authority is God-given, humans who make it into positions of authority in the Church do not automatically forsake self-will to permit the Holy Ghost to inform their work as 'fishers of men'. And you have to remember that my troops and I here in the Underworld have a special interest in corrupting these folks. Hence the scandals that have always plagued the *Sancta Ecclesia*!

"Everybody blubbers about the Divine Plan whose goal most of those who do couldn't even say if they were asked. If they really knew anything about that 'Plan', they would also know about another Plan - my Evil Plan!

"The strategy I follow in implementing my evil plan is to get poor forsaken children of Adam and Eve, who are starved for graces and are thirsty for the Word, to look at the Holy Church and mistake it for something else - for my work! It is a measure of our success here in the Pit that so many souls that are hungry for the Word of the Prime Mover actually believe that the pope is not just the Antichrist, but also the personification of me, Satan!

"And there is nothing that helps us in implementing the evil plan more than actions of priests and prelates that are reprehensible. And, guess what - as long as those 'fishers of men' are not perfect like the Deliverer Himself (which they can never be), they will always be contributing some to my cause - to bringing my evil plan to fruition! Meaning that they will be doing something that will make it seem as if the Holy Catholic Church, which was established by the Deliverer and is informed by the Holy Ghost, is actually my work."

Armageddon: a scenario...

"Even we pure spirits have instincts and hunches, and my hunch tells me that it will actually not be some super power that will be calling the shots as Armageddon approaches, but the so-called terrorists and their nests around the globe. Armed with brief-case nuclear bombs constructed with technology obtained by hacking into computers of the United States military, the terrorists will be roaming the world taking out cities at will, after successfully blackmailing and eventually rounding up leaders of the so-called 'nuclear club' and locking them up in a maximum security facility in Cuba!

"The great irony of it all is that it is the heavy-handed repression by governments of extremists so called and insurgents in places like Iraq, Afghanistan, Pakistan - yes, Pakistan because my hunch tells me that that is where everything is going to unravel - and a string of other countries that will be reeling under occupation that will be responsible for the unprecedented upsurge of 'terrorism'. It is for that self-same reason that the new crop of terrorists, as they go about the business of straightening out a world gone out of control, will be particularly merciless and uncompromising.

"The chaos and confusion in the world, particularly in the so-called advanced countries, as seething masses of humans scramble to get out of cities that are next on the list of destruction and as others attempt to flee urban centers in North America and Europe for the relative safety of Africa, will be unimaginable. In the chaos, ordinary Americans and Europeans will be begging the terrorists to spare them in return for cooperating in identifying and locating anyone who may have participated in the occupation of foreign lands or been complicit in the flagrant violation of human rights under the guise of fighting terrorism.

"The stock response of the terrorists will be predictable, namely that all they are doing is let the authors of the myth of terrorism and those who supported them have a taste of their own medicine. They will claim that agreeing to the reintroduction of the now discredited practice of resolving international disputes through negotiation and peaceful means will amount to surrender to the 'real terrorists'; and that it will be just a waste of their time to try and negotiate with those who could not understand that all humans were equal, and were inclined to the view that anyone who sought self-determination was not only an inferior human, but automatically also a terrorist or insurgent whose concerns did not merit any consideration.

"The end will come when a defiant American general and self-proclaimed 'Christian crusader', hoping to destroy the terrorists' leadership in one fell swoop after receiving reports that the leader of the 'holy war on the Great Satan' and his closest lieutenants were secretly gathered in the Pakistani city of Karachi for a convention, will level that city with up to fifty mega nukes from the remnant of America's nuclear arsenal.

"In response, hundreds of thousands of operatives for the terrorists, already positioned in all corners of the globe with their brief-case nuclear bombs, will do what they have to do. On a prearranged signal, they will grab the 'brief-cases' by their handles to trigger the nuclear holocaust. And that is how the nuclear 'monster' - the 'baby child' of the West which was christened the Manhattan Project and was successfully 'tested' over

Hiroshima and Nagasaki - will come back to haunt those who created it.

"Oh, my! Oh my! When my own pride set me on the unholy path of spiritual depravity and degradation at the beginning of time, little did I know that things would get so interesting…that generations of humans would follow me down that path, and then try to outdo each other in playing the part of human devils! The insincerity of humans and underhand dealings is not just the root cause of quarrels, bigotry, family break-ups, schisms and heresies, wars and other evils; but it is the reason those humans who bear the guilt for those evils think they can hoodwink the world and pass for blameless and innocent victims!

"Or, did you think that we would miss those details just because our reign is confined to the Underworld! Well, always just remember that the high priest who bragged that he was better that the tax collector - the high priest who represented Moses and the prophets and led prayers in the temple in Jerusalem - was closer to me, Beelzebub, than the 'blooming tax collector'! And, while 'pagans', former unbelievers, 'unsaved' people and others who join the Mystical Body of the Deliverer escape my tentacles in the process, you have to accept that my buddies in the Underworld and I do give the successors of the apostles a run for their money, and cannot be accused of abnegating our responsibilities in that particular respect.

"It is not the first time - mark you - that creatures that are made in 'the Image' and have been placed by the Prime Mover in positions of responsibility have chosen to stand out as 'princes'. In the beginning, during my own period of trial after the Prime Mover had deigned to bring me into existence, I immediately started aspiring to be a prince - the 'Prince of Light'! The 'Chief Prince of Light' to be precise! You know how things are when one is puffed up, and wants to stand out above the crowd.

"Because I had come into existence ahead of Michael the Archangel, Rafael and the rest, I despised them. Even though we were 'jewels' - all of us - in the Prime Mover's precious collection, I got this idea that I could perhaps maneuver myself into a position from which I would be able to make them feel small – as if they were just fake jewels, not real ones! Well, you know the rest of the story, don't you? If you were inquisitive about how the successors to the apostles ended up referring to themselves as 'Princes of the Church' even before they themselves had passed their Church Triumphant Entrance Test, there is your clue.

Human nature...

"We demons understand human nature a little bit better than humans themselves do. And humans themselves are so stupid! Instead of relaxing and praying always and, I might also add, taking their time to meditate on the words of the Lord's prayer, they are always jumpy and going off on a limb just like dumb, fledgling little kittens that venture out into the open, completely oblivious to the fact that hungry kites are lurking in the skies above.

"It is quite rare for demons to possess humans and have power over them on a full-time basis. We do not usually waste our time doing that. Instead, we merely bide our time, and look for opportunities to play the weakness of one human against the weaknesses of another one. And we will inspire and help one human to hurt another human by doing uncouth things like telling lies initially in small things and then gradually in big things. In the case of a married couple, we will quietly

765

infiltrate the first one who will provide us an opening, and form a partnership with him or her with a view to 'straightening up' the other party. Once we get one party losing his/her temper, we will capitalize on that and get them hurling words at each other and even getting physical with each other as the friction between them mounts.

"When that happens, the innocent party will be tempted to try and hit back by demonstrating that he/she can also be really bad, and even dishonest. Before they know it, the two humans will be shouting and screaming at each other, and calling each other names such as 'lying bitch' and 'dirty devil'.

"We know that once humans start pulling each other's legs or cheating, they make a habit of it; and quitting habits is, of course, not something that humans do easily. If anything, habits quickly become a part of human nature! And as humans become entrenched in their crooked ways, common sense and reason concurrently become commodities that are in very short supply.

"And so, before long, the couple will be swearing and blaming each other for all sorts of imaginary things. And it is not unusual for them to stop believing in the very God by whom they will be swearing, and to lose their faith. They will, of course, be completely unaware that it is us here in the Pit who were responsible for creating the turmoil between them; and they will have forgotten that it was they themselves who provided us a window of opportunity by neglecting the Lord's prayer.

"The fact that one of the parties might have persevered in praying and fasting unceasingly, of course, wouldn't have made things any easier for that individual. If anything, the life of the innocent party is almost guaranteed to be more hellish for that reason. We demons, working through the sinful humans, usually go all out to try and drive the faithful and holy soul to despair. What will save that poor soul will be his/her constancy in praying to the Prime Mover and his/her complete resignation to His will, and nothing else.

"Yes, eschewing acts of self-love and self-importance which are incompatible with the surrender of oneself to the will of the Almighty One, instead of putting on some quixotic performance that overlooks one's own failings and is driven by hypocrisy. But we know that the majority of humans end up seeking consolation in self-indulgence and completely abandoning prayer and self-mortification. They end up losing hope and eventually their faith in the Prime Mover.

"As expected, it is usually the party that suffers from having an inferiority complex that ends up as the most vicious in domestic and other conflicts. And, coincidentally, they are also the ones who are usually to blame for first poisoning the atmosphere with their unrealistic demands of the other party to the conflict, and then finally igniting it by 'throwing a spanner into the spokes' by suddenly doing something that really hurts the other party.

"The intensity of the antipathy for the other party usually corresponds to the conviction that the imaginary ills are inspired by us here in the hell. The end result is that a party that may be entirely innocent is effectively blamed for devilishness that is completely the figment of the complainant's own imagination. We ourselves derive enormous satisfaction from seeing things transpire that way - from seeing humans who are entirely innocent cast as devils and treated accordingly by the very humans who are dedicated to advancing our cause.

"Feelings of inferiority complex and feelings of insecurity are unlikely to be things that instill self-confidence. Humans who feel inferior do not usually expect things to take care of themselves. It is thus not surprising that it is the actions of the insecure party that in the end are largely to blame for the friction between two individuals going out of hand. Feelings of insecurity do not engender either calm or trust in Providence. That is the nature of the beast.

"We demons have instincts and hunches too, and I have a hunch that while hell may be overflowing with humans who became lost because they were over confident in life even as they suffered from an incurable inferiority complex and did not therefore have any excuse giving others a hell, the population in Purgatory at any one time is largely made up of humans who also suffered from an inferiority complex but now need special help in ridding themselves of that condition, stopping to clamor for sympathy and special treatment, and getting back on their feet again.

"More so than humans who exude confidence in themselves, insecure humans, have this tendency to blame others for perceived ills suffered by them and for imaginary ills as well. But what makes their posturing particularly upsetting to those who become their targets is their habit of acting meek and innocent even as they are fabricating lies or otherwise claiming that they have been short-changed. They love to cast themselves as victims out of a desire to satisfy some inordinate craving for attention. All of which explains the fact that all humans justify their sins by imagining that they genuinely aggrieved and deserve better from the Prime Mover! And that is all balderdash because the fact is that the more humans are pampered, the more they demand, and this is due to an evil streak in them that goes back to the sin of Adam and Eve. And their attempts to justify their sins lead to sins that are even more grievous.

"But whenever humans sin, they always also commit the sin of ingratitude, because they are oblivious to the many gifts that they have received from the Prime Mover, including the gifts of existence and human nature, and the invitation to be with the Prime Mover in eternity. And you would think that it is the poor, uneducated folks who are plagued by inferiority complex, rather than the educated and the well-to-do. Nothing could be further from the truth. If anything, those who grow up in so-called tradition-bound societies very rarely feel inadequate or inferior. The state of inferiority complex is in fact almost exclusively the preserve of those in society who are haughty, think they know too much, and are always trying to overreach without even knowing it.

"Any way - that is the extent to which humans seem determined to show that they are their own masters. Some of these nuts, not satisfied with carving out chunks of Planet Earth and claiming them for their own exclusive use, are already eyeing nearby planets like the moon and Mars. They now think that they can claim parts of these other planets also as their personal real estate! And this is after they have rigged Planet Earth with weapons of mass destruction to a point to which a tiny spark will cause it to catch fire and burn, and perhaps even disintegrate into pieces.

"But, talking about putting a spin on things, the opportunities for us here in the Underworld to manipulate innocent, unsuspecting humans ballooned instead of vanishing as we had feared, with the inauguration of the Church, and they now seem unlimited. Some folks like referring to the bounty or 'good' that came out of evil. Well, here is a clear case of the diametric opposite - of 'evil' being generated by something that is not just 'good' but priceless! Yes - you can say that we also try!

"And you can bet that I usually know when a human

769

is mine and I, in turn, am his or hers. It is when humans have changed sides and are under my control that they step up their vainglorious self-flattery, and try to cast themselves as righteous and holy devil haters who supposedly are also pals of the Prime Mover. It is when they sanctimoniously affirm their determination to 'fight evil'! I know that because I am the one who inspires them to act like that.

"When humans, after deliberately making a wrong turn, get off the narrow path and end up in my camp, I certainly do not go begging them to become composed and regain their wits. I urge them to tell their guardian angels to get lost so that they can enjoy life to the maximum while it lasts. True to form, they all invariably get the message from reading my lips; and, instead of imploring the mercies of the Prime Mover and His saving graces, they haughtily try to justify their actions and to redefine the Prime Mover's injunctions to suit their own purposes.

"That is very creative. It isn't something that we pure spirits could bring off! Humans are able to do that - to turn around and try to 'justify' their actions - because they have separate and distinct faculties of the imagination and intellect. In our case, those faculties are rolled into one, so that when we think, we automatically also imagine, and when we imagine, we automatically think. In the case of humans, the faculty of the imagination can and often does operate independently of the intellect, and vice versa. And that is a boon for us here in the Underworld as we try to woo humans to join our cause.

"Once humans kill, perhaps because of the way their imagination interacts with the intellect, they have this tendency to try and justify their actions when they really should be begging the Prime Mover for mercy - especially knowing that he forgives humans their sins. And the way they do so is by killing over and over again - by making a habit of it! And as they do so, they also start claiming self-righteously that they have a duty to rid the world of those amongst them who are 'bad apples' - as if they were any good themselves after committing murder and then trying to cover it up!

"What happens there is that humans let their faculties of the imagination have the upper hand in determining their next course of action. That is why, at one point it is 'kill, kill, kill!' and almost in the same breath, they are extolling their own 'virtues' and referring to anyone who disagrees with them as evil! But, while they might look on the surface as if they might be suffering from schizophrenia or some similar psychotic disorder, they remain on top of things and know perfectly well what they are up to.

"You will see a bunch of humans publicly confessing to murders and attempted murder one moment, and the next moment, their heads will be bowed down meekly, not as a prelude to begging for divine mercies, but to thank the Prime Mover for giving them the wherewithal to make progress in achieving their worldly ambitions - as though they had never heard of the Ten Commandments!

"To return to the so-called 'natural disasters' and 'acts of God', the Prime Mover allows humans to perish in the circumstances described to show that all humans are equal and also that the culture of death is, therefore, self-defeating; that one might be a 'death culture enthusiast' one moment and the next moment that individual himself or herself might be dead; that the fate of all humans is in the hands of the Prime Mover, not in the hands of self-appointed human 'gods'; and, above all, that the Prime Mover is quite capable of using - and in fact uses - wicked humans and their acts of 'treachery' to achieve His own ends and to fulfil His divine plan.

"And so, today as in the first century, the Church has its 'Judas Iscariots' and 'Ananiases'. And, talking about 'Ananiases', there is this fallacy that when humans heed the call to be 'fishers of men' or to some other form of 'religious life', they somehow become insulated from temptations of the flesh and from our wiles - that they become 'special'! Others even entertain the equally strange notion that being well versed in matters of philosophy and theology automatically propels individuals to spiritual heights.

"Nothing actually could be further from the truth. This is because anyone whom we observe starting to veer off Broadway onto the Narrow Path automatically becomes a very special target for us - let alone anyone who displays enthusiasm for joining the workforce in the field and an interest in helping with the harvest as a 'fisher of men'!

"As the Evil One, I can assure you here and now that a human soul becomes a special point of focus for my troops the moment it starts being drawn to anything that is positive and noble. And we ourselves get drawn towards candidates for the religious life just like magnets become drawn towards anything metallic. Is it, therefore, any wonder that it is the souls that are humble and steadfast in their love of the Prime Mover and in their self-abnegation that are likely to be found enduring dark nights of the soul and things of that sort!

"To return to the subject of mercenaries in the Church, just as was the case in the days of the early Church, so today they have no scruples in doing whatever they do in the name of the Prime Mover and in the name of the Church - until they get exposed (if they ever do). Many of those mercenaries of death have no scruples about trying to pass for 'people of God', and do their best to show that they are imbued with a messianic mission to change the world for the better and presumably also bring salvation to 'non-believers'. But, unfortunately for them (and also for us here in the Underworld whose duty it is to inspire and cheer them on), the strategies of 'world dominance and pre-emption' so-called betray them and unmask their 'messianic mission' for what it really is - naked worldly ambition!

"Now, you might know that when humans get caught up in 'messianic missions', the end also starts to justify the means from then on. It doesn't take much after that to get full-scale wars waged by the self-declared righteous against multiple evildoers and axes of evil going. Instead of seeing danger looming and making a U-turn, they tend to become fixated with the notion that they themselves are making history. You can bet that we take our job of planting notions like those into the heads of people in positions of responsibility very seriously.

"And as the nations led by the types who, having buckled in the face of temptation, wind up as 'demagogues' begin to get sucked slowly but surely down the black hole that transforms all once-powerful but expansionist nations of the world into history, the common sense that might have previously fueled 'anti-war' protests and the like ceases to be common altogether. This happens as the citizenry unite behind their 'great and glorious leaders' in the 'troubled times' when their country starts to look like it is indeed facing implacable and determined 'enemies'.

"That is also the time when the truism of the maxim that 'citizens *deserve* their leaders' becomes tested. It is the time when any protest begins to spell 'betrayal' of and 'treasonous conduct' against the motherland in the looming times of tragedy. But, of course, the citizenry of

773

an aggressor nation wouldn't be very different from their leaders. It is they themselves after all who choose to give the individuals who lead them the reins of power, and to keep and not just tolerate them but support them even after the murderous schemes they have hatched come to light.

"That is not at all surprising since there definitely would be a sprinkling of 'Mother Theresas' and 'Francises of Assisi' among them at the most, and the rest of the populace would be hoping that imperial power and expansionism will guarantee each one of them a retirement beach side cottage constructed to withstand any type of hurricane (thanks to the booty shipped back home from the pacified territories). And that after all is the basis of that truism which has been tested time and again in the course of human history.

"Talking about history - it is the actions humans do that over time constitute 'history'. And there is nothing that demonstrates the stupidity of humans as does history. It is most damning - this so-called history of humankind - even before the Judge has come into the picture. And it is all the more damning because it keeps repeating itself.

"Take the things hoodlums who paraded themselves as emperors and kings at some point in history did to other humans in the name of empires and kingdoms over which they held fief. These hoodlums conducted themselves like gods while they lived and the empires and kingdoms lasted. But, disregarding the myths about those kings and emperors and the cruel things they did which are banded around as 'history', where (one might ask) are those 'kings' and 'emperors' and their kingdoms and empires? The fact that they all are no more says something about the stupidity of my human friends, I tell you.

"The resources the regimes that are determined to 'dominate and conquer' employ *fortunately* are public resources that should be devoted to improving the living conditions of the citizenry and others who are in need instead of being wasted on armaments and the like. My folks and I in the Underworld certainly deserve a 'pat on the back' (even if only in the figurative sense) for the fact that the activities of those for whom the 'culture of death' is a necessary 'evil' are always dictated by 'practical considerations' like the prospects of winning an election!

"Those 'practical considerations' unfortunately have the effect of stopping well placed humans from aiming really high and taking over and subjugating as much of the world as the resources at their disposal permit. If planned well, a major offensive aimed at taking over and occupying huge swaths of territory typically results in the resources available to the aspiring super power swelling and becoming unmatched as the war chests of nations that are overrun become the property of the occupier. In a few instances, following a successful foray, operatives of the invading nation can even get to set up home in opulent palaces complete with golden domes! And that is not to mention other booty including precious artworks and the like.

"The temptation to take a gamble and dedicate a nation's available resources, both material and human, to an alluring 'project' that additionally promises limitless, albeit only 'temporal', returns can be just too great to withstand. Frequently megalomaniacs at the helm of an aspiring super power mortgage their nation's economy and (by getting the media to join in the spin) hoodwink the citizenry into making untold sacrifices just so they can give themselves and their close associates a shot at setting up home and/or an office in palatial surroundings in some exotic lands. But again it is those 'practical

775

considerations' that always interfere with our work.

"And then there is the problem of those 'peaceniks'. They are a real menace and the harm they do to our cause can be immeasurable. But that should change in time as money matters and militarism become accepted as good things in themselves. In any case, thanks to the good work of money lovers and the death culture enthusiasts, this planet is already ringed with enough explosives to send it smoldering in a ball of flames at the touch of a button. No, those idiots - the peaceniks - won't stop us
!

Predator nations...

"In the meantime, we need humans who can take risks and are not inhibited by 'public opinion polls' and things of that sort. We need more and more 'leaders' who can say 'to hell with pollsters' and public opinion; and 'to hell with democracy'! Look, we are offering ambitious folks the opportunity to own the whole world!

"The only qualification that is necessary is a genuine desire to dominate the world using any means - pre-emptive regime changes, nuclear strikes (limited or otherwise), colonization, occupation, *et cetera*. In this business, the end definitely justifies the means! Those humans who may be bothered that they may be turning a peaceful nation into one that preys on other nations and effectively becomes a 'predator' nation in the process are automatically disqualified.

"This culture of death is not confined to people of certain nations. Judging by the widespread support for warmongers, this is a culture of death that appeals to many, many folks in virtually every land. Hence the prospects for the rise of many as opposed to just a few predator nations. Under the circumstances, wars are, therefore, not unfortunate things that inevitably happen. They are a perfectly acceptable and lawful way of doing business in the world.

"The fascination with military science, which has as its objective the empowerment of 'nation states', might be described as a 'culture of death'. But it is a 'culture' that is honorable, if only because it is concerned with national 'security' in the short term as well as the long term.

"The actions of the first predator serve to draw the attention of other potential predator nations to the existence of booty within the territorial borders of some unfortunate country. The 'booty' can never be 'adequately' protected because, before long, alliances between nations, ostensibly for the purpose of advancing the human condition, are formed with a view to exploiting the resources deemed to be of 'vital national interest' to members of the alliance. The result is an ever-changing balance of power on the geopolitical scene, as the predator nations of today become the meat upon which newer alliances of nations feast.

"Even when united and resolute against the assault on their sovereignty, it is very rare that the citizenry of an occupied country succeeds in reversing the situation and regaining their right of self-determination and independence. That quite naturally emboldens the potential predator nations to be on the lookout for opportunities to invade, occupy, or (as it is usually put) 'liberate' selected countries from real or imaginary tyrants.

"Those nations that have the wherewithal would be remiss not to gear themselves up so that they too can actively seek out other resource rich nations to conquer and subjugate. And so, it is not a question of whether resource-rich nations will be 'occupied' and taken over by some more powerful 'predator' nations; but a question of when the takeovers will occur.

"To be sure, the change will often bring with it a respite of sorts, albeit temporary. But the suppressed citizenry usually soon learn that it is expecting too much that their new masters in fact came to 'liberate' them - that it is expecting too much even to think that international law over which the United Nations is guardian will protect them. That would certainly be expecting way far too much since that world body, whose decisions are subject to veto by certain select nations, was established for the specific objective of safeguarding the interests of those nations, and none other.

"As predator nations realize their goal of being the undisputed masters of some resource-rich corner of the globe, they simultaneously move to legitimize their positions by twisting the arms of any and all nations that might challenge their authority in those parts of the world, and will not hesitate to enforce their 'hard-worn' and sole right to exploit the available natural resources as they deem fit by imposing economic and other sanctions on those nations that refuse to become their allies and the use of force where necessary.

"The fact that it is not statesmanship or anything like that, but naked unbridled greed that drives geopolitics should serve as a reminder to you humans that it is I - not the Deliverer or anyone else - who will continue to hold sway over the fortunes of this planet until it disintegrates into fragments in a nuclear conflagration at the end of time! It should already be clear by now that the pursuit of happiness in disregard of the sanctity of life is worse than worshipping idols made by human hands out of stone. It constitutes worship of the Author of Death...Me!

"All agents of death worship me regardless of what they proclaim! There are times when it looks as if we have every soul on earth in our camp in this regard. It is

778

on those Heroes' Days - every country on earth has at least one every year - when celebrations are held to honor those who died in 'defense of freedom'. More often than not, that 'defense of freedom' amounted to nothing more than participation in naked aggression whose only purpose was to gain control of territory, waterways, and other assets belonging to other nations. It was either a successful looting expedition or a looting expedition gone awry; and, consequently, the displays of military might and victory parades are all a celebration of the death culture.

"In some cases it might, of course, also have been a nation's fight for survival, but a fight for survival that was triggered by hostile activity on the part of that nation. But then you have to remember that to the extent any nation on earth claims that its borders are 'sacred' and 'inviolable', to that extent my evil cause, whose objective is to drive a wedge between humans who are all made in the Image and are members of the same 'human' family, has succeeded!

"That does not alter the fact that the more I myself succeed, the more I hurt my cause. The more my troops succeed in corrupting those in leadership positions and getting governments, that are supposed to promote the commonweal, to shirk their responsibilities to the people of God and to instead become instruments for suppression while furthering the interests of a tiny manipulative minority, the more it becomes clear to an ever-growing number of humans that it is not their material but their spiritual wellbeing that really matters.

"In other words, the more we have been successful in recruiting folks to sow seeds of death, the more it becomes clear to other folks who care to stop and reflect that they are temples of the Prime Mover and not simply unfeeling animals that must be abandoned to greed and

779

other vices. The more I succeed, the easier it becomes for humans to see through my lies.

"Lacking any real legitimacy - because those who occupy the halls of power in the predator nations I control have essentially hijacked the powers of state with no real intention of using them for the common good - these quislings of mine do not require any urging to become believers in the doctrine that might is right, that it establishes the legitimacy they crave, and that any attempt to resist them automatically becomes illegitimate; and that anyone even remotely suspected of involvement in challenging them is fair game - hence the labels 'insurgent' and 'terrorist'.

"Acts of the *de facto* authority, regardless of how it came to be the *de facto* 'authority', that would themselves be regarded as 'aggression' or illegal under international conventions, become 'liberation' or legitimate 'occupation' and acceptable under those self-same conventions. The insurgents and the terrorists become eligible for a reprieve only as and when their country becomes denuded of its natural resources and stops being rated by the occupiers one that has any importance to their or any other would-be-predator-nation's 'national security'.

"Now, I could try and warn my hirelings that the adage that 'might is right' is a hollow one when applied to creatures. Might is really right only when it is the Almighty exercising his rightful might. That is because, in addition to being infinitely Good, the Almighty is also all knowing, and consequently also always right.

"And, even though the Almighty One is a 'Jealous God', because He created everything that exists outside of Himself out of nothing, and everything is His *ipso facto*, His jealousy cannot include any 'covetousness' or desire for what belongs to someone else. In any case, if I were to alert my lackeys that theirs is a hopeless cause, I would be doing a great disservice - nay, a great 'wrong' - to my own cause. First of all, as the devil incarnate, I myself also aspire to be 'Almighty' when it comes to evil matters - I mean matters that are sordid, foul and sickening, and ignoble.

"But humans are so stupid, they probably wouldn't believe me anyway. If I told them that in pursuing the philosophy that might is right, they were setting themselves up for failure, humans would think that I am going crazy. They are so stupid, they would think that I had gone nuts if I told them that they were actually hurting themselves each time they tried to 'liquidate' fellow humans they disliked, and that things didn't work that way. Humans are so stupid, they don't even learn from history.

"When Julius Caesar was planning his invasion of North Africa, he passed an edict to the effect that anything that looked like it could be melted and used to manufacture implements of war, by which he meant ramming rods, swords, javelins, spears, arrow heads, slings, catapults, shields, and helmets for the foot soldiers and cavalry, cuirasses for his generals, wheels for chariots, and so on and so forth to be so melted and employed. And he caused all well bodied Romans aged twenty-five to forty-five to be enlisted in his armies. He even commandeered the chariots of the noble men in Rome, Venice and other cities of the empire.

"But, as you can see, Caesar's conquest of North Africa was a mirage and, apart from the ruins of the amphitheater in Rome, there is absolutely nothing to show for sacrificing human lives in particular on that scale. If Julius Caesar had invested the treasures he squandered in the course of prosecuting his wars in Africa and in Gaul in uplifting the standards of living of Romans, the Roman Empire would probably have succeeded in withstanding the subsequent onslaught of the barbarians, and perhaps even survived as a force to be reckoned with to this day!

"Instead, even as his forays into Africa, Gaul and Britannia for the purpose of guaranteeing access to the world's scarce resources were faltering, too proud to admit defeat, Julius Caesar and those who stepped into his shoes after he was felled by his own friend Brutus tried to show that they were winning even in defeat! And it has been the same story with all demagogues. In modern times, honorable exits from debacles resulting from failed expansionist policies have sometimes taken the form of 'granting independence to member states of the commonwealth' and things like that.

"But, have you ever heard words of the Deliverer to the effect that what is spoken behind doors or in secret will be revealed to all and sundry? I myself know from my experience the shame of defeat; and I can tell you that the shame that awaits the demagogues, who have no scruples about sacrificing precious treasure and blood while seeking 'honorable' exits from their unsuccessful forays abroad in search of booty, will be so devastating, not even the most curious among humans will want to be a witness as the sentence is passed.

"In the meantime, it is not likely that the Prime Mover is going to send His legions to Earth to dislodge me, much less deal with those humans who are enthusiasts of the culture of death and stop them. He did not do so when His only begotten Son was 'neutralized' and effectively 'silenced' two thousand years ago. He did not do it when the death culture enthusiasts no longer 'tested' nuclear and hydrogen bombs over Hiroshima and Nagasaki.

"And it is unlikely that He will do so if the latest crop

782

of death culture enthusiasts and money lovers start by taking out those nations that form the so-called 'axis of evil' - as they seem quite prepared to do. I can't wait to see satellite pictures of these countries burning all at the same time.

"And it is not as if the Prime Mover does not value every single human life in these countries. He sent His Son into the world because of His infinite love for humans born or unborn, and Christian or non-Christian. And His Son, imploring His Father to 'take away the cup' if it were possible and sweating blood in the Garden of Gethsemane, was in fact grieving for all present, past and future victims of death culture enthusiasts. No, it is not the intention of the Prime Mover to interfere with my rule over the world at this point in the game!

Sissy...

"But it seems that the solution to the 'problem of terrorism' wouldn't have ended up costing so much in lives and money if the original concerns of the 'terrorists' had been addressed in an equitable manner, and if partiality in the resolution of international conflicts had not been sacrificed at that altar of 'vital national interests' and 'bull-shit' like that.

"I am the devil, and I can confirm to you here and now that, for all the hype, 'vital national interests' remain temporal worldly considerations, and a price has to be paid sooner or later when 'vital national interests' are permitted to take precedence over Natural Justice. Who, after all, inspired humans to get involved in 'empire building' projects and this foolish business of 'national security'!

"Natural justice is trampled underfoot, not promoted, when powerful nations are bent on world domination and their leaders will stop at nothing to try and achieve their misguided objective. And that spells more, not less trouble even for a super power. And this is precisely what gave rise to the grievances of present-day 'terrorists'. Then, repressive measures that overlook natural justice are definitely bound to breed new and even more deadly 'terrorism'. It is not really hard to create a multi-headed monster out of terrorism that could be solved by accepting that everybody is equal and listening to and addressing the genuine concerns of their fellow humans.

"Rooted as it is in greed and selfishness, this 'cycle of violence' is the evidence of our own continuing reign on earth. It is something we in the Underworld not only welcome but will do everything in our power to abet. But it also shows how dumb humans are. They are so dumb they do not see violence and the culture of death for the nasty things they are until they themselves are at the receiving end. But there is another dimension to the dumbness and stupidity. When humans are terrorized and murdered in their thousands in countries that are not regarded as 'vital' to the interests of the powerful nations of the world, these nations leaders have the habit of looking the other way - as if the massacres, which frequently have their roots in the policies those same powerful nations pursued - were occurring on a different planet.

"You humans are such 'amazing' creatures. Just fancy the world's so-called super powers united in fighting an 'invisible enemy' - an enemy who seems to 'know the terrain' very well, and who apparently understands that he can simply go on sapping the super powers' resources and energy at will, and bleeding the super powers to death by simply 'rearing his head' from time to time in different places before conveniently retreating underground.

"And imagine the super powers compounding the problem by fancying that they can deflect attention from the 'real problem' by staging pre-emptive strikes on 'rogue' states they imagine are an easier 'kill'. That is too bad. Pre-emptive forays by some nations against others automatically alert the nations that see themselves as likely targets of the emergence of potential 'trouble makers'. And just imagine what will go through the minds of military strategists of those nations that do not qualify as traditionally allies of the aggressor nations. It is just so reckless.

"When the Romans made their foray into Gaul and colonized it, they did it pre-emptively. But now where are there! When the Japanese crossed the Pacific Ocean and levelled Pearl Harbor, they did it pre-emptively. But now where are they as a military power! And when the Nazis made their land-grab and occupied Europe, North Africa and half of Russia, they did it pre-emptively. But all those efforts came to naught! Not only is the doctrine not new; it always appears to spell disaster for those nations that fall for it.

"Talking about spelling disaster, I was stupid enough myself to try and challenge the Prime Mover to a fight when I did. It did more than spell disaster for me and for the angelic hosts I persuaded to join me in mounting that challenge! And that is how we wound up here in Gehenna, my dear! You humans could learn from us, but you are so dumb.

"When nations imagine that they are powerful and can therefore pick fights, they forget that the more threatened the targeted nations feel, the more resolute they will be in taking measures to counter the threats to them. The nations that feel that they are powerful and can get away with anything forget that it is the survival instincts of the targeted nations that take over and start dictating the courses of actions they have to take to contain the threat. Unlike the nations that seek to pick fights, the nations that find their existence threatened will not be playing games at all, and will aim to rcmove the threat to themselves once and for all.

"It might, of course, not be possible for the first nations to be targeted by the imperialists, colonialists or foreign invaders intent on controlling the sources of any scarce resource to withstand the initial wave of attacks by the aggressor nations. And that will, of course, have the effect of emboldening the aggressor nations even more. The more nations an aggressor nation with the help of its allies succeeds in occupying and 'pacifying', the more emboldened that nation will be. And also the more wary the nations that sense that they are likely targets for future attack will be - and the greater the danger the aggressor nation will in fact be facing.

"Now, the world is a huge place, and wars are fought and ultimately won, not by the nations that initially had the edge at the beginning of conflicts, but by those that have the edge as the conflicts wind down and come to a close. Threatened nations will enter into secret pacts with other nations with which they have common cause; and together those nations will do whatever it takes to neutralize the emerging 'foe'.

"In this day and age, when weapons of mass destruction can cause so much ruin in such a short space of time, not only is the idea of an invincible 'super power' illusory; but any power, however 'super', that decides to pick fights with other nations in these circumstances takes risks that are plainly incalculable.

"Any member of the 'nuclear club' today can leave any nation on earth however powerful levelled and devastated. The winner is unlikely to be the nation with the largest stockpile of nukes, but with the motivation to use the nuke. And nations that feel threatened invariably have greater motivation to strike out and 'stop' the enemy cold.

"And creating enemies who become labeled as 'terrorists' or 'insurgents' is definitely not the way to go in this day and age in which individuals are known to own labs that are capable of producing functional nukes. Only those who feel insecure in a world in which everybody and every nation is equal, and who nevertheless think they know too much, can make the blunder of overreaching without even knowing it. It is simply reckless.

"We in the Underworld will naturally support the efforts of humans who seek to saw ruin regardless of whether it is on themselves alone or on themselves and others. History will tell you that ruin rarely will come on others alone; and that, while nations that stay clear of conflicts are occasionally spared ruin, the aggressor nation is never spared ruin (or the world would still be under the rule of Romans, Greeks, Egyptians, and what have you).

"It is a singular mark of our success that humans have also developed this strange complex which enables them to act weak and completely helpless one moment - 'sissy' is the word they themselves would use to describe this disposition - and to be all over the place claiming that they are powerful and invincible the next moment.

"Similarly, at any one moment, humans will be ranting against me - Satan - and blaming me for drawing them into the rebellion against the Prime Mover; and they will not accept any responsibility for their own part in it. Some even want you to believe that, if they wind up here in hell with me, it wasn't their fault - that they were just 'predestined' to end up here and really did nothing themselves to deserve it.

"And if they end up in heaven - well, the refrain changes. It is because they are terrific, godly and completely different from the thieves, plunderers, terrorists and others who were hell-bent and of course also hell-bound. But my advice to humans is that they should hold their breath and stop claiming that they are 'saved' until they actually see St. Peter opening the Gates of Heaven to let them in. In fact until then, all humans are equally thieves, terrorists, insurgents, and sinners who are in great need of the mercies of the Prime Mover.

"I may be 'evil personified'; but I am not about to accept responsibility for the willful acts of humans who take it upon themselves to groom dictators, arm them, and abet and even participate in their murderous adventures; and then have no qualms putting the lives of other innocent humans including women and children at risk as they seek to effect regime changes and install puppets in place of their old friends turned enemy.

"I do not issue any license to these folks to kill. All I do is merely tempt them - as I am supposed to do. And when I use humans as my minions - to lie and falsify and even kill - it is always only after they themselves agree to join 'the cause' as willing accomplices.

"These folks are endowed with intelligence and a free will just like us pure spirits. But, more than that, they have all these graces that are dispensed to them through the Church; and that Church operates in the open, not underground. For those of you who do not know, its headquarters is on a hill in Vatican City in Rome from where the Romans ruled the world, and not in some inconspicuous place. That is a second chance we pure spirits did not get, but which humans appear determined to fritter away.

"Humans who follow my example and kill will face

fireworks for their sins of commission and omission just as we ourselves have. The fact that I am the face of Evil did not stop Michael the Archangel and other spirits from rebuffing my attempts to draw them into the rebellion. So forget the myth that I, Beelzebub, must cuddle human 'devils' and assume responsibility for their misdeeds. Again, I simply do what I am supposed to do, and that is to tempt them.

"Humans are entirely responsible for the consequences of their actions and, whether they like it or not, will roast here in hell with us for their 'sins'. When they arrive here, we will stage a special 'welcome' for those humans who tried to hold me Satan and my troops responsible for the evils they themselves did to their fellow humans. There will be a separate, grand reception to celebrate their rebellion against the Prime Mover who has outlawed murder, stealing, lying and things of that nature.

"And, for those humans who are still determined to pick a fight with us, I say: 'We are ready. Bring it on!'"

Made in the USA
Middletown, DE
17 April 2022

64053489R00451